Henry Thomas Buckle, Henry, Thomas Buckle

# Miscellaneous and posthumous works of Henry Thomas Buckle

I0592360

Henry Thomas Buckle, Henry, Thomas Buckle

**Miscellaneous and posthumous works of Henry Thomas Buckle**

ISBN/EAN: 9783742848109

Manufactured in Europe, USA, Canada, Australia, Japa

Cover: Foto ©Andreas Hilbeck / pixelio.de

Manufactured and distributed by brebook publishing software
(www.brebook.com)

Henry Thomas Buckle, Henry, Thomas Buckle

# Miscellaneous and posthumous works of Henry Thomas Buckle

# MISCELLANEOUS

AND

# POSTHUMOUS

# WORKS

OF

# HENRY THOMAS BUCKLE

VOL. I.

# MISCELLANEOUS

### AND

# POSTHUMOUS

# WORKS

#### OF

# HENRY THOMAS BUCKLE

EDITED WITH A BIOGRAPHICAL NOTICE BY

HELEN TAYLOR

IN THREE VOLUMES

VOL. I.

LONDON·
LONGMANS, GREEN, AND CO.
1872

LONDON: PRINTED BY
SPOTTISWOODE AND CO., NEW-STREET SQUARE
AND PARLIAMENT STREET

# CONTENTS.

## VOL. I.

# CONTENTS.

## VOL. II.

## VOL. III.

# BIOGRAPHICAL NOTICE.

FEW men, perhaps, have been placed throughout life in circumstances more favourable to the development and utilisation of intellectual power than those which surrounded Henry Thomas Buckle, the author of the History of Civilization in England. He belonged by birth to that middle class of whose services to the world he himself entertained so high an estimate; and he had the good fortune also to belong to a family which seems to have united considerable taste for literature with sufficient fortune to place at his disposal, from an early age, such means of study or travel as he himself desired. These advantages he shared, it is true, with thousands of young men who never make any visible return to the world for their good fortune; nevertheless, it is probable that a larger proportion of young men so circumstanced do actually distinguish themselves, than of any other class in life.

But Mr. Buckle's good fortune consisted more especially in two other circumstances which fell to his lot. In the first place, his mother, who seems to have early formed a high estimate of her son's abilities, unceasingly stimulated and encouraged him to exertion. And, in the second place, the delicacy of his health, from childhood upwards, shut him out from schools, from the universities, and from the professions—from all those places and pursuits, in short, where boys and men learn to imitate one another; where they learn to accept conventional solutions to the problems which are sure to present themselves to every active intellect; or where they learn to limit their ambition to the acquirement of wealth or of worldly success. For his love of study, as well as for his undoubted ambition to distinguish himself, Mr. Buckle was probably indebted to his mother. But to the weak health which led him to solitary study, must be attributed much, not only of his universally admitted originality of thought, but also of that characteristic vigour of expression which enabled him to bring his thoughts home to the popular mind with such striking success. His standard of expression was formed, like that of most other people, by his mental companions; but these companions were, in his case (fortunately for his renown and his readers), composed of the great minds of all ages.

A life so uneventful as that of Mr. Buckle ought to be recounted either by himself or by some intimate companion of his studies and his thoughts. The growth of a mind like his would be a valuable study to those who are engaged either in stimulating or in training other minds. And there would also be great psychological interest in tracing the growth of his ideas, the changes in his opinions, his habits of mind, and methods of work. Unfortunately, the only person except himself who might have been in a position to make all this known to the world, was the dearly-loved mother whose death preceded his own by three years. That she would have possessed the power to do it, had she outlived him, may be inferred with probability, from the terms in which he has described his own sad experience in watching her last illness, for he speaks of watching "the noble faculties dwindling by degrees."[1] And there is additional evidence that she could understand his work as well as stimulate him to it, in another touching passage of his writings, written after her death. For the opinion of the world, he says, he cares nothing, "because, now at least, there is no one whose censure I fear, or whose praise I covet. Once, indeed, it was otherwise, but that is past and gone for ever."[2] There can be little doubt, moreover, that the opinion so often expressed by him in his writings, that great men have generally had mothers of exceptional talent, was not uninfluenced by his own experience.

The fact that in his mother's society he found all the aid and the sympathy he needed, and that she was his almost constant companion, has probably had an unfavourable effect on the value of such materials as could be collected for a biography.

[1] See his review of Mill on Liberty, *infra*, p. 67.
[2] See Letter to a Gentleman respecting Pooley's Case, *infra*, p. 72.

Fortunately, however, we may be tolerably sure that it would have been his own wish that a biography of him should be mainly concerned with his writings. "I live," says he, "only for literature; my works are my only actions; they are not wholly unknown, and I leave it to them to protect my name."[1] The present sketch, therefore, will be in the main confined to tracing, as far as his very dry and succinct Journals will allow, the preparatory studies which led up to his writings, and to preserving such remarks of his own upon their scope and purport as it has been possible to collect. Even for this the materials are but slight; but before entering upon them it will be well that the reader should be in possession of an outline of the facts of his life, for which we are indebted to his surviving sister :

"Henry Thomas Buckle was the son of Thomas Henry Buckle, a wealthy merchant, who was born 6th of October, 1779, died 24th of January, 1840, and who married Jane, daughter of Peter Middleton and Mary Dodsworth his wife, both of the county of York, in 1811, by whom he had three children : a son, Henry Thomas, and two daughters. Henry Thomas was born at Lee, in Kent, 24th of November, 1821, whilst his parents were on a visit to his father's only brother. Greatly beloved by his family, the author of the History of Civilization in England was a feeble and delicate infant. He had no pleasure in the society of children of his own age, nor did he care for children's books; his great delight was the Bible; he would sit for hours by the side of his mother to hear the Scriptures read. But although his mother bought him books without end, he felt no interest in any of them until one day she brought him home the Arabian Nights, which he greedily devoured, and from that time he loved books. His father was a staunch Tory, and at an early age his son took interest in politics, and held his father's views. When he was quite a youngster he and a cousin of about his own age, who was brought up with him as a brother, used to play at Parson and Clerk as they called it. Henry Thomas would always preach, and although quite a child his mother used to say that his eloquence was extraordinary. As a child he was never awkward or intrusive, but always did the right thing in the right place. From a child he had conversational powers, and made himself acquainted with everything that was going on. He was sent to school to a clergyman, it being thought that a change from home might be of service to him; but his health failed, and he was soon taken away. His father encouraged his love of reading, and he had many advantages at home. In the year 1837, being with his family at Tunbridge Wells, he indulged in billiards, and after three months lost a considerable sum of money, which his mother paid. He often alluded to this in after life, thinking it

[1] Letter to a Gentleman respecting Pooley's Case, infra, p. 71.

fortunate that he had lost rather than won. After this, his health improving, he was placed with a private tutor. He never learnt any lessons, but
he was always foremost in his class. Again, his health failing, he returned
home; and he now began to form a small library, and was in the habit of
walking all about London in search of cheap books. He had long been a
great reader of novels, and his father, who had a very retentive memory,
was fond of reciting Shakespeare in his evenings at home. On the 24th
of January, 1840, his father died, after an illness of four weeks, and his
last words were addressed to his son when he called him to his bedside, a
few minutes before his death, 'Be a good boy to your mother.' Young
Buckle was immediately seized with a fainting-fit and taken out of the
room. For some months after this he was attended by his physicians, and
had frequent attacks of fainting, with great prostration of strength. His
mother, then in delicate health, was advised both for herself and her son to
try entire change of scene and climate, and in July, 1840, his mother, his
unmarried sister, and himself left England, and remained a year abroad.
His health improved wonderfully, and during that time he studied the languages and the literature of the various countries he visited, was always at
his books, and kept regular and early hours. On his return to England
he continued to study languages, and in 1841, his mother writing to him,
says, 'I am glad that you continue your Dutch master.' In the spring of
1843 he was presented at the English court, and immediately afterwards
left England in company with a friend, and visited many of the capitals of
Europe. In the autumn of the same year his sister married, and immediately afterwards his mother left England to join her son in Munich,
where he had been laid up with a severe attack of rheumatic gout. She
remained with him until the spring of 1844, when they both returned to
England, and his mother again settled in London. He then began to collect
his extensive library, and his diary shows how regular his habits and hours
were. He delighted in dinner-company and good talk. He never danced;
had no taste for music. He disliked horse exercise, and though ordered
when he was young to ride for his health, would never ride alone, as he said
he forgot he was on horseback; and on one occasion, when riding with Mrs.
Hutchinson, one of his sisters, at Hastings, he was so entirely absorbed with
his own thoughts that he allowed his horse to take him into the library
on the Parade. He had no taste for the country or country pursuits; and
although his health was delicate he liked no place but London. He was
fond of walking alone, as he used to say that he could talk to himself. He
made few friends, and rather disliked strangers; and though he was affable
to every one, he only admired talent, and what he called 'good talk.' He
was fond of children, and would play with his own nephews and niece in
a simple and childlike way. His disposition was kind, and in many letters
written to one of his sisters there breathes much love, sympathy, and kind-
heartedness. He had an aunt, his mother's last surviving sister, to whom
he was much attached; also a favourite cousin; and though he disliked
letter-writing, and used to say it was great waste of time, he never forgot

his near relatives. He was very methodical, careful, scrupulously correct in accounts and all money matters, and could calculate the expenses of any household. He was just in all his dealings, and although he disliked being called charitable, as it is termed, there are many who can testify to his kindness. He was always ready 'to help those who helped themselves,' but he would never 'let his left hand know what his right hand doeth.' His mother died in April, 1859, and through her distressing illness she had but one thought—her children, and more especially her son, who was her friend and companion. In the frequent wanderings of her mind for many months before her death she was always cheerful and collected when her son came into her room, so that he could not see her imminent danger, and even on the day of her death he was unwilling to telegraph to the family; and when it was only a matter of hours or perhaps minutes, he was still sanguine. But the hour came; and the great man was prostrate. He had lost in that mother everything that made his home happy. During the remainder of that year he was a constant wanderer. He visited his friends, and later in the year his sister. A heavy domestic affliction which befell the family at that time weighed heavily on him. The following year his health from time to time was much enfeebled, and in 1861, feeling still wretched and unsettled, he made up his mind to leave England. On the 20th of October in that year he left Southampton for Alexandria; and on the 29th of May, 1862, died at Damascus of fever."

From this outline of Mr. Buckle's life it will be seen that at the age of nineteen he was free to choose a career for himself; and that he then spent a year on the Continent with his mother, and on his return to England continued the study of languages which he had begun abroad. He appears to have known something of Latin, nothing of Greek, and to have had some knowledge of French, German, Italian, Spanish, Dutch, Russian, and Danish. It was probably during this period, between the age of nineteen and twenty-one, that he formed a determination out of which grew, in time, the work by which he became known. The most interesting passage in the whole of his Journals is that in which he notes down this resolution :—

" *Saturday, October* 15, 1842.—Being this day settled in my new lodgings, No. 1, Norfolk Street, I determined to keep a journal of my actions —principally, for the sake of being able to review what I have read, and consequently to estimate my own progress. My reading has, unfortunately, been hitherto, though extensive, both desultory and irregular. I am, however, determined from this day to devote all the energies I may have, solely to the study of the history and literature of the Middle Ages. I am led to adopt this course, not so much on account of the interest of

the subject, though that is a great inducement, but because there has
been, comparatively speaking, so little known and published upon it.  And
ambition whispers to me the flattering hope that a prolonged series of
industrious efforts, aided by talents certainly above mediocrity, may at
last meet with success.'

Ten days afterwards he reviews his own progress in reading :—

" The sketch then of the history of France during the Middle Ages, has
occupied me just ten days.  But then on one of those days I did not read
at all, and, besides that, I am now in better train for reading than I was at
first, so that I think on an average I may say eight days will suffice in
future for each history. It is my intention to go first in this hasty and superficial way through European history of the Middle Ages, and then, reading
the more elaborate works, make myself as much a master of the subject
as is possible, considering the meagre information we at present possess."

The works from which he had during these ten days been
employed in gathering a general view of French history in the
Middle Ages (from Clovis to Charles VIII.) were Hallam, Gibbon,
and Lardner's Cabinet Cyclopedia, and this passage in his Journal
is remarkable, for it shows him anticipating, as it were, at the
very outset of his task, the remarks which fifteen years later were
so very generally made on the character of the authorities referred to in the notes to his published book—authorities which
are certainly not more, and are generally less deserving the name
of " elaborate" than Gibbon and Hallam.  This expression, too, of
" elaborate works," as indicating what at that time he expected to
find, is very curious, especially when taken in conjunction with his
thinking he could make himself master of the subject by reading
"elaborate " works.   He cannot have failed very soon to find out
that few or no more elaborate works than those of Gibbon and
Hallam exist in any literature, and accordingly it is precisely
these and works of the same description to which he ultimately
was content to refer in his own book.  And no reader even of
these works, can fail to be aware of the original authorities,
besides that we have plenty of evidence that he was acquainted
with their general characteristics even when he had not read
them.   It cannot, therefore, have been by accident or ignorance
that he paid so little attention to them.  It can scarcely have
been from negligence either, since in the fifteen years that
elapsed between this first serious devotion of himself to historical
study and the completion of the first volume of the work he
ultimately designed, we find him devoting time to subjects,—

such, for instance, as phrenology—a knowledge of which few historians would think necessary to fit them for writing history.[1] It seems likely that, in fact, he soon discovered that the bent of his own mind was deductive. There is little trace of his ever having exercised his mind much on facts at first hand : people, things and events, society, nature, art, science, and even politics, seem to have had their main interest for him after they had been chronicled, and even grouped for him by other minds. He evidently preferred to use his own original powers of thought on the materials that had been amassed by other thinkers; and we may conjecture that it was this preference, whether conscious or not, that led him to transform his early scheme of a history of the middle ages into a design for a history of civilization.

At what time it was that this change in his plan took place, I have not been able to meet with any evidence to show. There is some reason to suppose that he formed other and intermediate plans between the two, and that at one time he thought of writing a history of the sixteenth century, at another of writing a history of the reign of Elizabeth. It is plain that from the first he did not confine himself strictly to the Middle Ages, for on March 7, 1843, occurs the entry in his Journal, " Began my Life of Charles I." And he seems to have worked at this for several hours a day for three weeks. What he then wrote is, possibly, probably even, what will be found under the head " Charles I." in vol. ii. of the Common Place Books. In July, 1850, occurs the entry, " Finished that part of Somers' Tracts which relates to my history of Elizabeth." And in January, 1855, he mentions, " the account of Hooker and Chillingworth which I wrote about five years ago." Hence it is most probable that the chapters on the reign of Elizabeth, printed in the present volume, were written about the year 1850, when he was twenty-nine years of age ; but it is not certain whether he wrote them with the intention of their forming part of a larger work, or whether he meant them for a history of the reign of Elizabeth only. Already in 1842 he had begun the practice of writing those copious abstracts which constitute his Common Place Books, and at which he used to work for several hours a day. The reader will notice that, in these, verbatim extracts, abstracts of matter,

[1] "*January* 27, 1852.—I intend now to begin the study of phrenology, to deter-mine its bearings upon the philosophy of history."—*Journal.*

and  original  remarks  of  his  own  are  very  much  mixed  up
together,  and  in  making  these  on  one  point  of  interest  after
another,  he  may  have  been  sometimes  led  to  plan  writing  on  one
subject,  and  sometimes  on  another.   There  is,  however,  one  entry
in  his  Journal,  respecting  his  reading,  which  seems  to  point  to
the  direction  his  mind  was  taking :—

"*June* 24, 1850.—Read  Simon's  Animal  Chemistry.   The  more  I  read
of  this  great  work  the  more  delighted  I  am,  particularly  at  the  new  views
it  opens  to  me,  and  of  which  Simon  seems  to  have  no  idea,  I  mean  the
connection  between  his  researches  and  speculations,  and  the  philosophic
history  of  man."

From  this  it  may  be  inferred  with  tolerable  certainty  that  it
was  during  these  eight  years—from  1842  to  1850—that  his
gradually  amassed  knowledge  of  the  great  outlines  of  modern
history,  together  with  the  experience  he  was  acquiring  of  the
tendencies  of  his  own  mind,  led  him  to  the  choice  of  his  subject.
His  literary  style  seems  also  to  have  been  completely  formed  by
this  time,  for  all  its  main  characteristics  are  to  be  found  in  the
fragments  on  the  reign  of  Elizabeth,  written  at  least  as  early  as
1850.   One  of  its  most  marked  characteristics,  and  one  which
principally  contributes  to  its  energy  and,  above  all,  to  its
picturesque  charm,  is  his  frequent  use  of  those  metaphors  and
of  those  rhetorical  forms  of  speech  to  which  all  the  world  is
accustomed,  and  which  have  become  common-places  in  the
language.   In  the  last  century  this  was  more  common  than  it
is  now,  for  writers  then  talked  a  great  deal  more  about  "an
elegant  simplicity,"  or  a  "severe  taste,"  or  "purity  of  style"  than
they  practised  it.   But  at  the  present  time  the  dread  of  criticism
makes  the  style  of  most  of  our  writers  very  colourless;  and,
unfortunately,  when  anyone  has  a  taste  for  fine  language,  he
generally  thinks  it  necessary  to  invent  it  for  himself,  by  which
means  he  is  pretty  sure  to  be  incomprehensible  and  affected,
without  always  succeeding  in  being  fine.   There  is  much  to  be
said  in  favour  of  using,  in  prose  at  least,  the  metaphors,  the
pathos,  and  the  grandiloquence  to  which  all  the  world  is  accustomed,  and  to  which  all  the  world  attaches  much  the  same
sort  and  amount  of  meaning.   These  things  are,  like  legendary
and  religious  or  national  traditions,  common  ground  for  all
men's  imaginations ;  they  touch  that  second  nature  which  makes
all  who  speak  the  same  language,  kin.   Like  proverbs,  these

common-places have got into common use just because they were apt and happy expressions fitted to bring a meaning home to most people's minds; and a man may easily go farther and fare worse in seeking to replace them by some original turn of his own. When anyone talks, for instance, of " bearding the lion in his den," all the world knows what is meant to be conveyed; and (what is no less important) all the world receives at once an impression of something grand and uncommon. It is true we are so used to the phrase that we may forget to ask whether the lion has got any beard, and may apply it, as Mr. Buckle has done in the case of Queen Elizabeth, to someone who certainly had not. But a writer may very well trust to correcting these little over-sights when he revises his work, whereas certainly no one ever put vigour into his style as it passed through the press.

We know that Mr. Buckle was fond of reading aloud and reciting poetry, and that he was, in after years, fond of reading Shakespeare aloud, as his father had been, from whom, perhaps, he may have acquired the taste. We know also that he greatly admired and studied Burke; and it may be questioned whether a style so brilliant and so clear as his, is not always founded more or less on oratory. The Greeks—the greatest masters of style—produced the greatest orators, and must have formed their ideas of style rather upon spoken than on written speech. The master-pieces of French literature were immediately preceded by a series of great preachers, while in England, and in Germany the drama led the way to the most brilliant periods of the national literature. The wonderful group of English poets (Shelley, Wordsworth, Coleridge, Keats, and Byron, not to speak of lesser lights), who shone on the beginning of the nineteenth century, had been preceded by Garrick, Siddons, Kemble, Kean, Pitt, Fox, Burke, and Sheridan, who must have made it difficult for those who had heard them to forget altogether that language is meant to be spoken. The statement of Mr. Buckle's sister, that in his childhood he was addicted to preaching sermons, is in this point of view of interest in connection with his fondness for Burke and Shakespeare.

It is in the year 1851 that there occurs the first evidence of his having decided on the form his " book " was to take.

" *May* 12, 1851.—Went to talk to Petheram about publishing my History of Civilization, which I hope to bring out next year."

a

But although he must already have made considerable progress even to entertain such a hope, no one will be surprised that it was many years before his book was really ready for publication. During the next three years—from May, 1851, to November, 1854—he was continually occupied in writing and re-writing what subsequently appeared as the first volume of his History. Thus, for example, in 1853, he wrote as chapter iii. what afterwards appeared as chapter v.; in 1854 he re-wrote large portions, such, for instance, as "the beginning of the view of French civilization;" the "view of the influence of England on the French Revolution;" his "account of the connection between science and the confusion of ranks preceding the French Revolution;" and in July, 1854, he mentions that he "had long had in his mind" the "physical laws which made the old civilizations superstitious." At length, in November, 1854, he for the second time thought he had his work ready for publication, and on November 25 he says that he hopes to publish vol. i. of "my work next summer." Six months more, however, passed before he (in July, 1855) "began at length the great task of copying my work for the press;" and a few months later still he "began to revise spelling in MS." Copying, revising, and looking out notes, with some few additions to the original matter, occupied him for two years more after the work was substantially finished, before it actually appeared.

During these six years, which were probably the happiest of his life, he lived in London, at 59, Oxford Terrace, with the exception of occasional short visits to relations at Brighton, Boulogne, &c., and a few short excursions on the Continent. He led a very quiet and regular life, noting down day by day in his Journal, the number of hours during which he wrote or made entries in his Common Place Books; the titles of the books he read; the number of hours he gave to reading, and the number of pages he read in them. All this is put down in the fewest words and the minutest handwriting into which it is possible to compress it, and diversified only by an equally dry and minute statement of the hours at which he rose, took his meals, walked out, &c. Even when he was travelling the Journal is continued in exactly the same form, and never diverges into any remarks on what he saw. One or two examples will be sufficient to give the reader an idea of it.

*Monday, November* 24, 1851, *Brighton.*—Rose at 8. Walked half an hour and then breakfasted. From 10.5 to 12 read German. From 12 to 1.30 read Mill's Analysis of the Mind, i., 66–140. Walked one hour and a half, and from 3.40 to 4.30 made notes from Leigh Hunt's Autobiography. From 4.30 to 6.20 read Lord Lyttleton's Memoirs and Correspondence, i., 246, to vol. ii., p. 580 (the paging of the two volumes is continuous). Dined at 6.30. In bed at 10.20, and to 11.30 read Beattie's Campbell, ii. 61–236."

Another—

" *Saturday, May* 19, 1855, 59, *Oxford Terrace.*—Rose at 8.30. Walked half an hour, and then breakfasted. From 10.40 to 1.50 finished the chapter in which I pass from physical laws to inquire into metaphysical resources. Walked one hour and a half, and from 5.30 to 7.10 finished Transactions of Asiatic Society, iii., pp. 138–585. Dined at 7.15. In bed at 10.40, and to 11.40 read Journal Asiatique, i., serie x., 82–335."

The only entries I have found in any part of his Journals of his having taken the advice of a friend respecting any of his literary work, occur shortly before the publication of his first volume: " *April* 1, 1857.— Altered part of Chapter XII., which I had sent to Miss Shirreff to revise."

And again—" *April* 7, 1857.—Made some alterations in Chapter XIV. suggested by Miss Shirreff."

Even before the publication of his book his own health seems to have shown signs of over-work, and this, along with the gradually failing health of his mother, occasionally caused him some sad forebodings, as we find from some of his letters.

30 June [1856].

" I will not be so affected as to conceal from you that I am a little alarmed, and at times very depressed to think that with such large hopes I have such little powers. My head is at times weak and slightly confused, but it goes off (the feeling, *not* the head—I will have my joke) again directly. They tell me I have nothing to fear, and I am not apprehensive except of my future. To break down in the midst of what, according to my measure of greatness, is a great career—to pass away and make no sign— this, I own, is a prospect which I now, for the first time, see as possible, and the thought of which seems to chill my life as it creeps over me. Perhaps I have aspired too high, but I have had at times such a sense of power—such a feeling of reach and grasp—and, if I may so say, such a command over the realm of thought, that it was no idle vanity to believe that I could do more than I shall now ever be able to effect. I must contract my field—maybe I shall thus survey the ground the better, and

a 2

others may not miss what to me will be an irretrievable loss—since I forfeit my confidence in myself."

From this and from other passages in his letters, as well as from that we have already seen from his Journal, where he sets down his intention to devote himself to a great task, it is evident that the love of fame was very strong in him. There is another passage in a letter written by him from Jerusalem, little more than a month before his death, which throws some additional light on what his feelings were before the publication of his book, but which removes some of the sadness of his early death, as it shows that he himself was able to look back with complacency upon what he had achieved. Speaking of a friend whose health was much impaired, he said (Jerusalem, April 16, 1862), "Poor fellow! It is sad under any circumstances to feel the brain impaired; but how infinitely sadder when there is nothing to compensate the mischief; nothing to show in return. Nothing, if I may so say, to justify it." One cannot help seeing that he felt that in his own case there was, as he expresses it, something "to show in return."

Several of his letters written about this time—shortly before the publication of his book—are very interesting.

Tunbridge Wells, July 27 [1856].

"The air here is really so fine, and my mother is so much improving in it, that I am almost beginning to like the country. A frightful and alarming degeneracy! Pray God that my mind may be preserved to me and that the degradation of taste does not become permanent. I am as well as ever, and, I think, as busy as ever—deeply immersed in comparative anatomy, the dryness of which I enliven by excursions into free will and predestination. I find that physiology and theology correct each other very well, and between the two reason holds her own."

Boulogne sur Mer, 22 December [1856].

"Fortunately, I only feel weak physically, and am as fit for head work as I ever was. This is a great comfort to me, and I am only sorry not to get on with my first volume, though if I were in town I should probably feel the fatigue too much of moving and opening books, and verifying my notes. Dr. Allatt strongly urges my putting aside my first volume for the present. To lose another season would be a great vexation for me; and then too, these early checks make me think mournfully of the future. If I am to be struck down in the vestibule, how shall I enter the temple?"

[London] 19 January [1857].

"Being somewhat deranged, if not altogether mad, at finding I had time to spare, I went out in the afternoon to enjoy myself, which I

accomplished by playing chess for seven hours—and difficult games too.
I have not been so luxurious for four or five years, and feel all the better
for it to-day."

Brighton, 1 March [1857].

" Pray take example from your former state, and also from mine, and
proceed *gradually.* I should never have been as I am now but for an
eager desire to save this season. Indeed, I was getting half ashamed at
constantly putting off what I was perhaps too ready to talk about. However, all this is past, and comparing one month with another, I certainly
am not losing ground, so that I have every right to suppose that diminished
labour will be rewarded with increased strength."

It is also partly to this period of his life that some reminiscences refer, which have been furnished by the lady whose
judgment we have seen so highly valued by Mr. Buckle; and,
although these reminiscences will anticipate what I have to say
of a later period, I shall make no apology for offering them
to the reader as they were written, without either transposition or
alteration:

" It was in the spring of 1854 that we first made acquaintance with Mr.
Buckle. The intimacy became so close, and occupied so large a place in
our lives while it lasted, that it seems strange, on looking back, to realise
how short a time actually witnessed its beginning and its close. His
mother's death, in 1859, his altered mode of life in various ways subsequent to that, and serious illness in our own family, which withdrew us in
great measure from society, had indeed relaxed our intercourse even before
the great close of Death fell upon it; and thus the period during which
we were in the habit of frequently meeting or corresponding was little
more than five years. Three years later, he who had been the life of our
circle lay helpless and friendless among strangers, and the utterances of his
genius were hushed for ever in that silence nothing mortal can break.

" Never, perhaps, among men who have made a name and left their
stamp on the thought of their generation has any one enjoyed so sudden
a blaze and so brief a span of glory. From obscurity he sprang into
sudden fame, and before men had reached the point of dispassionate criticism or appreciation of what he had done he had passed away from among .
us. But with his fame in the world, with the brief record of his life, such
as the unusually scanty materials may allow it to be written, I have
nothing to do here; my purpose is only to comply, so far as I can, with
the request made to me to record a few personal recollections of him, a
few personal impressions of character; contributions, whose insufficiency
none can feel so strongly as I do myself, towards the portraiture of one
who, had he lived, would assuredly have stamped his image in inefface-
able characters on the memory of men.

" A valued friend of ours had known Mr. Buckle and his mother for
some time, and paid us the compliment of thinking we should appreciate

him, unknown as he then was to the world.  Accordingly he arranged a dinner-party for the purpose of making us acquainted.  It was a house in which good conversation was valued, and where consequently guests contributed their best.  Talk flowed on, mostly on literary or speculative subjects, and Mr. Buckle was brilliant and original beyond even what we had been led to expect.  His appearance struck us as remarkable, though he had no pretension to good looks.  He had fine eyes, and a massive, well-shaped head; but premature baldness made the latter rather singular than attractive; and beyond a look of power, in the upper part of the face especially, there was nothing to admire.  He was tall, but his figure had no elasticity; it denoted the languor of the mere student, one who has had no early habit of bodily exercise.  The same fact could be read in his hand, which was well-shaped, but had that peculiar stamp that marks one trained to wield a pen only.  Unfortunately, the delicacy that had kept him as a boy from school teaching had excluded him from school play as well; and while by his own indomitable perseverance he had made up in later years for the one loss, the other was never compensated for, and to the end of his life he could only do with effort, and often could not do at all, things that to other men are mere matters of course.  This want of active power was seen in his gait and movements.  In society his manner was very simple and quiet, though easily roused to excitement by conversation ; and we found later that in intimate intercourse a boyish playfulness often varied his habitually earnest conversation on the great subjects which were never long absent from his thoughts.

" That first meeting led to many others, at our own house or among friends ; quiet evenings or long afternoon talks, in which he sometimes was led to forget the rigid method of his hours.  It was less easy to know his mother, for she was even then an invalid ; but he was very eager to bring us together, and succeeded ere very long in doing so.  The acquaintence thus begun rapidly extended to all our familiar circle, grew into intimacy with other members of our family, and ripened into one of those friendships which are not reckoned by years, but are felt early in their growth to be beyond the power of time to alter.

" In the course of that spring we spent several weeks in the neighbourhood of London, and Mr. Buckle, like other friends, was invited from time to time to spend a day with us.  We did not know then what a rare exception he was making in his habitual life when he came down before luncheon and stayed with us till the late evening.  Pleasant days they were ; and, like a boy out of school, he seemed to enjoy strolling in the garden, rambling in Richmond Park, roaming also in conversation over every imaginable subject, and crowding into the few hours of his visit food for thought, and recollections of mere amusing talk, such as weeks of intercourse with others can seldom furnish.  Deeply do I regret, as I have often had occasion before to regret, that I am utterly devoid of that power which some possess of reproducing conversation ; even immediately afterwards I am unable to recall the exact words, or even to give the full bearing of what has passed ; and at this distance of time I feel that the least attempt to represent what such intercourse was would be colourless and vapid; an abstract of discussion or a dry repetition of anecdotes which *apropos* made delightful. The interest and the charm of conversation are like the fleeting lights and shadows on a landscape, and what they add to the beauty can never be rendered, however faithful the sketch; so perhaps it is no loss to the reader after all that the sketch itself is beyond my power.

"Another and still more unusual break in Mr. Buckle's habits was a day spent with us at the Crystal Palace, then lately opened, which he always said he never should have seen but for our taking him, and which he never re-visited. It was a day more rich in many ways than mortal days are often allowed to be. We were a large party, all intimates, and all ready for enjoyment, and for the kind of enjoyment which the Crystal Palace offered for the first time. It was a lovely summer's day, and the mere drive some miles out of London—for there was no noisy, whistling railway then—was a delight. The art collections were not so full, the flowers not in such rich luxuriance as they have been since; but there was a charm about the fresh beauty of the place, and in the new views of popular enjoyment that it offered, which added to the pleasure then, something which more than loss of novelty has since impaired.

" We were not altogether disabused at that time of the illusions of a new era of peaceful progress which the first Exhibition of 1851 had seemed to inaugurate. It is true that we were even then in the first stage of the Crimean war; but many still believed that the struggle would quickly end; the glorious days, the dark months of suffering yet to come were little anticipated. Still less did any prophetic vision disclose to us the dire future that was to bring the Indian Mutiny, the American war, the battle-fields of Italy and Denmark, of Germany and of France; or tell us that twenty years after nations had met in amity, and seemed pledged to run a new course of friendly emulation, we should be plunging deeper and deeper into the barbarism which turns the highest efforts of man's skill and inventive power towards producing instruments of destruction.

" None shared the illusions of that period more fondly than Mr. Buckle. He thought he had reached philosophically, and could prove as necessary corollaries of a certain condition of knowledge and civilization, the conclusion which numbers held, without knowing why; and it was this train of thought which made the opening of ' The People's Palace ' interesting to him. Habitually sanguine views of the future, combined with intense interest in every democratic movement to heighten his enjoyment of what might not otherwise have been greatly to his taste, for his love of art was not keen. This and a want of sensibility to the beauties of nature, always seemed to me strange deficiencies in a mind so highly imaginative in other respects; but so it was. He said he had been very sensitive to both in earlier youth, and had keenly enjoyed the various galleries as well as the grandest mountain scenery of Europe; but that year by year, as philosophical speculation engrossed him more and more, what only appealed through the outward senses lost its power to move him. It was only for music that he acknowledged never having had feeling or comprehension. But if imagination remained untouched by sound or form, it kindled to everything that roused a human interest. Antiquity, with its revelations of past modes of thought and feeling—historical associations—all moved him deeply; and when moved he turned to poetry as to the natural expression of great thoughts; and it was on that day that I first heard him quote Shakespeare. I knew later how often he did so, when carried beyond the tone of ordinary conversation. We had wandered through the different courts, reproducing in a manner as new then as it was striking, the memorials of the past. From Nineveh to Egypt—Greece—Imperial Rome—Moslem Granada, and Italy through her days of glory to her decline—all had been passed in review; and he then turned, as he loved to do, to the future, with its bright promise of reward to man's genius, and of continued triumph over the blind powers of Nature; and it seemed but a natural transition from his own speaking, as if still uttering his own thoughts, when he took up Hamlet's words: 'What a piece of work is man! How noble in reason! How infinite in faculty! . . . .'

" His voice and intonation were peculiar; his delivery was impassioned, as if another soul spoke through his usually calm exterior; and it has seemed to me of many a familiar passage, that I never had known its full power and beauty till I heard it from his lips.

" In the course of that summer I paid my first visit to Mrs. Buckle, who had taken a cottage at Highgate for a few months. Mrs. Buckle had had a severe illness the previous year, from the effects of which she was still suffering, and from which, indeed, she never entirely recovered. I may almost say that it permanently affected her son also. It had been his first acquaintance with grief, and with anxiety more trying to the health than grief, and in order to fight against them he had forced himself to work; but this double strain on the nerves was too much for an originally delicate organisation, and, when startled by some symptoms that occurred immediately after his mother's illness, he consulted her physician, he was ordered immediate and complete rest; and for the time he entirely recovered. When we made his acquaintance, there was no appearance of ill-health about him, but this attack was the forerunner of the state of utter prostration into which he fell a few years later, when the blow he then feared had actually fallen upon him.

" It was during my visit to Highgate that I made real acquaintance with Mrs. Buckle; and, apart from her being the mother of such a son, she was a very interesting person to know. It is curious how many people there are on whom their own lives seem to have produced no impression; they may have seen and felt much, but they have not reflected upon their own experience, and they remain apparently unconscious of the influences that have been at work around and upon them. With Mrs. Buckle it was exactly the reverse. The events, the persons, the books that had affected her at particular times or in a particular manner, whatever had influenced her actions or opinions, remained vividly impressed on her mind, and she spoke freely of her own experience, and eagerly of all that bore upon her son. He was the joy, even more than the pride of her heart. Having saved him from the early peril that threatened him, and saved him, as she fondly believed, in great measure by her loving care, he seemed twice her own; and that he was saved for great things, to do true and permanent service to mankind, was also an article of that proud mother's creed, little dreaming how short a time he was to be allowed even for sowing the seeds of usefulness. A few months at the utmost had been the limit of separation from her that he had ever known, thus the two lives had grown, as it were, one into the other. The ordinary state of things had been reversed in the family, and Mrs. Buckle had sent her daughters to school, while ill-health kept her son at home. Then, as both the daughters married early, no claim had arisen to interfere with her devotion to him. Once he went abroad alone, intending to stay for some time in Germany; but he was taken ill at Munich, and Mrs. Buckle hurried over to join him. Thus ended the first and last attempt at any real separation.

" When I said above that Mrs. Buckle spoke freely of her own experience, I should add that her conversation was the very reverse of gossip. It was a psychological rather than a biographical experience that she detailed. I rarely remember any names being introduced, and never unless associated with good. Of all her husband's family, the one she spoke of most often was his nephew, Mr. John Buckle, for whom she had great respect and affection. Henry Buckle also made frequent reference to his cousin's opinions, and had the highest esteem for his abilities and confidence in his friendship.

" One point in Mrs. Buckle's early experience that she spoke of more than once to me is worth mentioning, as it exercised probably no small influence later upon her son. She had lived at one time surrounded by persons who held strict Calvinistic opinions, which she felt compelled to adopt under their influence. The intense suffering caused by this she could hardly look back upon with calmness, even at the distance of half a lifetime. Views full of terror and despair, with their wild visions of vengeance and condemnation, which have shattered the peace of many a noble mind, wrought into hers a deep-seated misery which no external circumstances could alleviate, and which only passed away when she had conquered her own freedom through years of thought and study. Hence, when she had a young mind to train, her most anxious care was that no such deadly shadow should come near it. She appeared to me to be a person of a naturally strong religious temperament, and the sentiment remained untouched by the fierce struggle she had gone through. Such are, indeed, always the minds that suffer most cruelly under that dire form of creed which lighter natures profess without ever seeming to feel the awful scope of the tenets their tongues run so glibly over. In her horror of imposed doctrines, she refrained from teaching dogmatically even such views as were full of hope and consolation to herself. Where her son differed from her, she was content to wait. She had boundless faith in the final triumph of truth, and could trust to it, even when her best loved was in question; and that noble sentiment, so prominent in her son's writings, was first inspired by her.  If to this precious influence we add that his taste for metaphysical speculation and his love for poetry were also inherited from his mother, we may judge in some measure how much he owed to her.  And gladly and fondly at all times did he acknowledge the debt.  It was a theme he loved to dwell upon, and it always seemed to me that her presence brought out all that was best in him.  In his manner with her he had playful boyish ways, mixed with exquisite tenderness, and later, when the cloud of fear and sadness had fallen upon their intercourse, the feeling of what the past had been seemed to grow deeper still.  In one letter, written when she was ill, he says, ' You, who can form some idea, and only some, of what my mother has been to me, may imagine how unhappy I am.'

" All the notices of Mr. Buckle's life that have appeared have spoken more or less accurately of his delicate health as a boy, which caused him to be a self-educated man.  His mother spoke of it often, and in what follows I speak only of what I heard from her.  The subject is of importance from its bearing on his after life, which was more or less coloured throughout by the two facts of his self-acquired knowledge, and his comparative isolation ; both caused by his exclusion from school and college.  There was more threatening of evil than of present danger in the attacks which led, under medical advice, to his being taken at an early age away from school.  She was quite aware that many had thought her foolish at the time, and possibly that some believed she had influenced the medical opinion, or exaggerated its import; and she left me the impression that her husband had yielded the point, in part at least, as a concession to her feelings.  She was content to bear any blame that might be thrown upon her in this matter.  The doctors had ordered complete cessation of study; the brain, they said, was to remain absolutely fallow for a time,—and she followed their directions implicitly.  For years she persevered in the system, making her boy's health the first object, but never losing her hope —so well rewarded in the end—that with bodily vigour the mental power would assert itself, and overcome the manifold disadvantages entailed by the loss of regular occupation.  So complete was the idleness, that to keep him quiet at times, she had taught him to knit.  It does not appear from what he used to say of it himself, that he was impatient under this system, or that it was one of painful repression.  It may have been that a certain degree of mental lethargy accompanied the physical weakness, and mercifully shielded the faculties which, had they maintained the activity they displayed in early childhood, might never have reached maturity.

" Before he was trusted with books, his mother ventured to read to him, mostly travels, poetry, or the Bible, and it was from these readings that he dated his passionate love of Shakspeare.  Gradually, as time went on, his health improved, and his mind began to work upon many subjects, but not in any regular or studious fashion.  The newspapers, taken up casually, then began to stir his attention, and the powerful interest of politics grew upon him, and perhaps biassed the course of his after labours. His earliest efforts at connected thought took the shape of speculation on free-trade, the principle of which he seemed to have seized as soon as it was presented to him, in the discussions then rife in all the papers. He had no home bias or assistance in forming his opinion, for his father's views were, as I understood, quite different. On one occasion he even grew so excited on the subject as to sit up at night to write a letter to Sir Robert Peel, which, however, he had not courage to send.

" But the first thing in which he manifested real power was chess, and that to so remarkable a degree, that before he was twenty he had made a name in Europe by his playing. Through life it remained a great source of pleasure to him, and an afternoon devoted to it from time to time was the form of holiday he most often allowed himself.

" Seeing him fairly restored to health and giving promise of ability, his father thought it was time that he should begin life in earnest; and that life was destined by him to be spent, as his own had been, in City business. Mrs. Buckle more than once described to me her dismay when she found it impossible to move her husband from this resolution. Her own tastes were studious, she had watched the growing vigour of her son, and this was not the future she had dreamt for him ; but resistance was vain, and instead of repairing the loss of early education by some course of regular study, he was placed at eighteen in his father's counting-house. At times he looked back with shuddering to the period of weariness that he spent there, but he also owned that it had not been without its use as a strict discipline, after the desultory idleness of his boyhood.[1] What shape his mental activity would have taken had this compulsory drudgery continued, it is vain to conjecture, the restraint was removed by his father's death before any decided bent had shown itself. He was free then to choose his own path, for Mrs. Buckle's authority was exercised only to protect him from the interference of others. She was left in easy circumstances ; there was no necessity for him either to remain in business or to prepare for a profession ; and she resolved that the life and brain so narrowly rescued from destruction, should in their almost unhoped-for maturity, be devoted only to the career he might choose for himself. The first obvious step was to acquire instruction ; and it was proposed that, after some preliminary study, he should go to college, whence the opening to any liberal profession was secure. But the painful sense of his own ignorance made him most reluctant to adopt this course. His whole acquirements then consisting of little more than reading and writing English and proficiency in chess, it seemed indeed hopeless, within such limits of age as University education commonly embraces, to make up for lost time; and his growing sense of power, and the new ambition beginning to stir within him, would have ill-brooked defeat among his contemporaries. He knew that he had not only to acquire

---

[1] I have been lately told that Mr. Buckle only remained three months in the counting house. However short the time he attributed to it the effect spoken of above.

knowledge, but to learn to be taught—one of the most difficult things when the mind has attained a certain point of maturity without having followed any groove of teaching; and, thus hopeless of success upon the too-long neglected beaten tracks, he determined on choosing a path for himself.

"His first step was to persuade his mother to go abroad with him, to give him the opportunity of learning foreign languages; and they accordingly left England and travelled for a considerable time in France, Italy, and Germany. Of this very important period of Mr. Buckle's life there is absolutely no record, and though both of them frequently spoke of that time, I received no distinct impression of its external circumstances, though a strong one of the mental progress he was making. Often as Mrs. Buckle loved to dwell upon that subject, it would have been easy indeed to have learned all we now so much wish to know; but who then could dream that within a few short years we should be recording mere recollections of one so full then of life and hope, the youngest of our little knot of intimates? It was, perhaps, careless, and much do I regret it, but so it was. I learnt the history of his intellect, of the history of his outward life I learnt little. To study he gave himself with ever-increasing ardour. Languages, ancient and modern, were his first object; then history and metaphysics; finally, but not perhaps till later, mathematics and physical science. And as he studied, the bent of his mind became more and more marked; and his repugnance to enter into a profession that must claim his time and thought for other objects more and more decided. It was, as he said to me, a strange revelation to himself when he found that the knowledge he sought ceased to present itself as a means, and became an object in itself. And stronger and stronger the feeling grew in proportion as he cast the slough of his long-enforced ignorance. At first he probably grasped at all he could reach with the mere eager delight of the earnest mind seeking truth, but seeking it vaguely in all directions; gradually, however, as thought expanded, the sense of power grew, and the faculty of original speculation awoke. Then all his seemingly desultory studies were co-ordinated to one definite purpose, and that purpose, the gigantic project of setting forth in one connected view the various paths through which the human intellect has worked its way, and won for our practical life that fulness and freedom which we call civilization; seeking through the records of history to make manifest in the march of human progress that same empire of law which physical science discloses in the material universe.

"This immense undertaking appears to have dawned upon his mind ere yet he had completed the studies that were to supply the blank of early instruction; and a few years after he left England an ignorant boy he had begun in resolute earnestness to prepare for the work to which he devoted his whole after life, with unswerving conviction and energy of purpose. And if, in thus early framing such a scheme, we may think we see something of the vaulting ambition and sanguine self-confidence of untried youth, it was with no youthful neglect of means, no hasty or scanty preparation, that he contemplated beginning his task. And as he went on, no man was perhaps ever more fully prepared for labour on so extensive a field. He was reproached after the publication of his first volume with errors in this or that particular subject; and from Bacon to our own day the same has been said of all men who survey wide fields of knowledge to seek out the principles that underlie many different branches, or that may overarch the limited truths which seemingly keep them divided. Such men can rarely, if ever, possess the thorough knowledge of the specialist in the one department to which he devotes himself. It was necessary for Mr. Buckle not to linger over the details of science, but to range over extensive provinces; to master, if possible, every fruitful principle; to learn the methods of science and philosophy, in order to trace their influence on the progress of knowledge and civilization; and to find the basis of those wide generalisations on which his theory rested. Accordingly, within these limits there was perhaps no branch of science that he had not studied, of which he had not followed the history and tracked the important threads of discovery.

" In metaphysical research his purpose was the same; from the earliest Greek to the latest German he had read with this aim of seizing in each system the master thought which had influenced the minds of men, which had formed schools, or tended to shape the practical philosophy or political life of nations. In literature, in like manner, it was no mere scholarship that he sought or valued; but he desired to trace the peculiar development of intellect through the various forms of different languages and different social conditions. And for this purpose he made himself acquainted with most of the languages of Europe, and had thoroughly mastered, for the purposes of reading at least, all, whether ancient or modern, that possess a literature to be studied.[1] Of eastern languages Hebrew was the only one he had acquired. He always looked forward to the time when he should have leisure to study Sanscrit, which his intense interest in what a great master of the subject has called ' the science of language ' made him earnestly desire to learn. In our own literature he was profoundly versed, and though he seemed to read for the matter only, he could appreciate the prose as acutely as any who make literary criticism their principal aim. Pages of our great prose writers were impressed on his memory. He could quote passage after passage with the same ease that others quote poetry, while of poetry itself he was wont to say, ' it stamps itself on the brain.' Truly did it seem that without effort on his part, all that was grandest in English poetry had become, so to speak, a part of his mind. Shakespeare ever first, then Massinger, and Beaumont and Fletcher, were so familiar to him that he seemed ever

---

[1] Mr. Buckle had extreme difficulty in acquiring a foreign pronunciation. French, which he could speak fluently, it was painful to hear him attempt. In German, my own unpractised ear could not have detected this defect, but he used himself to laugh over his signal failure in speaking Dutch after he hoped that he was rather successful. Travelling in a railway-carriage in Holland, he ventured to try his powers of conversation with a gentleman, who, after a time, remarked that he was sorry he did not know Italian!

ready to recall a passage, and often to recite it, with an intense delight in
its beauty which would have made it felt by others even naturally indifferent.

"Whatever the subject of his study, it was always as part of the history
of human development that it acquired its chief interest to him.   Literature, science, philosophy, however engrossing singly, occupied him as
part of a great whole; and the mode of co-ordinating all those various
branches of knowledge was his chief concern.   Accordingly, all the great
masters of method had been his especial study, from Aristotle, Bacon, and
Descartes, to Comte and Mill.   The latter, of all living writers, he held in
highest esteem, and through his own work may be traced that great
thinker's influence, together with that of Comte, to whose faults he was
far from blind, but whose merits he had earnestly appreciated at a time
when he was little known in England.

"It may seem that in thus speaking of Mr. Buckle's aims and studies
I am departing from the sphere of mere personal recollections to which I
had limited my contribution to the present volume, but this is not really
so.   With himself and with his mother, conversation continually turned
upon these matters.   It is the impression left by those long hours of intimate intercourse that I strive, however feebly, to reproduce, and when I
remember that of all he hoped to achieve, an unfinished introduction—one
truncated fragment of the fair pyramid he trusted to erect—is all the world
has before it to pronounce judgment upon, I feel that some record of those
towering hopes and of the assiduous labours by which he thought to realise
them, is not out of place in a friend's personal recollections of him.

"Those were pleasant, quiet days in the little Highgate cottage !   Days
of unvarying routine, but a routine in which walks over a beautiful country,
and long evening hours of talking, and reading out loud, had their place,
and there seemed a new fulness of life to myself in coming in contact with
the overflowing vitality of Mr. Buckle's intellect.   He was then writing his
first volume, which was not published till nearly three years later.   Sometimes at his mother's suggestion he would read parts of it to us in the
evening, and there are passages of that volume which still read to me like
a chapter from that old life so utterly past and gone !

"The home routine with which I then became first acquainted, was
ordered with a view to study and to health.   He believed extreme regularity to be no less essential, in his own case at any rate, for the latter than
for the former.   Every hour was systematically disposed of, whether for
work, exercise, or relaxation; and he so carefully respected the rules he
laid down for himself, that they were in very rare cases departed from.
His health—always requiring care—made many things important to him
which others can easily dispense with, and thus gave an appearance of
somewhat effeminate ease to his daily life; but I am convinced that he
acted in these matters upon principle, though he may have been mistaken.
Exercise was essential to him.   He walked every morning for a quarter of
an hour only before breakfast, and used to say that having adopted this custom upon medical advice, it had grown such a necessary habit, that he could

not work till he had been in the air. Heat or cold, sunshine or rain, made no difference to him either for that morning stroll, or for the afternoon walk which had its appointed time and length, and which he rarely would allow himself to curtail, either for business or visits. He used to say that he did not know the sensation of mental fatigue, that he could have gone on working hours beyond his fixed time without any *immediate* discomfort; but previous illness had left its warning, and he knew that he dared not overtask his brain; thus he worked with his watch on the table, and resolutely laid aside his occupation when the appointed hour came. After his duly-measured walk he returned to his library to read till dinner-time; and he always retired early in the evening, reading again for a certain time, but not far into the night, for he required many hours' rest, and was fortunately a good sleeper. One of his curiously minute habits, which he appears never to have omitted for years, was that of recording in a diary the exact manner in which the day had been spent, even to the number of pages he had read in a given time. No doubt this practice was begun as a check upon early desultory habits, and was continued perhaps almost mechanically.

"He was a smoker, and though a very moderate one as compared with many, it was so imperious a necessity with him to have his three cigars every day, that he said he could neither read, write, nor talk, if forced to forego them, or even much to overpass the usual hour for indulging in them; and as he could not smoke when walking, the effort being too great for him, he never went to stay in any house where smoking in-doors was objected to. More than one house that never tolerated a cigar before, bore with it for his sake. But at the time I am speaking of he rarely paid any visits except to his own relations, to one of his sisters, married to Dr. Allatt, and living at Boulogne, with whom he and his mother generally spent some weeks every year; or to a sister of Mrs. Buckle's at Brighton, where, I believe, he became known in society earlier than in London. He also stayed several times in the country with some of my family, but it was not till after his mother's death that he visited more generally, and seemed glad to escape from his lonely home to be among those who knew and valued him enough to let him follow his own ways. When there were children in any house that he frequented, he noticed them very much, and they grew fond of him. His strong interest in education made him the confidant and counsellor of more than one anxious mother. The child he was most attached to was one of his own nephews, whose great promise he often spoke of; and the poor boy's death, which happened, soon after his mother's, grieved him most deeply.

"The method by which a man works is always interesting as an indication of character; it may be well, therefore, to mention what I remember of Mr. Buckle's. It was chiefly remarkable for careful systematic industry and punctilious accuracy. His memory appeared to be almost faultless; yet he took as much precaution against failure as if he dared not trust it. He invariably read with a paper and pencil in his hand, making copious references for future consideration. How laboriously this system was acted upon, can be appreciated only by those who have seen his note-books, in which the passages so marked during his reading were either copied or referred to under proper heads. Volume after volume was thus filled, written with the same precise neatness that characterised his MS. for the press; ranging over every subject to which his omnivorous appetite for knowledge had led him, and indexed with care, so that immediate reference might be made to any topic. But carefully as these extracts and references were made, there was not a quotation in one of the copious notes that accompanied his work that was not verified by collation with the original from which it was taken.

" Mr. Buckle had made a very close study of style with a view to forming his own. He had not only analysed the styles of our best English writers, but carefully compared the peculiarities and merits of the best French writers with our own. He was, accordingly, a severe critic, and it was a valuable lesson to hear him dissect an ill-constructed sentence, and point out how the meaning could have been brought out with full clearness by such or such changes. While studying style practically for his own future use, he had been in the habit of taking a subject, whether argument or narrative, from some author, Burke for instance, and to write himself, following of course the same line of thought, and then compare his passage with the original, analysing the different treatment so as to make it evident to himself when, and how, he had failed to express the meaning with the same vigour, or terseness, or simplicity. Force and clearness were his principal aim, and accordingly in his book, though eloquent passages are rare, there is not a feeble page, nor a sentence that requires a second glance to be understood. 'It is the most perfect writing I know for a philosophical work,' was the remark made to me by one of the most eminent men of our day, and I was proud to find such an opinion agreeing with my own.

" Industry and patience were the two qualities on which he prided himself, and which he unceasingly preached to others. In speaking of what he had done or intended doing there was little said or implied of confidence in superior power; systematic work and patient thought were, he said, the great engines by which he had conquered difficulties. I have before me now a letter that he wrote to a friend, who had consulted him about a projected work of wide scope, and requiring no small knowledge; it is characteristic both of his way of looking at an arduous undertaking, and also of his prompt kindness in responding to the call for advice. He writes :—' I shall keep your MS. (the scheme of the work in question) till I see you, and I want to turn over the subject in my mind. At present I see no difficulty which you cannot conquer. Great preliminary knowledge will have to be acquired ; but, speaking hastily, I should say ten or twelve years would suffice. The main thing will be to study *economically*, letting no time run to waste. I need not assure you that all that I know, and have, and can, will be at your disposition.' Nor was this an idle form of words. Nothing roused his sympathy more completely than the efforts of another mind to reach or to spread knowledge. This was to him the great pursuit of life, and he wearied not in giving

help to any who sought his aid with an equally earnest spirit. Time
books, advice, the result of his own studies, all would be freely given for
such a purpose. At a time when he was most fully engaged he voluntarily undertook the revision of a friend's MS., laying aside his own occupation for a considerable time daily, to go through a minute and tedious
labour of criticism. Mental sympathy had been to himself a blessing of
every hour; he sought it frankly, and seemed to depend on receiving it
with an almost *naïve* confidence which had a charm of its own, though it
perhaps denoted his scanty dealings with the world. But he also gave
sympathy in full measure, and his manner of showing it was among the
things that made his friendship as valuable as his society was delightful.

"Doubtless his mother's influence, the feeling of all he owed to her
intellectually, as well as for her devoted care and love, led him to value
the mental sympathy and companionship of women. He had learnt
through her a keen appreciation of what their peculiar intellectual
qualities—so commonly neglected—ought to do for society, and the feeling which prompted his choice of a subject, the only time he ever spoke
in public, was easy to be understood by all who had watched mother and
son together. But facts were strangely distorted when it was said that he
did not care for men's society because he was spoiled by women, who fed
his vanity. I can answer for the first of these statements not being true,
for I know how he delighted in the conversation of men who were the
least likely to concede a single point to him except in fair argument.
With regard to the latter, it is somewhat too vague to be met. I would
only remark, that if a man who has nothing of that brilliant exterior,
which might dazzle a certain class of women, is a favourite among us, it
must be for some qualities that we recognise as worthy, and do not often
find among men. Women may, and too often do, to their own bitter cost,
utterly mistake a man's character, because large phases of his life are
hidden from them. They may be as little able to estimate his virtues as
his vices; and, in ignorance of the world, are liable to condemn too
severely as well as to praise too highly. But in what comes within their
ken they are not so easily deceived, for women are close observers, and
they more often pity and forgive the faults of men than remain blind to
them. When, therefore, a mere student is welcomed and valued among
women, we may be sure there is a solid foundation for it. In Mr.
Buckle's case one attaching quality may have been extreme gentleness,
which, when united with power, whether mental or physical, always has
a peculiar charm for women. Whatever the cause, however, of Mr.
Buckle being a favourite with women (a fact generally adduced, I remark,
by other men as a sort of reproach), he did not owe it to the halo of fame,
which is supposed to be so irresistible to our hero-worshipping sex; for
his most valued female friendships were, with one exception, formed before
his name was known to the world; and I may venture to assert that the
intercourse with those friends was on that footing of perfect confidence
and freedom which excludes the base idea of flattery as completely as
any other treachery to friendship; and letters might be published proving

b

the candid spirit in which he met criticism freely offered, and even grave
disapproval, expressed with all the frankness of honest regard.

"Mr. Buckle's rigid mode of life, his frequent refusal to break through
it for any of the claims of society, was often the subject of comment; and
he was not spared the reproach of selfishness, so lavishly brought against
all, whose self requires something different from the self of those who are
criticising. I am writing no panegyric, and could not if I would decide
how far he really was amenable to the reproach; but I will say that in
this respect, at any rate, his selfishness was of a rare and high order,
and might rather be called by a better name. He would not allow anything to interfere with the course he had laid down for himself; but that
course was one which he felt to be worth his best efforts, and he knew
how much care was requisite to enable him to sustain those efforts. And
if he set aside the claims of society and the pleasure of others, he set
aside no less rigidly things that afforded the highest gratification to himself. For instance, from the time he began to write he never allowed
himself to play a match at chess. One that he had played against
the famous Löwenthal, and in which he won four games out of seven,
took more out of him, he said, than he would give to any such frivolous
triumph again. I happened to be staying in the same house with him—I
think in 1858—when earnest solicitation was made to him to play a match
at some great chess congress that was to take place shortly, and I witnessed
the severe struggle it was to refuse it. I mention this as an illustration of
the principle on which his rigid habit was founded: namely, the determination to shape his own life, as far as an originally feeble constitution
would allow; never, as he said himself, to be the slave of habits such as
men drift into without knowing why, but to avail himself of the whole
force of habit to work out his own purposes. And the purpose of his life
was his book. It had been the dream of his youth, gradually assuming
shape through years of solitary study; it was the task of his manhood,
for which every other object that might have tempted his ambition was
renounced, and it dwelt in his last conscious thoughts when life, with all
its unfulfilled hopes and baffled schemes, was passing away! Though at
the time I am speaking of years seemed to stretch out before him, he
knew that his tenure of health was such as to make many a sacrifice
necessary in order to attain that object, and he was willing to make every
sacrifice except that of his mother's comfort. To conform himself to his
mode of life was no sacrifice to her, though many may doubtless have
thought so; but they forgot that she also lived for his book with a singleness of devotion which was touching to witness.

"This intense earnestness of pursuit was part of his power. It might
offend the idle, or occasionally weary at a dinner-table, where lighter
subjects of conversation would have been more acceptable; but it
seized upon those who lived with him more intimately, and it may safely
be said that no mind at all alive to intellectual impressions, ever was
brought into much communion with his, without being in some small
measure interpenetrated with his spirit; without feeling the grandeur and

power of truth, and the littleness of mere worldly success compared with the lofty objects to which the lover of knowledge may aspire. His life was a standing protest against the low views of knowledge which so widely prevail in this country, which taint our systems of education from the highest to the lowest, and gauge every exertion of man's intellect by its market price. What the real worth of Mr. Buckle's speculations, and whether he overrated them or not, is not for me to examine; but I do know that having, as he believed, attained some valuable principles, some glimpses of truth not hitherto recognised, such a possession was to him the call to an apostleship in as true and earnest a sense as ever was realised by missionary or philanthropist. He believed, as they do, that men should not ' put their light under a bushel,' but rather so toil as to place it where it shall light up the dark corners of the earth. Widely, indeed, did he differ from them as to the means of doing good among men, but he was not the less kindled by the noble desire that by his labours he might leave the world better than he found it.

" I have wandered far from my visit to Mrs. Buckle at Highgate. Our life there was too quiet to afford anything to relate, and impressions of character, not events, really constitute all I have to recall. When we met again, it was in London; and the next time I was staying with them it was there. They had been settled for some years in the house in Oxford Terrace which he occupied till he left England on his last fatal journey. It was small, but all the space at the back had been built over, making one good-sized room, lighted by a skylight, and this was Mr. Buckle's library. There were indeed books all over the house, but in this room was arranged the largest part of his splendid collection, perhaps the largest any private student ever made in a few years for his own use. For his library was for use only ; he did not seek rare editions, or any of the curiosities of literature that have such a charm for the book collector, and he was often content with a cheap second-hand copy, and delighted with a bargain at a bookstall. His tastes would naturally have led him to form a library, but his health made it almost a necessity. His high-strung nerves required absolute quiet and privacy while he worked, and reading in public libraries was almost unendurable to him. This reminds me to notice a point on which some slighting remarks have been made about his book. He is reproached with never quoting original documents, ranging among well-known authors and neglecting the sources of historical knowledge. I will answer first what my remarks above recalled to my mind, that he confessed he never could have borne the fatigue of studying MSS. The effect upon his sight, and through the eyes on the brain, was such that a short time of such work would have unfitted him for anything, therefore he doubly rejoiced to feel that no such labour was needful for his purpose. It was not tried and laid aside, but deliberately neglected, because printed matter supplied in abundance all the materials he wanted. It was not his province to examine into the accuracy of this or that particular document, or to search for proofs for or against the received version of individual conduct or national transactions. All he wanted was the great outline of history, which furnished him with the data for some of his speculations, and the proof of others. It was the broad history of nations that he sought to illustrate, and erudite researches would have afforded him no assistance. The accusation has been brought against him as a slight upon his literary industry; but it only proves that those who brought it knew neither the man, nor the scope of his work.

"Mr. Buckle was very fond of society, and, as long as his mother's health permitted her to do so, she gathered pleasant parties in their house, where talk flowed freely, and wit and wisdom were equally appreciated. Later, when Mrs. Buckle could no longer receive, he had occasional dinner-parties of men alone; but the numbers were larger, and I used to hear from himself and others that they lacked the charm of the former social meetings. The brilliancy of Mr. Buckle's conversation was too well known to need mention; but what the world did not know, was how entirely it was the same among a few intimates with whom he felt at home as it was at a large party where success meant celebrity. His talk was the outpouring of a full and earnest mind, it had more matter than wit, more of book-knowledge than of personal observation. The favourite maxim of many dinner-table talkers, ' *Glissez, mais n'appuyez pas,*' was certainly not his. He loved to go to the bottom of a subject, unless he found that his opponent and himself stood on ground so different, or started from such opposite principles, as to make ultimate agreement hopeless, and then he dropped or turned the argument. His manner of doing this unfortunately gave offence at times, while he not seldom wearied others by keeping up the ball, and letting conversation merge into discussion. He was simply bent on getting at the truth, and if he believed himself to hold it, he could with difficulty be made to understand that others might be impatient while he set it forth. On the other hand, it is fair to mention that if too fond of argument, and sometimes too prone to self-assertion, his temper in discussion was perfect; he was a most candid opponent, and an admirable listener.

"The faults of his conversation, such as they were, might be traced, like many other peculiarities, to his secluded life. He did not possess that knowledge of society which comes from practical intercourse with men, and which often gives such zest to the talk of barristers or politicians, or even mere men of the world. He had lived too much alone, or at least his graver life had been too solitary. He knew most of what was written, he often did not know enough of what was said and done. He was versed in the tenets of philosophical and religious and political sects, as they have existed and worked in the past; he was not always sufficiently awake to the various forms of life and opinion existing around him. He had not been forced, as most men are, in the actual contact of the working world, to see, and learn to appreciate at their real value, influences foreign to his own life. And what his own experience did not teach him, he could not learn through others, as he might have done had he possessed that wide circle of familiar acquaintance which surrounds a man who has passed through school and college, and belongs to a profession or a party. This social disadvantage, entailed by his early ill-health, told even in graver matters; and some things by which he gave offence would perhaps never have been said or done had he lived in the close intimacy of school or college friends, where the frankness of boyish days often lives as a privilege long after it has ceased to be the natural habit of life.

"In many ways, the influence of self-education and of a retired home-life was apparent in the tone of Mr. Buckle's opinions and character. Had it been possible to write a real biography of him, it must have afforded the most interesting illustrations of two important points—the influence of self-training on a powerful mind, and the influence of a mother on her son. As it is, those who knew them can feel how much there was of both, but have no means of making it evident to others. Having won everything by his own exertions, and never tried his strength against others, he sometimes appeared to underrate, sometimes to overrate, the common average of ability and of attainments. Accordingly, in his work we occasionally find points elaborately dwelt upon and enforced by repeated quotation, which few would have been inclined to dispute; and occasionally, on the other hand, a belief in the ready acceptance of some principle which the majority of men are still far from acknowledging. A man who had gone through the normal routine of education and of life would not, even with half his ability, have fallen into these mistakes.

"On another point he judged others too much by his own standard. To himself, recognising a truth and accepting it as a principle to be acted upon, were one and the same thing; and I believe it was his ignorance of the world that made it hard for him to admit how feebly in general men are stirred by an appeal to their understanding. The very common inconsistency between opinions and practice which perhaps saves as much evil in one direction as it causes in another, was so foreign to his own mind that he often failed to allow for it. The profession, for instance, of intolerant views in religion or politics made him look upon the persons who professed them, as if they were prepared to carry them into practice, as perhaps they might have done in times when the symbols of their religious or political allegiance had a living power among men. He gave one signal proof of his uncompromising mode of judging matters of this kind in his severe strictures on Sir John Coleridge,[1] which caused deep pain to many of his friends, and to none more than to myself. Every form of intolerance roused the intolerant spirit in him; for he could not forgive that anyone should pretend in dealing with his fellow-men to abridge that perfect freedom of thought and speech which, to himself, was the most precious inheritance of an era of knowledge and civilisation.

"On one other point only I have known Mr. Buckle to depart from his habitually indulgent view of the conduct of others. This was extrava-

---

[1] In a review upon J. Stuart Mill's work on Liberty, published in Fraser's Magazine, May 1859. The earnest letters of remonstrance that I wrote to him at the time were, I suppose, destroyed; his answers I kept, and portions of them at least will be published here; they give what he considered his own justification; they also illustrate the spirit in which he met opposition.

gance or disorder in money matters. A man who could endure debt was
to him not only wanting in rigid uprightness, but almost incurred his contempt for the unmanly feebleness he thought it indicated. His strong
feeling on this subject, and his adherence to the maxims of political
economy as regards charity, were perhaps partly the cause of his being
considered close, and fond of money. It requires a very accurate
acquaintance with a man's private affairs to substantiate or rebut such an
accusation, and it does not concern me to do either. I speak of my own
recollection only, and I have known of kind and liberal offers made by
Mr. Buckle, which, in the case I allude to, were repeatedly urged in spite
of refusal. It must also be remembered that his delicate health enhanced
the value of money to him by rendering a certain scale of comfort and even
of luxury so indispensable that without it no mental exertion would have
been possible. At any rate, if he loved money, he loved knowledge more.
With his abilities none can doubt that golden success might have been his
had he gone to the bar, for instance, or turned his attention to any lucrative employment; but he deliberately preferred the moderate independence
which left him free to follow his own pursuits. And never yet did such
pursuits pay any man the money's worth of the time he has devoted to
them. The public hearing now and then of large sums paid to an author,
straightway forms a magnificent notion of the profits of literary labour, and
yet never, perhaps, except to the successful novelist, was literary labour
profitable. Even in the few cases which form apparent exceptions to this
rule, the element of time is left out in the popular estimate. But if we
consider the men who alone are capable of producing a great work, and
remember what such men might probably have made in business or in a
profession during the ten, fifteen, or twenty years of life that have been
spent in studious preparation, and in the slow ripening of thought and
speculation, it is evident that no work of real value ever can find its money
price. The writer may be paid in coin more precious to him than gold
and silver, but at least let no such man be reproached with a sordid love
of wealth.

"In the summer of 1855 I had promised to pay a visit to Mrs. Buckle at
Hendon, where they had moved according to their annual custom of
leaving London early in the season; their choice of a summer residence
being governed generally by consideration of an easy journey for her, and
easy access for him to his library whenever some fresh supply of books
should be needed. But my visit was hindered by Mrs. Buckle being
taken seriously ill. His letters at that time were full of alarm for her and
of general discouragement; he was not strong enough to react against depression, and it was fortunate, therefore, that in the ordinary state of
things after this illness, he got used to his mother's invalid condition, and
only at times was roused from his false security by some fresh symptom.
I went abroad for some months, and we did not meet till the winter; the
painful change in Mrs. Buckle was very apparent then to unaccustomed eyes.

"In 1856 he began to prepare his first volume for publication. Whether
this volume should or should not appear alone, had been the subject

of much discussion, and it was Mrs. Buckle's earnest wish, founded
on her own sense of her precarious term of life, that finally prevailed.
His own intention had been at least to finish the Introduction before he
gave any portion of his work to the public. He felt no impatience about
it. Engrossed with his labour, and confident of power, he was content to
wait. In the words of one, who, though strenuously opposed to his opinions,
yet paid a graceful tribute to his memory, 'he knew that whenever he
pleased he could command personal distinction, but he cared more for his
subject than for himself. He was content to work with patient reticence,
unknown and unheard of, for twenty years, thus giving evidence of qualities as rare as they are valuable.' [1]   But his mother knew too well that
she could not afford to wait. During the spring and summer of 1856 she
was more ill, and had a more general sense of failing than she would allow
him to know. She kept up her courage and her spirits for his sake, lest
he should be diverted from his work. I was staying with them for a short
time at Tunbridge Wells, and daily she betrayed to me her knowledge that
her days were numbered, and her anxiety to see her son take his right
place in the world. She had had no vulgar ambition for him; she had
been content that he should hide his bright gifts in their quiet home so
long as the serious purpose of his life required it, but now that it was
partly attained, that a portion of his work was ready, she grew eager to
see those gifts acknowledged before she herself went forth to be no more
seen on earth. Chapter by chapter, almost page by page, had that first
volume been planned with her, commented by her; every speculation as
it arose talked over with her; and now her mind was oppressed with the
fear that she might never know how those pages, so unutterably precious
to her, would be welcomed by those whose welcome would crown her
beloved with fame. Yet, to spare him, she never would betray in his
presence the real secret of her growing impatience; only when we were
alone she would say to me, 'Surely God will let me live to see Henry's
book;' and she did live to see it, and to read the dedication to herself, the
only words there that she was unprepared to meet. Mr. Buckle told me
he bitterly repented the rash act of laying the volume before her to enjoy
her surprise and pleasure; for he was alarmed at her agitation. Even the
next day, when showing it to me, she could not speak, but pointed with
tears to the few words that summed up to her the full expression of his
love and gratitude. She thus saw her ardent wish gratified, and her impatience was but too well justified. The second volume was dedicated to
her memory alone !

    " But to return to the motives which determined Mr. Buckle to publish
a single volume. I wish to speak of them, for probably these were never
understood; but to do so I must say a few words of the book itself. The
plan of his Introduction required that, after laying down the principles of
his method, and enumerating the laws he believed to have governed the

_____

[1] Froude lecture, delivered at the Royal Institution, February, 1864, and published
in the volume of Short Studies on Great Subjects.

course of human progress, he should illustrate these principles from the history of those nations in which certain tendencies had predominated. The first volume—the only one then ready—contained his theory. The histories of Spain and of Scotland were to furnish a portion of the requisite illustrations of the theory, and the remainder were to be drawn from the social condition and intellectual development of Germany on the one hand, and of the United States on the other. For the portion relative to Spain and Scotland he was prepared; but he held that he was not competent to work out the other without spending some time in the countries to be studied. This, however, would have involved a lengthened separation from his mother, which, in her condition, he could not encounter; and this consideration finally decided him to publish what was ready, and wait for the remainder till he should be able to accomplish his purpose. Friends combated his view of the necessity of this delay; they reminded him of the mass of information he had collected and might yet collect from books; but he was not to be moved. The United States especially could not, as he believed, be studied thoroughly through books, and no argument could induce him to hurry over his work or be content with any less laborious investigation than he himself felt to be desirable. Neither would he leave England in the precarious state of his mother's health. He would wait and work, if needs be, for years; he had work enough before him, but he would not slur it over, nor, on the other hand, bring upon her and himself the bitter anxiety of a long separation. Thus it happened that the materials which he considered necessary for completing the mere introduction to his work never were collected; for when he was, all too soon, free to follow his own wishes, he was too much broken down to travel for any serious purpose. And of a plan so gigantic an unfinished introduction was all he lived to accomplish. It has been judged as a work—it was only a fragment. Of the body of the work itself, for which he had amassed considerable materials, he wrote nothing, though doubtless some fragments found among his papers, and since given to the public, were roughly sketched out for it.

"It was in the summer of 1856 that Mr. Buckle determined to publish his first volume. So little did the sagacity of publishers foresee its success, that no admissible offer was made for it, and he resolved on publishing it at his own cost. He did so, and the volume appeared early in 1857.

"Sanguine as had been the anticipations of friends who had seen the MS., the result far exceeded them. His circle of acquaintance had been gradually enlarging, still it was a comparatively small one, and strictly private; he did not till some time after belong even to a club. He had never tried his strength in reviews or magazines; once only, to help a friend, he had offered to review a work, but the offer of the unknown writer was refused, and thus not a line from his pen had ever been seen till this volume of 800 pages, purporting to be the first of a long work, took the public by surprise. He sprang at once into celebrity; and singularly enough, considering the nature of the book, he attained not merely to literary fame, but to fashionable notoriety. To his own great amusement, he became the lion of the season ; his society was courted, his library besieged with visitors, and invitations poured in upon him, even from houses where philosophical speculation had surely never been a passport before. To himself, as to the public, his previous obscurity added to the glare of his sudden triumph ; but it is pleasant to remember that he was unaltered by his changed position. Such as he was before, such he remained afterwards. He enjoyed it, indeed, freely and frankly, all the more, probably, because no school or college competition, no professional struggles, had given him before an assured place among his contemporaries. He had been proudly confident in his own power, and he felt a natural pleasure in seeing it for the first time publicly acknowledged ; but his mind was too earnestly bent on what he yet hoped to achieve to dwell with complacent satisfaction on the social distinction won by past exertion ; and in the first flush of his triumph he refused the most flattering invitations to different parts of the country, in order to spend the few weeks of absence from his mother with friends in a small country parsonage, where his time was divided between study, playing and talking with children, and long evening conversations, into which he threw the same richness and animation as if the most brilliant circle had been gathered round him.

" It was the same the following summer (1858), when I was again, and for the last time, staying in the same house with him. The intervening months, while he was enjoying the new and valuable society to which his book had introduced him, entering into correspondence with eminent men at home and abroad, preparing a second edition which was rapidly called for, and working at his second volume—these months so spent had been very bright and happy but for the increasing anxiety about his mother. She had now given up all society, even intimate friends rarely saw her, and gradually she was unable more and more to join in any conversation with him, or even to hear him talk. Some of his letters during this time were full of gloomy despondency ; then again he seemed to persuade himself that she would yet recover. It was during a bright interval that we met, as I said above, and I never saw him more full of fun and spirits, more eager about his work, or more ready to take an interest in that of others. In the following spring the long-dreaded blow fell at last ; Mrs. Buckle died, and he seemed stunned as by an unexpected calamity. But it is needless to dwell upon that dark time, especially as I scarcely saw him. After a while he went among strangers, but it was long before he could bear to be with those who had been the chosen companions of happier days. In some painful letters he expressed that feeling so strongly as to make us cease to press him.

" From that time I have little to record. He prepared and published his second volume, he returned to the world, he went more into general society, and accepted invitations into the country now that no home considerations fettered his movements ; but our old frequent intercourse had been altered, partly by circumstances in our own family, which made us live more retired, while he was a great deal out of town ; and all through

both the summers of 1860 and 1861, wandering about from place to place
in hopes of recovering the effect of over-work that he was suffering from.
He had been severely tried by preparing his second volume for the press,
and would not rest till it was done. It was published early in 1861, and
then it seemed for a time as if he could never rally working-power again.

"In the autumn of that year he began to talk of going to the United
States, but all who cared for him felt that he was unfit for a journey which
was to be connected with serious study; and partly to divert him from it,
a friend suggested Egypt, that he had often wished to visit. The plan
delighted him from the first; his arrangements were soon made, and vainly
did we protest against some of them, which we felt were incompatible with
his state of health. He dined with us the last night but one that he passed
in London, and we parted, never to meet again!

"The story of that fatal journey has been often told. At first all went
well. He wrote little, but his few letters spoke of intense enjoyment.
We measured the benefit he had derived by the physical exertion he was
able to make, and especially by his willingly encountering the extreme
fatigue of crossing the Desert of Sinai. Such an exertion was so contrary
to all his former habits, that his successful accomplishment of that expedition seemed like the promise of renewed and more vigorous youth. The
spring of 1862 came; we looked forward to the pleasure of seeing him
among us again, and to the far deeper pleasure of seeing him resume his
interrupted labours, when the fatal news reached us, and we knew that a
solitary grave in the far East had closed over all our hopes—over all his
visions of earthly fame!"

———————

We must now return to the epoch of the publication of the
first volume of the History of Civilization in England. Early in
the year 1857, the author made arrangements with Mr. Parker,
the publisher, to publish his work on commission, and at length,
on June 9, 1857, he entered in his Journal: "Looked into my
Volume I., of which the first complete and bound copy was sent
to me this afternoon." His own account of the intended scope
of the book, and his own estimate of various passages in it, have
been preserved in several letters and in one or two passages of
his Journal:

"The fundamental ideas of my book are: 1st. That the history
of every country is marked by peculiarities which distinguish it from
other countries, and which, being unaffected, or slightly affected, by individual men, admit of being generalised. 2nd. That an essential preliminary to such generalisation is an enquiry into the relation between
the condition of society and the condition of the material world surrounding such society. 3rd. That the history of a single country (such as
England) can only be understood by a previous investigation of history

generally. And the object of the Introduction is to undertake that investigation.

. . . . .

"I may fairly say that I have bestowed considerable thought on the general scheme, and I think I could bring forward arguments (too long for a letter) to justify the apparently disproportionate length of the notices of Burke and Bichat.[1] As to the French Protestants, I am more inclined to agree with you, though even here it is to be observed that general historians represent the struggle between Protestants and Catholics as *always* a struggle between toleration and intolerance; and as I assert that the triumph of the Catholic party in France has increased toleration, I thought myself bound to support with full evidence what many will deem a paradoxical assertion. . . . . I have also worked this part of the subject at the greater length because I thought it confirmed one of the leading propositions in my fifth chapter, to the effect that religious tenets do not so much affect society as they are affected by it. I wished to show how much more depends on circumstance than on dogma. It was therefore useful to prove that though the Catholics are theoretically more intolerant than the Protestants, they were, in France, practically more tolerant, and that this arose from the pressure of general events."[2]

. . . . .

"I want my book to get among the mechanics' institutes and the *people;* and to tell you the honest truth, I would rather be praised in popular and, as you rightly call them, vulgar papers than in *scholarly* publications. . . . . They are no judges of the *critical* value of what I have done, but they are admirable judges of its *social* consequences among their own class of readers. And these are they whom I am now beginning to touch, and whom I wish to move.

. . . . .

[September, 1857.]

"You remind me that I have not answered your former questions respecting transcendental convictions and the relation between them and religious belief; the reason of my silence is the impossibility of treating such subjects in a letter. In conversation you would raise difficulties and ask for further information on what seemed obscure, but you cannot *cross-examine* a letter, and on subjects of such immense difficulty I fear to be misunderstood; and I shrink from saying anything that might give a painful direction to your speculations. In regard to books, on this

---

[1] "*October* 1. 1852.—Continued writing my account of Burke, which I think will be one of the best parts of the Introduction."—*Journal.*

[2] "*January* 17*th*, 1853.—Wrote in my book what I think a fine comparison between Calvinism and Arminianism, as illustrating the influence of Jansenism on the French Revolution.

"*February* 2*nd*, 1853.—Read Comte's Traité de Législation; a profound work, which has anticipated some views that I thought original upon the superiority of intellect over morals as a *directing* principle of society."—*Journal.*

there is nothing in English, and what perhaps I should most recommend
are the minor works of Fichte, which I could lend you if you find yourself
strong enough in German to master them. The difference between the
transcendental operations of the reason and the empirical operations of the
understanding is also worked out by Kant, and at the end of my first
chapter you will find all the passages collected in which that wonderful
thinker applies the theory of their difference to solve the problem of free
will and necessity. Coleridge saw the difficulty, but *dared* not investigate
it. Miserable creatures that we are, to think that we offend God by using
with freedom the faculties that God has given us! There is only one
safe maxim on these questions, viz., that if we strive honestly after the
truth we satisfy our conscience, and having done all that lies in our
power, may wash our hands of the result. If this maxim be neglected
then investigations will only lead to a life of misery, and had far better be
left alone.

 •         •         •         •         •         •

[January, 1858.]

" You ask me how I reply to the charge of not taking into consideration
the effect produced by the passions of men on the course of history. My
answer is that we have no reason to believe that human passions are *mate-
rially* better or worse than formerly—nor that they are smaller or greater.
If, therefore, the amount and nature of the passions are unchanged, they
cannot be the cause either of progress or of decay—because an unchangeable
cause can only generate an unchangeable effect. On the other hand, it is
true that the manifestation, and, as it were, the *shape* of the passions, is
different in different periods; but such difference not being innate, must
be due to external causes. Those causes propel and direct the passions of
men, and these last are (in so far as they are changeable), the products of
civilisation and not the producers of it. In my book I always examine the
causes of events as high up as I can find them, because I consider the
object of science is to reach the largest and most remote generalisations.
But my critics prefer considering the immediate and most proximate
causes—and in *their* way of looking at the subject they naturally accuse
me of neglecting the study of emotions, moral principles, and the like.
According to my view the passions, &c., are both causes and effects, and
I seek to rise to *their* cause—while if I were a practical writer I should confine myself to their effects. But I despair of writing anything satisfactory
in the limits of a letter on this subject."

 •         •         •         •         •         •

[December, 1859.]

" It is impossible in a letter to answer fully your questions on the utilitarian theory of morals. But I do not think that you separate rigidly
two very different matters, viz., what morals *do* rest upon, and what
they *ought* to rest upon. All very honest people who have not any reach
of mind, regulate the greater part of their moral conduct without attend-

ing to consequences; but it does not follow that they *ought* to do so. The doctrine of consequences is only adopted by persons of a certain amount of thought and culture, or else by knaves, who very likely have no thought or culture at all, but who find the doctrine convenient. Thus it is that the science of political economy perpetually leads even disinterested and generous men to conclusions which delight interested and selfish men. The evil of promiscuous charity, for instance, and the detriment caused by foundling hospitals and similar institutions, is quite a modern discovery, and is directly antagonistic to that spontaneous impulse of our nature which urges us to *give*, and always to relieve immediate distress. If there ever was a moral instinct, this is one, and we see it enforced with great pathos in the New Testament, which was written at a period when the evil of the instinct (as shown by a scientific investigation of the theory of consequences) was unknown. I have no doubt that when our knowledge is more advanced, an immense number of other impulses will be in the same way proved to be erroneous; but even when the proof is supplied there are only two classes who will act upon it: those who are capable of understanding the argument, and those who, without comprehending it, are pleased with the doctrine it inculcates. What is vulgarly called the moral faculty is always spontaneous—or at least always appears to be so. But science (i.e. *truth*), is invariably a *limitation* of spontaneousness. Every scientific discovery is contrary to common sense, and the history of the reception of that discovery is the history of the struggle with the common sense and with the unaided instincts of our nature. Seeing this, it is surely absurd to set up these unaided instincts as supreme ; to worship them as idols ; to regret the doctrine of consequences, and to say, ' I will do this because I feel it to be right, and I will listen to nothing which tempts me from what I know to be my duty ; ' to say this is well enough for a child, or for an adult who has the intellect of a child ; but on the part of a cultivated person it is nothing better than slavery of the understanding, and a servile fear of that spirit of analysis to which we owe our most valuable acquisitions.

"I wish I could publish an essay on this ! How I pine for more time and more strength ! Since I have been here I have read what Mill says in his Essays, and, like everything he writes, it is admirable—but I think that he has done better things. He does not make enough of the historical argument of *unspontaneous* science encroaching on *spontaneous* morals, and the improvement of moral conduct consequent on such encroachment. I saw this when I wrote my fourth chapter on the impossibility of moral motives causing social improvement. But here I am getting into another field, and it is hopeless . . . ."

.       .       .       .       .       .

Almost directly after the publication of his first volume, he applied himself to the preparation of the second, for which, indeed, he had prepared some matter several years before, since in October, 1855, he noted in his Journal that he had "begun and finished" a "notice of the history of Spain and the Inquisition, to prove that morals cannot diminish persecution." He interrupted this work in January, 1858, in order to prepare the lecture, on the Influence of Women on the Progress of Knowledge, which he delivered at the Royal Institution on March 19 of the same year. On January 19 he entered in his Journal, that he "began to write a lecture on the Influence of Women;" and he continued to enter, nearly every day, the number of hours (generally from two to four), that he gave to writing it until February 21, when he notes "finished writing lecture on women." On the following day he enters "studied lecture on women;" and this entry is repeated several times a week until March 19, when he notes, "From 10·10 to 1·30 studied Lecture ——. At 9 I delivered at the Royal Institution a lecture on the Influence of Women on the Progress of Knowledge. I spoke from 8·55 to 10·25 without hesitation and without taking my notes out of my pocket." His self-gratulation on not requiring the aid of his notes appears to have produced the mistaken impression in some quarters that he spoke extempore.

The next event in his life was the loss of his mother, an event the coming shadow of which had already been gathering for many years. In 1857 he had written to a friend on the occasion of the death of a mother:—

"I have more than once undergone in anticipation what you are suffering in reality, and it has always seemed to me that consolation may be for the dead, but never for the living. Still, you are not as I shall be—you have not lost all—you do not stand alone in the world."

In the same year he writes of his mother in other letters:—

"Month after month she is now gradually altering for the worse; at times slightly better, but on the whole perceptibly losing ground . . . Nothing remains of her as she once was except her smile and the exquisite tenderness of her affections. I while away my days here, doing nothing and caring for nothing, because I feel that I have no future.

·        ·        ·        ·        ·        ·

"In the last three weeks I have been unable to write a single line of my history, and I now confine myself to reading and thinking, which I can do as well as ever, though I am too unsettled to compose. My mother is just the same as when I wrote last, caring for nothing but seeing me, though she is too unwell to converse. . . . While she is in this state, nothing could induce me to leave her, even for a day, without absolute necessity. She has no pleasure left except that of knowing that I am near her, and as long as that remains she shall never lose it. . . . I want change, for besides my anxiety I am vexed, and, to say the truth, a little frightened at my sudden and complete inability to compose."

[February, 1859.]

" I am still immersed in Scotch theology, for I am more and more convinced that the real history of Scotland in the seventeenth century is to be found in the pulpit and in the ecclesiastical assemblies. A few days ago I tried to compose, and with better success than previously. I wrote about three pages that morning, and this has given me fresh courage. But it is only after the great excitement of conversation that I can write in the morning. Nothing now stirs me but talk. Every other stimulus has lost its power. I am dining out a good deal, and hear much of my own success ; but it moves me not. Often could I exclaim with Hamlet, ' They fool me to the top of my bent.' "

On February 6 and 7, 1859, he notes in his Journal that he " read Mill on Liberty ; " and two days afterwards he " began to arrange notes with a view to reviewing, in Fraser, Mill's new work on Liberty." With this view he re-read the same writer's System of Logic, Principles of Political Economy and Thoughts on Parliamentary Reform ; and the writing of his own review occupied him for several hours every day for upwards of two months. It was while he was thus engaged that the death of his mother took place. " April 1, 1859. At 9·15 P. M. my angel mother died peacefully without pain," is the record in his diary on that day, on which he had been occupied in the morning in writing his account of the Pooley case ; and it was under the immediate impression of his loss that he wrote what he calls " the evidence of immortality supplied by the affections," which forms part of his Essay on Mill. In spite of this blow he continued steadily at his work, and did not leave London till he had finished his Essay. Soon after it was published (in Fraser's Magazine) he writes to a friend, who had remonstrated with him on the violence of his attack in it on Mr. Justice Coleridge.

10 May [1859].

" What you say about my notice of Justice Coleridge does a little surprise me. I knew at the time that most persons would think I had shown too much virulence ; but I believed then, and I believe now, that in this case, as in other cases where I have taken an unpopular view (such, for instance, as the absence of *dynamical* power in morals), those who object to my treatment have not taken as much pains to inform themselves as I have done. You know that I have no personal animosity against Coleridge, and yet I say that, to the best of my judgment, his sentence on Pooley is the most criminal act committed by an English judge since the seventeenth century. Most acts of religious cruelty have been in *compliance* with the temper of the age; but here we have a man going out of his way and running counter to the liberal tendencies of the time in order to gratify that malignant passion—a zeal for protecting religion. I have felt all I have written; and I should be ashamed of myself if on such a subject, and with my way of looking at affairs, I had expressed less warmth. Of course I may be wrong; but it seemed to me that the influence, the name, and the social position of the Judge made it the more necessary to be uncompromising, and to strike a blow which should be felt. . . . . I believe that the more the true principles of toleration are understood the more alive will people be to the magnitude of that crime. At all events, I know that even if I had used still stronger language, I should only have *written* what a powerful and intelligent minority *think*. And I have yet to learn that there are any good arguments in favour of a man concealing what he does think. I never have and never will attack a man for speculative opinions; but when he translates these opinions into acts, and in so doing commits cruelty, it is for the general weal that he should be attacked. A poor, ignorant, half-witted man, sentenced to be imprisoned for a year and nine months, for writing and speaking a few words against the Author of the Christian religion! And when I express the loathing and abomination with which I regard so monstrous an act, you, my dear friend, 'regret the extreme violence' of my expressions. To me it appears that your doctrine would root out indignation from my vocabulary; for if such an act is not to rouse indignation, what is? With all honesty do I say that I attach the highest value to your judgment, and therefore it is that I should really be glad if you will let me know *why* you dislike these remarks on Coleridge."

13 May [1859].

"Although I admit the force of all your reasoning, I am not convinced by it, simply because our premises are different. We look at affairs from an opposite point of view, and therefore adopt opposite methods. My habits of mind accustom me to consider actions with regard to their consequences—you are more inclined to consider them with regard to their motives. You, therefore, are more tender to individuals than I am, particularly if you think them sincere; and you hold that moral principles *do* hasten the improvement of nations; I hold that they do *not*. From these fundamental differences between us, it inevitably happens that we estimate differently such an act as the sentence on Pooley. We are both agreed that the sentence was wrong; but you consider that the Judge, not having bad motives (but who can penetrate the heart and discern motives?), and not being a bad man, diminishes the *criminality* of the sentence, and therefore should have prevented me from using such strong language.

"However, I should prefer resting my view upon grounds still broader than these. As a public writer (not as a private or practical man) I estimate actions solely according to their *consequences*. The consequence of this sentence I deem far more pernicious than I have been able to state in my essay, because I could not, for want of space, open up all the topics connected with it. Dealing, as I always do, with the interest of masses, and striving to reach the highest view of the subject, I hold that when an act is pernicious, when it is done in the teeth of the liberal tendencies of the time, when the punishment far exceeds the offence, when it is not only cruel to the victim but productive of evil consequences as a public example—when these qualities are combined in a single transaction, I call that transaction a great crime, and therefore the author of it a great criminal.

"Now in commenting upon such an act, how should the principal actor be treated? You say that I should not have used language which one 'gentleman' would not have used to another in conversation. Here we are altogether at issue. My object was not merely to vindicate the principle of toleration (for that, to all persons of competent understanding and knowledge, was done before I was born), but to punish a great and dangerous criminal. Whether I am able to punish is another question. If I am not able, my remarks are ridiculous from their impotence, and I have been foolish from incapacity and not wrong as to intention. That is to say, not wrong in intention unless my way of looking at affairs is wrong; and this is the very point on which we disagree. At all events, starting with this view (which is precisely the theory of method that underlies everything I have ever written) it formed no part of my plan to use nice and dainty words. Instead of confining myself to writing like a *gentleman*, I aimed at writing like a *man*. . . . . Is it the business of literature to chastise as well as to persuade? I think it is; and I follow the example of many who have done the greatest good and left the greatest names. You would have me expose the crime and yet spare the criminal. But I cannot stop at the act of oppression; my mind goes on to the oppressor. And yet you say, 'the personality of the attack is the only thing I regret.' Most truly do I know that you speak out of the very fulness and kindness of your heart; and I value more than I can tell you, a frankness which proves your friendship, if I needed new proof. But I cannot conceal from you that we are in this matter as far asunder as the poles. As an author, I will always say what I think; and when an act of cruelty comes across my path perpetrated by a powerful and influential man, I will never let conventional and '*gentlemanly*' considerations restrain the indignation which I feel.

"You also think that I weaken my own influence and consideration by making such an attack; and in that respect I am inclined to agree with you in part. Many will be offended, but it is not the verdict of London drawing-rooms that can either make or mar a man who has a great career to run, and a consciousness of being able to run it. I would not willingly seem arrogant, but I think you will understand me when I

c

say that I feel that within me which can sweep away such little obstacles, and force people to hear what I have to offer them."

For a short time after his mother's death he seems to have been sustained by the excitement of composition; but the letters he wrote during the following year show that, as is usual where a loss is very great, the sense of it became deeper with time:—

[April, 1859].

"Do not be uneasy about me. I am quite well, and within such limits as are left to me, I am happy. I can work freely and well; beyond this there is nothing for me to look for except the deep conviction I have of another life, and which makes me feel that all is not really over."

[April, 1859].

"I remain quite well, but my grief increases as association after association rises in my mind, and tells me what I have lost. One thing alone I cling to—the deep and unutterable conviction that the end is not yet come, and that we never really die. But it is a separation for half a life, and the most sanguine view that I can take is that I have a probability before me of thirty years of fame, of power and of desolation."

[Brighton] 19 May [1859].

"Here I am, working hard; and it is my only pleasure, just as the capacity of work and of thought is the only part of me that has not deteriorated. Strange, that the intellect alone should be spared! but so it is. The feeling of real happiness I never expect again to know, but I am perfectly calm."

The next letter was written in the midst of illness, and about the time of the death of a young nephew to whom he was attached:—

[Boulogne, December, 1859].

"I cannot tell you how I dread the idea of going to London, to that dull and dreary house which was once so full of light and of love! On the other hand, my ambition seems to grow more insatiate than ever, and it is perhaps well that it should, as it is my sheet-anchor."

He continued to work steadily at his new volume, and while it was passing through the press he wrote to a friend to whom he sent the proofs: 'I hope you will like the peroration (of Chap. I. vol. ii.). I am hardly a fair judge; but as a mere piece of English composition, I think it is much the best thing I have written." But at the very time that he was writing this "peroration," with which he was so much pleased, he seems to have been suffering, more even than he had done a year before, from the low spirits and weakened health consequent on the loss of his mother.

[November, 1860].

" I see too surely how changed I am in every way, and how impossible it will be for me to complete schemes to which I once thought myself fully equal. My next volume is far from being ready for the press, and when it is ready, it will be very inferior to what either you or I expected."

After the publication of his second volume (in May, 1861), his health gave way still more completely, and in the following autumn he determined to lay aside all literary work for a time, and to try the effect of a winter in Egypt and Syria.

This journey seems to have been begun under favourable auspices, and if we may trust his own letters, it would appear that all his hopes of invigorated strength were realised by it, and that the fever by which it was cut short was purely fortuitous, and not at all the result of his previously weakened health. He was accompanied by the two young sons of a friend, of whom he writes; ' They are very pleasant, intelligent boys, and I delight in young life.' That the friendly feeling was reciprocated we may infer from a sentence in a letter home, in which the boys enunciate the opinion that ' Bucky's a brick ' !

" I cannot tell you," writes he a few days before leaving England, " I cannot tell you the intense pleasure with which I look forward to seeing Egypt—that strange mutilated form of civilization. For years nothing has excited me so much." He left England towards the end of October, and early in November he writes from Alexandria : " I feel in better health and spirits than at any time during the last three years. Especially I am conscious of an immense increase of brain-power, grasping great problems with a firmness which at one time I feared had gone from me for ever. I feel that there is yet much that I shall live to do." And again, ten days later from Cairo ; " I am better than I have been for years, and feel full of life and thought. How this country makes me speculate ! " To the friend whose sons accompanied him he wrote from Cairo :—

Cairo, 15 November, 1861.

" I feel the responsibility of your dear children perhaps more than I expected ; but I am not anxious, for I am conscious of going to the full extent of my duty and neglecting nothing, and when a man does this, he must leave the unknown and invisible future to take care of itself."

And in the same letter he wrote in reply to some questions which had been addressed to him :—

e 2

"All I can say is, that the true Utilitarian philosophy *never* allows anyone, for the sake of present and temporary benefits, either to break a promise or tell a falsehood. Such things degrade the mind, and are therefore evil in themselves. . . . The other point is more difficult; but *I* would not hesitate to tell a falsehood to save the life of any one dear to me, though I know that many competent judges differ as to this; and in the present state of knowledge, the problem is perhaps incapable of scientific treatment. It is, therefore, in such cases, for each to act according to his own lights."

## From Thebes he writes, on January 15, 1862 :—

"We arrived at Thebes this morning. We have all been, and are, remarkably well. The journey into Nubia, notwithstanding its many discomforts, was in the highest degree curious and instructive. Not one Egyptian traveller in ten enters Nubia, but, as you see, I felt confident in bringing us all well out of it; and now that we have been there, I would not have missed it for five hundred pounds. I feel very joyous, and altogether full of pugnacity, so that I wish someone would attack me—I mean, attack me speculatively—I have no desire for a practical combat."

## On his return to Cairo he writes :—

Cairo, 7th February, 1862.

"We have returned to Cairo all quite well, after a most interesting journey to the southern extremity of Egypt and on into Nubia, as far as Wady Halfeh (the Second Cataract). I feel better and stronger than I have done for years. In about ten days we leave here for Mount Sinai, and intend proceeding thence through the desert to Gaza, and then to Jerusalem by way of Hebron. Fancy me travelling on the back of a camel for seven or eight hours a day for from four to six weeks, and then travelling on horseback through Palestine and Southern Syria! That I have not already been thrown is a marvel, seeing that among other audacious feats I went from the Nile to Abydos on a donkey with a cloth for a saddle and two pieces of rope for stirrups, and in this wretched plight had to ride between eight and nine hours.

"To give you any, even the faintest idea of what I have seen in this wonderful country, is impossible. No art of writing can depict it. If I were to say that the temple of Karnac at Thebes can even now be ascertained to have measured a mile and a half in circumference, I should perhaps only tell you what you have read in books; but I should despair if I were obliged to describe what I felt when I was in the midst of it, and contemplated it as a living whole, while every part was covered with sculptures of exquisite finish, except where the hieroglyphics crowded on each other so thickly that it would require many volumes to copy them. There stood their literature, in the midst of the most magnificent temples ever raised by the genius of man. I went twice to see it by moonlight, when the vast masses of light and shade rendered it absolutely appalling. But I fear to write like a guide-book, and had rather abstain from details till we meet. One effect, however, I must tell you that my journey has produced upon me. Perhaps you may remember how much I always preferred form to colour ; but now, owing to the magical effect of this, the driest atmosphere in the world, I am getting to like colour more than form. The endless variety of hues is extraordinary. Owing to the transparency of the air, objects are seen (as nearly as I can judge) more than twice the distance that they can be seen in England under the most favourable circumstances. Until my eye became habituated to this, I often over-fatigued myself by believing that I could reach a certain point in a certain time. The result is a wealth and exuberance of colour which is hardly to be credited, and which I doubt if any painter would dare to represent. . . .

" If you were here, and felt as I do what it is to have the brain every day over-excited—be constantly drunk with pleasure—you would easily understand how impossible much letter-writing becomes, and how impatient one grows of fixing upon paper ' thoughts that burn.' But, as you know of old, if my friends were to measure my friendship by the length of my letters, they would do me great injustice."

He reached Jerusalem on April 13, 1862, and in a letter written a few days later, he gives the following account of the journey :—

Jerusalem, 16 April [1862].

" We arrived here three days ago, after a most fatiguing and arduous journey through the *whole* desert of Sinai and of Edom. We have traversed a deeply-interesting country, visited by few Europeans and by none during the last five years, so dangerous was the latter part of the journey reputed to be. But I had taken my measures before venturing to go beyond Sinai, and, gradually feeling my way, secured, as I went on, the protection of every leading sheik, having studied at Cairo their relative power and position. Having an ample stock of provisions, I was prepared at any moment to fall back and return, if need be, to Egypt. Three other parties, chiefly Americans, joined us at Sinai, each having their separate establishment arranged with their own dragoman, but all, for greater safety, keeping together till we reached Hebron. We were in all sixteen persons, and with our servants and escort we numbered 110 armed men. Nothing but a combination of tribes could hurt us ; and such a combination I considered to be morally impossible in the face of the precautions which I suggested, and to which, after some demur, the other parties agreed. When I say ' morally impossible,' I mean the odds were so large as not to be worth the consideration of a prudent man. There were several alarms, and there was undoubted danger ; but, in my deliberate judgment, the danger was not greater than would be encountered in a rough sea with a good vessel and a skilful captain. Some of our fellow-travellers were in great fear two or three times, and assured me that they had no sleep on those occasions. For my own part I never was kept awake ten minutes. . . . . The result is that we have seen Petra—as wonderful and far more beautiful than anything in Egypt. Burkhardt, about forty years ago, was the first

European who ever set foot there, and since then, not more, probably,
than a hundred persons have seen it—that is to say, have really seen it as
we did, at leisure, and spending three whole days there.  Occasionally
gentlemen without tents and with no food but what they can carry on
their own horse, gallop from Hebron to Petra (about one hundred and
twenty miles) in two days and a half, reaching Petra in the evening,
seeing it by moonlight, and then gallop back again before the Bedouins
and Fellahin are aware of their presence.  The English and other consuls
and the Governor of Cairo, with other persons of influence, all declared
that this was the only way I could see Petra; but the hardship of the
journey, and the risk of sleeping in the open air, prevented me from
thinking for a moment of such a plan.  Among the English here
the journey has created quite a sensation, and the result is one of
many proofs which have convinced me of the profound ignorance of
officials in the East of everything which their eyes do not see.  I had to
collect all my facts through an interpreter, but I analysed and compared
them with something more than official care and precision.  Having done
so, I acted; and I look back to this passage through Petra from Egypt as
by far the greatest practical achievement of my life.  I believe that you
are both laughing, and I am almost inclined to laugh myself.  But I am
conceited about it, and I think I have reason to be so.  For I must
moreover tell you that nearly all our party were more or less ill with
fatigue, anxiety and the extraordinary vicissitudes of temperature, . . .
but we three had not once the least pain or inconvenience of any kind. . .
The dear little kids are now the picture of health, and we are all as brown
as Arabs. . . .   The fact is, that we were the only ones who had
proper food, and were properly clothed. . . . . I am far stronger
both in mind and body than I have been since you knew me, and I
feel fit to go on at once with my work.  But I neither read nor write;
I think, I see, and I talk.  Especially I study the state of society and
habits of the people."

Cheerfully as he speaks of this journey by Petra, it is probable
that the fatigue, excitement, and anxiety he underwent in the
course of it, laid the foundation of the fever which was so soon
to carry him off.

He spent eleven days at Jerusalem, and three days after
commencing his journey from Jerusalem to Beyrout he was
attacked by the first symptoms of illness.  He ought at once
to have returned to Jerusalem and rested until every sign of
illness had disappeared, but unfortunately his energetic and
hopeful disposition prompted him to struggle on, in spite of
suffering, until the malady had too tight a hold on him ever to
be shaken off.  From the first attack, at Nazareth, to his death a
month later at Damascus, his diary records all the vicissitudes of

illness, brought on by fatigue and exhaustion. At Nazareth he was attended by an American doctor, and at Sidon by the French resident doctor, of whom he says that he " turns out to be an intelligent man," and who told him that what he wanted was rest. Had he taken this advice his life would probably have been saved, but he continued his journey to Beyrout, where he arrived on May 14, thinking himself cured, although " still very weak." From Beyrout he wrote cheerfully and full of plans for the future. " We arrived here to-day, all well ; " and then he goes into minute details of his plans for spending the summer at Gratz. Nor was it only in his letters, but also in his Journal, that he spoke of himself as " feeling better" at Beyrout, and even there rest might yet have saved him. But directly he re-commenced his journey his illness returned, and on the day he arrived at Damascus (May 18), he spoke of himself as " utterly prostrate."

At Damascus he received the utmost kindness from Mr. Sand-with, the English consul, but from this time the fever never left him, and he sank under it on May 29, 1862. His last words were words of kindness to his two young companions.

# INTRODUCTION.

THE CONTENTS of the following volumes may be divided into three portions. Firstly, the Miscellaneous Works published by the author during his lifetime, consisting of a lecture on the Influence of Women on Knowledge, of a review of Mr. Mill's work on Liberty, and of a short defence of this review under the name of " A Letter to a Gentleman on Pooley's Case."

Secondly, of the contents of Mr. Buckle's Common Place Books, which fill the second and third volumes of the present work. These have been printed precisely as they were left by the author, with the exception of the omission of a few articles on account of the subjects of which they treated. The numbering has, however, been carried on as in the original, both on account of references to the articles by number in other places, and that those who care to do so, may see where omissions have occurred. The Index to the Common Place Books was made by the author himself, and has been printed verbatim; it therefore contains references to the omitted articles.

A large proportion of the Common Place Books, even when substantially extracted from other writers, is in Mr. Buckle's own words, especially towards the latter part. On this account it has been thought best to make as few alterations as possible in them as they originally stood, although the reader may observe many mistakes which the author would probably have corrected had he himself given the books to the press. But they have been left unaltered because some statements which may appear mistakes to the editor or reader might have proved to be deliberate opinions of the writer, which he might have been able to substantiate; while the alteration or omission of others, about which there seems no room for doubt, would have diminished the autobiographical value of the remains—a great part of their value to the general reader.

The third part consists of the Fragments, the most connected portions of which (on the reign of Elizabeth) appeared in Fraser's Magazine about five years after the author's death.  So much of the Common Place Books is original and so much of the Fragments consists of little more than abstracts of books, that the difference of character between the two is not very great.  But the Common Place Books were so called by their author, and their contents were entered by him in consecutive numbers.  The Fragments seem to consist partly of notes from books such as he afterwards might have entered in his Common Place Books, partly of the first rough form in which he was in the habit of putting his ideas upon paper,[1] and partly of those portions of the original sketches of his published work which he had not incorporated into it.  Not one is a completed paper ; and to have presented any of them in a connected form would have been in fact to have re-written them.  Even to alter the order in which the disjointed fragments are thrown together would often have been to run a considerable risk of substantially misrepresenting the author's ideas.  For, in the first place, it would be to represent opinions as settled and matured, which were in fact only tentative suggestions and provisional hypotheses.  There are instances where he seems to have worked in one direction, and then, convinced by the results beginning to come out from his own labour, he seems to have begun again upon a totally different track.  We cannot tell how often this was the case, and it is due to a mind at once so bold and so laborious, carefully to avoid presenting his guesses in a form that might lead to the impression that they were his convictions.

There is another reason why no attempt has been made to work up these materials into any connected form.  The originality of the author's mind was shown in a great degree in the arrangement of his materials, and it would be as rash as presumptuous for anyone but himself to disturb the order in which he has himself thrown together even the most apparently disconnected facts.  This order may be, in many cases, entirely accidental ; but it also may be the result of some of the writer's most characteristic powers, destined, had he lived, to throw new light on the relations of history.  To disturb it therefore might not only be unfair

---

[1] This is shown by the numerous notes of interrogation which he was in the habit of putting where he was not quite sure of the statements made.

to Mr. Buckle, it might also be unfair to the studious among his readers. To some of these the apparently accidental order of some of the great heap of facts and ideas here thrown together may be like a flash of light, and may lead the way to new combinations. To have meddled with this order might have been to destroy their chief value to kindred minds.

# MISCELLANEOUS WORKS.

---

## THE INFLUENCE OF WOMEN
## ON THE PROGRESS OF KNOWLEDGE.[1]

THE subject upon which I have undertaken to address you is the influence of women on the progress of knowledge, undoubtedly one of the most interesting questions that could be submitted to any audience. Indeed, it is not only very interesting, it is also extremely important. When we see how knowledge has civilized mankind; when we see how every great step in the march and advance of nations has been invariably preceded by a corresponding step in their knowledge; when we moreover see, what is assuredly true, that women are constantly growing more influential, it becomes a matter of great moment that we should endeavour to ascertain the relation between their influence and our knowledge. On every side, in all social phenomena, in the education of children, in the tone and spirit of literature, in the forms and usages of life; nay, even in the proceedings of legislatures, in the history of statute-books, and in the decisions of magistrates, we find manifold proofs that women are gradually making their way, and slowly but surely winning for themselves a position superior to any they have hitherto attained. This is one of many peculiarities which distinguish modern civilization, and which show how essentially the most advanced countries are different from those that formerly flourished. Among the most celebrated nations of antiquity, women held a very subordinate place. The most splendid and durable monument of the Roman empire, and the noblest gift Rome has bequeathed to posterity, is her jurisprudence—a vast and harmonious system, worked out with consummate skill, and from which we derive our purest and largest notions of civil law. Yet this, which, not to mention the immense

[1] A Discourse delivered at the Royal Institution, on Friday, the 19th of March, 1858. (Reprinted from 'Fraser's Magazine,' for April, 1858.)

B

sway it still exercises in France and Germany, has taught to our most enlightened lawyers their best lessons; and which enabled Bracton among the earlier jurists, Somers, Hardwicke, Mansfield, and Stowell among the later, to soften by its refinement the rude maxims of our Saxon ancestors, and adjust the coarser principles of the old Common Law to the actual exigencies of life; this imperishable specimen of human sagacity is, strange to say, so grossly unjust towards women, that a great writer upon that code has well observed, that in it women are regarded not as persons, but as things; so completely were they stripped of all their rights, and held in subjection by their proud and imperious masters. As to the other great nation of antiquity, we have only to open the literature of the ancient Greeks to see with what airs of superiority, with what serene and lofty contempt, and sometimes with what mocking and biting scorn, women were treated by that lively and ingenious people. Instead of valuing them as companions, they looked on them as toys. How little part women really took in the development of Greek civilization may be illustrated by the singular fact, that their influence, scanty as it was, did not reach its height in the most civilized times, or in the most civilized regions. In modern Europe, the influence of women and the spread of civilization have been nearly commensurate, both advancing with almost equal speed. But if you compare the picture of Greek life in Homer with that to be found in Plato and his contemporaries, you will be struck by a totally opposite circumstance. Between Plato and Homer there intervened, according to the common reckoning, a period of at least four centuries, during which the Greeks made many notable improvements in the arts of life, and in various branches of speculative and practical knowledge. So far, however, from women participating in this movement, we find that, in the state of society exhibited by Plato and his contemporaries, they had evidently lost ground; their influence being less then than it was in the earlier and more barbarous period depicted by Homer. This fact illustrates the question in regard to time; another fact illustrates it in regard to place. In Sparta, women possessed more influence than they did in Athens; although the Spartans were rude and ignorant, the Athenians polite and accomplished. The causes of these inconsistencies would form a curious subject for investigation: but it is enough to call your attention to them as one of many proofs that the boasted civilizations of antiquity were eminently one-sided, and that they fell because society did not advance in all its parts, but sacrificed some of its constituents in order to secure the progress of others.

In modern European society we have happily no instance of
this sort; and, if we now inquire what the influence of women
has been upon that society, every one will allow that on the whole
it has been extremely beneficial.  Their influence has prevented
life from being too exclusively practical and selfish, and has saved
it from degenerating into a dull and monotonous routine, by infusing into it an ideal and romantic element.  It has softened
the violence of men; it has improved their manners; it has lessened their cruelty.  Thus far, the gain is complete and unde-
niable.  But if we ask what their influence has been, not on the
general interests of society, but on one of those interests, namely,
the progress of knowledge, the answer is not so obvious.  For, to
state the matter candidly, it must be confessed that none of the
greatest works which instruct and delight mankind have been
composed by women.  In poetry, in painting, in sculpture, in
music, the most exquisite productions are the work of men.  No
woman, however favourable her circumstances may have been, has
made a discovery sufficiently important to mark an epoch in the
annals of the human mind.  These are facts which cannot be
contested, and from them a very stringent and peremptory inference has been drawn.  From them it has been inferred, and it is
openly stated by eminent writers, that women have no concern
with the highest forms of knowledge; that such matters are altogether out of their reach; that they should confine themselves to
practical, moral, and domestic life, which it is their province to
exalt and to beautify; but that they can exercise no influence,
direct or indirect, over the progress of knowledge, and that if
they seek to exercise such influence, they will not only fail in their
object, but will restrict the field of their really useful and legitimate activity.

Now, I may as well state at once, and at the outset, that I
have come here to-night with the intention of combating this
proposition, which I hold to be unphilosophical and dangerous;
false in theory and pernicious in practice.  I believe, and I hope
before we separate to convince you, that so far from women exercising little or no influence over the progress of knowledge, they
are capable of exercising and have actually exercised an enormous
influence; that this influence is, in fact, so great that it is hardly
possible to assign limits to it; and that great as it is, it may with
advantage be still further increased.  I hope, moreover, to convince you that this influence has been exhibited not merely from
time to time in rare, sudden, and transitory ebullitions, but that
it acts by virtue of certain laws inherent to human nature; and
that although it works as an under-current below the surface, and

is therefore invisible to hasty observers, it has already produced the most important results, and has affected the shape, the character, and the amount of our knowledge.

To clear up this matter, we must first of all understand what knowledge is. Some men who pride themselves on their common sense—and whenever a man boasts much about that, you may be pretty sure that he has very little sense, either common or uncommon—such men there are who will tell you that all knowledge consists of facts, that everything else is mere talk and theory, and that nothing has any value except facts. Those who speak so much of the value of facts may understand the meaning of fact, but they evidently do not understand the meaning of value. For, the value of a thing is not a property residing in that thing, nor is it a component; but it is simply its relation to some other thing. We say, for instance, that a five-shilling piece has a certain value; but the value does not reside in the coin. If it does, where is it? Our senses cannot grasp value. We cannot see value, nor hear it, nor feel it, nor taste it, nor smell it. The value consists solely in the relation which the five-shilling piece bears to something else. Just so in regard to facts. Facts, as facts, have no sort of value, but are simply a mass of idle lumber. The value of a fact is not an element or constituent of that fact, but is its relation to the total stock of our knowledge, either present or prospective. Facts, therefore, have merely a potential and, as it were, subsequent value, and the only advantage of possessing them is the possibility of drawing conclusions from them; in other words, of rising to the idea, the principle, the law which governs them. Our knowledge is composed not of facts, but of the relations which facts and ideas bear to themselves and to each other; and real knowledge consists not in an acquaintance with facts, which only makes a pedant, but in the use of facts, which makes a philosopher.

Looking at knowledge in this way, we shall find that it has three divisions—Method, Science, and Art. Of method I will speak presently; but I will first state the limits of the other two divisions. The immediate object of all art is either pleasure or utility: the immediate object of all science is solely truth. As art and science have different objects, so also have they different faculties. The faculty of art is to change events; the faculty of science is to foresee them. The phenomena with which we deal are controlled by art; they are predicted by science. The more complete a science is, the greater its power of prediction; the more complete an art is, the greater its power of control. Astronomy, for instance, is called the queen of the sciences, because it is the most advanced of all; and the astronomer, while he abandons all hope of controlling or altering the phenomena, frequently knows what the phenomena will be years before they actually appear; the extent of his foreknowledge proving the accuracy of his science. So, too, in the science of mechanics, we predict that, certain circumstances being present, certain results must follow; and having done this, our science ceases. Our art then begins, and from that moment the object of utility and the faculty of control come into play; so that in the art of mechanics, we alter what in the science of mechanics we were content to foresee.

One of the most conspicuous tendencies of advancing civilization is to give a scientific basis to that faculty of control which is represented by art, and thus afford fresh prominence to the faculty of prediction. In the earliest stages of society there are many arts, but no sciences. A little later, science begins to appear, and every subsequent step is marked by an increased desire to bring art under the dominion of science. To those who have studied the history of the human mind, this tendency is so familiar that I need hardly stop to prove it. Perhaps the most remarkable instance is in the case of agriculture, which, for thousands of years, was a mere empirical art, resting on the traditional maxims of experience, but which, during the present century, chemists began to draw under their jurisdiction, so that the practical art of manuring the ground is now explained by laws of physical science. Probably the next step will be to bring another part of the art of agriculture under the dominion of meteorology, which will be done as soon as the conditions which govern the changes of the weather have been so generalized as to enable us to foretell what the weather will be.

General reasoning, therefore, as well as the history of what has been actually done, justify us in saying that the highest, the ripest, and the most important form of knowledge, is the scientific form of predicting consequences; it is therefore to this form that I shall restrict the remainder of what I have to say to you respecting the influence of women. And the point which I shall attempt to prove is, that there is a natural, a leading, and probably an indestructible element, in the minds of women, which enables them, not indeed to make scientific discoveries, but to exercise the most momentous and salutary influence over the method by which discoveries are made. And as all questions concerning the philosophy of method lie at the very root of our knowledge, I will, in the first place, state, as succinctly as I am able, the only two methods by which we can arrive at truth.

The scientific inquirer, properly so called, that is, he whose object is merely truth, has only two ways of attaining his result. He may proceed from the external world to the internal ; or he may begin with the internal and proceed to the external. In the former case he studies the facts presented to his senses, in order to arrive at a true idea of them ; in the latter case, he studies the ideas already in his mind, in order to explain the facts of which his senses are cognizant. If he begin with the facts his method is inductive ; if he begin with the ideas it is deductive. The inductive philosopher collects phenomena either by observation or by experiment, and from them rises to the general principle or law which explains and covers them. The deductive philosopher draws the principle from ideas already existing in his mind, and explains the phenomena by descending on them, instead of rising from them. Several eminent thinkers have asserted that every idea is the result of induction, and that the axioms of geometry, for instance, are the product of early and unconscious induction. In the same way, Mr. Mill, in his great work on Logic, affirms that all reasoning is in reality from particular to particular, and that the major premiss of every syllogism is merely a record and register of knowledge previously obtained. Whether this be true, or whether, as another school of thinkers asserts, we have ideas antecedent to experience, is a question which has been hotly disputed, but which I do not believe the actual resources of our knowledge can answer, and certainly I have no intention at present of making the attempt. It is enough to say that we call geometry a deductive science, because, even if its axioms are arrived at inductively, the inductive process is extremely small, and we are unconscious of it ; while the deductive reasonings form the great mass and difficulty of the science.

To bring this distinction home to you, I will illustrate it by a specimen of deductive and inductive investigation of the same subject. Suppose a writer on what is termed social science wishes to estimate the influence of different habits of thought on the average duration of life, and taking as an instance the opposite pursuits of poets and mathematicians, asks which of them live longest. How is he to solve this? If he proceeds inductively he will first collect the facts, that is, he will ransack the biographies of poets and mathematicians in different ages, different climates, and different states of society, so as to eliminate perturbations arising from circumstances not connected with his subject. He will then throw the results into the statistical form of tables of mortality, and on comparing them will find, that notwithstanding the immense variety of circumstances which he has investigated, there is a general average which constitutes an empirical law, and proves that mathematicians, as a body, are longer lived than poets. This is the inductive method. On the other hand, the deductive inquirer will arrive at precisely the same conclusion by a totally different method. He will argue thus: poetry appeals to the imagination, mathematics to the understanding. To work the imagination is more exciting than to work the understanding, and what is habitually exciting is usually unhealthy. But what is usually unhealthy will tend to shorten life; therefore poetry tends more than mathematics to shorten life; therefore on the whole poets will die sooner than mathematicians.

You now see the difference between induction and deduction; and you see, too, that both methods are valuable, and that any conclusion must be greatly strengthened if we can reach it by two such different paths. To connect this with the question before us, I will endeavour to establish two propositions. First, That women naturally prefer the deductive method to the inductive. Secondly, That women by encouraging in men deductive habits of thought, have rendered an immense, though unconscious, service to the progress of knowledge, by preventing scientific investigators from being as exclusively inductive as they would otherwise be.

In regard to women being by nature more deductive, and men more inductive, you will remember that induction assigns the first place to particular facts; deduction to general propositions or ideas. Now, there are several reasons why women prefer the deductive, and, if I may so say, ideal method. They are more emotional, more enthusiastic, and more imaginative than men; they therefore live more in an ideal world; while men, with their colder, harder, and austerer organisations, are more practical and more under the dominion of facts, to which they consequently ascribe a higher importance. Another circumstance which makes women more deductive, is that they possess more of what is called intuition. They cannot see so far as men can, but what they do see they see quicker. Hence, they are constantly tempted to grasp at once at an idea, and seek to solve a problem suddenly, in contradistinction to the slower and more laborious ascent of the inductive investigator.

That women are more deductive than men, because they think quicker than men, is a proposition which some persons will not relish, and yet it may be proved in a variety of ways. Indeed, nothing could prevent its being universally admitted except the fact, that the remarkable rapidity with which women think is obscured by that miserable, that contemptible, that preposterous system, called their education, in which valuable things are carefully kept from them, and trifling things carefully taught to

them, until their fine and nimble minds are too often irretrievably injured.  It is on this account, that in the lower classes the
superior quickness of women is even more noticeable than in the
upper; and an eminent physician, Dr. Currie, mentions in one of
his letters, that when a labourer and his wife came together to
consult him, it was always from the woman that he gained the
clearest and most precise information, the intellect of the man
moving too slowly for his purpose.  To this I may add another
observation which many travellers have made, and which any one
can verify: namely, that when you are in a foreign country, and
speaking a foreign language, women will understand you quicker
than men will; and that for the same reason, if you lose your way
in a town abroad, it is always best to apply to a woman, because a
man will show less readiness of apprehension.

These, and other circumstances which might be adduced—such,
for instance, as the insight into character possessed by women,
and the fine tact for which they are remarkable—prove that they
are more deductive than men, for two principal reasons.  First,
Because they are quicker than men.  Secondly, Because, being
more emotional and enthusiastic, they live in a more ideal world,
and therefore prefer a method of inquiry which proceeds from
ideas to facts; leaving to men the opposite method of proceeding
from facts to ideas.

My second proposition is, that women have rendered great
though unconscious service to science, by encouraging and keeping
alive this habit of deductive thought; and that if it were not for
them, scientific men would be much too inductive, and the progress of our knowledge would be hindered.  There are many here
who will not willingly admit this proposition, because, in England,
since the first half of the seventeenth century, the inductive
method, as the means of arriving at physical truths, has been
the object, not of rational admiration, but of a blind and servile
worship; and it is constantly said, that since the time of Bacon
all great physical discoveries have been made by that process.  If
this be true, then of course the deductive habits of women must,
in reference to the progress of knowledge, have done more harm
than good.  But it is not true.  It is not true that the greatest
modern discoveries have all been made by induction; and the
circumstance of its being believed to be true is one of many
proofs how much more successful Englishmen have been in
making discoveries than in investigating the principles according
to which discoveries are made.

The first instance I will give you of the triumph of the deductive method, is in the most important discovery yet made re-

specting the inorganic world; I mean the discovery of the law of gravitation by Sir Isaac Newton. Several of Newton's other discoveries were, no doubt, inductive, in so far as they merely assumed such provisional and tentative hypotheses as are always necessary to make experiments fruitful. But it is certain that his greatest discovery of all was deductive, in the proper sense of the word; that is to say, the process of reasoning from ideas was out of all proportion large, compared to the process of reasoning from facts. Five or six years after the accession of Charles II., Newton was sitting in a garden, when (you all know this part of the story) an apple fell from a tree. Whether he had been already musing respecting gravitation, or whether the fall of the apple directed his thoughts into that channel is uncertain, and is immaterial to my present purpose, which is merely to indicate the course his mind actually took. His object was to discover some law, that is, rise to some higher truth respecting gravity than was previously known. Observe how he went to work. He sat still where he was, and he thought. He did not get up to make experiments concerning gravitation, nor did he go home to consult observations which others had made, or to collate tables of observations: he did not even continue to watch the external world, but he sat, like a man entranced and enraptured, feeding on his own mind, and evolving idea after idea. He thought that if the apple had been on a higher tree, if it had been on the highest known tree, it would have equally fallen. Thus far, there was no reason to think that the power which made the apple fall was susceptible of diminution; and if it were not susceptible of diminution, why should it be susceptible of limit? If it were unlimited and undiminished, it would extend above the earth; it would reach the moon and keep her in her orbit. If the power which made the apple fall was actually able to control the moon, why should it stop there? Why should not the planets also be controlled, and why should not they be forced to run their course by the necessity of gravitating towards the sun, just as the moon gravitated towards the earth? His mind thus advancing from idea to idea, he was carried by imagination into the realms of space, and still sitting, neither experimenting nor observing, but heedless of the operations of nature, he completed the most sublime and majestic speculation that it ever entered into the heart of man to conceive. Owing to an inaccurate measurement of the diameter of the earth, the details which verified this stupendous conception were not completed till twenty years later, when Newton, still pursuing the same process, made a deductive application of the laws of Kepler: so that both in the beginning and in the end, the greatest discovery of the greatest natural philosopher the world has yet seen, was the fruit of the deductive method. See how small a part the senses played in that discovery! It was the triumph of the idea! It was the audacity of genius! It was the outbreak of a mind so daring, and yet so subtle, that we have only Shakspeare's with which to compare it. To pretend, therefore, as many have done, that the fall of the apple was the cause of the discovery, and then to adduce that as a confirmation of the idle and superficial saying "that great events spring from little causes," only shows how unable such writers are to appreciate what our masters have done for us. No great event ever sprung, or ever will spring, from a little cause; and this, the greatest of all discoveries, had a cause fully equal to the effect produced. The cause of the discovery of the law of gravitation was not the fall of the apple, nor was it anything that occurred in the external world. The cause of the discovery of Newton was the mind of Newton himself.

The next instance I will mention of the successful employment of the *à priori*, or deductive method, concerns the mineral kingdom. If you take a crystallised substance as it is usually found in nature, nothing can at first sight appear more irregular and capricious. Even in its simplest form, the shape is so various as to be perplexing; but natural crystals are generally met with, not in primary forms, but in secondary ones, in which they have a singularly confused and uncouth aspect. These strange-looking bodies had long excited the attention of philosophers, who, after the approved inductive fashion, subjected them to all sorts of experiments; divided them, broke them up, measured them, weighed them, analysed them, thrust them into crucibles, brought chemical agents to bear upon them, and did everything they could think of to worm out the secret of these crystals, and get at their mystery. Still, the mystery was not revealed to them. At length, late in the eighteenth century, a Frenchman named Haüy, one of the most remarkable men of a remarkable age, made the discovery, and ascertained that these native crystals, irregular as they appear, are in truth perfectly regular, and that their secondary forms deviate from their primary forms by a regular process of diminution; that is, by what he termed laws of decrement—the principles of decrease being as unerring as those of increase. Now, I beg that you will particularly notice how this striking discovery was made. Haüy was essentially a poet; and his great delight was to wander in the *Jardin du Roi*, observing nature, not as a physical philosopher, but as a poet. Though his understanding was strong, his imagination was stronger; and it was for the purpose of filling his mind with ideas of beauty that he directed his attention at first to the vegetable kingdom, with its graceful forms and various hues. His poetic temperament luxuriating in such images of beauty, his mind became saturated with ideas of symmetry, and Cuvier assures us that it was in consequence of those ideas that he began to believe that the apparently irregular forms of native crystals were in reality regular; in other words, that in them, too, there was a beauty—a hidden beauty—though the senses were unable to discern it. As soon as this idea was firmly implanted in his mind, at least half the discovery was made; for he had got the key to it, and was on the right road, which others had missed because, while they approached minerals experimentally on the side of the senses, he approached them speculatively on the side of the idea. This is not a mere fanciful assertion of mine, since Haüy himself tells us, in his great work on Mineralogy, that he took, as his starting point, ideas of the symmetry of form; and that from those ideas he worked down deductively to his subject. It was in this way, and of course after a long series of subsequent labours, that he read the riddle which had baffled his able but unimaginative predecessors. And there are two circumstances worthy of note, as confirming what I have said respecting the real history of this discovery. The first is, that although Haüy is universally admitted to be the founder of the science, his means of observation were so rude that subsequent crystallographers declare that hardly any of his measurements of angles are correct; as indeed is not surprising, inasmuch as the goniometer which he employed was a very imperfect instrument; and that of Wollaston, which acts by reflection, was not then invented. The other circumstance is, that the little mathematics he once knew he had forgotten amid his poetic and imaginative pursuits; so that, in working out the details of his own science, he was obliged, like a schoolboy, to learn the elements of geometry before he could prove to the world what he had already proved to himself, and could bring the laws of the science of form to bear upon the structure of the mineral kingdom.

To these cases of the application of what may be termed the ideal method to the inorganic world, I will add another from the organic department of nature. Those among you who are interested in botany, are aware that the highest morphological generalisation we possess respecting plants, is the great law of metamorphosis, according to which the stamens, pistils, corollas, bracts, petals, and so forth, of every plant, are simply modified leaves. It is now known that these various parts, different in shape, different in colour, and different in function, are successive

stages of the leaf—epochs, as it were, of its history.   The question
naturally arises, who made this discovery?   Was it some inductive investigator, who had spent years in experiments and minute
observations of plants, and who, with indefatigable industry, had
collected them, classified them, given them hard names, dried
them, laid them up in his herbarium that he might at leisure
study their structure and rise to their laws?   Not so.   The discovery was made by Göthe, the greatest poet Germany has produced, and one of the greatest the world has ever seen.   And he
made it, not in spite of being a poet, but because he was a poet.
It was his brilliant imagination, his passion for beauty, and his
exquisite conception of form, which supplied him with ideas,
from which, reasoning deductively, he arrived at conclusions by
descent, not by ascent.   He stood on an eminence, and looking
down from the heights generalised the law.   Then he descended
into the plains, and verified the idea.   When the discovery was
announced by Göthe, the botanists not only rejected it, but were
filled with wrath at the notion of a poet invading their territory.
What! a man who made verses and wrote plays, a mere man of
imagination, a poor creature who knew nothing of facts, who had
not even used the microscope, who had made no great experiments
on the growth of plants; was he to enter the sacred precincts of
physical science, and give himself out as a philosopher?   It was
too absurd.   But Göthe, who had thrown his idea upon the world,
could afford to wait and bide his time.   You know the result.
The men of facts at length succumbed before the man of ideas:
the philosophers, even on their own ground, were beaten by the
poet; and this great discovery is now received and eagerly welcomed by those very persons who, if they had lived fifty years
ago, would have treated it with scorn, and who even now still go
on in their old routine, telling us, in defiance of the history of
our knowledge, that all physical discoveries are made by the
Baconian method, and that any other method is unworthy the
attention of sound and sensible thinkers.

One more instance, and I have done with this part of the subject.   The same great poet made another important physical
discovery in precisely the same way.   Göthe, strolling in a ceme-
tery near Venice, stumbled on a skull which was lying before
him.   Suddenly the idea flashed across his mind that the skull
was composed of vertebræ; in other words, that the bony covering
of the head was simply an expansion of the bony covering of the
spine.   This luminous idea was afterwards adopted by Oken and
a few other great naturalists in Germany and France, but it was
not received in England till ten years ago, when Mr. Owen took it

up, and in his very remarkable work on the " Homologies of the Vertebrate Skeleton," showed its meaning and purpose as contributing towards a general scheme of philosophic anatomy. That the discovery was made by Göthe late in the eighteenth century is certain, and it is equally certain that for fifty years afterwards the English anatomists, with all their tools and all their dissections, ignored or despised that very discovery which they are now compelled to accept.

You will particularly observe the circumstances under which this discovery was made. It was not made by some great surgeon, dissector, or physician, but it was made by a great poet, and amidst scenes most likely to excite a poetic temperament. It was made in Venice, that land so calculated to fire the imagination of a poet; the land of marvels, the land of poetry and romance, the land of painting and of song. It was made, too, when Göthe, surrounded by the ashes of the dead, would be naturally impressed with those feelings of solemn awe, in whose presence the human understanding, rebuked and abashed, becomes weak and helpless, and leaves the imagination unfettered to wander in that ideal world which is its own peculiar abode, and from which it derives its highest aspirations.

It has often seemed to me that there is a striking similarity between this event and one of the most beautiful episodes in the greatest production of the greatest man the world has ever possessed; I mean Shakspeare's " Hamlet." You remember that wonderful scene in the churchyard, when Hamlet walks in among the graves, where the brutal and ignorant clowns are singing and jeering and jesting over the remains of the dead. You remember how the fine imagination of the great Danish thinker is stirred by the spectacle, albeit he knows not yet that the grave which is being dug at his feet is destined to contain all that he holds dear upon earth. But though he wists not of this, he is moved like the great German poet, and he, like Göthe, takes up a skull, and his speculative faculties begin to work. Images of decay crowd on his mind as he thinks how the mighty are fallen and have passed away. In a moment, his imagination carries him back two thousand years, and he almost believes that the skull he holds in his hand is indeed the skull of Alexander, and in his mind's eye he contrasts the putrid bone with what it once contained, the brain of the scourge and conqueror of mankind. Then it is that suddenly he, like Göthe, passes into an ideal physical world, and seizing the great doctrine of the indestructibility of matter, that doctrine which in his age it was difficult to grasp, he begins to show how, by a long series of successive changes, the head of Alexander might have been made to subserve the most ignoble purposes; the substance being always metamorphosed, never destroyed. "Why," asks Hamlet, "why may not imagination trace the noble dust of Alexander?" when, just as he is about to pursue this train of ideas, he is stopped by one of those men of facts, one of those practical and prosaic natures, who are always ready to impede the flight of genius. By his side stands the faithful, the affectionate, but the narrow-minded Horatio, who, looking upon all this as the dream of a distempered fancy, objects that—"'Twere to consider too curiously to consider so." O! what a picture! what a contrast between Hamlet and Horatio; between the idea and the sense; between the imagination and the understanding. "'Twere to consider too curiously to consider so." Even thus was Göthe troubled by his contemporaries, and thus too often speculation is stopped, genius is chilled, and the play and swell of the human mind repressed, because ideas are made subordinate to facts, because the external is preferred to the internal, and because the Horatios of action discourage the Hamlets of thought.

Much more could I have said to you on this subject, and gladly would I have enlarged on so fruitful a theme as the philosophy of scientific method; a philosophy too much neglected in this country, but of the deepest interest to those who care to rise above the little instincts of the hour, and who love to inquire into the origin of our knowledge, and into the nature of the conditions under which that knowledge exists. But I fear that I have almost exhausted your patience in leading you into paths of thought which, not being familiar, must be somewhat difficult, and I can hardly hope that I have succeeded in making every point perfectly clear. Still, I do trust that there is no obscurity as to the general results. I trust that I have not altogether raised my voice in vain before this great assembly, and that I have done at least something towards vindicating the use in physical science of that deductive method which, during the last two centuries, Englishmen have unwisely despised. Not that I deny for a moment the immense value of the opposite or inductive method. Indeed, it is impossible for any one standing in this theatre to do so. It is impossible to forget that within the precincts of this building great secrets have been extorted from nature by induction alone. Under the shadow and protection of this noble Institution, men of real eminence, men of power and thought have, by a skilful employment of that method, made considerable additions to our knowledge, have earned for themselves the respect of their contemporaries, and well deserve the homage of posterity. To them all honour is due; and I, for one, would say, let that honour be paid freely, ungrudgingly, and with an open and bounteous heart. But I venture to submit that all discoveries have not been made by this, their favourite process. I submit that there is a spiritual, a poetic, and for aught we know a spontaneous and uncaused element in the human mind, which ever and anon, suddenly and without warning, gives us a glimpse and a forecast of the future, and urges us to seize truth as it were by anticipation. In attacking the fortress, we may sometimes storm the citadel without stopping to sap the outworks. That great discoveries have been made in this way, the history of our knowledge decisively proves. And if, passing from what has been already accomplished, we look at what remains to be done, we shall find that the necessity of some such plan is likely to become more and more pressing. The field of thought is rapidly widening, and as the horizon recedes on every side, it will soon be impossible for the mere logical operations of the understanding to cover the whole of that enormous and outlying domain. Already the division of labour has been pushed so far that we are in imminent danger of losing in comprehensiveness more than we gain in accuracy. In our pursuit after special truths, we run no small risk of dwarfing our own minds. By concentrating our attention, we are apt to narrow our conceptions, and to miss those commanding views which would be attained by a wider though perhaps less minute survey. It is but too clear that something of this sort has already happened, and that serious mischief has been wrought. For, look at the language and sentiments of those who profess to guide, and who in some measure do guide, public opinion in the scientific world. According to their verdict, if a man does something specific and immediate, if, for instance, he discovers a new acid or a new salt, great admiration is excited, and his praise is loudly celebrated. But when a man like Göthe puts forth some vast and pregnant idea which is destined to revolutionise a whole department of inquiry, and by inaugurating a new train of thought to form an epoch in the history of the human mind; if it happens, as is always the case, that certain facts contradict that view, then the so-called scientific men rise up in arms against the author of so daring an innovation; a storm is raised about his head, he is denounced as a dreamer, an idle visionary, an interloper in matters which he has not studied with proper sobriety.

Thus it is that great minds are depressed in order that little minds may be raised. This false standard of excellence has corrupted even our language, and vitiated the ordinary forms of speech. Among us a theorist is actually a term of reproach, instead of being, as it ought to be, a term of honour; for to theorise is the highest function of genius, and the greatest philosophers must always be the greatest theorists. What makes all this the more serious is, that the farther our knowledge advances, the greater will be the need of rising to transcendental views of the physical world. To the magnificent doctrine of the indestructibility of matter, we are now adding the no less magnificent one of the indestructibility of force; and we are beginning to perceive that, according to the ordinary scientific treatment, our investigations must be confined to questions of metamorphosis and of distribution; that the study of causes and of entities is forbidden to us; and that we are limited to phenomena through which and above which we can never hope to pass. But, unless I greatly err, there is something in us which craves for more than this. Surely we shall not always be satisfied, even in physical science, with the cheerless prospect of never reaching beyond the laws of co-existence and of sequence? Surely this is not the be-all and end-all of our knowledge. And yet, according to the strict canons of inductive logic, we can do no more. According to that method, this is the verge and confine of all. Happily, however, induction is only one of our resources. Induction is, indeed, a mighty weapon laid up in the armoury of the human mind, and by its aid great deeds have been accomplished, and noble conquests have been won. But in that armoury there is another weapon, I will not say of a stronger make, but certainly of a keener edge; and, if that weapon had been oftener used during the present and preceding century, our knowledge would be far more advanced than it actually is. If the imagination had been more cultivated, if there had been a closer union between the spirit of poetry and the spirit of science, natural philosophy would have made greater progress, because natural philosophers would have taken a higher and more successful aim, and would have enlisted on their side a wider range of human sympathies.

From this point of view you will see the incalculable service women have rendered to the progress of knowledge. Great and exclusive as is our passion for induction, it would, but for them, have been greater and more exclusive still. Empirical as we are, slaves as we are to the tyranny of facts, our slavery would, but for them, have been more complete and more ignominious. Their turn of thought, their habits of mind, their conversation, their influence, insensibly extending over the whole surface of society, and frequently penetrating its intimate structure, have, more than all other things put together, tended to raise us into an ideal world, lift us from the dust in which we are too prone to grovel, and develop in us those germs of imagination which even the most sluggish and apathetic understandings in some degree possess. The striking fact that most men of genius have had remarkable mothers, and that they have gained from their mothers far more than from their fathers; this singular and unquestionable fact can, I think, be best explained by the principles which I have laid down. Some, indeed, will tell you that this depends upon laws of the hereditary transmission of character from parent to child. But if this be the case, how comes it that while every one admits that remarkable men have usually remarkable mothers, it is not generally admitted that remarkable men have usually remarkable fathers? If the intellect is bequeathed on one side, why is it not bequeathed on the other? For my part, I greatly doubt whether the human mind is handed down in this way, like an heir-loom, from one generation to another. I rather believe that, in regard to the relation between men of genius and their mothers, the really important events occur after birth, when the habits of thought peculiar to one sex act upon and improve the habits of thought peculiar to the other sex. Unconsciously, and from a very early period, there is established an intimate and endearing connection between the deductive mind of the mother and the inductive mind of her son. The understanding of the boy, softened and yet elevated by the imagination of his mother, is saved from that degeneracy towards which the mere understanding always inclines; it is saved from being too cold, too matter-of-fact, too prosaic, and the different properties and functions of the mind are more harmoniously developed than would otherwise be practicable. Thus it is that by the mere play of the affections the finished man is ripened and completed. Thus it is that the most touching and the most sacred form of human love, the purest, the highest, and the holiest compact of which our nature is capable, becomes an engine for the advancement of knowledge and the discovery of truth. In after life other relations often arise by which the same process is continued. And, notwithstanding a few exceptions, we do undoubtedly find that the most truly eminent men have had not only their affections, but also their intellect, greatly influenced by women. I will go even farther; and I will venture to say that those who have not undergone that influence betray a something incomplete and mutilated. We detect, even in their genius, a certain frigidity of tone; and we look in vain for that burning fire, that gushing and spontaneous nature with which our ideas of genius are indissolubly associated. Therefore, it is, that those who are most anxious that the boundaries of knowledge should be enlarged,

*c

ought to be most eager that the influence of women should be increased, in order that every resource of the human mind may be at once and quickly brought into play. For you may rely upon it that the time is approaching when all those resources will be needed, and will be taxed even to the utmost. We shall soon have on our hands work far more arduous than any we have yet accomplished; and we shall be encountered by difficulties the removal of which will require every sort of help, and every variety of power. As yet we are in the infancy of our knowledge. What we have done is but a speck compared to what remains to be done. For what is there that we really know? We are too apt to speak as if we had penetrated into the sanctuary of truth and raised the veil of the goddess, when in fact we are still standing, coward-like, trembling before the vestibule, and not daring, from very fear, to cross the threshold of the temple. The highest of our so-called laws of nature are as yet purely empirical. You are startled by that assertion, but it is literally true. Not one single physical discovery that has ever been made has been connected with the laws of the mind that made it; and until that connection is ascertained our knowledge has no sure basis. On the one side we have mind; on the other side we have matter. These two principles are so interwoven, they so act upon and perturb each other, that we shall never really know the laws of one unless we also know the laws of both. Everything is essential; everything hangs together, and forms part of one single scheme, one grand and complex plan, one gorgeous drama, of which the universe is the theatre. They who discourse to you of the laws of nature as if those laws were binding on nature, or as if they formed a part of nature, deceive both you and themselves. The laws of nature have their sole seat, origin, and function in the human mind. They are simply the conditions under which the regularity of nature is recognised. They explain the external world, but they reside in the internal. As yet we know scarcely anything of the laws of mind, and therefore we know scarcely anything of the laws of nature. Let us not be led away by vain and high-sounding words. We talk of the law of gravitation, and yet we know not what gravitation is; we talk of the conservation of force and distribution of forces, and we know not what forces are; we talk with complacent ignorance of the atomic arrangements of matter, and we neither know what atoms are nor what matter is; we do not even know if matter, in the ordinary sense of the word, can be said to exist; we have as yet only broken the first ground, we have but touched the crust and surface of things. Before us and around us there is an immense and

untrodden field, whose limits the eye vainly strives to define ; so
completely are they lost in the dim and shadowy outline of the
future.   In that field, which we and our posterity have yet to
traverse, I firmly believe that the imagination will effect quite as
much as the understanding.   Our poetry will have to reinforce
our logic, and we must feel as much as we must argue.   Let us,
then, hope that the imaginative and emotional minds of one sex
will continue to accelerate the great progress, by acting upon and
improving the colder and harder minds of the other sex.   By this
coalition, by this union of different faculties, different tastes, and
different methods, we shall go on our way with the greater ease.
A vast and splendid career lies before us, which it will take many
ages to complete.   We see looming in the distance a rich and
goodly harvest, into which perchance some of us may yet live to
thrust our sickle, but of which, reap what we may, the greatest
crop of all must be reserved for our posterity.   So far, however,
from desponding, we ought to be sanguine.   We have every reason
to believe that when the human mind once steadily combines the
whole of its powers, it will be more than a match for the difficulties presented by the external world.   As we surpass our fathers,
so will our children surpass us.   We, waging against the forces of
nature what has too often been a precarious, unsteady, and un-
skilled warfare, have never yet put forth the whole of our strength,
and have never united all our faculties against our common foe.
We, therefore, have been often worsted, and have sustained many
and grievous reverses.   But even so, such is the elasticity of the
human mind, such is the energy of that immortal and god-like
principle which lives within us, that we are baffled without being
discouraged, our very defeats quicken our resources, and we may
hope that our descendants, benefiting by our failure, will profit by
our example, and that for them is reserved that last and decisive
stage of the great conflict between Man and Nature, in which,
advancing from success to success, fresh trophies will be constantly won, every struggle will issue in a conquest, and every
battle end in a victory.

If a jury of the greatest European thinkers were to be impannelled, and were directed to declare by their verdict who, among our living writers had done most for the advance of knowledge, they could hardly hesitate in pronouncing the name of John Stuart Mill. Nor can we doubt that posterity would ratify their decision. No other man has dealt with so many problems of equal importance, and yet of equal complexity. The questions which he has investigated concern, on the one hand, the practical interests of every member of society, and, on the other hand, the subtlest and most hidden operations of the human mind. Although he touches the surface he also penetrates the centre. Between those extremes lie innumerable subjects which he has explored, always with great ability, often with signal success. On these topics, whether practical or speculative, his authority is constantly evoked; and his conclusions are adopted by many who are unable to follow the arguments by which the conclusions are justified. Other men we have, remarkable for their depth of thought; and others again who are remarkable for the utility of their suggestions. But the peculiarity of Mr. Mill is, that both these qualities are more effectively combined by him than by any one else of the present day. Hence it is, that he is as skilful in tracing the operation of general causes, as in foreseeing the result of particular measures. And hence, too, his influence is far greater than would otherwise be possible; since he not only appeals to a wider range of interests than any living writer can do, but by his mastery over special and practical details he is able to show that principles, however refined they appear, and however far removed from ordinary apprehension, may be enforced, without so dangerous a disturbance of social arrangements, and without so great a sacrifice of existing institutions, as might at first sight be supposed. By this means he has often disarmed hostility, and has induced practical men to accept conclusions on practical grounds, to which no force of scientific argument and no amount of scientific proof would have persuaded them to yield. Securing

[1] Reprinted from 'Fraser's Magazine' for May, 1859.

by one process the assent of speculative thinkers, and securing by
another process the assent of working politicians, he operates on
the two extremes of life, and exhibits the singular spectacle of one
of the most daring and original philosophers in Europe, winning
the applause of not a few mere legislators and statesmen who are
indifferent to his higher generalizations, and who, confining themselves to their own craft, are incapable of soaring beyond the safe
and limited routine of ordinary experience.

This has increased his influence in more ways than one.   For
it is extremely rare to meet with a man who excels both in practice and in speculation ; and it is by no means common to meet
with one who desires to do so.   Between these two forms of excellence, there is not only a difference, there is also an opposition.
Practice aims at what is immediate ; speculation at what is remote.
The first investigates small and special causes ; the other investigates large and general causes.   In practical life the wisest and
soundest men avoid speculation, and ensure success because by
limiting their range they increase the tenacity with which they
grasp events ; while in speculative life the course is exactly the
reverse, since in that department the greater the range the greater
the command, and the object of the philosopher is to have as
large a generalization as possible ; in other words, to rise as high
as he can above the phenomena with which he is concerned.   The
truth I apprehend to be that the immediate effect of any act is
usually determined by causes peculiar to that act, and which, as
it were, lie within it ; while the remote effect of the same act is
governed by causes lying out of the act ; that is, by the general
condition of the surrounding circumstances.   Special causes produce their effect quickly ; but, to bring general causes into play,
we require not only width of surface but also length of time.   If,
for instance, a man living under a cruel despotism were to inflict
a fatal blow upon the despot, the immediate result—namely, the
death of the tyrant—would be caused solely by circumstances
peculiar to the action, such as the sharpness of the weapon, the
precision of the aim, and the part that was wounded.   But the
remote result—that is, the removal, not of the despot but of the
despotism—would be governed by circumstances external to the
particular act, and would depend upon whether or not the country
was fit for liberty, since if the country were unfit, another despot
would be sure to arise and another despotism be established.   To
a philosophic mind the actions of an individual count for little ;
to a practical mind they are everything.   Whoever is accustomed
to generalise, smiles within himself when he hears that Luther
brought about the Reformation ; that Bacon overthrew the ancient

philosophy; that William III. saved our liberties; that Romilly humanised our penal code; that Clarkson and Wilberforce destroyed slavery; and that Grey and Brougham gave us Reform. He smiles at such assertions, because he knows full well that such men, useful as they were, are only to be regarded as tools by which that work was done which the force and accumulation of preceding circumstances had determined should be done. They were good instruments; sharp and serviceable instruments, but nothing more. Not only are individuals, in the great average of affairs, inoperative for good; they are also, happily for mankind, inoperative for evil. Nero and Domitian caused enormous mischief, but every trace of it has now disappeared. The occurrences which contemporaries think to be of the greatest importance, and which in point of fact for a short time are so, invariably turn out in the long run to be the least important of all. They are like meteors which dazzle the vulgar by their brilliancy, and then pass away, leaving no mark behind. Well, therefore, and in the highest spirit of philosophy, did Montesquieu say that the Roman Republic was overthrown, not, as is commonly supposed, by the ambition of Cæsar and Pompey, but by that state of things which made the success of their ambition possible. And so indeed it was. Events which had been long accumulating and had come from afar, pressed on and thickened until their united force was irresistible, and the Republic grew ripe for destruction. It decayed, it tottered, it was sapped to its foundation; and then, when all was ready and it was nodding to its fall, Cæsar and Pompey stepped forward, and because they dealt the last blow, we, forsooth, are expected to believe that they produced a catastrophe which the course of affairs had made inevitable before they were born.

The great majority of men will, however, always cling to Cæsar and Pompey; that is to say, they will prefer the study of proximate causes to the study of remote ones. This is connected with another and more fundamental distinction, by virtue of which, life is regarded by practical minds as an art, by speculative minds as a science. And we find every civilised nation divided into two classes corresponding with these two divisions. We find one class investigating affairs with a view to what is most special; the other investigating them with a view to what is most general. This antagonism is essential, and lies in the nature of things. Indeed, it is so clearly marked, that except in minds, not only of very great power, but of a peculiar kind of power, it is impossible to reconcile the two methods; it is impossible for any but a most remarkable man to have them both. Many even of the greatest thinkers have been but too notorious for an ignorance of ordinary affairs, and for an inattention to practical every-day interests. While studying the science of life, they neglect the art of living. This is because such men, notwithstanding their genius, are essentially one-sided and narrow, being, unhappily for themselves, unable or unaccustomed to note the operation of special and proximate causes. Dealing with the remote and the universal, they omit the immediate and the contingent. They sacrifice the actual to the ideal. To their view, all phenomena are suggestive of science, that is of what may be known ; while to the opposite view, the same phenomena are suggestive of art, that is, of what may be done. A perfect intellect would unite both views, and assign to each its relative importance ; but such a feat is of the greatest possible rarity. It may in fact be doubted if more than one instance is recorded of its being performed without a single failure. That instance, I need hardly say, is Shakspeare. No other mind has thoroughly interwoven the remote with the proximate, the general with the special, the abstract with the concrete. No other mind has so completely incorporated the speculations of the highest philosophy with the meanest details of the lowest life. Shakspeare mastered both extremes, and covered all the intermediate field. He knew both man and men. He thought as deeply as Plato or Kant. He observed us closely as Dickens or Thackeray.

Of whom else can this be said ? Other philosophers have, for the most part, overlooked the surface in their haste to reach the summit. Hence the anomaly of many of the most profound thinkers having been ignorant of what it was shameful for them not to know, and having been unable to manage with success even their own affairs. The sort of advice they would give to others may be easily imagined. It is no exaggeration to say that if, in any age of the world, one half of the suggestions made by the ablest men had been adopted, that age would have been thrown into the rankest confusion. Plato was the deepest thinker of antiquity ; and yet the proposals which he makes in his "Republic," and in his " Treatise on Laws," are so absurd that they can hardly be read without laughter. Aristotle, little inferior to Plato in depth, and much his superior in comprehensiveness, desired, on purely speculative grounds, that no one should give or receive interest for the use of money : an idea which, if it had been put into execution, would have produced the most mischievous results, would have stopped the accumulation of wealth, and thereby have postponed for an indefinite period the civilisation of the world. In modern as well as in ancient times, systems of philosophy have been raised which involve assumptions, and seek to compel consequences, incompatible with the practical interests of society. The Germans are the most profound philosophers in Europe, and it is precisely in their country that this tendency is most apparent. Comte, the most comprehensive thinker France has produced since Descartes, did in his last work deliberately advocate, and wish to organise, a scheme of polity so monstrously and obviously imprac- ticable, that if it were translated into English the plain men of our island would lift their eyes in astonishment, and would most likely suggest that the author should for his own sake be imme- diately confined, Not that we need pride ourselves too much on these matters. If a catalogue were to be drawn up of the prac- tical suggestions made by our greatest thinkers, it would be im- possible to conceive a document more damaging to the reputation of the speculative classes. Those classes are always before the age in their theories, and behind the age in their practice. It is not, therefore, strange that Frederick the Great, who perhaps had a more intimate and personal knowledge of them than any other prince equally powerful, and who moreover admired them, courted them, and, as an author, to a certain slight degree belonged to them, should have recorded his opinion of their practical inca- pacity in the strongest terms he could find. " If," he is reported to have said, " if I wanted to ruin one of my provinces, I would make over its government to the philosophers."

This neglect of the surface of things is, moreover, exhibited in the peculiar absence of mind for which many philosophers have been remarkable. Newton was so oblivious of what was actually passing, that he frequently overlooked or forgot the most neces- sary transactions, was not sure whether he had dined, and would leave his own house half-naked, appearing in that state in the streets, because he fancied all the while that he was fully dressed. Many admire this as the simplicity of genius. I see nothing in it but an unhappy and calamitous principle of the construction of the human mind, which prevents nearly all men from successfully dealing both with the remote and the immediate. They who are little occupied with either, may, by virtue of the smallness of their ambition, somewhat succeed in both. This is the reward of their mediocrity, and they may well be satisfied with it. Dividing such energy as they possess, they unite a little speculation with a little business; a little science with a little art. But in the most eminent and vigorous characters, we find, with extremely rare ex- ceptions, that excellence on one side excludes excellence on the other. Here the perfection of theory, there the perfection of practice; and between the two a gulf which few indeed can bridge. Another and still more remarkable instance of this unfortunate peculiarity of our nature is supplied by the career of Bacon, who, though he boasted that he made philosophy practical, and forced her to dwell among men, was himself so unpractical that he could not deal with events as they successively arose. Yet he had everything in his favour. To genius of the highest order he added eloquence, wit, and industry. He had good connections, influential friends, a supple address, an obsequious and somewhat fawning disposition. He had seen life under many aspects, he had mixed with various classes, he had abundant experience, and still he was unable to turn these treasures to practical account. Putting him aside as a philosopher, and taking him merely as a man of action, his conduct was a series of blunders. Whatever he most desired, in that did he most fail. One of his darling objects was the attainment of popularity, in the pursuit of which he, on two memorable occasions, grievously offended the Court from which he sought promotion. So unskilful, however, were his combinations, that in the prosecution of Essex, which was by far the most unpopular act in the reign of Elizabeth, he played a part not only conspicuous and discreditable, but grossly impolitic. Essex, who was a high-spirited and generous man, was beloved by all classes, and nothing could be more certain than that the violence Bacon displayed against him would recoil on its author. It was also well known that Essex was the intimate friend of Bacon, had exerted himself in every way for him, and had even presented him with a valuable estate. For a man to prosecute his benefactor, to heap invectives upon him at his trial, and having hunted him to the death, publish a libel insulting his memory, was a folly as well as an outrage, and is one of many proofs that in practical matters the judgment of Bacon was unsound. Ingratitude aggravated by cruelty must, if it is generally known, always be a blunder as well as a crime, because it wounds the deepest and most universal feelings of our common nature. However vicious a man may be, he will never be guilty of such an act unless he is foolish as well as vicious. But the philosopher could not foresee those immediate consequences which a plain man would have easily discerned. The truth is, that while the speculations of Bacon were full of wisdom, his acts were full of folly. He was anxious to build up a fortune, and he did what many persons have done both before and since: he availed himself of his judicial position to take bribes from suitors in his court. But here again, his operations were so clumsy, that he committed the enormous oversight of accepting bribes from men against whom he afterwards decided. He, therefore, deliberately put himself in the power of those whom he deliberately injured. This was not only because he was greedy after wealth, but also because he was injudiciously greedy. The error was in the head as much as in the heart. Besides being

a corrupt judge, he was likewise a bad calculator. The consequence was that he was detected, and being detected was ruined.
When his fame was at its height, when enjoyments of every kind
were thickening and clustering around him, the cup of pleasure
was dashed from his lips because he quaffed it too eagerly.   To
say that he fell merely because he was unprincipled, is preposterous,
for many men are unprincipled all their lives and never fall at all.
Why it is that bad men sometimes flourish, and how such apparent injustice is remedied, is a mysterious question which this is
not the place for discussing; but the fact is indubitable.   In
practical life men fail, partly because they aim at unwise objects,
but chiefly because they have not acquired the art of adapting
their means to their end.   This was the case with Bacon.   In
ordinary matters he was triumphed over and defeated by nearly
every one with whom he came into contact.   His dependents
cheated him with impunity ; and notwithstanding the large sums
he received he was constantly in debt, so that even while his
peculations were going on he derived little benefit from them.
Though, as a judge, he stole the property of others, he did not
know how to steal so as to escape detection, and he did not know how
to keep what he had stolen.   The mighty thinker was, in practice,
an arrant trifler.   He always neglected the immediate and the
pressing.   This was curiously exemplified in the last scene of his
life.   In some of his generalisations respecting putrefaction, it
occurred to him that the process might be stopped by snow.   He
arrived at conclusions like a cautious and large-minded philosopher : he tried them with the rashness and precipitancy of a
child.   With an absence of common sense which would be incredible if it were not well attested, he rushed out of his coach
on a very cold day, and, neglecting every precaution, stood shiver-
ing in the air while he stuffed a fowl with snow, risking a life in-
valuable to mankind for the sake of doing what any serving-man
could have done just as well.   It did not need the intellect of a
Bacon to foresee the result.   Before he had finished what he was
about he felt suddenly chilled : he became so ill as to be unable
to return to his own house, and his worn-out frame giving way,
he gradually sank and died a week after his first seizure.

Such events are very sad, but they are also very instructive.
Some, I know, class them under the head of martyrdom for
science : to me, they seem the penalty of folly.   It is at all events
certain that in the lives of great thinkers they are painfully
abundant.   It is but too true that many men of the highest power
have, by neglecting the study of proximate causes, shortened their
career, diminished their usefulness, and, bringing themselves to a

premature old age, have deprived mankind of their services just at the time when their experience was most advanced, and their intellect most matured. Others, again, who have stopped short of this, have by their own imprudence become involved in embarrassments of every kind, taking no heed of the morrow, wasting their resources, squandering their substance, and incurring debts which they were unable to pay. This is the result less of vice than of thoughtlessness. Vice is often cunning and wary; but thoughtlessness is always profuse and reckless. And so marked is the tendency, that "Genius struggling with difficulties" has grown into a proverb. Unhappily, genius has, in an immense majority of cases, created its own difficulties. The consequence is, that not only mere men of the world, but men of sound, useful understandings, do, for the most part, look upon genius as some strange and erratic quality, beautiful indeed to see, but dangerous to possess: a sparkling fire which consumes while it lightens. They regard it with curiosity, perhaps even with interest; but they shake their heads; they regret that men who are so clever should have so little sense; and, pluming themselves on their own superior sagacity, they complacently remind each other that great wit is generally allied to madness. Who can wonder that this should be? Look at what has occurred in these islands alone, during so short a period as three generations. Look at the lives of Fielding, Goldsmith, Smollett, Savage, Shenstone, Budgell, Charnock, Churchill, Chatterton, Derrick, Parnell, Somerville, Whitehead, Coombe, Day, Gilbert Stuart, Ockley, Oldys, Boyse, Hasted, Smart, Thomson, Grose, Daws, Barker, Harwood, Porson, Thirlby, Baron, Barry, Coleridge, Fearne, Walter Scott, Byron, Burns, Moore, and Campbell. Here you have men of every sort of ability, distinguished by every variety of imprudence. What does it all mean? Why is it that they who might have been the salt of the earth, and whom we should have been proud to take as our guides, are now pointed at by every blockhead as proofs of the inability of genius to grapple with the realities of life? Why is it that against these, and their fellows, each puny whipster can draw his sword, and dullards vent their naughty spite? That little men should jeer at great ones is natural; that they should have reason to jeer at them is shameful. Yet, this must always be the case so long as the present standard of action exists. As long as such expressions as "the infirmities of genius" form an essential part of our language—as long as we are constantly reminded that genius is naturally simple, guileless, and unversed in the ways of the world—as long as notions of patronising and protecting it continue—as long as men of letters are regarded

with pitying wonder, as strange creatures from whom a certain
amount of imprudence must be expected, and in whom it may be
tolerated—as long as among them extravagance is called generosity, and economy called meanness—as long as these things
happen, so long will the evils that correspond to them endure, and
so long will the highest class of minds lose much of their legitimate influence.   In the same way, while it is believed that authors
must, as a body, be heedless and improvident, it will likewise be
believed that for them there must be pensions and subscriptions ;
that to them Government and society should be bountiful ; and
that, on their behalf, institutions should be erected to provide for
necessities which it was their own business to have foreseen, but
which they, engaged in the arduous employment of writing books,
could not be expected to attend to.   Their minds are so weak and
sickly, so unfit for the rough usages of life, that they must be
guarded against the consequences of their own actions.   The
feebleness of their understandings makes such precautions necessary.   There must be hospitals for the intellect, as well as for the
body ; asylums where these poor, timid creatures may find refuge,
and may escape from calamities which their confiding innocence
prevented them from anticipating.   These are the miserable
delusions which still prevail.   These are the wretched infatuations
by which the strength and majesty of the literary character are
impaired.   In England there is, I rejoice to say, a more manly
and sturdy feeling on these subjects than in any other part of
Europe ; but even in England literary men do not sufficiently
appreciate the true dignity of their profession ; nor do they sufficiently understand that the foundation of all real grandeur is a
spirit of proud and lofty independence.   In other countries, the
state of opinion is most degrading.   In other countries, to have a
pension is a mark of honour, and to beg for money is a proof of
spirit.   Eminent men are turned into hirelings, receive eleemo-
synary aid, and raise a clamour if the aid is not forthcoming.
They snatch at every advantage, and accept even titles and decorations from the first foolish prince who is willing to bestow them.
They make constant demands on the public purse, and then they
wonder that the public respects them so little.   In France, in
particular, we have within the last year seen one of the most
brilliant writers of the age, who had realised immense sums by
his works, and who with common prudence ought to have amassed
a large fortune, coming forward as a mendicant, avowing in the
face of Europe that he had squandered what he had earned, and
soliciting, not only friends, but even strangers, to make up the
deficiency.   And this was done without a blush, without any sense

of the ignominy of the proceeding, but rather with a parade of glorying in it. In a merchant, or a tradesman, such a confession of recklessness would have been considered disgraceful; and why are men of genius to have a lower code than merchants or tradesmen? Whence comes this confusion of the first principles of justice? By what train of reasoning, or rather, by what process of sophistry, are we to infer, that when men of industry are improvident they shall be ruined, but that when men of letters are improvident they shall be rewarded? How long will this invidious distinction be tolerated? How long will such scandals last? How long will those who profess to be the teachers of mankind behave like children, and submit to be treated as the only class who are deficient in foresight, in circumspection, in economy, and in all those sober and practical virtues which form the character of a good and useful citizen? Nearly every one who cultivates literature as a profession can gain by it an honest livelihood; and if he cannot gain it he has mistaken his trade, and should seek another. Let it, then, be clearly understood that what such men earn by their labour, or save by their abstinence, or acquire by lawful inheritance, that they can enjoy without loss of dignity. But if they ask for more, or if they accept more, they become the recipients of charity, and between them and the beggar who walks the streets, the only difference is in the magnitude of the sum which is expected. To break stones on the highway is far more honourable than to receive such alms. Away, then, with your pensions, your subscriptions, your Literary Institutions, and your Literary Funds, by which you organise mendicancy into a system, and, under pretence of increasing public liberality, increase the amount of public imprudence.

But before this high standard can be reached, much remains to be done. As yet, and in the present early and unformed state of society, literary men are, notwithstanding a few exceptions, more prone to improvidence than the members of any other profession; and being also more deficient in practical knowledge, it too often happens that they are regarded as clever visionaries, fit to amuse the world, but unfit to guide it. The causes of this I have examined at some length, both because the results are extremely important, and because little attention has been hitherto paid to their operation. If I were not afraid of being tedious I could push the analysis still further, and could show that these very causes are themselves a part of the old spirit of Protection, and as such are intimately connected with some religious and political prejudices which obstruct the progress of society; and that in the countries where such prejudices are most powerful, the mischief is most serious and the state of literature most unhealthy.  But to prosecute that inquiry would be to write a treatise rather than an essay; and I shall be satisfied if I have cleared the ground so far as I have gone, and have succeeded in tracing the relation between these evils and the general question of philosophic Method.  The divergence between speculative minds and practical minds, and the different ways they have of contemplating affairs, are no doubt encouraged by the prevalence of false notions of patronage and reward, which, when they are brought to bear upon any class, inevitably tend to make that class unthrifty, and therefore unpractical.  This is a law of the human mind which the political economists have best illustrated in their own department, but the operation of which is universal.  Serious, however, as this evil is, it only belongs to a very imperfect state of society, and after a time it will probably disappear.  But the essential, and, so far as I can understand, the permanent cause of divergence, is a difference of Method.  In the creation of our knowledge, it appears to be a fundamental necessity that the speculative classes should search for what is distant, while the practical classes search for what is adjacent.  I do not see how it is possible to get rid of this antithesis.  There may be some way, which we cannot yet discern, of reconciling the two extremes, and of merging the antagonistic methods into one which, being higher than either, shall include both.  At present, however, there is no prospect of such a result.  We must, therefore, be satisfied if from time to time, and at long intervals, a man arises whose mind is so happily constructed as to study with equal success the surface and the summit; and who is able to show, by his single example, that views drawn from the most exalted region of thought, are applicable to the common transactions of daily life.

The only living Englishman who has achieved this is Mr. Mill. In the first place, he is our only great speculative philosopher who for many years has engaged in public life.  Since Ricardo, no original thinker has taken an active part in political affairs.  Not that those affairs have on that account been worse administered; nor that we have cause to repine at our lot in comparison with other nations.  On the contrary, no country has been better governed than ours; and at the present moment, it would be impossible to find in any one European nation more able, zealous, and upright public men than England possesses.  In such extremely rare cases as those of Brougham and Macaulay, there are also united to these qualities the most splendid and captivating accomplishments, and the far higher honour which they justly enjoy of having always been the eager and unflinching advocates of popular liberty.  It

cannot, however, be pretended that even these eminent men have
added anything to our ideas; still less can such a claim be made
on behalf of their inferiors in the political world.  They have
popularised the ideas and enforced them, but never created them.
They have shown great skill and great courage in applying the
conceptions of others; but the fresh conceptions, the higher and
larger generalizations, have not been their work.  They can attack
old abuses; they cannot discover new principles.  This incapacity
for dealing with the highest problems has been curiously exemplified
during the last two years, when a great number of the most active
and eminent of our public men, as well as several who are active
without being eminent, have formed an Association for the promotion of Social Science.  Among the papers published by that
Association will be found many curious facts and many useful
suggestions.  But Social Science there is none.  There is not even
a perception of what that science is.  Not one speaker or writer
attempted a scientific investigation of society, or showed that
in his opinion, such a thing ought to be attempted.  Where
science begins the Association leaves off.  All science is composed
either of physical laws, or of mental laws; and as the actions of
men are determined by both, the only way of founding Social
Science is to investigate each class of laws by itself, and then,
after computing their separate results, co-ordinate the whole into
a single study, by verifying them.  This is the only process by
which highly complicated phenomena can be disentangled; but
the Association did not catch a glimpse of it.  Indeed, they reversed the proper order, and proceeded from the concrete to the
abstract, instead of from the abstract to the concrete.  The reason
of this error may be easily explained.  The leading members of
the Association being mostly politicians, followed the habits of
their profession; that is to say, they noted the events immediately
surrounding them, and, taking a contemporary view, they observed
the actual effects with a view of discovering the causes, and then
remedying the evils.  This was their plan, and it was natural to
men whose occupations led them to look at the surface of affairs.
But to any mind accustomed to rise to a certain height above
that surface, and thoroughly imbued with the spirit of scientific
method, it is obvious that this way of investigating social phenomena must be futile.  Even in the limited field of political
action, its results are at best mere empirical uniformities; while
in the immense range of social science it is altogether worthless.
When men are collected together in society, with their passions
and their interests touching each other at every point, it is clear
that nothing can happen without being produced by a great

variety of causes. Of these causes, some will be conflicting, and their action being neutralized they will often disappear in the product; or, at all events, will leave traces too faint to be discerned. If, then, a cause is counteracted, how can you ascertain its existence by studying its effect? When only one cause produces an effect, you may infer the cause from the effect. But if several causes conspire to produce one effect this is impossible. The most persevering study of the effect, and the most intimate acquaintance with it, will in such case never lead to a knowledge of the causes; and the only plan is to proceed deductively from cause to effect, instead of inductively from effect to cause. Suppose, for example, a ball is struck on different sides by two persons at the same time. The effect will be that the ball, after being struck, will pass from one spot to another; but that effect may be studied for thousands of years without any one being able to ascertain the causes of the direction the ball took; and even if he is told that two persons have contributed to produce the result, he could not discover how much each person contributed. But if the observer, instead of studying the effect to obtain the causes, had studied the causes themselves, he would have been able, without going farther, to predict the exact resting-place of the ball. In other words, by knowing the causes he could learn the effect, but by knowing the effect he could not learn the causes.

Suppose, again, that I hear a musical instrument being played. The effect depends on a great variety of causes, among which are the power possessed by the ear of conveying the sound, the power of the ear to receive its vibrations, and the power of the brain to feel them. These are vulgarly called conditions, but they are all causes, inasmuch as a cause can only be defined to be an invariable and unconditional antecedent. They are just as much causes as the hand of the musician; and the question arises, could those causes have been discovered merely by studying the effect the music produced upon me? Most assuredly not. Most assuredly would it be requisite to study each cause separately, and then, by compounding the laws of their action, predict the entire effect. In social science, the plurality of causes is far more marked than in the cases I have mentioned; and therefore, in social science, the method of proceeding from effects to causes is far more absurd. And what aggravates the absurdity is, that the difficulty produced by the plurality of causes is heightened by another difficulty—namely, the conflict of causes. To deal with such enormous complications as politicians usually deal with them, is simply a waste of time. Every science has some hypothesis which underlies it, and which must be taken for granted. The hypothesis on which social science rests, is that the actions of men are a compound result of the laws of mind and the laws of matter; and as that result is highly complex, we shall never understand it until the laws themselves have been unravelled by a previous and separate inquiry. Even if we could experiment, it would be different; because by experimenting on an effect we can artificially isolate it, and guard against the encroachment of causes which we do not wish to investigate. But in social science there can be no experiment. For, in the first place, there can be no previous isolation; since every interference lets into the framework of society a host of new phenomena which invalidate the experiment before the experiment is concluded. And, in the second place, that which is called an experiment, such as the adoption of a fresh principle in legislation, is not an experiment in the scientific sense of the word; because the results which follow depend far more upon the general state of the surrounding society than upon the principle itself. The surrounding state of society is, in its turn, governed by a long train of antecedents, each linked to the other, and forming, in their aggregate, an orderly and spontaneous march, which politicians are unable to control, and which they do for the most part utterly ignore.

This absence of speculative ability among politicians, is the natural result of the habits of their class; and as the same result is almost invariably found among practical men, I have thought the illustration just adduced might be interesting, in so far as it confirms the doctrine of an essential antagonism of Method, which, though like all speculative distinctions, infringed at various points, does undoubtedly exist, and appears to me to form the basis for a classification of society more complete than any yet proposed. Perhaps, too, it may have the effect of guarding against the rash and confident assertions of public men on matters respecting which they have no means of forming an opinion, because their conclusions are vitiated by the adoption of an illogical method. It is, accordingly, a matter of notoriety that in predicting the results of large and general innovations, even the most sagacious politicians have been oftener wrong than right, and have foreseen evil when nothing but good has come. Against this sort of error, the longest and most extensive experience affords no protection. While statesmen confine themselves to questions of detail, and to short views of immediate expediency, their judgment should be listened to with respect. But beyond this, they are rarely to be heeded. It constantly, and indeed usually happens, that statesmen and legislators who pass their whole life in public affairs, know nothing of their own age, except

*D

what lies on the surface, and are therefore unable to calculate, even approximatively, remote and general consequences. Abundant evidence of their incapacity on these points will present itself to whoever has occasion to read much of State Papers or of Parliamentary discussions in different ages, or, what is still more decisive, the private correspondence of eminent politicians. These reveal but too clearly that they who are supposed to govern the course of affairs are utterly ignorant of the direction affairs are really taking. What is before them they see ; what is above them they overlook. While, however, this is the deficiency of political practitioners, it must be admitted that political philosophers are, on their side, equally at fault in being too prone to neglect the operation of superficial and tangible results. The difference between the two classes is analogous to that which exists between a gardener and a botanist. Both deal with plants, but each considers the plant from an opposite point of view. The gardener looks to its beauty and its flavour. These are qualities which lie on the surface ; and to these the scientific botanist pays no heed. He studies the physiology ; he searches for the law ; he penetrates the minute structure, and rending the plant, sacrifices the individual that he may understand the species. The gardener, like the statesman, is accustomed to consider the superficial and the immediate ; the botanist, like the philosopher, inquires into the hidden and the remote. Which pursuit is the more valuable is not now the question ; but it is certain that a successful combination of both pursuits is very rare. The habits of mind, the turn of thought, all the associations, are diametrically opposed. To unite them requires a strength of resolution and a largeness of intellect rarely given to man to attain. It usually happens that they who seek to combine the opposites fail on both sides, and become at once shallow philosophers and unsafe practitioners.

It must, therefore, be deemed a remarkable fact that a man who is beyond dispute the deepest of our living thinkers, should, during many years, not only have held a responsible post in a very difficult department of government, but should, according to the testimony of those best able to judge, have fulfilled the duties of that post with conspicuous and unvarying success. This has been the case with Mr. Mill, and on this account his opinions are entitled to peculiar respect, because they are formed by one who has mastered both extremes of life. Such a duality of function is worthy of especial attention, and it will hardly be taken amiss if I endeavour to show how it has displayed itself in the writings of this great philosopher. To those who delight in contemplating the development of an intellect of the rarest kind, it will not appear unseemly that, before examining his latest work, I should compare those other productions by which he has been hitherto known and which have won for him a vast and permanent fame.

Those works are his " Principles of Political Economy," and his " System of Logic." Each of these elaborate productions is remarkable for one of the two great qualities of the author; the Political Economy being mostly valuable for the practical application of truths previously established; while the Logic contains an analysis of the process of reasoning, more subtle and exhaustive than any which has appeared since Aristotle.[1] Of the Political Economy, it is enough to say that none of the principles in it are new. Since the publication of the "Wealth of Nations," the science had been entirely remodelled, and it was the object of Mr. Mill not to extend its boundaries, but to turn to practical account what had been achieved by the two generations of thinkers who succeeded Adam Smith. The brilliant discovery of the true theory of rent, which though not made by Ricardo, was placed by him on a solid foundation, had given an entirely new aspect to economical science ; as also had the great law, which he first pointed out, of the distribution of the precious metals, by means of the exchanges, in exact proportion to the traffic which would occur if there were no such metals, and if all trade were conducted by barter. The great work of Malthus on Population, and the discussions to which it led, had ascertained the nature and limits of the connection which exists between the increase of labour and the rate of wages, and had thus cleared away many of the difficulties which beset the path of Adam Smith. While this threw new light on the causes of the distribution of wealth, Rae had analysed those other causes which govern its accumulation, and had shown in what manner capital increases with different speed,

[1] I do not except even Kant; because that extraordinary thinker, who in some directions has perhaps penetrated deeper than any philosopher either before or since, did, in his views respecting logic, so anticipate the limits of all future discovery, as to take upon himself to affirm that the notion of inductively obtaining a standard of objective truth was not only impracticable at present, but involved an essential contradiction which would always be irreconcilable. Whoever upon any subject thus sets up a fixed and prospective limit, gives the surest proof that he has not investigated that subject even as far as the existing resources allow; for he proves that he has not reached that point where certainty ends, and where the dim outline, gradually growing fainter, but always indefinite, teaches us that there is something beyond, and that we have no right to pledge ourselves respecting that undetermined tract. On the other hand, those who stop before they have reached this shadowy outline, see everything clearly because they have not advanced to the place where darkness begins. If I were to venture to criticise such a man as Kant, I should say, after a very careful study of his works, and with the greatest admiration of them, that the depth of his mind considerably exceeded its comprehensiveness.

in different countries, and at different times. When we, more-over, add that Bentham had demonstrated the advantages and the necessity of usury as part of the social scheme; that Babbage had with signal ability investigated the principles which govern the economy of labour, and the varying degrees of its productiveness ; and that the abstract but very important step had been taken by Wakefield of proving that the supposed ultimate division of labour is in reality but a part of the still higher principle of the co-operation of labour; when we put these things together, we shall see that Mr. Mill found everything ready to his hand, and had only to combine and apply the generalisations of those great speculative thinkers who immediately preceded him.

The success with which he has executed this task is marvellous. His treatise on Political Economy is a manual for statesmen even more than for speculators ; since, though it contains no additions to scientific truths, it is full of practical applications. In it, the most recondite principles are illustrated, and brought to the sur-face, with a force which has convinced many persons whose minds are unable to follow long trains of abstract reasoning, and who re-jected the conclusions of Ricardo, because that illustrious thinker, master though he was of the finest dialectic, lacked the capacity of clothing his arguments in circumstances, and could not adapt them to the ordinary events of political life. This deficiency is supplied by Mr. Mill, who treats political economy as an art even more than as a science.[1]  Hence his book is full of suggestions on many of the most important matters which can be submitted to the legislature of a free people. The laws of bequest and of in-heritance ; the law of primogeniture ; the laws of partnership and of limited liability ; the laws of insolvency and of bankruptcy; the best method of establishing colonies; the advantages and dis-advantages of the income-tax ; the expediency of meeting extra-ordinary expenses by taxation drawn from income or by an increase of the national debt : these are among the subjects mooted by Mr. Mill, and on which he has made proposals, the majority of which are gradually working their way into the public mind. Upon these topics his influence is felt by many who do not know from whence the influence proceeds. And no one can have at-tended to the progress of political opinions during the last ten years, without noticing how, in the formation of practical judg-

[1] Thereby becoming necessarily somewhat empirical ; for directly the political economist offers practical suggestions, disturbing causes are let in, and trouble the pure science which depends far more upon reasoning than upon observation. No writer I have met with has put this in a short compass with so much clearness as Mr. Senior. See the introduction to his *Political Economy*, 4th edit. 1858, pp. 2–5.

ments, his power is operating on politicians who are utterly heed-less of his higher generalisations, and who would, indeed, in the largest departments of thought, be well content to sleep on in their dull and ancient routine, but that from time to time, and in their own despite, their slumbers are disturbed by a noise from afar, and they are forced to participate in the result of that pro-digious movement which is now gathering on every side, un-settling the stability of affairs, and sapping the foundation of our beliefs.

In such intellectual movements, which lie at the root of social actions, the practical classes can take no original part, though, as all history decisively proves, they are eventually obliged to abide by the consequences of them. But it is the peculiar prerogative of certain minds to be able to interpret as well as to originate. To such men a double duty is entrusted. They enjoy the ines-timable privilege of communicating directly with practitioners as well as with speculators, and they can both discover the abstract and manipulate the concrete. The concrete and practical ten-dency of the present age is clearly exhibited in Mr. Mill's work on Political Economy; while in his work on Logic we may see as clearly the abstract and theoretical tendency of the same period. The former work is chiefly valuable in relation to the functions of government; the latter in relation to the functions of thought. In the one the art of doing, in the other the science of reasoning. The revolution which he has effected in this great department of speculative knowledge will be best understood by comparing what the science of logic was when he began to write with what it was after his work was published.

Until Mr. Mill entered the field there were only two systems of logic. The first was the syllogistic system which was founded by Aristotle, and to which the moderns have contributed nothing of moment, except the discovery during the present century of the quantification of the predicate.[1] The other was the inductive system, as organised by Bacon, to which also it was reserved for our generation to make the first essential addition; Sir John

---

[1] Made by Sir William Hamilton and Mr. De Morgan about the same time and, I believe, independently of each other. Before this, nothing of moment had been added to the Aristotelian doctrine of the syllogism, unless we consider as such the fourth figure. This was unknown to Aristotle; but it may be doubted if it is essential; and, if I rightly remember, Sir William Hamilton did not attach much importance to the fourth syllogistic figure, while Archbishop Whately (*Logic*, 1857, p. 5) calls it 'insignificant.' Compare Mansell's *Aldrich*, 1856, p. 76. The hypo-thetical syllogism is usually said to be post-Aristotelian; but although I cannot now recover the passage, I have seen evidence which makes me suspect that it was known to Aristotle, though not formally enunciated by him.

Herschel having the great merit of ascertaining the existence of four different methods, the boundaries of which had escaped the attention of previous philosophers.[1] That the word logic should by most writers be confined to the syllogistic, or, as it is sometimes called, Formal method, is a striking proof of the extent to which language is infested by the old scholastic prejudices; for as the science of logic is the theory of the process of inference, and as the art of logic is the practical skill of inferring rightly from given data, it is evident that any system is a system of logic which ascertains the laws of the theory, and lays down the rules of the practice. The inductive system of logic may be better or worse than the deductive; but both are systems.[2] And till nearly the middle of the present century, men were divided between the Aristotelian logic which infers from generals to particulars, and the Baconian logic which infers from particulars to generals.[3]

[1] This is acknowledged by Mr. Mill, who has stated and analysed these methods with great clearness.—Mill's *Logic*, 4th edit. 1856, vol. i. p. 451.

[2] Archbishop Whately, who has written what is probably the best elementary treatise existing on formal logic, adopts the old opinion that the inductive "process of inquiry" by which premises are obtained, is "out of the province of logic."—Whately's *Logic*, 1857, p. 151. Mr. De Morgan, whose extremely able work goes much deeper into the subject than Archbishop Whately's, is, however, content with excluding induction, not from logic, but from formal logic. "What is now called induction, meaning the discovery of laws from instances, and higher laws from lower ones, is beyond the province of formal logic."—De Morgan's *Logic*, 1847, p. 215. As a law of nature is frequently the major premiss of a syllogism, this statement of Mr. De Morgan's seems unobjectionable. The point at issue involves much more than a mere dispute respecting words, and I therefore add, without subscribing to, the view of another eminent authority. "To entitle any work to be classed as the logic of this or that school, it is at least necessary that it should, in common with the Aristotelian logic, adhere to the syllogistic method, whatever modifications or additions it may derive from the particular school of its author."—Mansell's Introduction to Aldrich's *Artis Logicæ Rudimenta*, 1856, p. xlii. See also Appendix, pp. 194, 195, and Mr. Mansell's *Prolegomena Logica*, 1851, pp. 89, 169. On the other hand, Bacon, who considered the syllogism to be worse than useless, distinctly claims the title of "logical" for his inductive system. "Illud vero monendum, nos in hoc nostro organo tractare logicam, non philosophiam."—*Novum Organum*, lib. ii. aphor. lii. in Bacon's *Works*, vol. iv. p. 382. This should be compared with the remarks of Sir William Hamilton on inductive logic in his *Discussions*, 1852, p. 158. What strikes one most in this controversy is, that none of the great advocates of the exclusive right of the syllogistic system to the word "logic" appear to be well acquainted with physical science. They, therefore, cannot understand the real nature of induction in the modern sense of the term, and they naturally depreciate a method with whose triumphs they have no sympathy.

[3] To what extent Aristotle did or did not recognise an induction of particulars as the first step in our knowledge, and therefore as the base of every major premiss, has been often disputed; but I have not heard that any of the disputants have adopted the only means by which such a question can be tested—namely, bringing together the most decisive passages from Aristotle, and then leaving them to the judgment of the reader. As this seems to be the most impartial way of proceeding, I have gone through Aristotle's logical works with a view to it; and those who are interested in these matters will find the extracts at the end of this essay.

While the science of logic was in this state, there appeared in 1843 Mr. Mill's "System of Logic;" the fundamental idea of which is, that the logical process is not from generals to particulars, nor from particulars to generals, but from particulars to particulars. According to this view, which is gradually securing the adhesion of thinkers, the syllogism, instead of being an act of reasoning, is an act, first of registration, and then of interpretation. The major premiss of a syllogism being the record of previous induction, the business of the syllogism is to interpret that record and bring it to light. In the syllogism we preserve our experience, and we also realise it; but the reasoning is at an end when the major premiss is enunciated. For after that enunciation no fresh truth is propounded. As soon therefore as the major is stated, the argument is over; because the general proposition is but a register, or, as it were, a note-book, of inferences which involve everything at issue. While, however, the syllogism is not a process of reasoning, it is a security that the previous reasoning is good. And this in three ways. In the first place by interposing a general proposition between the collection of the first particulars and the statement of the last particulars, it presents a larger object to the imagination than would be possible if we had only the particulars in our mind. In the second place, the syllogism serves as an artificial memory, and enables us to preserve order among a mass of details; being at once a formula into which we throw them, and a contrivance by which we recall them. Finally, the syllogism is a protection against negligence; since when we infer from a number of observed cases to a case we have not yet observed, we, instead of jumping at once to that case, state a general proposition which includes it, and which must be true if our conclusion is true; so that by this means if we have reasoned erroneously, the error becomes more broad and conspicuous.

This remarkable analysis of the nature and functions of the syllogism is, so far as our present knowledge goes, exhaustive; whether or not it will admit of still further resolution we cannot tell. At all events it is a contribution of the greatest importance to the science of reasoning, and involves many other speculative questions which are indirectly connected with it, but which I shall not now open up. Neither need I stop to show how it affords a basis for establishing the true distinction between induction and deduction, a distinction which Mr. Mill is one of the extremely few English writers who has thoroughly understood, since it is commonly supposed in this country that geometry is the proper type of deduction, whereas it is only one of the types, and though an admirable pattern of the deductive investigation of coexistences, throws no light on the deductive investigation of sequences. But, passing over these matters as too large to be discussed here, I would call attention to a fundamental principle which underlies Mr. Mill's philosophy, and from which it will appear that he is as much opposed to the advocates of the Baconian method as to those of the Aristotelian. In this respect he has been, perhaps unconsciously, greatly influenced by the spirit of the age; for it might be easily shown, and indeed will hardly be disputed, that during the last fifty years an opinion has been gaining ground that the Baconian system has been overrated, and that its favourite idea of proceeding from effects to causes instead of from causes to effects, will not carry us so far as was supposed by the truly great, though somewhat empirical, thinkers of the eighteenth century.

One point in which the inductive philosophy commonly received in England is very inaccurate, and which Mr. Mill has justly attacked, is, that following the authority of Bacon, it insists upon all generalisations being conducted by ascending from each generalisation to the one immediately above and adjoining; and it denounces as hasty and unphilosophic any attempt to soar to a higher stage without mastering the intermediate steps.[1] This is an undue limitation of that peculiar property of genius which, for want of a better word we call intuition; and that in this respect Bacon's philosophy was too narrow, and placed men too much on a par[2] by obliging them all to use the same method is now frequently though not generally admitted, and has been perceived by several philosophers.[3] The objections raised by Mr. Mill on this ground, though put with great ability, are, as he

---

[1] "Ascendendo continentor et gradatim, ut ultimo loco perveniatur ad maxime generalia; quæ via vera est, sed intentata."—*Novum Organum*, lib. i. aphor. xix. in Bacon's *Works*, vol. iv. p. 268. London, 1778; 4to. And in lib. i. aphor. civ. p. 294—"Sed de scientiis tum demum bene sperandum est, quando per scalam veram et per gradus continuos et non intermissos, aut hiulcos, a particularibus ascendetur ad axiomata minora, et deinde ad media, alia aliis superiora, et postremo demum ad generalissima."

[2] "Nostra vero inveniendi scientias ea est ratio, ut non multum ingeniorum acumini et robori relinquatur; sed quæ ingenia et intellectus fere exæquet."—*Novum Organum*, lib. i. aphor. lxi.; Bacon's *Works*, vol. iv. p. 275. And in lib. i. aphor. cxxii. [*Works*, vol. iv. p. 301], "Nostra enim via inveniendi scientias exæquat fere ingenia, et non multum excellentiæ eorum relinquit; cum omnia per certissimas regulas et demonstrationes transigant."

[3] And is noticed in Whewell's *Philosophy of the Inductive Sciences*, 1847, vol. ii. p. 240; though this celebrated writer, so far from connecting it with Bacon's doctrine of gradual and uninterrupted ascent, considers such doctrine to be the peculiar merit of Bacon, and accuses those who hold a contrary opinion, of "dimness of vision," pp. 126, 232. Happily, all are not dim who are said to be so.

would be the first to confess, not original ; and the same remark may be made in a smaller degree concerning another objection— namely, that Bacon did not attach sufficient weight to the plurality of causes,[1] and did not see that the great complexity they produce would often baffle his method, and would render another method necessary. But while Mr. Mill has in these parts of his work been anticipated, there is a more subtle, and, as it appears to me, a more fatal objection which he has made against the Baconian philosophy. And as this objection, besides being entirely new, lies far out of the path of ordinary speculation, it has hardly yet attracted the notice even of philosophic logicians, and the reader will probably be interested in hearing a simple and untechnical statement of it.

Logic, considered as a science, is solely concerned with induction ; and the business of induction is to arrive at causes ; or, to speak more strictly, to arrive at a knowledge of the laws of causation.[2] So far Mr. Mill agrees with Bacon ; but from the operation of this rule he removes an immense body of phenomena which were brought under it by the Baconian philosophy. He asserts, and I think he proves, that though uniformities of succession may be investigated inductively, it is impossible to investigate, after that fashion, uniformities of co-existence ; and that, therefore, to these last the Baconian method is inapplicable. If, for instance, we say that all negroes have woolly hair, we affirm an uniformity of co-existence between the hair and some other property or properties essential to the negro. But if we were to say that they have woolly hair in consequence of their skin being black, we should affirm an uniformity not of co-existence, but of succession. Uniformities of succession are frequently amenable to induction : uniformities of co-existence are never amenable to it, and are consequently out of the jurisdiction of the Baconian philosophy. They may, no doubt, be treated according to the simple enumeration of the ancients, which, however, was so crude an induction as hardly to be worthy the name.[3] But the powerful induction of

[1] Mill's *Logic*, fourth edition, vol. ii. p. 321. I am almost sure this remark had been made before.

[2] "The main question of the science of logic is induction, which however is almost entirely passed over by professed writers on logic."—Mill's *Logic*, vol. i. p. 309. "The chief object of inductive logic is to point out how the laws of causation are to be ascertained."—Vol. i. p. 407. "The mental process with which logic is conversant, the operation of ascertaining truths by means of evidence, is always, even when appearances point to a different theory of it, a process of induction."—Vol. ii. p. 177.

[3] The character of the Aristotelian induction is so justly portrayed by Mr. Maurice in his admirable account of the Greek philosophy, that I cannot resist the pleasure of transcribing the passage. "What this induction is, and how entirely it differs from that process which bears the same name in the writings of Bacon, the reader will

the moderns, depending upon a separation of nature and an elimination of disturbances, is, in reference to co-existences, absolutely
impotent.   The utmost that it can give is empirical laws, useful
for practical guidance, but void of scientific value.   That this has
hitherto been the case the history of our knowledge decisively
proves.   That it always will be the case is, in Mr. Mill's opinion,
equally certain, because while, on the one hand, the study of
uniformities of succession has for its basis that absorbing and
over-ruling hypothesis of the constancy of causation, on which
every human being more or less relies, and to which philosophers
will hear of no exception; we, on the other hand, find that the
study of the uniformities of co-existence has no such support, and
that therefore the whole field of inquiry is unsettled and indeter-
minate.   Thus it is that if I see a negro suffering pain, the law of
causation compels me to believe that something had previously
happened of which pain was the necessary consequence.   But I am
not bound to believe that he possesses some property of which his
woolly hair or his dark skin are the necessary accompaniments.   I
cling to the necessity of an uniform sequence; I reject the necessity of an uniform co-existence.   This is the difference between
consequences and concomitants.   That the pain has a cause, I am
well assured.   But for aught I can tell, the blackness and the
woolliness may be ultimate properties which are referrible to no
cause;[1] or if they are not ultimate properties, each may be
dependent on its own cause, but not be necessarily connected.
The relation, therefore, may be universal in regard to the fact,
and yet casual in regard to the science.

    This distinction when once stated is very simple; but its con-
sequences in relation to the science of logic had escaped all previous thinkers.   When thoroughly appreciated, it will dispel the
idle dream of the universal application of the Baconian philo-

perceive the more he studies the different writings of Aristotle.   He will find, first,
that the sensible *phenomenon* is taken for granted as a safe starting point.   That
phenomena are not principles, Aristotle believed as strongly as we could.   But, to
suspect phenomena, to suppose that they need sifting and probing in order that we
may know what the fact is which they denote, this is no part of his system."—Maurice's
*Ancient Philosophy*, 1850, p. 173.   Nothing can be better than the expression that
Aristotle did not *suspect* phenomena.   The moderns do suspect them, and therefore
test them either by crucial experiments or by averages.   The latter resource was
not effectively employed until the eighteenth century.   It now bids fair to be of
immense importance, though in some branches of inquiry the nomenclature must
become more precise before the full value of the method can be seen.

    [1] That is, not logically referrible by the understanding.   I say nothing of causes
which touch on transcendental grounds; but, barring these, Mr. Mill's assertion
seems unimpeachable, that "co-existences between the ultimate properties of things"
. . . "cannot depend on causation," unless by "ascending to the origin of all things."—
Mill's *Logic*, vol. ii. p. 106.

sophy; and in the meantime it will explain how it was that even during Bacon's life, and in his own hands, his method frequently and signally failed. He evidently believed that as every phenomenon has something which must follow from it, so also it has something which must go with it, and which he termed its Form.[1] If he could generalise the form—that is to say, if he could obtain the law of the co-existence—he rightly supposed that he would gain a scientific knowledge of the phenomenon. With this view he taxed his fertile invention to the utmost. He contrived a variety of refined and ingenious artifices, by which various instances might be successfully compared, and the conditions which are essential distinguished from those which are non-essential. He collated negatives with affirmatives, and taught the art of separating nature by rejections and exclusions. Yet, in regard to the study of co-existences, all his caution, all his knowledge, and all his thought, were useless. His weapons, notwithstanding their power, could make no impression on that stubborn and refractory topic. The laws of co-existences are as great a mystery as ever, and all our conclusions respecting them are purely empirical. Every inductive science now existing is, in its strictly scientific part, solely a generalisation of sequences. The reason of this, though vaguely appreciated by several writers, was first clearly stated and connected with the general theory of our knowledge by Mr. Mill. He has the immense merit of striking at once to the very root of the subject, and showing that, in the science of logic, there is a fundamental distinction which forbids us to treat co-existences as we may treat sequences; that a neglect of this distinction impairs the value of the philosophy of Bacon, and has crippled his successors; and finally, that the origin of this distinction may be traced backward and upward until we reach those ultimate laws of causation which support the fabric of our knowledge, and beyond which the human mind, in the present stage of its development, is unable to penetrate.

While Mr. Mill, both by delving to the foundation and rising to the summit, has excluded the Baconian philosophy from the investigation of co-existences, he has likewise proved its incapacity for solving those vast social problems which now, for the first time in the history of the world, the most advanced thinkers

[1] "Etenim forma naturæ alicujus talis est, ut, ea posita, natura data infallibiliter sequatur. Itaque adest perpetuo, quando natura illa adest, atque eam universaliter affirmat, atque inest omni. Eadem forma talis est, ut ea amota, natura data infallibiliter fugiat. Itaque abest perpetua quando natura illa abest, eamque perpetuo abnegat, atque inest soli."— *Novum Organum,* lib. ii. aphor. iv.; *Works,* vol. iv. p. 307. Compare also respecting these forms, his treatise on *The Advancement of Learning,* book ii.; *Works,* vol. i. p. 57, 58, 61, 62.

are setting themselves to work at deliberately, with scientific purpose, and with something like adequate resources. As this, however, pertains to that domain to which I too, according to my measure and with whatever power I may haply possess, have devoted myself, I am unwilling to discuss here what elsewhere I shall find a fitter place for considering; and I shall be content if I have conveyed to the reader some idea of what has been effected by one whom I cannot but regard as the most profound thinker England has produced since the seventeenth century, and whose services, though recognised by innumerable persons each in his own peculiar walk, are little understood in their entirety, because we, owing partly to the constantly increasing mass of our knowledge, and partly to an excessive veneration for the principle of the division of labour, are too prone to isolate our inquiries and to narrow the range of our intellectual sympathies. The notion that a man will best succeed by adhering to one pursuit, is as true in practical life as it is false in speculative life. No one can have a firm grasp of any science if, by confining himself to it, he shuts out the light of analogy, and deprives himself of that peculiar aid which is derived from a commanding survey of the co-ordination and interdependence of things and of the relation they bear to each other. He may, no doubt, work at the details of his subject; he may be useful in adding to its facts; he will never be able to enlarge its philosophy. For, the philosophy of every department depends on its connection with other departments, and must therefore be sought at their points of contact. It must be looked for in the place where they touch and coalesce; it lies not in the centre of each science, but on the confines and margin. This, however, is a truth which men are apt to reject, because they are naturally averse to comprehensive labour, and are too ready to believe that their own peculiar and limited science is so important that they would not be justified in striking into paths which diverge from it. Hence we see physical philosophers knowing nothing of political economy, political economists nothing of physical science, and logicians nothing of either. Hence, too, there are few indeed who are capable of measuring the enormous field which Mr. Mill has traversed, or of scanning the depth to which in that field he has sunk his shaft.

It is from such a man as this, that a work has recently issued upon a subject far more important than any which even he had previously investigated, and in fact the most important with which the human mind can grapple. For, Liberty is the one thing most essential to the right development of individuals and to the real grandeur of nations. It is a product of knowledge when know-

ledge advances in a healthy and regular manner; but if under
certain unhappy circumstances it is opposed by what seems to be
knowledge, then, in God's name, let knowledge perish and Liberty
be preserved. Liberty is not a means to an end, it is an end itself.
To secure it, to enlarge it, and to diffuse it, should be the main
object of all social arrangements and of all political contrivances.
None but a pedant or a tyrant can put science or literature in
competition with it. Within certain limits, and very small limits
too, it is the inalienable prerogative of man, of which no force of
circumstances and no lapse of time can deprive him. He has no
right to barter it away even from himself, still less from his
children. It is the foundation of all self-respect, and without it
the great doctrine of moral responsibility would degenerate into
a lie and a juggle. It is a sacred deposit, and the love of it is a
holy instinct engraven in our hearts. And if it could be shown
that the tendency of advancing knowledge is to encroach upon it;
if it could be proved that in the march of what we call civilization, the desire for liberty did necessarily decline, and the exercise of liberty become less frequent; if this could be made
apparent, I for one should wish that the human race might halt
in its career, and that we might recede step by step, so that the
very trophies and memory of our glory should vanish, sooner than
that men were bribed by their splendour to forget the sentiment
of their own personal dignity.

But it cannot be. Surely it cannot be that we, improving in
all other things, should be retrograding in the most essential.
Yet, among thinkers of great depth and authority there is a fear
that such is the case. With that fear I cannot agree; but the
existence of the fear, and the discussions to which it has led and
will lead, are extremely salutary, as calling our attention to an
evil which in the eagerness of our advance we might otherwise
overlook. We are stepping on at a rate of which no previous
example has been seen; and it is good that, amid the pride and
flush of our prosperity, we should be made to inquire what price
we have paid for our success. Let us compute the cost as well as
the gain. Before we announce our fortune we should balance our
books. Every one, therefore, should rejoice at the appearance of
a work in which for the first time the great question of Liberty
is unfolded in all its dimensions, considered on every side and
from every aspect, and brought to bear upon our present condition with a steadiness of hand and a clearness of purpose which
they will most admire who are most accustomed to reflect on this
difficult and complicated topic.

In the actual state of the world, Mr. Mill rightly considers

that the least important part of the question of liberty is that
which concerns the relation between subjects and rulers.  On this
point, notwithstanding the momentary ascendancy of despotism
on the Continent, there is, I believe, nothing to dread.  In France
and Germany the bodies of men are enslaved, but not their minds.
Nearly all the intellect of Europe is arrayed against tyranny, and
the ultimate result of such a struggle can hardly be doubted.  The
immense armies which are maintained, and which some mention
as a proof that the love of war is increasing instead of diminishing,
are merely an evidence that the governing classes distrust and
suspect the future, and know that their real danger is to be found
not abroad but at home.  They fear revolution far more than invasion.  The state of foreign affairs is their pretence for arming;
the state of public opinion is the cause.  And right glad they are
to find a decent pretext for protecting themselves from that punishment which many of them richly deserve.  But I cannot understand how any one who has carefully studied the march of the
European mind, and has seen it triumph over obstacles ten times
more formidable than these, can really apprehend that the liberties of Europe will ultimately fall before those who now threaten
their existence.  When the spirit of freedom was far less strong
and less universal, the task was tried, and tried in vain.  It is
hardly to be supposed that the monarchical principle, decrepit as
it now is, and stripped of that dogma of divine right which long
upheld it, can eventually withstand the pressure of those general
causes which, for three centuries, have marked it for destruction.
And, since despotism has chosen the institution of monarchy as
that under which it seeks a shelter, and for which it will fight its
last battle, we may fairly assume that the danger is less imminent
than is commonly imagined, and that they who rely on an old and
enfeebled principle, with which neither the religion nor the affections of men are associated as of yore, will find that they are
leaning on a broken reed, and that the sceptre of their power will
pass from them.

I cannot, therefore, participate in the feelings of those who
look with apprehension at the present condition of Europe.  Mr.
Mill would perhaps take a less sanguine view; but it is observable that the greater part of his defence of liberty is not directed
against political tyranny.  There is, however, another sort of
tyranny which is far more insidious, and against which he has
chiefly bent his efforts.  This is the despotism of custom, to
which ordinary minds entirely succumb, and before which even
strong minds quail.  But custom being merely the product of
public opinion, or rather its external manifestation, the two prin-

ciples of custom and opinion must be considered together; and I will briefly state how, according to Mr. Mill, their joint action is producing serious mischief, and is threatening mischief more serious still.

The proposition which Mr. Mill undertakes to establish, is that society, whether acting by the legislature or by the influence of public opinion, has no right to interfere with the conduct of any individual for the sake of his own good. Society may interfere with him for their good, not for his. If his actions hurt them, he is, under certain circumstances, amenable to their authority; if they only hurt himself, he is never amenable. The proposition, thus stated, will be acceded to by many persons who, in practice, repudiate it every day of their lives. The ridicule which is cast upon whoever deviates from an established custom, however trifling and foolish that custom may be, shows the determination of society to exercise arbitrary sway over individuals. On the most insignificant as well as on the most important matters, rules are laid down which no one dares to violate, except in those extremely rare cases in which great intellect, great wealth, or great rank enable a man rather to command society than to be commanded by it. The immense mass of mankind are, in regard to their usages, in a state of social slavery; each man being bound under heavy penalties to conform to the standard of life common to his own class. How serious those penalties are is evident from the fact that though innumerable persons complain of prevailing customs, and wish to shake them off, they dare not do so, but continue to practise them, though frequently at the expense of health, comfort, and fortune. Men, not cowards in other respects, and of a fair share of moral courage, are afraid to rebel against this grievous and exacting tyranny. The consequences of this are injurious, not only to those who desire to be freed from the thraldom, but also to those who do not desire to be freed; that is, to the whole of society. Of these results, there are two particularly mischievous, and which, in the opinion of Mr. Mill, are likely to gain ground, unless some sudden change of sentiment should occur.

The first mischief is, that a sufficient number of experiments are not made respecting the different ways of living; from which it happens that the art of life is not so well understood as it otherwise would be. If society were more lenient to eccentricity, and more inclined to examine what is unusual than to laugh at it, we should find that many courses of conduct which we call whimsical, and which according to the ordinary standard are utterly irrational, have more reason in them than we are disposed to imagine. But, while a country or an age will obstinately insist upon condemning all human conduct which is not in accordance with the manner or fashion of the day, deviations from the straight line will be rarely hazarded. We are, therefore, prevented from knowing how far such deviations would be useful. By discouraging the experiment, we retard the knowledge. On this account, if on no other, it is advisable that the widest latitude should be given to unusual actions, which ought to be valued as tests whereby we may ascertain whether or not particular things are expedient. Of course, the essentials of morals are not to be violated, nor the public peace to be disturbed. But short of this, every indulgence should be granted. For progress depends upon change; and it is only by practising uncustomary things that we can discover if they are fit to become customary.

The other evil which society inflicts on herself by her own tyranny is still more serious; and, although I cannot go with Mr. Mill in considering the danger to be so imminent as he does, there can, I think, be little doubt that it is the one weak point in modern civilization; and that it is the only thing of importance in which, if we are not actually receding, we are making no perceptible advance.

This is, that most precious and inestimable quality, the quality of individuality. That the increasing authority of society, if not counteracted by other causes, tends to limit the exercise of this quality, seems indisputable. Whether or not there are counteracting causes is a question of great complexity, and could not be discussed without entering into the general theory of our existing civilization. With the most unfeigned deference for every opinion enunciated by Mr. Mill, I venture to differ from him on this matter, and to think that, on the whole, individuality is not diminishing, and that so far as we can estimate the future, it is not likely to diminish. But it would ill become any man to combat the views of this great thinker, without subjecting the point at issue to a rigid and careful analysis; and as I have not done so, I will not weaken my theory by advancing imperfect arguments in its favour, but will, as before, confine myself to stating the conclusions at which he has arrived, after what has evidently been a train of long and anxious reflection.

According to Mr. Mill, things are tending, and have for some time tended, to lessen the influence of original minds, and to raise mediocrity to the foremost place. Individuals are lost in the crowd. The world is ruled not by them, but by public opinion; and public opinion, being the voice of the many, is the voice of mediocrity. Affairs are now governed by average men,

who will not pay to great men the deference that was formerly
yielded. Energy and originality being less respected, are becoming more rare; and in England in particular, real energy has
hardly any field, except in business, where a large amount of it
undoubtedly exists.[1] Our greatness is collective, and depends not
upon what we do as individuals, but upon our power of combining. In every successive generation, men more resemble each
other in all respects. They are more alike in their civil and political privileges, in their habits, in their tastes, in their manners,
in their dress, in what they see, in what they do, in what they
read, in what they think, and in what they say. On all sides the
process of assimilation is going on. Shades of character are
being blended, and contrasts of will are being reconciled. As a
natural consequence, the individual life, that is, the life which
distinguishes each man from his fellows, is perishing. The consolidation of the many destroys the action of the few. While we
amalgamate the mass, we absorb the unit.

The authority of society is, in this way, ruining society itself.
For the human faculties can, for the most part, only be exercised
and disciplined by the act of choosing; but he who does a thing
merely because others do it, makes no choice at all. Constantly
copying the manners and opinions of our contemporaries, we
strike out nothing that is new; we follow on in a dull and monotonous uniformity. We go where others lead. The field of
option is being straitened; the number of alternatives is diminishing. And the result is, a sensible decay of that vigour and
raciness of character, that diversity and fulness of life, and that
audacity both of conception and of execution which marked the
strong men of former times, and enabled them at once to improve
and to guide the human species.

Now all this is gone, perhaps never to return, unless some
great convulsion should previously occur. Originality is dying
away, and is being replaced by a spirit of servile and apish imitation. We are degenerating into machines who do the will of
society; our impulses and desires are repressed by a galling and
artificial code; our minds are dwarfed and stunted by the checks
and limitations to which we are perpetually subjected.

How, then, is it possible to discover new truths of real importance? How is it possible that creative thought can flourish
in so sickly and tainted an atmosphere? Genius is a form of

---

[1] " There is now scarcely any outlet for energy in this country except business.
The energy expended in that may still be regarded as considerable."—Mill *On Liberty*,
p. 125. I suppose that, under the word business, Mr. Mill includes political and the
higher class of official pursuits.

originality; if the originality is discouraged, how can the genius remain? It is hard to see the remedy for this crying evil. Society is growing so strong as to destroy individuality; that is, to destroy the very quality to which our civilization, and therefore our social fabric, is primarily owing.

The truth is, that we must vindicate the right of each man to do what he likes, and to say what he thinks, to an extent much greater than is usually supposed to be either safe or decent. This we must do for the sake of society, quite as much as for our own sake. That society would be benefited by a greater freedom of action has been already shown; and the same thing may be proved concerning freedom of speech and of writing. In this respect authors, and the teachers of mankind generally, are far too timid; while the state of public opinion is far too interfering. The remarks which Mr. Mill has made on this, are so exhaustive as to be unanswerable; and though many will call in question what he has said respecting the decline of individuality, no well-instructed person will dispute the accuracy of his conclusions respecting the need of an increased liberty of discussion and of publication.

In the present state of knowledge the majority of people are so ill-informed as not to be aware of the true nature of belief; they are not aware that all belief is involuntary, and is entirely governed by the circumstances which produce it. They who have paid attention to these subjects, know that what we call the will has no power over belief, and that consequently a man is nowise responsible for his creed, except in so far as he is responsible for the events which gave him his creed. Whether, for instance, he is a Mohammedan or a Christian, will usually resolve itself into a simple question of his geographical antecedents. He who is born in Constantinople will hold one set of opinions; he who is born in London will hold another set. Both act according to their light and their circumstances, and if both are sincere both are guiltless. In each case, the believer is controlled by physical facts which determine his creed, and over which he can no more exercise authority than he can exercise authority over the movements of the planets or the rotation of the earth. This view, though long familiar to thinkers, can hardly be said to have been popularised before the present century;[1] and to its diffusion, as well as to other larger and more potent causes, we must ascribe the increasing spirit of toleration to which not only our literature but even our statute-book bears witness.

[1] Its diffusion was greatly helped by Bailey's *Essays on the Formation of Opinions*, which were first published, I believe, in 1821, and being popularly written, as well as suitable to the age, have exercised considerable influence.

But, though belief is involuntary, it will be objected, with a certain degree of plausibility, that the expression of that belief, and particularly the formal and written publication, is a voluntary act, and consequently a responsible one.  If I were arguing the question exhaustively, I should at the outset demur to this proposition, and should require it to be stated in more cautious and limited terms; but, to save time, let us suppose it to be true, and let us inquire whether, if a man be responsible to himself for the publication of his opinions, it is right that he should also be held responsible by those to whom he offers them?  In other words, is it proper that law or public opinion should discourage an individual from publishing sentiments which are hostile to the prevailing notions, and are considered by the rest of society to be false and mischievous?

Upon this point, the arguments of Mr. Mill are so full and decisive that I despair of adding anything to them.  It will be enough if I give a summary of the principal ones; for it would be strange, indeed, if before many months are past, this noble treatise, so full of wisdom and of thought, is not in the hands of every one who cares for the future welfare of humanity, and whose ideas rise above the immediate interests of his own time.

Those who hold that an individual ought to be discouraged from publishing a work containing heretical or irreligious opinions, must, of course, assume that such opinions are false; since, in the present day, hardly any man would be so impudent as to propose that a true opinion should be stifled because it was unusual as well as true.  We are all agreed that truth is good; or, at all events, those who are not agreed must be treated as persons beyond the pale of reason, and on whose obtuse understandings it would be idle to waste an argument.  He who says that truth is not always to be told, and that it is not fit for all minds, is simply a defender of falsehood; and we should take no notice of him, inasmuch as the object of discussion being to destroy error, we cannot discuss with a man who deliberately affirms that error should be spared.

We take, therefore, for granted that those who seek to prevent any opinion being laid before the world, do so for the sake of truth, and with a view to prevent the unwary from being led into error.  The intention is good; it remains for us to inquire how it operates.

Now, in the first place, we can never be sure that the opinion of the majority is true.  Nearly every opinion held by the majority was once confined to the minority.  Every established religion was once a heresy.  If the opinions of the majority had

always prevailed, Christianity would have been extirpated as soon
as Christ was murdered. If an age or a people assume that any
notion they entertain is certainly right, they assume their own
infallibility, and arrogantly claim for themselves a prerogative
which even the wisest of mankind never possess. To affirm that
a doctrine is unquestionably revealed from above, is equally to
affirm their own infallibility, since they affirm that they cannot
be mistaken in believing it to be revealed. A man who is sure
that his creed is true, is sure of his own infallibility, because he
is sure that upon that point he has committed no error. Unless,
therefore, we are prepared to claim, on our own behalf, an immunity from error, and an incapability of being mistaken, which
transcend the limits of the human mind, we are bound not only
to permit our opinions to be disputed, but to be grateful to those
who will do so. For, as no one who is not absurdly and im-
modestly confident of his own powers, can be sure that what he
believes to be true is true, it will be his object, if he be an honest
man, to rectify the errors he may have committed. But it is a
matter of history that errors have only been rectified by two
means; namely, by experience and discussion. The use of discussion is to show how experience is to be interpreted. Experience alone has never improved either mankind or individuals.
Experience, before it can be available, must be sifted and tested.
This is done by discussion, which brings out the meaning of experience, and enables us to apply the observations that have been
made, and turn them to account. Human judgment owes its
value solely to the fact that when it is wrong it is possible to
set it right. Inasmuch, however, as it can only be set right by
the conflict and collision of hostile opinions, it is clear that
when those opinions are smothered, and when that conflict is
stopped, the means of correcting our judgment are gone, and
hence the value of our judgment is destroyed. The more therefore that the majority discourage the opinions of the minority,
the smaller is the chance of the majority holding accurate views.
But if, instead of discouraging the opinions, they should suppress
them, even that small chance is taken away, and society can have
no option but to go on from bad to worse, its blunders becoming
more inveterate and more mischievous, in proportion as that
liberty of discussion which might have rectified them has been
the longer withheld.

Here we, as the advocates of liberty, might fairly close the
argument, leaving our opponents in the dilemma of either asserting their own infallibility, or else of abandoning the idea of interfering with freedom of discussion. So complete, however, is

our case, that we can actually afford to dispense with what has been just stated, and support our views on other and totally different grounds. We will concede to those who favour restriction all the premises that they require. We will concede to them the strongest position that they can imagine, and we will take for granted that a nation has the means of knowing with absolute certainty that some of its opinions are right. We say then, and we will prove that, assuming those opinions to be true, it is advisable that they should be combated, and that their truth should be denied. That an opinion which is held by an immense majority, and which is moreover completely and unqualifiedly true, ought to be contested, and that those who contest it do a public service, appears at first sight to be an untenable paradox. A paradox indeed it is, if by a paradox we mean an assertion not generally admitted; but, so far from being untenable, it is a sound and wholesome doctrine, which if it were adopted, would to an extraordinary extent facilitate the progress of society.

Supposing any well-established opinion to be certainly true, the result of its not being vigorously attacked is, that it becomes more passive and inert than it would otherwise be. This, as Mr. Mill observes, has been exemplified in the history of Christianity. In the early Church, while Christianity was struggling against innumerable opponents, it displayed a life and an energy which diminished in proportion as the opposition was withdrawn. When an enemy is at the gate the garrison is alert. If the enemy retires the alertness slackens; and if he disappears altogether, nothing remains but the mere forms and duty of discipline, which, unenlivened by danger, grow torpid and mechanical. This is a law of the human mind, and is of universal application. Every religion after being established loses much of its vitality. Its doctrines being less questioned, it naturally happens that those who hold them scrutinise them less closely, and therefore grasp them less firmly. Their wits being no longer sharpened by controversy, what was formerly a living truth dwindles into a dead dogma. The excitement of the battle being over, the weapons are laid aside; they fall into disuse; they grow rusty; the skill and fire of the warrior are gone. It is amid the roar of the cannon, the flash of the bayonet, and the clang of the trumpet, that the forms of men dilate; they swell with emotion; their bulk increases; their stature rises, and even small natures wax into great ones, able to do all and to dare all.

So indeed it is. On any subject universal acquiescence always engenders universal apathy. By a parity of reasoning, the greater the acquiescence the greater the apathy. All hail therefore to those who, by attacking a truth, prevent that truth from slumbering. All hail to those bold and fearless natures, the heretics and innovators of their day, who, rousing men out of their lazy sleep, sound in their ears the tocsin and the clarion, and force them to come forth that they may do battle for their creed. Of all evils, torpor is the most deadly. Give us paradox, give us error, give us what you will, so that you save us from stagnation. It is the cold spirit of routine which is the nightshade of our nature. It sits upon men like a blight, blunting their faculties, withering their powers, and making them both unable and unwilling either to struggle for the truth, or to figure to themselves what it is that they really believe.

See how this has acted in regard to the doctrines of the New Testament. When those doctrines were first propounded, they were vigorously assailed, and therefore the early Christians clung to them, realised them, and bound them up in their hearts to an extent unparalleled in any subsequent age. Every Christian professes to believe that it is good to be ill-used and buffeted; that wealth is an evil, because rich men cannot enter the kingdom of heaven; that if your cloak is taken, you must give your coat also; that if you are smitten on your cheek, you should turn round and offer the other. These, and similar doctrines, the early Christians not only professed, but acted up to and followed. The same doctrines are contained in our Bibles, read in our churches, and preached in our pulpits. Who is there that obeys them? And what reason is there for this universal defection, beyond the fact that when Christianity was constantly assailed, those who received its tenets held them with a tenacity, and saw them with a vividness which cannot be expected in an age that sanctions them by general acquiescence? Now, indeed, they are not only acquiesced in, they are also watched over and sedulously protected. They are protected by law, and by that public opinion which is infinitely more powerful than any law. Hence it is, that to them, men yield a cold and lifeless assent; they bear them and they talk about them, but whoever was to obey them with that scrupulous fidelity which was formerly practised, would find to his cost how much he had mistaken his age, and how great is the difference, in vitality and in practical effect, between doctrines which are generally received and those which are fearlessly discussed.

In proportion as knowledge has advanced, and habits of correct thinking been diffused, men have gradually approached towards these views of liberty, though Mr. Mill has been the first to bring them together in a thoroughly comprehensive spirit, and to concentrate in a single treatise all the arguments in their behalf.

How everything has long tended to this result must be known to whoever has studied the history of the English mind. Whatever may be the case respecting the alleged decline of individuality, and the increasing tyranny of custom, there can, at all events, be no doubt that, in religious matters, public opinion is constantly becoming more liberal. The legal penalties which our ignorant and intolerant ancestors inflicted upon whoever differed from themselves, are now some of them repealed, and some of them obsolete. Not only have we ceased to murder or torture those who disagree with us, but, strange to say, we have even recognised their claim to political rights as well as to civil equality. The admission of the Jews into Parliament, that just and righteous measure, which was carried in the teeth of the most cherished and inveterate prejudice, is a striking proof of the force of the general movement; as also is the rapidly increasing disposition to abolish oaths and to do away in public life with every species of religious tests. Partly as cause, and partly as effect of all this, there never was a period in which so many bold and able attacks were made upon the prevailing theology, and in which so many heretical doctrines were propounded, not only by laymen, but occasionally by ministers of the church, some of the most eminent of whom have, during the present generation, come forward to denounce the errors in their own system, and to point out the flaws in their own creed. The unorthodox character of physical science is equally notorious; and many of its professors do not scruple to impeach the truth of statements which are still held to be essential, and which, in other days, no one could have impugned without exposing himself to serious danger. In former times, such men would have been silenced or punished; now, they are respected and valued; their works are eagerly read, and the circle of their influence is steadily widening. According to the letter of our law-books, these, and similar publications, which fearless and inquisitive men are pouring into the public ear, are illegal, and Government has the power of prosecuting their authors. The state of opinion, however, is so improved, that such prosecutions would be fatal to any Government which instigated them. We have, therefore, every reason to congratulate ourselves on having outlived the reign of open persecution. We may fairly suppose that the cruelties which our forefathers committed in the name of religion, could not now be perpetrated, and that it would be impossible to punish a man merely because he expressed notions which the majority considered to be profane and mischievous.

Under these circumstances, and seeing that the practice of prosecuting men for uttering their sentiments on religious

matters has been for many years discontinued, an attempt to
revive that shameful custom would, if it were generally known,
be at once scouted. It would be deemed unnatural as well as
cruel: out of the ordinary course, and wholly unsuited to the
humane and liberal notions of an age which seeks to relax penalties rather than to multiply them. As to the man who might be
mad enough to make the attempt, we should look upon him in
the light in which we should regard some noxious animal, which,
being suddenly let loose, went about working harm, and undoing
all the good that had been previously done. We should hold him
to be a nuisance which it was our duty either to abate, or to warn
people of. To us, he would be a sort of public enemy; a dis-
turber of human happiness; a creature hostile to the human
species. If he possessed authority, we should loathe him the
more, as one who, instead of employing for the benefit of his
country the power with which his country had entrusted him,
used it to gratify his own malignant prejudices, or maybe to
humour the spleen of some wretched and intolerant faction with
which he was connected.

Inasmuch, therefore, as, in the present state of English society,
any punishment inflicted for the use of language which did not
tend to break the public peace, and which was neither seditious
in reference to the State, nor libellous in reference to individuals,
would be simply a wanton cruelty, alien to the genius of our
time, and capable of producing no effect beyond reviving intolerance, exasperating the friends of liberty, and bringing the administration of justice into disrepute, it was with the greatest
astonishment that I read in Mr. Mill's work that such a thing
had occurred in this country, and at one of our assizes, less than
two years ago. Notwithstanding my knowledge of Mr. Mill's
accuracy, I thought that, in this instance, he must have been mistaken. I supposed that he had not heard all the circumstances,
and that the person punished had been guilty of some other
offence. I could not believe that in the year 1857, there was a
judge on the English bench who would sentence a poor man of
irreproachable character, of industrious habits, and, supporting
his family by the sweat of his brow, to twenty-one months' imprisonment, merely because he had uttered and written on a gate
a few words respecting Christianity. Even now, when I have
carefully investigated the facts to which Mr. Mill only alludes,
and have the documents before me, I can hardly bring myself to
realise the events which have actually occurred, and which I will
relate, in order that public opinion may take cognisance of a
transaction which happened in a remote part of the kingdom, but

which the general welfare requires to be bruited abroad, so that men may determine whether or not such things shall be allowed.

In the summer of 1857, a poor man, named Thomas Pooley, was gaining his livelihood as a common labourer in Liskeard, in Cornwall, where he had been well known for several years, and had always borne a high character for honesty, industry, and sobriety. His habits were so eccentric, that his mind was justly reputed to be disordered; and an accident which happened to him about two years before this period had evidently inflicted some serious injury, as since then his demeanour had become more strange and excitable. Still, he was not only perfectly harmless, but was a very useful member of society, respected by his neighbours, and loved by his family, for whom he toiled with a zeal rare in his class, or indeed in any class. Among other hallucinations, he believed that the earth was a living animal, and, in his ordinary employment of well-sinking, he avoided digging too deeply, lest he should penetrate the skin of the earth, and wound some vital part. He also imagined that if he hurt the earth, the tides would cease to flow; and that nothing being really mortal, whenever a child died it reappeared at the next birth in the same family. Holding all nature to be animated, he moreover fancied that this was in some way connected with the potato-rot, and, in the wildness of his vagaries, he did not hesitate to say that if the ashes of burnt Bibles were strewed over the fields, the rot would cease. This was associated, in his mind, with a foolish dislike of the Bible itself, and an hostility against Christianity; in reference, however, to which he could hurt no one, as not only was he very ignorant, but his neighbours, regarding him as crackbrained, were uninfluenced by him; though in the other relations of life he was valued and respected by his employers, and indeed by all who were most acquainted with his disposition.

This singular man, who was known by the additional peculiarity of wearing a long beard, wrote upon a gate a few very silly words expressive of his opinion respecting the potato-rot and the Bible, and also of his hatred of Christianity. For this, as well as for using language equally absurd, but which no one was obliged to listen to, and which certainly could influence no one, a clergyman in the neighbourhood lodged an information against him, and caused him to be summoned before a magistrate, who was likewise a clergyman. The magistrate, instead of pitying him or remonstrating with him, committed him for trial and sent him to jail. At the next assizes, he was brought before the judge. He had no counsel to defend him, but the son of the judge acted as counsel to prosecute him. The father and the son performed their parts with zeal, and were perfectly successful. Under their auspices, Pooley was found guilty. He was brought up for judgment. When addressed by the judge, his restless manner, his wild and incoherent speech, his disordered countenance and glaring eye, betokened too surely the disease of his mind. But neither this, nor the fact that he was ignorant, poor, and friendless, produced any effect upon that stony-hearted man who now held him in his gripe. He was sentenced to be imprisoned for a year and nine months. The interests of religion were vindicated. Christianity was protected, and her triumph assured, by dragging a poor, harmless, and demented creature from the bosom of his family, throwing him into jail, and leaving his wife and children without provision, either to starve or to beg.

Before he had been many days in prison, the insanity which was obvious at the time of his trial ceased to lurk, and broke out into acts of violence. He grew worse; and within a fortnight after the sentence had been pronounced he went mad, and it was found necessary to remove him from the jail to the County Lunatic Asylum. While he was lying there, his misfortunes attracted the attention of a few high-minded and benevolent men, who exerted themselves to procure his pardon; so that, if he recovered, he might be restored to his family. This petition was refused. It was necessary to support the judge; and the petitioners were informed that if the miserable lunatic should regain his reason, he would be sent back to prison to undergo the rest of his sentence. This, in all probability, would have caused a relapse; but little was thought of that; and it was hoped that, as he was an obscure and humble man, the efforts made on his behalf would soon subside. Those, however, who had once interested themselves in such a case, were not likely to slacken their zeal. The cry grew hotter, and preparations were made for bringing the whole question before the country. Then it was that the authorities gave way. Happily for mankind, one vice is often balanced by another, and cruelty is corrected by cowardice. The authors and abettors of this prodigious iniquity trembled at the risk they would run if the public feeling of this great country were roused. The result was, that the proceedings of the judge were rescinded, as far as possible, by a pardon being granted to Pooley less than five months after the sentence was pronounced.

By this means, general exposure was avoided; and, perhaps, that handful of noble-minded men who obtained the liberation of Pooley, were right in letting the matter fall into oblivion after they had carried their point. Most of them were engaged in political or other practical affairs, and they were, therefore,

obliged to consider expediency as well as justice. But such is
not the case with the historian of this sad event. No writer on
important subjects has reason to expect that he can work real
good, or that his words shall live, if he allows himself to be so
trammelled by expediency as to postpone to it considerations of
right, of justice, and of truth. A great crime has been committed, and the names of the criminals ought to be known. They
should be in every one's mouth. They should be blazoned abroad,
in order that the world may see that in a free country such things
cannot be done with impunity. To discourage a repetition of the
offence the offenders must be punished. And, surely, no punishment can be more severe than to preserve their names. Against
them personally, I have nothing to object, for I have no knowledge of them. Individually, I can feel no animosity towards men
who have done me no harm, and whom I have never seen. But
they have violated principles dearer to me than any personal
feeling, and in vindication of which I would set all personal
feeling at nought. Fortunate, indeed, it is for humanity, that
our minds are constructed after such a fashion as to make it impossible for us, by any effort of abstract reasoning, to consider
oppression apart from the oppressor. We may abhor a speculative principle, and yet respect him who advocates it. This distinction between the opinion and the person is, however, confined
to the intellectual world, and does not extend to the practical.
Such a separation cannot exist in regard to actual deeds of cruelty.
In such cases, our passions instruct our understanding. The same
cause which excites our sympathy for the oppressed, stirs up our
hatred of the oppressor. This is an instinct of our nature, and
he who struggles against it does so to his own detriment. It
belongs to the higher region of the mind; it is not to be im-
peached by argument; it cannot even be touched by it. Therefore it is, that when we hear that a poor, a defenceless, and a
half-witted man, who had hurt no one, a kind father, an affectionate husband, whose private character was unblemished, and
whose integrity was beyond dispute, is suddenly thrown into
prison, his family left to subsist on the precarious charity of
strangers, he himself by this cruel treatment deprived of the
little reason he possessed, then turned into a madhouse, and
finally refused such scanty redress as might have been afforded
him, a spirit of vehement indignation is excited, partly, indeed,
against a system under which such things can be done; but still
more against those who, in the pride of their power and wickedness of their hearts, put laws into execution which had long fallen
into disuse, and which they were not bound to enforce, but of

which they availed themselves to crush the victim they held in their grasp.

The prosecutor, who lodged the information against Pooley, and had him brought before the magistrate, was the Rev. Paul Bush. The magistrate, who received the information, and committed him for trial, was the Rev. James Glencross. The judge who passed the sentence which destroyed his reason and beggared his family, was Mr. Justice Coleridge.

Of the two first, little need be said. It is to be hoped that their names will live, and that they will enjoy that sort of fame which they have amply earned. Perhaps, after all, we should rather blame the state of society which concedes power to such men, than wonder that having the power they should abuse it. But with Mr. Justice Coleridge we have a different account to settle, and to him other language must be applied. That our judges should have great authority is unavoidable. To them, a wide and discretionary latitude is necessarily entrusted. Great confidence being reposed in them, they are bound, by every possible principle which can actuate an honest man, to respect that confidence. They are bound to avoid not only injustice, but, so far as they can, the very appearance of injustice. Seeing, as they do, all classes of society, they are well aware that, among the lower ranks, there is a deep, though on the whole a diminishing belief that the poor are ill-treated by the rich, and that even in the courts of law equal measure is not always meted out to both. An opinion of this sort is full of danger, and it is the more dangerous because it is not unfounded. The country magistrates are too often unfair in their decisions, and this will always be the case until greater publicity is given to their proceedings. But, from our superior judges we expect another sort of conduct. We expect, and it must honestly be said we usually find, that they shall be above petty prejudices, or at all events, that whatever private opinions they may have, they shall not intrude those opinions into the sanctuary of justice. Above all do we expect, that they shall not ferret out some obsolete law for the purpose of oppressing the poor, when they know right well that the anti-Christian sentiments which that law was intended to punish are quite as common among the upper classes as among the lower, and are participated in by many persons who enjoy the confidence of the country, and to whom the highest offices are entrusted.

That this is the case was known in the year 1857 to Mr. Justice Coleridge, just as it was then known, and is now known, to every one who mixes in the world. The charge, therefore, which I bring against this unjust and unrighteous judge is, that he passed a

sentence of extreme severity upon a poor and friendless man in a
remote part of the kingdom, where he might reasonably expect
that his sentence would escape public animadversion ; that he
did this by virtue of a law which had fallen into disuse, and was
contrary to the spirit of the age ;[1] and that he would not have
dared to commit such an act, in the face of a London audience,
and in the full light of the London press. Neither would he,
nor those who supported him, have treated in such a manner u
person belonging to the upper classes. No. They select the
most inaccessible county in England, where the press is least
active and the people are most illiterate, and there they pounce
upon a defenceless man and make him the scapegoat. He is to
be the victim whose vicarious sufferings may atone for the offences
of more powerful unbelievers. Hardly a year goes by without
some writer of influence and ability attacking Christianity, and
every such attack is punishable by law. Why did not Mr. Justice
Coleridge, and those who think like him, put the law into force
against those writers? Why do they not do it now? Why do
they not have the learned and the eminent indicted and thrown
into prison? Simply because they dare not. I defy them to it.
They are afraid of the odium ; they tremble at the hostility they
would incur, and at the scorn which would be heaped upon them,
both by their contemporaries and by posterity. Happily for
mankind, literature is a real power, and tyranny quakes at it.
But to me it appears, that men of letters perform the least part
of their duty when they defend each other. It is their proper
function, and it ought to be their glory, to defend the weak
against the strong, and to uphold the poor against the rich. This
should be their pride and their honour. I would it were known
in every cottage, that the intellectual classes sympathise, not with
the upper ranks but with the lower. I would that we made the
freedom of the people our first consideration. Then, indeed, would
literature be the religion of liberty, and we, priests of the altar,
ministering her sacred rites, might feel that we act in the purest
spirit of our creed when we denounce tyranny in high places, when
we chastise the insolence of office, and when we vindicate the
cause of Thomas Pooley against Justice Coleridge.

For my part, I can honestly say that I have nothing exaggerated,
nor set down aught in malice. What the verdict of public opinion
may be I cannot tell. I speak merely as a man of letters, and do

---

[1] Or rather by virtue of the cruel and persecuting maxims of our old Common Law,
established at a period when it was a matter of religion to burn heretics and to drown
witches. Why did not such a judge live three hundred years ago ? He has fallen
upon evil times and has come too late into the world.

not pretend to represent any class. I have no interest to advocate; I hold no brief; I carry no man's proxy. But unless I altogether mistake the general feeling, it will be considered that a great crime has been committed; that a knowledge of that crime has been too long hidden in a corner; and that I have done something towards dragging the criminal from his covert, and letting in on him the full light of day.

This gross iniquity is, no doubt, to be immediately ascribed to the cold heart and shallow understanding of the judge by whom it was perpetrated. If, however, public opinion had been sufficiently enlightened, those evil qualities would have been restrained and rendered unable to work the mischief. Therefore it is, that the safest and most permanent remedy would be to diffuse sound notions respecting the liberty of speech and of publication. It should be clearly understood that every man has an absolute and irrefragable right to treat any doctrine as he thinks proper; either to argue against it, or to ridicule it. If his arguments are wrong, he can be refuted; if his ridicule is foolish, he can be out-ridiculed. To this there can be no exception. It matters not what the tenet may be, nor how dear it is to our feelings. Like all other opinions, it must take its chance; it must be roughly used; it must stand every test; it must be thoroughly discussed and sifted. And we may rest assured that if it really be a great and valuable truth, such opposition will endear it to us the more; and that we shall cling to it the closer in proportion as it is argued against, aspersed, and attempted to be overthrown.

If I were asked for an instance of the extreme latitude to which such licence might be extended, I would take what, in my judgment, at least, is the most important of all doctrines, the doctrine of a future state. Strictly speaking, there is, in the present early condition of the human mind, no subject on which we can arrive at complete certainty; but the belief in a future state approaches that certainty nearer than any other belief, and it is one which, if eradicated, would drive most of us to despair. On both these grounds it stands alone. It is fortified by arguments far stronger than can be adduced in support of any other opinion; and it is a supreme consolation to those who suffer affliction, or smart under a sense of injustice. The attempts made to impugn it have always seemed to me to be very weak, and to leave the real difficulties untouched. They are negative arguments directed against affirmative ones. But if, in transcendental inquiries, negative arguments are to satisfy us, how shall we escape from the reasonings of Berkeley respecting the non-existence of the material world? Those reasonings have never been answered, and our knowledge must be infinitely more advanced than it now is, before they can be answered. They are far stronger than the arguments of the atheists; and I cannot but wonder that they who reject a future state, should believe in the reality of the material world. Still, those who do reject it, are not only justified in openly denying it, but are bound to do so. Our first and paramount duty is to be true to ourselves; and no man is true to himself who fears to express his opinion. There is hardly any vice which so debases us in our own esteem, as moral cowardice. There is hardly any virtue which so elevates our character, as moral courage. Therefore it is that the more unpopular a notion, the greater the merit of him who advocates it, provided, of course, he does so in honesty and singleness of heart. On this account, although I regard the expectation of another life as the prop and mainstay of mankind, and although I cannot help thinking that they who reject it have taken an imperfect and uncomprehensive view, and have not covered the whole field of inquiry, I do strenuously maintain, that against it every species of attack is legitimate, and I feel assured that the more it is assailed the more it will flourish, and the more vividly we shall realise its meaning, its depth, and its necessity.

That many of the common arguments in favour of this great doctrine are unsound might be easily shown; but until the entire subject is freely discussed, we shall never know how far they are unsound, and what part of them ought to be retained. If, for instance, we make our belief in it depend upon assertions contained in books regarded as sacred, it will follow that whenever those books lose their influence the doctrine will be in peril. The basis being impaired the superstructure will tremble. It may well be, that in the march of ages, every definite and written creed now existing is destined to die out, and to be succeeded by better ones. The world has seen the beginning of them, and we have no surety that it will not see the end of them. Everything which is essential to the human mind must survive all the shocks and vicissitudes of time; but dogmas, which the mind once did without, cannot be essential to it. Perhaps we have no right so to anticipate the judgment of our remotest posterity as to affirm that any opinion is essential to all possible forms of civilization; but, at all events, we have more reason to believe this of the doctrine of a future state than of any other conceivable idea. Let us then beware of endangering its stability by narrowing its foundation. Let us take heed how we rest it on the testimony of inspired writings, when we know that inspiration at one epoch is often different from inspiration at another. If Christianity

should ever perish, the age that loses it will have reason to
deplore the blindness of those who teach mankind to defend this
glorious and consolatory tenet, not by general considerations of
the fundamental properties of our common nature, but by traditions, assertions, and records, which do not bear the stamp of
universality, since in one state of society they are held to be true,
and in another state of society they are held to be false.

Of the same fluctuating and precarious character is the argument drawn from the triumph of injustice in this world, and the
consequent necessity of such unfairness being remedied in another
life.   For it admits of historical proof that, as civilization
advances, the impunity and rewards of wickedness diminish.
In a barbarous state of society virtue is invariably trampled upon,
and nothing really succeeds except violence or fraud.   In that
stage of affairs, the worst criminals are the most prosperous men.
But, in every succeeding step of the great progress, injustice
becomes more hazardous ; force and rapine grow more unsafe ;
precautions multiply ; the supervision is keener ; tyranny and
deceit are oftener detected.   Being oftener detected, it is less
profitable to practise them.   In the same proportion, the rewards
of integrity increase, and the prospects of virtue brighten.   A
large part of the power, the honour, and the fame formerly
possessed by evil men is transferred to good men.   Acts of injustice which at an earlier period would have escaped attention,
or, if known, would have excited no odium, are now chastised,
not only by law, but also by public opinion.   Indeed, so marked
is this tendency, that many persons by a singular confusion of
thought, actually persuade themselves that offences are increasing
because we hear more of them, and punish them oftener ; not
seeing that this merely proves that we note them more and hate
them more.   We redouble our efforts against injustice, not on
account of the spread of injustice, but on account of our better
understanding how to meet it, and being more determined to
coerce it.   No other age has ever cried out against it so loudly ;
and yet, strange to say, this very proof of our superiority to all
other ages is cited as evidence of our inferiority.   This I shall
return to elsewhere ; my present object in mentioning it, is partly
to check a prevailing error, but chiefly to indicate its connection
with the subject before us.   Nothing is more certain than that,
as society advances, the weak are better protected against the
strong ; the honest against the dishonest ; and the just against
the unjust.   If, then, we adopt the popular argument in favour
of another life, that injustice here must be compensated hereafter,
we are driven to the terrible conclusion that the same progress

of civilization which, in this world, heightens the penalties inflicted on injustice, would also lessen the need of future compensation, and thereby weaken the ground of our belief. The inference would be untrue, but it follows from the premises. To me it appears not only sad, but extremely pernicious, that on a topic of such surpassing interest, the understandings of men should be imposed upon by reasonings which are so shallow, that, if pushed to their legitimate consequence, they would defeat their own aim, because they would force us to assert that the more we improve in our moral conduct towards each other, the less we should care for a future and a better world.

I have brought forward these views for the sake of justifying the general proposition maintained in this essay. For, it is evident that if the state of public opinion did not discourage a fearless investigation of these matters, and did not foolishly cast a slur upon those who attack doctrines which are dear to us, the whole subject would be more thoroughly understood, and such weak arguments as are commonly advanced would have been long since exploded. If they who deny the immortality of the soul, could, without the least opprobrium, state in the boldest manner all their objections, the advocates of the doctrine would be obliged to reconsider their own position, and to abandon its untenable points. By this means, that which I revere, and which an overwhelming majority of us revere, as a glorious truth, would be immensely strengthened. It would be strengthened by being deprived of those sophistical arguments which are commonly urged in its favour, and which give to its enemies an incalculable advantage. It would, moreover, be strengthened by that feeling of security which men have in their own convictions, when they know that everything is said against them which can be said, and that their opponents have a fair and liberal hearing. This begets a magnanimity, and a rational confidence, which cannot otherwise be obtained. But such results can never happen while we are so timid, or so dishonest, as to impute improper motives to those who assail our religious opinions. We may rely upon it that as long as we look upon an atheistical writer as a moral offender, or even as long as we glance at him with suspicion, atheism will remain a standing and a permanent danger, because, skulking in hidden corners, it will use stratagems which their secrecy will prevent us from baffling; it will practise artifices to which the persecuted are forced to resort; it will number its concealed proselytes to an extent of which only they who have studied this painful subject are aware; and, above all, by enabling them to complain of the treatment to which they are

*F

exposed, it will excite the sympathy of many high and generous natures who, in an open and manly warfare, might strive against them, but who, by a noble instinct, find themselves incapable of contending with any sect which is oppressed, maligned, or intimidated.

Though this essay has been prolonged much beyond my original intention, I am unwilling to conclude it just at this point, when I have attacked arguments which support a doctrine that I cherish above all other doctrines. It is, indeed, certain that he who destroys a feeble argument in favour of any truth, renders the greatest service to that truth, by obliging its advocates to produce a stronger one. Still, an idea will prevail among some persons that such service is insidious; and that to expose the weak side of a cause, is likely to be the work, not of a friend but of an enemy in disguise. Partly, therefore, to prevent misinterpretation from those who are always ready to misinterpret, and partly for the satisfaction of more candid readers, I will venture to state what I apprehend to be the safest and most impregnable ground on which the supporters of this great doctrine can take their stand.

That ground is the universality of the affections; the yearning of every mind to care for something out of itself. For, this is the very bond and seal of our common humanity; it is the golden link which knits together and preserves the human species. It is in the need of loving and of being loved, that the highest instincts of our nature are first revealed. Not only is it found among the good and the virtuous, but experience proves that it is compatible with almost any amount of depravity, and with almost every form of vice. No other principle is so general or so powerful. It exists in the most barbarous and ferocious states of society, and we know that even sanguinary and revolting crimes are often unable to efface it from the breast of the criminal. It warms the coldest temperament, and softens the hardest heart. However a character may be deteriorated and debased, this single passion is capable of redeeming it from utter defilement, and of rescuing it from the lowest depths. And if, from time to time, we hear of an apparently well attested case of its entire absence, we are irresistibly impelled to believe that, even in that mind, it lurks unseen; that it is stunted, not destroyed; that there is yet some nook or cranny in which it is buried; that the avenues from without are not quite closed; and that, in spite of adverse circumstances, the affections are not so dead but that it would be possible to rouse them from their torpor, and kindle them into life.

Look now at the way in which this godlike and fundamental principle of our nature acts.    As long as we are with those whom we love, and as long as the sense of security is unimpaired, we rejoice, and the remote consequences of our love are usually forgotten.    Its fears and its risks are unheeded.    But, when the dark day approaches, and the moment of sorrow is at hand, other and yet essential parts of our affection come into play.    And if, perchance, the struggle has been long and arduous; if we have been tempted to cling to hope when hope should have been abandoned, so much the more are we at the last changed and humbled.    To note the slow, but inevitable march of disease, to watch the enemy stealing in at the gate, to see the strength gradually waning, the limbs tottering more and more, the noble faculties dwindling by degrees, the eye paling and losing its lustre, the tongue faltering as it vainly tries to utter its words of endearment, the very lips hardly able to smile with their wonted tenderness;—to see this is hard indeed to bear, and many of the strongest natures have sunk under it.    But when even this is gone; when the very signs of life are mute; when the last faint ⸱ tie is severed, and there lies before us nought save the shell and husk of what we loved too well, then truly, if we believed the separation were final, how could we stand up and live?    We have staked our all upon a single cast, and lost the stake.    There, where we have garnered up our hearts, and where our treasure is, thieves break in and spoil.    Methinks, that in that moment of desolation, the best of us would succumb, but for the deep conviction that all is not really over; that we have as yet only seen a part; and that something remains behind.    Something behind; something which the eye of reason cannot discern, but on which the eye of affection is fixed.    What is that, which, passing over us like a shadow, strains the aching vision as we gaze at it?    Whence comes that sense of mysterious companionship in the midst of solitude; that ineffable feeling which cheers the afflicted?    Why is it that at these times, our minds are thrown back on themselves, and being so thrown, have a forecast of another and a higher state?    If this be a delusion, it is one which the affections have themselves created, and we must believe that the purest and noblest elements of our nature conspire to deceive us.    So surely as we lose what we love, so surely does hope mingle with grief.    That if a man stood alone, he would deem himself mortal I can well imagine.    Why not?    On account of his loneliness, his moral faculties would be undeveloped, and it is solely from them that he could learn the doctrine of immortality.    There is nothing, either in the mechanism of the material universe, or in

the vast sweep and compass of science, which can teach it. The
human intellect, glorious as it is, and in its own field almost omni-
potent, knows it not. For, the province and function of the intellect is to take those steps, and to produce those improvements,
whether speculative or practical, which accelerate the march of
nations, and to which we owe the august and imposing fabric of
modern civilization. But this intellectual movement which de-
termines the condition of man, does not apply with the same
force to the condition of men. What is most potent in the mass,
loses its supremacy in the unit. One law for the separate elements; another law for the entire compound. The intellectual
principle is conspicuous in regard to the race; the moral principle in regard to the individual. And of all the moral sentiments which adorn and elevate the human character, the instinct
of affection is surely the most lovely, the most powerful, and the
most general. Unless, therefore, we are prepared to assert that
this, the fairest and choicest of our possessions, is of so delusive
and fraudulent a character that its dictates are not to be trusted,
we can hardly avoid the conclusion that, inasmuch as they are
the same in all ages, with all degrees of knowledge, and with
all varieties of religion, they bear upon their surface the impress
of truth, and are at once the conditions and consequence of
our being.

It is, then, to that sense of immortality with which the affections inspire us, that I would appeal for the best proof of the
reality of a future life. Other proofs perhaps there are, which it
may be for other men or for other times to work out. But
before this can be done, the entire subject will have to be re-
opened, in order that it may be discussed with boldness and yet
with calmness, which however cannot happen as long as a stigma
rests on those who attack the belief; because its assailants, being
unfairly treated, will for the most part be either timid or passionate. How mischievous as well as how unjust such a stigma is,
has, I trust, been made apparent, and to that part of the question
I need not revert. One thing only I would repeat, because I
honestly believe it to be of the deepest importance. Most
earnestly would I again urge upon those who cherish the doctrine
of immortality, not to defend it, as they too often do, by arguments which have a basis smaller than the doctrine itself. I long
to see this glorious tenet rescued from the jurisdiction of a narrow
and sectarian theology, which, foolishly ascribing to a single religion the possession of all truth, proclaims other religions to be
false, and debases the most magnificent topics by contracting
them within the horizon of its own little vision. Every creed

which has existed long and played a great part, contains a large amount of truth, or else it would not have retained its hold upon the human mind. To suppose, however, that any one of them contains the whole truth, is to suppose that as soon as that creed was enunciated the limits of inspiration were reached, and the power of inspiration exhausted. For such a supposition we have no warrant. On the contrary, the history of mankind, if compared in long periods, shows a very slow, but still a clearly marked, improvement in the character of successive creeds; so that if we reason from the analogy of the past, we have a right to hope that the improvement will continue, and that subsequent creeds will surpass ours. Using the word religion in its ordinary sense, we find that the religious opinions of men depend on an immense variety of circumstances which are constantly shifting. Hence it is, that whatever rests merely upon these opinions has in it something transient and mutable. Well, therefore, may they who take a distant and comprehensive view, be filled with dismay when they see a doctrine like the immortality of the soul defended in this manner. Such advocates incur a heavy responsibility. They imperil their own cause; they make the fundamental depend upon the casual; they support what is permanent by what is ephemeral; and with their books, their dogmas, their traditions, their rituals, their records, and their other perishable contrivances, they seek to prove what was known to the world before these existed, and what, if these were to die away, would still be known, and would remain the common heritage of the human species, and the consolation of myriads yet unborn.

---

Note to p. 38.

"Ὅτι δὲ ἐκ τῶν πρότερον εἰρημένων οἱ λόγοι, καὶ διὰ τούτων, καὶ πρὸς ταῦτα, μία μὲν πίστις ἡ διὰ τῆς ἐπαγωγῆς. Εἰ γάρ τις ἐπισκοποίη ἑκάστην τῶν προτάσεων καὶ τῶν προβλημάτων· φαίνοιτ' ἂν ἢ ἀπὸ τοῦ ὅρου, ἢ ἀπὸ τοῦ ἰδίου, ἢ ἀπὸ τοῦ συμβεβηκότος γεγενημένη.—*Aristotelis Topicorum*, lib. i. cap. vi., Lipsiæ, 1832, p. 104.

Διωρισμένων δὲ τούτων, χρὴ διελέσθαι, πόσα τῶν λόγων εἴδη τῶν διαλεκτικῶν. Ἔστι δὲ τὸ μὲν ἐπαγωγή, τὸ δὲ συλλογισμός. Καὶ συλλογισμὸς μὲν τί ἐστιν, εἴρηται πρότερον. Ἐπαγωγὴ δὲ ἡ ἀπὸ τῶν καθέκαστα ἐπὶ τὰ καθόλου ἔφοδος· οἷον, εἰ ἐστι κυβερνήτης ὁ ἐπιστάμενος κράτιστος, καὶ ἡνίοχος· καὶ ὅλως ἐστὶν ὁ ἐπιστάμενος περὶ ἕκαστον ἄριστος.—*Aristot. Topic.* lib. i. chap. x. p. 108.

Ἐὰν δὲ μὴ τιθῇ, δι' ἐπαγωγῆς ληπτέον, προτείνοντα ἐπὶ τῶν κατὰ μέρος ἐναντίων. Ἡ γὰρ διὰ συλλογισμοῦ, ἢ δι' ἐπαγωγῆς τὰς ἀναγκαίας ληπτέον· ἢ τὰς μὲν ἐπαγωγῇ, τὰς δὲ συλλογισμῷ· ὅσαι δὲ λίαν προφανεῖς εἰσι, καὶ αὐτὰς προτείνοντα. Ἀδηλότερόν τε γὰρ ἀεὶ ἐν τῇ ἀποστάσει καὶ τῇ ἐπαγωγῇ τὸ συμβιβόμενον· καὶ ἅμα τὸ αὐτὰς τὰς χρησίμους προτεῖναι καὶ μὴ δυνάμινον ἐκείνως λαβεῖν, ἕτοιμον. Τὰς δὲ παρὰ ταύτας εἰρημίνας ληπτέον μὲν τούτων χάριν. ἑκάστῳ δὲ ὧδε χρηστέον· Ἐπάγοντα μὲν ἀπὸ τῶν καθέκαστα ἐπὶ τὰ καθόλου, καὶ τῶν γνωρίμων ἐπὶ τὰ ἄγνωστα.—*Aristot. Topic.* lib. viii. cap. i. pp. 253, 254.

Ἐπεὶ δὲ πᾶσα πρότασις συλλογιστικὴ ἢ τούτων τίς ἐστιν, ἐξ ὧν ὁ συλλογισμός, ἢ τινος τούτων ἕνεκα· δῆλον δ', ὅταν ἑτέρου χάριν λαμβάνηται τῷ πλείῳ τὰ ὅμοια ἐρωτᾷν· (ἢ γὰρ δι' ἐπαγωγῆς, ἢ δι' ὁμοιότητος, ὡς ἐπὶ τὸ πολὺ τὸ καθόλου λαμβάνουσι·) τὰ μὲν καθίκοστα πάντα θετέον, ἂν ᾖ ἀληθῆ καὶ ἔνδοξα.—*Aristot. Topic.*, lib. viii. cap. vii. p. 267.

Τῇ μὲν οὖν καθόλου θεωροῦμεν τὰ ἐν μέρει, τῇ δὲ οἰκεία οὐκ ἴσμεν. Ὥστ' ἐνδέχεται καὶ ἀπατᾶσθαι περὶ αὐτά· πλὴν οὐκ ἐναντίως, ἀλλ' ἔχειν μὲν τὴν καθόλου, ἀπατᾶσθαι δὲ τῇ κατὰ μέρος.—*Aristotelis Analytica Priora*, lib. ii. cap. xxiii., Lipsiæ, 1832, p. 134.

Ἅπαντα γὰρ πιστεύομεν ἢ διὰ συλλογισμοῦ, ἢ ἐξ ἐπαγωγῆς. Ἐπαγωγὴ μὲν οὖν ἐστι καὶ ὁ ἐξ ἐπαγωγῆς συλλογισμός τὸ διὰ τοῦ ἑτέρου θάτερον ἄκρον τῷ μέσῳ συλλογίσασθαι.—*Aristot. Analyt. Prior.* lib. ii. cap. xxv. p. 138.

Φανερὸν δὲ καί, ὅτι, εἴ τις αἴσθησις ἐκλέλοιπεν, ἀνάγκη καὶ ἐπιστήμην τινὰ ἐκλελοιπέναι, ἣν ἀδύνατον λαβεῖν· εἴπερ μανθάνομεν ἢ ἐπαγωγῇ, ἢ ἀποδείξει. Ἐστι δ' ἡ μὲν ἀπόδειξις ἐκ τῶν καθόλου· ἡ δ' ἐπαγωγὴ ἐκ τῶν κατὰ μέρος· ἀδύνατον δὲ τὰ καθόλου θεωρῆσαι, εἰ μὴ δι' ἐπαγωγῆς· (ἐπεὶ καὶ τὰ ἐξ ἀφαιρέσεως λεγόμενα ἔσται δι' ἐπαγωγῆς γνώριμα, ἐάν τις βούληται γνώριμα ποιεῖν, ὅτι ὑπάρχει ἑκάστῳ γίνει ἔνια, καὶ εἰ μὴ χωριστά ἐστιν, ᾖ τοῖον δι' ἕκαστον·) ἐπαχθῆναι δὲ μὴ ἔχοντας αἴσθησιν ἀδύνατον. Τῶν γὰρ καθίκαστον ἡ αἴσθησις· οὐ γὰρ ἐνδέχεται λαβεῖν αὐτῶν τὴν ἐπιστήμην· οὔτε γὰρ ἐκ τῶν καθόλου ἄνευ ἐπαγωγῆς, οὔτε διὰ τῆς ἐπαγωγῆς ἄνευ τῆς αἰσθήσεως.—*Aristotelis Analytica Posteriora*, lib. i. cap. xviii., Lipsiæ, 1832, p. 177.

Καὶ ἡ μὲν καθόλου νοητή· ἡ δὲ κατὰ μέρος εἰς αἴσθησιν τελευτᾷ.—*Analyt. Post.* lib. i. cap. xxiv. p. 101.

All that Aristotle knew of induction is contained in these passages. What he says in his Metaphysics is more vaguely expressed, or perhaps the text is more corrupt. The early part of the first book may, however, be looked at.

# LETTER TO A GENTLEMAN

## RESPECTING POOLEY'S CASE.[1]

London : June, 1859.

Sir,—You are quite right in supposing that I have read a letter which is signed " John Duke Coleridge," and published in " Fraser's Magazine " for the present month. But you are wrong in thinking that the tone of the letter surprises me. When I held up to public opprobrium that, for our time, almost incredible transaction in which the name of Coleridge was painfully conspicuous, the indignation which I felt prevented me from measuring my language, and I did not care to search for soft and dainty words in relating how, under shelter of the law, an outrage had been perpetrated upon a poor, an honest, a defenceless, and a half-witted man. I wrote as I thought it behoved me to write, and I rejoice that I did so. Since, however, I did not spare the principal actors of that deed, I could not expect that Mr. Coleridge should wish to spare me. And I must, in common justice, acquit him of any such intent. He has done his utmost. He is so anxious to be severe that he has not only expressed anger, he has even tried to express contempt. He has imputed to me nearly every kind of baseness and of folly. He has ascribed to me sentiments which I never entertained, and language which I never used. He has charged me with ignorance, cowardice, malignity, and slander. He has attempted to ruin my reputation as an author, and to blast my character as a man, by representing me as a perverter of facts, a fabricator of falsehoods, a propagator of libels, and a calumniator of innocence. To all this I shall make no reply. Whatever I have done in the matter of Sir John Coleridge, or in other matters, is open and before the world. I live merely for literature ; my works are my only actions ; they are not wholly unknown, and I leave it to them to protect my name. If they cannot do that, they are little worth. I have never written an essay, or even a single line anonymously, and nothing would induce me to do so, because I deem anonymous writing of every kind to be an evasion of responsibility, and

[1] London: J. W. Parker and Son, 1859.

consequently unsuited to the citizen of a free country. Therefore it is that I can easily be judged. I have myself supplied the materials, and to them I appeal. So far from despising public opinion, I regard it with great, though not with excessive respect; and I acknowledge in it the principal source of such influence as I have been able to wield. But this respect which I feel for public opinion is only when I consider it as a whole. For the opinion of individuals I care nothing, because, now at least, there is no one whose censure I fear, or whose praise I covet. Once, indeed, it was otherwise, but that is past and gone for ever. Desiring rather to move masses than to influence persons, I am nowise troubled by accusations before which many would shrink. They who dislike my principles, and who dread that boldness of inquiry, and that freedom of expression which this age desires, and which I seek to uphold, have already taken their course, and done what they could to bring me into discredit, and prevent my writings from being read. If I say that they have failed, I am not speaking arrogantly, but am simply stating a notorious fact. Yet they employed the resources with which Mr. John Duke Coleridge is familiar. They, too, impugned my veracity, aspersed my motives, and denied my honesty. You know, sir, that I have never in the slightest degree noticed these charges, though some of them were prepared with considerable skill. You will hardly suppose that having refused to defend myself against men of ability, I should now, at the eleventh hour, put myself on my trial at the bidding of this new assailant. Mr. John Duke Coleridge is quite welcome to publish his sentiments respecting me, and I do not wish to disturb them. But, though I shall not answer his accusations, I shall examine his defence.

An act of cruelty has been committed by an English judge, and I have arraigned the perpetrator before the bar of public opinion, because that is the only tribunal to which he is amenable. His son, by pleading on his behalf, has recognised the jurisdiction. It remains for me to consider his reply; it will finally remain for the public to decide on its validity. If it is valid, the charge falls to the ground; the accused is absolved; and I, as the accuser, am covered with confusion. If it is not valid, the failure of the defence will strengthen the force of the accusation, and even they who wished to favour the judge will be compelled to allow, that what they would fain have palliated, as the momentary ebullition of an arbitrary temper, swells into far graver matter, when, instead of being regretted, it is vindicated with stubborn pertinacity, and in an obstinate and angry spirit.

The first thing which strikes me in Mr. Coleridge's apology for
his father is, that some of the most serious charges which I have
brought are passed over in complete silence.  They are not only
unanswered, they are not even noticed.  On the other hand,
several charges which I did not bring are satisfactorily refuted.
Indeed the greater part of Mr. Coleridge's letter is occupied with
repelling imaginary accusations.  He ascribes to me assertions
which I neither made nor intended to make ; and then he decisively proves that those assertions are false.  His victory is
complete, but it is gained over himself, and not over me.  He
takes infinite pains to show that I am altogether wrong in supposing that Sir John Coleridge, an English judge, could refuse to
try a prisoner who was brought before him.  I am equally wrong
in supposing that he could try one who was not brought before
him.  I am either ignorant or malicious, when I affirm that he
could have determined what laws should be enforced, and what
laws should not be enforced.  I ought to have been aware that
judicial power is different from legislative power ; that the judge,
instead of making laws, merely administers them ; and that he
is, in fact, unable to fix on the county in which the trial shall be
held.  It is no part of his duty to collect evidence for the prosecution ; nor is he expected to concert measures with the counsel
in order to convict the prisoner.  These things are not done in
England, and it is scandalous for me to assume that they are
done.  It is still more scandalous that upon such assumptions
I should have presumed to impeach the conduct of Sir John
Coleridge.  The audacity is monstrous.  How dare I thus assail
a blameless and immaculate man whose fame has hitherto been
unsullied?  Before I could bring these charges I must have
been lost to all shame.  What I have alleged respecting the existence of a conspiracy between the clergy, the judge, and the
government, is equally preposterous, and is of itself enough to
ruin the reputation of a writer who pretends to be an historian.
The clergy were in Cornwall ; the Home-Office is in London ; and
the judge is a traveller, who, going from place to place, has no
means of ascertaining beforehand what causes he will have to
try.  How wicked, and yet how foolish I am, to say that these
distant and discordant parties conspired together against a poor
well-sinker!  Moreover, if I had enquired into the facts, I
should have learnt that these proceedings were in the latter
half of 1857, and that from July to December in that year,
the Home Minister was Sir George Grey, and the Under Secretaries at the Home-Office were Mr. Massey and Mr. Waddington,
most worthy, and indeed distinguished men, utterly incapable

of entering into that nefarious compact with which I have taunted them.[1]

It is after this fashion that Mr. Coleridge defends his father. All these charges, he rebuts with a closeness and minuteness of argument deserving the highest praise, but where he found the charges I cannot tell. Certainly they are not in my Essay, and they never were in my mind. Meanwhile, the real accusation remains. To that he makes no reply. Perhaps he was right. Perhaps he found it easier to answer what I had not said than what I had said. A compact between a Cornish clergyman and a Cabinet Minister. A private understanding between an English barrister and an English judge![2] A judge trying a case in which he had got up evidence for the prosecution! A judge having guilty foreknowledge of the depositions of witnesses! A dark and wicked conspiracy between Sir George Grey, Sir John Coleridge, Mr. Massey, and Mr. Waddington, the sole object of which was to punish a poor labourer! Truly Mr. Coleridge must be very confident of the goodness of his cause, if he thinks that it will bear handling in this way. I appeal to you, sir, and to every one who has read my Essay, whether or not these things are in it. If they are in it let the passages be produced. If they are not in it, I submit that the zeal of Mr. Coleridge has carried him a little too far, and that he has been rather indiscreet in laying himself open to so obvious a challenge.

The first charge against Sir John Coleridge is that he committed an act of cruelty. In determining whether or not his sentence upon Pooley was cruel, it is necessary to consider what the sentence was. But this, Mr. Coleridge, in the whole of his long letter, carefully abstains from mentioning. He does not tell his readers that poor Pooley, a man exemplary in all the relations of life, and of unstained character, was ordered to be imprisoned for a year and nine months simply because he wrote and uttered words which neither hurt nor traduced any living being. In those words there was neither calumny against in-

---

[1] See at the end of this letter, extracts from Mr. Coleridge's apology for his father.

[2] The following is the only passage in which I even allude to Mr. Coleridge: "He (Pooley) had no counsel to defend him, but the son of the judge acted as counsel to prosecute him. The father and the son performed their parts with zeal, and were perfectly successful. Under their auspices Pooley was found guilty." Every word of this is literally and strictly true. Mr. Coleridge did prosecute Pooley; he did perform his part with zeal, as also did his father; he succeeded; and Pooley was found guilty in consequence of his address, and of the summing-up of the judge. Yet out of these simple and irrefutable statements Mr. Coleridge has constructed a charge of "private understanding" between himself and the judge. See extracts at the end of this letter.

dividuals, nor disaffection towards government. There was nothing
to set man against man, or to set men against their rulers. All
this, Mr. Coleridge knows, and does not attempt to deny. He
also knows that on this ground, and on no other, Pooley was
condemned to an imprisonment of twenty-one months. Why does
he keep this fact back? How is it that he never chances to mention
what the punishment was? How is it that, though he frequently
quotes passages from my Essay, he by no accident ever quotes
one in which the act is clearly set forth? Why does he, when
professing to defend his father against a particular charge,
conceal the charge, and then labour hard to defend him against
other charges which no one brought? If Pooley had not been
punished, Sir John Coleridge would not have been accused.
Surely, then, the amount of the punishment is an essential part
of the accusation, and is more pertinent to the issue than those
speculative enquiries in which Mr. Coleridge, with great ingenuity, has proved how unlikely it is that there should have
been a conspiracy between Sir George Grey, Sir John Coleridge,
Mr. Massey, and Mr. Waddington.

But this is of a piece with the rest of Mr. Coleridge's letter.
For with other and most important items in my accusation he
deals in the same manner; that is to say, he does not deal with
them at all. I charged Sir John Coleridge with passing a sentence
which, independently of the other objections against it, was alien
to the spirit of the age. To this I find no reply. I charged
him with bringing the administration of justice into disrepute,
by encouraging the prevailing and most dangerous notion that
the poor are more harshly treated than the rich. Again, I find
no reply. I charged him with doing this on the person of an
unhappy, but most industrious man, whose family were, consequently, left either to starve or to beg. Still, no reply. I
charged him, and the result has proved that I charged him
truly, with exasperating the friends of liberty, and rekindling
old animosities. No reply. I charged him with taking as his
victim an undefended prisoner, whom our law humanely supposes
to have the judge for his counsel, but who on this occasion had
the judge for his oppressor. No reply. I charged him with
inflicting a punishment which, severe at any period, is particularly
so in our time, when all humane and thinking men aim at
lessening penalties, rather than the increasing them. This, too,
Mr. Coleridge being unable to deny, passes over in silence.

Such is his plan. It is a cunning artifice with which the
rhetoricians of old were long since familiar. With them, as with
him, taciturnity was a favourite stratagem, but taciturnity in

order to be effective, should be invariable. Otherwise there is danger that when a man does speak, he will speak at the wrong time, and say the wrong things; and certainly one of the pleas which Mr. Coleridge has set up is so eccentric, that it will expose him to this imputation. He does not question my assertion that penalties are becoming milder, but he meets the consequences of that assertion in a way peculiar to himself. He says that Sir John Coleridge being employed to administer the law, and not to make it, was obliged to administer it as he found it. The judge, says Mr. Coleridge, could not choose "what laws he would or would not put in force."[1] Unhappy judge! he had no choice. His hands were tied. His leaning was on the side of humanity; he longed to be merciful; but he was in the melancholy position of being obliged to enforce an odious law. He was so straitened and circumscribed that he was, in fact, a victim rather than an oppressor. Really, sir, it is humiliating to read such arguments; it is still more humiliating to have to answer them. What! no choice! Has an English judge no option? Has he no latitude? Is no discretion vested in him? Must he always exact the letter of the bond, and take the last ounce of flesh? Mr. Coleridge is indeed in difficulties if this is his best defence. The fact is that an assize is rarely held without an instance of the judge imposing a light, and often a mere nominal, punishment, when the law allows him to impose a severe one. That part of our common law which coerces the expression of opinion, was established in a barbarous and ignorant age, when the very amusements of men were brutal, and when they delighted in inflicting pain and in seeing it inflicted. It was an age in which human life was disregarded, and human suffering made a jest. To suppose that an English judge is bound to follow with servile acquiescence all the decisions of such a period, is to suppose what is not only absurd in itself, but is contradicted by the judicial history of this country. In England the abrogation of a law is gradual, and usually passes through three stages. First, it is reasoned against or ridiculed; then it falls into discredit; and finally, it is either repealed, or else by common consent it is disused. This is the history of those cruel laws which our ancestors cherished; such, for example, as the laws relating to heresy, witchcraft, and slavery, which, before they were done away with, were opposed by public opinion and discountenanced by our judges. All these things are part of the same scheme;

---

[1] I quote Mr. Coleridge's own words; but the entire passage will be found in the extracts at the end of this letter. Mr. Coleridge had probably forgotten his previous admission, "that the sentence is a perfectly fair ground for observation."

they belong to the same turn of mind, and must stand or fall together. It is natural that when slavery was legal, heresy should have been illegal. It is also natural that, in such a state of society, heretical or blasphemous expressions should be punished. We have, however, long been outgrowing those views, not because we love blasphemy, but because we love liberty. We look upon impious language as proof of a vulgar mind; but we are not to cast into prison an honest man and beggar his family, on account of his mind being vulgar. Even if the blasphemy is of such a kind as to indicate depravity on the part of the utterer, no one is concerned with it unless it tends to produce a breach of the peace. If the public peace is in danger, he who endangers it should be restrained. But to punish blasphemy irrespectively of these wider considerations is a thing which this age will not tolerate, and which is contrary to the whole tone and scope both of modern literature and of modern legislation. The charge against Thomas Pooley was that he uttered blasphemy. On this charge he was committed; on this he was indicted; and on this he was sentenced. The crime alleged was not that he injured men's property, nor that he insulted them, nor that he provoked them to violence. He wrote upon a private gate, which he had no right to do, and for which, therefore, redress might have been reasonably exacted. That was an offence; and if his conduct was likely to disturb the public peace, that was another offence. But instead of receiving such slight punishment as these offences would justify, he was punished as a blasphemer; and a judge was found capable of sentencing this poor, helpless, and ignorant man to twenty-one months' imprisonment. Shame! shame on it! In compliance with the humane and enlightened spirit of this age, the practice of punishing men for words which calumniate no individual and imperil no government, was fast falling into disuse when it was revived by Sir John Coleridge. This is his offence, and a most serious and, so far as he is concerned, irreparable offence it is. It is a revival of cruelty; it is a revival of bigotry; it is a revival of the tastes, the habits, and the feelings of those days of darkness which we might have hoped had gone for ever.

I have only one more point to notice in Mr. Coleridge's apology for his father. Mr. Coleridge assures us that, when Pooley was sentenced, the judge was not aware of the state of his mind. I rejoice to hear it; I am most willing to accept any explanation which can soften so terrible a transaction and deprive it of some of its horrors. Consider the sentence as we may, it is enormous, and posterity will hardly believe that, in the existing state of public opinion, it could have been passed. For the honour of the judicial character and for the honour of human nature, let us make what abatement we can, and be glad to think that this heavy article in the impeachment may be withdrawn. That Pooley was deranged is certain. We have the concurrent testimony of his neighbours; we have eminent medical opinion; we have the observations of reporters who were present at his trial; we have the fact of his having been sent to a lunatic asylum; and we have the additional fact of his being pardoned on the ground of insanity. Against such evidence, the unsupported assertions of the attorney for the prosecution are not worth a straw. I had supposed that what was so clearly marked as to excite the attention of the reporters for the press, could hardly have escaped the notice of the presiding judge.

But Mr. Coleridge declares that it did escape him. Be it so. It says little for his perspicacity that he should have overlooked what was obvious to less practised eyes. This, however, I pass over; and I leave the other facts, respecting which there is neither doubt nor cavil, to speak for themselves. Upon those facts I have elsewhere delivered my mind, and delivered it freely. The circumstances to which I have directed public attention were not sought for by me. I did not go out of my road to find them. I had never heard of the case of Pooley until I came across it in the book which I was reviewing. As it had fallen in my way, I thought it my duty first to investigate it, and then to expose it. In exposing it, I denounced the principal actors, especially him who gave the finishing touch to the whole.

By doing so I have incurred the hostility of his friends, and I have, moreover, displeased a large class of persons who consider that an English judge occupies so elevated a position that he ought not to be made the object of personal attack. To me, however, it appears that his elevation, and his name, and the pomp and the dignity and the mighty weight of that office which he held, are among the circumstances which justify the course I have taken. If he had been a man of no account, it would hardly have been worth while for me to pause, in the midst of my solitary labours, that I might turn aside and smite him. For, what is he to me? Our ways of life and our career are so completely different, that between us there can be no rivalry; and the motives which commonly induce one man to attack another can have no place. I cannot envy him, for I see nothing to envy. Neither can I fear him; nor can I expect to derive any benefit from hurting him. Unless, therefore, it is supposed that I am actuated by a spirit of pure, naked, and motiveless malignity, I have a right to be believed when I say that in this matter my sole object has been to promote the great and, to me, the sacred cause of liberty of speech and of publication. This, indeed, lies near to my heart. And it is this alone which gives to the present case its real importance, and will prevent it from sinking into oblivion. Yet a few years, and Sir John Coleridge and Thomas Pooley will be numbered with the dead. But though the men will die, the principles which they represent are immortal. The powerful and intolerant judge seeking to stop the mouth of the poor and friendless well-sinker is but the type of a far older and wider struggle. In every part of the civilized world the same contest is raging, and the question is still undecided, whether or not men shall say what they like ; in other words, whether language is to be refuted by language, or whether it is to be refuted by force. Disguise it as you will, this is the real issue. In this great warfare between liberty and repression, Sir John Coleridge has chosen his side and I have chosen mine. But he, being armed with the power of the executive government, has been able to carry matters with a high hand, and to strengthen his party, not indeed by arguments, but by violence. Instead of refuting, he imprisons. My weapons are of another kind, and shall I not use them ? Am I for ever to sit by in silence ? Are all the blows to be dealt from one side, and none from the other ? I think not. I think it is but right and fitting that Sir John Coleridge, and those who agree with him, should be taught that literature is able to punish as well as to persuade, and that she never exercises her high vocation with greater dignity than when, upholding the weak against the strong, she lets the world see that she is no respecter of persons, but will, if need be, strike at the highest place, and humble the proudest name.

I have now finished the task which I set to myself, and which I undertook simply because I thought it ought to be done, and I could not learn that any one more competent was likely to do it. The accusation and the defence being both before the world, we may fairly suppose that the matter is thoroughly sifted, and the circumstances which are essential separated from those which are casual. It remains for the public to form their opinion ; and I trust that in doing so they will not hear one side only, but will carefully read Mr. Coleridge's apology for his father. In asking this, I am by no means disinterested ; since his letter, by leaving the principal charges untouched, is a tacit assumption that they cannot be rebutted. His defence fully justifies my attack ; and, if he is willing to agree to the proposal, I wish for nothing better than that both attack and defence should be reprinted side by side, and circulated together as widely as possible, so that they ·

may be read wherever the English people are to be found, or wherever the English tongue is known.

I am, Sir,

Yours faithfully,

HENRY THOMAS BUCKLE.

Although I have expressed a hope that every one who reads this pamphlet will also read Mr. Coleridge's letter, I think it advisable, as a further precaution, to reprint the following passages. They are all to be found in "Fraser's Magazine" for June, and are copied word for word from the letter which Mr. Coleridge addressed to the editor:—

"Mr. Buckle's libel. . . . I need not tell you that it is a libel, nor need I offer you any opinion as to the effect on the character of your Magazine of publishing a tissue of what I must call coarse personal malevolence. . . . Intolerable licentiousness of speech. . . . Licence of slander. . . . His many columns of slander. . . . The base charges which he has insinuated, but has not had the courage to set down in plain and simple words. . . . It is certainly hard that a person like Mr. Buckle should be able to put a blameless man on his defence by reckless accusation. . . . Dirt thrown by the meanest hand. . . . Imputations of the basest kind. . . . Dirty stuff. . . . Mr. Buckle does not comprehend the common feelings of a gentleman. . . . Of me he says he knows nothing; yet he insinuates of a man whom he does not know, that he, a barrister, was party to a private understanding with the judge (that judge his own father) in a criminal case, to oppress a poor undefended criminal, and pervert the course of justice. . . .

"That Mr. Buckle should have thought such conduct possible in an English advocate of any standing, that he should have made such a charge without evidence and without inquiry, is a proof that his learning (if he be a learned man) is not education, and has not raised him above the feelings and prejudices of a thoroughly vulgar mind. . . . . The man (Pooley) was there to be tried on a charge which neither Sir John Coleridge nor I had any more to do with, nor knew any more about before the assizes took place at Bodmin, than Mr. Buckle himself. That a judge selects whom he will try, and where he will try them; that he can try or not try at his pleasure persons who are arraigned before him; that he can refuse, if he pleases, to put in force the law he is sent to administer, and choose which laws he will enforce and which he will not; that he or the counsel for the prosecution, or both of them, have anything whatever to do with getting up cases against prisoners, are matters which Mr. Buckle really seems as if he believed, but as to which he displays ignorance to a degree hardly credible. . . . . It is familiar to all persons of ordinary education that a judge in the position of Sir John Coleridge had and could have no choice whether he would try a particular prisoner or not, in what county he would try him, and what laws he would or would not put in force. . . . . From July to December 1857, the Home Secretary was Sir George Grey, and the Under Secretaries at the Home Office were Mr. Massey and Mr. Waddington. The notion that these distinguished men, or any of them, would join in a conspiracy in order to please Sir John Coleridge and two Cornish clergymen, to suppress freedom of speech, crush liberty, and do injustice to a poor man till they were terrified by the petitioners mentioned by Mr. Buckle, is a notion so excessively ridiculous, that, except for the total absence of humour from Mr. Buckle's composition, one might suspect him of attempting a gloomy joke."

# POSTHUMOUS WORKS.

## REIGN OF ELIZABETH.

### I.

#### POLITICAL.

AT the accession of Elizabeth the position of England was more pregnant with danger than it had been at any period since the Danish invasion. Indeed, the hordes of ferocious savages who in the eighth and ninth centuries ravaged the kingdom, were not more formidable than those enemies who now threatened it from every quarter. It would not be consistent with the object of this work to enter at length into the mere political events of civil history, but it will be impossible fully to understand the real magnitude of this crisis without giving some account, not only of the internal state of the country, but also of those peculiar foreign hazards which, during many years, were so imminent. And to the adoption of this course I am decided, not so much by the obvious interest of the struggle as by the consideration that during the reign of this great queen not only was every obstacle surmounted and every danger repulsed, but that, by the application of principles hitherto unknown or neglected, England was raised to a position which made her the envy and wonder of Europe ; that the way was paved for the establishment of a prosperity which not even the wretched misgovernment of her immediate successor could seriously disturb; that a prodigious impulse was given to all the great branches of manufacture and commerce; that all the arts which minister to the comfort of man, and lend a charm to civilized life, were cultivated and encouraged ; and, what is more important than all these, that there was laid the foundation of a literature which is by far the proudest boast of this mighty people, which will long survive the country that has given it birth, and which will be read with astonishment by nations yet unborn, even when the very name of England has almost faded from the memory of man.

The chief danger to the new Queen arose from the agitation of those religious disputes by which, for nearly forty years, Europe had been convulsed. In all the other great countries there was a decided majority on the side either of the Protestants or of the Catholics. But in England the nation, in point of numbers, was about equally divided between the two great religions; and though, under ordinary circumstances, the Government could, perhaps, easily have turned the scale, yet the Catholics were at this time even more formidable than might have been supposed from their mere numerical force, for they counted among their adherents an immense majority of the aristocracy, who exercised over their dependents an almost unlimited authority. England was thus split into two hostile sects, each of which had its martyrs and its miracles: each of which was equally confident of the truth of its own tenets, and of the damnable errors of its adversary: and each of which thirsted for the other's blood. Of these great parties, one occupied the north and the other the south. The Catholics of the north were headed by the great families of [the Percies and Nevilles] and had on their side all those advantages which the prescription of ages alone can give. To the south were the Protestants, who, though they could boast of none of those great historical names which reflected a lustre on their opponents, were supported by the authority of Government, and felt that enthusiastic confidence which only belongs to a young religion.

While the nation was thus severed in twain by the accursed spirit of religious faction, the aspect of Europe was so threatening that it might well have appalled the stoutest heart. For half a century the Spanish power had been supreme. Francis I., defeated in the field and baffled in the closet, was at length taken prisoner by his great rival, and could only purchase his liberty by the most degrading concessions. After his ignominious reign was brought to a close, the languishing fortunes of the French monarchy were, with the greatest difficulty, sustained by his son and successor; (?) but on his death the last symptoms of vigour disappeared from the national councils, and everything fell into disorder. In the meantime the power of Spain was rapidly progressing. The reign of Philip II. was ushered in by the battle of St. Quentin, at which Philibert of Savoy cut in pieces the chivalry of France, and shook the throne of Henry.[1] Then followed the battle of Gravelines, at which the star of Philip was again in the

---

[1] At the very same moment the Spanish troops pushed forward to the gates of Rome, and compelled the Pope to sign a peace under the walls of his own capital.

ascendant; and at the accession of Elizabeth the Spanish empire, which had been built up by three generations of statesmen and of warriors, had reached a height of alarming grandeur. Even at the present day such a power would be formidable : in the middle of the sixteenth century it seemed irresistible. The population and the revenues of the European dominions of Philip were more than double those of France and England put together. The only power that could in the least pretend to balance so prodigious a preponderance was France : but France, during thirty years of the reign of Elizabeth, was governed by three ignorant and pro- fligate boys, was torn by the agitations of civil war, and was hemmed in by Philip at every quarter, with the single exception of the side of Germany, and even there the throne was occupied by the uncle, and afterwards by the cousin, of the Spanish monarch.

If anything is wanting to complete this picture, we have only to consider the neglected and, indeed, the almost defenceless condition of the nation which had to contend against such immi- nent perils.

During the whole of the fourteenth and fifteenth centuries, the power and reputation of England had been steadily advancing, and the national resources, though not developed with any extra- ordinary skill, were found more than equal to meet those emer- gencies which occasionally arose. But during the latter years of Henry, and under the extremely feeble government of Edward, everything went to ruin. The throne of the sickly and bigoted boy was surrounded by advisers who were too much occupied with caring for the souls of men to trouble themselves much about their bodies. It could hardly be expected that statesmen who were busied in the exalted functions of drawing up canons for a church and forms for a sacrament should stoop so low as to pro- vide for the national prosperity : still less was it likely that they should be anxious for the national honour. Indeed, whatever may have been the other merits of the English Reformation, it is re- markable that during the early period of its progress it did not produce a single man of genius. There were some expert rea- soners, there were many able scholars, but there was not one original thinker ; there was not even one competent statesman. Even when Mary came to the throne, and called to her councils two advisers of unquestionable ability, Gardner and Pole, still the frenzy of religion had so occupied the minds of men, that there was no room left for the realities of government. All the energies of the executive were directed to burning heretics and refuting schismatics. The foolish and bigoted queen thought that she had fulfilled one of the first of her royal duties so soon as she had converted an apostate, or even comforted a repentant sinner. It may be easily imagined that during the heat of this religious fervour the real interests of the nation were entirely forgotten. Indeed, it would be difficult to find in modern Europe an instance of a country worse governed than England was during the generation that elapsed between the fall of Wolsey and the death of Mary. The men who ruled the State were profoundly ignorant of the affairs of Europe, of which, indeed, they took no trouble to instruct themselves. At many courts there was no English representative, and even when there did happen to be one, his information was as bad as it could possibly be. The consequence was that their foreign policy was a continued succession of perpetual blunders. During the eleven years which were occupied by the contemptible reigns of Edward and Mary, we endured a series of disgraceful disasters such as even now it is painful to remember. Whenever we made a claim it was sure to be rejected; whenever we put forward a pretension it was sure to be spurned. If we attacked a city, it was always too strong to be taken; if we defended one, it was always too weak to be held.

.         .         .         .         .

But this was only a precursor of what was to follow, and just before Mary died we sustained a loss more serious than any of the others. For more than two hundred years Calais had been an English possession, and was considered as part of the national domain. And yet this most important city, which was so strong by nature and by art as to be considered almost impregnable, was wrested from us in the middle of winter in three weeks, and almost without resistance.[1]

.         .         .         .         .

Scarcely was Elizabeth seated on the throne when she began to feel the alarming embarrassment of her position. The bishops unanimously refused to crown her. The Pope denied her legitimacy, and would not recognise her as queen. The two universities of Oxford and Cambridge, which at that time had immense influence, united with Convocation in presenting to the House of Lords a solemn declaration in favour of the Papal supremacy. This was almost tantamount to a declaration in favour of the pretensions of Mary, and those pretensions were openly supported by her father-in-law, Henry II. of France, who caused her not only to assume the arms and title of Queen of England and

---

[1] No standing army; no navy. Gunpowder had been in general use for two centuries, but the English were entirely ignorant of the art of making it. The Crown was overwhelmed with debt.

Ireland, but to execute a solemn instrument transferring to him the right of succession in case she should die without issue.

With the risk of a rebellion hanging over head, and exposed at any moment to the presence on her shores of a foreign army, it seemed that Elizabeth had only one escape that was yet left to her. Philip had already saved her life; he now offered her his hand. With him for her husband, there would be no fear of foreign aggression; and his power, combined with that of the English Catholics, would afford ample protection against any insurrection which the Protestants might be willing to excite. The offer was indeed tempting, and the ministers of Elizabeth advised her to accept it; but the queen herself, with a magnanimity of which history furnishes few examples, rejected his proposal, and determined to trust entirely to the resources of her own enfeebled and divided kingdom. Philip, deeply mortified by an answer which he had little expected, determined to ruin the presumptuous heretic who had ventured to repulse his addresses. He proceeded with singular and characteristic cunning. Fearing that by a declaration of war against England he would compel Elizabeth to throw herself into the arms of Henry, he endeavoured to cut away that resource by inducing her to continue [?] the hostilities with France into which Mary had so imprudently embarked. He knew that in England men of all parties eagerly desired the restitution of Calais, the loss of which they considered as a national disgrace, and he now proposed that Spain and England should jointly carry on the war until that city was restored. But Elizabeth suspected the snare. Doubtful of the sincerity of Philip, and certain that the kingdom, such as Mary had bequeathed it, could hardly support the efforts of a single campaign, she determined to give it rest, even though Calais should be the price of the peace. She had already sent ministers to the different foreign courts, and to them she now issued the necessary instructions. The result was the treaty of Château Cambresis, which was signed only [five] months after her accession to the throne, and which, for a time at least, secured to the nation the tranquillity that was necessary to recruit its wasted energies. Relieved for a moment from the open hostility of France, Elizabeth now concentrated her attention upon domestic affairs. Her first care was to put the country into a state of proper defence.

.          .          .          .          .

[Here Mr. Buckle has marked in pencil in his MS. the word "Military," and at a short distance "Toleration," as though it had been his intention to insert at this stage of the history, a

chapter on each of these subjects.  For the first of these, how-
ever, there remain no materials, the notes in his Common Place
Books upon it having too little reference to the reign of Queen
Elizabeth to be in place here.  His materials for the chapter on
Toleration are as follows.—EDITOR.]

————— —— —— ——

## II.

### TOLERATION.

WHILE she was thus actively employed in developing the neglected resources of the country, her conduct in matters of religion
was still more admirable.  It is the peculiar trait of this great
queen that she was the first sovereign in Europe who publicly
tolerated the exercise of a religion contrary to that of the State.
Indeed for many years she showed a disposition not only to tolerate, but even to conciliate.  Her first act of authority was to
form a council for the management of public affairs.  Of the
members of this council thirteen were Catholics, and eight only
were Protestants.

Even the administration of foreign diplomacy was entrusted by
her to the professors of an adverse religion.  In 1564, she sent a
commission to Bruges to treat with Philip respecting some affairs
of great importance.  One of the members of this commission
was the celebrated Dr. Wotton : but at the head of it we find the
name of Lord Montague, a zealous and well-known Catholic.
Several years later (in 1572) she sent the earl of Worcester as
her proxy to Paris, to stand in her room as godmother to the
daughter of the French king.  The earl who was selected for this
honourable office was brother-in-law to that foolish rebel, the earl
of Northumberland, and was himself a prominent and notorious
Catholic.[1]

But without accumulating similar instances, I need only mention that several years, and indeed shortly before the arrival of
the armada, Sir Philip Stanley, a Catholic, received charge during
the time of war of the important town of Deventer.

Indeed, so anxious was Elizabeth to avoid even the semblance
of religious bigotry, that on the death of Cardinal Pole she not
only adopted the unusual course of issuing an order in council
that all debts due to him should be at once paid to his executors,
but she actually caused letters to be written to the same effect to

[1] In 1586, when Leicester was in Holland, the queen wrote to rebuke him for
having, by his intolerance, discouraged the Catholics.

all the bishops, and, where there were no bishops, to the deans and chapters of all the cathedral churches throughout England. In another instance she acted in a similar way, though in a manner entirely opposed to the genius of that bigoted age. Sir Francis Englefield had been a privy councillor to Mary, and had taken an active part in her proceedings against the heretics. (?) He, apprehensive of the consequences, and conceiving that his fortunes were irretrievably ruined, abjured the realm. He not only corresponded with the enemies of Elizabeth, but wrote to Leicester an insolent letter respecting her. But, notwithstanding this, the queen allowed him to receive abroad all the revenues of his English estate, only reserving a small portion for the support of his wife, who still remained in her own country, and who had brought him a large fortune.

In all her public acts she displayed the same spirit. The oath of supremacy was that which most offended the conscience of the Catholics. Of this the queen was well aware, and she in 1562, ordered that if it was once refused no bishop should presume to tender it a second time to the same person, but should wait for express instructions for each particular case. The ministers of Edward, with that tendency to excess so characteristic of apostates, had inserted a clause in the Litany, " From the tyranny of the bishop of Rome and all his detestable enormities, good Lord deliver us." This blasphemous language, in which the Reformers invoked the name of the great God of love and peace as a pander to their own malignant passions was, by the order of Elizabeth, immediately expunged from the services of the church.

In the same way, and in a spirit which might teach a salutary lesson to the contemptible polemics of our own time, she issued a proclamation forbidding " the use of opprobrious words, as papist, papistical, heretic, schismatic, or sacramentary."

Even towards the Irish, who, ever since they have been connected with England, have suffered so bitterly from Protestant intolerance, she displayed a similar spirit. In a remarkable letter written in 1573, which is yet extant, the earl of Essex gives an account of an interview which he had with the queen just before going to Ireland, in which she particularly charged him " not to seeke too hastely to bring people that hath bene trayned in another religion, from that which they have bene brought up in."

In the meantime the Catholics, presuming upon her forbearance, or perhaps merely instigated by a spirit of mischievous activity, were so far from aiding the government that they did everything to throw it into confusion. White, bishop of Winchester, publicly delivered in London a most inflammatory sermon, in which, with an obvious allusion to Elizabeth, he reminded his hearers of the address which Trajan had made to one of his officers when he delivered to him the sword—" If my commands are just, use this sword for me; if unjust, against me." During the reign of Henry such language would have cost the bishop his head. Elizabeth merely ordered him to keep his house, and at the end of a month dismissed him without further punishment. In the same year the well-known Dr. Story, in his place in the House of Commons, publicly boasted of the number of Protestants he had caused to be burnt: and he not only expressed his regret that he had left so many alive, but pointedly added that " it grieved him that they laboured only about the young and little twigs, whereas they should have struck at the root."

The bishops, all of whom were Catholics, had, as I have already mentioned, unanimously refused to crown her; and it was with the greatest difficulty that one of the meanest of them was at length induced to perform the necessary ceremony. It is, however, remarkable that this open hostility from the heads of the Catholic Church did not cause the least change in her conduct towards them. Dr. Kitchin, who alone of all the bishops would take the oath of allegiance (?), was allowed to retain his see; the others, who openly avowed the supremacy of the papal power, were of course deprived, but only one of them was punished; and Heath, who was one of the most prominent, and who during the last reign had been Lord Chancellor, was allowed to retire to his estate, where at a later period he was often visited by Elizabeth.

We have the statement of the Catholics themselves that no less than one thousand priests were allowed to remain with their patrons in different parts of England, and perform for them the ordinary functions of their religion. Indeed, a Protestant author who wrote eight years after the accession of Elizabeth, states that at that time the number of Catholic priests in England exceeded the entire number of the Protestant clergy, a statement which, however incredible it may appear, is confirmed by other independent and contemporary evidence.

In 1569, the year of the great northern rebellion, an inquiry was instituted at the Temple with the view of testing the loyalty of the lawyers. The question put to them was, not whether mass was celebrated nor whether they attended it, but merely " whether at mass they prayed for the queen." [1]

It may, perhaps, appear to some that such instances as these

<hr />

[1] Soames (*Elizabethan Religious History*, p. 251) quotes Stubbes' *Gaping Gulf* to show that mass was commonly performed in London.

are by no means remarkable, and that a sovereign who merely obeys the dictates of an ordinary charity is scarcely deserving of an extraordinary praise. But those who by such an objection think to lessen the merits of Elizabeth, must have a very scanty knowledge of the real history of the sixteenth century. The broad and general features of intolerance which distinguished the governments of that age are no doubt familiar to every reader: but only those who are acquainted with the lighter literature of the time, its biographies, its correspondence, even its very poetry and its tales, can form an adequate notion of the fearful extent to which the spirit of bigotry had possessed the minds of men. The Reformation, so far from assuaging the passions, had roused them to a fury which is hardly to be conceived. Men exemplary in every relation of domestic life, and of the most unblemished purity of morals, not only habitually inculcated the necessity of extirpating heresy by the sword, but, the moment they had the power, showed themselves prompt to put their own principles into execution. Even the few who at an earlier period had dared while in their closets to speculate on the propriety of toleration, soon changed their ideas when they emerged into the world. Sir Thomas More, in a philosophical romance, laid down the noblest sentiments in the clearest language; and yet the same man, whose private virtues, amenity of manners, and boundless hospitality made him the darling of the nation, attempted to convert heretics by whipping, by torturing, and by burning.

In the generation which followed the death of More, there arose men who, without the humanity of his principles, enforced all the cruelties of his practice. Under Edward, the Protestants burnt the Catholics; under Mary, the Catholics burnt the Protestants. And although in the struggle of rival cruelties the Catholics had the advantage in the greater number of their opponents whom they were able to immolate; yet, if we fairly distinguish the natural temper of the men and the circumstances in which they were placed, there is not much 'to choose in point of wickedness between Cranmer and Bonner, between the advisers of Edward, and the advisers of Mary. Indeed, if we estimate their intentions by their professions, and if we judge their private opinions by their public creed, there can be no doubt that intolerance is a greater crime among Protestants, whose very existence is founded upon the right of private judgment, than it is among Catholics, who are bound to renounce such right, and to accept with humility all the traditions of the Church. But without attempting to parcel out that monstrous load of guilt, which must be shared by the rival religions, it is sufficient to state the undoubted fact, that when Elizabeth came to the throne, no civil or religious ruler, no governor either of State or Church in any part of Europe, had ventured on what would have been considered the blasphemous experiment of allowing men to settle their religion as a private question between themselves and their God.

It was under such circumstances as these that Elizabeth not only conceived the scheme of a religious toleration, but for several years actually enforced its principles. In an age when the smallest offences were habitually corrected by the severest punishments, and when the slightest whisper of toleration had never been heard to penetrate the walls of a palace, this great queen publicly put forward opinions which in our own days have become obvious truisms, but which in the sixteenth century were considered damnable paradoxes : " We know not nor have any meaning to allowe that any our Subjects should be molested either by Examination or Inquisition, in any matter either of Faith, as long as they shall profess the Christian Fayth, not gaynsayeng the Authority of the holly Scriptures, and of the Articles of our faith contained in the Creeds Apostolic and Catholic : or for matter of ceremony or any other external matter appertaining to Christian religion, as long as they shall in their outward conversation show themselves quiet and conformable and not manifestly repugnant and obstinate to the Laws of the realm, which are established for Frequentation of divine service in the ordinary churches, in like manner as all other Laws are whereunto Subjects are of duty and by allegiance bound." She proceeds to add, " in the word of a Prince and the Presence of God," that there shall be no " molestation to them by any person by way of Examination or Inquisition of their secret opinions in their consciences for matters of Faith." Such were the sentiments put on record by Elizabeth in a public proclamation after she had been eleven years on the throne : and it may be confidently asserted that there was not any sovereign then living in Europe from whose mouth such language had been heard. And without accumulating instances of the general spirit in which such principles had been carried out by her Government, it is sufficient to state that her bitterest enemies have never been able to point out a single instance of persecution for religion during the eleven years which elapsed between her accession to the throne and the date of the proclamation which I have just quoted.

Those who are acquainted with the theological literature of the sixteenth century will form some idea of the horror and disgust which these proceedings excited in the minds of the bishops and superior clergy. They regarded such toleration not only as a dangerous experiment, but as a most impious contrivance.

Sandys, who was consecrated bishop of Worcester the year after the death of Mary, endeavoured to expel all the Catholics from his diocese; and several years later, Aylmer, bishop of London, advised the government at once to throw into prison all the principal English Catholics. Whitgift declared that "if papists went abroad unpunished, when by law they might be touched, surely it was a great fault and could not be excused, and he prayed God it might be better looked to."[1] Whittingham, dean of Durham, wrote to the earl of Leicester in 1564, bitterly complaining of the "great lenity towards the papists."

But the queen easily penetrated the designs of these men. She saw that, under the pretence of purifying the Church, they were bent on the double object of gratifying their own bigotry and extending their own influence. Determined to prevent this, she took every opportunity of repressing their specious interference. Indeed, if she had not done so there would soon have been established in England an ecclesiastical tyranny not inferior to that which was already established in Spain. One or two instances may serve as a specimen to show the spirit of the chiefs of the Protestant Church. At the Portuguese embassy, mass was publicly said, and it was well known that many English Catholics were always present at its celebration. In 1576 the Recorder of London, the prying and impudent Fleetwood, who was intimately connected with many of the Protestant clergy, was scandalised by such an exhibition of idolatry, and on one occasion ventured forcibly to interrupt the religious ceremonies. But the queen, so far from applauding his zeal, reprimanded him for his interference, and actually committed him to prison.

There is yet extant a letter which was written in 1562, to the Lords of the Council, by the bishops of London and Ely, complaining of some Catholics that they "will neither accuse themselves nor none other." These Christian prelates suggest as a remedy that one of them, who was a priest, should be tortured in order to compel him to confess; and in order to enlist on their side the poverty of Elizabeth, they add that by such means a large sum of money may also be wrung from him. In 1564, Nowel, Dean of St. Paul's, in a sermon before Elizabeth, violently attacked some Catholic work which had just been published; but the queen, to his great amazement, instead of corresponding to his ardour, sharply rebuked him for his intemperate language. The only serious blot upon the character of Elizabeth is the exe-

---

[1] This was in 1572.

cution of Mary of Scotland.   But many years before she was put
to death, and therefore many years before she was even tried,
some of the bishops advised that she should be executed.


# III.

### POLITICAL.

WHILE this struggle was still pending between a tolerant government and an intolerant clergy, there suddenly occurred an
event which, though apparently unimportant, led the way to a
complete change in the religious policy of Elizabeth.   Mary of
Scotland, after suffering a series of insults for which her conduct
had given but too much cause, suddenly fled from her own country
and crossed the English border.   She came as a fugitive : she was
treated as a prisoner.   But from this moment Elizabeth had no
peace.   The English Catholics, confident in their numbers and in
the goodness of their cause, had been for some time husbanding
their strength until a favourable opportunity should arrive.   That
opportunity was now afforded to them by the presence of Mary.
Her youth, her beauty, and her misfortunes made her popular ;
and a belief that she was suffering for her religion raised her to
the dignity of a martyr.   At the same time, the old aristocracy
felt themselves aggrieved by the preference which Elizabeth displayed for men of inferior rank.   They had already formed a combination to drive Cecil from her councils ; and failing in that,
they now united with the Catholics, and both parties suddenly
flew to arms.   Thus the aristocratic influence and the Catholic
influence, either of which when unsupported was formidable, were
now united against the government of the queen.   Their combined forces were headed by the earls of Westmoreland and
Northumberland ; and they naturally selected as the first scene
of hostilities the north of England, which I have already described
as being almost entirely occupied by the adherents of the old religion.   The progress of the rebellion was frightfully rapid ; and
as the tide of insurrection rolled on towards the south, the country
became rife with the most alarming reports.   The government entertained serious apprehensions of a rising in Wales, where the
Catholics formed an immense majority of the population ; and it
was even said that in the other parts of England no less than a
million of men were ready to take arms for their religion, and
only waited the signal of their leaders.
   If such an outbreak had taken place a few years before, the

government would certainly have fallen, and the sovereign would probably have been deposed. But the efforts which Elizabeth had made to organise a military establishment, although they were necessarily slight, were now the means of protecting her crown, and perhaps of saving her life. However, even with this advantage, the matter for a time remained in suspense. At first her troops only endeavoured so to hold the rebels in check, as to prevent their advance on the capital; but when they perceived the utter incapacity of the Catholic and aristocratic leaders, to whose management the rebellion was happily entrusted, they ventured on more decisive steps, and after a short but hazardous struggle, the insurrection was at length put down. The Catholics, who felt that they had played their game and lost their stake, now became desperate. As soon as the news reached the Vatican [1] the pope, mad with passion, signed a bull depriving Elizabeth of her crown and absolving her subjects from their allegiance : and there was found an Englishman bold enough to nail the bull on the very gates of the palace of the bishop of London. The queen, who saw herself thus bearded in her own capital, even before she had time to forget the terrors of the rebellion, determined to revenge herself on a party which had shown so restless and so implacable a spirit. As soon as she perceived that there was a body of men among her subjects who not only maintained the deposing power of the pope, but who were ready to carry out that power to its utmost consequence, it became evident to her that the whole ground of the question was suddenly changed. It became evident to her that the matter was no longer a mere dispute between two rival religions, but that it had risen to a deadly struggle between the temporal authority and the ecclesiastical authority. The choice did not now lie between the superstitions of Popery and the superstitions of Protestantism; but the question was, whether the people of England were to be governed by their own civil magistrate, or by the deputies of the bishop of Rome. The question was soon decided; but, unhappily for the reputation of Elizabeth, and, what is much more important, unhappily for the interests of England, the decision was followed up by measures which strongly savoured of the intolerant spirit of that barbarous age. I will not relate the infamous cruelties which the Protestants now practised on their Catholic countrymen; the pilloryings, the whippings, the torturings; but it is enough to mention that during a period of thirty years nearly two hundred Catholics were publicly executed as martyrs to their

[1] Lingard, iv. 120.

religion, many of them cut down while they were yet living, and
their hearts torn from their bodies in the presence of a savage
mob, who delighted to witness their dying agonies.

It is, indeed, distressing to observe how Elizabeth had thus
allowed herself to be drawn out of that noble policy in which,
for so long a time, she had steadily persisted.  But while, with all
the force which language allows, we must reprobate the conduct
of the queen, what shall we say to those modern Protestant
writers who, to their eternal disgrace, have attempted to palliate
so infamous a massacre ?   To punish men for their religion was a
great crime in Elizabeth, of which she is perhaps even now
paying the penalty.  It was a much greater crime in those
bishops and archbishops who had for so many years been urging
her on to the evil work.  But there can be no doubt that, in a
high moral point of view, the greatest crime of all is committed
by those persons of our own time who, in a comparatively enlightened age, and without the stimulus of danger, are constantly
exerting their puny abilities to excite that bigotry with which
English Protestants are but too apt to regard their Catholic
countrymen, and who, in order to do this, are not ashamed to
defend the conduct of Elizabeth, which on this occasion was as
contrary to good policy as it was abhorrent to the spirit of all.
true religion.  Happily, however, for the progress of civilization,
the influence of these men is now on the wane ; and, without
detaining the reader by the consideration of their petty schemes,
I will now return to the more important matters of general
history.

While these things were passing in England, the aspect of
foreign affairs had gradually become more favourable.  The Dutch,
smarting under the cruel exactions of the Spanish government,
and knowing that they could reckon on the support of Elizabeth,
had turned on their oppressors, and it seemed likely that they
would be able to hold at bay all the power of Philip, distracted
as he was by a fresh insurrection of the Moors. . . . .

At the moment when Spain was thus weakened by the open
revolt of the most flourishing of its dependencies, there were
gradually accumulating in an adjoining country the materials for
the most deliberate and bloody tragedy that has ever yet disgraced the history of men.  The French government, which had
for some years been a laughing-stock to its neighbours, at length
distinguished itself by the commission of a crime which, considered in all its parts, stands alone, a solitary and instructive
monument of the frightful extent to which religious bigotry can
aggravate the natural malignity of our mean and superstitious

nature. It will be understood that I allude to the massacre of St. Bartholomew, which, while it caused in our own country a panic fear, produced the beneficial effect of inducing every Englishman to rally round the throne of Elizabeth. Whatever might be the natural discontents of the Catholics and Puritans, they were conscious that this was not the time to embarrass the government of the queen. Indeed, the alarm that was felt in England was so great that it showed itself in the most exaggerated rumours. It was currently reported that this was only the beginning of a series of similar acts; that all the lands of the French Protestants were to be sold, and the proceeds to be used for achieving the conquest of heretical countries.[1]

Even in France the assassins did not reap the fruits of their crime. Rochelle still held out, and the Huguenots, with varying success, were able to keep their ground until, seventeen years later, their liberties were secured to them by the accession of Henry IV.

While France and Spain were thus weakened by intestine feuds, England was rapidly rising into greatness. For nearly twenty years after the great northern rebellion, Elizabeth was at peace with all the world, and was enabled to mature her plans for enriching and civilizing her people. The leading characteristics of her policy will be unfolded under their respective heads in a subsequent part of this volume; but I may here mention some of those minor and yet important improvements which we owe to her fostering care.

.          .          .          .          .

In the midst of these great and pacific exertions, the country was again startled by the rumours of impending danger. Relieved for a time from the threat of foreign aggression, Elizabeth had now to guard against the insidious projects of domestic treason. Such projects were the natural result of the antagonism of two great conflicting parties, and they were furthered by several circumstances which had conspired to raise the hopes of the Catholics. On the side of Scotland, the queen had for several years considered herself perfectly secure so long as the regency was possessed by Morton, who was a creature of her own, and who acted entirely under her guidance. But he was now suddenly arrested, tried for his life, sentenced to die, and, in spite of the active intercession of the English government, was publicly brought to the block. This[2] was immediately followed by a visit to James by Waytes, a priest, and Creighton, a Jesuit. Their reception by the king and the court

[1] See Strype's *Annals*, vol. ii. pt. i. p. 238.
[2] "This sentence is too abrupt."—[Marginal note by Mr. Buckle.]

was such as to inspire them with the expectation of changing
the religion of the country. The whole Catholic party was now
alive. Within a year of the death of Morton its most influential
members held a great meeting at Paris, in which it was proposed
that James and Mary should be associated on the [Scottish]
throne. To this Mary of course agreed, and James not only gave
in his adherence to the proposal, but caused a letter to be written
to his mother expressing his approval of a plan of invading
England, formed by the duke of Guise. The government, whose
information nothing could escape, intercepted the letter. The
spirit of the English Protestants, which even in our own time has
boiled over at much slighter insults, was roused to indignation at
this attempt to introduce a foreign army into the heart of the
kingdom. Looking upon Mary as the real author of the conspiracy, they rose almost as one man, and signed an association
binding themselves to pursue to the death any one by whom or
even *for* whom an attempt should be made on the life of Elizabeth. While the nation was thus exasperated, its irritability was
fomented into madness by the discovery of a plot formed by
Babington, Ballard, and others, to assassinate the queen. The
people, always ill-judging and always in extremes, considered this
a fresh evidence of a deeply-laid scheme to extirpate their religion ; and their fury, excited partly by fear and partly by hatred,
rose to such a pitch that the Catholics in and about London were
apprehensive of becoming the victims of a general massacre.
Indeed, at one moment there was reason to fear that the horrors
of St. Bartholomew's day were about to be imitated on the English
soil. Happily we were saved from so foul a blot ; but the fate of
Mary was sealed. Within a month after the execution of Babington, a commission was appointed to try her. She was sentenced
to die. Elizabeth hesitated, but parliament and the country
clamoured for her head. The queen signed the fatal warrant :
recalled it : signed it again : and again recalled it. Whether
these were compunctions of conscience or whether they were mere
tricks of state is uncertain, and until the publication of further
evidence than is yet in our hands will remain unknown. At all
events, mistaken views of policy, aided no doubt by feelings of
personal jealousy, at length induced her to bring Mary to the
block. All Europe thrilled with horror ; and Philip, whose re-
sentment against Elizabeth had been accumulating for thirty
years, determined to avail himself of the general feeling by
striking against her a great and decisive blow. The queen had
the earliest intelligence of his designs, and bestirred herself with
all her wonted energy. Her first care was for Scotland. James,

on hearing of Mary's execution, talked big and loud.  He would raise troops from every part of his kingdom.  He would put himself at the head of his nobility, and inflict the most signal vengeance on the murderer of his mother.  But all this was not the grief of a bereaved son: it was not even the injured dignity of a king: it was nothing but the idle vapouring of a noisy bully.  Elizabeth knew her man.  First she cajoled him, and then she bribed him.  She wrote him an affectionate letter, and she sent him four thousand pounds.  The affection he might have withstood, but the money was irresistible; and Elizabeth felt that from the north she had nothing to fear.

But in another quarter the clouds gathered thick and blackened the horizon.  The king of Spain had received a vast accession of strength from the conquest of Portugal, and with increased energy now pushed his preparations for war.  Not even the fear of the establishment of a universal monarchy could prevent the Catholic powers from openly sympathising with this stupendous design.  The pope not only promised him a million of crowns, but with infinite difficulty actually collected that sum, which was ready to be paid the moment the invading army should have landed in England. . . . .

To these immense preparations Elizabeth had to oppose a power which, though now prodigiously strengthened, was still affected by the curse of religious schism.  At home she was able to keep that spirit in check; but abroad it now produced some very alarming results.  Holland was with reason considered a great bulwark of England; and the queen had sent forces to aid the Dutch in that noble struggle which they were now making against the power of Spain.  But news was now brought to England that in that very country Sir William Stanley with all his troops had deserted to Philip, and had given up the important town of Deventer, with the government of which he, although a Catholic, had been entrusted. . . . .

And in order that these examples might not be lost on the other subjects of Elizabeth, they were held up for imitation in the works of two of the most influential of the English Catholics. It is, indeed, a remarkable proof of the havoc which superstition can commit, even in superior intellects, that these infamous and cowardly treasons were, on the pretence of religion, publicly justified (?) in written documents, not only by the coarse and turbulent Parsons, but also by Cardinal Allen, a man of amiable character, and, considering the time in which he lived, of a most enlightened mind.

Such conduct, shameful as it must appear, is rather to be

ascribed to the general workings of religious bigotry than to any circumstances peculiar to the Church of Rome. But this was not the view taken by the English hierarchy. The bishops, so soon as they had heard of what had happened, availed themselves of it to effect their own ends; and, with redoubled zeal they now urged Elizabeth to revenge the acts of a few incendiaries upon the great body of her Catholic subjects.[1]

But Elizabeth well knew that, under the mask of loyalty, these men only sought to gratify the hatred with which they regarded their Catholic countrymen, and she indignantly rejected those cruel precautions which they sought to impose upon her. And as if to show her dislike, she appointed Catholics to offices of trust.

.          .          .          .          .          .

While the queen was thus employed, there were assembling in the Spanish ports the materials for an armament the like of which had never been seen in Europe since the day [of] Xerxes.

When the expedition was almost ready to sail, Philip consecrated it by a form of solemn prayer: but Elizabeth, heedless of such precautions, only laboured to infuse into her people a portion of her own intrepid spirit. Having done this, and having, by her rejection of the intolerant advice of the bishops, attempted to unite all England into a bulwark for her throne, she calmly waited for the dreadful crisis. It was indeed not only a time of agonising suspense, but it was a great moment in the history of the world. In a deadly contest between the two first of living nations, there was now to be put to the issue everything that is dearest to man. If the army of Philip could once set its foot on the English soil, the result was not a matter of doubt. The heroism of Elizabeth and the chivalrous loyalty of her troops would have been as nothing when opposed by that stern and disciplined valour which had carried the Spanish [flag] through a hundred battles. And when the irregular forces of England had once been dispersed, the people of England would then have risen, and there would have followed another unavailing struggle, which even at this distance of time it is frightful to consider. It would have been a struggle of race against race, in which the descendants of a Latin colony would have gloried in avenging upon a Teutonic people the cruel injuries which had been heaped on their fathers by the savage tribes of Alaric and Attila. It would have been the struggle of religion against religion, in

[1] Just after the Armada, Cooper, Bishop of Winchester, urgently demanded more stringent laws against the Catholics and Puritans. See Cooper's *Admonition to the People of England*. 1589, pp. 72, 107, 108; London, 1817.

which the fiendish passions of a ferocious priesthood would have glutted themselves to satiety in the blood of the heretic. It would have been a struggle which would have decided the fate, not merely of England, not merely of Protestantism, but, what was far more important, the fate of the liberties of Europe, and of that young and brilliant civilization which was now beginning to shine in an almost meridian splendour.

If the prodigious power of the Spanish empire had been wielded by a sovereign at all competent to the task, these probabilities would have become matters of almost absolute certainty. But Philip was one of those men who seem to be always in the wrong. After the battle of St. Quentin, an excess not of caution, but of timidity, prevented him from pushing his troops into the heart of France. And yet now, when he was meditating the capital enterprise of his long reign, when he was about to undertake the subjugation of a country whose resources had been developed during thirty years by the greatest sovereign that had been seen since the death of Charlemagne, at this moment it was that the commonest calculations of an ordinary prudence seem suddenly to have deserted him. Flushed by the hope of an immortal renown, he spurned the advice of his ablest councillors. It was in vain that the duke of Parma urged the necessity of first taking Flushing, which, in case of adverse fortune, would secure a certain retreat. It was in vain that this great commander insisted on the danger of sailing through a narrow sea which was girdled by hostile ports. Philip, urged on by his priests, who told him that he was the chosen minister of God, determined at once to strike the blow. The armada sailed from the coast of Spain. The results I need not stop to relate, for they form a part of those heroic traditions of our glory by which the infant was once rocked in the cradle, by which the man was once spurred on to the fight.

From this time everything prospered under the hands of Elizabeth. After much hesitation she had at length determined openly to protect the Netherlands against the power of Spain. Those unfortunate provinces had, by the assassination of the Prince of Orange (in 1584), been deprived not only of their greatest general, but of their only statesman, and they now saw their government thrown into the hands of an inexperienced boy. The consequence was that the duke of Parma had carried everything before him. Brussels and Sluys had successively fallen into his hands. Antwerp, after a stubborn resistance, had met with the same fate, and it seemed likely that Philip would regain everything which had for so many years been lost to him. Indeed, immediately after the failure of the armada, the duke of Parma determined to wipe out that disgrace by the entire conquest of the Low Countries. Having already reduced the whole of Brabant with the single exception of Bergen-op-Zoom, he at once with his entire army laid siege to that important town, the possession of which would have thrown open to him those rich and flourishing provinces which lay to the north of the Waal. But on the land, as well as on the ocean, Philip was to be foiled by the hand of Elizabeth. The Dutch, with the aid that the queen had sent to them, succeeded in baffling all his attempts, and he, unquestionably the greatest general in Europe, was compelled to effect a sudden and disastrous retreat. The duke, still acting under the orders of Philip, then marched into France, hoping by this sudden movement to effect a junction with the rebels, and with their united forces overthrow Henry IV., the friend and ally of Elizabeth. But there also the troops of England were at hand, and contributed not a little to the complete defeat of the Spanish army.

While the fortunes of Philip were thus declining abroad, Elizabeth suddenly determined to attack him at home. Having already insulted his fleet, intercepted his treasure on its way from America, and even destroyed his ships as they sailed from port to port, she at length sent an expedition which cut out his navy under the very guns of Cadiz, captured the city, burnt it to the ground, and inflicted an irretrievable injury on the Spanish empire.

The most powerful of her enemies being thus crippled, and her position being still further secured by the accession of a Protestant prince to the throne of France, Elizabeth was now at leisure to direct her attention to a country which has always been the disgrace as well as the curse of England, and which, even at the present day, is as a foul and ulcerous excrescence deforming the beauty and weakening the energy of this mighty empire. For three centuries ( ? ) Ireland had been a source of constant anxiety to the English government. Its wild and desperate population was constantly rising in arms, and within the last few years there had broken out a fresh and dangerous rebellion, headed by a man of no common abilities—the proud but subtle Tyrone. The queen, with that knowledge of men which, except in two instances,[1] never deceived her, now selected Mountjoy for the difficult task of reducing this turbulent country. He, after a desperate struggle, completely suppressed the rebellion : compelled Tyrone to surrender at discretion, and sent him to London to be disposed

---

[1] Leicester and Essex.

of at the discretion of the queen. This was the last act of this great and glorious reign; but the news of it was not to meet the ears of her to whom it was owing. Indeed, the powers of Elizabeth, which had been for some time declining, were now worn out. After nearly half a century of incessant labour, the life of the great queen began to ebb. The death of her oldest and wisest councillors, the sensible diminution of her energies, and perhaps a prophetic vision of the future, preyed on her mind. Weary of life, which for her had lost its charms, her shattered body yielded to the first summons, and she died full of years and of glory. The people were not fully sensible of the loss they had sustained, and indeed they had no means of fairly estimating it until they had compared her with that contemptible buffoon who was now to fill her place. Still it was a blow which they felt bitterly; and there is not the slightest foundation for the assertion so confidently made by modern writers, that Elizabeth outlived her popularity. Camden indeed tells us, what we know from other sources, that many of the courtiers deserted her in order to pay their homage to James. This is likely enough of that debased and unmanly tribe. It is likely enough that those wretched creatures who are always fluttering in a palace should be the first to desert the falling ruin. It is likely enough that those who are so servile as to humble themselves before the sovereign when she is living, should be so treacherous as to desert her when she is dying. But the people at large knew nothing of such grovelling intrigues, and they could not fail to admire that intellect which had conducted them unscathed through such constant and pressing dangers. They respected Elizabeth as a sovereign: they loved her as a friend: and they took good care that she should not have the last agonies of death embittered by the sharp sting of national ingratitude.

The reader will perhaps be surprised that I should as yet have taken no notice of the Puritans, who during the last years of the sixteenth century began seriously to embarrass the government, and but for the prudence of Elizabeth would perhaps have succeeded in impeding its operations. But I have designedly made this omission, because I feel that in this, which is but a preliminary sketch, it would be impossible to do justice to so important a subject, and because it has appeared to me that the proper period for attempting a philosophic estimate of their tendencies will be the moment of their final success. That moment was indeed now at hand, and under the reign of James we shall find this obscure sect rapidly swelling into a mighty party, whose power swept away the throne and the Church, and whose influence is still perceptible in our laws, in our institutions, and in many of the strokes of our national character. But the causes and extent of their influence, which form one of the most important and difficult branches of English history, will be discussed at length in the next volume : and I now turn with pleasure from the relation of mere political events to consider the moral and economical state of England during the reign of Elizabeth.

<hr />

## IV.

### CLERGY.

THE two great principles which Elizabeth kept steadily in view, and from which she never swerved, were to repress the arrogance of the ecclesiastical power, and to diminish the influence of the great landed aristocracy. As these were the leading points in her domestic policy during more than forty years, and as it is to the success with which she pursued them that we owe no small share of our unprecedented advance in liberty, in morals, and in wealth, I shall endeavour to examine them at a length somewhat commensurate with their importance. I therefore propose in this and the succeeding chapter to inquire into the state and conditions of the ecclesiastical power ; and, in the two remaining chapters of this book, I shall in the same way examine the aristocratic power, and show the connection between its decline and the rise of those middle classes, to whom the most brilliant peculiarities of modern civilization are chiefly owing.

In the second book I shall trace the development of civilization in other matters, and in the third book I shall examine manners.

The ecclesiastical history of England during the sixteenth century is so intimately connected with the general history of Protestantism, that it would be highly unphilosophical to attempt to estimate either of these events by considering them as separate phenomena. But, for the convenience of analytic investigation, I shall, in the first place, endeavour to set in a clear light the general causes of the Reformation, and then I shall descend to that narrower and more practical view which will connect the whole with the particular history of our own country.

It is a very remarkable circumstance that no one has yet succeeded in writing the history of that great revolution which, three hundred years ago, changed the face of the civilized world. This, no doubt, is partly to be ascribed to the backward state of the moral sciences, which in their present unformed condition render such a task eminently difficult; but it is, as I should suppose, quite as assignable to the feelings of extreme prejudice with which nearly all men approach the consideration of so irritating a subject. To me it appears undoubted, that while the effects of the Reformation have, on the whole, been beneficial to mankind, they have been, and still are, greatly exaggerated: the evil effects exaggerated by the Catholics, the good effects exaggerated by the Protestants. The truth is, that the Reformation, until it had been curbed and modified by the strong hand of the temporal power, effected little for any part of Europe. One great merit, indeed, it had; it roused the European mind. It taught man to know his own power. But how that power was to be employed, whether it was to be used in accelerating the march of the human species or in building up another spiritual tyranny in the place of that which it had overthrown, these were questions to which there was nothing in the general aspect of Europe early in the sixteenth century, or in the spirit of the first Reformers, which could have enabled an observer of that time to give a satisfactory answer. Indeed, the bigotry of the Protestants was not at all inferior to the bigotry of the Catholics; and, although their cruelty was necessarily less, because its exercise was bounded by the more limited extent of their power, yet whenever the Reformed clergy obtained the upper hand, there were committed excesses as obnoxious to humanity as any of those with which they perpetually taunted their opponents.

And yet there is, I know, an opinion very prevalent among those who are but little acquainted with the sources of history, that it was the Reformation which gave a death-blow to superstition, and that to it alone we are indebted for our emancipation from the trammels of priestly authority. To this it would perhaps be sufficient to answer that in most Protestant countries no such emancipation has ever taken place: that every instance in which a Catholic nation is enslaved by its clergy is merely the effect of the ignorance of the people, and would equally occur if those people were Protestants; and that in France, for example, where there has been no reformation, there is among the higher classes less superstition than in England. But, without entering into these general considerations, it will be sufficient to show by an historical analysis how the establishment of Protestantism was the effect and not the cause of the decline of ecclesiastical power; and how the decline of that power was in the first instance brought about by the mere force of political combinations.

It must, I think, at the present day be clear to every well-informed person, that the Reformation was the result, not so much

of the desire of purifying religion as of the desire of lightening
its pressure.  There is, indeed, no doubt that some of the founders
of Protestantism were actuated by the purest and most dignified
motives ; but it may be broadly laid down that neither in the
sixteenth century nor at any other period has any great revolution
been permanently effected, except with the view of remedying
some palpable and physical evils.   Among barbarous tribes there
can, I should suppose, be little doubt that the influence of the
clergy is an almost unmixed benefit, and that within certain
limits the greater the power of the priests, the greater the happiness of the people.   In such a state of society it is the ministers
of religion alone who are able to temper the ferocity of the
passions, and even the fictions of superstition may be employed
in ameliorating the condition of the savage.   But in a civilized
country, when property has begun to be accumulated, and when
the arts of peace are already cultivated, the existence of such an
ecclesiastical power produces two serious evils, it wrings from the
people the fruits of their industry, and it checks the progress of
inquiry, and therefore the progress of knowledge.   To the latter
of these evils the majority of even the most civilized nations is
always indifferent.   How, indeed, can it be expected that those
who sweat at the plough or toil at the loom should trouble themselves about the impediments which are opposed to the advance
of science or to the progress of society?   How can it be expected
that the peasant and the mechanic, drooping under the weight
of incessant labour, should band together to uphold liberty of
thought and freedom of discussion?   But when these same men
perceive that the clergy is wresting from them a part of their
scanty earnings; when they see a lazy priesthood fattening on the
products of their industry, their indignation is soon aroused, and
nothing but the constant efforts of the ecclesiastical power will
prevent that indignation from finding a destructive vent.   In such
a case the safety of the hierarchy will depend, not on any moral
considerations, but solely on their ability to resist the aggression
with which they are threatened.   Thus it is that a careful survey
of history will prove that the Reformation made the most progress, not in those countries where the people were most enlightened ; but in those countries where, from political causes,
the clergy were least able to withstand the people.   It is, therefore, in the investigation of those causes that we must seek the
solution of this question.

In every nation in Europe the power of the clergy at an early
period bore an inverse ratio to the power of the sovereign.   In
countries such as France, where the feudal system had succeeded

in eradicating every vestige of representative government, and where the authority of the king was not sufficient to supply the deficiency, the councils of the church were the only links which knit together the discordant elements, and bound up in one nation a multitude of independent fiefs. The church, by thus stepping in and remedying isolated abuses, prevented feudalism from denationalising France. At the same time the circumstances which gave the church this power, tended to increase it. The sovereigns of France, seeing the flowers of their prerogative droop one by one, and sorely pressed by the arrogance of the great feudal proprietors, looked around them for a counterpoise to the aristocratic power. That counterpoise they found in the church. From the time of Charlemagne we see a growing disposition on the part of the kings of France to increase the power of the priesthood. Thus that power reached such a height that when the Reformation broke out, it found the French clergy so compact and so well organised as to be able to resist a movement which shook Europe to the centre.

But in England the matter was far different. During the rule of the Anglo-Saxons we find, indeed, causes in operation similar to those which took place in France. We find the aristocratic power constantly rising, and the royal power constantly declining. We find the consequence, that even the wisest of our kings thought it necessary to court the church in order to secure themselves against the nobles. But, in the middle of the eleventh century, the whole course of affairs was suddenly diverted. The Norman conquest, by making the king the granter of baronies, at once threw the great nobles under his control. The feudal system was never developed, and except during the turbulent reign of Stephen, national assemblies were constantly held. The first five (?) kings of England possessed a power such as no sovereign of Europe then possessed. In consequence of the existence of this central power, the want of church councils in our own country was never felt; the Plantagenets never found it worth their while to encourage the ecclesiastical authority: on the contrary, they exerted themselves to repress it: and when, at the end of the fourteenth century, the rapid decline of the royal power made it the interest of our kings to court the church, it was then too late to establish an authority, the chains of which can only be firmly riveted in times of the grossest ignorance. The history of Germany is in this respect very analogous to the history of England.[1] After the death of Charlemagne, Germany

---

[1] Protestantism rose and flourished in North Germany: compare that with South Germany.

remained in the hands of his family for nearly a century; but on the death of his grandson the throne became elective, and custom, and afterwards positive law, limited the number of electors. The result was, that the government was turned into an oligarchy, and the supreme power vested in the hands of the electoral princes, who, unembarrassed by any rival authority in their own states, were in this respect like our Norman kings, and did not court the church because they had no occasion for its aid. The consequence was, that in England the clergy were less efficient, either for good or evil, than in any country of Europe, except Germany. Hence we can easily understand why the Reformation began in Germany and spread in England. In both countries religious men welcomed it as the means of averting national infidelity; ambitious men welcomed it as the means of extending their own power.

It would be easy to extend the view I have here taken to the other great countries of Europe : and to show how, in Spain, the Visigothic code, drawn up by the clergy before the consolidation of the monarchy, became by their arts so incorporated with the kingly institutions.[1]

    .        .        .        .        .        .

In the same way, I might show how, on the other side of the Rhine, the constant struggle between the bishops of Utrecht and Counts of Holland resolved itself into a struggle between the spiritual and temporal power.[2]

But I may safely leave such further application to the knowledge of the reader; and I will now resume the general thread of the ecclesiastical history of England.

The circumstances which I have just stated explain the facility with which the foundations of the Reformation were laid by Henry. They also explain the little resistance which the clergy

---

[1] It was remarked at the Council of Trent, as a peculiarity of the Spaniards, that they claimed for the bishops a power independent of the popes (Ranke, *Päpste*, band i. pp. 331-341). Vamba, King of Spain, was deposed by the clergy in A.D. 681 ; and this is the first instance of the ecclesiastical authorities assuming such a power (Fleury, *3me Discours* in *Histoire ecclésiastique*, tome xiii. p. 22 ; Paris, 1758). In Spain, the Inquisition itself had not the power of imprisoning bishops (see Geddes' *Miscellaneous Tracts*; Lond. 1730; vol. i. p. 389). And although there were at one time signs that the indifference of Charles V. would weaken the ecclesiastical power (M'Crie's *Reformation in Spain*), yet the spread of the Jesuits (Ranke, *Päpste*, i. 233), who rose in Spain and flourished in Spain, saved it—and so did the bigotry of Philip IV.

[2] On the spirit of hostility to the church which appeared in the Low Countries during the fourteenth century, see Van Kampfen, *Geschiedenis der Lattere in de Nederlander* ; Gravenhaye, 1821 ; Deel. i. blad 24-25). He truly says, 'de dageraad der Hervorming brak aan.'

were able to make, even to the incompetent ministers of his immediate successor.[1]

Towards the very close of the reign of Edward, the government, impelled partly by avarice, and partly, as we may hope, by higher views of general policy, determined to deal the clergy a sudden and, as it afterwards appeared, a most severe blow. As the results of this were of great moment, I shall consider them in reference to the general question of the sources of ecclesiastical power. Among the many contrivances of the clergy to increase their own authority, the adornment of churches has always occupied a prominent place; and there are few better measures of the superstition of a nation, than the proportion which the money spent in them bears to the general wealth of the country. But in England the proportion had, in the middle ages, always been greater than would be supposed probable by those who only take into account the low state of our clergy as compared with their more flourishing condition in other countries. This peculiarity arose from circumstances which I will now endeavour to explain.

As soon as the fine arts began to revive in Europe, the Church laid hold of them, and used them for her own purposes. Poetry, painting, architecture, nay, even music itself, were employed by her as engines to exalt the senses and subjugate the reason of mankind. The degree of her success in the different arts depended on the laws, on the climate, and perhaps on the physical condition of the different nations of Europe. Among the luxurious and indolent inhabitants of the south, painting and music were the means which she chiefly employed. In the north, where the brilliant imagination which the great tribes of Scandinavia owed to their recent migration from Asia, was as yet unchecked by their laws, but was tempered by the severity of their climate, poetry was the vehicle in which the Church taught her dogmas to a credulous people. But in England, where a higher degree of civilization had to some extent checked the first exuberance of the fancy, neither poetry, nor painting, nor music were able to attain to such precocious maturity; and the only art left to the clergy was the art of building temples which, by their beauty, should charm the taste of the refined, and by their splendour gratify the senses of the vulgar. It is not surprising that the English clergy, thus concentrating upon a single art their wealth and their energies, should have succeeded in raising it to a height which no other modern nation has been able to attain. The

---

[1] In the first year of Edward VI., lampoons on the sacrament were stuck on the doors of many of the cathedrals. In 1531, Cranmer writes that the people 'now begin to hate priests' (Todd's *Life of Cranmer*, i. 34).

beauty of their churches is sufficiently attested by those splendid remains which are yet standing.

But the age which could consider such trifles as important matters was soon to pass away, and one of the most decisive symptoms of approaching civilization was the decline of church architecture. As the business of life became more complicated : as the knowledge of men became more extensive, and their views more enlarged, just in that proportion increased their disinclination to build churches, and to encourage architects by whom those churches were planned. It is, indeed, an instructive fact, that the first decline of ecclesiastical architecture dates in our own country from the fourteenth century : that great century in which the House of Commons first laid the foundations of its power : in which the first great steps were taken towards relieving our slaves from their serfdom : in which Wickliff began to preach and Chaucer began to write : and in which the barbarous energy of our Saxon tongue was effectually tempered by the chaste elegance of the Norman-French, and, by the combination, gave rise to that great and noble dialect, which now, so rapid is its progress, bids fair, before many centuries are passed, to supersede the other languages of the earth, and, by uniting civilized man under one speech, realise the wildest schemes of the most Utopian philologists.

As civilization rapidly advanced, our ecclesiastical architecture as rapidly declined ; and in the fifteenth and sixteenth centuries reached its lowest point of debasement, from which it only rose for a moment during the superstitious government of the first English Stuarts. But these remarks only apply to the external form; and the pictures, the costly ornaments, the glittering plate, even the very shrines on which superstition loved to heap its wealth, still retained all their mediæval splendour, and, by attracting worshippers to the sanctuary, swelled the numbers of the admirers of the church. Captivated by the gorgeousness of the temple, men were inclined to look up with respect to the priests by whom the services of the temple were conducted, and this reflected homage served not a little to check the downfall of the clergy. But even this resource was at length to be torn from them ; and only six years before the accession of Elizabeth orders were issued by the government of Edward to strip all the churches in England of their plate, their jewels, and indeed all their ornaments ( ? ). The results of this measure, executed as it was with unsparing severity, it is difficult for a reader at the present day fully to estimate. In an age when reading was a scarce accomplishment, and when the few who could read found little worth the trouble of reading; when public amusements were exceedingly rare: when no theatre had yet been built in England, and when the wretched dramas that were in existence were acted in churches and performed by priests; when there were no operas, and neither reviews nor newspapers; when all these frivolities, with which ignorance now disports its leisure, were entirely unknown, the splendid services of the church offered a daily amusement, of the excitement of which we, in our time, can hardly form a conception. When these were withdrawn, men ceased to flock to churches, which for them had lost their charms. A great link which bound together the clergy and the laymen was suddenly severed, and the results were so remarkable, that even intelligent foreigners who visited our country were struck by them.

The clergy, who had long forfeited the love of the people, now even lost their respect. During the reign of Mary, not even the utmost pressure of the municipal authority could protect them from popular expressions of undisguised contempt. In London the very chaplains of the queen were pelted and mobbed as they walked in the streets; and though the fires were yet blazing in Smithfield, a dog was publicly exposed, with his head shaved in mockery of the ecclesiastical tonsure. Even the most sacred ordinances of the church were not spared. In Cheapside a cat was hung up with a wafer in its paws, to ridicule the sacrament.[1]

If the clergy were thus handled, in spite of the protection given them by Mary, it was not likely that her death would improve their position. Indeed, after the accession of Elizabeth, their influence went on declining with an accelerated velocity; for besides the general causes which I have pointed out, there were now some specific causes which tended to the same end, and by lessening their wealth, degraded them still further in the ranks of society. This diminution of income appears to have been effected in three different ways: first, by an alteration of their special fees; second, by the abolition of clerical celibacy; third, by a fall in the value of the precious metals. I will consider each of these three methods in the order in which I have stated them.

The Catholic Church, with a due regard for the temporal prosperity of her priests, had in every country secured to them fees, which were paid by those who received their spiritual aid. Some of these fees, such as those on marriage, burials, and the like, lapsed, after the fall of the Catholic clergy, into the hands of

[1] Only four months after the death of Edward VI. a clergyman, who had sold his wife to a butcher, was punished by being driven through London in a cart. In the first year of the reign of Mary a priest was nearly pulled to pieces by the people at St. Bartholomew's, and on the next Sunday, when Dr. Watson preached at St. Paul's Cross, he was protected from a similar indignity by the queen's guards.

their Protestant successors. But some of the most onerous and lucrative charges, particularly those made on the performance of prayers for the dead, &c., were considered too superstitious to be inherited by the priests of a purer religion, and the laity, of course, gladly acquiesced in a change by which they alone were the gainers. Although we are not in possession of precise statistical evidence on this subject, it is nevertheless certain that the alteration must have caused a serious defalcation in the revenue of the clergy; and the effects of this loss were the more important on account of the other causes which I have now to consider, and which operated in the same direction.

The operation of these circumstances was such as it is easy to imagine. The clergy, already degraded in character, were now ruined in fortune, and they rapidly sunk into that state which was natural to their fallen position. When any class of men cease to be respected by the nation, they soon cease to respect themselves. Treated as the outcasts of society, they betook themselves to the meanest and most grovelling amusements. Amid the refuse of mankind, they passed their time by dicing, and carding, and drinking in petty ale-houses, which they seldom left except in a state of beastly intoxication.

The impurity of their morals formed a fitting counterpart to the coarseness of their manners. No father would trust his daughter, no husband would trust his wife, alone in the company of one of these men. Indeed their depravity was so great and notorious, that when Archbishop Cranmer drew up his system of Ecclesiastical Law (in 1552), he was obliged to order that " unmarried clergymen were not to retain as housekeepers any women under sixty years of age, except their own near relations." But the scandal still increasing, this regulation was, within twenty years, renewed by one of the heads of the church, and the archbishop of York circulated orders through the whole of his diocese for " no minister (being unmarried) to keep in his house any woman under the age of sixty years, except she be his mother, aunt, sister, or niece."

Such regulations, however, availed nothing to control the unbridled licentiousness of these men. Several of the London clergy are stated by a contemporary to have kept a harem, and although we may hope that this is an unfounded assertion, for the expense would have been a serious obstacle, yet we have other evidence against them of the fullest and most painful character. A well known clergyman of the name of Barton was detected in London in an act of fornication under circumstances of singular infamy; and was dragged off to Bridewell under the groanings and hootings of the mob.

While the clergy were thus falling into contempt, it was not likely that competent men would be willing to engage in so despised a profession. The highest offices of the church, shorn as they were, still presented attractions for vain and avaricious men. But such offices could only be occupied by a few; and with the inferior departments, scarcely any one of decent character was willing to meddle. The consequence was that all over the kingdom an immense number of cures were entirely unoccupied, and whole parishes were left without the slightest religious instruction. To supply this deficiency, a somewhat strange expedient was adopted, and only two years after the accession of Elizabeth, it was found advisable to license common mechanics to read the services to the people in the different churches. This, though perhaps a necessary measure, tended still further to depress the character of the sacred profession. At length the evil reached such a pitch that the bishops, in order to recruit the diminished numbers of the clergy, were compelled not only to license such men as readers, but even to confer upon them the holy rite of ordination. Tradesmen and artisans, mechanics, alehouse-keepers, tinkers, cobblers, nay, even common serving-men, now formed a considerable portion of the clergy of the established church of England. As every Sunday came round, these men, ignorant of the rudiments of literature, might be seen to mount the pulpit, from whence they enlightened their hearers by declaiming against the abominations of popery, and not unfrequently by explaining the abstrusest subtleties of Calvinistic metaphysics. Such monstrous absurdities revolted even that ignorant age. Out of every part of the kingdom addresses flocked in from the indignant and outraged parishioners. The inhabitants of Essex presented a petition to the council, complaining that their clergy were " men of occupation, serving-men, the basest of all sorts; . . . risters, dicers, drunkards, and of offensive lives." The parishioners of Maidstone complained that their curate was " a person of a most scandalous life: frequenting alehouses, retreating thither ordinarily from the church; and a common player of cards and dice."

Elizabeth, unable to remedy such a state of things, to which she herself was personally indifferent, could only return evasive answers; and in many places the people, who now began to loathe their clergy, took the law into their own hands. At Westenden, they, of their own authority, put their vicar into the common stocks. In another parish, the name of which is not mentioned, the unfortunate clergyman was subjected to the same indignity,

*I

and was otherwise ill treated. In 1574, the clergyman at Manchester, who, as we are carefully informed, was a "bachelor of divinity," was attacked on his way to the church, when he was about to preach, was beaten, wounded, and almost killed. One of the magistrates of Surrey directed the vicar of Chertsey to appear before him respecting some pecuniary deficit. This the reverend gentleman declined to do; but his disobedience was immediately punished: he was at once put into the public stocks, and when he appealed for redress to the quarter sessions, his appeal was rejected.

The clergy, thus beggared, despised, and assaulted, resorted to expedients which will astonish a modern reader. With the view of increasing their incomes, they not unfrequently publicly sold beer, wine, and other provisions; and in order that they might do this with the greater facility, they converted their rectories into alehouses and taverns.

Their wives, who had been mostly servant-girls, were still less scrupulous than themselves. A woman married to one of the clergymen of Cardiganshire was, in 1584, publicly tried for administering potions to young girls, with the view of causing abortion.

The evils attendant on such a state of things had now become so palpable that the government was at length compelled to notice them. In 1584, the Lords of the Council, whose interest it must have been to conceal the nakedness of the church, wrote to the archbishop of Canterbury that "great numbers of persons that occupy cures are notoriously unfit, most for lack of learning; many chargeable with great and enormous faults, as drunkenness, filthiness of life, gaming at cards, haunting of ale-houses."

It does not, however, appear that the rebuke was attended with any advantage, and from the contemporary documents which I have seen, I believe that during the whole of the sixteenth century the situation of the clergy went on degenerating. But the painful details into which as an historian I have been compelled to enter, refer almost entirely to their moral character; and it will now be necessary to bring forward such other evidence as will enable the reader to judge of their intellectual accomplishments.

In the course of nearly three centuries an immense amount of evidence has of course perished; but the proofs which are yet extant of the gross ignorance of the clergy in the reign of Elizabeth, are such as would stagger the most incredulous, even if they were not confirmed by every description of historical testimony which has come down to us. We have it on the most unimpeachable evidence that twenty-one years after the death of

Mary, there were in the county of Cornwall alone one hundred and forty clergymen who, if they succeeded with infinite difficulty in reading the prayers, were quite incapable of preaching a sermon. Nor must this be considered as a peculiarity confined to that distant county. In 1584, the celebrated Sampson stated in a formal address to parliament that many of the clergy "neither can nor will speak anything in the congregation where they be resident more than they are compelled to read out of a printed book;" and he adds, "a number of them do read in no better sort than some young scholars could do which were newly taken out of some English school. Truely this their reading is so rude in some places among us, that they seem themselves scarce to understand that which they do read." In the year 1563, an official (?) list was drawn up of the clergy in the archdeaconry of Middlesex; and to the name of each man there was appended an account of his acquirements. The number of the clergy thus characterised was one hundred and sixteen, and out of the entire number three only were acquainted with Latin and Greek.

If from such general cases we now descend to particular instances, we shall find the evidence still more remarkable, and, if possible, still more irrefragable: nor will I bring forward anything except what is related by contemporary writers, who only record that which was passing before their eyes, and which was to them a matter of daily and familiar observation. Early in the reign of Elizabeth, the chaplain to the archbishop of Canterbury had occasion to examine the curate of Cripplegate, and by way of testing his knowledge asked him the meaning of the word *function*. To this difficult question the reverend gentleman, not having paid much attention to the niceties of language, was unable to make a satisfactory reply. Several years later the clergyman of Farnham, All Saints, was examined by the bishop of Norwich. The conversation which ensued is deserving attention; and it is preserved by Strype, whose devotion to the Church of England no one will think of questioning. "The bishop asked him the contents of the third chapter of Matthew: he answered nothing: and the contents of the eleventh chapter; neither could he answer to that. He asked him how many chapters the Epistle to the Romans contained, and what the subject of that Epistle was. To neither of these could he answer. And when he adventured to answer, he showed his ignorance as much as by his silence."

But I might fill a volume with similar instances, and I can only afford room for one or two more examples. In 1574, a certain William Ireland was presented to the rectory of Harthill. The archbishop of York directed his chaplain to examine him.

The chaplain first desired him to translate an easy Latin sentence. This he was unable to do; but as such knowledge was not very common in the clerical profession, the absence of it did not amount to a disqualification, and the examiner proceeded in his inquiry. He asked the reverend gentleman "who brought up the people of Israel out of Egypt?" He answered, King Saul. And, being asked who was first circumcised, he could not answer.

It was not to be expected that men such as these should display any remarkable ability when they had occasion to mount the pulpit. Indeed, their apostolic deficiencies were so glaring that it was found necessary to draw up sermons which they might read to the people. But some of the more adventurous of the sacred order, disdaining to shine by such borrowed light, ventured to address their parishioners in their own language, and with their own ideas. One of them, with the view, as I suppose, of moderating the presumption of his flock, preached in favour of mediocrity, and his sermon was considered such a masterpiece of theology that it was repeated in two or three different parishes. "God," says this great divine, "delighted in mediocrity by these reasons: viz. man was put *in medio paradisi*: a rib was taken out of the *midst* of man. The Israelites went through the *midst* of Jordan; and the *midst* of the Red Sea. Samson put firebrands in the *middlest* between the foxes' tails. David's men had their garments cut off by the *middlest*. Christ was hanged in the *middlest* between two thieves."

I am really ashamed of quoting such incoherent follies, but the reader must remember that they refer to the history of a very important body of men, whose peculiarities can only be elucidated by the assemblage of such instances. I will, however, only add two or three more out of the immense abundance of those materials which I have collected. It is stated by Aylmer, who was afterwards raised to the episcopal bench, that upon one occasion the vicar of Trumpington, in the course of divine service, fell upon the text, "Eli, Eli, lama sabacthani." Being much struck by what appeared to him so strange a repetition, the reverend gentleman could not restrain his wonder. "When he came to that place,"— I quote the words of the bishop,—"he stopped, and calling the churchwardens, said: Neighbours, this geare must be amended. Here is Eli twice in the book, I assure you if my lord of Ely come this way and see it, he will have the book. Therefore, by mine advice we shall scrape it out, and put in our own town's name, Trumpington, Trumpington, lamah zabacthani." The bishop adds what we should scarcely believe on any inferior authority, that to this strange suggestion the churchwardens acceded, and that the proposed alteration was actually made in the Bible of the church. In the country, which is the natural abode of ignorance, the clergy, low as they were sunk, were in points of acquirements not so very inferior to many of the laymen; but in the towns, which are always far advanced beyond the rest of the kingdom, the difference was most striking, and it was not to be expected that these more cultivated inhabitants should pay much attention to the spiritual exhortations of men such as I have described. Indeed, so far from receiving respect, they were considered as legitimate marks for popular derision; and they could hardly stir from their houses without being jeered at, and even assaulted by the apprentices and serving-men as they passed through the streets of London.

The churches themselves were not only neglected, they were actually profaned. . . . .

The consequence was, that in the towns the clergy were even more scarce than in the country. An official inquiry made in the middle of the reign of Elizabeth, brought to light the startling fact that in the whole of London there were only to be found nineteen "resident preachers."

Nor were the universities themselves much better supplied. Even in these great nurseries of religion there were not clergy sufficient to perform the most ordinary functions of the church; and on one occasion, when the congregation were assembled in St. Mary's, Oxford, there was no one to be found who was able to preach the sermon. The high sheriff of the county, indeed, mounted the pulpit with the view of supplying the deficiency, but his discourse was not much calculated to edify the audience. "I have brought you," said the orator, "some biscuits baked in the oven of charity, carefully conserved for the chickens of the church, the sparrows of the spirit, and the sweet swallows of salvation."

While such theology as this was preached in the pulpits of the Protestant Church of England, and while the morals and learning of the clergy were such as I have described, the queen, with a rare forbearance, never expressed by any general measure the contempt which she must have felt for the entire order. This is the more remarkable when compared with the active steps which we shall afterwards see she took against the episcopal hierarchy; and I have sometimes thought that she might have in view a scheme of balancing against each other the different orders of the church, and of reigning over them in virtue of their mutual rivalries. However this may be, it is at least certain that the laws respecting the clergy were as all laws ought to be—something in the rear of the general feeling of the age.  One of the most striking anomalies of this sort was the existence of unrepealed statutes respecting the benefit of the clergy.  This I need scarcely say was a privilege conceded to a certain class of men, of withdrawing the jurisdiction of their offences from the temporal courts and carrying it to the spiritual courts, where a trifling punishment, or no punishment at all, was usually imposed.  This privilege was at first only allowed to those who had the clerical dress and tonsure, but was afterwards extended to all who could read.  When the art of reading became 'more generally diffused, an act was passed which drew a distinction, and only allowed to lay-scholars the benefit of clergy *once*, directing that to prevent them from having it a second time, they should be burnt in the hand when they first received it.  This distinction was abolished by two subsequent statutes, but is supposed, though as appears to me on no good authority, to have been restored during the reign of Edward VI.  However this may be, it is at least certain that long before the accession of Elizabeth, and indeed during several years of her reign, when a clergyman was convicted in a court of common law of the most grievous offences, the ecclesiastical court took him out of their hands, allowed him to purge himself, and, after a great deal of idle form, generally pronounced him innocent, and let him loose on society.  The results of such a system may be easily imagined.  The clergy, ignorant, poor, and dissolute, had every inducement which men can have to commit crime, while they felt none of those checks by which crime is generally repressed.  Whenever there was a fray in the country, or a riot in the town, a clergyman was nearly always to be found at the bottom of it.  Whenever an act of violence was characterised by more than common audacity, it was to them that general suspicion invariably pointed.  This was a state of things not only opposed to good government, but even contrary to the commonest ideas of social order.  Still that love of old laws and old customs which, in the sixteenth century was so strong, and which even in our own time still lingers among ignorant men, long stood in the way of the necessary alteration.  At length, after Elizabeth had been many years at peace, she directed her attention to this important subject, and procured an Act which ordered that after conviction the clerical offender should not be delivered over to the ordinary, but that the judge should have the power of punishing his crime with imprisonment.

# V.

### BISHOPS.

In the preceding chapter I have stated the causes which, long before the Reformation, brought about a diminution of the influence of the clergy. It might have been expected that the bishops, as being the heads of the clergy, should in a certain degree have shared their fate; and that whatever tended to lessen the power of the one, should also have tended to lessen the power of the other. And there is no doubt that this was the natural course of events; and that if particular circumstances had not intervened, the whole fabric of ecclesiastical power would, before the end of the sixteenth century, have been so completely undermined, that the bishops would not have been able to lend their aid in supporting the rebellion of the Stuarts against the authority of the nation. What the particular circumstances were which, contrary to the general experience of history, enabled the bishops to maintain their ground in the face of an advancing civilization, is in itself a matter of very curious inquiry: and as it particularly concerns the object of this work, I shall examine it at some length.

When the baronial power was, at the end of the eleventh century, reduced almost to its last gasp, the authority of the bishops of course received a corresponding check.[1]  But in less than two hundred years the crown, which had been gradually losing ground, reached its lowest point of debasement during the long reign of Henry III.: and as that power declined, in the same proportion the opposite power of the nobles and bishops began to rise. In the first half of the thirteenth century, the royal authority, owing partly to the incapacity of John and Henry III., partly to the loss of the French possessions, and partly to the growing spirit of liberty, began rapidly to decline; and even the great abilities of Edward I. were scarcely able to avert its fall. In the meantime the bishops had taken care to place themselves on the winning side. They joined the barons (?) in forcing John to grant the great boon of Magna Charta; and when, ninety years later, an attempt was made to evade one of its most important provisions, Archbishop Winchelsey was one of the three great leaders who compelled the king to abandon his purpose. Stephen de Langton, Archbishop

---

[1] The early Norman kings, who were for the most part men of considerable ability, treated the hierarchy with supreme contempt. William I. kept many of the episcopal sees vacant for entire years, with the view of receiving their revenues; and he sometimes on the death of a bishop seized all his property.

of Canterbury, aided the barons in 1213 in forcing the great Charta upon John. In proportion as the people were ignorant, the power of the bishops was naturally greater. This was a legitimate source of power, but to this was soon added the power which the kings gave them for *political* purposes. The advance of knowledge, which was so fatal to the inferior clergy, did not affect the bishops in the same manner; and this seems to have been owing, partly to the character of the bishops, who were for the most part men of energy, generally able warriors, sometimes learned scholars, and partly to the advantages of their position as members of the imperial parliament. To this last circumstance I am inclined to ascribe a very high importance. In the present day the episcopal bench only forms one-fourteenth of the House of Lords; in the eighteenth century it formed one-eighth, and in the twelfth it formed six-sevenths of the entire House. Their moral influence must have been still greater than we should suppose from the numerical proportion. For more than half a century the episcopal bench, with one brilliant living exception, has not been occupied by any man of genius; scarcely by any man whose learning has gained him a European reputation. But in an age when laymen could rarely read, the bishops, as the only educated men among the peers, were naturally looked up to with considerable respect. Under these circumstances it seemed an obvious policy on the part of the crown to conciliate the bishops. Such was the course adopted by the German emperors: and such was the course adopted by the English kings. This was the policy of Henry I., who first subjected the diocese of St. David's and indeed a great part of South Wales, to the jurisdiction of the Archbishops of Canterbury. Hence it was that when our kings began to be pressed by the hereditary nobility, and by the growing power of the chartered towns, no expedient seemed more feasible to them than to strike an alliance with the bishops. This was the policy of Stephen, who in a great measure owed his throne to the archbishop of Canterbury, and to the bishops of Winchester and of Salisbury. Henry II., although he nearly lost his crown in the struggle with Becket, could think of no better means of consummating the conquest of Wales than that of allowing his successor, Baldwin, to travel through the country with all the pomp and authority of a metropolitan. Henry IV., whose doubtful title to the crown made him feel the insecurity of his position, conciliated the episcopacy by a very remarkable concession. By the old law of England, the bishops were not allowed the luxury of burning heretics, except by the authority of a writ issued by the king in council. But Henry IV. procured a law ordering that all heretics were to be judged by the bishop of the diocese, and, if found guilty, were to be burnt without any reference to the consent or even to the knowledge of the crown.[1]

Henry VIII., who to the advantage of a good title, added an indomitable will, was able to impose a yoke which the bishops bore with great repining. After the death of Wolsey, Henry prosecuted in the King's Bench the whole of the clergy, for having submitted to the legatine authority: and by holding out the terrors of a præmunire, compelled them to acknowledge him as supreme head of the Church.[2] But even Henry VIII. erected six new bishoprics—those of "Westminster, Oxford, Bristol, Gloucester, Chester, and Peterborough;" although, "after the incumbency of a single prelate, episcopal honours were denied to Westminster."[3] The respect paid to Wolsey was perhaps rather due to his legatine than to his archiepiscopal authority. But after his death Henry's chief advisers were Cranmer, archbishop of Canterbury, and Gardiner, bishop of Winchester (?). In a curious paper of instructions which the bishop of Chichester drew up for his clergy (in the reign of Henry VIII.), he distinctly tells them that disobedience to the king will be followed not only by punishment in this world, but also by damnation in the next.[4] His execution of Fisher impressed the bishops with an awe which that haughty body had not felt for centuries. But so far as principles are concerned, the most important of all his ecclesiastical measures was the nomination of Thomas Cromwell as Vicar General to the crown. By this appointment he set the example of elevating a layman above the heads of the church. But scarcely was this Rehoboam of England gathered to his fathers when the bishops made vigorous efforts to recover from the temporary depression in which he had held them. In this they were eminently successful. Henry had deprived them of nearly every vestige of their civil jurisdiction (?), but almost immediately after the accession of Edward an Act was passed to punish those who should speak disrespectfully of the sacrament; and it was carefully provided that the trial of such offenders should not be left to the ordinary jurisdiction of the courts of law; but that either the bishop or a deputy appointed by him should sit on the bench, and have a jurisdiction co-ordinate with that of the justices.

[1] At the very moment they were raising the bishops, they were also depressing the clergy.—[Memorandum by Mr. Buckle.]

[2] Soames' History of the Reformation, vol. i. pp. 279–281.

[3] Ibid. vol. ii. pp. 285, 286; also Strype's Ecclesiastical Memorials, vol. i. part i. p. 539.

[4] Strype's Ecclesiastical Memorials, vol. i. part ii. pp. 375, 376.

The great contriver of these measures was Cranmer, one of
those supple and designing characters in which revolutionary
periods are always fertile. This man, so long as Henry was
alive, never ventured to interfere in temporal, scarcely even in
spiritual concerns; but on his death, the minority of the prince,
and the factions into which the government was notoriously
divided, emboldened the archbishop to measures of unusual
energy. His first object was to control the clergy, which, from
the state of weakness into which they had fallen, he had little
difficulty in doing. It was [with] this view that he procured an
order forbidding all clergymen to preach without a license either
from the protector or from himself.[1] He drew up articles of
religion which all churchwardens, school-masters, and clergymen
were compelled to sign,[2] and he even prepared a complete body
of ecclesiastical law, the publication of which was only prevented
by the sudden death of Edward.[3] Cranmer usurped all the
functions of the state. When the celebrated question was agitated
as to the validity of the marriage contracted by the Marquis of
Northampton, the matter, instead of being tried by the ordinary
courts, was referred to a commission, of which Cranmer was the
president and the mouth-piece. During the reign of Henry VIII.
Cranmer, even after he had been raised to the archbishopric, had
so little power that he was more than once in want of money.
When Henry VIII. broke up the monasteries, the courtiers were
greatly enriched by the plunder. The archbishop, naturally
anxious to have some share in the spoil, solicited a part for one
of his own friends. But this request Henry refused to grant. In
the same spirit, when the bill for attainting Cromwell was presented to parliament, Cranmer would not risk the favour of the
king by voting against the judicial murder of a man whom he
knew to be innocent, and whom in the days of his prosperity he
had been glad to call his friend.

The canons most peremptorily ordered that the clergy should
on no account participate in judgments of blood; but the anxiety
of the archbishop to extend his political power, caused him to
disregard this humane law, and to sign the warrant for the execution of Seymour. Barton, bishop of Bath and Wells, had, for
some cause which is not mentioned, deprived his dean, John
Goodman. The dean, acting upon the advice of his lawyers,
sued him upon a præmunire, but the bishop, to make himself
perfectly secure, obtained from the king a full pardon for what he
had done. The judges, with their usual spirit, still persisted in
proceeding to trial, and when summoned before the Privy Council,

[1] Wilkins, iv. 27–30.        [2] Lingard, vii. 91, 92.        [3] Lingard, vii. 92.

represented that they were bound by their oaths to suffer the law to have its course. This, however, availed them nothing, for the government, determined to uphold the episcopacy, would not wait for a legal decision, but they deprived Goodman of his deanery, and not content with that, actually threw the unfortunate dean into prison, " for his disobedience and evil behaviour to the bishop."

By these and similar artifices, the archiepiscopal power was at length raised to so high a pitch that it seemed as if nothing could shake it; and the authority of Cranmer was as great under the administration of Warwick as it had been under that of Somerset, the great enemy of Warwick.

Mary, whose feeble mind naturally inclined towards the church, followed up with success the policy of Edward. Cranmer, indeed, paid with his life the penalty of his crimes; but the episcopal power, though it changed hands, did not lose ground. Mary found it impossible to restore the inferior clergy to their former position, but she at least determined to make every effort to consolidate the power of the bishops.[1] She made Gardiner knight of the garter, president of the council, and lord high chancellor of England, and on his death gave the seals to Archbishop Heath. What Edward had done for the Protestant bishops, that did Mary, and more also, for the Catholic bishops. Into their hands she threw all the powers of the state. She procured an act which rendered them independent of the crown (?), and sent to every diocese forbidding them to insert in any instrument the clause, " Regiâ authoritate fulcitus." She not only resigned the barren title of Supreme Head of the Church, but gave up its lands which were in the possession of the crown, and restored the first fruits and the tenths. The foreign ministers residing at her court complained that no business could be transacted except through the medium of the bishops. Every description of honour was lavished on the bishops. Immediately after her marriage with Philip was celebrated in the cathedral of Winchester, the royal pair regaled themselves by a splendid banquet, at which Gardiner, and Gardiner alone, was permitted to take his seat. If the life of Mary had been spared, it is probable that she would have built up the whole fabric of ecclesiastical tyranny, and Convocation had the audacity to propose that the statute of mortmain, which had been in force for nearly three centuries, should be repealed. To this indeed, even Mary did not dare to consent;

[1] A contemporary writer notices the contemptuous way in which, in the first year of Mary's reign, the bishops in Convocation treated the lower clergy. See Strype's Ecclesiastical Memorials, vol. iii. part i. pp. 75, 76.

but she caused the execution of them to be suspended for twenty years.

The people were accustomed to look on the bishops as the natural depositaries of political power. The Catholic bishops had been supreme under Mary, why should not the Protestant bishops be supreme under Elizabeth? If Pole and Gardiner were fit councillors for the first, why should not Parker and Grindal be fit councillors for the other? The very year after the accession of Elizabeth, a celebrated preacher, named Vernon, delivered a sermon before the queen, in which he publicly told her that the lands and revenues of the bishops must on no account be curtailed. Such reasonings, indeed, were natural; but the conduct of Elizabeth soon dispelled the illusion. The first step of her ecclesiastical policy was one at which Mary or Edward would have stood aghast with fear. She issued a commission for a royal visitation addressed to fourteen persons. The powers which by this commission were intrusted to the visitors were immense, and, as concerned the church, were supreme; but of the entire fourteen visitors, thirteen were laymen. In the very same year (?) she procured an Act of Parliament reannexing the tenths, first-fruits, &c., to the crown; and she immediately followed this up by another law, authorising the crown, on the vacancy of any see, to seize certain of its lands. The bishops had been in the habit of granting long leases, which bound their successors and enriched themselves; while the country was not unfrequently (?) called upon to make good the deficiency in the revenue of the succeeding bishops. But to this the queen determined to put an end, and the disabling or restraining statute, as it was not inaptly called, declared that all grants made by bishops for more than twenty-one years, or three lives, should be absolutely void.

These decisive measures were all adopted by Elizabeth within the first [twelve] months of her reign, and inspired the bishops with feelings of the most lively alarm. The statute by which the queen was to seize certain of their lands seems to have been that which most affected their minds. Scarcely had the bill become law, when they earnestly entreated Elizabeth not to enforce it. But the arguments which they used were not precisely such as would recommend themselves to her mind. They told her that when Egypt was pinched [by] famine, even Pharaoh would not touch the property of the priests; that when Artaxerxes had ordered the Jews to contribute towards the expenses of building the Temple, he had especially exempted the Levites from all charge; that Isaiah had distinctly prophesied that kings were to be nursing fathers, and queens nursing mothers of the church,

and that these circumstances had been particularly recorded by
the Holy Ghost, in order that they might serve as an example
for all future princes. Doubting, perhaps, whether these arguments would be quite conclusive, they added others of a still
weightier description, and the bishops of the Protestant church
of England were not ashamed to offer bribes to their sovereign
in order to induce her not to enforce a measure which had been
just passed by both Houses of Parliament, and had with every
circumstance of form received the assent of the crown. But the
queen remained firm: and the bishops, finding that they could
neither convince her nor bribe her, became anxious to force on
an immediate rupture with the Church of Rome; hoping that if
this was once achieved, she would be unable to hold the balance,
and would be obliged to throw herself into their arms. Sandys,
bishop of Winchester, had already remonstrated with her for
keeping a crucifix in her chapel. To this remonstrance she only
replied by threatening to punish his interference by deprivation;
but now the whole hierarchy (?) had fairly taken the alarm, and
they presented to her a formal address, requesting that images
should be removed from all the churches. But the queen saw
their drift, and determined not to be hurried into measures which
would drive the Catholics to despair, replied to their address by
a proclamation, forbidding the displacement of any image of
Christ or of his apostles.[1] Within a year after the death of
Henry VIII., Cranmer had obtained an order for having all
images removed from churches.[2]

The indignation of the bishops was great. Foiled at every
turn, they could scarcely restrain themselves within the bounds
of decency. "As far as my reading and information reaches,"
says Archbishop Parker, "it has been the custom of all ministers,
both Christian and Pagan, to countenance the ministers of religion; . . . . . but now it is our misfortune to be singled out
from the rest of mankind for infamy and aversion." His grace,
warming with his subject, even intimates a threat of resistance,
in language very familiar to the readers of ecclesiastical history.
"It would trouble me if the clergy should be forced upon in-
compliance, and declare, with the apostles, that we must obey God
rather than man." In 1582, the bishop of Coventry, in a complaining letter to the lord treasurer, writes: "I speak it with
grief; I receive injuries, and yet dare not complain, for fear of
the exasperation of men's minds, and mine own further trouble."
Archbishop Sandys reminded his hearers that "we must obey

[1] Collier's Ecclesiastical History, vol. vi. p. 322.
[2] Soames's History of the Reformation, vol. iii. p. 227.

princes, *usque ad aras*, as the proverb is; so far as we may, without disobeying God." In 1575, Whitgift indignantly declared "that the temporalty sought to make the clergy beggars, that they might depend upon them." In 1588, Sandys, archbishop of York, pathetically said: "These be marvellous times. The patrimony of the church is laid open as a prey unto all the world; the ministers of the Word, the messengers of Christ, are become despised by all people, and are esteemed as the excrements of the world." In 1573, Sandys, who was then bishop of London, writes to the lord treasurer: "But I am too weak; yea, if all of my calling were joined together, we are too weak. Our estimation is little; our authority is less. So that we are become contemptible in the eyes of the basest sort of people." The bishop of Ely, having greatly suffered from the determination of the queen to reduce his revenues, wrote to her in 1575, a very pathetic remonstrance, in which he humbly inquires "whether it was not troublesome enough that her Majesty's priests everywhere were despised and trodden upon, and were esteemed as the offscourings of the world, unless the commodities which they possessed were thus licked and scraped away from them?" In a sermon preached at St. Paul's in the middle of the reign of Elizabeth, Archbishop Sandys indignantly says: "Was there ever any time, any age, any nation, country, or kingdom when and where the Lord's messengers were worse entreated, more abused, despised, and slandered than they are here at home, in the time of the gospel in these our days? We are become in your sight, and used as if we were the refuse and parings of the world."

But all this availed nothing, except to confirm the queen in her views of the necessity of humbling the episcopal power. In these views she was warmly seconded by the Lower House of Parliament, where the spirit of liberty, which for nearly a century (?) had been completely stifled, was again beginning to rear its head. I have already mentioned some of the statutes which were particularly directed against the bishops, and they were now succeeded by others hardly inferior in importance.

.        .        .        .

While these great measures were in the course of being recognised as the law of the land, the queen was not slow to apply to the bishops individually the same principles which governed her general policy towards them. The bishops of Durham had for centuries enjoyed the privilege of receiving all estates within their see which were forfeited for high treason. This privilege was [now] first taken from them, and vested in the crown, *pro hac vice* as it was pretended; but I need hardly add that Elizabeth never allowed the right to slip from her (?).

The archbishops of Canterbury had always been in the habit,
much to their own profit, of felling timber in Long Beech Wood,
in Westwell.  But this, in strictness, belonged to the crown, and
when Parker began to cut the wood the queen caused a suit to be
commenced against him in the Exchequer, and the terrified
prelate was obliged, not only to abandon his claims, but to write
a most submissive letter to Elizabeth.[1]  Indeed, in order to
mortify the bishops, she did not hesitate to interrupt the ordinary course of law.  The bishop of Norwich deprived a certain
Dr. Willoughby of his benefice for not having subscribed the
Articles of Religion.  This, though perhaps a harsh proceeding,
was strictly legal ; but the queen caused a letter to be written to
the bishop, ordering him to restore Willoughby, and sharply rebuking him for this exercise of episcopal authority.[2]  Even in
the slightest affairs of life she exercised a similar authority, and
kept them in a thraldom which, to men of any spirit, would have
been insupportable.  Fletcher, bishop of London, married a
widow, the sister of Sir George Gifford.  The character of the
lady was unexceptionable, but the bishop had omitted to ask the
consent of the queen, and Elizabeth not only banished Fletcher
from the court, but obliged the archbishop of Canterbury to
suspend him from his episcopal jurisdiction.[3]  Only a few years
later (i.e. after Parker had been forbidden to cut down wood), a
precisely similar circumstance occurred to the bishop of London.
He, uninstructed of the treatment which Parker had received,
thought to enrich himself by selling some of the timber in his
diocese (?), and he actually felled a great number of trees.  But
he was immediately called before the council, in whose presence
the lord treasurer publicly and sharply rebuked him ; and, as
he showed some disposition to persevere in a conduct which he
had found so lucrative, the queen herself sent him a peremptory
order to cut down no more of the wood belonging to his see.

A few years later she ordered Grindal, archbishop of Canterbury, to suppress the prophesyings, as they were absurdly called.
His grace hesitated, and modestly wrote to her not to " interpose
your prerogative in ecclesiastical matters."  Elizabeth, who had
heard such language before, knew how to meet it.  She immediately sequestered the archbishop from his jurisdiction, confined
him to his house, and would most assuredly have deprived him
if he had not written a letter acknowledging the justice of the
punishment inflicted upon him.  And although the humbled
prelate thus preserved his see, the queen did not remove the

[1] Strype's Parker, ii. 43–46.            [2] Strype's Parker, ii. 158, 159.
[3] Strype's Whitgift, ii. 215, 216.

sequestration until he had made another and still more precise submission. Elizabeth, not content with this triumph over the head of the church, sent a circular letter to all the bishops, threatening them with punishment unless they immediately obeyed those orders about which Grindal had ventured to hesitate. In 1576, the bishop of Gloucester, being unable or unwilling to pay the queen 500*l.* which he owed her, she did not hesitate to order the sheriff to seize his lands and goods for satisfaction of the debt.

Even the ministers of Elizabeth caught something of her spirit, and used language to the bishops which half a century before, not even the proudest layman would have dared to employ. When the bishops ventured to resent such treatment from men whom twenty years before they would have almost scorned to notice, the queen never failed to support her ministers with all the power of her prerogative. The earl of Leicester had procured for a certain Dr. Gardiner a nomination to the archdeaconry of Norwich; but the bishop of that place, having already granted the presentation to one of his own friends, not only refused to admit Gardiner, but wrote to him a very scurrilous and threatening letter. The queen hearing this, adopted her usual course, and made so peremptory a communication to the bishop, that he, to his great mortification, was actually compelled to admit his opponent to the disputed archdeaconry in his own episcopal city.

When, on one occasion, the archbishop of Canterbury wrote an apologetic letter to Leicester, the earl, with marked contempt, took the letter from the hands of the messenger and put it in his pocket without reading it: " which contempt," says his pious biographer, " might justly be resented by him, being a person of such high dignity and honour as that of an archbishop of Canterbury." In 1584 Beal, clerk of the queen's counsel, a man of considerable and known ability, wrote a work, in which he treated the bishops with the greatest severity; and as if to show his utter indifference to episcopal authority, he sent what he had written as an acceptable present to Whitgift, archbishop of Canterbury. His grace, greatly moved, wrote to the lord treasurer, demanding redress for the insult which had been thus publicly put upon him. But little or no attention was paid to his complaints: Beal was allowed to retain his office; and I have not met with any evidence to show that he was ever reprimanded for his conduct.

Blackstone (*Commentaries*, 1809, iii. p. 54) says, that from 1373 all the chancellors were ecclesiastics or statesmen (but never lawyers), until Henry VIII., in 1530, promoted Sir Thomas More. After this, the great seal was entrusted to lawyers, courtiers, and churchmen indifferently, until, in 1592, Sergeant Puckering was made lord keeper; " from which time to the present the court of Chancery has always been filled by a lawyer, excepting the interval from 1621 to 1625," when the seal was entrusted to Williams, dean of Westminster, afterwards bishop of Lincoln.

By a long course of these and similar measures the inordinate pretensions of the bishops were at length reduced to something like a rule of reason. But the process was slow and onerous. There is a concentrated energy in ecclesiastical power, which renders it so tenacious of life that, when at all supported by public opinion, nothing but the most resolute conduct of the civil authority will prevent it from gradually arrogating to itself the entire function of the state. Indeed, if the episcopal bench of the sixteenth century could have boasted a single man of genius, or even of powerful will: if there had been seated on it an Ambrose or a Becket, the result of the struggle might have been fatal to the liberties of England. But it was not given to the feeble intellects of men like Parker and Grindal and Sandys to wrestle with success against a woman such as she who now occupied the throne. Within twenty years of the death of Mary, we begin to observe a marked change in the tone of their language. Forgetting the lofty language of apostolic authority, they adopted a tone of entreaty to which even the meanest of their predecessors would hardly have descended. The bishop of London complained to the council, "that the authority of the Church signified little; that the bishops themselves were sunk and lamentably disvalued by the meanest of the people." The bishop of Winchester declared that his order was treated with " loathsome contempt, hatred, and disdain."

At the same time, the execution of Mary, and consequent firm establishment of a Protestant prince on the throne of Scotland; the defeat of the Armada, the accession of Henry IV., the decline of the Spanish branch of the house of Austria, the consolidation of the Dutch republic, all these things, which followed each other in rapid succession, so strengthened the hands of Elizabeth, that the bishops despaired of recovering their power. Within [seven] months of the defeat of the Armada, Bancroft, who was one of the most violent persecutors of the Puritans, and who was afterwards raised to the archbishopric of Canterbury, delivered a very remarkable sermon.[1] This set discourse was not preached to

---

[1] In February 1588-9.

K

any mean assembly, but was delivered at St. Paul's Cross, where the Privy Council, the judges, and the bishops who might happen to be in town, formed part of the audience. Indeed, this sermon was looked upon as so important, that it was printed by authority (?); and in it we find a most distinct recognition of the supremacy of the civil power.

In the preceding reigns, the judges, with a few noble exceptions, had displayed towards the bishops a servility which was but too natural to their relative positions. But now, stimulated by the conduct of Elizabeth, they began to adopt a very different tone. In 1592 the judges solemnly affirmed that the supremacy of the sovereign was both spiritual and temporal, and that the regale, in its fullest extent, is inherent to the English crown. In individual cases they displayed the same spirit. In 1596 a clergyman named Allen was tried by Anderson, one of the assize judges at the city of Lincoln. According to the provisions of the statute law (?), the bishop of the place was seated on the bench, and some point of divinity being at issue, Allen appealed to him as his ordinary. But the days when such things were allowed had now passed by, and the judge—I quote the words of a contemporary—"entertained that speech with marvellous indignation, affirming that he was his ordinary and the bishop both, in that place, and daring all that should take his part."

The pretensions of the bishops, thus beaten back by the strong hand of the queen, now took refuge in one of the most impudent fictions which the hierarchy have ever attempted to palm upon the people. Compelled to relinquish the practice of power, they compensated their loss by exaggerating its theory. It will be understood that I allude to the divine right of episcopacy, a doctrine which first assumed a definite form towards the end of the sixteenth century. At present it will not be necessary for me to give any account of the rise and progress of this monstrous dogma, for as long as Elizabeth was alive there was no fear of its producing any injurious result. But under the wretched administration of her successor the doctrine was put forward with renewed confidence; and by infusing new life into the now wasted frame of episcopacy, it enabled the bishops to support the extravagant pretensions of the feeble pedant who then sat on the throne. How, in those evil days, the bishops loved the king, and how the king loved the bishops, until, in the next generation both king and bishops were swallowed up in that whirlwind of national rage which was excited by their united tyranny; these things, though deeply interesting, are connected with subjects which it does not fall within the compass of the present volume to describe.

But before Elizabeth died, her government, aided by the now rising class of common lawyers, had succeeded in erecting another barrier against the encroachments of these ambitious men.

.        .        .        .        .        .

I have thus endeavoured to convey to the reader an idea of the manner in which, during nearly half a century, the bishops were treated by the greatest sovereign that ever sat on the English throne. It may perhaps be brought as a charge against Elizabeth, that her proceedings towards them were marked by an appearance of passion which somewhat lowered her personal dignity. But although such a charge would be by no means devoid of truth, we must at the same time remember the peculiar circumstances in which she was placed in relation to them. The immense influence which, in an ignorant age, they naturally possessed, made them objects of legitimate suspicion to the executive government; while those who are best acquainted with their personal habits, will reluctantly confess that their moral qualities were not calculated to conciliate attachment, or even to disarm distrust. It is at all events certain, that while Elizabeth only despised the inferior clergy, she actually hated the bishops. She hated them for their meddling inquisitorial spirit, for their selfishness, for their contracted and bigoted minds. Indeed, this feeling in her was so strong that it showed itself at a moment when even the most violent of the passions are usually lulled. Only a few hours before her death, the archbishop of Canterbury, with some of the other bishops, waited upon her with the view of obtruding that spiritual advice which, from such men, she little cared to receive. Concentrating into a single moment the indignation of an entire life, she treated them, in the face of her court, with marked and biting scorn. " Upon the sight of them," says an eyewitness ( ? ) of this striking scene, " she was much offended, cholerically rating them, bidding them be packing, saying she was no atheist, but knew full well that they were hedge priests, and took it for an indignity that they should speak to her."

Into this and the preceding chapter I have endeavoured to compress the substance of an inquiry into the fortunes of the ecclesiastical power in England; and I have collected the materials for that inquiry from original documents of unquestioned authenticity. Those who owe their opinions to the traditions of education rather than to the exercise of their independent reason, will be seriously shocked at the picture which I have found it necessary to draw; and even among those who take a much higher view of human affairs, there are many who still conceive, not only

κ

that a national church paid by the state supplies a cohesive principle to the great fabric of society, but that whatever tends to
weaken the authority of the church tends in the same proportion
to diminish the prosperity of the nation.  This last opinion is
indeed so rapidly disappearing under the influence of extending
knowledge, that it will be hardly necessary to spend any time in
refuting it ; but we must treat with more respect the theory of those
who consider the church as a conservative principle, and who, without affirming that it has any necessary connection with the happiness of the people, are yet deeply concerned at the attacks which
are now constantly made upon it.  This theory, which is in itself
temperate, and which is advocated by men of undoubted ability,
is one which, with the most unfeigned respect for many of its
supporters, I can by no means adopt ; and as the discovery of
general principles, by an appeal to history, forms a part of my
original plan, I shall now endeavour to explain the circumstances
under which this theory has arisen, and to show how far it is
capable of general application.

The opinion, then, with which we have now to do, appears to
me to owe its rise to the principle of association, or, what in this
case is the same thing, to the operation of imperfect induction.
Because the institution of an endowed church has, in nearly every
European country, performed the most undoubted services to
civilization, men, with their natural proneness to generalisation,
have supposed that it has done this in virtue of some original
principle, which will produce the same results under any combination of events : and having made this natural assumption, they
look with alarm on any proposition for destroying an institution
which has caused such beneficial effects.  It might be a sufficient
answer to this to appeal to the history of England in the sixteenth
and seventeenth centuries, when we find the power and reputation
of the established church almost always bearing an inverse ratio
to the power and reputation of the country at large : rapidly
sinking under the brilliant and orderly administration of Elizabeth, and as rapidly rising under the disgraceful and disorderly
government of the first English Stuarts.  Indeed, in the course of
this work I shall show that the horrible wars which, in the middle
of the seventeenth century, devastated England were quite as much
owing to the impudent pretensions of the ecclesiastical hierarchy
as to the weakness and perfidy of that bad man who then sat on
the throne.  But without thus anticipating views which I have
not yet offered to the world, it will be more agreeable to the
scope of this work if I attempt to draw my arguments from a
wider survey of general history.

In all countries which have not reached a high point of civilization there is a marked tendency either to despotism or to anarchy.
In the former case, when the government is too strong, an
endowed church does much to neutralise power; and I do not
remember a single instance in history of a secure and durable
despotism, in which the sovereign was not priest as well as king.
The institution of castes, by separating the two powers, tempered
despotism. It is thus that in ancient Rome the liberties of the
people were not finally destroyed until the emperor was worshipped as a god. In the other case, when the government is
too weak, an endowed church performs many of the functions of
the ordinary executive. This was seen in Spain in the fifth
century, and in France in the tenth and eleventh centuries, when
the councils of the church were alone strong enough to protect
the civil power against the inroads of a great oligarchy. In
these two instances, then, when the sovereign is likely to tyrannise
over the people, or when the people are likely to oppress the
sovereign, we find that an endowed church is highly useful in
maintaining the balance; and, as we know from history, it has
generally adopted the wise and benevolent policy of supporting
the weaker side. In the middle ages the influence of the church
was almost invariably exerted on the side of order and peace. It
was the church which encouraged the liberation of slaves.

.            .            .            .            .            .

Such are the obligations which Europe owes to the church; and
for such obligations Europe should be grateful, but she should
not be superstitious. Such, however, is the natural propensity
of man to cling to what has once supported him, that we must
not be surprised if the church is reaping the benefit of her
former acts, and if whole nations are willing to believe that what
has already protected them is able and willing to protect them
again. When the idea of the utility of an established church
became firmly [rooted] in the popular mind, it was strengthened
by the influence of tradition and the habits of education, and by
a feeling, not devoid of truth, that whatever has long existed
must have a certain merit, since experience has shown that it is
capable of meeting some of the exigencies of mankind. The
great majority of men, who never think on such difficult
questions, are always content with that which their ancestors have
handed down to them; and even among the few who are in the
habit of reflecting, there is a marked indisposition to admit, or
even to discuss, new conceptions.

When society has advanced beyond a certain point there grow
up a number of checks, which perform those offices which the

church had before performed. These checks, by which the great organism of society is kept in repair, are a free press, a constitutional jealousy of the public towards the governing powers, the general diffusion of education, and the like. These checks are amply sufficient to supply the place of the old ecclesiastical checks; and this, which I suppose will be universally admitted, leads us to some very important considerations.

The great principle that every man is the best judge of his own interests was, in the hands of Beccaria and Adam Smith, fertile of the most splendid results. This principle, which is only suitable to an educated nation, has not yet been carried out to its legitimate consequences; and if we apply it to the theory of an established church, it is not easy to see how that theory can stand the test. The perfection of government is the maximum of security with the minimum of interference : and everything which unnecessarily lessens the responsibility of individuals checks the progress of civilization. The great majority even of the most civilized nations, have no real education, except that which is forced on them by the bustle and friction of life: if these difficulties of life are too much softened, if the alternatives of choice are too much straitened,

.          .          .          .          .

The state, by holding up one form of religion as particularly excellent, lessens the responsibility of those who still have a religion to choose ; and whatever diminishes responsibility must check inquiry. If the state thinks too much, the people will think too little. This, independently of those economical reasonings, which of themselves amount to demonstration, is a strong argument against those foolish men who, under the name of Protectionists, are seeking to force upon the country a return to the barbarous maxims of a superannuated policy.

The opinions which will be formed on this subject will of course be regulated in the great majority of cases, not by reason, but by prejudice. I cannot, however, avoid noticing one remarkable circumstance which, as connected with the subject, is of considerable value. The two greatest events of modern times in which the two chief nations in the world first fairly felt their own strength, are separated by a period of 150 years; but in both instances they were immediately preceded by the entire destruction of the national churches of their respective countries. In the English Revolution of 1640, and in the French Revolution of 1790, it was found impossible to retrieve the ancient liberties of man without first sweeping away the whole of the ecclesiastical hierarchy. In both cases the next generation, smarting under

the sting of anarchy, thought it advisable to restore that which
had just been destroyed. But as they restored it in a mitigated
form its pressure has not been so obvious; yet I am inclined to
consider that it has been and still is injurious. The time is now
not far distant when the whole question of an endowed church
will be reconsidered. Whatever may be the solution of this
great and difficult problem, this much at least is certain: that
the fanatical attempts which are now making in this country to
exaggerate the power of the church tend to strengthen the hands
of its opponents, and if persevered in will insure its final overthrow. These attempts proceed from a faction which, though
under the name of Puseyism it has earned an ignominious
celebrity, is in reality nothing but a malignant developement of
the worst form of Arminianism. Indeed, there is not to be
found, even in the black records of ecclesiastical history, a single
instance of opinions so unsocial, so subversive of all order, as
those which these men are now shamelessly obtruding upon the
world. The mischief they have done is incalculable. They
hang like an incubus on the frame of society, paralysing its
movements, corrupting its morals, and like a canker eating into
the very organs of its life. In the present unformed state of
philosophic history, it is perhaps impossible to predict with
absolute certainty what will be the fate of these conspirators
against the liberties of mankind. But it is at least certain that
unless they are able to beat back that tide of knowledge which is
now so quickly flowing, they will not succeed in inducing men to
bow the neck before the throne of an ambitious priesthood. For
my own part I feel confident that we shall be able to wipe out
this plague-spot from among us; and when that is done, when
we have succeeded in beating back the enemy from the gate, we
shall know the place that these men will occupy in the annals [of
the country].

# FRAGMENTS.

## POSSIBILITY OF HISTORY.

I WRITE the history of England because it is *normal*: Government has little interfered, and our insular position has prevented intellectual disturbance.

.   .   .   .   .   .   .

In the same way, not only has great light been thrown upon human anatomy by the study of comparative anatomy, but we have actually discovered several principles respecting the physiology of man, by applying to it laws suggested by a general study of organic life, even in its vegetable form.

.   .   .   .   .   .   .

After giving an account of the different opinions about free will, say : it might seem from these considerations that history is a *fatalism* ; and so it would be if we knew the statical laws as well as the dynamical. Then give a view of statical desiderata, and then say everything is referrible to intellectual and moral phenomena. Then add that the intellect of a people overrides all ; or, perhaps I ought *first* to say this, and then add : " From these considerations we might think history fatalism ; and so it would be if we knew statics ; but, as we do not know statics, we must lay the foundations of them by detailing manners, which are residual phenomena. To raise history to a science, we should have to take in the universe, which it is impossible for one man to do. And although this may eventually be done by a series of successive generalisations, there is a still greater difficulty, viz., the want of *statical science*.

.   .   .   .   .   .   .

Mind most important. It might, therefore, have been supposed that mind should be first studied ; but the difficulties are too great. . . .

It has been generally supposed by the very few persons to whom the idea of a philosophic history has occurred, that the proper method for creating it [is] to assemble the principal external facts, and discover their laws by treating them according to the ordinary resources of inductive logic. But there is one circumstance which will convince us that in this subject such a method is impracticable. All the inductive sciences have been created from materials which are under our immediate control. They have been raised by a series of experiments in which, by successively varying the circumstances and by carefully noting the facts, we have been able to eliminate the disturbances, and thus discover the law. For the inductive method, therefore, two things are necessary: first, that we should vary the experiment, and, secondly, that we should note the particulars. But in history we can do neither. We can never, with a merely scientific object, perform upon any nation a series of experiments; and even if we could do this, the complication would be found so enormous that no single intellect could seize the whole of the facts to which the experiment would give birth. Since, therefore, the inductive method of treating history is impossible, we are driven to deduction, which is the only other resource for the discovery of truth with which we are acquainted.

In induction we study the effect in order to learn the causes. In deduction we study the causes in order to learn the effects. This last is the method which has been pursued in geometry, which is the science of co-existences; and in astronomy, which is the science of successions. In both these instances the phenomena are beyond our reach. We have, therefore, been compelled to set out from certain principles, and by a syllogistic process bring under them those facts which we can observe, but upon which we can by no means experiment. It only, therefore, remains for us to treat the phenomena of history in the same way as we have treated those of astronomy; and, with a view to this, our first inquiry must be, how we are to get at those principles from which we must pursue our synthetic reasonings This, which to some metaphysicians would appear a very easy task, does, in reality, present the most formidable difficulties.

Since the movements of human nature, so far from being capricious, are always the same under the same circumstances, it would seem that the proper method is to learn first the laws of the mind, and deductively bring under them all the great phenomena which society presents to our view. But here we are met by a difficulty which, in the present state of our knowledge, is, I think, insurmountable.

.   .        .   .

Dugald Stewart has defended at greater length than any other writer the capacity of metaphysics for being inductively investigated; and it is curious to find that he even supposes that the mind can be not only observed but experimented on. His remarks are by way of reply to the Edinburgh Review.[1] He says[2] that in his metaphysical inquiries he has pursued the method of "imitating, as far as I was able, in my reasonings, the example of those who are allowed to have cultivated the study of natural philosophy with the greatest success." At p. xxvii. he speaks of "the analogy between the inductive science of mind and the inductive science of matter." At p. xxxvi. he strangely says that, even in external nature, "the difference between experiment and observation consists merely in the comparative rapidity with which they accomplish their discoveries, or rather in the comparative command we possess over them as instruments for the investigation of truth. The discoveries of both, when they are actually effected, are so precisely of the same kind, that it may safely be affirmed there is not a single proposition true of the one which will not be found to hold equally with respect to the other." And yet at p. xliii. he says that analysis of association, memory, &c., is an experiment, and that "the whole of a philosopher's life, indeed, if he spends it to any purpose, is one continued series of experiments on his own faculties and powers;" and yet again, at pp. xlv., xlvi., he explains away this boasted experiment as a mere observation ! ! !    At p. xlv. he says, "Hardly, indeed, can any experiment be imagined which has not already been tried by the hand of Nature;" and at p. xlv. he says, "that above all the records of thought preserved in those volumes which fill our libraries, what are they but *experiments* by which Nature illustrates, for our instruction, on her own grand scale, the varied range of man's intellectual faculties, and the omnipotence of education in fashioning his mind." It is singular that Cousin, who often says that metaphysics is an inductive science, tells us in one place[3] that the inductive method of Bacon and Newton is insufficient, because it will only give us the causes of phenomena.

.        .        .        .        .        .

On these grounds I have most unwillingly arrived at the conclusion that the resources of metaphysicians are at present inadequate to grapple with those great problems which history presents us for solution.

[1] Vol. iii. p. 269 et seq.
[2] Stewart's Philosophical Essays, Edinburgh, 1810, 4to. p. 111.
[3] Histoire de la Philosophie, 1er série, tome iv. pp. 390, 391.

But it appears to me that there is another mode of proceeding, which has escaped the notice of that small number of eminent thinkers who have paid attention to this great subject, but which I believe to be the only one that is practicable in the present state of our knowledge.

The method to which I allude, and which I shall adopt in the present work, is this: I shall, in the first place, by a general survey of modern universal history, arrive at certain conclusions, which, although they cannot be looked upon as scientific truths, will constitute uniformities of succession or of co-existence which will be of the nature of empiric laws, increasing in value in proportion as we increase the extent of the surface from which they are collected. These laws I then propose to employ deductively, and, descending in[to] a particular period of history, verify them by a special investigation. Their verification will consist of two parts. In the first place, I shall convert them into those principles of the mind which are not only admitted by metaphysicians, but which are obvious to every man of ordinary understanding. The other part of the verification of those laws will consist in showing that they are compatible with the moral, economical, and physical phenomena which characterise the period under examination. With this view I propose, for the sake of clearness, to divide what I have called the special history of society into certain classes, not according to any arbitrary standard, but according to the actual condition of things—as, for instance, clergy, aristocracy, agriculturists, manufacturers, and the like. This division will only be adopted as a scientific artifice, and with the view of showing [that] the principles which I have arrived at from a general observation of history are applicable to all the different classes of a special period. If such a proof can be made out, it is evident that such a series of parallel reasonings will be more confirmatory of the original principle than the ordinary method of investigation. If, for instance, I can show that a certain law which I have arrived at by a general consideration of history, is in any large period separately applicable to all the great classes of society, I shall have made out a case very analogous to that in which the general laws of natural philosophy are applied to mechanics, hydrostatics, acoustics, and the like. This is also the way in which general physiological principles collected from the whole of organic nature have been applied to man, and the nutrition of plants throws light on the functions of human nutrition. At the same time, and by way of further precaution, I shall, while investigating periods of special history, take occasion, when very important principles are at stake, to recur to general

history, and I shall not hesitate to collect evidence from other
countries, in order to prove that it holds good under the most
different conditions.   If this is accomplished with any degree of
success, I shall not only have pointed out some of the great
laws which regulate the movements of nations, but I indulge
a hope that, by a reflex process, some light will be thrown
upon the general constitution of the human mind, and that
some contribution will have been made towards the formation of a basis on which metaphysical science can be hereafter
erected.

It appears then to me that history can only be satisfactorily
treated by applying to its special periods those general principles
which have been derived from a comprehensive survey of it as a
whole; and that before making this application, it will be advisable to simplify the phenomena of the smaller periods by breaking
them into divisions, which will correspond to those classes that
are always found in every civilized society.   Having laid down
these preliminary views, the next thing is to consider what those
branches of knowledge are with which we must be acquainted in
order to apply the general principles to the particular period.   It
is evident that, looking upon society as a whole, it admits of two
sorts of divisions : a division into classes, and a division into
interests.   The nature of the first set of divisions is very obvious,
because it is constantly passing before our eye.   But the nature
of the division into interests is much more obscure ; and this
seems to arise partly from the circumstance that men generally
love their interest more than they love the class to which they
belong, and partly because, to understand the different interests,
it is necessary to have a much more comprehensive knowledge
than is required in understanding the feelings of the different
classes by which those interests are put in movement.   And yet,
since it will be necessary, after having viewed society analytically
in reference to classes, to complete the process by viewing it
synthetically in reference to the aggregate of its interests, it is
evidently important to come to a preliminary understanding as to
what those interests are, and as to the nature of those sciences by
which their workings are explained.

There are, so far as I can perceive, in every civilized society,
six great interests, in the preservation of which a wise government will be careful to interest the whole of its subjects, but
which will from selfish motives be always especially protected by
certain classes.   These interests are, Religion, Science, Literature,
Wealth, Liberty, and the great principle of Order, by which I
understand a conserving impulse, which is exceedingly dangerous

in the contracted minds of ordinary politicians, because it makes them oppose themselves to the healthy development of society, but which, notwithstanding, has more than once saved this country, and is the only protection we possess against the anarchical licence into which, unhappily, liberty is so prone to run. It is evident that the most perfect society will be that in which each of these great interests is developed to the highest possible pitch that is compatible with the free existence of the others; and that the great problem in politics is to effect this for the benefit of the entire nation, which will be done occasionally though vigorously by administering here a little check and there a little aid; but that, upon the whole, the general opinion is correct, that a wise government will employ the smallest possible interference which is compatible with the preservation of the entire fabric. But without entering into a consideration which will be made very apparent in the course of this work, we must now consider those great interests in the order in which I have stated them, and inquire into the nature of those resources which the present state of our knowledge supplies for their general elucidation.

1st. *Religion.*—The view I have given of the progress of the intellect in France, in England, and in Germany, will, I think, have established this important principle—that there is no necessary connexion between the clergy as a class and religion as an interest; and that scepticism is a preliminary condition necessary to the reception among nations of the most important truths of religion, by which I understand toleration, charity, and peace. Every man who is not interested in the subversion of his country must desire that these opinions should be universally received in their fullest extent; but the concurrent experience of universal history will show that their promulgation has always been preceded by a marked diminution of the ecclesiastical power. These are the two great principles which we learn from history respecting the great interest of religion; but if, for additional information, we turn to theology, we shall find that it has been treated in so contracted a spirit as to furnish us with the materials indeed for a science, but not with any of the laws of the science itself. It is quite possible for a man to have mastered all that immense learning which is connected with ecclesiastical history, and still remain without the knowledge of a single law respecting the rise and fall of religion; unless, indeed, he possess a mind of sufficient power to enable him to make out those laws from the resources of his own understanding. This backward and infantine condition of theology arises partly from the fact that it has been

nearly always monopolised by that class who think that they have
an interest in making reason yield to tradition, and partly from
the fact that, even among laymen, no one has yet arisen who is
competently acquainted with all the great religions of the earth,
from a large study of which we can alone expect to discover those
general principles which, when verified by special applications,
would rise to the dignity of scientific truths. But, besides these
two causes of the imperfection of theological science, there is yet
a third, which, though under the advance of knowledge it is
becoming less powerful, still produces most injurious results.
This is the habit of looking upon theology as an exceptional
branch of knowledge, which is not to be treated according to the
ordinary methods of discovery. This miserable superstition, by
which men voluntarily renounce the exercise of their reason, will,
so long as it exists, render us incapable of understanding the influence of religions upon nations, and the reaction of nations upon
religions. And yet so strong is the dominion of ancient prejudice,
that men, even in our own times, writers of ability and of undoubted
honesty, are not ashamed in professedly scientific works to lay
down the maxim that no one should presume to attack the national religion, or in any way to disturb the acknowledged principles of an established faith. To me it appears that this arbitrary
interference with the jurisdiction of the human reason is not only
injurious to the formation of scientific habits, but is unworthy of
the relation which we bear to that Great Being who is the cause
and the centre of created things. I am as firm a believer in the
truths of religion as any of those men who are afraid of letting
in the light of day upon their opinions. But I know of no ultimate object in inquiry except the discovery of truth, to which
everything else must be subordinate. And this I do say, that not
only traditions and dogmas, but even the awful question of the
existence or non-existence of the Deity, blasphemous as it is if
conceived in a jeering spirit, should be handled, with tenderness
indeed, but with unlimited freedom. It will, of course, be op-
tional with us to reject the argument, and to recur to that individual and transcendental belief which has often been the last
resource of the subtlest minds. But we must never attempt to
stifle what we suspect that we are unable to answer: nor can I
conceive anything more repugnant to the primary principles of
religion than a belief that the Almighty First Cause can regard
with displeasure the exercise of that great and lofty curiosity of
which He first implanted the seeds, and under whose protection
we reap the fruits.

The method of History must be to study the phenomenon separately in that country where it has been most developed. Thus, for instance, to construct a theory of the Fine Arts. The country most celebrated for music is Bohemia.[1] The question must then be put, what is there peculiar in Bohemian history which is not found in other nations? Talvi only mentions[2] that Bohemia was the only country where the Reformers did not oppose themselves to the Fine Arts.[3] He also says[4] that the Bohemians are the only Slavic race to whom the institution of chivalry was known.

## TRIUMPH OF INTELLECTUAL OVER PHYSICAL LAWS.

Tocqueville[5] says, " En même temps que les Américains se mêlent, ils s'assimulent; les différences que le climat, l'origine et les institutions avaient mises entre eux, diminuent; ils se rapprochent tous de plus en plus d'un type commun." The greater facility of travelling and diminution of national and religious prejudices helps this. We are less dependent on seasons since we have repealed our absurd corn-laws, and since harvest and carriage is easier, and freight less expensive. In the same way the progress of chemistry will eventually equalise all soils. Before the Fire of London, in 1666, the most unhealthy months were August and September, because the plague and dysentery were so fatal. But dysentery is now rarely fatal, or plague either, so that "the most fatal months in London are now January, February, and March."[6] Government by attempting to diminish poverty has increased it. It is, I think, probable that the original directions of national character were the result of physical laws; but that now the European intellect is so active as to have overbalanced those laws; and I shall hereafter show that the salient differences in national character are traceable to intellectual antecedents.

Without pretending to anything like an exhaustive survey of physical agents, I will show that their influence is diminishing, by taking the most prominent, as climate, food, soil, pestilence, famine. In many cases physical phenomena, like coal and iron, are *occult*, and then their influence depends on the *knowledge* men have of them. In other instances phenomena are not occult,

[1] See Talvi's Slave Nations, New York and Lond. 1850, pp. 148, 149, 389.
[2] P. 183.    [3] See also p. 184.    [4] P. 159.
[5] Démocratie en Amérique, vol. iii. p. 232.
[6] Journal of the Statistical Society, vol. iii. p. 267 and vol. viii. p. 182.

but still their influence depends on the *opinion* we form about them. By increased protection against climate, in houses and clothes, we are neutralising its effect. We are also introducing from other countries non-indigenous food, and thus assimilating the diet of men. The excess of male over female births does not depend on climate : but the excess is less in towns than in the country ;[1] and among legitimate births the proportion of boys is greater than among illegitimate ones.[2] In France the excess of male births is greater in muscular employments—as in agriculture—than in the more sedentary occupations of commerce and manufactures.[3] It is doubtful whether hot or cold climates are most favourable to fecundity ;[4] so that we may abstract climate and broadly say that the number of births depends on the number of marriages. Births are influenced by the seasons; but, it is observable that this and all other influences of climate are more felt in the country than in towns; the latter having, as Quetelet observes, more means of correcting the inequality of temperature.[5] National character must depend on mental laws because we find that savages who are still entirely under the dominion of the physical world, have no national character ; all of them being equally vain, crafty, cruel, superstitious, and improvident. The mortality in the different parts of Paris is determined, not by the physical condition of the different parts, but by the state of wealth and comfort of the inhabitants.[6] The average length of life is evidently of the greatest importance, for on it depends the nature of crime, since violent offences are committed by the young, fraudulent ones by the old. On age also depends the spirit of accumulation ; hence interest of money ; hence wages ; hence increased democracy ; and this depends more on man himself than on climate. Thus we find that in the same places, i.e. where nature is the same, mortality has diminished, and some of the worst parts of European India are now less unhealthy than three centuries ago even the best parts of Europe. Man has increased his longevity by his intellect ; i.e. by cultivating the ground, and thus changing the temperature ; drying morasses ; giving himself more healthy food and plenty of it ; ventilation ; improved medicine. It used to be supposed by Montesquieu that the use of fish increased fecundity, but this is now known to be false.[7] And the same thing was formerly supposed of potatoes ;[8] but the truth is, we know of no physical influence

---

[1] Quételet, Sur l'Homme, tome i. pp. 42, 43, 45.
[2] Ib. pp. 49, 50.
[3] Ibid. tome i. pp. 99, 180. See also tome ii. pp. 321, 323.
[4] Ibid. tome i. pp. 152, 153.
[5] Ben Jonson and Shakespeare.
[6] Ib. pp. 46, 47, 48.
[7] Ib. pp. 72, 75, 76.
[8] Ib. tome i. p. 106.

that increases population; it depends on foresight and habits of caution. Compare the increase in America and Ireland. Population should be increased, not by increasing the births, but by diminishing the deaths. And this on two grounds. In the first place every child costs an enormous sum of money before he can *repay* society.[1] So that the prosperity of a country depends not on multiplication but on conservation. In the second place, the more adults there are the greater the chance of intellectual discovery. The effect the great plague in the fourteenth century had upon every branch of morals may be learnt from Boccacio and Villani and Hecker. But now the most frightful plague causes fewer deaths than the ordinary mortality of diseases did formerly. The same remark holds good of famine. Comte says that as nations advance the differences between individuals increase.[2] This, if true, I may perhaps use as an argument for the increased influence of mental laws. Famines are now extinct. Charles Comte[3] has brought forward evidence to show that those tribes which, from the badness of their country are most exposed to famines, are precisely the most treacherous, suspicious, and cruel. Montesquieu thinks drunkenness peculiar to hot climates, but this is an error.[4] Whatever be the natural difference of soils, the progress of knowledge is assimilating them to one common standard by chemical manures, &c. We correct climate and food; as Liebig shows, this begins early in history by an excess of carbon. It is said that owing to the activity of the English and the increasing improvement of the country, wild beasts, and particularly tigers, are rapidly becoming extinct in the North of India. This was observed by Bishop Heber in 1824 and 1825.[5] Heber distinctly ascribes this to the English. The inevitable law is non-assimilation. In America the Red Indians are becoming extinct. We are conquering India, and Russia invading Turkey; and we and [the] French are meeting in Africa. Our command over nature is now so great that famines and pestilences, in the old sense of the word, are impossible. Coffee, the great cause of temperance, is now commonly grown. Mr. Stephens, when in Costa Rica in 1840, says that " Potatoes, though indigenous and now scattered all over Europe, are no longer the food of the natives, and but rarely found in Spanish America."[6] Liebig[7] pithily says, " Science

[1] See curious estimate in Quételet Sur l'Homme, tome i. pp. 144, 145.
[2] Traité de Legislation, tome i. pp. 291, 292.　　[3] Ib. tome ii. pp. 274, 275.
[4] Ibid. tome ii. p. 318.
[5] See Heber's Journey through India, vol. ii. pp. 14, 15, 127, 193, 232.
[6] Stephens's Central America, vol. i. p. 302.
[7] Letters on Chemistry, p. 23.

L

renders the powers of nature the servants of man, whilst empiricism subjects man to their service." Liebig says,[1] " The clearing of the primæval forests of America, facilitating the access of art to that soil, so rich in vegetable remains, alters gradually but altogether its constitution." He says,[2] " The origin of epidemic diseases may often be referred to the putrefaction of great masses of animal and vegetable matters." Notwithstanding the grandeur of nature, the people of North America are not more superstitious than the English, and are less so than the Scotch and Irish. Wealth has only two elements, the physical element of the productions of nature and the intellectual one of skilled labour. In the earlier stages of the world the physical element triumphed, as in India, &c., but now the intellectual one is in the ascendant, and Europe is richer than Asia.

It is a familiar remark that now men suffer little in cold climates from cold, in hot climates from heat. By our precautions we have baffled nature. This is said of Russia.[3] From the Institutes of Menu there is " ground for a suspicion that the famines which even now are sometimes the scourge of India, were more frequent in ancient times."[4] The progress of knowledge, by explaining the most marvellous phenomena, is *equalising* the wonders of nature, so that even in the United States there is not more superstition than in England. In North Africa the French are advancing, in South Africa the English; and in Asia the Russians are advancing in North West Asia. " The outposts of Anglo-Saxon civilization have already reached the Pacific."[5] " The total amount of steam power in Great Britain is equal to about 4,000,000 men,"[6] and " a bushel of coals which costs only a few pence in the furnace of a steam-engine, generates a power which in a few minutes will raise 20,000 gallons of water from a depth of 360 feet, an effect which could not be accomplished in a shorter time than a whole day by twenty men working with the common pump."[7] Read Babbage's Economy of Manufactures. Ireland is far better supplied with rivers than England, but, says Somerville,[8] " There are 2,990 miles of canal in Britain. . . . . It is even said that no part of England is more than fifteen miles distant from water communication." The laws of earthquakes, &c., are being discovered ; hence one great cause even in tropical countries, is dying away, and our wealth depends

[1] Letters on Chemistry, p. 211.
[2] P. 230.
[3] Custine's Russia, tome iii. p. 310.
[4] Elphinstone's History of India, p. 49.
[5] Somerville's Physical Geography, vol. i. p. 223.
[6] Ib. vol. i. p. 300.
[7] Ib. p. 313.
[8] Ib. vol. i. p. 380.

less on our mines than on our own energy. Tea being brought into Europe has diminished intoxication.[1] The first civilized parts of Europe were the most fertile—Greece, Turkey, Italy, and Spain; but now improved agriculture bears the palm. The potato is now generally cultivated in Asia and Africa.[2] Even in Ireland, the strongest case of all, the potato, has been remedied by the pestilence, and one physical evil thus counteracted another.

Begin account of triumph of intellectual laws by saying that the chemical, physiological, and economical laws I have laid down are *certain*, whether or no any illustrations from history are good or bad. But, like all laws, they in their applications become *tendencies*; and I shall now prove that as civilization advances, although the law remains intact, the tendency becomes fainter. End the chapter by saying that we and the French are even civilizing Africa—not from love of war, but from energy.[3] Wheat is now grown in India, and so are potatoes. The progress of knowledge has made barren land fertile, and turned unwholesome marshes and sand into populous cities. The old civilization of North Africa was Phœnician, now it is French. As to food affecting character nothing is known, and there is reason to think that food only acts by those large social laws I have pointed out. In some parts of Soudan, Mahommedanism has only recently penetrated, but now it has reached to 'Zinder, west of Lake Tchad.[4] Richardson, whose experience is well known, says,[5] " only foreign conquest by a power like Great Britain or France can really extirpate slavery from Africa." In Mandara, south of Lake Tchad, the inhabitants are Mahommetans.[6] "The greater part of the natives of Kordofan prefer Islamism."[7] Pallme says,[8] "I have heard through several authentic sources that there are but few provinces in the interior of Africa where Mahommedanism has not already begun to gain a footing."[9] The Arabs, now driven back into their old quarters, have relapsed into their old state. On the entire absence of mechanical skill, even in the Hedjaz, see Burckhardt's Travels in Arabia, vol. i. p. 266. Burckhardt says[10] even of their holy city, "Not a bookshop or a bookbinder is found in Mecca." And

---

[1] See an inaccurate remark in Somerville's Physical Geography, vol. ii. p. 156, and on coffee, p. 171.

[2] See Common-Place Book, Art. 1486.

[3] On the probability of the French civilizing the desert of Sahara, see Richardson's Travels in the Sahara, vol. i. p. xxix.

[4] Richardson's Mission to Central Africa, vol. ii. pp. 105, 205, 219.

[5] Ib. vol. ii. p. 275.

[6] Denham's Central Africa, p. 117.

[7] Pallme's Travels in Kordofan, p. 184.                     [8] Ib. p. 190.

[9] See p. 350.                                               [10] Vol. i. p. 302.

at vol. ii. p. 275, a similar state of things at their other holy city, Medina. On the other side, namely, in Oman, there is no sort of literature.[1] In Europe, nature more languid and less extreme; soil less fertile; climate less hot; nature less majestic, and thus inspires less awe. The so-called Republics of South America are not democratic.[2] Now the accumulated energies of Europe are forcing themselves upon the faded remnants of old civilization and destroying them. "Egypt formerly fed 7,000,000 of people, and provided grain for exportation; now she with difficulty sustains 2,500,000."[3] In Europe, mild and healthy climate lowers profits and raises wages; hence democracy. Then show that this industrial energy is also aided by nature being generally less *grand* and oppressive; and that in Europe the physical laws are constantly in abeyance, and intellect more and more continues its encroachment on matter. The wheat of Europe is a dear food.[4] Without the least evidence wheat is supposed to have originated in Palestine.[5] In Italy and in Spain most (?) earthquakes and volcanoes, and there have been nurtured worst forms of Christian superstition. Azara[6] well says that in America nature is larger and more powerful than in Europe. The whole of America absorbed by the United States an offshoot of Peru. Wheat is grown in Thibet.[7] In 1852, it is said[8] that "printing-presses have been set up all through the East India Company's territories." No part of Europe is within the tropics, nor is [there] anywhere cheap food. The soil is not too fertile, and it is certain that rain diminishes as we advance from the Equator.[9] European civilization the first in which both men and women had influence; though in the case of Greece the Asiatic contact somewhat weakened the influence of women. When I mention the superstition of Spain and Italy, say that in America high wages are one of the causes of democracy. Darwin[10] says, "I think there will not in another half century be a wild Indian northward from the Rio Negro" (the Negro is in east of Patagonia). On approaching extinction of other barbarous races see Darwin, pp. 520, 534. In Italy and Spain superstitions, the arts, painting, but *not*

[1] See Wellsted's Travels in Arabia, vol. i. pp. 318, 319. And Niebuhr's Description de l'Arabie, pp. 161, 188, 189.
[2] See on the Republics of La Plata, M'Culloch's Geographical Dictionary, vol. ii. p. 516.
[3] Journal of Asiatic Society, vol. vii. p. 280.
[4] See Meyer's Geography of Plants, pp. 292, 294, 295.
[5] See Lyell's Geology, p. 585.         [6] Amérique Méridionale, vol. i. p. 75.
[7] Journal of Asiatic Society, vol. xii. p. 377.
[8] Ib. vol. xiii. p. 211.
[9] See the table in Prout's Bridgewater Treatise, p. 296.
[10] Journal, p. 122.

poetry. The only remedy to this *deductiveness* is physical studies, which no Asiatics ever had—nothing but astronomy. Even Alison [1] confesses that after Napoleon's expedition to Egypt our decisive superiority over barbarians is no longer a disputable matter. On the great mineral treasures of Spain see Liebig's "Letters on Chemistry," p. 499. The Esquimaux are "gradually wasting away." Simpson's Discoveries on North Coast of America, p. 309. Sadler [2] says, "The most prolific surface beyond all comparison in Central Europe was, on the unanimous authority of all writers, especially agricultural ones, originally and naturally one of the most sterile. I need not say I allude to the Netherlands;" and *now* Belgium is the most thickly peopled. "The annual produce of iron in round numbers is in Great Britain 1,500,000 tons," or about 500,000 made in England, 500,000 in Wales and Monmouthshire, 500,000 in Scotland." [3] But it availed little that those things were in the bosom of the earth until the skill of men drew them forth. It is said that we could grow silk in England and Ireland, so as to be independent of foreign supply. [4] Plenty of coals in China; [5] and so there always were in North America.

Famine is now " impossible." [6]

---

## DISPUTES AMONG DIFFERENT BRANCHES OF KNOWLEDGE.

AFTER giving an account of the use of statistics, political economy, metaphysics, &c., add the following:—

It might have been supposed that as soon as these important accessions to history began to be studied, history itself would receive a corresponding increase of strength and dignity. But, unhappily for the interests of knowledge, these subjects had scarcely assumed a distinct form when men, not seeing the connection between them, committed the serious error of treating them as separate and independent sciences. We thus have metaphysicians, political economists, statisticians, writers on jurisprudence, writers on the history of philosophy, on the history of

[1] History of Europe, vol. iv. pp. 652, 653.
[2] Law of Population, vol. i. p. 95.
[3] Report of British Association for 1848, p. 15.
[4] Report of British Association for 1849, p. 82. And see Report for 1839, Transactions of Sections, pp. 87–89.
[5] See Davis's Chinese, vol. iii. p. 133.
[6] Herschel On Natural Philosophy, p. 65.

literature, on civil history, on military history, on ecclesiastical
history. All these we have in abundance. (Speak here of European literature generally. In England there is a great deficiency
of original writers on many of these subjects.) But all of them
exaggerate the utility of their own pursuits, and undervalue those
in which they are not engaged. Instead of working together as
friends and allies, they struggle together as rivals and enemies.
Instead of showing how all knowledge converges, they do everything to increase its divergence. The consequence of all this
has been most mischievous, and that in two different ways. Not
only has much been left undone, which, by a more comprehensive
process might have been achieved, but men of large and philosophic minds have been so offended by the contracted spirit in
which these studies are pursued that they have neglected them
for the more attractive pursuits of physical science. This explains
what would otherwise appear a very unnatural feature in the literature of this great age, that a vast majority of the finest living
intellects are occupied in interrogating the phenomena of the
inorganic world and the laws by which those phenomena are regulated. The result has been that topics of the most surpassing
importance—the extent and functions of the human mind, the
origin and condition of human knowledge and the degree of certainty to which it may pretend, the foundation of morals and
religion, the action of law and customs upon religion and its reaction upon them, the connection between the riches of a country
and the virtue of a country, the diffusion of education, the causes
of an increase of crime, the accumulation and the distribution of
wealth,—many of these subjects which form the top and pinnacle
of all knowledge, have been, with a few well-known exceptions,
abandoned to those inferior men who conduct the practical business of the country, and fondly expect that they will receive their
final solution amidst the agitations of a popular assembly.

A few instances of the contracted spirit in which some of the
most important topics have been treated by some of the ablest
writers will serve to illustrate my meaning. It is an undoubted
truth that everything which tends to hamper the movements and
limit the responsibilities of individual men is in itself a serious
evil; but, like all other evils, should be practised if the balance
of advantage is on its side. Now it will be generally admitted
that men who have power are likely to abuse it, and that the
tendency of the upper classes is to oppress the lower classes.
Bearing these facts in mind, we will suppose that we are called
on to give an opinion upon what seems a very simple question—
the propriety of landlords inserting clauses in their leases which

shall bind the tenants as to the management of their farms. Now, on the one hand, we have the fact that landlords being better educated than their tenants, and having a more permanent interest in the land, are more likely to know and recommend the best course for increasing the productiveness of the soil. Here then we have a strong argument in favour of the insertion of stringent clauses in leases. But, on the other hand, there arise grave moral and political doubts as to the propriety of any measure which not only increases the power of landlords, but, by diminishing the responsibility of the tenant, lessens the necessity which he would be under, if his choice were unconditional, of informing himself as to the best modes of cultivation. A sound opinion can only be given by weighing these conflicting arguments and comparing the moral gain with the economical loss. (I by no means admit that there would necessarily be an economical loss if leases were unfettered; but I concede it in order to simplify this illustration.) But instead of doing this, the moralist obstinately shuts his eyes to the argument in favour of controlling the tenant; and supposes that he shows the whole question when he shows the folly of limiting the alternatives of men, and thus depriving them of what may be called the practical education of life. Just in the same way the political economist as obstinately refuses to recognise the moral argument, and tests the whole question by an inquiry as to which method will most increase the productiveness of the land. The consequence is that moralists and political economists, instead of combining together with a common aim, despise each other's objects; and by this lamentable disunion the breach between these two great sciences is every year becoming more hopelessly irreparable. In the same spirit some eminent authors have estimated different epochs by drawing the standard from their private studies. Even in the more abstract branches of moral knowledge a similar course has been adopted. M. Cousin, who is beyond all comparison the greatest metaphysician that France has possessed since the death of Descartes, has struck out a very beautiful theory of the philosophy of history, of which I shall presently give a detailed account. It now only concerns me to mention that this great thinker despises statistical and physiological science.

. . . . . . .

The real causes of the rise of Holland are not yet known. It is idle to ascribe it merely to liberty and industry, for other nations have been free and laborious without being great. A celebrated German writer ascribes their great wealth to the augmented demand for commodities caused by the influx of gold into

Europe, the price of which commodities he supposes the Dutch were able to fix.[1]  This is a striking instance of the impossibility of writing history without a knowledge of political economy.

. ... .

## PHYSIOLOGY.

THE strong prejudices that exist against systems which even savour of materialism are, perhaps, a natural reaction against the exaggerated philosophy of such writers as Mandeville, Helvetius, and Lamarck.  And yet it cannot be denied that such prejudices are very unfavourable to the general progress of knowledge. Because the supporters of a particular school of metaphysics have laid down that the habits of man are entirely the result of his physical organisation, modern writers, indignant at such a dogma, have fallen into the opposite extreme, and have denied the existence of any such influence.  It has always appeared to me that the metaphysician is incapable of deciding this question without calling in the aid of the physiologist.  A single instance will illustrate my meaning.  It is well known that the great object of food is to remedy the waste of the body, which it does by supplying fibrine to the tissues, and hematine, globuline, and serum to the blood.  The greater part of the process by which this is accomplished is perfectly understood ; but the effect produced on the tissues and on the blood by different food still remains to be ascertained.  That, supposing other things equal, the state of the chyme is regulated by the nature of the food, is now universally admitted ; and there is great reason to believe that the chyle is equally susceptible.  If this is the case, if the chyle is really modified by the nourishment which supplies it, then it seems hardly possible to believe that the blood can escape the contagion. A few well directed experiments would set the question at rest ; and, should it appear that the blood of a single man is affected by his food, it will follow that the blood of an entire people must be affected by their national food.  The chemist would then step in, and would show that certain states of the blood are incidental to certain diseases.  Having proceeded thus far, we should inquire into the connection between diseases of the body and peculiarities of the mind—we should inquire, for instance, to what diseases the poet was most subject, and to what the mathematician—he who most cultivated the imagination as compared with him who most

[1] Schiller's Werke, band viii. pp. 15, 16, Stuttgart, 1838.

cultivated the intellect, popularly so called. Having thus built up a chain of facts, the possibility of which none who have studied the subject can deny, we should be in possession of some main principles by which we could eliminate the influence of national food upon national character. It would then only remain for the antiquary to furnish us with a history of the different foods to enable us to apply our principles to elucidate the history of the human mind.

.    .    .    .    .    .    .    .

M. Damiron observes, " La philosophie de M. de Tracy ne saurait être considerée comme une théorie satisfaisante, elle pèche par sa base en se fondant sur la physiologie." [1]  Now this may or may not be true. All that I say is that in the present state of our knowledge it is not yet certain what *is* the real base of philosophy.

Except by the means of physiology, we shall never be able to estimate the effects, if effects there are, caused by the difference of races.

In 1804, Sir James Mackintosh, who had received a medical education, writes from Bombay, "Dr. Moseley's paradox I now perfectly understand—that the diseases of hot countries arise chiefly from cold. No doubt cold is the immediate cause of most of them ;" i.e., he means people are too eager to enjoy the coolness when it comes.[2]

The result of Sir James Mackintosh's observations in India were to make him believe that the Hindoos were of an inferior race.[3]

Lawrence[4] says, " To lay down the laws of the animal economy from facts furnished by the human subject only, would be like writing the natural history of our species from observing the inhabitants of a single town or village."

We have some very curious evidence of the physical effects of moral degradation in Ireland.[5]

Fletcher, in his elaborate essays on Moral and Educational Statistics, supposes that there is in different races a different tendency to crime.[6]  It has been observed[7] that in all parts of the world there is a great mortality among the negro troops.

[1] Damiron, Histoire de la Physiologie, tome i. p. 113.
[2] Memoirs of Sir James Mackintosh, edited by his Son, 8vo, 1835, vol. i. p. 211.
[3] See his letter to Degerando, in Memoirs of Sir James Mackintosh, by his Son, 1835, i. 294, 295.
[4] Lectures on Man, &c., 1844, p. 60.
[5] See Prichard's Physical History of Mankind, vol. ii. p. 349.
[6] Journal of the Statistical Society, vol. x. 203, and vol. xii. pp. 226-228.
[7] Ibid. vol. i. pp. 428, 429.

A remarkable fact is that " the proportion of boys born among the Jews is much larger than among Christians." [1]

Whatever may be the influence of race, all our evidence shows that intellect is equal. As to the negroes, Gregorie first showed this. As to the Hindoos, no one will doubt their power who has looked into their profound metaphysical inquiries; and for their *present* ability, see Journal of Statistical Society, vol. viii. pp. 109, 236, 255.

The climate of Mauritius is " unfavourable to the negro constitution, while it does not appear to have any decidedly evil influence on that of Europeans." [3] The fecundity of the Icelandic women is extraordinary, they often having twenty children.[3] In India, unlike Europe, there is an " immense excess of males over females." [4]

Fletcher has no doubt of the influence of race on crime.[5]

---

## CLIMATE.

TOCQUEVILLE[6] observes that in the southern states of North America the climate makes labour very unpleasant; hence slavery, and hence, I may add, all the evils that slavery brings. And Tocqueville remarks[7] that in those hot countries the culture of rice is dangerous to health, and would hardly be undertaken by free men. Besides this,[8] tobacco, cotton, and sugar require in their cultivation *constant* care: there is a premium on domestic slavery. In hot climates the phenomena are more sudden, alarming, and startling—hence men are more superstitious. An important effect of climate is that when it lowers the mortality, it diminishes the accumulating spirit, raises profits, and lowers wages. Hence no democracy in hot climates and no scepticism. Lunacy rare in tropical climates.[9] The decline of Rome has been accompanied by a change in the climate.[10] " We believe, indeed, that it will be found wholly impossible, except under peculiar circumstances, to carry on the culture of sugar on its present

[1] Journal of the Statistical Society, vol. ii. p. 268; see also ix. p. 81.
[2] Ibid. xii. 390.
[3] Ibid. xiv. 8, 10.                                [4] Ibid. xv. 327.
[5] Ibid. xii. 236.
[6] Démocratie en Amérique, vol. iii. p. 170.       [7] Ibid. p. 171.
[8] Ibid. p. 172.
[9] Statistical Society, vol. viii. pp. 62, 63.      [10] Ibid. xv. 173.

plan in tropical countries by the agency of *really* free labourers." [1]

In England the temperature does not produce much effect in
determining the relation of the different classes of disease, "with
the exception perhaps of those which form a measure of the activity of the sexual passion, which were in excess during the
hottest months of the year, a fact which corresponds with and
corroborates our experience of the influence of the seasons on
crime against the person." [2] More rape, I suppose, in summer.
Montesquieu, I think, says that in the East the intellectual and
physical advantages of women occur at different times. In the
tropics, the earthquakes, tempests, constant danger from wild
beasts, &c., alarm men; and they even deify wild beasts. In hot
climates, nature being favourable, invention is not necessary. But
to this, slavery being added, there arose that apparent civilization
found in Arabic palaces. While a warm climate renders labour
painful, it also renders thought and invention unnecessary. Hence
a low standard of comfort, which lowers wages and perpetuates
tyranny. But as the fertility of the ground secures *some* leisure at
an earlier period of society than men can find in cold climates, we
find that the Asiatics produce *some* thinkers and philosophers at
an earlier period than cold countries.

Climate does not affect strength, causes danger, and therefore
superstition. In cold climates men too busy in getting food to
think.

In hot [cold?] countries it is believed that hell is cold: and it
has been ingeniously doubted whether metempsychosis could have
risen in a hot climate. Comte [3] says that Montesquieu did not,
properly speaking, consider the influence of climate, but merely
the immediate influence exercised by the temperature of the
atmosphere. Comte never notes the *indirect* influence of climate,
which Laing has so well pointed out. In hot climates, nature
being bountiful, man is not obliged to use foresight. He says [4]
that Montesquieu borrowed his remarks from Chardin, and he
himself got it from Hippocrates, Diodorus Siculus, and Bodin.
In hot countries men are short lived. Heber [5] says drunkenness is
rare in India. And in 1824 he writes: [6] "The general sobriety of
the Hindoos, a virtue which they possess in common with most
inhabitants of warm climates."

Symes, when at a great public festival at Pegu, observed with
surprise that the Burmese of all classes were assembled in great

[1] Journal of Statistical Society, vol. xv, p. 232.   [2] Ibid. vi. 148.
[3] Traité de la Législation, vol. ii. p. 122.   [4] Ibid. 116.
[5] Journey through India, vol. ii. p. 486.   [6] Ibid. vol. iii. p. 355.

numbers, " without their committing one act of intemperance, or
being disgraced by a single instance of intoxication."[1]  Climate
does not affect strength.  Look at Laplanders and Esquimaux, and
the powerful Galla.  Kohl[2] says of the Baltic provinces of Russia,
" In countries where the different seasons glide mildly into one
another, there are always a hundred resources and make-shifts to
supply a particular scarcity.  Nowhere, consequently, is the agriculturist tormented by so many anxious cares as in these countries ; and nowhere does the population fluctuate so continually
between plenty and want."  Neander[3] says of Egypt : " From
hence Monachism spread to Palestine and Syria, where the climate
was more favourable to such a mode of life, and where too, even
at an earlier period, among the Jews much that was analogous had
already existed."  The American climate is said to be favourable
to the increase of nervous diseases.  Connect this with my notes
on the way nervous diseases and plague caused superstition.  Unhealthy climates shorten life : hence an excess of young men :
hence a cause of the ardour and imprudence of the Americans.
See my America.  Unhealthy climates weaken the energies and
desire of accumulation.  See on this Political Economy.  Bancroft[4] observes that there is no country where work can be carried
on out of doors so regularly all through the year.  Wright[5] says
of the eighth century, " In the legends of this period the craters
of volcanoes were believed to be entries to hell."  Custine[6] observes that the Russians are great imitators, but have no originality.  In the Penny Cyclopædia (article *Climate*) it is said[7] that,
as a general rule, the temperature of countries *between* the tropics
and the poles depends on latitude ; but that *in* the tropics this
rule does not apply.  For this reasons are given, and " this reasoning is not contradicted by experience.  The countries in which
the greatest degree of heat is experienced lie near the Tropic of
Cancer.  They are the countries on the banks of the Senegal, the
Tehama of Arabia, and Mekran in Beloochistan."  Feuchters-
leben[8] says, " There are numerous examples of the reciprocal
action of the respiratory and psychical functions.  The courageous
and cheerful disposition of the inhabitants of mountains, in comparison with that of the inhabitants of lowlands, and especially of

---

[1] Symes's Embassy to Ava, vol. ii. p. 35.
[2] Russia, 8vo, 1844, p. 363.
[3] History of the Church, vol. iii. p. 333.
[4] History of American Revolution, vol. ii. pp. 55–59.
[5] Wright, Biog. Brit. Lit., i. 342.
[6] Russie, iv. 317, 318.
[7] Vol. vii. p. 260.
[8] Medical Psychology, p 178.

those who breathe the close air of towns, is well known."
Broussais [1] says that, having practised and made autopsies in the
north, as well as in the south, he has found that the more men
live indoors the more numerous are the aberrations of nutrition,
as great tumours and other organic alterations. But by living out
of doors, and inhaling and excreting in open air, the body becomes condensed and less liable to those "monstrueuses déforma-
tions" and "aussi les cadavres sont ils en general secs et maigres
dans les pays chauds." Mrs. Somerville [2] says, "The average age of
a nation, or the mean duration of life, has a considerable influence
on the character of a people. The average age of the population
of England and Wales is twenty-six years seven months. By the
census the average age of the population of the United States of
North America is twenty-two years two months. In England
there are 1365 persons in every 10,000 who have attained fifty
years of age, and, consequently, of experience: while in the
United States only 830 have arrived at that age: hence in the
United States the moral predominance of the young and passionate is greatest." [3]

The thunder, the hurricane, and whirlwind, the imposing
majesty of nature, forests, mountains, and deserts. There is an
interesting note on the Law of Hurricanes in Somerville's
Physical Geography, vol. ii. p. 52. Mrs. Somerville [4] says, "Whirl-
winds in tropical countries occur in all kinds of weather, by
night as well as by day, and come without the smallest notice."
At vol. ii. p. 31, she says, "Professor Dove has shown from a
comparison of observations that northern and central Asia have
what may be termed a true continental climate, both in summer
and in winter, that is to say, a hot summer and cold winter; that
Europe has a true insular or sea climate in both seasons, the
summers being cool and the winters mild." Connect this with the
*immense size* of Asia, Africa, and America; hence men become
irregular, fitful, and capricious—as everyone may understand by
noticing the *impetus* of habit and beauty of undeviating method.
Get Johnson's Physical Atlas, highly praised by Mrs. Somerville. Wilkinson observes that in hot countries vegetables are
more wholesome than meat; but he evidently knows not why.
In hot climates *perhaps* women are precocious; but at all events
experience is wanting in very young wives. In hot climates
clothes, &c., are less costly. [5] End the laws of climate and pre-

[1] Examen des Doctrines médicales, vol ii. p. 311.
[2] Physical Geography, vol. ii. p. 401.
[3] See my America. [4] Physical Geography, vol. ii. p. 55.
[5] Guizot, Civilization en Europe, p. 97.

cedo the laws of religion by saying that in Europe accumulation
of wealth was, until the intellect came into play, much slower
than in Asia; but this fully compensated by the fact that in
Europe climate makes men more hardy, more methodical, and
more intellectual.    Diodorus Siculus,[1] describing a volcanic
irruption, says, "The violent irruption of the fiery matter is so
wonderful, that it seems to be the immediate effect of some
Divine power."    Hot climate shortens life, and thus raising
interest, will, if other things are equal, lower wages.    The very
vague and contradictory opinions respecting the influence of
climate, which have been put forward by different writers, from
Hippocrates to our own time, are collected in two elaborate
Dissertations by Sir W. Ainslie.[2]    Elliotson[3] says, "The average
life of all ranks in the Peninsula in India falls one-eighth below
what it is in Europe, and the sixtieth year is seldom attained
there."    On the fear caused by thunder, see Erman's Travels in
Siberia, vol. i. p. 101.

—  —

## CRIME.

Mr. FLETCHER, in his valuable Essays in vols. x. xi. xii. of The
Statistical Society's Journal, has proved that in England there
is a correspondence between the increase of education and diminution of crime.    But this, I believe, is because with us education is not compulsory.    In France,[4] Sweden, and Prussia it
*is* compulsory, and therefore produces no good, for force cannot
check a disease by attacking its symptoms.    Even if it were to be
shown that education and diminished crime *did* go together, it
would be doubtful which is the cause :  but we know from Guerry
that in France the reverse is the case.    The real thing is the
increased comfort of men, and then their increased independence
and foresight.    It is not that crime is more common now than
formerly, but that it is more commonly punished.    Formerly the
people sympathised with the offender ;  now they sympathise with
the law, because it is more merciful.    Besides this, we have a
better police.    Education is *evidence* of comfortable circumstances ;  but what is the use of *simulating* the symptom, as the
French and Prussians do.    We might as well think that we could

[1] Book xi. chap. 27, by Booth, vol. i. p. 430.
[2] Journal of Asiatic Society, vol. ii. pp. 13-42 ; vol. iii. pp. 55-93.
[3] Human Physiology, p. 1038.
[4] Error.—[Ed.]

give a corpse the ruddy glow of health by painting its face. Who ever heard of a merchant or a banker picking a pocket or stealing a fowl ? but no one will say that all merchants are moral men. They have no temptation. Crimes apparently increasing are in reality diminishing. For, in the first place, we only register a few crimes, and those not the most important. 2nd. The real measure of crime in a moral point of view is temptation, and temptation is now greater than it ever was. The most active cause of crime is drunkenness, and this is caused partly by misery, partly by ignorance, which makes men think it a *remedy*, and partly by a want of intellectual occupation. Crime may be considered socially or morally. In the last case, it has not increased so fast as temptation. In the former case, society is certainly *safer* now than it ever was, as any man must know who has read light literature, &c. Game-laws, which have made poachers in order to amuse gentlemen. On crimes indirectly caused by poaching, see Journal of Statistical Society, vol. x. p. 58. In vol. xii. pp. 231–236, Mr. Fletcher sums up the results of his elaborate Essays on Moral Statistics.

For a remarkable instance of a regular ratio between crime and education see Quételet, Sur l'Homme, vol. ii. p. 180. For tables of crime in France and Belgium see Quételet, Sur l'Homme, vol. ii. pp. 167, 169, 174, 214, 298, 313.

In the same country the difference in crime will depend on the changes of society, the price of food, &c. In different countries we must make allowance for the different state of the police, the difference in manners, morals, and knowledge ; and, above all, the fact that some countries punish as crimes those acts which other countries allow to pass with impunity.

On the influence *age* exercises over crime see Quételet, tome i. p. 20; tome ii. pp. 227–234, 238, 239, 242. Journal of Statistical Society, ix. pp. 224–226 ; xiv. p. 356; ii. pp. 329–330.

On the influence of *seasons* over crime, see Quételet, Sur l'Homme, tome ii. pp. 211, 212, 244.

The chaplain of a great prison in Connecticut told Mr. Abdy "that the generality of convicts were in point of intellect below mediocrity."[1] Laing[2] well says that no men are so moral as the Londoners, for they have to struggle more with temptation ; and what is virtue but temptation conquered ? Should we praise a savage for not committing burglary where there are no houses—for not being a pickpocket where men wear no clothes? The

[1] Abdy's United States, Lond. 1835, vol. i. p. 94.
[2] Laing's Notes of a Traveller, 1st series, pp. 281, 282.

diminution of crime is solely due to the people, and depends on them far more than on government. Thus in America the police is wretched, but such is the sympathy of the people with the government that in *no country*, says Tocqueville, does crime so rarely escape.[1]

In England, in 1838, we hear,[2] "It will probably excite some astonishment that one child of eight years old, two of nine, and eight of ten, should be imprisoned, even under commuted sentences, for three years." Crime committed for the sake of finding a home in prison see Statistical Society, vol. ii. p. 103. Very few young criminals have both parents alive.[3] Drunkenness caused by an *ignorant* belief that without spirits and beer strength to work cannot be kept up.[4] And yet most crime is caused by drunkenness.[5]

In an able and interesting paper on Norfolk Island, it is said that the convicts there have no fear of death, never having an idea that they have committed any moral offence;[6] and "not to have committed some great offence is often considered to indicate a want of spirit."[7] In England and Wales, from 1805 to 1842, crime continued constantly to increase; but in 1843, 1844, and 1845, steadily decreased.[8] This was the result of prosperity. Even in 1846, it is admitted that the lower orders were goaded into crime because in London they had no civil rights, the practical operation of the law leaving them "wholly remediless."[9] Tables of crime afford no evidence of its increase, but only of its detection.[10] More females are acquitted than males.[11]

The greater the amount of misery and depression, the greater the amount of drunkenness.[12] "The tendency to crime in the male sex five times greater than in the female sex."[13] Crime diminishes as education increases.[14] Crime caused by want of employment,[15] and by poverty;[16] and it is greater where there are large farms and the lower classes have no land.[17]

Mr. Fletcher, in summing up the result of his elaborate Essays

[1] Tocqueville, Démocratie en Amérique, tome i. pp. 170, 307.
[2] Journal of Statistical Society, vol. i. p. 242.  See also note at vol. ii. p. 89.
[3] Ib. vol. vi. pp. 153-254.          [4] Ib. vol. vii. p. 241.
[5] Ib. vol. i. p. 124; vol. iii. p. 335.     [6] Ib. vol. viii. p. 29.
[7] Ib. vol. viii. p. 48.              [8] Ib. vol. ix. pp. 177, 179, 180.
[9] Ib. vol. ix. p. 298; vol. x. p. 47.   [10] Ib. vol. x. p. 39.
[11] Ib. vol. x. p. 43.                [12] Ib. vol. xi. pp. 133, 134.
[13] Ib. vol. xi. p. 153.
[14] Ib. vol. ii. p. 98; vol. iii. p. 332; vol. ix. pp. 233, 234, 235, 236; vol. x. pp. 197, 316, 327; vol. xi. pp. 141, 143, 146, 155; vol. xii. pp. 152, 154, 202, 219, 229, 230.
[15] Ib. vol. v. p. 266.
[16] Ib. vol. iii. pp. 289, 200; vol. xiii. pp. 64, 70; vol xiv. p. 233.
[17] Ib. vol. xiii. pp. 64, 68.

on Crime and Education in England says, " A great excess of crime is observed to follow every considerable *access* to the price of food."[1]

I can scarcely entertain the doctrine enunciated by Socrates and defended by Plato, that " no one is voluntarily wicked."[2]

---

## MIDDLE STATE OF EUROPEAN HISTORY BEFORE THE SIXTEENTH CENTURY.

THE first great improvement was the Crusades, which, by making Europe *one*, accustomed the chroniclers to take a large view of affairs. Then came the Scholastic Philosophy, which made Europe *logical.* The rise of poetry *drew off* the imaginative men from history, and thus there became less fiction and more dryness, i.e. chronicles. Observe on this that *all* history is at first poetry, i.e. ballads. Then came the rise of towns and civic corporations in the thirteenth and fourteenth centuries, which first made historians aware of the importance of *men.* Then, in the fifteenth century, we have in Commines the first historian who cast a penetrating eye on human affairs; the first who separated them from the speculations of the cloister. Carlyle[3] says, " The Troubadour period in general literature, to which the *Swabian* era in German answers"; and[4] he says, " The era of the Troubadours, who in Germany are the Minnesingers, gave place in that country, as in all others, to a period which we might name the didactic; for literature now ceased to be a festal melody, and addressing itself rather to the intellect than to the heart, became, as it were, a school lesson." This then was the epoch of the understanding, when men became *logical* and *practical*; and, as Carlyle says,[5] " Fable, indeed, may be regarded as the earliest and simplest product of didactic poetry, the first attempt of instruction clothing itself in fancy. . . . But the fourteenth century was the age of fable in a still wider sense; it was the age when whatever poetry there remained took the shape of apologue and moral fiction. Hence," says Carlyle,[6] " the tales of Boccaccio, the fables of Boner, and the narrations of Hugo." Schlegel[7] says that early in the sixteenth

[1] Journal of Statistical Society, vol. xii. p. 233.
[2] Ritter's Hist. of Ancient Philosophy, vol. ii. pp. 139, 195; vol. iv. p. 589.
[3] Miscellanies, 3rd edit. Lond. 1847. Vol. ii. p. 274.
[4] Ibid. p. 282.       [5] Ibid. p. 300.       [6] Ibid. p. 301.
[7] Lectures on the History of Literature, vol. ii. p. 100.

M

century it became usual to turn "the subjects of the old chivalric
romances into epic poems;" but "in Spain things took a different
turn, and poetry became daily more and more historical in its
theme." This we find in Ercilla and in Camoens. This, I suspect, arose from the fact that in Spain poets and historians
were military men and nobles. Poets were also actors. There
was no division of labour, and history remained in a chronicle
state. Commines was to Froissart what Macchiavelli was to the
Italian chroniclers, and what Thucydides was to Herodotus, i.e.
the psychological began to triumph over the descriptive. This
was the consequence of the *division of labour*, a step which
it was necessary to take in history, but which has been carried
too far. Another corruption of history is the development of
*invention*, for savages rarely have *imagination*. The study
of classical literature injured superstition by showing the superiority of the Pagan writers to the Christian writers, and this
first told in Italy where the associations were more fresh, and
where scepticism therefore arose. Whewell observes that architecture made men *clear*, and I may add that it, like poetry and
painting, *drew* off from history imaginative men. But in Spain
this *drawing* off never took place. Why not? The crusades
increased the stock of fables, and all the fictions of the East were
suddenly let loose upon Europe. Mr. Laing [1] has noticed the
greater spirit of *adventure* introduced into literature since the
first crusades. The crusades stimulated the European imagination, the last faculty developed among civilized people, and thus
prepared the way for the rise of an independent imaginative class,
as architects, painters, &c. This was the greatest service done
by the crusades; for generally the imagination is a late form of
intellectual development, but the crusades, by accelerating it,
quickened the progress of Europe. Blanco White, who was
learned in such matters, says that in the different legends the
same miracles are ascribed to different saints.[2] In Kemble's
Saxons in England,[3] there are some instances of the same story
being related on different occasions in different countries, ·and
among others the tale of Dido and Byrsa is related of Ragnor
Lodbrog, and the Hindoos declare that we obtained possession of
Calcutta by similar means. Kemble says,[4] "Had Ivanhoe not
appeared, we should not have had the many errors which disfigure
Thierry's Conquête de l'Angleterre par les Normands.[5] The

---

[1] Sweden, p. 52.
[2] White's Evidence against Catholicism, p. 191.　　　　[3] Vol. i. pp. 16, 17.
[4] Saxons in England, vol. i. p. 373.
[5] For William Toll, see Kemble's Saxons, vol. i. p. 422.

formation of towns encouraged, as I shall presently state, the progress of scepticism, and besides this, gave scope to architects, which drew off the fancy, and, as Whewell shows, first made men's ideas steady. Raymond Lully, in the thirteenth century, is one of the very first who attacked the Aristotelian and scholastic philosophy.[1] But Roger Bacon, born in 1214, was still more remarkable.[2] Roger Bacon himself says that it was in A.D. 1230 that the Aristotelian philosophy first became generally known and, as it were, fashionable.[3] But Whewell strangely says,[4] that the adoption of this philosophy by the Dominican and Franciscan orders "in the form in which the angelical doctor had systematised it, was one of the events which most tended to defer for three centuries the reform which Roger Bacon urged as a matter of crying necessity in his own time." Another circumstance which aided the increasing precision of men's minds was the study of law. Whewell says,[5] "Gratian published the Decretals in the twelfth century, and the Canon and Civil Law became a regular study in the Universities soon afterwards." He says,[6] "The indistinctness of ideas was first remedied among architects and engineers;" for if their mechanical ideas had not been correct their works would have failed. Leonardo da Vinci, who died in 1520, aged 78, is the first instance of this. Flassan[7] observes that the crusades increased geographical and statistical knowledge. Flassan says,[8] that Louis XI. first introduced the custom of having *permanent* ministers at foreign courts—"Avant lui les ministres n'avaient que des missions temporaires et determinées." See some very striking remarks in Vico.[9] Vico says that barbarians always aggrandise and extend *particular ideas,* and thus while the poets make their gods and heroes bigger than other men (and I may add make the patriarchs long lived), so in the middle ages the features of Jesus Christ and the Virgin are of a colossal grandeur. In such times, says Vico,[10] men do not *reflect,* and therefore they cannot *invent*; and even so great a man as Dante represented in the Divina Commedia *real* persons. And, says Vico,[11] "Jamais les grecs et les latins ne prirent un *personnage imaginaire* pour sujet principal d'une tragedie." And [12] "Chez les latins *mémoire* est synonyme d'*imagination* (*mémorable* imaginable dans Terence); ils disent *comminisci* pour feindre, imaginer: *commentum* pour une fiction, et en italien *fantasia* se prend de même pour *ingegno.*"

[1] See Whewell, Philosophy of the Inductive Sciences, vol. ii. p. 157.     [2] Ibid. p. 160.
[3] Ibid. pp. 164, 165.     [4] Ibid. p. 173.     [5] Ibid. p. 175.     [6] Ibid. pp. 205, 206.
[7] Histoire de la Diplomatie française, vol. i. p. 99.     [8] Ibid. p. 247.
[9] Philosophie de l'Histoire, pp. 269–272.     [10] Ibid. p. 270.
[11] Ibid. p. 271.     [12] Ibid. p. 272.

The inaccuracy of men was shown by their ignorance of the measurement of time, of space, of weight, and of number. They had no clocks; and in France, in the fourteenth century, when the sun did not appear, it was necessary to send into the town a messenger to know the time.[1] They had no good balances; they were ignorant of distances; they had no hereditary names. In the fourteenth century parents often did not know the age of their own children.[2] The want of a division of labour is a proof of this indistinctness.[3] Mention of epitomes, compendiums, &c., which appeared in the fourteenth century. In the fourteenth, and even in the fifteenth century, it was generally believed, and was laid down in the maps, that Jerusalem was exactly in the middle of the world.[4]

The spread of the art of writing among laymen began to deprive history of the exclusively theological character which it had hitherto possessed. Even in the fifteenth century, in France, paper, though used in family archives, was little employed in books.[5] The absurd forgeries of Isidore were believed; and so were the wildest miracles. The invention of gunpowder equalised all men on the field of battle.

M. de Tocqueville says[6] that the mania for centralisation in France began in the reign of Philip the Fair, " l'époque où les légistes sont entrés dans le gouvernement." (Connect this with the rise of the lawyers.) In the first chapter of the third volume Tocqueville has some very interesting remarks on the spirit of the " légistes." He says,[7] that for 500 years " les légistes " have been mixed up with political movements, and that while in the middle ages they always aided the royal power, they have since then attacked it. In England they are the friends of the aristocracy; in France its enemies. They are naturally lovers of *form* and *order*, and they prefer equality to liberty;[8] and " Le légiste appartient au peuple par son intérêt et par sa naissance et à l'aristocratie par ses habitudes et par ses goûts. Il est comme la liaison naturelle entre ces deux choses, comme l'anneau qui les unit."[9] From this it would seem that the rise of law did good, first, by making men *precise* and orderly; and then by raising up a class which *linked* the aristocracy with the people, and thus

[1] Monteil, Histoire des Français des divers États, tome i. pp. 97, 98.
[2] The natives of Bengal never know their age; but until the age of ten their mothers know it. See the Journal of the Statistical Society, vol. xv. p. 131. See Monteil, Histoire des Français, tome ii. pp. 7, 17, and tome iv. pp. 30, 31.
[3] Monteil, Histoire des Français, tome i. p. 104, note.
[4] Ibid. tome ii. p. 76.          [5] Ibid. tome iii. p. 230.
[6] Démocratie en Amérique, tome i. p. 307.          [7] Ibid. tome iii. pp. 4, 5.
[8] Ibid. pp. 6, 8, 9.          [9] Ibid. p. 10.

increased *sympathy* and contact. The increasing knowledge of law increased the *wants* of men, and thus *compelled* their contact, while the improvements in travelling facilitated it; and we find in the progress of society that the *contact* increases. Thus feudality was a great step, because it knit men together in clans. Then came the despotism of kings, and *pressed* men into one country. Indeed, Tocqueville [1] makes the interesting remark, that so broken up was France by feudality, that "le mot patrie lui-même ne se rencontre dans les auteurs français qu'à partir du seizième siècle." The next step is, I think, to diminish patriotism in favour of general benevolence, just as patriotism has diminished *personal fidelity*. Tocqueville [2] observes, that when the chroniclers of the middle ages relate the death of a noble, their words are full of grief; but they relate with indifference the sufferings of the lower orders. This, I think, was caused by want of *contact* and *sympathy*. Tocqueville says, [3] that as society becomes democratic, the relation between father and son becomes more friendly and less austere. The same increased *contact* is, I think, shown in the relation between master and servant; at all events, it is between the upper and lower orders. The settlements made by the Normans in the tenth century in France, and in the eleventh century in England, formed the last great external change, and society began to settle. Scarcely had this been effected, when the increased *contact* of men gave rise to the crusades, which made Europe *one*. After the breaking up of the Roman Empire, each state, and almost each village, had separate theological caprices—their separate saints, superstitions, &c.; and this gave rise, says Tocqueville, [4] to that spirit of idolatry which even Christianity assumed directly after the breaking-up of the Roman Empire.

I think I may say that we were then in danger of relapsing into an idolatry worse than that of the ancients. The destruction of feudality by Philip the Fair gave the crown great power, and *forced* France into fusion and *contact*. Ranke [5] observes the eminently "modern" and secular character of Philip the Fair. The abolition of slavery was an evidence of the increased sense of the dignity of man. Ranke [6] says that under Louis XII. and Francis I. Italian civilization had a great influence in France. In the fifteenth century there were sixteen universities in France, half of which (i.e. eight), were founded in the fifteenth century. [7]

[1] Démocratie en Amérique, tome v. p. 113.   [3] Ibid. p. 4.
[2] Ibid. p. 52.       [4] Ibid. tome iv. pp. 39, 40.
[5] Civil Wars of France, Lond. 1852, vol. i. p. 57.   [6] Ibid. pp. 116, 155.
[7] See Monteil, Histoire des divers États, tome iv. p. 145.

In the sixteenth century it is said[1] that there were ancient parish books, which, however, mentioned neither births nor deaths. The art of printing, by making books cheap, increased the number of readers, and thus gave History a more social and sympathetic air. Men gradually became more exact. See the history of Mathematics. In 1556, Forcadel's book on Arithmetic reduced to four rules the old two hundred and forty rules of arithmetic.[2] Commerce first made nations sympathise with each other; and then came consuls before ambassadors. Until the twelfth or thirteenth century there was no means of any kind of sending letters, &c. from one part of France to another.[3] From the middle of the fifteenth century to 1521, more than three thousand works were published upon the theology and philosophy of antiquity.[4] Capefigue[5] says that most of the municipal charters are placed under the "protection d'un saint patronage." Capefigue[6] says that in the fourteenth century there arose the lawyers, a middle class between the nobles and the people. Capefigue[7] says that in the feudal times each province formed a separate polity with different laws, each divided into great fiefs; but that when the religious wars broke out at the Reformation, "les antiques rivalités des barons se transformaient en haine du prêche ou de la messe."[8] Capefigue[9] says that the spirit of feudality "s'était éteint avec les prouesses des paladins du treizième siècle." Ibn Batuta was one of the most celebrated travellers of the fourteenth century. Read his travels and those of Mandeville for the opinions of educated men. Read the accounts of Ireland and Wales by Giraldus Cambrensis, which, as Cooley says,[10] was extremely popular and greedily received at Oxford. In the old maps, mentioned in British topography, Scotland is represented as an island.[11] An extraordinary map is preserved at Turin, and is mentioned by Cooley.[12] It is, indeed, extraordinary that men in such a state should ever have become accurate. But without pretending to write a history of the middle-age civilization, I will now trace some of the causes. The monks were almost the only historians of the middle ages. Some doubts having been expressed respecting the legal majority of the French kings, there was issued in 1383 a constitution of Charles V. fixing it at the age of fourteen, and assigning as precedents the cases of Joash, of Josiah, of David,

---

[1] Monteil, Histoire des divers États, tome v. p. 108.
[2] Ibid. tome vi. p. 104.  [3] Ibid. tome vii. p. 254.
[4] See Capefigue, Histoire de la Réforme, tome i. p. 31.  [5] Ibid. pp. 249, 250.
[6] Ibid. tome ii. p. 23.  [7] Ibid. tome iv. pp. 31, 32.
[8] See also tome v. p. 78.  [9] Histoire de la Réforme, tome iv. p. 120.
[10] History of Maritime Discovery, vol. i. p. 228.
[11] Cooley, vol. i. p. 230.  [12] Ibid. p. 232.

of Solomon, and of Hezekiah.   In Smedley's Reformed Religion
in France, pp. 380, 381, there is an account of a mythological
morality performed at Paris in 1572, which is not worth quoting,
but which I may refer to.   The canonical laws, first drawn up
about 1107 by Gratian, a monk of Bologna, consist of canons of
the councils, writings of the fathers, constitutions of the popes,
and some of the imperial laws.[1]   Lerminier[2] says the "établisse-
mens" of St. Louis, " sont après les assises de Jérusalem, fruit des
Croisades, importation de la loi chrétienne en Asie, le premier
monument de la législation française; car Charlemagne et ses
capitulaires appartiennent autant à l'Allemagne qu'à la France."
The first great intellectual and democratic movement was shown
by the use of the modern languages.   Formerly intellect was
wasted on theological and military matters.   The first step was
to divert it to secular subjects, and this was done in the eleventh
century by the rise of schools and of educated laymen, and in the
thirteenth century by gunpowder, which gave rise to a *separate*
military class.   In the middle of the reign of Elizabeth, according to one account, the population of England was estimated at
nine hundred thousand; according to other accounts the number
of men capable of bearing arms was nearly twelve hundred thousand, which of course would give a population of from four and
a half to five millions.   In and after the fourth century men
became ignorant because they were exclusively theological.[3]
Early in the ninth century schools first arose.   About the seventh
century the barbarians *entered* Christianity, and though they
added to it fresh superstitions, they began to *temper* it with their
secular and independent spirit.   Pilgrimages and missionaries
began the *contact* and *fusion*; then came the crusades, when for
the first time we see the *secular* element of conquest.   Another
proof of this spirit of contact and condensation is to be found in
the great collections, &c., which Whewell, who calls it the commentatorial spirit, wrongly supposes to be a retrogression.   The
papal power aided the process of condensation, *contact*, and *unity*.
This began with Hildebrand immediately before the crusades, or
perhaps by Leo IX. in A.D. 1049.[4]   The power of the bishops was
succeeded by the power of the popes, just as alodial proprietors
were succeeded by the great feudal landlords.   Scarcely was
Christianity established when monasticism sprang up.   The revival of classical literature taught men for the first time that there
was something more beautiful than legends.   This gave rise to a

[1] Lerminier, Philosophie du Droit, tome i. pp. 259, 260.     [2] Ibid. p. 267.
[3] See Neander's History of the Church, vol. iv. p. 41, 128.     [4] Ibid. vol. vi. p. 47.

sense of *beauty*, which is never found among nations altogether
barbarous ; and to this we owe the rise of the fine arts which
*chastised* credulity and *drew off* imaginative men from history.
In the eleventh century the French clergy began to oppose the
church.[1]  Neander[2] says that the revived study of the ancient
Latin authors in the ninth, and particularly in the eleventh century, " injured the church and encouraged heresy." In the sixth
century the Greek schools were shut and men became theological.
Arnold of Brescia and Abelard aided the great movement, and
*style* became better, for clear thinkers always have a clear style.
In the middle of the twelfth century arose the canon law.[3] Abelard attacked the stories of "miraculous cures."[4]  There were,
indeed, the schools of Charlemagne and of Ireland; but until
the Pilgrimages and the Crusades Europe never *pulled together*. In
vain did the church by monastic and mendicant orders try to in-
vigorate her dying frame.  The hostility between Reason and Faith
only became more marked.  In the thirteenth century the mendicant monks alone were considered *religious* men; their mode of
life being called *religio*.[5]  The antagonism increased and the church
became more and more superstitious.  Then transubstantiation
was fixed in A.D. 1215 ;[6] and hence the superstitious festival of
Corpus Christi, ordered in 1264, and again in A.D. 1311.[7]  In the
thirteenth century the clergy first openly and peremptorily withdrew the cup from the laity, and this was the work of the mendicant monks, *all* of whom, except Albert, declared that the clergy
alone should take the wine.[8]  In 1215, auricular confession was
first made imperative.[9]  Neander[10] mentions " the worldly culture
which began to flourish from the time of the twelfth century,
and particularly the speculative bent which set itself in hostility
against the faith."  According to the old notions universal ideas
were considered as *real*, but late in the eleventh century Roscelin
founded Nominalism ; and "he maintained that all knowledge
must proceed from experience, individuals only had real existence ;
all general conceptions were without objective significance;"[11]
and even Anselm, the great opponent of Roscelin[12] did nevertheless feel " constrained to account to himself by a rational knowledge for that which in itself was to him the most certain of all
things."[13]  Abelard held " that faith proceeds first from enquiry."[14]

[1] Neander, History of the Church, vol. vi, p. 348.
[2] Ibid. p. 362.          [3] Ibid. vol. vii. p. 282.          [4] Ibid. p. 355.
[5] Ibid. p. 304.          [6] Ibid. p. 466.          [7] Ibid. pp. 473, 474.
[8] Ibid. pp. 476, 477, 479.          [9] Ibid. p. 491.          [10] Ibid. p. 450.
[11] Ibid. vol. viii. p. 3.          [12] Ibid. p. 10.
[13] Ibid. p. 19.          [14] Ibid. p. 35.

Abelard first attacked the old story about Dionysius.[1] In the middle of the twelfth century Peter Lombard's Book of Sentences shows the commentatorial spirit;[2] and fifty years later Peter Cantor drew up his "Summa."[3] As to Aquinas's love for novelty, see Neander, vol. viii. p. 86. In the thirteenth century the Arabian school began to exercise great influence.[4] The theological tendency of Roger Bacon's works is considered by Neander;[5] their scientific tendency by Whewell. Bacon was in the thirteenth century. He opposed tradition and advocated inquiry.[6] In the thirteenth century it was forbidden to write theological books in French.[7] "In the twelfth century traces of the influence of the Aristotelian dialectic may already be discerned; though at first only single logical writings of that great philosopher could have been known."[8] At p. 242, Neander gives a curious instance of the way in which Thomas Aquinas was influenced by Aristotle. The disputes of nominalism and realism rescued many subjects from theology and brought them under the jurisdiction of metaphysics. In the eleventh century that accumulation of absurdities called the Fathers came to a close, Bernard being generally considered the last. A very learned writer[9] strangely speaks of the "antecedent improbability of the Crusades." But they were the natural result partly of the theological spirit, partly of the increased contact of nations. Sir W. Hamilton[10] says that in the middle ages, and even by the scholastic philosophers, philosophy was always made subordinate to theology. In the twelfth and thirteenth centuries law, medicine, and philosophy were studied by immense numbers at the universities. See an interesting Essay on the History of Universities in Sir W. Hamilton's Discussions on Philosophy, p. 403. Where shall we find finer intellects than Erigena, Lanfranc, and Abelard? men far greater than any modern metaphysician since Descartes —certainly far superior to Locke, and to the whole Scotch school from Hutcheson to Hamilton. The finest minds were occupied with theology, ontology, law; in France, feudal law; in England, the law of real property. The genuineness of William Tell was first attacked in 1760.[11] The invention of the compass and of posts *fused* Europe and enlarged the views of historians. In the

[1] Neander, History of the Church, vol. viii. p. 40. On Abelard's heretical and imaginative tendencies, see Ibid. pp. 50, 51.
[2] Ibid. p. 77      [3] Ibid. p. 84.
[4] Ibid. p. 127.      [5] Ibid. pp. 97, 100, 112, 114.
[6] Ibid. p. 98.      [7] Ibid. p. 132.      [8] Ibid. p. 88.
[9] Grote, History of Greece, vol. i. p. 572.
[10] Discussions in Philosophy, p. 197.
[11] Koch, Tableau des Révolutions, tome i. p. 255.

middle of the fifteenth century there rose the idea of balance of power;[1] and just after this we find, I think, the first ambassadors. The first school of medicine was founded at the end of the eleventh century.[2]

---

## CAUSES OF BACKWARD STATE OF HISTORY BEFORE A.D. 1200.

*Method.*—After giving, in the East, and then in the Edda, an account of the corruption of history by the change of religion, say that religion was not only changed but became supreme. This was because in Europe the conquerors adopted the religion of the conquered Romans, who being now civilized, had on that account influence; and who on account of their weakness were compelled to substitute subtlety for force. Hence theology, being the only literature, became supreme. The schools of Greece were shut up, and credulous men believed everything. Then relate *isolated* absurdities and say these were not mere stray and popular opinions, but the ideas of grave historians. Give an account of Gregory of Tours, Bede, &c.

.          .          .          .          .

In the fourth century there arose monachism, and in the sixth century the Christians succeeded in cutting off the last ray of knowledge, and shutting up the schools of Greece. Then followed a long period of theology, ignorance, and vice. Then arose those legends of the saints of which the size and number are even more remarkable than the absurdity. About 1120, Philip de Thuan published a poem called Livre des Créatures, which is a treatise on astronomy, as far as it was cultivated by the priesthood as a means of calculating the movable times and seasons observed by the church.[3] Grote[4] quotes Ampère, Histoire littéraire de la France, to the effect that in the sixth century the pagan *scientific view* being destroyed, everything became theological, and the legend first arose. Broussais[5] notices the same servile spirit in medicine. "On commenta Galien, Avicenne, Aristote, Averrhoes, et l'on négligea l'observation et l'expérience." The first Christian physician of any reputation was Ætius, who flourished at the end of the fifth and beginning of the sixth century; and his

---

[1] Koch, Tableau des Révolutions, vol. i. p. 315.          [2] Ibid. p. 156.
[3] Wright's Biographia Britannica Literaria, vol. ii. p. 87.
[4] Grote's History of Greece, vol. i. p. 627.
[5] Broussais, Examen des Doctrines médicales, tome i. p. 260.

notions of medicine were miserably superstitious.[1]  Anatomical
dissections were entirely abandoned, owing to the anathema of
the church.  And besides this, says Renouard,[2] medicine declined,
owing to the rapid spread of Christianity, " qui désorganiza les
écoles païennes, discrédita les sciences profanes, et ruina leur enseignement. . . . L'histoire de la médicine ne trouve qu'un seul
nom à citer durant cet espace d'environ sept cents ans."[3]  And
that name is John, son of Zachariah, late in the thirteenth century.  Paul Ægineta, late in the sixth and in the first half of
the seventh century, is the last Greek physician of importance.[4]

---

## ABSURDITIES AS SPECIMENS OF HISTORIANS.

*Gildas.*[5]—Geoffrey of Monmouth calls the history of Gildas
" what so great a writer has so eloquently related," and " Gildas
in his elegant treatise." [6]  William of Malmesbury[7] says " Gildas,
an historian neither unlearned nor inelegant, to whom the Britons
are indebted for whatever notice they obtain among other nations."
The French boast of Gregory of Tours as their first historian.[8]

*The Saxon Chronicle.*—No part of this chronicle was composed
so early as A.D. 890 ;[9] but Wright says [10] that Plegmund, archbishop
of Canterbury, " one of Alfred's " learned men, *did* compile the
early part; though he strangely adds that Plegmund did this
" down to the year 981 "—a chronological impossibility, because
Alfred died in 901.  Wright adds,[11] " from that period the narrative of contemporary events was continued from time to time in
the Anglo-Saxon tongue by different writers, until the entire
breaking up of the language in the middle of the twelfth century."

*William of Malmesbury* died in or after 1143 ; and his " Modern History " (which is a continuation of his History of the
Kings of England) " terminates at the end of the year 1142."[12]
His History of the Kings, and History of the Prelates, both
of which are in *Scriptores post Bedam*, were completed in
1125.[13]  William of Malmesbury says of Bede, " After him you

---

[1] See Renouard, Histoire de la Médicine, tome i. p. 386.      [2] Ibid. p. 408.
[3] Ibid. p. 431.          [4] Ibid. pp. 391-392.
[5] We may pass over the wretched Gildas and Nennius.  [Author's marginal note.]
[6] Six Old Chronicles, pp. 108, 187.          [7] Chronicle, edit. Bohn, p. 22.
[8] See Dacier, Rapport sur les Progrès de l'Histoire, p. 168.
[9] Wright's Biog. Brit. Literaria, vol. i. p. 415.
[10] Ibid. p. 63.                    [11] Ibid. p. 63.
[12] William of Malmesbury's English Chronicle, edit. Bohn, 1847, p. vii.
[13] Ibid. p. vii.

will not, in my opinion, find any person who has attempted to
compose in Latin the history of this people;"[1] and "with this
man was buried almost all knowledge of history down to our
times, inasmuch as there has been no Englishman either emulous
of his pursuits or a follower of his graces, who could continue
the thread of his discourse, now broken short."[2] "But be these
matters as they may, I especially congratulate myself on being
through Christ's assistance, the only person, or at least the first
who since Bede has arranged a continued history of the English."[3] "And as the moderns greatly and deservedly blame our
predecessors for having left no memorial of themselves or their
transactions since the days of Bede."[4] All this William of
Malmesbury says with reason. Yet he was usually credulous, bom-
bastic in his style, and relates nothing of real importance. So
low, however, is the standard by which the merit of that age
is to be estimated that on him the most extravagant praises have
been lavished. It would, however, be unjust to forget one other
writer of much higher rank in the church, and who in his life, as
well as for some time after his death, enjoyed a still higher reputation. This is Geoffrey of Monmouth.

The splendour of all preceding historians was eclipsed by this
celebrated man. His History of the Britons was published in
1147, when he was archdeacon ; and, says Wright,[5] "it was partly
perhaps the reputation of this book which procured the author
the bishopric of St. Asaph."[6] It was Walter Mapes, archdeacon of
Oxford, who brought over the materials from Armorica and communicated them to Geoffrey of Monmouth;[7] and the book when
finished was dedicated to Robert earl of Gloucester, son of
Henry II.[8] Wright[9] says of Geoffrey's History, "Within a century after its first publication it was generally adopted by writers
on English history, and during several centuries only one or two
rare instances occur of persons who ventured to speak against its
veracity." In 1148 or 1150, it was translated into Anglo-Norman
by Gaimar;[10] and just at the same time a Latin abridgement of
it was published by Alfred of Beverley, one of our historians.[11]
About 1170 to 1180, it was translated into Anglo-Norman verse
by Wace, and into English by Layamon.[12] Soon after, or in 1183,
Gervase of Tilbury, in his work Otia Imperialia, gives a history

[1] William of Malmesbury's English Chronicle, edit. Bohn, 1847, p. 3.
[2] Ibid. pp. 60, 61.   [3] Ibid. p. 77.   [4] Ibid. p. 613.
[5] Biog. Brit. Lit. vol. ii. p. 144.   [6] See Borlase, Antiq. of Cornwall, 1768, p. 402.
[7] Six Old Chronicles, p. xii.
[8] Wright, Biog. Brit. Lit vol. ii. p. 144, and Six Old Chronicles, p. xii.
[9] Biog. Brit. Lit. vol. ii. p. 146.          [10] Ibid. pp. 151, 152.
[11] Ibid. p. 156.                    [12] Ibid. p. 439.

of the Britons, in which he follows Geoffrey of Monmouth.[1]
Geoffrey relates that when Troy was taken, Ascanius fled from the
city and sailed to Italy, of which, on the death of Æneas, he
obtained the kingdom.   In the course of time Ascanius begat a
son named Brutus,[2] who after various adventures in different parts
of Europe[3] crossed over to England, which was then called Albion,
but which Brutus named after himself Briton; and hence it is
that the inhabitants are still known as Britons.[4]   When Brutus
arrived in Albion the only inhabitants were a few giants,[5] but
these the invader, aided by a certain Corinæus (one of the descendants of the Trojan warriors)[6] easily conquered.[7]   Brutus
having settled the affairs of his new kingdom, built a city on the
Thames which he called New Troy, but which, being afterwards
improved by Lud, became known as Lud-town; hence the name
of London.[8]   After the death of Brutus there came a long line of
kings, even to the period of the Saxon invasion, most of whom
were remarkable for their abilities, and some were famous for the
prodigies which occurred in their reign.   Thus during the government of Rwallo it rained blood for three consecutive days;[9] and
when Morndas was on the throne the coasts were infested by a
cruel sea-monster, who, having devoured innumerable persons, at
length swallowed the king himself.[10]   And when the Saxons
actually invaded England, the royal race, though defeated, were
not left without resources.   For there was raised up a certain
Merlin, the son of a virgin, or all events who had no father,[11] for
on this nice point the archdeacon seems to have had his doubts.
He performed several miracles,[12] and brought over from Ireland
certain stones which had a magical virtue;[13] and this it is said in
a note[14] is the origin of Stonehenge.   After Merlin there was
raised up Arthur, born under strange circumstances,[15] who not only
slew great numbers of Saxons, but conquered Norway, invaded
Gaul, fixed his court at Paris, and made preparations to effect the
conquest of Europe.[16]   Arthur killed a giant in single combat,[17]
and performed various other feats, but was at length killed.[18]
Geoffrey of Monmouth says[19] that what he relates respecting
Arthur he " heard from that most learned historian Walter, archdeacon of Oxford."   I give a long account of Geoffrey of Monmouth, because his work was highly valued and procured for

[1] Wright, Biog. Brit. Lit. vol. ii. pp. 284, 285.
[2] Six Old Chronicles, p. 91.     [3] Ibid. pp. 92-106.     [4] Ibid. pp. 106, 107.
[5] Ibid. p. 106.     [6] Ibid. p. 102.     [7] Ibid. p. 107.     [8] Ibid. p. 108.
[9] Ibid. p. 120.     [10] Ibid. p. 133.     [11] Ibid. p. 193.
[12] Ibid. pp. 194-225.     [13] Ibid. pp. 216, 217.
[14] Ibid. p. 218.     [15] Ibid. p. 225.     [16] Ibid. pp. 239, 241.
[17] Ibid. pp. 253, 254.     [18] Ibid. p. 271.     [19] Ibid. p. 268.

himself great honour, and also because it was the last elaborate historical absurdity. For a great change was now at hand, which was to transfer history into the hands of laymen, and even temper the theological spirit of ecclesiastics themselves.

---

## ABSURDITIES IN EARLY HISTORY TO BE CONSIDERED ISOLATED.

GEOFFREY DE VINSAUF has written a chronicle of the crusade of Richard I. (A.D. 1187–1192), *at which he was himself present.*[1] In the prologue to his history he says[2] that he ought to be believed as being an eyewitness in the same way as "Dares Phrygius is more readily believed about the destruction of Troy, because he was an eyewitness of what others related only on hearsay." Vinsauf says of Godfrey de Lusignan's achievements in the Crusades that "no one since the time of those famous soldiers Roland and Oliver could lay claim to such distinction;[3] and[4] he says of Richard I. "to whom even famous Roland could not be consideredo qual." See also William of Malmesbury's Chronicle of Kings, p. 277. Geoffrey de Vinsauf says[5] the Turks "abominate swine as unclean, because swine are said to have devoured Mahomet."

Gildas distinctly states[6] that all the older native histories of Britain had perished; and yet Nennius says[7] "the island of Britain derives its name from Brutus, a Roman consul;" and he gravely says, "Respecting the period when this island became inhabited subsequently to the flood, I have seen two distinct relations."[8]

Nennius wrote his History of the Britons in the eighth, ninth, or tenth century.[9] He gravely relates that Vortigern, king of Britain, at the time of the Saxon invasion, fortunately discovered a boy who was born of a woman without the intervention of man, and whom on that account he was directed to put to death and thus escape from his difficulties. But the boy saved himself by performing the most astonishing miracles.[10] He also says[11] that Saint Patrick "gave sight to the blind, cleansed the lepers, gave hearing to the deaf, cast out devils, raised nine from the dead."

[1] Chronicles of Crusades, Bohn, 8vo, 1848, pp. iii, iv.          [2] Ibid. p. 65.
[3] Ibid. p. 203.          [4] Ibid. p. 326.          [5] Ibid. p. 319.
[6] Six Old English Chronicles, p. 301.          [7] Ibid. p. 386.          [8] Ibid. p. 387.
[9] Ibid. pp. vii, 384.          [10] Ibid. pp. 402, 403.          [11] Ibid. p. 410.

See Geoffrey of Monmouth's account of the eleven thousand virgins.[1] At Marseilles, in 1646, Monconys[2] was told that seven out of the eleven thousand virgins were buried. Prichard, Physical History of Mankind, pp. 111, 172, 173.

On Gog and Magog, see Chronicles of Crusaders. Bohn, 1848, p. 476.

Asser, in his Life of Alfred, traces Alfred's genealogy back to Seth and Adam.[3]

Froissart[4] says, "At last king Robert of Scotland arrived with red bleared eyes of the colour of sandal-wood, which clearly showed he was no valiant man, but one who would rather remain at home than march to the field."

Judas had *red* hair. This is perhaps an eastern superstition. In the institutes of Menu, chap. iii. sec. viii.[5] it is said of the pious man, "Let him not marry a girl with reddish hair, nor with any deformed limb." The ancient Egyptians had a great contempt for " red-haired men."[6] Blanco White[7] says that in Spain it is understood that Judas had red hair, and that Peter was bald; and the former opinion, he observes, is alluded to by Shakespeare : "His hair," says Rosalind, in As you like it, "was of the dissembling colour—something browner than Judas's."

Froissart[8] says that Arthur's principal residence was at Carlisle.

It was believed "that leap year had been caused by Joshua, when he made the sun stand still." A writer of the tenth century notices this as the opinion of " some unlearned priests."[9]

"The real city of the Seven Sleepers was Ephesus; but the story is attached traditionally to many other places in the East."[10]

Shakespeare, in King John, act ii. scene 1, alludes to Richard the First's combat with a lion.[11]

For a curious instance of story repeated by classical writers, see Grote, History of Greece, iv. 394.

There is good evidence for the story of Tamerlane and the Iron Cage.[12]

De Thou, the first historian of his age, relates as an undoubted

[1] Six Old Chronicles, pp. 171–173, and Maury, Légendes pieuses, p. 214.
[2] Voyages, vol. i. p. 195.　　　　[3] Six Old Chronicles, pp. 43, 44.
[4] Chronicles, 8vo. 1839, vol. ii. p. 48.　　[5] Works of Sir W. Jones, vol. iii. p. 120.
[6] Wilkinson, Ancient Egyptians, vol. v. pp. 344, 345.
[7] Doblado's Letters from Spain, p. 289.　　[8] Chronicles, vol. ii. p. 54.
[9] Wright, Biog. Brit. Literaria, vol. i. p. 89.
[10] Rawlinson in Journal of Geographical Society, vol. ix. p. 72. See also William of Malmesbury Chronicles of English Kings, pp. 250, 251.
[11] See also Keightley's Mythology of Greece and Rome, pp. 10, 11.
[12] See Works of Sir W. Jones, vol. v. pp. 547, 548.

fact that, among other prodigies which occurred in the wonderful year of 1588, a woman was delivered of twins within five days one of the other.

When the ancient painters in the middle ages had occasion to represent the siege of Troy, they always inserted some artillery.[1]

Charles IV., in his Bull, in the fourteenth century, says that there must be seven electors to oppose the seven mortal sins.[2]

The extent to which such feelings governed the minds of men is hardly to be believed. Pope Paul III. was unwilling to form an alliance with Francis I., because there was no conformity between their nativities.

Melancthon, one of the most enlightened men of his time, was a prey to superstition of which a washerwoman would now be ashamed. When the gravest events were being discussed at the diet of Augsburg, he declared that the results would certainly be favourable to his own party, because the Tiber had overflowed its banks, and because there was born at Rome a mule with a crane's foot.

I say nothing of their belief in witchcraft, in palmistry, and astrology.

In 1545, at the opening of the council of Trent, a sermon was preached by the bishop of Bitonto [ ? ], in which he undertook to prove the necessity of the council being held. Among other reasons, one is that, in the Æneid, Jupiter is represented as holding a council of the gods.[3]

------

## PROGRESS IN EUROPEAN HISTORY AS SHOWN IN HISTORIANS.

Read Rishanger's Chronicle, written early in the fourteenth century, in *Camden Society's publications.* Fabian was a merchant, and Sir T. More a lawyer.

Late in the fourteenth century, Richard of Cirencester wrote a treatise on the geography and history of Britain, which has only been published by Betram, at Copenhagen, in 1757.[4] He was a Benedictine monk. In his History we find no miracles nor

[1] See Sainte Palaye, Mém. sur L'Ancien Chevalerie, tome ii. p. 127.
[2] Essai sur les Mœurs, chap. lxx. in Œuvres de Voltaire, tome xvi. p. 277.
[3] Ibid chap. clxxii. in Œuvres de Voltaire, tome xviii. p. 21.
[4] Six Old English Chronicles, Bohn, pp. xviii-xx, where no doubt is hinted as to its genuineness, which, however, from no one having seen the MS. is suspected in Macray's Manual of British Historians, 8vo. 1845. pp. 46, 48.

martyrdoms. He says of the early inhabitants of Britain,[1]
" Writers are not wanting who assert that Hercules came hither
and established a sovereignty ; but it is needless to dwell on such
remote antiquities and idle tales." At p. 464 he ironically says,
" Nor are those wanting who believe that London was shortly
after built by a king called Bryto." At p. 468 he apologises for
the meagreness of the early history of Britain, because, " conforming myself closely to the rules and laws of history, I have
collected all the accounts of other persons which I found most
accurate and deserving of credit. The reader must not expect
anything beyond an enumeration of those emperors and Roman
governors who had authority over this island." Bede gives a long
and dull account of the martyrdom of St. Alban ; but Richard,
speaking of Verulamium, simply says " St. Alban, the martyr, was
here born."[2] I may first give an account of Joinville and Froissart, and then say that the pressure of the age was so strong as to
be felt even by monks like William of Malmesbury and Richard
of Cirencester, both of whom were naturally inferior to Bede.

*Joinville* was a layman, and published his Memoirs of
Louis IX. in 1309.[3] It is said in the Penny Cyclopædia that
he "and his predecessor, Villehardouin, are among the oldest of
the French chroniclers who wrote in the vernacular tongue."
Although Joinville's work is the history of an eminently religious
undertaking, there are fewer miracles in it than in any preceding
history. Indeed, he only mentions three miracles.[4] And he
shows his anti-theological spirit by the general character of his
narrative. Ducange[5] says he laughs "at those who, having committed atrocious acts of plunder during their lives, imagine they
may acquit themselves before God by giving alms to some monasteries or churches." Joinville also refused to wash the poor on
Holy Thursday ; "never will I wash the feet of such fellows."

Giles[6] says, " The story of Brute and the descent of the Britons
from the Trojans was universally allowed by Giraldus Cambrensis
and others, and was opposed for the first time by John of
Wellhamstede,[7] who lived in the fifteenth century."

*Froissart.*--Froissart, a layman, wrote in the latter half of the
fourteenth century. After the end of the thirteenth century there
is no instance of any historian of note relating long miracles. In
Froissart we seem carried into a new world, the old theological
spirit being destroyed. He relates the deeds of noble knights,

[1] Six Old Chronicles, p. 422.
[2] Ibid. p. 445.
[3] Chronicles of Crusades, by Bohn, p. 347.
[4] Ibid. pp. 434, 502, 512.
[5] Ibid. Note. p. 356.
[6] Preface to Six Chronicles, p. xi.
[7] Nicholson's English Hist. Library, 2nd edit. p. clv.

N

and love of lovely ladies, but ecclesiastics are altogether subordinate. He was naturally a man of great credulity (one of the
most remarkable proofs of this is the extraordinary account he
gives of the island of Cephalonia, which he believed to be governed by women, who kept up a communication with fairies)[1];
but the spirit of the age forbad his credulity running into a
theological channel. The prevalence of feudality in *polity*, and
chivalry in *manners*, though they were great evils, did, as I
shall hereafter show, check and divert the theological spirit. It
was not that Froissart wanted the moral element. Among many
other instances, he says,[2] after relating the death of Aymerigot
Marcel, " Had Aymerigot turned his mind to virtue, he would
have done much good, for he was an able man at arms and of
great courage; but, having acted in a different manner, he came
to a disgraceful death." This is a proof that Froissart did not,
as is often said, *exclusively* look at warlike and military virtue.
But the great object of his history was war. Thus, very early in
his History, he says, " The real object of this history being to
relate the great enterprises and deeds of arms achieved in these
wars; "[3] and, having nearly finished his history, he says of it,
" The more I labour at it, the more it delights me; just as a
gallant knight or squire at arms, who loves his profession, the
longer he continues it, so much the more delectable it appears." [4]
He represents a battle as being decided, not by Providence, but
by the courage of soldiers and skill of generals. I do not remember a single passage in his History in which he speaks of a
lost battle as a divine retribution; and there are several passages
where in guarded language he seems to imply an opposite opinion.
Thus,[5] " It always happens that in war there are gains and losses :
very extraordinary are the chances, as those know well who follow
the profession; " and again, " Good or evil fortune depends on a
trifle."[6] He says of the crusade undertaken by Philip of France
about 1333, " The croisade was preached and published over the
world, which gave much pleasure to many, especially to those who
wished to spend their time in feats of arms, and who at that time
did not know where otherwise to employ themselves." [7] He par-
ticularises no miracles. The only exception to this is[8] where he
says of Thomas, earl of Lancaster, " many miracles have been performed at his tomb in Pomfret, where he was beheaded." Observe this is of a layman, not of a saint. He says that in a battle

[1] Froissart, vol. ii. pp. 650, 651.     [2] Ibid. vol. ii. p. 465, chap. xix.
[3] Ibid. vol. i. p. 5, chap. iv.          [4] Ibid. vol. ii. p. 548.
[5] Ibid. vol. ii. p. 1.                   [6] Ibid. vol. ii. p. 287.
[7] Ibid. vol. i. p. 39.                   [8] Ibid. vol. i. p. 6.

everyone would have been slain, " if it had not been, *as it were,* a miracle of God."[1] Again, " who by divine inspiration (*as one may well suppose it*) gained information that Paris was to be sacked and destroyed."[2] At vol. ii. p. 312, beginning of chap. ci. he says, "About this period *there were many rumours* that the body of St. Peter de Luxembourg, who had been a cardinal, showed miraculous powers in the city of Avignon."

Froissart and Monstrelet, who wrote forty-five years later, are the first French writers who took an extensive view of foreign history, and who saw the necessity of *filiating* the order of events. Froissart's is the most voluminous and comprehensive history that had yet appeared in Europe. He relates the affairs of England, France, Scotland, Spain, and Portugal. Froissart says,[3] "If I were merely to say such and such things happened at such times, without entering fully into the matter, which was grandly horrible and disastrous, it would be a chronicle, but no history." He says,[4] " It should be known that in the year 1390, I had laboured at this history thirty-seven years, and at that time I was fifty-seven years old."

William of Newbury, who died in 1208, is one of the best historians of his age, and in his History of his own Time, he, "in a preface of some length, protests against the absurdity of the fabulous history of King Arthur, and the prophecies of Merlin, and treats very contemptuously the authority of Geoffrey of Monmouth."[5] Newbury was a monk.

Campbell[6] says Sir Thomas More's Edward V. and Richard III. " has the merit of being the earliest historical composition in the English language." If so, this is another proof of how much later history was developed in England than in France.

In the sixteenth century, notwithstanding the preceding progress, little was done. In Italy, indeed, where, as we shall hereafter see, scepticism first arose, we find the beginning of their illustrious thinkers, which extend from Guicciardini and Macchiavelli to Vico and Giannone, but in other countries gross credulity. Then give some instances of that credulity.

[1] Froissart, vol. i. p. 30.                  [3] Ibid. vol. i. p. 246.
[2] Ibid. vol. ii. p. 239.               [4] Ibid. vol. ii. p. 258.
[5] Wright's Biog. Brit. Lit. vol. ii. p. 408.
[6] Lives of the Chancellors, vol. i. p. 586.

## BALLADS, ETC.

I. The very sermons which the ignorant preachers addressed to their ignorant audience were enlivened not only by the introduction of the fables of Æsop, all of which were looked upon as strictly true, but also by various tales of much more questionable merit ; and the custom became so general that the tales which were related on these occasions were thrown into various collections in order to refresh the memory of the clergy. These stories, which formed a large part of the spiritual instruction of the people, are such as were natural to the ignorance of barbarians depraved by the superstition of priests. In them we learn how an Indian girl of exquisite beauty, having been fed on serpents, was sent to Alexander as a fatal gift; how a certain empress, becoming pregnant by her own son, was moved to repentance by the sudden appearance of the Virgin Mary, &c. See Swan's Gesta Romanorum.

II. William of Malmesbury made a step in advance, but even in his time the influence of ballads remained, and, as Warton says,[1] "It is remarkable that almost all the professed writers in prose of this age made experiments in verse." Giraldus Cambrensis, who wrote at the end of the twelfth century, was also a poet.[2] At the end of the thirteenth century, Robert of Gloucester put Geoffrey of Monmouth into rhyme ;[3] and early in the fourteenth century, Robert de Brunne wrote a Metrical Chronicle of England.[4] This I suspect was the first sign of improvement, for he tells the reader that he has avoided the language of minstrels and harpers.[5] Warton says,[6] that Richard I. "is the last of our monarchs whose achievements were adorned with fiction and fable." Saxo-Grammaticus wrote in the twelfth century. A very competent authority says, " The history of Ireland by Jeffrey Keating is not one whit more true than that of Britain by his namesake of Monmouth."[7] Bede could not describe accurately even external objects. Among the Hindoos, mythological fables have arisen out of confusion of *language*.[8]

III. Bede, the most celebrated and perhaps the most judicious collector of such early traditions, makes liberal additions to them

---

[1] History of English Poetry, vol. i. pp. cxx, cxxi.
[2] Ibid. vol. i. pp. cxxiv, cxxv.　　[3] Ibid. vol. i. p. 47.　　[4] Ibid. p. 58.
[5] Ibid. pp. 67, 68.　　　　　　　　[6] Ibid. pp. 125, 126.
[7] Keightley on the Transmission of Tales and Fictions, 1834, p. 178.
[8] See Wilson's Vishnu Purana, pp. 280, 380. Read Walker's Memoirs of Irish Bards. Evan's Welsh Ballads. Miss Brooke's Reliques of Ancient Irish Poetry. See Prichard's Physical History of Mankind, vol. iii. pp. 140, 141.

In the account, for instance, of the Magi who worshipped Christ, he enters into the fullest details, from which we learn that Melchior was an old man with a long beard; that Gaspar, the second of the Magi, was young, and that, though he had no beard, it was he who offered the frankincense. Neander[1] says that St. Patrick first gave the Irish an alphabet.

IV. . . . . In the same way the famous Olaf, king of Norway, is said to have disappeared in the middle of battle, to have never returned, but to have been anxiously expected during five centuries. This myth has crept into a history of the south, and we are assured that exactly the same thing happened to Sebastian of Portugal.[2] Wraxall, who was in Lisbon in 1773, says that many persons still believed that Sebastian had appeared at Venice in 1598.[3]

Respecting Whittington and his Cat, see *Common-Place Book*, ART. 854. At Sleswick, as "in most Protestant towns," there is a tradition of the eyes of an artist being put out by the priests that he might not surpass his own work.[4]

V. . . . . Ctesias corrupted history by copying monuments. The poverty of invention in the middle ages is shown by the fact that "many of the Roman Catholic legends are taken from Apuleius."[5] Middleton and Blunt have shown this of the Christian ceremonies. Read Panizzi on the Poetry of the Italians, quoted by Lewis.[6] Read also Eichhorn, Geschichte der Literatur, quoted by Lewis.[7]

VI. (See No. 1.) In a celebrated French mystery performed by the clergy on Christmas Day, the principal characters were Moses in an alb and cope, Balaam with large spurs, and David in a green waistcoat, to whom was added Virgil, who in monkish rhymes carried on a conversation with these sacred persons.

VII. The modes in which, at this stage of society, history became falsified, are too various to be enumerated. Sometimes the apparent improbability of an event caused its rejection, and there was substituted for it an occurrence which, though it never happened, seemed better to harmonise with the other circumstances which accompanied it. Sometimes an accidental peculiarity in the name of a hero gave rise to the relation of an imaginary adventure. . . . Sprat, bishop of Rochester, mentions

---

[1] History of the Church, vol. iii. p. 176.
[2] See Crichton's Scandinavia, vol. i. p. 153.
[3] Historical Memoirs of my own Time, 8vo, 1818, vol. i. p. 73.
[4] Laing's Denmark, p. 222.
[5] Coleridge's Literary Remains, vol. i. p. 188.
[6] Observations on Politics, vol. i. p. 280.          [7] Ibid. pp. 312, 320.

as a vulgar story, " Kentish men having long tails, for the murder
of Thomas Becket."[1]

VIII. The first historian in Dutch seems to have been Miles
Stoke at the very end of the thirteenth century.[2]    But there was
one who wrote in *Latin* (Sigbert of Genblonus) in the middle of
the twelfth century.[3]    However, " Zyn werk is vol de fabelen in
de oude lyden."[4]    Early in the fourteenth century, Lodewyk van
Villhelm published his Spiegel Historiaal, a continuation of the
History of Maerlant, in which he places together the predictions
of Daniel, of St. John, of the conjuror Merlin, and of the Abbot
Hildegard.[5]    Did not Maerlant write history ?    In the Netherlands
in the fourteenth century there were *Sprekers*, the same as our
minstrels.[6]    I might extend considerably these specimens of
almost incredible anachronisms, but I will only mention one more,
which is sufficiently striking, and which applies to a so-called
Universal History, written just after the invention of printing.[7]
Daniel in his History of France, says that Louis VIII. when
very ill, was ordered by his physician to admit to his bed a young
woman, which the pious king refused, and therefore died.    This
story, says Voltaire, has been related of other kings.[8]    It is said
that the only man who escaped the Sicilian Vespers in 1282
was named Porcellet ; and it is also said that Porcellet saved
Richard Cœur de Lion when surrounded by Saracens.[9]

IX.  Historical ballads, or at all events political songs, were very
common in the time of the Fronde.[10]    I think their importance
after this period rapidly declined.

Another source of error consists in applying to individuals what
has been said of cities.    This is done in the Old Testament, and
is said to have been done in French history.[11]    It is thus that in
metaphysical philosophy Hartley and Condillac almost at the same
moment and without any knowledge of each other's labours, arrived
at similar conclusions upon some of the highest and most difficult
branches of abstract knowledge.

The story of the eleven thousand virgins is very commonly
related.[12]    A story similar to the myth which relates how Dido got

[1]  Observations on Sorbiere's Voyage to England, p. 129, Lond. 1709.
[2]  See Van Kampen, Geschiedenis der Letteren in de Niederlanden, deel i. blad 14.
[3]  Ibid. blad 28.                    [4]  Ibid. blad 29.
[5]  Ibid. blad 22.                    [6]  Ibid. blad 26.
[7]  Kampen, deel i. blad 43.
[8]  See Essai sur les Mœurs, chap. li. at end. (Œuvres de Voltaire, tome xvi. pp. 102,
103, and tome xl. p. 211.
[9]  See Œuvres de Voltaire, 1826, tome xv. p. 208.
[10]  See Grimm's Correspondance littéraire, tome vi. pp. 244, 245.
[11]  See Sorel, Bibliothèque française, p. 300.
[12]  See Prichard's Physical History of Mankind, vol. iii. pp. 172, 173, note.

Carthage is common in the East.[1] Wright[2] says, "But it was a peculiar trait in the character of the middle ages to create imaginary personages and clothe them with the attributes of a class —types as it were, of popular belief, or of popular attachment or glory."[3] And Wright says that, perhaps from the associations with the remains of ancient art, "The people of the middle ages first saw the type of the magician in the poets and philosophers of the classic days. The physician Hippocrates, under the corrupted name of Ypocras, was supposed to have effected his cures by magic, and he was the subject of a legendary history certainly as old as the twelfth century, containing incidents which were subsequently told of a more celebrated conjuror, Virgil." He adds,[4] "It is not impossible that the equivocal meaning of the Latin word *carmen* (which means a poem and a charm) may have contributed to the popular reputation of poets;"[5] and again, "Down to a very recent period, if not at the present day, the people in the neighbourhood of Palestrina have looked upon Horace as a powerful and benevolent wizard." Mr. Wright has given[6] a very curious account of the myths in the middle ages respecting Virgil. Vico[7] says that the French nation "a conservé une sorte de poëme homérique dans l'histoire de l'archévêque Turpin, qu'ont ensuite embelli tant de poëmes et de romans." Vico says,[8] "Au moyen-âge les historiens latins furent des poètes héroïques comme Guntérus, Guillaume de Pouilles, et autres." He says[9] that the Greek singers or rhapsodists learnt pieces of Homer.

Frankfort-on-the-Main, so called because the Franks discovered a ford there to cross the river Main.

The forged writings of Dionysius the Areopagite were particularly influential in the Greek monasteries.[10]

In the tenth century a missionary called Bruno was surnamed Boniface, and "two different persons having been made out of these two names, a missionary Boniface was invented, who is to be wholly stricken out of the list of historical persons."[11]

. . . . . . .

Coryat, who was in Switzerland in 1609, heard the story of Tell, all of which he devoutly believed.[12] Archdeacon Hare believes all about Tell.

Mackay says,[13] "It has been ingeniously surmised that the

[1] See Malcolm's History of Persia, vol. i. p. 242.
[2] Narratives of Sorcery and Magic, Lond. 1850, vol. i. p. 99.    [3] Ibid. p. 100.
[4] Ibid.    [5] Ibid.    [6] Ibid. pp. 101-121.
[7] Philosophie de l'Histoire, p. 34.    [8] Ibid. p. 162.    [9] Ibid. pp. 274, 275.
[10] Neander's History of the Church, vol. v. p. 234.    [11] Ibid. vol vii. p. 57.
[12] See Coryat's Crudities, vol. ii. pp. 193-196.
[13] Progress of the Intellect, Lond. 1850, vol. i. p. 402.

genealogy from Shem to Abraham is in part significant of geographical localities, or successive stations occupied by the
Hebrews," &c. As to the origin of St. Luke being believed to
be a painter, see Swinburne's Courts of Europe at close of last
Century, vol. i. pp. 231, 232. Read Blunt's Vestiges of Ancient
Manners in Italy. Kemble,[1] speaking of Saxo-Grammaticus,
gently notices "Saxo's very extraordinary mode of rationalising
ancient mythological traditions." Because there was no tide in
the Baltic we are told that Canute ordered his chair to be taken
to the coast to show that the tide would not retire at his command.[2] On the Niebelungen Lied, note that Laing[3] says that
while all tradition of it is lost in Germany, fragments exist in the
oral state at the present day in the Færo Islands. Laing[4] says
that Saxo-Grammaticus employed "historical Saga different from
those used by his contemporary Snorro." Another source of confusion was that the church and clerical historians introduced the
Latin language, in which Laing says[5] the *spirit* of old events
perished. And "*Philology*" shows that a new language will
introduce errors. Ranke[6] says, "As in all countries the legend of
the Wild Huntsman has been connected with the most renowned
names, Arthur, Waldemar, and Charlemagne, so in France it was
associated with that of Hugh Capet. Compare Grimm, German
Mythology, p. 894.

A great source of error has been that poets have copied in their
works engravings or sculptures. Göthe relates that when a youth
he made poems to suit some engravings with which he met.[7]
Marsden[8] says of the Sumatrans, "The country people can very
seldom give an account of their age, being entirely without any
species of chronology."[9]

For a singular instance of a strange story told twice of the same
person, see Autobiography of the Emperor Iehanguein, pp. 68,
69. In the Russian account of Kamtschatka it is said of the
natives, "They keep no account of their age, though they count
as far as one hundred."[10]

There was a very important sect known as the Paulicians, said
to be Manichæan. Those men by whom in the middle ages

[1] Saxons in England, vol. i. p. 340.
[2] Laing's Denmark, p. 286.
[3] Ibid. pp. 347, 348.
[4] Ibid. p. 340.
[5] Ibid. p. 369.
[6] Civil Wars of France in the Sixteenth and Seventeenth Centuries, Lond. 1852. vol. i. p. 259.
[7] See the curious passage in Wahrheit und Dichtung, in Göthe's Werke, band ii. theil ii. p. 98, and Bohn's translation, vol. i. p. 267.
[8] History of Sumatra, p. 248.
[9] Ibid. p. 248.
[10] Grieve's History of Kamtschatka. p. 177, 4to.

ecclesiastical history was written laid hold of this and declared
that the sect must owe its origin to a man named Paul, who
must be not the apostle but a heretic. And on this ground they
ascribe the sect to various Pauls, all without reason. (Paulicians
are said to be an offshoot of Manicheism.)

On the confused notions of the Greeks, Neander[1] observes from
Ritter that they called Ethiopia and Arabia Felix part of India.
The north point of Yucatan is now called Cape Cotoche, having
its origin from the Indians having said to the Spaniards " Conex
cotoch," " Come to our town."

## PRELIMINARY FOR REIGN OF ELIZABETH.

THE spirit of chivalry, which during the middle ages had greatly
hastened the progress of civilization, not only ceased to produce
good, but tended to retard what it had before accelerated. The
sterner features of knightly sentiment are incompatible with true
civilization—with that civilization which humanises, not a single
class, but an entire people. It is to the lingering spirit of chivalry
that we owe some of the most absurd enactments which disgrace
our statute-book, and the last operation of that spirit may be
traced in the present day in the sentiment of those mad enthu-
siasts who extol the superior virtues of barbarism, and look on
the increase of wealth and luxury as the sure sign of a declining
civilization.[2]

The history of England from the fourteenth to the sixteenth
centuries, inclusive, is the history of a continual struggle between
the middle class, who represent the modern civilization, and the
upper classes, who represent the ancient civilization of chivalry.
Everything which tended to increase the comfort, and therefore
to ameliorate the condition of men, was stigmatised, not only as
an impertinent novelty, but as a demoralising luxury. Hence
even coaches were on their first introduction denounced as effeminate, and as ill suited to the manly character of Britons.    It is
to this spirit that we owe the sumptuary laws.[3]

[1] History of the Church, vol. i. p. 113.
[2] For the absurdity of supposing that wealth has an uncivilizing tendency, see the
admirable remarks of Whately (Political Economy, Lond. 1831, pp. 42, 43, 58, 64).
The fourteenth century which is the dawn of civilization is the period when chivalry
began to decline.  See C. P. D. art. 1236.
[3] See some amusing instances of this given by Mr. Maitland in his interesting paper
on the early use of carriages in England, in Archæologia, vol. xx. pp. 443–476, and in
particular the quotation at p. 469.

When did the middle classes arise ?   Of course when chivalry
declined.   Probably the rebellion of 1569 was the last instance
in this country of the spirit of chivalry producing such an effect.
Wright has observed[1] that probably all the families who took
share in it " were allied by blood or intermarriage with the two
families of the Percies and Nevilles."

----

## SIXTEENTH CENTURY.

At the end of the fifteenth century there occurred two most
important events which gave a new direction to the current of
European thought.   To the West a new world was found.   To
the East a new passage was discovered, by which thousands of
inquisitive men hastened to the cradle of the human race.   To
America, to Asia, and to Africa, there poured a stream of travellers, whose relations of what they had seen were read with an
eager curiosity of which we can now scarcely form an idea.

The field of history thus suddenly enlarged as to space, was
necessarily contracted as to time.   Instead of tracing the annals
of a people back to their supposed origin, the views of historians
became concentrated on the marvellous events of their own age.
The effect of this spirit was soon apparent in a general disposition
to break those imaginary links by which Europe was connected
with the most remote antiquity.   Towards the end of the reign
of Henry VIII., Polydore Virgil, the best writer on English
history that had yet appeared, boldly denied the existence of
Brute, and even ventured to hint his suspicions as to the value of
that romance by Geoffrey of Monmouth, which the world had
long considered as a work of unimpeachable veracity.
    *         *         *         *         *

It is possible, though I think it is scarcely probable, that the
tendency to purge history of its fables would under ordinary
circumstances have worn itself out, and have been succeeded by
some newer fashion.   But towards the end of the sixteenth, and
during great part of the seventeenth century, it was still further
confirmed by the revolutions which broke out in every part of
Europe, and which fixed the attention even of speculative men
upon the momentous events that were passing around them.
Macchiavelli and Guicciardini, De Thou and Sully, Davila and
Bentivoglio, Clarendon and Burnet, were certainly superior to any

----

[1] Wright's Elizabeth, Lond. 1838, vol. i. p. xxxiv.

historian who had yet appeared. But they were so deeply impressed with the important events of their own generation that they had little inclination to busy themselves with those of a former age. This explains the fact that during more than a century the greatest historians in Europe were those who occupied themselves in writing the history of their own times. And that this is the real explanation becomes still more probable from the circumstance that in Spain, where, after the expulsion of the Moors there was no great revolution, there is not to be found any eminent contemporary historian.

If we require any further confirmation of the accuracy of these views, we shall find it in the circumstance that the first man of genius who studied history with anything like comprehensive views, was a native of that country where the insurrectionary spirit was first decisively quelled. The revolutions of France had in the middle of the seventeenth century been brought to a close before the people had succeeded in obtaining their liberties. The ultimate consequences of this were most disastrous, and were afterwards felt during many generations, but in a mere literary point of view the effect was at first beneficial. The splendid successes of Louis XIV. soon conciliated his subjects, and his power was such as to render hopeless even the idea of popular resistance. The versatile intellect of France, diverted from politics, took refuge in letters, and produced a literature which, so far as polish and beauty are concerned, it would be difficult to match in any country or any age. Of the ornaments of that time, Bossuet, Bishop of Meaux, was in many respects one of the most remarkable. This great man, wonderful as an orator, still more wonderful as a divine, is perhaps the finest theological genius that Christianity has yet produced. It is, however, with his work on Universal History that we are now more immediately concerned. In this most remarkable fragment he has displayed a sublimity and a grandeur which is unrivalled in the whole compass of historic literature.

But it had great faults, which perhaps were natural to his character, and which certainly were natural to the circumstances under which he was placed. His powerful mind was hampered by the prejudices of his profession, and this made him the more willing to refer all matters of difficulty to authority rather than to reason. This affection for tradition is indeed still characteristic of the clergy, but in his admiration for what is called classical antiquity, Bossuet was also influenced by feelings which he held in common with nearly every man of his time. It is indeed difficult for us at the present day to understand the extraordinary

veneration with which even the wisest of men formerly regarded
the ancient world.   As such a feeling, by exaggerating the
achievements of the past, was of course very prejudicial to the
progress of history, I shall now give some evidence of the extent
to which it had spread in the sixteenth and seventeenth centuries,
and I will then endeavour to trace those circumstances which led
to its decline.

Among the many benefits which Europe owes to the Reformation, the right of the exercise of private judgment would, if it had
been persisted in, have been unquestionably the most important.
As long as the reformers admitted that right, it is evident that
the antagonistic principle of submission to authority in matters of
opinion must have been proportionably weakened: and with it
must also have been weakened that veneration for antiquity which
can only be felt by men who prefer the submission of faith to the
exercise of reason.   It is not, therefore, surprising to find in the
writings of the earliest Protestants innumerable passages expressing their contempt of form and tradition, and even their
disregard for the most accredited opinions of the ancient fathers.
But as soon as the first heat of Protestantism had subsided, its
leaders found it advisable to recur to that principle of faith which
they had somewhat hastily discarded.   They found that opinions
which were convenient enough for a rising sect were by no means
suitable for a wealthy church.   The results are but too well
known to the readers of ecclesiastical history.   Those men who
had risen to power by professing the right of private judgment
did not hesitate to abrogate this right as soon as they had gained
the power.   Aided by the civil magistrate, they emulated the
tyranny of her whom they loved to call the Man of Sin, and the
whore of Babylon.   Without the slightest regard to the independent judgment of individuals, they framed articles and canons
and dogmas which under the severest penalties they expected to
be implicitly received.   As these proceedings could scarcely be
defended by reason, it was necessary to defend them by authority;
and both Catholics and Protestants eagerly appealed to antiquity
to justify their respective measures.   If a theological tenet was at
stake, the question to be decided was not whether it was rational,
or whether it was suited to the exigencies of society, but the
question was if it could be found in the writings of Irenaeus or
Cyprian, if it was mentioned by Tertullian before he became a
Montanist, or if it was to be discovered in the works of the
apostolic fathers.   This is the way in which, in the sixteenth century, disputes were conducted; and this is what we are expected
to admire as the model of controversial theology.   By common

consent both parties spurned anything like an attempt at independent reasoning; and questions of the deepest interest were
decided by an appeal to writers whose works are defaced by the
most contemptible puerilities, and whose antiquity was the only
possible claim they could have to respect. While such was the
spirit in which men handled the sublimest dogmas of religion, it
was hardly to be expected that they would adopt a better course
in the inferior department of profane history. If an argument
was to be constructed, or an illustration to be found, it was always
to the history of Greece, of Rome, or of Judæa, that men turned
their eyes. The annals of modern people were considered to
labour under some inherent disadvantage, and not to possess that
dignity which entitled them to the attention of the learned. Not
only was everything of value written in the Latin language, but
the minds of men seemed unable to support the idea of anything
beyond a servile imitation of the ancients. The writings of
Cicero, which, beautiful as they are, too often by their redundance
transcend the bounds of a severe taste, were the delight of men
who admired the sparkle but could not see the gold. A number
of these authors would only use Ciceronian phrases; and, when
Erasmus ventured to ridicule this folly, he was attacked with the
most indecent fury. Macchiavelli was a man of the most unquestionable capacity, and, considering the age in which he lived, of
large views; but he drew all his illustrations from antiquity.

At the end of the sixteenth century the two great English historians were Camden and Hayward. Camden, indeed, was a mere
antiquary, and even in that branch of knowledge was very careless, as those who have made much use of his Britannia will
readily allow. As an historian, he was still more inaccurate; and
his history of Elizabeth, though it will always possess value as a
contemporary relation, literally swarms with blunders, and does
not contain a single observation which is worthy of being remembered. Hayward was a writer of somewhat superior intellect, and
is the first of our historians who attempted to investigate the
causes of particular actions and the motives of statesmen. His
history of part of the reign of Elizabeth was written early in the
seventeenth century, and shows the usual respect for antiquity.
Thus, on the occasion of the siege of Leith by the English, Hayward inquires into the propriety of their attacking some churches
in which the French had posted their artillery. The mere existence of a doubt on such a question shows the superstition of the
age; but, as the English determined to fire into the churches,
Hayward thinks it necessary to justify their resolution by quoting
passages from Livy, from Florus, from Josephus, from Tacitus,

and from Isocrates. Indeed, several years later, we find a similar method employed by men of much superior powers. Selden was not only an able politician, but was unquestionably the most learned Englishman of his time. He in the year 1640 published a work upon the Law of Nations, but, so far from condescending to settle that intricate matter by human reason, he founds the whole of his arguments upon a lying invention of the Rabbis, called the Seven Precepts of Noah.

Even De Thou, whose justly celebrated history appeared early in the seventeenth century, was by no means free from the prevailing spirit.

Bayle's work on The Comet, which was written in 1681, was not allowed to be printed in France. His reply to Maimbourg was publicly burnt in Paris. He himself was driven from his native country, and compelled to take refuge in Holland, where he published his Critical Dictionary, the most celebrated and elaborate of all his works. He died while Louis XIV. was yet on the throne; and he was not destined to see that great moral revolution to which he was the first contributor. In 1690, Perrault, in his celebrated Parallel between the Ancients and Moderns, not only preferred the last, but placed Scudery and Chapelain above Homer. In 1715, Terrasson published an elaborate attack upon Homer. La Motte published an abridgment of the Iliad, and considered that by doing so he had greatly improved the original. Indeed, he stated in an essay that the merits of Homer were, in his opinion, greatly overrated. This outbreak against the ancient celebrities was conducted by men very incompetent [to] the task; but there never before was an age in which such things would have been even dreamt of. It was natural that the same spirit which attacked classical prejudice should also attack theological prejudices. This was now done by Fontenelle, a very remarkable man, whose long life connected two great ages of French literature. The Fathers, who were not very good judges of evidence, had generally taken for granted the supernatural origin of the pagan oracles. They, however, took care to add that the priests were inspired by Satan, who hoped by this stratagem to put to confusion the people of God. Such was the superstition among even the best informed of European scholars, that this theory was very generally believed until the end of the seventeenth century.

## SEVENTEENTH CENTURY.

GROTIUS, the first great historical thinker after Macchiavelli, was in Holland, the first great republic in Europe. Men were still very ignorant. The population of France was differently estimated at from five to twenty millions.[1] Monteil[2] observes how few works there were in the seventeenth century on politics. Capefigue[3] says that after the defeat of the Armada in 1588, the prosperity and *revolutionary freedom* of Holland began. Capefigue says[4] that "les gazettes hollandaises" first began in the seventeenth century. The kingly *character* even declined. Olivarez, Richelieu, and Buckingham were supreme, and Europe had such miserable sovereigns as James I., Louis XIII., and Philip III. Then the Fronde, Massaniello, Retz, Cromwell. Spain lost Naples and Catalonia. All this was aided by the change in the value of money. Spain, the last great ecclesiastical monarchy the world has ever seen, was now falling to pieces; and, as I shall hereafter show, the sceptical movement was seizing all the departments of politics. The independent and *personal* method of Bacon and Descartes, which, so far from being different, are identical. Hallam[5] says that Hakewill in his Apology, or Declaration of the Power of God, in 1627, " seems to be one of the first" who claimed for modern literature a superiority over the ancient. In a pamphlet published in 1652, the population of Paris is estimated at 6,000,000.[6] There was as yet no real community of nations and little sympathy. The execution of Charles I. was not known in Paris till three weeks after it occurred. The memoirs of Retz, a great demagogue, are the first that show political penetration; they are the first that, like Clarendon and Burnet, sketch *character*, thus showing the increasing sense of the importance of [the] people and individual [s]. Retz[7] speaks with the greatest contempt of the "vulgar historian." See also tome ii. p. 114, where he thinks historians can only know what they *see* and *do*. Patin was so struck by the revolutionary character of the age, that in 1649 he writes,[8] " Il y a quelques constellation en rigueur contre les têtes couronnées." In 1650, Patin writes from Paris,[9] "Il y a içi un Jésuite qui a conçu un nouveau dessin touchant la géographie. Il s'appelle le père

[1] See Monteil, Histoire des Français, tome viii. p. 278.    [2] Ibid. p. 290, note.
[3] Histoire de la Réforme, tome v. p. 102.
[4] Richelieu, Mazarin et la Fronde, tome ii. p. 30.    [5] Literature, vol. iii. p. 236.
[6] Sainte-Aulaire, Histoire de la Fronde, tome ii. p. 247.
[7] Mémoires, vol. i. pp. 448, 453.
[8] Lettres, tome i. p. 151.    [9] Ibid. tome ii. p. 251.

Laurent le Brun ; il nous veut donner une géographie universelle in-folio." Oliver St. John, one of the most influential
members of the Long Parliament, was the first Englishman who
seriously laboured to establish an English democracy, an idea
which he is said to have acquired when in Holland. Horoscope
of Louis XIV.[1] In the seventeenth century the great movement
for *independence,* hitherto theological, now first became *secular*
and *philosophical,* and Luther and Calvin were succeeded by
Bacon, Descartes, Grotius, and Leibnitz. It was Holland that
resisted the dangerous force of Louis XIV. and gave us a free
king, William III. Bayle and Quesnel fled to Holland, and so
did Jurieu, who, as Capefigue well says,[2] " appartenait à ces
reformateurs qui proclamaient l'empire des masses sur les rois, de
l'élection sur les droits de race." The Dutch published all sorts
of caricatures against Louis XIV.[3] Many of their pamphlets
were even circulated in Paris, and made the people discontented
with Louis XIV.[4] The abdication of James II. was not known
in the Orkney Islands till three months after it occurred. It is
said that Brienne, who visited Lapland in 1654, was the first
Frenchman who had ever been there. The characteristics of the
seventeenth century were political revolution, speculative legislation, and the rise of geography as connected with history. The
Eastern nations, even at the present day, have no idea of numbers.[5] Wilkinson[6] says, " It is remarkable that in the East no
one knows his exact age ; nor do they keep any registers of births
or deaths." In 1724, M. de Moivre published the first edition of
his Tract on Annuities on Lives. In an elaborate description of
London written in 1643, it is estimated that London contains
500,000 houses, and more than 3,000,000 people.[7] Bunsen says,
"Towards the close of the sixteenth century, Joseph Scaliger
commenced his great undertaking, the restoration of ancient
chronology." See Bunsen's Egypt, vol. i. p. 231, *et seq.,* where the
highest praises are bestowed upon Scaliger. Carlyle says, " Lord
Clarendon, a man of sufficient unveracity of heart, to whom
indeed whatsoever has direct veracity of heart is more or less
horrible."[8] In 1686 there were great disputes about the population of London and Paris.[9] Even in the middle of the reign of

---

[1] Mémoires de Lenet, tome ii. p. 48.          [2] Louis XIV., tome i. pp. 215, 279, 328.
[3] See specimens in Capefigue, Louis XIV., tome i. pp. 147, 176, 408, 464.
[4] Ibid. p. 377.          [5] See Grote's History of Greece, vol. v. p. 53.
[6] Ancient Egyptians, vol ii. p. 34.
[7] See Lethgore's Survey of London in Somers Tracts, vol. iv. p. 541.
[8] Carlyle's Cromwell, vol. i. p. 106.
[9] See Ray's Correspondence, edited by Lankester, p. 189.

George II., it was a common dispute whether London or Paris were the more populous.[1] Even ninety years ago it was an unsettled question "whether London or Paris is the larger city."[2]

## PHILOLOGY.

THE historical importance of the study of languages has during the present century been made peculiarly apparent. By it we have ascertained the movements of nations at a time when written records were not in existence. Thus we know that the great Gothic nations and the great Celtic nations have a common origin, and that both of them came from Asia. In a general view of the history of mankind, these two facts are of course of immense importance, but we know of no means except by Philology by which they could have been discovered. The origin of language was the naming of our sensations, and this forms what are commonly called Nouns-Substantive. These, it is clear, must be the names of the most important sensations. Mr. James Mill[3] says, "Sensations being infinitely numerous, all cannot receive marks or signs. A selection must be made. Only those which are the most important are named." He adds[4] that most nouns-substantive are first names of sensations, and "are afterwards employed as names also of the ideas or copies of these sensations." If therefore we have a list of the nouns-substantive of any people, we may tell what sensations they considered most important. If, for instance, every record of the Arabs had perished except a dictionary of their language, we should know that they were jealous of their women when we found that they had several names for eunuchs. Another remark is that we may ascertain the extent to which a people have pushed the process of abstraction, by noting the number of abstract words to be found in their language. In the same way, the extent to which commercial expressions have crept into a language show the extent to which the people have become commercial. Here then we have another consideration of great moment. Since the association of ideas is intimately connected with language, and since there can be little doubt that the firmest

[1] Le Blanc's Lettres d'un Français, tome i. p. 385.
[2] The Police of France, Lond. 4to. 1763, p. 123.
[3] Analysis of the Phenomena of the Human Mind, Lond. 1829, vol. i. p. 93.
[4] Ibid. p. 90.

O

belief is only a case of indissoluble association, it follows that the
speech of every people must greatly modify their beliefs, or, in
other words, their opinions. Nor can this be answered by objecting
that the language of nations would follow their ideas, and not
precede them. For in the first place, without adopting the extravagance of the Nominalists, it is certain that, even if we
suppose a people to have entirely worked out their own language,
there can be no doubt that in some instances such language
would precede and govern the order of their ideas. But in the
second place, this supposition is an unnecessary concession, for
there probably never existed any people whose natural speech
was free from foreign elements, which have been forced upon
them by external circumstances unconnected with their own intellectual development. In England, for instance, there can be
no doubt that the introduction by the Normans of a refined, and,
comparatively speaking, a philosophic language must, so soon as
it became interwoven into the Saxon, have produced considerable
effect upon the trains of ideas of our countrymen, and therefore
upon their opinions. The advantage we thus received is an advantage over and above that which we gained from such knowledge as the Norman race were able to impart. The knowledge
itself is now useless. In every respect we have far outstripped
that savage race who were only civilized, inasmuch as they were
less barbarous than their neighbours. But by the communication
of their language, they have laid the foundation of a dialect
which, at the present time, influences every Englishman in his
own despite during every moment of his existence, and which
has contributed to fix our national associations, and to regulate
our national opinions. Supposing other things equal, if in any
language we find one word having five synonyms, and another
word having only two synonyms, we may rely upon it that the
sensation represented by the first word is considered more important than the sensation represented by the second. In the
same way it will always be found that when two correlatives
represent ideas nearly equal in importance, a word will be invented
for each; but that when there is no sort of equality between
them, there will be a word for the smaller correlative and one
for the greater. Mill notices this,[1] but this remark had already
been made in Hume's Essay on the Populousness of Ancient
Nations. Sir J. Mackintosh, says Leibnitz, "seems to have been
the first philosophical etymologist, and to have rightly estimated
the importance of the Teutonic nations and languages. That he

---

[1] Analysis of the Mind, Lond. 1829, vol. ii. p. 87.

called them Celtic was a mistake which can appear important
only to Mr. Pinkerton."[1] Mr. Rogers, in his Essay upon Leibnitz,
says that great man " was probably the first to predict the important connection—so fruitful of results—which would be found
to subsist between philological and historical researches, and the
light which the former might be made to shed on the latter."[2]
In India the monsoon being an ordinary phenomenon, there is no
name for it.[3]

---

## EIGHTEENTH CENTURY.

I HAVE thus brought down to the close of the seventeenth century a general view of the progress of historical literature, in
which, passing over matter of minor importance, I have endeavoured to confine myself to those changes which mark the
great epochs through which the human mind has successively
passed. The leading nations of Europe, though steadily advancing, had hitherto, with the exception of the mathematical
and a few of the physical sciences, effected nothing of much value
in any of the departments of knowledge, and some of the most
powerful minds were still corrupted by foolish and grovelling
superstition. There was, however, now at hand a great movement,
which, though it first appeared in England, displayed its great
activity in France, where it eventually overturned an ancient
monarchy, a corrupt nobility, and a licentious priesthood. But
long before it accomplished this, it effected what was much more
important, a complete change in the tone and spirit of men.
Such was at that time the sudden audacity of the French intellect,
that feelings and prejudices which from their extreme antiquity
seemed to form a necessary part of the human mind were in a
moment rooted up and destroyed. Unhappily this great work was
towards its close defaced by a cruel spirit of revenge. But in
its early stage, when the intellectual revolution was nearly completed, and before the political revolution had begun, there was
accomplished for philosophic history in the short space of two
generations more than had yet been done from the earliest commencement of written records. Not only were views originated
far more comprehensive than any which had yet been put forward,

[1] Memoirs of Sir J. Mackintosh, edited by his Son, 1835, vol. i. pp. 397, 398.
[2] Rogers, Essays, Lond. 1850, vol. i. pp. 191, 192.
[3] See Crawfurd's History of the Indian Archipelago, vol. i. pp. 316, 317, Edinb. 8vo,
1820.

o 2

but several branches of knowledge which are indispensable to history were suddenly developed, and began to take their stand in the rank of sciences. Political economy, statistics, jurisprudence, physiology, and several branches of metaphysics were studied with such success that many of their laws were for the first time satisfactorily established. Nor was this great movement confined to a single nation. There were indeed, as I shall endeavour to explain, some circumstances which prevented it from producing much effect in England, from whence it had, in its mildest form, originally proceeded; but in other countries it caused very important results. In Italy it gave rise to a great school, from which Europe has learned some of its most valuable lessons in the science of jurisprudence. Its greatest effects were, however, produced in Germany, where it rescued a whole people from the depths of superstition, and enabled them to rear up that wonderful literature to which, as we shall presently see, the intellectual regeneration of Europe is in no small degree to be ascribed.

It may be easily supposed that in this great field of inquiry which we are now about to enter, I shall not be able to preserve that conciseness to which I have hitherto carefully adhered. The grandeur with which, in the eyes of all thinking men, the eighteenth century is naturally invested, has stimulated me to a more than ordinary diligence, and I should be doing justice neither to myself nor to my readers if I were to suppress too many of the materials which have suggested those views that will form the basis of the future volumes of this history. As it is possible that some of these views may be considered original, and as it is, I fear, certain that many of them will give offence, I have deemed it right to fortify them by every description of evidence which study and reflection enable me to supply. If therefore anyone is inclined to be offended by the variety of topics into which I have entered, or by the number and length of the notes, he will, I trust, have the candour to ascribe them, not to a pedantic desire of displaying my own reading, nor to the wish of diverging upon matters which are alien to the object of this work. I can say, with the most perfect confidence, that my only anxiety has been to state with fairness the grounds upon which my opinions have been formed, in order that if they are wrong, they may be the more easily refuted, and that if they are right, they may be the more readily believed. I should not have made this remark if I had not observed in this country of late years a growing disposition on the part of authors to conceal the immediate sources of their information, and a corresponding disposition on the part of critics to form their opinions with great rapidity, and to content themselves on many subjects of difficulty and importance with the most meagre and imperfect evidence.

The first and most important peculiarity of the great historians of the eighteenth century is the view which they took of subjects connected with religion. Not only did they enforce by every means in their power the great principle of toleration, but they pushed it to so extreme a point that even at the present day many enlightened men have found occasion to blame their conduct. The five writers to whose genius we owe the first attempt at comprehensive views of history were Bolingbroke Montesquieu, Voltaire, Hume and Gibbon.[1] Of these, the second was but a cold believer in Christianity, if, indeed, he believed in it at all; and the other four were avowed and notorious infidels. Nor were they content with preserving what they would have considered a philosophic indifference upon so important a subject. Hume, indeed, whose fine, clear, but cold mind seemed incapable of enthusiasm, always kept his attacks upon Revelation within those limits which the decencies of the age seemed to require. But Montesquieu, during a considerable part of his life, and Voltaire and Gibbon during the whole of their lives, never cared to conceal their opinions, and employed all their energies in attacking Christianity with every weapon which their learning and genius could supply. This has always appeared to me to suggest some very important considerations. That he who believes Christianity to be false should endeavour to expose its errors, is but fair and natural. Nor would anyone properly instructed in the real principles of toleration attempt to interfere with so undoubted a right. But that men of genius and learning and great benevolence should hate and ridicule a religion which, whether true or false, is certainly the mildest and most beneficent that has been yet seen in the world; that, not content with arguing, they should jibe and jeer at a system on which alone millions of their countrymen repose all their hopes of a future life; that these things should be publicly done, is at first sight so utterly incomprehensible as to suggest a suspicion either that the authors were professing principles which they did not entertain, or else that the merits of their personal character must have been grossly exaggerated. And yet, so far is this from being true, that it is certain from their private correspondence that their dislike to Christianity was even stronger than that which they

[1] Vico, indeed, attempted to show the way, but he made no attempt to apply principles.

expressed in their works.  And it is as certain that all of them
were beloved by those who knew them, and were of the warmest
and most kindly affections.  We have full and undoubted evidence that Voltaire, who was by far the most scurrilous of these
great writers, was a man of the most lively sensibility, that he
passed his long life in acts of unwearied benevolence, that he
was the friend of the oppressed and the father of the orphan, and
that he even squandered a large income on acts of private and
unostentatious charity.  Unless therefore we are prepared to
believe that men remarkable for their abilities and their virtues
were governed by the most criminal and contemptible caprice,
we must refer their conduct to some general principle which influenced them in their own despite, and which gave to their works
that appearance with which many of us are so justly offended.
What that principle was, I will now endeavour to explain, with
the aid of such lights as history will enable me to supply.

It may I think be laid down as a law of the human mind that
in every country where religious toleration is established, scepticism must

    *        *        *        *        *

In the eighteenth century our own literature first assumed its
popular character and formed a part of the intellectual polity of
Europe.  Then, too, the literature of Denmark arose, in 1720,
under Holberg.[1]

In law Beccaria, Bentham, Anquetil, Du Perron, Sonnerat, and
Genht studied the laws of the Brahmins.  Egypt explored by
Bruce, Arabia by Volney.  Cook and Bougainville explored the
world.  Now it was that the great brotherhood of nations became
knit together in one polity.  Before Lord Hardwicke, international
law was scarcely known in England.[2]  Bunsen[3] says, " No school
of Coptic theology was instituted till the beginning of the
eighteenth century. . . . The founder was David Wilkins, who
published the New Testament at Oxford (1716), and the Penta-
teuch (1730)."  The Rosetta stone was discovered in 1799.[4]  Since
Young and Champollion, the only *discoverers* in hieroglyphics are
Lepsius and Leemans.[5]  Bunsen says,[6] " Sylvester de Sacy, that
great man who brought Arabic philology, neglected since the
time of Reiske, to its true historical position."

Until the eighteenth century there was no history, and in
England the people only knew history from ballads.

[1] See Laing's Denmark, p. 355.       [2] Storey's Conflict of Laws, p. 12.
[3] Egypt, vol. i. p. 260.          [4] Ibid. pp. 309, 310.
[5] Ibid. pp. 332, 333.           [6] Ibid. p. 315.

It was in the eighteenth century that medicine, the most important of all the arts, was first able to throw off those superstitious fancies which had long impeded its progress. At the end of the century there was put forward that great undulatory theory of light which in the opinion of an eminently competent [authority] is hardly inferior to Newton's discovery of universal gravitation.

The influence of French literature was even slightly felt in Spain.

Although the power of the clergy was one of the proximate causes of the backward state of history, facility of belief was the primary one; and I have shown from speculative arguments that this was also the cause of intolerance. I will now prove the same thing historically, and show that as scepticism advanced toleration did, and does of necessity increase. This I shall prove in French history; and first I will give *condensed* evidence in English history. The people must diminish their inordinate confidence in government and clergy, i.e. inquire in politics and religion, and before inquiring doubt. Here, then, we have the starting point of progress—*scepticism*. I broadly assert that there is no progressive principle except the increasing experience of mankind, which stores up practical truths which, being generalised, become scientific truths. All, therefore, that men want is, *no hindrance* from their political and religious rulers. But the absence of hindrance can only be caused by pressure from without, hence the first step is *scepticism*. Until common minds doubt respecting religion they can never receive any new scientific conclusion at variance with it,—as Joshua and Copernicus.

Civilization depends on knowing the future, which can only be done by the intellect. When men are left alone, each succeeding generation first perceives more facts and then discovers more relations or laws. If government will only be quiet, increasing experience will suggest increasing thought. The main point in history to which everything else is subordinate is to trace the course of the human intellect and the way the ignorant and selfish ruling classes have tampered with it.

. . . . . . .

A writer of considerable reputation, Warton, draws a strange distinction between history and philosophy.[1]

The absurdity of talking about the descendants of Japhet and the Gomerites has been continued in England to our own time; which is the more remarkable, for even in 1771 it was exposed by

[1] Warton's History of English Poetry, vol. i. p. cxciii.

Schlözer in his Allgemeine Geschichte.[1]  There is too much truth
in Mr. Blackwell's generalisation that in matters of knowledge
" the Germans are nearly half a century in advance of us."

In the meantime comparative philology, from which we have
already been able to make many remarkable discoveries, was for
the first time cultivated.  The learned men of the seventeenth
century, the Vossiuses, the Scaligers, and the Casaubons were
mere pedants without any idea of the psychological importance
of their subject.  Indeed the first great step in European philology was made in 1770 by Percy, a writer of considerable miscellaneous knowledge and acuteness, but by no means remarkable
for his learning.  He however was, I believe, the first who
showed that there was a fundamental difference between the two
great families of European languages, the Teutonic and the
Celtic.

One of the most eminent historians of that age, the celebrated
Robertson, though totally ignorant of the German language,
undertook to write the history of a German emperor.

A celebrated traveller, who had also a good deal of reading,
talks familiarly about the descendants of Shem and Japhet.[2]

A writer of extensive reading says, but without quoting any
authority, that the theories of Wolf and Niebuhr were anticipated in the Scienza Nuova of Vico; but that "neither of them
certainly knew anything of that work."[3]

Another stimulus to the philosophy of history was the increase
of materials.  The study of Sanscrit opened to our view the treasures of Brahmanical lore and the subtleties of the Veda and
the Puranas.  The study of Pali, and later of Tibetan, gave us
the theology of Buddhism.  The energy of a single man—the
noble-minded Du Perron—opened the Zendavesta and the religion of Zoroaster.  The accounts of travellers brought before us a
strange state of society.  The results of the contact of the German
mind were soon seen in the rise of a larger and more comprehensive method of treating history.  Without entering into prolonged details, I may mention some instances in which this spirit
is very apparent, such as the great subjects of the feudal system,
the middle ages considered as a whole, &c.

I.  The new school certainly produced no man at all comparable
in knowledge or in general powers to Blackstone, still less to

[1] Blackwell's note in Mallet's Northern Antiquities, Lond. 1847, p. 26.
[2] Clarke's Travels, vol. ix. p. 41, Lond. 1824.
[3] Keightley. On the Resemblance and Transmission of Tales and Fictions, Lond.
1834, p. 18.

Montesquieu.  And yet both these writers, having occasion to
inquire at great length into the feudal system, were so misled by
the contracted spirit of their time, as to consider this wonderful
institution as entirely the result of the Germanic invasions.  The
extreme inadequacy of the cause did not in the least startle them,
and subsequent authors were content to repeat their cónfident
assertions.  It was reserved for a young Scotchman of fine genius,
and himself one of the earliest students of German literature, to
expose this singular error.  Sir Walter Scott was, I believe, the
first in Europe, and certainly the first in this country, to subject
the feudal system to anything like a philosophic analysis.  He
not only pointed out in an essay the similarity between many of
the feudal phenomena and those found in Asiatic countries, but
he even attempted to trace them all to general causes.

Schiller, perhaps the most eloquent and popular of all the
German writers, wrote in 1788, an elaborate history of the revolt
of the Netherlands, but he openly avows his ignorance of the
Dutch language, and, mistaking the mere form of history for its
spirit, seems to think that he will have done sufficient if he
amuses the reader by an artistic arrangement of striking events.

(Before the account of the ignorance of the middle ages in the
eighteenth century put the following).

That foolish veneration for antiquity so characteristic of the
seventeenth century had now generally subsided; but, unfortunately it was replaced by a not less foolish contempt.  Because
one generation admired the past too much, the next generation
admired it too little.  The real value and the matchless beauty
of the classic literature soon rescued it from this passing contempt.
But the middle ages had no such recommendation, and they were
now despised by every writer who affected to be raised above the
level of his time.  It was in vain that men of unrivalled knowledge brought before the world their history and their literature.
It was in vain that Muratori, Maffei, Ducange, Bouquet, and the
Benedictines of France published gigantic folios which hardly
anybody bought, and which nobody read.  The treasures of learning, accumulated by these modest and useful men, were spurned
aside in that sceptical and audacious age.  Those who were considered to be the great historians of the day, spoke and wrote of
the middle ages with wild and ignorant presumption.

.        .        .        .        .        .        .

After giving an account of the rise of Political Economy, &c.,
and their divergence, I may preface my account of Germany as
follows,—" While these great branches of knowledge were thus

isolating themselves into comparative insignificance, there were
springing up a race of men, who, neglecting the mere details of
inquiry, were attempting by great efforts of general reasoning, to
discover the laws to which all knowledge is itself subject.

Voltaire declared that the history of the middle ages deserved
to be written as little as did the history of bears and wolves.

In France, at the head of financial affairs, was Law, a Scotchman of great ability, whose schemes were received rather by the
fickleness of the Regent than by their own imperfections. Lavallée, I think inaccurately, accuses Law of having confused
[credit?] and money, and of supposing that by increasing the
circulating medium of the country he necessarily increased its
wealth.[1]

I think that Butler was almost the only Englishman who in
the eighteenth century adopted a larger creed of ethics than
La Rochefoucault.

In England, Toland, Tindal, Collins, Chubb, Mandeville, and
even Shaftesbury and Bolingbroke, were no match for men like
Warburton, Waterland, Lardner, and Clarke. *Before Gibbon, the
only Englishman who took a comprehensive view of history was
Bolingbroke, an avowed Deist.* All the pedants of England combined to write the *Universal History.*

---

## ENGLAND—FOR INTRODUCTION.

Ferguson insists on the importance of investigating history inductively.[2] But, after all, Ferguson's book is very poor. The
illustrations are all of the tritest character, and, indeed, in point
of learning, the whole work might have been written by a clever
schoolboy. Ferguson rejects the theory of a cycle in history, that
is, he opposes those who talk of the *necessary* decay of society.[3]
He supposes[4] that one cause of decay is that, from caprice, nations
become *tired* of practising the arts, &c. This of course is absurd ;
but another cause which he mentions[5]—over-division of labour—
must have been very efficacious ; though I suspect he got it from
Adam Smith. He says,[6] "From the tendency of these reflections
then, it should appear that a national spirit is frequently transient,

· [1] Lavallée, Histoire des Français, tome iii. p. 393.
  [2] See Ferguson's Essay on the History of Civil Society, Lond. 1768, pp. 3–4, and
for his attack on the opinions of Rousseau, pp. 7, 8, 12.
  [3] Ibid. pp. 346, 391, and p. 347.          [4] Ibid. p. 350.
  [5] Ibid. p. 362.                              [6] Ibid. p. 372.

not on account of any incurable distemper in the nature of mankind, but on account of their voluntary neglect and corruptions." Ferguson enthusiastically says,[1] "When I recollect what the President Montesquieu has written, I am at a loss to tell why I should treat of human affairs."

Then we had also Tindal's wretched history. If during the first half of the eighteenth century we compare the historic literature of France and England, it will be hardly possible to conceive a greater contrast. In the one country, the finest geniuses of the age—Montesquieu, Voltaire—were engaged in the successful cultivation of what our ancestors seemed to consider too trifling a pursuit to occupy the attention of superior minds. In England, men of the dullest intellects and of the meanest acquirements busied themselves with writing history, because history was supposed to be the only thing which they were able to write. It is not too much to assert that during this period all the English historians who were not totally ignorant of their subject were at best but zealous antiquaries, who collected facts which they did not know how to use, and who were as inferior to the great French authors as the mason who carries the materials is inferior to the architect who schemes the edifice. Carte, for example, was a man of great industry, and, until the appearance of Dr. Lingard, his work was the best history of England which had been published. But so contracted was his mind that he thought it necessary to enter into a long examination of the important question of touching for the king's evil, a prerogative well known to be peculiar to the Lord's anointed. Carte, after considering at great length this difficult question, modestly asserted that God had not granted to our Hanoverian kings the power of miraculously curing the scrofula, but that he had allowed that power to remain in the hands of the Pretender.[2] The discussion of this trumpery superstition was considered so important that it excited in England a storm of angry controversy, and this at the very moment when the great historians of France were actively employed in purifying their literature from the remains of bigotry by which it was still encumbered. Besides Carte's, the only celebrated history of England was that of Rapin, an author now only to be found in the libraries of country gentlemen, who believe him to be honest because they know him to be dull. Indeed, to say the truth, his dulness, intolerable as it is, is the smallest of his faults. Even when men of genius wrote

---

[1] Ferguson's Essay on the History of Civil Society, Lond. 1768, p. 106.
[2] Carte did *not* discuss this question. I think he does not *deny* the power of touching of George II.: but only says that the Pretender had it. [Author's note.]

history, they seemed suddenly to have lost their powers. Gold-smith is certainly one of the most delightful of all our writers. But no sooner did he sit down to his histories of Greece and Rome, than he seemed to be suddenly smitten with an incurable dull-ness. Ancient history was in the hands of Leland and Mitford.

On the history of foreign countries our literature was, if pos-sible, still more deficient. The first thing that strikes us is the extreme presumption of men who supposed that they could under-stand the history of a people of whose literature, and, indeed, of whose speech they were perfectly ignorant. Thus there is Dr. Harte, who, though entirely unacquainted with the Swedish language, wrote a well-known history of the greatest of the Swedish kings, and it is remarkable that his work, dull, and in-accurate as it is, still remains the best life of Gustavus Adolphus that has yet been published in this country. Johnson, the most celebrated, and, in some respects, the most able critic of the day, declared that the best history extant was Knolles' History of the Turks, which had appeared a century before his time. And yet the work of Knolles is not only disfigured by a pompous and inflated style; but the author, though writing the adventures of a powerful Eastern people, did not feel himself called upon to study any of the Eastern tongues except the Hebrew, a language which, except for the philologist, is of no possible importance, and the scanty literature of which has always displayed a marked defi-ciency in historical productions.

As the eighteenth century advanced, there seemed little likeli-hood of a change for the better. Indeed, the immense increase of the national wealth, which was almost entirely owing to a successful application of the physical sciences to the economy of manufactures,[1] tended still further to lessen the interest which men felt in the moral sciences. It was natural that the wonder-

---

[1] The South Sea Company was the first proof of the desire of wealth.

Navigable canals were first constructed by Brindley, an engineer of original genius, employed by the Duke of Bridgewater; and they were at the end of the eighteenth century greatly improved by Telford.

In 1763, Wedgwood made his remarkable improvements in the manufacture of earthenware.

In 1774, the first steam engine of Watt was exhibited at the Soho Works, near Bir-mingham, under the auspices of Boulton; and in a single mine at Cornwall the saving of coals was so large that the proprietors agreed to pay 800l. a year for the use of each engine. These steam engines greatly increased the productiveness of the Corn-wall tin mines; and tended also to the improvement and extension of coal mines.

The spinning jenny, invented by Hargreaves, in 1764, was in operation before 1768.

In 1771, Arkwright "erected the first spinning mill worked by water power."

In 1776, the mule-jenny of Crompton combined the spinning-jenny of Hargreaves, and the water power of Arkwright.

ful inventions of Arkwright, Watt, &c., and the immense fortunes
by which in most cases the inventors were rewarded, should diminish the reputation of those still higher branches of knowledge
from which no such results were to be expected.  Even Political
Economy, which in a mercantile country ought to find the most
successful cultivators, was in England entirely neglected, and the
greatest statesman of the eighteenth century declared that he
never could understand Smith's Wealth of Nations.  If this was
the case with a science which has only to do with the accumulation and distribution of wealth, we may well imagine that those
sciences of which the utility is less evident would fare still worse.
In Ethics, we did not produce during the whole of the eighteenth
century one original writer.  In Psychology we were equally
deficient, for Berkeley, the author of perhaps the most important
discovery that has ever been made in that noble science, was born
in Ireland, lived in Ireland, and died in Ireland.  In Æsthetics,
the only work of the least merit was by Burke, who was also an
Irishman,[1] whose ingenious but imperfect Essay was the work of
a very young man (he was only twenty-six when he wrote on what
is, after ethics, the most obscure branch of metaphysics); nor did
this great writer ever after think it worth his while to return to
so unprofitable a subject.[2]  The consequence was that the English
mind seemed gradually hardening itself to everything except the
accumulation of wealth and the acquisition of military power.  The
German literature, which at a later period did so much to correct
this evil state, was then only in the first dawn of its splendour,
and had not yet gained any reputation.  The French literature, as
I have already described, had after the middle of the eighteenth

At the end of the reign of George II. the Taylors effected the first great improvement in the manufacture of blocks for the rigging of ships.

The travels in England of Saint Fond contain some curious details respecting arts
and manufactures in the latter half of the eighteenth century.  They are often quoted
in the Pictorial History of England.

Just before the French Revolution, Cartwright invented a machine for combing
wool, by which there was effected a wonderful saving of labour.

In Pictorial History of England, vol. vii. p. 714, reference is made to an estimate
by Sir Frederic Eden, in Annals of Commerce, vol. iv. pp. 548, 550.  According to
which the value of "machinery, such as steam-engines, spinning works," &c., was in
England, 40,000,000l.

In the middle of the reign of George II., Harrison, by combining different metals
in the pendulum, and by other contrivances, constructed chronometers of such accuracy as greatly to lessen the risk of sea voyages.  These improvements were followed
up by Thomas Mudge who, in 1774, completed the first chronometer.  See M'Culloch's
Commercial Dictionary, article Hardware.

[1] But Reynolds and Payne Knight.  [Author's note.]

[2] Burke did intend to continue metaphysics, but his noble mind became empirical.
[Author's note.]

century, begun to deteriorate, and was losing every year something of that influence which it had formerly possessed. But happily there had for some time been forming in a long neglected country a school which did much to restore to England a higher tone of thought, and which soon produced the happiest effect upon the study of history. As this movement is one of great importance in the history of the human mind, and as we are still reaping the benefit of it, I shall not scruple to examine it at considerable length.

.        .        .        .        .        .        .

In literature, the supreme chief was Johnson, a man of some learning and great acuteness, but overflowing with prejudice and bigotry. The little metaphysical literature which we did possess went on deteriorating at each stage of its progress from Hartley to Priestley, and from Priestley to Darwin. While the wretched work of De Lolme on the English Constitution was read with avidity, the profound and yet practical inquiries of Hume were almost neglected. In ecclesiastical literature, the most prominent names were Warburton the bully and Hurd the sneak. When the Duchess of Marlborough wished a life to be written of her celebrated husband, whose genius had changed the face of Europe, she could find no one more competent than Mallet, a miserable adventurer who lived by plundering the booksellers and cheating the public. And yet this man, whom the French would hardly have thought worthy of dusting the manuscripts of one of their great historians, was in England a very considerable person, and actually received 1,000*l.* for promising to write the history of those great events by which France had been suddenly degraded from the pinnacle of her military fame. In 1776, Hume writes to Gibbon, "But among many other marks of decline, the prevalence of superstition in England prognosticates the fall of philosophy and decay of taste."[1] And in the same year he writes to Adam Smith in a similar strain.[2] The fear entertained of the French Revolution gave an influence to such women as Hannah More, and they tended still further to depress our literature. Mrs. Montague's wretched Dissertation on Shakespeare was considered a masterpiece of criticism. In 1785, Beattie writes to Arbuthnot that Mrs. Montague's Essay on Shakespeare is "one of the best, most original, and most elegant pieces of criticism in our language, or in any other."[3]

We produced no historian. Gibbon indeed was an exception, but he was a Frenchman in everything except the accident of his birth.

[1] Burton's Life of Hume, vol. ii. p. 485.                    [2] Ibid. p. 487.
[3] Forbes's Life of Beattie, Lond. 1824, vol. ii. p. 164.

His early studies were carried on in Switzerland, in the house of a French Calvinist. His first work was written in the French language, which for many years was more familiar to him than his own tongue. His first literary correspondence was with Crevier, a well-known professor in the University of Paris. The whole of his great history was composed abroad, while his mind was influenced by the associations and traditions of foreign society, and he only visited England at such intervals as were necessary to make arrangements for its publication. When, after having wasted several years on the formation of projects which were never accomplished, he at length began to write the history of the Roman Empire, he still retained his old habits.

Rousseau's Prize Discourse before the Academy of Dijon was translated into English in 1751, and accompanied with an absurd preface by Bowyer, which is reprinted in Nichols's Literary Anecdotes of the Eighteenth Century, vol. ii. pp. 226–227. In 1771, there was translated into English Millot's wretched History of England.[1] It might have been expected that we should have brought from Asia some of those great treasures of learning which even now have by no means been thoroughly explored. But such was the want of energy, that, although we possessed a settlement in India since early in the seventeenth century, it was not until near the end of the eighteenth that Sanscrit was first studied in England, and during one hundred and fifty years of our dominion there were only to be found in the whole of the East India Company two persons acquainted with the Chinese language. While France, with scarcely any intercourse with China, had established a Chinese professorship in Paris, our own Government, intent on nothing but wealth and military power, had not taken a single step in that direction.

The history of the Papacy is a great and important subject. The only history of the Popes was that of the wretched Bower, a liar and a swindler, who apostatized from the Church of Rome. While such was the state of bigotry little could be expected, and it is a melancholy consideration that the only great historian we produced in the eighteenth century was Gibbon, a notorious Deist. On the question of the Regency in 1788, Parr gravely writes, " What is meant by the word '*right*'? Look into Burlamaque and there you will find a clear, sound, metaphysical explanation ; in conformity to which I maintain the Prince's '*right*,'" &c.[2] In 1787, Burke writes to Parr, " If we have any priority over our neighbours, it is in no small measure owing to the early care we take

[1] Nichols's Literary Anecdotes, vol. ii. p. 347.
[2] Johnstone's Life of Parr, Lond. 1829, vol. i. p. 330.

with respect to a classical education." [1]  The most celebrated Whig
historian was Mrs. Macaulay, a foolish and restless democrat, and
while she was still alive, Dr. Wilson erected in the chancel of St.
Stephen's, Walbrook, a statue to her.   In Nichols's Literary
Anecdotes, vol. viii. p. 54, there is a very severe but accurate
criticism on Leland's History of Ireland, which was published
in 1773.

It may in some degree be esteemed a misfortune that so great
a man as Bacon should have flourished when the sciences were
still in their infancy, and were therefore unable to supply him
with an instance of the triumphs of *Deduction*.   The ancient
philosophy had been in the habit of laying down general principles, and then treating them as if they were laws, without
sufficiently attending to the process of verification, by which alone
their truth could be ascertained.   The real merit of Bacon was
to have shown the impropriety of this, and not to have pointed
out induction, which must always have been practised from the
remotest antiquity.   But at the same time he committed a serious
error.   He supposed that scientific knowledge was only to be
acquired inductively, that is to say, that we must proceed from
the lowest to the highest generalizations.   This, as Mill well says,
was the consequence of the backward state of the sciences. [2]   To
this I may add that in Scotland and Germany there was no great
man before the sciences were advanced—hence the method became deductive—and this was also aided by the fact that sensualism made no head here.   But in France Descartes, and afterwards,
Condillac, insured the reputation of induction; for it is quite a
mistake to oppose Descartes to Bacon ; both were inductive, and
Descartes did for metaphysics exactly what Bacon did for physics.

Davis received a pension from the crown for his wretched
attack on Gibbon. [3]

George III., a mean and ignorant man, did everything in his
power to ruin literature by patronising it.   But happily he had
neither the wealth nor the power of Louis XIV.   It is a curious
instance of the gross ignorance of political economy, even in the
nineteenth century, that Christian, Chief Justice of Ely, in his
notes to so respectable a book as Blackstone's Commentaries,
should think it necessary formally to refute the assertion that our
national debt increased our wealth. [4]   Blackstone himself [5] thought
it a " very good regulation " to authorise the justices at sessions

[1]  Johnstone's Life of Parr, Lond. 1829, vol. i. p. 200.
[2]  Mill's Logic, 2nd edit., 8vo, 1846, vol. ii. pp. 531, 532.
[3]  See the note in Walpole Letters, 8vo, 1840, vol. vi. pp. 30, 41.
[4]  Blackstone's Commentaries, 8vo, 1809, vol. i. p. 328.        [5]  Ibid. p. 427.

to fix the rate of wages ; and he thinks[1] that marriages should be
encouraged. As to our laws at the end of the eighteenth century,
their bigotry and their cruelty are too well known.

Warburton thought little of Milton. In 1776, Dr. Kampe, a
learned physician, wrote in favour of alchemy. Mr. Stephens's
medicine for gout was popular. In 1771 the celebrated Fox
writes to George Selwyn, " I am reading Clarendon, but scarcely
get on faster than you did with your Charles the Fifth. I think
the style bad, and that he has a good deal of the old woman in his
way of thinking, but hate the opposite party so much that it
gives me a kind of partiality for him."[2] In a note Jesse says,
" This is a very curious passage from the pen of Charles Fox."
Priestley, whose mind was admirably adapted for physical inquiries, insisted on becoming a metaphysician and introducing
into *morals* and psychology his empirical method.

Warburton was, I think, the founder of that new school which
considers history in a large point of view. He denied the argument of Middleton that the similarity of Popish and Pagan
ceremonies was an evidence that the first was derived from the
other ; and he referred such similarity to similar conditions of
human nature. See his two letters to Lyttleton, dated October
and November, 1741, printed in Phillimore's Memoirs and Correspondence of Lord Lyttleton, 8vo, 1845, vol. i. p. 163-175.
For the foolish notions of Johnson about history, and in favour
of Knolles' History of the Turks, see the Rambler, No. 122.
(Dryden in the preface to his Translation of Plutarch, complains
that the English had no historians.)

Soon after the middle of the eighteenth century, the writer
who was respected as the greatest living historian was Lord
Lyttleton, whose History of Henry II. was published in 1764.
To this work, which was the labour of thirty years, it would be
unfair to deny the praise of considerable research. But this is all
that can be possibly said in its favour. The materials are so ill-
arranged, and the style is so insufferably prolix, that it is now never
looked into except by those who read for the purpose of writing,
and who amid so much dross hope to find a little gold. The
author himself was a man of some industry, but of a narrow and
superstitious mind. Of his public life but little is known, and
that little is very unfavourable. In politics it is now only
remembered that he was the friend of an ignorant and dissolute
prince, whom nothing but an accident prevented from ascending
the throne of England; that during several years he directed all

[1] Blackstone's Commentaries, Lond. 1809. vol. i. p. 438.
[2] Jesse's Selwyn and his Contemporaries, vol. iii. p. 11.

P

his efforts against Walpole and Chatham, who were beyond all
comparison the greatest statesmen of his time; and that when
his ambition was rewarded by receiving an appointment in the
Exchequer, his incapacity was so notorious as to raise a report
that this manager of finance was unacquainted with the common
rules of arithmetic.    In theology, in which, according to the
measure of that age, he was considered to make a figure, he is
only remembered as the author of an Essay on the Conversion of
St. Paul, a lame and ill-reasoned work, in which the greatest
men are treated with contempt.    From such a man as this it
would be idle to expect anything like a great conception of
history.   Indeed, his opinion was that in the writings of Bolingbroke and Warburton, history had reached the highest point of
perfection which it was capable of attaining.   (Then give
instances of Littleton's incapacity.)   These instances, which
it would be easy to multiply, will give the render some idea of
what in those days was considered a masterpiece of historic composition.    This was the writer in whose favour Hume and Adam
Smith were rejected ; and this was the work which Bishop Warburton—whose mere opinion was fame—declared to be unrivalled
since the time of Clarendon.

Perhaps Burke abandoned his metaphysical pursuits in obedience
to the foolish prejudice that an abstract thinker is unfit to be a
statesman.   In 1785 the celebrated caricaturist, Sawyer, published
a print of him which is entitled Burke on the Sublime and
Beautiful.[1]   "The celebrated Anti-Jacobin was established in the
latter part of November 1797."[2]   For Grecian history we had
the wretched production of Mitford, who attempted to use ancient
history as the means of defending his own political prejudices.

The sensualist philosophy, though it has, I think, more truth
in it than the idealist, has by its prevalence in England caused
one great detriment.   It has aided the Baconian system by
making men bigoted to induction, and the progress of what may be
called our *economic* civilization has further aided this.   (J. S. Mill
is the only sensualist whose mind has been large enough to
escape this.)   Cousin[3] quotes Lord Bacon to the effect that it is
absurd to *observe* the mind.   See also Cousin's contemptuous
notice of Bacon's metaphysical efforts.[4]

Descartes was never popular in England.   His physical errors,
his theory of vortices, &c., were not calculated to inspire confidence
in his method.   What Cousin says of the eighteenth century in

[1] Wright's England under the House of Hanover, Lond. 1848, vol. ii. p. 126.
[2] Ibid. p. 282.
      stoire de la Philosophie, 2ᵐᵉ série, tome ii. p. 69          [4] Ibid. p. 72.

general, is particularly true of England. "Le XVIII⁰ siècle a
généralisé l'analyse. La philosophie, devenue plus scrupuleuse
encore par le faux pas du Cartesianisme, s'est empressée de re-
doubler de circonspection."¹ When at length, in the progress of
civilization, some attention began to be paid to the philosophy of
the mind, the method of Bacon was followed by Hobbes and
Locke, who said that we knew nothing except by the senses. At
the end of the seventeenth century there was, indeed, a faint
attempt made by Cudworth and Clarke to erect an ideal school.
But empiricism soon became again supreme, and its method was
carried out by Tooke; but in the nineteenth century Donaldson,
taught by the German school, introduced a better method. (More,
the platonist, was deductive.)

The success of Gibbon's history, immense as it was, could not
protect the author from the attacks of ignorant and bigoted men.
Bishop Newton, in his Life of himself, makes some insolent
remarks on Gibbon, to which the great historian admirably
replies.² Gibbon printed his history in 1787.³ Voltaire, who
was in England in 1726, says of Bacon: "Aujourd'hui les Anglais
revèrent sa mémoire au point qu'à peine avouent-ils qu'il a été
coupable," i.e. of bribery, &c.⁴ This is like Basil Montague.
Voltaire⁵ has some admirable remarks on our absurd compilation,
The Universal History, which show the immense superiority of
his own historical views.

Bacon directed a too exclusive attention to *externals*. This
benefited us theologically—but in a more advanced state of
knowledge it has injured us *scientifically*. Archdeacon Hare⁶
says that if Warburton, bishop of Gloucester, had "been born in
the twelfth century, no man would have been more zealous in
kindling fires to consume the Waldenses." In England, puritanism,
as I shall have occasion to show, has left the clearest traces of its
presence. Its influence, by encouraging accumulation, has greatly
increased the national wealth, but until the present century it
has corrupted philosophy with its own mechanical and prosaic
spirit. It is probable that the dislike to speculation would have
become fainter as the power of puritanism declined; but it
was fostered by what we in the present unformed state of our
knowledge, must, I suppose call, an accidental event. Towards
the end of the seventeenth century, perhaps the most wonderful

¹ Histoire de la Philosophie, Part II., tome ii. p. 75.
² See Gibbon's Miscellaneous Works, Lond. 1837. pp. 101, 102.     ³ Ibid. p. 107.
⁴ Lettre XII. sur les Anglais in Œuvres de Voltaire, tome xxvi. p. 58.
   Fragments sur l'Histoire, Œuvres, tome xxvii. p. 160.
   The Mission of the Comforter, Lond. 1850, p. 271.

genius that has ever been seen began to dazzle Europe with a
continual succession of the most amazing discoveries. In the
course of a few years Sir Isaac Newton changed the surface of
physical science. It was natural that the intellect of Europe
intoxicated, and as it were bribed, by his unprecedented success,
should have supposed that his method of investigation was of
universal applicability. In England, this erroneous notion was
particularly conspicuous, and it gave rise to a low empirical
practical spirit, the injurious effects of which are, as I shall show
in another place, apparent in nearly the whole of our literature
during the eighteenth century. It was not to be expected that
while men looked at morals as they looked at matter, and thought,
like ethics and chemistry, that they would be able to make any
discoveries of real and permanent value; and during one entire
century we did not produce a single great man. The powers of
Hume, indeed, were great, and if he had possessed learning
there can be no doubt that he would have effected great things.
The only other writer is Gibbon—a man of the most surprising
reading, of great sagacity, and of matchless integrity, but—if I
may state my opinion—of a genius incomparably inferior to that
of Hume.

Niebuhr, at the end of the eighteenth century, visited London,
well supplied with introductions from his father, the celebrated
traveller, and although greatly prepossessed before his arrival in
favour of the English, he could not conceal his surprise at the
narrow views of our most eminent men. Hallam says[1] that
Burnet's History of the Reformation is the first history in English
"which is fortified by a large appendix of documents." Daniel
published in 1618 a History of England.[2] Bacon, the great
sceptical philosopher, was the first who wrote history. Then we
have Herbert's History of Henry VIII. He too was a sceptic.
Coleridge[3] notices the deficiencies of Mitford; but the suggestions
he offers would hardly improve him. Even Coleridge, in his
Lectures, gravely traces mankind from Shem, Ham, and Japhet.[4]
The formation of the Royal Society encouraged our too inductive
tendencies. It was the opinion of Bishop Warburton that the
absurd speculations of Stukely would "be esteemed by posterity
as certain, and continue as uncontroverted as Harvey's discovery
of the circulation."[5] The proposals for Carter's History were at
first munificently welcomed by subscription; see Nichols's Literary

[1] Literature of Europe, vol. iii. p. 695.        [2] Ibid. p. 149.
[3] Literary Remains, vol. i. p. 153.        [4] Ibid. pp. 69, 70.
[5] Nichols's Literary Illustrations of the Eighteenth Century, vol. ii. p. 57. See also
at vol. iii. p. 682, an absurd eulogy of Speed.

Illustrations, vol. v. p. 159. Wesley[1] says, Lord Herbert of Cherbury is "the author of the first system of Deism that ever was published in England."

In England physical science not only *drew off* men from history, but gave them a *wrong pattern* to write it by. They said that in physics external and visible phenomena were everything, and they fancied the same held good in history. They did not know that the most important facts in history are invisible. The external world is governed by *acts*, the internal world by opinions. In physics actions produce their effects whether they are known or not; in history they only produce their effects *if* they are known. Every great historical revolution has been preceded by a corresponding intellectual revolution. The first edition of Speed's History of Great Britain was published *not* in 1614 but in 1611.[2] Lingard very unfairly quotes MS. authorities, which no one but his own party can see. One of these was an important Life of Lord Arundel; and when the Camden Society offered to publish it, the late Duke of Norfolk refused "for reasons arising out of the character of certain facts of the narrative."[3] Our English historians continue to quote as a picture of England in the middle of the sixteenth century, Harrison's description prefaced to Holinshed; but this is said by no less an authority than Hearne, to be copied from Leland.[4] Coleridge, *after* Hallam had written, calls Sharon Turner "the most honest of our English historians, and with no *superior* in industry and research."[5] Archdeacon Echard, in his History, tells a story which he gravely defended, of Cromwell selling himself to the devil.[6] Gibbon filled the chasm between the ancient and modern world. Indeed so notorious was our want of historical power, that when in 1766 a miserable adventurer named Champigny issued in London a prospectus for publishing a history of England, numerous subscriptions were attracted, but the history never appeared. Goldsmith as an historian had the carelessness of Hume, without his genius, and yet when the Royal Academy was instituted, he was appointed Professor of History. Even Johnson, so slow in praising, declared that not only as a comic writer, but even as an historian "he stands in the first class." In 1757 Burke published part of his English History.[7] Such was the poverty of our historians that in the middle of the eighteenth century, the elder

[1] Journal, p. 682.
[2] See Ellis, Original Letters of Literary Men. Camden Society, pp. 108, 109.
[3] Ibid. p. 114.     [4] Ibid. p. 355.
[5] Coleridge on Church and State, p. 61.
[6] See Calamy's Own Life, Lond. 1829, vol. ii. p. 399.
[7] Prior's Life of Burke, p. 45.

Pitt could find no better historians to recommend to his nephew than Bolingbroke, Rapin, and Witwood. Ockley's History of the Saracens is fabulous.[1]

Sir William Temple gravely says that Paolo's great work, a History of the Council of Trent, cannot properly be called a history; and yet Temple had been engaged in public affairs, and wrote a book on the history of England, which in value is equal to Mrs. Trimmer or Lord Lyttleton. Sir Thomas Browne[2] says that Rycaut's History, added to Knollys, is "one of the best histories that we have in English." Browne says that history has only to do with memory, and poetry with imagination. In 1743, Ralph was "esteemed one of the best political writers in England."[3] Burke had large views of history.[4] Guthrie wrote on history. We were taunted by foreigners with not writing history. Sir J. Reynolds[5] takes it for granted that "the historian takes great liberties with fact, in order to interest his readers and make his narrative more delightful." Alison says,[6] "Till the era of the peninsular war, when a cluster of gifted spirits arose, there are no writers on English affairs at all comparable to the great historical authors of the continent." I have not been able to learn the name of these "gifted spirits" to whom Mr. Alison alludes. We have had no history of English literature—no history of English science—no history of England—that is to say, of the English people—except the compilation Pictorial History of England.

Göthe, in his autobiography, complains bitterly of the labour he wasted on that dull book, Bower's History of the Popes.[7] Sir R. Walpole said there could be no truth in history.[8] Coxe, in his Life of Sir R. Walpole, takes no notice of Walpole's second marriage to his mistress, Miss Skerrit; and in the same spirit Coxe never mentions Walpole's secret message to the Pretender in 1739, though he had the *very letter* in his possession.[9]

[1] See note in Hallam's Middle Ages, vol. i. p. 479.    [2] Works, vol. i. p. 272.
[3] Life of Franklin, by Himself, vol. i. p. 215.
[4] See Burke's Works, vol. ii. p. 275, and Rogers's Introduction to Burke's Works, pp. lxii, lxiii.
[5] Ibid. p. 306.    [6] History of Europe, vol. i. p. xxii.
[7] Wahrheit und Dichtung in Göthe's Werke, band ii. theil ii. p. 45.
[8] Parliamentary History, vol. xxvii. p. 600.
[9] Mahon's History of England, vol. ii. p. 263 ; vol. iii. p. 23.

## GENERAL REFERENCES FOR INTRODUCTION.

1. WHEN did the Scotch schools begin to favour Rousseau? Adam Smith says, "that cowardice and pusillanimity so natural to man in his uncivilized state."[1] See these notes, nos. 8–23.

2. Adam Smith[2] observes that Polytheism only ascribes irregular events to the gods. This remark is an anticipation of Comte.

3. In 1755 appeared the Edinburgh Review, of which only two numbers were published.[3]

4. In 1759 appeared Robertson's History of Scotland.[4]

5. In 1769 appeared Robertson's Charles V.[5]

6. "The writings of Dr. Hutchison certainly produced a considerable effect; but it was the publications of that extraordinary man, David Hume, that called forth the energies of the Scottish philosophers,"[6] &c.

7. Beaufort's République Romaine is in the Mémoires de l'Académie.

8. Hume speaks boldly against the supposed virtues of barbarians.[7]

9. Hume tells the story of Elizabeth's famous letter to the bishop of Ely, "Proud prelate," &c.[8]

10. In 1757, Home published Douglas, which raised the fury of the church.[9]

11. Klopstock, besides "Messiah," wrote poems upon Adam, Solomon, and David.[10]

12. As to the absurd assertion of the Quarterly Review that the Scotch clergymen in the eighteenth century were deists and hypocrites, see Burton's Life and Correspondence of Hume, vol. i. pp. xi. xii.

13. In 1749, Middleton had a reputation in Paris.[11]

14. In 1758, Hume notices the great sale of Smollett's History.[12]

15. Gibbon was ignorant of German.[13]

16. Hume, in a letter written in 1776, speaks of Gibbon as a remarkable exception to the low state of knowledge in England.[14]

[1] Smith's Essays on Philosophical Subjects, p. 23, 4to, 1795.     [2] Ibid. p. 25.
[3] Bower's History of the University of Edinburgh, vol. iii. p. 69.
[4] Ibid. p. 78.          [5] Ibid. p. 84.          [6] Ibid. p. 175.
[7] Hume's History of England, vol. i. p. 222.          [8] Ibid. vol. v. p. 472.
[9] Stewart's Life of Robertson, p. 4, prefixed to Robertson's Works.
[10] Schlosser's Eighteenth Century, vol. ii. p. 55.
[11] Burton's Life of Hume, vol. i. p. 457.          [12] Ibid. vol. ii. p. 115.
[13] Ibid. p. 410.          [14] Ibid. p. 484.

17. It has been said that Rousseau took the greater part of his Dissertation on the Dangers of Science from a letter by Giraldi to Picus Mirandolus.[1]

18. An author, who will certainly not be accused of indifference to religion, says "the orthodoxy of the seventeenth century lay like an incubus upon the whole of northern Germany."

19. This spirit [admiration for England] extended to the aristocracy; and for many years nothing was so fashionable in France as English dress and English manners. See some amusing instances in Scott's Life of Napoleon, edit. Paris, p. 17.

20. The mingled spirit of admiration for theology and antiquity, at the end of the seventeenth century, and the decline of that spirit, is strikingly displayed in Grimm's Correspondance littéraire, tome ix. p. 392.

21. In 1782, Grimm writes from Paris, "Malgré la décadence trop bien reconnue de la littérature nationale, on dédaigne plus que jamais la littérature étrangère."[2]

22. In 1759 appeared Smith's Theory of Moral Sentiments.

23. Lord Kames says "that the savage state was the original condition of man."[3]

24. Villemain[4] says that Diderot was the first Frenchman who gave a separate place to the history of philosophy.

25. Villemain[5] mentions the influence of French scepticism on Germany and on Joseph II.

26. Voltaire[6] says that Duclos was persecuted in consequence of his Louis XI.; but this is not mentioned in the Biographie universelle.

27. Lavallée[7] happily calls Descartes the Luther of philosophy.

28. Voltaire[8] says, "L'Abbé de Prades traité comme Arius par les Athanasiens."

29. Sismondi[9] says he was so fond of the middle ages that he had almost determined not to continue his history to a modern period.

[1] Menzel's German Literature, vol. i. p. 174.
[2] Grimm, Correspondance, tome xiii. p. 32.
[3] Tytler's Memoirs of Kames, vol. ii. p. 185.
[4] Villemain, Littérature au dixhuitième siècle, tome ii. p. 130.
[5] Ibid. tome iii. pp. 155, 158.      [6] Voltaire, Œuvres, tome lviii. p. 546.
[7] Lavallée, Histoire des Français, tome iii. p. 130.
[8] Voltaire, Œuvres, tome lxv. p. 327.
[9] Sismondi, Histoire des Français, tome xxii. p. 4.

# INFLUENCE OF GERMAN LITERATURE IN ENGLAND.

SHELLEY was born in 1792, and even when at Eton began to study German.[1] Medwin adds[2] that when Shelley first went to Oxford, "Göthe was only known by the Sorrows of Werther, and Canning and Frere had in the Anti-Jacobin thrown ridicule on the poetry of that country which they hated. Indeed, the spirit of his Æsthetics has somewhat, though not so much, of the daring of Schiller." Medwin then gives[3] some parallel instances from Schiller and Shelley, the former in German. Shelley had a very small library; but among his books were the works of Göthe and Schiller.[4] Medwin says,[5] "Shelley showed me a treatise he had written of some length on the Life of Christ, and which Mrs. Shelley should give to the world. In this work he differs little from Paulus, Strauss, and the rationalists of Germany." Shelley made some translations from Faust, of which "Göthe expressed his entire approbation."[6] Not even the disturbed state of Europe could now prevent men from satisfying their curiosity. In 1800, Campbell visited Germany, in order to study its language, with which, however, he seems to have had some small acquaintance before he left England. He attempted to understand Kant, and, though he failed in this, he studied the writings of Schiller, Wieland, and Bürger; and there is great reason to believe that his beautiful poem of Gertrude of Wyoming owes its origin to one of the German novels of La Fontaine. At all events, it is certain that the first idea of the erection of the London University sprung up in the mind of Campbell, when he was conversing with the German professors and noticing the system of German education. Early in the nineteenth century, Sir John Sinclair sent his son into Germany to learn German; and the young man was arrested on the charge of being a spy in 1806, and brought before Napoleon.[7] In 1814, Mrs. Grant writes of Wordsworth's Excursion. "His piety has too much of what is called Pantheism, or the worship of nature, in it. This is a kind of German piety too; they look to the sun, moon, and flowers for what they should find in the Bible."[8] In vol. ii. of Blanco White's Life of Himself, 8vo. 1845, there are several letters from Mr. White to Mr. J. S. Mill,

[1] See Medwin's Life of Shelley, Lond. 1847, vol. i. p. 45.   [2] Ibid. p. 60.
[3] Ibid. p. 278.   [4] Ibid. vol. ii. p. 31.
[5] Ibid. p. 50.   [6] Ibid. p. 267.
[7] Sinclair's Correspondence, Lond. 1831, vol. i. pp. 43, 44.
[8] Memoirs and Correspondence of Mrs. Grant of Laggan, Lond. 1844, vol. ii. p. 59.

respecting the Westminster Review, to which White was a contributor.

In 1799, Wordsworth and his highly-gifted sister went abroad, in order to learn German ; and in 1803 he borrowed from a celebrated German poem the stanza he employed in his exquisite ballad of Ellen Irwin. With Coleridge, who was still more intimately acquainted with German literature, Wordsworth had a long and intimate friendship, and he must have been greatly influenced by him.

In 1804, Sir James Mackintosh first began carefully to study German, of which he already had some slight knowledge ; and in 1805 he writes that he will not begin his intended work upon morals until he has matured its philosophic. Miss Smith, who was dead in 1811, translated Klopstock's Letters. The German school arose at Edinburgh, where the fanatical party had never been able to dispossess the philosophy. This was natural. The country and not towns is the place for bigotry. The German school was introduced by the Scotch, and by those who had not had an university education. The *highest* branches of German literature were, I think, first studied by Mackintosh and Coleridge, who exercised more influence by their conversation than by their writings.

In 1781, William Taylor, then very young, went into Germany to learn German. He, before the end of the eighteenth century, published several translations from the German, and, what was more important, he with indefatigable industry familiarised the English mind through reviews with the opinions of many eminent Germans. He published translations from Lessing in 1791 ; from Göthe in 1793 ; from Gleim in 1794 ; from Bürger in 1796 ; and the influence of his example was so great that early in the nineteenth century a literary society was formed at Norwich, where he ived, of which one of the chief objects was the study of German. Unfortunately, Taylor, though a man of most undoubted ability, had but little taste for metaphysics, and consequently little knowledge of them. This caused him almost entirely to neglect the highest branches of German literature in favour of its lighter branches. But this deficiency was soon compensated by the studies of two of the most remarkable men of the present century—Mackintosh and Coleridge. Coleridge in 1799 projected a Life of Lessing. In 1799, Walker writes that the Royal Irish Academy had issued a gold medal to the author of the best essay on German literature.[1]

[1] Pinkerton Correspondence, Lond. 1830, vol. ii. pp. 61, 62. Was this Essay published ?

Gibbon, in enumerating the classes of works in his own library, says nothing of German.[1] Little was known about the middle ages until the German influence made us study them. Even Gibbon calls the sixteenth century a period when the "world, awaking from a sleep of a thousand years," &c.[2] Dugald Stewart had no notion of German, and was so ignorant as to despise Kant. The influence of Coleridge's conversations was even greater than that of his writings. There is no doubt that Coleridge, with great carelessness, copied long passages from Schelling without making the least acknowledgment.[3] As to the charge of intentional plagiarism, which some English reviewers have brought against him, no one will believe for a moment that a man like Coleridge was capable of such things. If they do believe, they may see[4] what Schelling himself thought of the matter. Coleridge began to study German in 1796.[5] On the influence of German literature on Sir Walter Scott's poetry, see Gillies' Memoirs of a Literary Veteran, 8vo, 1851, vol. i. pp. 226, 227. Gillies adds, vol. ii. pp. 222-227, that even in 1817 there was only one person in Edinburgh who could teach German, and he was an Englishman. In 1799, Niebuhr writes from Edinburgh that German was much studied there. "In this place especially, a great number are learning German."[6] In 1799 Coleridge was at Göttingen.[7]

---

## ENGLISH LITERATURE IN THE NINETEENTH CENTURY.

DURING the whole of the eighteenth century the Scotch literature produced scarcely any effect upon England. The only great historical work which we produced was that by Gibbon, of which the first volume was published in 1776. The author, as might have been expected, was a sceptic, and was intimately acquainted with the two greatest Scotchmen of his time, Adam Smith and Hume. . . . . Johnson despised Hume and Adam Smith, and, I think, Robertson. Cousin says that Price, who just after the middle of the eighteenth century revived the Platonic idealism of Cudworth, is almost the only idealist that England produced in the eighteenth century.[8] Swedenborg, during his residence in

---

[1] See Gibbon's Miscellaneous Works, Lond. 1837, p. 323.    [2] Ibid. p. 447.
[3] See Coleridge's Biographia Literaria, Lond. 1847. vol. i. pp. vii, ix, 255.
[4] Ibid. p. xxxviii.    [5] Ibid. vol. ii. p. 364.
[6] Life and Letters of Niebuhr, Lond. 8vo, 1852, vol. i. p. 137, see also p. 138.
[7] See the Friend, vol. i. p. 39.
[8] Cousin, Histoire de la Philosophie, 11me série, tome iii. p. 16.

England, must have done much to encourage idealism. Lord Shaftesbury had, I think, been one of the very few who in England followed the deductive method. See the flattering opinion expressed of him in Cousin.[1] Lord Brougham says that the great Fox possessed "a minute and profound knowledge of modern languages."[2] It is said, though I know not on what authority, that even the infamous Marat taught French in Edinburgh about 1774.[3] In 1830 we are told that in Scotland "there is no gentleman of liberal education" who had not read the Wealth of Nations.[4]

In 1783, Hutton published the Theory of the Earth; and its views were adopted by Professor Playfair.[5]

Sir James Mackintosh says of Brown's philosophy, "It is an open revolt against the authority of Reid;"[6] he accuses Brown of supposing that he had made a *discovery* when he reduced Hume's principle of association to the *one* principle of contiguity.[7]

The German school rose at Edinburgh, where the last remains of philosophical party had fled. They were always strong there, and when in 1773, the chair of Professor of Natural and Experimental Philosophy in the University of Edinburgh was offered to Beattie, he refused to accept it on account of the dislike which he knew was felt for him there.[8] . . . .

The Quarterly Review, which was a mere bookseller's speculation, was begun in 1809, and of the nature of its authors some idea may be formed from the circumstance that Sir John Barrow, a painstaking and meritorious man, but certainly of no remarkable powers, was one of the chief contributors, and, indeed, wrote in it upwards of one hundred and ninety different articles.

Mr. Prescott[9] has some able remarks upon the nature and progress of history, but evidently has not the least idea of it as a *science*. He says,[10] "The personage by whom the present laws of historic composition may be said to have been first arranged into a regular system was Voltaire." And[11] he strangely says of Gibbon, "He was, moreover, deeply versed in geography, chronology, antiquities, verbal criticism; in short, in all the sciences

[1] Cousin, Histoire de la Philosophie, première série, tome iv. pp. 7, 8, 13.
[2] Brougham's Historical Sketches of Statesmen, vol. i. pp. 218, 219, Lond. 18mo, 1845.
[3] Ibid. vol. v. p. 131.
[4] Bower's History of the University of Edinburgh, vol. iii. p. 181.
[5] Ibid. p. 253.
[6] Dissertation on Ethical Philosophy, edit. Whewell, p. 345.      [7] Ibid. p. 347.
[8] Forbes's Life of Beattie, vol. i. pp. 292–313.
[9] Biographical and Critical Miscellanies, Lond. 1845, pp. 77–94.
[10] Ibid. p. 84.          [11] Ibid. p. 90.

in any way subsidiary to his art." This is equivalent to saying that moral and economical sciences are *not* subsidiary to history. Mr. Prescott says, perhaps too strongly, " The same extended philosophy which Montesquieu initiated in civil history, Madame de Stael has carried into literary." [1]

Respecting the dispute between Fearn and Stewart from 1818 to 1827, see Barker's Parriana, vol. i. pp. 556–622. Fearn's own theory was that " perceived extension and figure, when perceived, are demonstrated to be states or affections of the perceiving mind itself, and when not perceived are nowhere, that is, have no existence whatever; " and that, consequently, we have no evidence for the existence of *dead matter* in the world." [2] But his quarrel with Dugald Stewart stands thus. In 1812, Fearn stated that " a variety of colour is necessary for the perception of visible outline," [3] which *discovery* Stewart mentioned as a *known* fact, without stating Fearn's name. [4] On the other hand, Stewart says it *is* mentioned by several authors, but he only quotes Lord Monboddo, who, however, does not say anything of the sort. [5] The beginning of a sounder philosophy is shown by Brown, who *lessens* the number of original principles. Thus he reduces the laws of association to *one*. Damiron strangely says that Brown has added nothing to Dugald Stewart.

In the nineteenth century there was a general intellectual revival. Southey, in 1837, notices that this was the case in poetry. An increased love of the middle ages sprung up. At the end of the eighteenth century Hayley and Darwin were our greatest poets. The first editor of the Quarterly Review was Gifford, a learned but peevish and narrow-minded man. There is an extremely severe, but I should think not unjust character of Gifford in Leigh Hunt's Autobiography. [6] He says [7] that Gifford had " not a particle of genius." Lord Byron seduced Miss Clara C——, " a near connection, not as Mr. Moore says, a near relative of Mrs. Shelley." [8] Medwin adds [9] that Miss C. was in consequence brought to bed, and " some foul and infamously calumnious slander relating to this *accouchement* gave rise to the dark insinuations afterwards thrown out in the Quarterly Review by the writer of the critique on the Revolt of Islam." In 1818 this article was published in the Quarterly, and seen by Shelley, who was then at Florence. It was on his Laon and Cythna, now

[1] Biographical and Critical Miscellanies, Lond. 1845, p. 424.
[2] Barker's Parriana, vol. i. p. 568.     [3] Ibid. p. 598.
[4] Ibid. p. 590.                          [5] Ibid. pp. 592, 599, 614.
[6] Leigh Hunt's Autobiography, Lond. 1850, vol. ii. pp. 81–92.    [7] Ibid. p. 87.
[8] Medwin's Life of Shelley, Lond. 1847, vol. i. p. 280.    [9] Ibid. p. 284.

" better known as the Revolt of Islam."[1] Medwin truly adds[2] of the Quarterly, that it is "a Review, be it here said, that has always endeavoured to crush rising talent—never done justice to one individual whose opinions did not square with its own in religion or politics." Medwin[3] says that the attack on Shelley " in the April number" of the Quarterly (Is this the article before referred to?) was written by Milman. The effect of this attack on Shelley was terrible.

In 1802, Campbell was engaged in writing the " Annals of Great Britain," which he considered a degrading occupation. " Such," says his friend and biographer, " was his apprehension of losing *caste* by descending from the province of lofty rhyme to that of mere historical compilation, that he bound his employers to secrecy, and did not wish the fact to be known even among his intimate friends."[4]

One of the greatest and most valuable characteristics of Hallam is *scepticism*. Sydney Smith used, with pleasant good nature, to ridicule this scepticism in Hallam.[5] Campbell gives an account of a conversation he had with Schlegel in 1814, which will illustrate the rage for *induction*. He says, " I in vain endeavoured to vindicate that since the time of Lord Bacon the method in philosophy pointed out by that great man had been very properly pursued in England, which was to collect particular truths, and then combine them into general principles or conclusions."[6]

It is not, therefore, surprising that in 1813, Campbell should say of Reid, " He in the moral world has always seemed to me to be of the same order of minds as Newton in material philosophy."[7] In 1819, Mrs. Grant writes from Edinburgh that " all the wits " in Blackwood's Magazine are " from the west of Scotland." She mentions John Lockhart, Thomas Hamilton, John Wilson, and Robert Sym.[8] In the same year, 1819, she writes[9] that Blackwood " is supported by a club of young wits, many of whom are well known to me; who I hope in some measure fear. God, but certainly do not regard man. Four thousand of this cruelly witty magazine are sold in a month." After the death of Gifford, the Quarterly Review fell into the

[1] Medwin's Life of Shelley, Lond. 1847, vol. i. p. 357.

[2] Ibid. pp. 357, 358.                    [3] Ibid. p. 360.

[4] Beattie's Life and Letters of Campbell, Lond. 1849, vol. i. p. 414. See also vol. ii. p. 19.

[5] See an amusing anecdote of this in Beattie's Life of Campbell, vol. iii. p. 315.

[6] Beattie's Life and Letters of Campbell, vol. ii. p. 262.          [7] Ibid. p. 227.

[8] Correspondence of Mrs. Grant of Laggan, Lond. 1844, vol. ii. pp. 223, 224.

[9] Ibid. p. 236.

hands of Mr. Lockhart, a gentleman valued by his friends, but who has never displayed powers to justify an attempt to direct the public taste. He is no doubt well intentioned, but the Review has become very bigoted, and if it had influence, would be very dangerous. Mrs. Grant, who was personally well acquainted with Sir Walter Scott, says of his work on Demonology. "I was amused at Sir Walter's caution in keeping so entirely clear of the second sight; like myself, I am pretty confident he has a glimmering belief of, though not the same courage to own it."[1]

At the end of the eighteenth century there was no good poetry, nor was there any taste for it. In 1798 were published Wordsworth's Lyrical Ballads, which were received with coldness, and indeed were scarcely noticed. Early in the nineteenth century various circumstances, hereafter to be treated, had almost completed the amalgamation of the Scotch and English. This was aided by the extreme bitterness with which party politics were managed. The question no longer was put whether a man was Scotch or English, but whether he was Whig or Tory. Scott, moved by a personal pique, joined the Quarterly, and Southey hated the Scotch provided they were Whigs. In 1812, Pinkerton having a desire to settle at Edinburgh, Young writes to dissuade him; for, he says, "I know of no literary situations in Scotland which do not in a manner appertain to the clergy and professors, who have the eyes of a hawk for them."[2]

Pinkerton's great scheme for editing our national historians was in 1814 addressed by him to the Prince Regent, but that virtuous prince appears not even to have returned an answer.[3]

For a specimen of the infamous falsehoods of the Anti-Jacobin in 1798, see note in Coleridge's Biographia Literaria, 1847, vol. i. pp. 65, 66. The Edinburgh Review has been blamed for the bitter language it has sometimes employed.[4] This charge is not devoid of truth, but we should remember that this journal had to oppose [writers] most of whom were impervious to reasoning, and could only be reached by ridicule. Such writers as Hannah More and John Styles could feel the lash, though they could not understand the argument. The influence of the German literature was soon seen. Even Hume had put in an appendix his account of our laws, and in the text the vices of kings and ministers. But Hallam now put forward his great work on Con-

---

[1] Correspondence of Mrs. Grant of Laggan, Lond. 1844, vol. iii. p. 187.
[2] Pinkerton's Literary Correspondence, Lond. 1830, vol. ii. p. 403.
[3] Ibid. p. 456.
[4] See, for instance, Coleridge's Biographia Literaria, vol. ii. pp. 117, 128.

stitutional History, in which the philosophy of Hume is combined
with a learning far superior to that of Blackstone.    Alison's
ideas of history are perfectly childish.[1]

There are some extremely interesting remarks in Tocqueville's
Démocratie en Amérique.[2]    He says that the English hate generalisation ; the French love it ; and that this arises from their
aristocratic prejudices which *narrow* their notions, though their
knowledge of itself would make them generalise.    But now that
the old English government is falling to pieces, there is growing
up an increased love of generalisation.    For when classes are
very unequal it is difficult for the mind to bring them in the
same field so as to cover them by one law.    But in a democracy it
is more evident that the truths applicable to one are applicable
to all.    Besides this there is in a democracy no *obviously* moving
power, and therefore men can only explain social changes by
generalisation from the *general will*.    And Tocqueville[3] observes,
" Les historiens qui écrivent dans les siècles aristocratiques font
dépendre d'ordinaire tous les évènements de la volonté particulière et de l'humeur de certains hommes, et ils rattachent volon-
tiers aux moindres accidents les révolutions les plus importants."
Lord Mahon, a Tory who thinks we have [been] ruined by the
reform bill, takes the most superficial view of history, and even
talks of its dignity.    With the exception of what he says about
the Methodists, and a superficial account of literature, he tells
nothing worth remembering ; no account of manners, or of comforts of the people, or wages, or mode of living, &c.[4]

Humboldt[5] speaks with the greatest contempt of Pinkerton's
geographical knowledge.

---

# GEORGE III.

Of these leading and conspicuous events, the American War was
the earliest ; and for several years it almost entirely absorbed the
attention of English politicians.    It is well known that upon the
question of taxation, on which this contest entirely hinged, the

[1] See Alison's History of Europe, vol. i. pp. xxix, 3, 171.
    Tome iv. pp. 23, 27.                              [3] Ibid. p. 133.
[4] See Mahon's History of England, Lond. 1853, vol. i. pp. 46, 181, 182, 296 ;
vol. ii. pp. 24, 29, 138, 210 and seq., 235 ; vol. iii. pp. 89, 270, 357.
    [5] Humboldt, La Nouvelle Espagne, tome i. p. 146.

opinions of the greatest statesmen of the eighteenth century were unanimous. Sir R. Walpole, Lord Chatham, Burke, Fox, Lord Camden, Lord Shelburne, the Marquis of Rockingham, the Duke of Grafton, were all agreed respecting the absurdity of taxing colonies which had no representatives in the English legislature; and to this most of these celebrated men, moreover, added that, under such circumstances, the mother-country had no right to tax.

Such were the first fruits of the policy of George III. But the mischief did not stop there. The opinions which it was necessary to advocate, in order to justify this innovation, reacted upon ourselves. In order to defend the attempt to destroy the liberties of America, principles were laid down which, if carried out, would have subverted the liberties of England. Before the struggle actually began, and while it was in progress, doctrines were heard in the English parliament hardly less mischievous than those for which Charles I. had lost his head. It was even proposed in 1773 to contract the constituencies.[1]

In Brougham's Political Philosophy[2] it is said that in 1765 the pretension of taxing America was first put forward.[3] In 1765, Grenville proposed the resolutions preliminary to his Stamp Act. "This famous bill, little understood even at that time, was less attended to."[4] Such was the ignorance of the House of Commons that this great measure attracted no notice! In 1779 the king would have no minister who would not sign a declaration that America should never be independent.[5] Even Lord North was unwilling to continue the war.[6] In 1777, Markham, archbishop of York, attacked the revolution of 1688[7]; and this very man was tutor to the Prince of Wales.[8]

Lord Lyttleton declared that the king was the vicegerent of God. In 1769, Lord North denied the right of the people to petition for a dissolution of Parliament. Jenkinson, the minister (?), said that the authority of the House of Commons did not depend on the people. In 1770 it was held that the king's prerogative was sufficient to support government. When the people petitioned against the monstrous decision respecting Wilkes, Rigby said that such petitions were not to be regarded; for that even the freeholders themselves were, for the most part, "no

[1] Chatham Correspondence, vol. iv. p. 280.
[2] Nichols, Literary Anecdotes, vol. viii. p. 62.
[4] Walpole's Mem. of George III., vol. ii. p. 68.
[5] Russell, Mem. of Fox, vol. i. pp. 236, 237.
[7] See Parliamentary History, vol. xix. p. 327.
[8] See Walpole's Mem. of George III., vol. iv. p. 311.

[3] Part III. p. 328.

[6] Ibid. pp. 247, 254.

Q

better than an ignorant multitude." Lord North contemptuously
called the petitioners "the multitude;" they were the "drunken
ragamuffins of a vociferous mob." They were "rustics and
mechanics;" they were "ignorant;" they were "drunken;"
they had been taught, "in the jollity of their drunkenness, to
cry out that they were undone." The petitions themselves were
"treasonable." The petitioners were "a few factious, discontented
people;" they were "the rabble;" they were "the base born;"
they were "the scum of the earth;" and because the magistrates
of the City of London joined the petitioners against the minister,
they were denounced by the attorney-general, who, in the House
of Commons, called one of them "an ignorant mayor," another "a
turbulent alderman." The rights of the City of London were
"paltry corporation charters;" "little chartered grant of a city."
(This was because the magistrates interfered with privilege of
parliament.) Of many petitions the king took no notice; and to
some presented by the City of London he returned what Lord
Chatham declared in parliament to be an answer, for the harsh-
ness of which our history afforded no parallel. In 1769, the freeholders of Middlesex who returned Wilkes were called "the scum
of the earth."

These were the principles which in the reign of George III. it
was hoped to impress upon the English nation. Nor were they
intended for mere maxims to amuse the leisure of speculative
men. It cannot indeed be denied that there then existed in our
country all the political elements necessary to put them into
execution. The throne was filled by an arbitrary and active
prince. The House of Lords, as we have already seen, soon lost
that love of liberty by which it had once been characterised; and
the House of Commons, so far from being a popular assembly,
was almost entirely constructed by three classes of men, none of
whom were likely to have much sympathy with the popular
interests. These were men of great wealth, which was then illiberal, being rarely made in commerce—officers of the revenue,
&c., appointed by Government—and men of great family or county
interests. The consequence was that, with extremely few exceptions, it was hardly possible for any one to be a member of the
House of Commons unless he had a fortune sufficiently large to
enable him to buy a seat, or a spirit mean enough to wheedle
one.

On such a composition as this, arbitrary principles could hardly
fail to produce their effect, and what gave them fresh strength
was the French Revolution. The first open step of the king was
an attempt to ruin those Whig nobles who, though too full of

the vanity of their order, had done much for the country.[1] The House of Commons denied to the people the right of electing their own representatives.[2]

Owing to these things, and owing to absurd laws (46 George III.), wages greatly fell,[3] and the people were ripe for rebellion. H. Walpole says,[4] " On March 11, 1768, the Parliament was dissolved. Thus ended that Parliament, uniform in nothing but its obedience to the Crown." [5]

Such was the state of the government and legislature of England when the French Revolution suddenly broke loose on the world, and now it was that we felt the full effects of that political retrogression which I have attempted to trace. An event more fortunate for that party which was then in the ascendant could not possibly have occurred. The fact that a great people had risen against their oppressors could not fail to disquiet the consciences of those in high places. The remains of that old faction which supported Charles I. and wished to retain James II. were now kindled into activity. A new courage was infused into those creeping things which the corruption of the state is sure to nourish into life. The clergy, who had aided the

[1] In 1763, General A'Court was deprived of his regiment because he voted in favour of Wilkes. In 1762, the Duke of Newcastle, the Duke of Grafton, and the Marquis of Rockingham were dismissed from Lord Lieutenancies. The Duke of Devonshire, in 1762, was personally insulted by the King. . . . In 1762, one of the leaders of the Whigs, the Duke of Devonshire, was so offended by the new policy that he resigned the office of Lord Chamberlain ; a few days after this the King in council struck off his name from the list. In 1765, General Conway, Parl. History, vol. xvi. p. 45 ; Burke's Works, vol. i. p. 109. In 1767, the Whig Duke of Portland was robbed. Cooke, Hist. of Party, vol. iii. p. 103 ; Adolphus, George III., vol. i. pp. 307, 310 ; Parl. Hist. vol. xvi. p. 406 ; vol. xvii. pp. 1, 16, 302, 304, 307 ; Walpole's Mem. of George III., vol. iii. pp. 143, 146. The dismissal of Conway was the more shameful, for William III. refused to dismiss an officer under similar circumstances. See Mahon's England, vol. ii. pp. 173, 174, where the quotation is wrong; for it ought to be Parl. Hist. vol. ix. p. 312 and *not* p. 132, and see vol. xi. p. 1105.

[2] In [1769?] the House of Commons, in [the] case of Wilkes, disfranchised a whole county, and assuming the functions of electors as well as [of] elected, constituents and representatives, they opposed the people from whom their power was derived. The King personally hated Wilkes. See Walpole's Mem. of George III., vol. iii. pp. 200, 256. In 1785, the Marquis of Carmarthen and the Earl of Pembroke were deprived of their Lord Lieutenancies; the first, because he favoured the York petition ; the other, for his votes in Parliament. Parl. Hist. vol. xxi. pp. 212, 219, 220. It is said (Parl. Hist. vol. xxviii. p. 615) that when Onslow was Speaker he was obliged to resign because he gave a casting vote against Government. In 1782 (or 1783), the King used his personal influence with the Peers to induce them to vote against his own ministers. Burke's Works, vol. i. pp. 308, 309 ; Parl. Hist. vol. xxiv. p. 207. In 1763, Lord Temple, because he was the friend of Wilkes, was dismissed from his post of Lord Lieutenant of Buckingham.

[3] Hallam, vol. ii. p. 446.

[4] Mem. of George III., vol. iii. p. 163.

[5] Pitt admitted the decline of usages. Parl. Hist. vol. xxxii. p. 705.

king in the American war, were also very active in this new and still more serious error. The clergy excited a drunken mob to attack Priestley, and obliged that great man to emigrate to America, although his private character was spotless.[1] The Rev. Mr. Jones shows very amusingly his bitter hatred of Priestley. See Jones's Life of Bishop Horne, Lond. 1795, pp. 141, 145. In 1790, in consequence of the French Revolution, "the High Church party" revived. Parl. History, xxviii. 394. See at p. 399 the interference of Horsley, bishop of St. David's, in 1789, to throw out a candidate for Parliament who wished to repeal the Test Acts. In 1787, the clergy were greatly alarmed at the effort to repeal the Test Acts (Parl. Hist. xxvi. 822). The French Revolution was just like the American Revolution, with the exception that the provocation being greater the crimes were greater. And both were opposed in England by the same men—men who grow rich and fatten on the public distress. In 1792, Captain Gauler was dismissed because he belonged to the Society for Constitutional Information (Parl. Hist. xxx. 172). In 1793, " Reeves' Association at the Crown and Anchor" received anonymous letters, and acted on them, (Parl. Hist. xxx. 313).

There now rose a war the most monstrous that can possibly be conceived, a war in which we attempted to dictate to a great people, not their external policy, but their internal government. no wonder the French still burn with hatred against us. All the selfishness of the most selfish class, the greediness of wealth, the fears of rank, were stimulated into a new and preternatural activity. In 1795 the people desired peace (Parl. Hist. xxxi. 1347). Comte [2] truly says that the war with France would have ruined us if it had not been for the increase of our wealth by Watt's steam discovery. And now it was that the consequences of a war raised by the aristocracy were averted by the genius and energy of the middle classes, whose activity had been stimulated by scepticism.

The most contemptible and the meanest artifices were employed by the agents of the Government. They declared that French emissaries had poisoned with arsenic the water of the New River. The Traitorous Correspondence Bill was brought forward in 1793. For Fox's opinion of it, see Parl. Hist. xxx. 600, 634 ; Treasonable Practices Bill in 1795, xxxii. 246, 498, xxxiii. 615 ; in 1795, the Seditious Meetings Bill, xxxii. 275, 419. Read these three Bills in Statute Book. These scandalous measures, in spite of the

---

[1] See Adolphus, Hist. of George III., vol. v. pp. 71, 119, and Parl. Hist. vol. xxix. pp. 774, 775, 1378, 1397, 1434, 1435, 1437, and pp. 1450, 1451, 1453, 1457, 1512.
[2] Traité de Législation, tome iii. p. 298.

strenuous opposition of the people, became law, and were put into vigorous operation, so that Fox truly said, in 1795, and even before this monstrous system reached its height, resistance was only a question of prudence.[1]

The end of my view of tyranny must be that Fox, who had been minister and was minister again, gave it us his deliberate opinion that the time had now come when resistance was only a matter of prudence. While by an insane war the funds out of which wages are paid were diminishing, the claimants of wages were increasing, partly by the *spread* of poverty, which compelled even respectable men to become labourers, and partly from laws to stimulate population and supply troops for the field. By these and similar measures the country before the end of the eighteenth century fell to the brink of ruin. Wages fell, corn rose, discontent spread, country drained of specie, a run on the bank, the fleet mutinied at the Nore, the funds fell to 47. These were the effects on the material interests of the country. The effects on its political interests, and on the liberty of its inhabitants, were still more alarming. Our wealth was saved by the application of science to manufactures; our liberties were secured by the same energy being carried into politics.

## REACTION IN ENGLAND LATE IN EIGHTEENTH CENTURY.

THE loss of America, which in France assisted liberal opinions, in England damaged them. By our gross injustice we lost America. See in Campbell's Lives of the Chancellors, vi. 104, a striking account of the disgraceful pleasure with which the Privy Councillors listened to the infamous speech of Loughborough against Franklin. The injudicious, and in some respects criminal, coalition between Fox and North ruined the Whigs, and strengthened the hands of the retrogressive party. The king, by his insensate bigotry, nearly lost us Ireland. Quote Campbell's Lives of the Chancellors, vi. 281. Even Lord Campbell admits that in 1792–1793, the liberties of England were in danger, and of this he gives some strong instances in Lives of the Chancellors, vi. 243, 251, 252, 448, 449. This was done by the king and Pitt, aided by an apostate Chancellor. Campbell (vi. 244, 255) ascribes the greatest share in these infamous prosecutions to Lord Loughborough (see vii. 105). Directly after the death of Pitt, Fox was

---

[1] Parl. Hist. vol. xxxii. p. 383, and compare vol. xxxiii. p. 576.

made minister, and Erskine, whose matchless eloquence had roused the English juries, was made chancellor.[1] While the prosecutions in 1793–1794 were going on, it was seen how superior the people were to their rulers. This was the result of education. In 1806 the Whigs abolished the slave-trade, and this was "the great glory of the Fox and Grenville administration."[2] In 1807, their leader in the Commons brought in a Bill to allow Roman Catholic officers in England to hold commissions in the army ; but at this George III. was so angry that not only were ministers obliged to withdraw the Bill, but the king called on them for a written promise "never again to propose any measure for further relaxing the penal laws against the Roman Catholics," which they refusing to do, were dismissed.[3] In 1808, the Attorney-General, Sir Vicary Gibbs, carried a Bill to enable him to arrest any one "against whom he had filed an *ex officio* information for a libel," which, "though it still disgraces the Statute-Book, certainly no attorney-general since his time has ever thought of putting in force."[4] In 1811, the Prince Regent "continues the tory ministers in office."[5] In 1812, "Lord Liverpool, certainly one of the dullest of men, was now prime minister."[6] In 1817, 1818, 1819, 1820, most stringent acts were passed against the people.[7] In 1807, "a parliament was chosen in which the Whigs were not much more numerous than when they were vainly struggling against the ascendency of Pitt."[8] In 1808, the Tories carried a monstrous bill to prevent the exportation to the enemy of Jesuit's Bark.[9] In defiance of the whole authority of the executive government and the combined power of both Houses of Parliament, the English people protected an English queen against that bad man who sought to punish as crimes those levities which his own vices had provoked. In 1806, "the elections went strongly in favour of the Whigs."[10] Lord Campbell[11] says that in 1807 "the nominal head of the government was the Duke of Portland, never a very vigorous statesman, and now enfeebled by age and disease." Lord Eldon, a man in his own field of immense learning, but ignorant of even such political science as was then known—even Lord Eldon would not defend the infamous "Jesuit's Bark Bill" in 1808, though of course he voted for it.[12] In 1809, proceedings

---

[1] Campbell, vol. vi. pp. 526, 527.                      [2] Ibid. p. 560.
[3] Ibid. pp. 562, 563, 564. See the original letters on this in Pettor's Life of Sidmouth, vol. ii. pp. 451–465.
[4] Ibid. pp. 576, 577.          [5] Ibid. p. 585.          [6] Ibid. p. 598.
[7] Ibid. pp. 609, 610.          [8] Ibid. p. 573.          [9] Ibid. p. 574.
[10] Ibid. vol. vii. p. 189.      [11] Ibid. p. 210.         [12] Ibid. pp. 213, 214.

for corruption against the Duke of York.[1] George, directly he became Regent in 1812, renounced the Whigs.[2]

After the death of Pitt, the crown, and for a long time a great majority of the legislature, struggled in vain against the advancing intelligence of the English people. Cooke[3] well says that Pitt was guilty of a coalition as bad as that of Fox and North. Indeed he was so very popular because he was looked upon in 1783 as an ultra Whig.[4] It was in 1787, and therefore *before* the French Revolution, that Pitt, on the question of the Corporation and Test Acts, first abandoned the cause of toleration.[5] At the end of the eighteenth century we were saved by juries. Cooke[6] says, " When the minister attempted to prosecute his political opponents to the death, it became necessary to adduce evidence before an audience less tractable than a House of Commons." Cooke[7] says that the charges against the duke of York encouraged the general belief of corruption. Even Wilberforce, the intimate friend and great admirer of Pitt, separated from him in politics on account of his going to war in 1793,[8] and because he moved an amendment on this subject in the Commons, the king with characteristic bitterness took no notice of him at the next levée.[9] Wilberforce[10] ascribes the war to the influence Dundas had on Pitt. Wilberforce[11] was very dissatisfied with the improper letter which in 1800 Lord Grenville wrote when Buonaparte applied for peace. In 1803, the French hated the English.[12] Pitt, in 1803, patriotically aided Fox in turning out the incompetent Addington.[13] In 1805, Pitt though *not* a friend of Dundas, unflinchingly defended him,[14] and even quarrelled with Addington's party on the subject.[15] In 1804, such was the unsupportable arrogance of the English ministry that new countries which had not suffered from France wished us to be beaten.[16] A dangerous, or at all events a threatening, reaction took place of ascetic religion, headed not only by such persons as Hannah More, but also even by Wilberforce. This methodistic movement Sydney Smith, and in 1808 the Edinburgh Review, sensibly checked.[17] The war was persevered in by Pitt, in spite of the better judgment of the people. In 1796, " the war was now becoming universally unpopular." [18] In 1803,

[1] Campbell, vol. vii. p. 214.
[2] History of Party, vol. iii. pp. 332, 334.
[3] Ibid. p. 266.
[4] Ibid. pp. 341, 342.
[5] Ibid. p. 358.     [6] Ibid. p. 427
[7] Ibid. p. 470.
[8] See Life of Wilberforce, vol. iii. p. 16.
[9] Ibid. p. 72.
[10] Ibid. p. 391.     [11] Ibid. vol. ii. p. 354.
[12] Ibid. vol. iii. p. 69.
[13] Ibid. p. 142.     [14] Ibid. pp. 217, 219, 220.
[15] See Petter's Life of Sidmouth, vol. ii. pp. 368, 374.
[16] Life of Wilberforce, vol. iii. pp. 243, 244.
[17] Ibid. p. 364, see also vol. iv. p. 290, and vol. v. p. 47.     [18] Ibid. vol. ii. p. 169.

"all are distrustful of the duke of York's military talents."[1]  In 1812, Wilberforce was apprehensive that the church should be injured if it did not display an activity in education greater than the Methodists did.  In 1794, administration was *tempered* by Whigs.[2]  In 1794, Addington, on occasion of Hardy's trial, complains of "Erskine's strange doctrine upon the law of treason."[3]  Compare this with Lord Campbell's eulogy.  In 1796, general desire for peace.[4]  On the danger to Ireland in 1796, see *Petter's Life of Sidmouth*, vol. i. p. 174, 220.  In 1797, the mutiny at the Nore had also spread to an extent not generally known at Plymouth.[5]  Immense taxes.[6]

It is certain from Pitt's own account that Lord Grenville's letter in 1800 was written as an European manifesto, and with the *desire of continuing the war*.[7]  There can be no doubt that even if Pitt had not died nothing could have saved his ministry.[8]

Happily for the fortunes of England that great intellectual movement which I have already described had diffused among the middle classes an increased desire for liberty.  A very few years after the accession of George III. the first public meetings were held.  Then came associations for parliamentary reform.  We were benefited by the government being headed by men of such notorious incapacity as Addington and Liverpool.

## BAD POINTS UNDER GEORGE III.

### NEARLY LOST IRELAND—BIGOTRY.

It is often said that the court of George III. was very simple and paternal, but setting aside the unkind treatment of Miss Burney, even Mrs. Siddons, when reading before the queen, was obliged to stand till she nearly fainted.

In 1780, the rejection by the Upper House of the contractors' bill "rendered the Lords very odious."[9]

Laws became more severe.  In 1803, Lord Ellenborough's Act against cutting and maiming.[10]

In 1780, Turner in the House of Commons, violently attacked the clergy as friends to arbitrary power.[11]

[1] Life of Wilberforce, vol. iii. p. 120.
[2] Potter's Life of Lord Sidmouth, vol. i. p. 120.
[3] Ibid. p. 132.
[4] Ibid. p. 162; vol. ii. p. 2.
[5] Ibid. vol. i. p. 190.
[6] Ibid. vol. i. pp. 197, 358; vol. ii. p. 47.
[7] Ibid. vol. i. pp. 247, 248, 249.
[8] Ibid. vol. ii. p. 402.
[9] Campbell's Chancellors, vol. v. p. 308.
[10] Adolphus, vol. vii. p. 693.
[11] Adolphus, George III., vol. iii. p. 115.

Franklin was insulted by Wedderburn in presence of the judge.[1]

Bad judges.[2]

Charles Butler, who knew Wilkes, says, " In his real politics he was an aristocrat, and would much rather have been a favoured courtier at Versailles than the most commanding orator in St. Stephen's chapel."[3] In 1801, the peace of Amiens, and therefore in 1802 a great excess in the value of British exports ; but this being followed by war in 1803, our exports again fell.[4] The " Berlin Decree " would not have hurt us but for our foolish " Orders in Council " in 1807 (Porter, ii. 146). Porter (Progress of the Nation, iii. 183–186) notices the mischievous opposition made by Eldon and Ellenborough and the peers against Romilly and Mackintosh. George III. did wrong to make so many judges legislators, and raise them to high office in the state. Lord Camden was one of the greatest of all our judges. Lord Eldon was indifferent to truth. Kenyon, Lord Chief Justice of the King's Bench, in his advice on the coronation oath, confused the legislative with the executive capacity of the king ; and on another occasion he, as late as 1800, complimented a jury on their having found a man guilty of forestalling grain.[5] In 1770, Sergeant Glynn, in a motion said " that a general belief prevailed of the judges being unfriendly to juries, encroaching on their constitutional power, and laying down false law to mislead them in their verdicts."[6] Lord Ellenborough was able.[7] Lord Eldon, whose very virtues made bigotry more dangerous by making it more respectable. Lord Mansfield always opposed the Americans.[8] Campbell[9] says Lord Kenyon hated his predecessor, Mansfield, who opposed his appointment. Lord Mansfield wished Bullar to be his successor ; but this Pitt refused.[10] Eldon, Kenyon and Lord Redesdale despised Mansfield.[11] Lord Mansfield, the greatest judge ever seen in England, received his appointment a few years before George III. came to the throne, and directly the king ascended he openly avowed those principles which, under a better government, he had been glad to conceal. He favoured the monstrous pretensions of the House of Commons to disqualify Wilkes, and he, like

[1] Chatham Correspondence, vol. iv. p. 322.
[2] Campbell's Chancellors, vol. v. pp. 341, 344, 345, 508, 509, and vol. vi. pp. 210, 493.
[3] Butler's Reminiscences, vol. i. p. 73.
[4] Porter's Progress of the Nation, vol. ii. p. 145.
[5] Adolphus, vol. vii. pp. 406, 445.
[6] Adolphus. vol. i. p. 475, and still stronger in Parl. Hist. vol. xvi. pp. 1212, 1216.
[7] Brougham's Statesmen, vol. vi. p. 6.          [8] Adolphus, vol. ii. p. 145.
[9] Lives of the Chief Justices, vol. ii. p. 394.          [10] Ibid. p. 549.
[11] Campbell's Chief Justices, vol. ii. pp. 437, 438, 550 note.

all the judges, opposed the right of the jury to decide libels. He
opposed the extension of the Habeas Corpus. Lord Camden was
made Chief Justice of the Common Pleas in 1762, having already
been three years attorney-general.[1] He was chancellor from 1766
to 1770.[2] He opposed general warrants.[3] He was the only
friend to liberty among the judges. During the last fifty years
of the eighteenth century there was no chance of law reform.
Lord Camden, the only popular judge, openly opposed the ministry by whom he was appointed. Unscrupulous judges like
Bullar, and Gibbs, and Eldon, and even really eminent magistrates like Grant and Stowell, were narrow. Kenyon, Holroyd,
Littledale, Loughborough. Whenever the king had his way, all
the great judicial appointments were given to men who had distinguished themselves as enemies of the popular liberties. Lord
Camden, indeed, held for a time the office of chancellor, but he
was the open opponent of the ministers by whom he was appointed, and after his dismissal the great seal, which had been
held by Somers, Cowper, and Hardwicke, fell into the hands of
Loughborough, Thurlow, and Eldon. It was not to be supposed
they would do anything to cleanse the law from its impurities,
and all idea of law reform was lost. The chancellors were weak
men like Bathurst, or hypocrites like Thurlow and Eldon. In
1770, it was said by Townshend[4] that a judge, Sir Joseph Yates,
received a letter from the king desiring him to favour the court
in certain trials, but that he sent back the letter unopened. In
1770, Burke[5] speaks with great severity of the judges. Even the
judicial appointments were regulated by the same unhappy spirit.
It is now universally admitted that among the lawyers of that
age the largest and most enlightened minds were those of Mackintosh and Romilly. Romilly is perhaps chiefly known by his
noble efforts to soften those cruel laws for which our penal code
was then remarkable; but his other law reforms were in advance
even of our time. As to Mackintosh, it would be idle to praise
a man who, in addition to other merits, was the first to investigate
our laws on general principles.

But these were precisely the kind of men for which, in the
reign of George III., no honour could be found. While there
were such Chief Justices as Kenyon, and such Chancellors as
Bathurst and Thurlow, Romilly was made Solicitor-General, and
the Recordership of Bombay was conferred on Mackintosh. This
was natural in an age when North and Addington were the

[1] Brougham, vol. v. p. 192.                    [3] Ibid. pp. 198, 202, 203.
[2] Ibid. pp. 196, 201, 210.
[4] Parl. Hist. vol. xvi. pp. 1228, 1229.        [5] Ibid. p. 1270.

favourites, and Burke and Grenville excluded.[1] In 1778, the earl of Shelburne complained of the judges being politicians,[2] and then it was[3] that the pernicious custom first became general of mixing up the executive and legislative branches.[4]

Lord Mansfield opposed the Contractors' Bill in 1780,[5] by which it was attempted to limit the enormous influence of the Crown.

Lord Loughborough was chiefly recommended to the king by his hatred of the Americans.

The best guarantee in any country for the sound administration of justice is not the ability of the judges, but the extent to which they feel themselves under the control of public opinion. *Therefore* under George III., justice was pure but not liberal. Campbell, Denman, and Brougham could never have been appointed. The ability with which justice is administered depends on the ability of the judge, its purity and honesty on the control of the people. In 1782, George III. of his own authority added 1000*l.* a year to the pay of the Chief Justice of Common Pleas; thus, as the Duke of Richmond said, setting a bad example of inducing the judges to look up to the Crown.[6] In 1784, Lord Kenyon, then Master of the Rolls, asserted that the High Bailiff of Westminster was justified in not making a return when Fox brought forward the celebrated Libel Bill, now admitted to be one of the greatest improvements ever made; the judges universally opposed it.[7] Lord Mahon[8] says that George III. at his accession secured the independence of the judges. In 1761, Pratt, afterwards Lord Camden, was very ill-treated by Government.[9] "In 1794, the majority of the House of Commons for England and Wales was computed to be chosen by less than eight thousand out of eight millions."[10]

---

## DESPOTISM UNDER GEORGE III.

I. In 1763, the king deprived Wilkes of his commission as colonel in the Buckinghamshire militia, and as Lord Temple complimented Wilkes, he was dismissed from the lord-lieutenancy and his name expunged from the list of privy councillors.[11] In

[1] See Brougham, vol. ii. p. 13.  [2] Parl. Hist. vol. xix. pp. 924, 925.
[3] Ibid. p. 1318.  [4] See also vol. xxix. p. 1420.  [5] Ibid. vol. xxi. pp. 447, 451.
[6] Ibid. vol. xxiii. p. 961.  [7] See ibid. vol. xxix. pp. 1294, 1428, 1537, 1536.
[8] Hist. of England, vol. iv. p. 217.
[9] See Walpole, Mem. of George III., vol. i. pp. 125, 126.
[10] Note in Burton's Diary, vol. iii. p. 149.
[11] Adolphus, Hist. of George III., vol. i. p. 125.

1763, General Conway, who usually supported the Government, voted on one occasion against them, and was consequently " deprived of his civil and military employments."[1]

II. In 1769, the House of Commons, assuming the functions of representatives and constituents, expelled Wilkes from the House. The remark of Adolphus[2] is very pleasant.

III. In 1771, the Lord Mayor was sent to the Tower,[3] and even Adolphus[4] allows the purity of his conduct.

IV. In 1773, Colonel Barré and Sir Hugh Williams were passed over in some military promotion on account of their votes in Parliament.[5]

V. The king tampered with the peers to induce them to throw out Fox, his own minister. This Adolphus[6] seems inclined to doubt.

VI. In 1793, it was laid down by the Solicitor-General that during war the king had a right by proclamation to forbid " the return to the country of any subject not convicted of a crime."[7]

VII. In 1793 booksellers punished.[8]

VIII. Read Howell's Trial, xxii. 909, in Adolphus v. 529.

IX. In 1793, Lord Chief Justice Clark said that only " landed property " should be represented. Quote his amusing remarks in Adolphus, v. 539, 540.

X. In 1798, the duke of Norfolk was dismissed from the Lord-Lieutenancy for proposing the " majesty of the people." See Adolphus vi. 692, where it is said Pitt opposed this paltry act.

XI. In 1795, a bill was brought forward extending the statute of treason.[9] And another bill, against seditious meetings, forbad *any* meeting to be held without consent of the magistrate.[10] These two bills in popular speech were called respectively " the Treason and the Sedition Bills."[11] They made Fox say that obedience was only a question of prudence.[12] The consequence of all this violence was the mutiny at the Nore in 1797, of which there is an account in Adolphus at vi. 560–588. In 1799, Pitt *proposed* a measure to put an end to debating societies.[13]

XII. In 1799, the political prisoners were shamefully treated.[14]

XIII. Allen[15] says that on Hardy's trial the Attorney-General

---

[1] Adolphus, Hist. of George III., vol. i. p. 141.          [2] Ibid. p. 347.
[3] Ibid. pp. 489. 490.          [4] Ibid. p. 492.          [5] Ibid. p. 569.
[6] Ibid. vol. iv. p. 61.          [7] Ibid. vol. v. 395, 397.
[8] Ibid. vol. v. pp. 525, 526, and vol. vi. p. 695.
[9] Ibid. vol. vi. pp. 359, 360.          [10] Ibid. p. 364.          [11] Ibid. p. 368.
[12] Ibid. p. 373.  On their provisions, see p. 378.
[13] Ibid. vii. pp. 140, 141.          [14] Ibid. p. 134.
[15] Inquiry into the Royal Prerogative, p. 25.

claimed for the king of England power equal to that claimed for Louis XIV.

XIV. Read Wyvill's Correspondence, in five or six volumes, often quoted by Adolphus.

---

## DISASTERS UNDER GEORGE III.

I. The duke of Buckingham[1] says, in 1797, "the Bank had stopped payment. Two mutinies had broken out in the fleet, one at Spithead and another at the Nore. An organisation of malcontents had been formed in Ireland under the name of the United Irishmen."[2] On the Mutiny at the Nore in 1797, see Adolphus, vi. 560, 588.

II. Taxes; national debt; prices rose and wages fell.

III. Wages fell, see Hallam, ii. 446. Parl. Hist. xxxii. 705, 712.

IV. The people desired peace.

V. The country was drained of specie.

---

## AFTER FRENCH REVOLUTION.

The bank stopped payment and otherwise would have been bankrupt.[3] The directors of the bank told Pitt what the consequence would be of sending so much money out of the kingdom.

In 1797 the country had "long wished for" peace.[4]

In 1798 the Bishop of Durham made some silly remarks on the short petticoats of the opera women;[5] the minute knowledge displayed by the bishop on such a subject gave rise to some natural mirth, and the Morning Chronicle spoke of it in a way far milder than it would be now noticed if a bishop were to be so foolish. It will hardly be believed that Lambert and Perry were for this called to the bar of the House of Lords, fined 50l., and in addition to the fine, imprisoned in Newgate, each for three months.[6] In 1799, Mr. Flower, in a Cambridge newspaper, made some criticisms on a speech delivered by Watson, bishop of

---

[1] Adolphus, Mem. of George III., vol. ii. p. 362.    [2] Ibid. p. 384.

[3] Parl. Hist. vol. xxxiii. p. 51.

[4] Ibid. pp. 406, 414, 417, 718, and vol. xxxv. p. 413.

[5] Ibid. vol. xxxiii. p. 1308.    [6] Ibid. pp. 1311, 1313.

Llandaff. For this he was brought before the House of Lords, fined 100*l.*, and thrown into Newgate for six months.[1] In 1798 the attorney-general brought in a bill to "regulate newspapers."[2]

In 1799 Pitt brought in a bill to check debating societies.[3]

In 1798 the standing orders for excluding strangers were twice enforced.[4]

In 1798 Windham, Secretary of War, expressed a desire to prevent the proceedings of the House of Commons being published in the newspapers.[5]

In 1800 Sheridan said that the scarcity of provisions was partly caused by the *waste* arising from the increased consumption of men manning our navy in active service, who ate more than those at home.[6] And Grey adds:[7] "Thousands are taken from laborious occupations to consume what is produced by the labour of others." Read Tooke's History of Prices. In 1800 Jones said, "In Worcester numbers lived upon turnips, and in York numbers lived upon greens."[8] In 1800, bread was eighteen pence "the quartern loaf."[9]

In 1800, the wages of agricultural labour were 8*s.* to 9*s.* a week.[10] The increase of the poor widened the labour market, by throwing into it men who before had never been obliged to work. On the enormous increase of the poor rates see Parliamentary History, vol. xxxv. pp. 1064–1065; and read Eden's History of the Labouring Classes.

The trials of Muir and Palmer in Scotland, and Wakefield and Lord Thanet in England. Mem. of Fox, iii. 60, 165.

In 1793, the English people were tired of the war.[11]

In 1795, the Earl of Lauderdale said of the Treasonable Practices Bill, "In the old government of France there was nothing more despotic than what this bill went to create. It was the introduction of the system of terror into this country."[12] And Fox said[13] that "under it Locke would have been exiled for his writings."

[1] Parl. Hist. vol. xxxiv. p. 1000.
[2] Ibid. vol. xxxiv. p. 987.
[3] Ibid. vol. xxxiv. pp. 152, 153, 157, 158, 159.
[4] Ibid. vol. xxxv. p. 532.
[5] Ibid. p. 697.  [6] Ibid. p. 710, 711.
[7] Ibid. vol. xxxiii. p. 1415.
[8] Ibid. vol. xxxiii. pp. 1513, 151
[9] Ibid. p. 535.
[10] Ibid. p. 833.
[11] See Russell's Memoir of Fox, vol. iii. p. 39.
[12] Parl. Hist. vol. xxxii. p. 246.
[13] Ibid. vol. xxxiii. p. 615.

## IMPROVEMENTS UNDER GEORGE III.

Early in the eighteenth century political economy was first publicly taught. But in 1714 despised. In 1794, the attorney-general failed in five prosecutions, and was mobbed by the people.

Priestley, in 1768, lays down the right of cashiering the sovereign.[1]

The fortunate neglect of literary men by George II. and Walpole, assisted in establishing the independence of literature.[2]

In literature the Watsons, and in art West, opposed the classical school. See a curious account in Galt's Life of West. On the stage Garrick succeeded Quin. See Life of Cumberland and Macklin.

At the end of the seventeenth century the scientific spirit first attacked the classics. Compare the dispute of Sir W. Temple, &c. In 1708, Burnet[3] attacks Latin. In the middle of the eighteenth century it declined; and was discountenanced by both the Pitts. In 1730, all law pleadings were altered from Latin to English. Prejudices of Johnson. Lord Monboddo said no one ignorant of Greek could write English. Harris, in Hermes, derived from Latin our beautiful language. This was remedied by Horne Tooke, a *liberal*. Fusion of society. Coleridge[4] complains of the diminished respect for the ancients.

Anglo-Saxon even was neglected in that busy and spirited age. The increase of physical knowledge under Charles II. was the first blow to the ancients. The disloyalty of Oxford brought it into disrepute. Even Cambridge fell off. Hence private schools increased; then came Bell and Lancaster. *Dress* became careless; before then it was stiff. Like the Chinese, politeness and *rank* were known by dress. *Now* the dress is gone and only titles remain, which *will* go.

In 1771, Calcraft writes to Lord Chatham[5] "the ministers own Wilkes too dangerous to meddle with." In 1771, "mob even of the better class."[6] In the middle of the reign of George II. Le Blanc,[7] after mentioning the freedom of our press, says that government dare not act against it even legally. The acquittal of Tooke, &c., must have greatly weakened the government. That great authority, Lord Mansfield, laid it down " that a court prosecution should never be instituted without certainty of success."[8]

Franklin[9] writes in 1773, from London, that *all* the dissenters

[1] See Thomson's Hist. of Chemistry, vol. ii. p. 12.
[2] Ibid. pp. 61, 62.
[3] Works, vol. vi. pp. 200, 201.
[4] The Friend, vol. iii. p. 106.
[5] Chatham Correspondence, vol. iv. p. 122.
[6] Ibid. pp. 133, 134.
[7] Lettres d'un Français, vol. ii. pp. 313, 314.
[8] Butler's Reminiscences, vol. i. p. 125.
[9] Correspondence, vol. i. p. 237.

favoured the Americans ; and see Adolphus, History of George III.,
vol. ii. p. 331.

Middle class, in the middle of the eighteenth century, were
called *Esquire.*

Walpole, remaining a commoner, assisted their fame.

*Aristocracy.*—They lost ground early in the reign of George
III. by settling in London, instead of merely taking lodgings as
formerly. In 1708 Burnet (vi. 214), notices that the sessions of
Parliament, became longer, and caused an increased residence
of nobles in London.

George III. was ridiculed for his manners.

-----

## PROGRESS IN EIGHTEENTH CENTURY.

I. INCREASE of mercantile [intercourse] and manufactures lessened
superstition, as I have shown, under Charles II. In 1740 the
merchants were making great head.[1] In 1708 Burnet [2] says " as
for the men of trade and business, they are, generally speaking,
the best body in the nation, generous, sober, and charitable."
Thus early did they secure the character they have ever since
possessed. Between 1750 and 1796 a wonderful increase in
bankers.[3] The increasing *curiosity* and *wealth* of the commercial classes first induced them to buy seats in parliament,
and thus weakened the territorial influence.[4] The French war
in 1793, the landowners fancied was the cause of their own
ruin ; for, says Alison,[5] during the war the commercial and
manufacturing interest had so greatly increased, that they " had
become irresistible." By the beginning of the eighteenth century the people were becoming so powerful that the Tories as
well as the Whigs appealed to them. The " clamour " for parliamentary reform first rose late in the American war.[6] After
1688, the crown, terrified by the example of two Revolutions, began
to use corruption instead of threats. See the admirable remarks
of Erskine in Parl. Hist. xxx. 829. Locke, in his Essay on Government,[7] recommends doing away with rotten boroughs. Under
Charles II. it was first legal to present petitions to parliament.

II. Scarcely had the Revolution swept away the Stuarts and

Correspondence of Countess Pomfret and Harford. vol. i. p. 300.
[2] Own Times, vol. vi. p. 202.     [3] Burke's Works, vol. ii. p. 292.
[4] Hallam, vol. ii. p. 447.        [5] Hist. of Europe, vol. xiv. p. 188.
[6] Parl. Hist. vol. xxix. p. 1505.   [7] Works, vol. iv. pp. 432, 433.

humbled the Church, when Locke put forward the first proposal to change the electoral system. In 1710, newspapers first interfered in politics, and cheap political pamphlets first arose. In 1720, political caricatures first became common.

III. *Petitions.*—In 1717, the first political petitions.[1] In 1767, petitions to the king first became general. In 1780, Society for Constitutional Information, London Reforming Society, and the Society of the Friends of Liberty. In 1771 the "Society of the Bill of Rights." In 1765, *all* men were politicians.[2] Under the reign of George II. the power of the people continued rapidly to increase.

In 1779, the Yorkshire Association was formed for Parliamentary Reform. About 1770 an attempt was first made to increase the power of the electors by exacting pledges from candidates. There were debating clubs for political tradesmen. Even tradesmen met at the Robin Hood.[3] In 1792, the "Friends of the People" formed to get Parliamentary Reforms. In 1791, the London Corresponding Society.

IV. Even such dissolute men and demagogues as Paine and Fox were popular. The writings of Paine produced immense effect, solely because they opposed the tyranny of the Court and Church. The people knew that Wilkes was persecuted from revenge. In 1780, county meetings were attacked in Parliament.[4] In 1743, caricatures were becoming common.[5] Lord Mahon,[6] on the authority of Hallam, says in 1761, "the sale of boroughs to any wide extent may be dated from this period;" but Mahon[7] gives instances of this bribery as early as 1714.[8] Paine's works were popular, not that the people of this country had a taste for the apish buffoonery of Wilkes or scurrility of Paine, but because they saw them struggling against a bad government, and they sympathised, not with the martyrs, but with the cause. In 1738, even the lowest classes were greedy of political news.[9] In 1740, the sale of boroughs was notorious;[10] and in 1741, it is observed[11] that bribery and corruption had succeeded the excesses of authority. The great patriots of the time of Charles I. never thought

---

[1] Hallam, vol. ii. p. 419. Vernon Correspondence, vol. iii. p. 146.

[2] Grosley's London, vol. i. p. 189.

[3] Prior's Life of Burke, p. 75, and on Robin Hood Societies, Prior's Goldsmith, vol. i. pp. 419, 420, and Campbell's Chancellors, vol. vi. p. 373. Grosley's London, i. 150.

[4] Parl. Hist. vol. xx. p. 1352; vol. xxi. pp. 80, 265.

[5] Mahon's England, vol. iii. p. 187.

[6] Ibid. vol. iv. p. 220.      [7] Ibid. vol. i. p. 46.

[8] See also Hallam, vol. ii. p. 447.

[9] Parl. Hist. vol. x. p. 378.      [10] Ibid. vol. xi p. 376.      [11] Ibid. p. 1125.

of the doctrine of representation, nor was it claimed in the Bill
of Rights in 1688. Dr. Parr[1] says the American war made
Englishmen inquire into *political* rights. It was the strength of
public opinion which put an end to the American war.[2] Late in
the seventeenth century I find a complaint[3] that a republican
party was "reprinting Harrington's Oceana, the works of Milton,
Ludlow, and Sidney, all on the same subject, and tending to
promote the design of lessening and reproaching monarchy."
The impetus given by the Puritans remained after the Restoration an undercurrent—only showing itself in scepticism and
dissent.

Meetings for Parliamentary reform, see Albemarle's Memoirs
of Lord Rockingham, ii. pp. 93, 94.

In 1769, Chatham advises the nobles to unite with the people.[4]

V. *Newspapers.*—Their real power rose under Wilkes, when
the House of Commons ceased to be the popular organ.[5] Immense
increase of newspapers between 1724 and 1792. And on the
increasing power of the press, see Prior's Life of Burke, p. 275.

VI. Notwithstanding bad judges, the juries did their duty. In
1794, they acquitted Hardy, Tooke, and Thelwall; and in 1796,
Stone.[6] In Adolphus, Hist. of George III. vol. vi. pp. 48–71,
there is a summary of the trials of Hardy, Tooke, and Thelwall.
In 1794, Tooke was acquitted in a few minutes. The acquittal
of Hone in 1817 was a great gain. It became known that no
jury would bring in Junius guilty. At the accession of George II.
the Jacobite and High Church faction were nearly extinct. The
government of William III. avowedly relied on the consent of
the nation, and neither Anne nor George I. and II. dared to
oppose liberties to which they owed their crown. In 1721, the
first question was put in Parliament to a minister of the crown.

VII. *Nineteenth Century.*—By the end of the eighteenth century the social and intellectual movement had become so strong
that the political reaction could no longer bear up against it. See
in Life of Wilberforce, iii. p. 12, some very remarkable evidence
on the change in 1801, coming over the minds of men, and their
desire for reform. See also p. 227, respecting the increasing
power of "popular opinion." This notwithstanding the apostacy
of the Regent. The French Revolution diminished the inordinate
respect for rank. (See paper on Education.) As the nine-

[1] Works, vol. ii. p. 329.   [2] Ibid. vol. vii. p. 14.
[3] Somers Tracts, vol. xi. p. 155.
[4] Bancroft's American Revolution, vol. iii. p. 354.
[5] Arnold's Lectures on Modern History, pp. 261, 266.
[6] Campbell's Chancellors, vol. vi. pp. 450, 462, 470, 481.

teenth century advanced the progress became evident. The Whigs formerly were forced to call in the aristocracy to balance the Crown, but now the people were called in, and there arose Radicals, and even Tories were *mitigated* into Conservatives. The principles of Reform, invigorated by the American Revolution, were now reinvigorated by the French Revolution. In 1800, the monied interest, by loans, &c., had greatly benefited by the war at the expense of the "landed interest."[1] At the same time, the mean men whom Pitt made peers weakened the aristocratic element. At the same time, the anti-ecclesiastical movement rapidly proceeded. In 1801, the clergy were finally expelled the House of Commons, thus preparing the way for their ultimate removal from the Upper House. And, although this was really a party measure it supplied one of those precedents by which men are much influenced.

---

## CIRCUMSTANCES FAVOURABLE TO THE ENGLISH PEOPLE EARLY IN THE NINETEENTH CENTURY.

ALISON[2] says that in 1803 the violent conduct of Napoleon and his arrest of the English, reduced even the opposition to be in favour of a war with France, and thus turned a social struggle into a national contest. Indeed, it was now shown that the Whigs were really patriotic.[3] Pitt was for the first time supported by Fox and Sheridan; the incompetent ministry of Addington was turned out A.D. 1804.[4] Alison[5] says that the defeat of Austerlitz "made a deep impression on the public mind" of England, and caused men to desire a *fusion* of the two political parties, to make common cause against so dangerous an enemy. The result was that the miserable prejudices of George III. against the greatest statesman of his age were forced to give way, and in 1806 Fox and his party were admitted into the cabinet.[6] The new ministry, in the same year, introduced a bill for "enlistments for a limited period of service."[7] In 1806 they also abolished the slave trade.[8] However, in April, 1807, a Tory ministry came in.[9] When, in 1808, the news arrived that

[1] Parl. Hist. vol. xxxv. p. 699.
[2] Alison's History of Europe, vol. vi. p. 209.
[3] Ibid. pp. 237, 238; vol. viii. p. 455.
[4] Ibid. vol. vii. p. 85.
[5] Ibid. pp. 380, 387, 391.
[6] Ibid. pp. 456.

[4] Ibid. vol. vi. pp. 250, 251.
[5] Ibid. p. 88.
[6] Ibid. pp. 395, 403.

the Spanish *people* had risen against Napoleon, all classes in
England were mad with delight.[1]  As Napoleon's troops, after
beating the Spanish *government* had been beaten by the Spanish
*people*, it was believed that a new era had begun in which
military discipline would be conquered by popular energy.[2] Alison
says[3] that Canning's love of popularity made him "encourage
the insurrection of the South American colonies, but in so doing
he established a precedent of fatal application in future times to
his own country."

The Edinburgh Review did much.  Pitt was succeeded by
Perceval, Thurlow by Eldon, and thus the Tories were themselves
inferior men; but so, it may be added, were the Whigs.  However, now it was that the Whigs first began to study political
economy.  This must have aided our liberty by showing the
injury of that mischievous system which is called protective
government.  Pitt would have ruined us if there had not come
into play that enormous mechanical and physical knowledge
which I have already pointed out as one of the results of
diminished superstition, and which so increased our wealth that
we bore up against the pressure.

- - - - - - - - -

## ENGLAND IN THE NINETEENTH CENTURY.

.        .        .        .        .        .        .

. . . Opposition to the spirit of the age.  When sentence has
been passed upon it by a large majority of the nation, its doom
is inevitably fixed.  It may for a time be preserved by violence,
but that same violence must eventually react against those who
employ it, and in its ravages will destroy what under a more
pliant policy would probably have been preserved.  This is the
law of the physical world, and it is likewise the law of the moral
world. . . . .  And thus it always is with those statesmen
and legislators who are so ignorant of their calling as to think it
lies within their function to anticipate the march of affairs and
to provide for far distant contingencies.  In trifling matters this,
indeed, may be done without danger, though—as the constant
changes in the laws of every country abundantly prove—it is
also done without benefit.  But, in reference to those large and
fundamental measures which bear upon the destiny of a people,
such anticipation is worse than idle; it is highly injurious.  In

---

[1] Alison's History of Europe, vol. viii. p. 451.          [2] Ibid. pp. 497, 498.
[3] Ibid. vol ix. p. 254.

the present state of knowledge politics, so far from being a science, is one of the most backward of all the arts, and the only safe course for the legislator is to look upon his craft as consisting in the adaptation of temporary contrivances to temporary emergencies. His business is to follow the age, and not at all to attempt to lead it. He should be content to study [what] is passing before his eyes, and modify his schemes, not according to . the traditional theory, but according to the actual exigencies of his own time, of which society itself is the sole judge. But with extremely few exceptions, his practical habits and his ignorance of great speculative truths will always disqualify him from forming that philosophic estimate of his own time by which alone he could be able to anticipate the wants, and facilitate the progress, of distant generations.

These are among those broad and general views which will hardly be disputed by any man who, with a competent knowledge of history, has reflected much on the nature and conditions of modern society. But, during the reign of George III., not only were such views unknown, but the very end and object of government was entirely mistaken. It was then believed that government was made for the minority, to whose interests the majority were bound humbly to submit. In those days it was believed that the power of making laws must always be lodged in the hands of a few privileged classes: that the nation at large had no concern with those laws except to obey them; and that a wise government would secure the obedience of the people by preventing education from spreading among them. It is surely a remarkable circumstance that the people who had been withheld from their own now began to re-enter on their original rights. Political empire declined, and the intellectual empire rose up. And what is still more remarkable is, that this great change should have been effected, not by any great external event nor by a sudden insurrection of the people, but by the unaided action of moral force: the silent but effective pressure of public opinion which an arbitrary government had been able to stop but not to destroy. This has always appeared to me to be a decisive proof of the natural and, if I may so say, the healthy march of English civilization. It is a proof of an elasticity and yet a sobriety of spirit which no other nation has ever displayed. No other nation could have escaped from such a crisis except by a revolution, of which the cost might well have exceeded the gain. But in our country the progress of those principles which I have endeavoured to trace, had diffused among the people a caution and a spirit of wisdom which made them pause before

they cared to strike, taught them to husband their strength, and
which enabled them to reserve their force for those better days
when, for their benefit, a party began again to be organised in
the state, by whom their interests were successfully advocated,
even within the walls of parliament. For thirty-five years no
parliament has ventured to sanction, no minister has even dared
to propose, any measure hostile to the interests of the people.
Whigs have become Radicals, Tories have become Conservatives.
The Radicals avoid the monarchical and theologic prejudices of
the Tories and the aristocratic prejudices of the Whigs. In 1808
the Examiner, the first influential newspaper in favour of Reform.
Public meetings were held. Then came Associations for Parliamentary Reform. Then education, by Bell, &c. This was owing
to the Dissenters, who also favoured the Americans. Then came
the acquittal of Hardy and Tooke. . . .

The circumstances which accompanied this great reaction are
too complicated, and have been too little studied for me to
attempt in this Introduction to offer even a sketch of them.
It is, however, sufficient to say, what must be generally known,
that for nearly fifty years the movement has continued with
unabated spirit; everything which has been done has increased
the power of the people. Blow after blow has been directed
against those classes which were once the sole depositaries of
power. The Reform Bill, the Emancipation of the Catholics,
and the Repeal of the Corn Laws, are admitted to be the three
greatest political achievements of the present generation. Each
of these vast measures has depressed a powerful party. The
extension of the suffrage has lessened the influence of hereditary
rank, and, what is equally important, has broken up that great
oligarchy of landowners by whom both Houses of Parliament had
long been ruled. The abolition of protection still further enfeebled the territorial aristocracy, and by diminishing in many
instances the value of tithes has curtailed the incomes of the
clergy. At the same time those superstitious feelings, by which the
ecclesiastical order is mainly upheld, received a severe shock:
firstly, by the repeal of the Test and Corporation Acts, and afterwards by the admission of Catholics to the legislature; .steps
which are with reason regarded as supplying a precedent of
mischievous import for the interests of the Established Church. . .

.    .    .    .    .    .    .    .

There is no more danger of political reaction, for crown, church,
and nobles are weakened, [the] press is supreme, and the people
have a hold over public affairs, so that even the most imperious
minister defers to those whom half a century ago he would have

despised.    Great suffering was caused by the policy which
governed England during the reign of George III.   But those
sufferings will not be wasted if they teach our politicians the
lessons of modesty and inculcate the great truth that the art of
the statesman is to *wait* and bide his time—the servant of knowledge and the handmaid of great thinkers.

.        .        .        .        .        .        .

The spirit of practical benevolence is so strong and so active
that there is scarcely a corner of the kingdom where it is not
doing its work.  Even the judicial and legislative bodies of the
country have felt the general contagion.  Juries are unwilling to
condemn, and judges are anxious to pardon.  Less is thought of
punishing the offence, and more is thought of reforming the
offender.  Our prisons have been purged of those foul and infamous
abuses which gaolers once practised with impunity on their unhappy captives.  Madhouses have ceased to be receptacles for the
lust and cruelty of the keepers, and the insane themselves have
been treated with mercy.  Degrading and infamous punishments,
the pillory and personal mutilation, are obsolete, and even in the
army and navy flogging is going out.  In our schools less cruelty.
.   .   .   Ameliorations have been effected in our criminal code,
which the most humane legislator would formerly have considered
impossible, and penalties have been abolished which were once
deemed absolutely necessary.  And if we take a more general
view, we cannot fail to observe that at no period has our country
remained so long at peace.  This, I think, is one of the most
unequivocal features of the present age.  It is eminently the
result of a diminished ferocity in our temper, and of an increased
sense of the importance of human life.  Among the most civilised
people a growing contempt for warlike pursuits is gradually
extirpating that lust of military glory which is one of the most
diseased appetites of a barbarous nation.  Indeed, so clearly
marked is this tendency, that when recently, in an adjoining
country, an untoward combination of events hurried into the field
immense bodies of troops, the movement, at first so threatening,
ended in a spectacle for which the history of the world affords no
parallel.  Great armies, furnished with all the appliances of war,
and burning with national hatred, confronted each other for
months, and then, amid every variety of mutual provocation, were
disbanded without striking a blow, because their respective
governments did not dare to outrage the feelings of Europe by
giving that signal which the military leaders so eagerly expected.[1]

[1] The author probably refers to the position of Austria and Prussia in 1850.  [Ed.]

These are among the results of that increased sense of the value and dignity of man which, as we know from the experience of every country, is intimately connected with the decay of superstition. But while such have been the moral effects, the physical effects have been hardly less important. Whatever explanation we may give, it stands recorded in history as a fact beyond the possibility of dispute, that during the last five centuries the progress of knowledge has been everywhere accompanied by a decline of the ecclesiastical influence. To me the explanation of the pheno-menon appears very simple. As the theological spirit becomes more feeble, the secular spirit must become more powerful. In every successive generation the attention of men has been less attracted by dogmatic and ritual pursuits, and has therefore had more leisure for the acquisition of real and positive knowledge. What has been lost by the clergy has been gained by mankind. The English intellect, exulting in its freedom, has only in these latter times put forth its unshackled powers. The minds of our countrymen have become larger in their scope and more definite in their aim. The consequence has been that since the Revolu-tion of 1688 there has been effected in this little island alone more permanent good than had been accomplished before by the aggregate wisdom of the human race.

The laws of sound have been discovered, and to their aggregate the name of acoustics given. Bradley discovered the aberration of light. By the two Herschels the heavens have been surveyed in both hemispheres, and so jealously have they been, as it were, swept by the telescope, that discoveries are now being constantly made of the bodies which lie in their immeasurable space. By the discoveries of Young and Champollion the learning of Egypt has been restored : a silence of two thousand [years] has been broken. During that sceptical movement in the reign of Charles II. which I have already traced, Newton had begun, and in the reign of William III. had completed, that series of amazing dis-coveries any one of which would have immortalised his name. The law of gravitation was carried by him to the furthest boundaries of the solar system, and there is now a growing disposition to push it still further, so as to include the furthest limits of the physical universe. By the continued efforts of different countries there has been made that vast series of magnetic observations which almost cover the circuit of the globe, and from which it now remains for some great thinker to work out the laws of terres-trial magnetism. Since the death of Newton, electricity has been raised to a science. The geologists have begun and almost com-pleted their magnificent design of mapping out the globe. Bell,

Hall, and Mayo on the nerves. Prichard, Newman, and Donaldson on language. Hallam and Macaulay, the only two historians we have had since Gibbon. Sanscrit literature first known in 1785. The diseases of the mind, Pinel, Esquirol, and Pritchard. Political economy by Adam Smith, Ricardo, and Mill. The laws of population by Malthus, and at a great distance below by Sadler. In logic, the revival by Whately, and the discoveries by Herschel and Mill. We have in a few years created numerous manufactures, one of which is equal to all the manufactures of the ancient world put together. The enormous increase in our material wealth. The great revolution, begun by Bacon and Descartes, was completed; and the study of the mind became secular.

A long line of illustrious thinkers, from Newton to Davy, and from Davy to Faraday, have successfully laboured in their glorious vocation to push even into the depths of nature the intellectual empire of man. Laws, the very existence of which had never been suspected, have been made plain to the lowest understanding; and are now the common property of the civilized world. Innumerable varieties of physical phenomena have been observed, collected, and referred to those general principles by which the harmony of their movements is explained. Nor has this restless energy confined itself to those things by which we are more immediately surrounded. There is now hardly a spot in the globe where man has not planted his foot. In the pursuit of knowledge he has scaled the highest mountains and crossed the most dangerous deserts. He has ransacked the furthest extremities of the earth with the vain hope of glutting a curiosity that nothing can satiate. By him Nature, even in her inmost recesses, has been rifled of her choicest productions. All that she, in the exuberance of her wealth, can supply, has been gathered up and made to minister to the happiness of man. It is by him and for him that all this has been done. To multiply his pleasures, and to increase his powers, there have been lavished in boundless profusion all the inventions of art and all the discoveries of science. Nor is there in these unrivalled efforts the least symptom of approaching decline. Wonderful as are the things which have been accomplished, there is every reason to believe that they are as nothing compared to what will hereafter be attained. Indeed, the success of the present is the best guarantee for the hopes of the future. Within the memory of most men who are now living, there have been introduced improvements, the mere mention of which would have provoked the derision of our ancestors. The meanest peasant who tills the soil can now wield resources which, only one generation ago, neither wealth nor power could hope to

procure.   By the force of the human intellect the very conditions
under which Nature exists have been suspended.   By the application of steam we have diminished space.   By controlling the
motion of a subtle and imponderable fluid, we have, I do not say
facilitated communication, but without an hyperbole we have anticipated time.   But the powers of individual men have not only
been rendered greater, they have also been made more durable.
By discoveries in the arts of healing, and, what is more important, by discoveries respecting the prevention of disease, we have
diminished the total amount of pain; and we have in an extraordinary degree increased the average length of life.   Thus it is
that the resources of even the lowest unit of the human race have
become more numerous, more powerful, and more permanent.   At
the same time there have been wonderfully extended those intellectual enjoyments by which we are so eminently distinguished
from the rest of the animal creation.   Not only have the sources
of these mental pleasures been widened ; they have also been
multiplied.   New branches 'of knowledge are being constantly
opened, and the field of thought has been so incredibly enlarged
that even the most sluggish mind may well be lost in amazement
at the boundless expanse by which it is surrounded.

This is what has been done by the intellect of man.   This is
what has been done by those noble faculties which a class that
yet lingers among us is constantly labouring to vilify and to
fetter.   There are, indeed, various circumstances incidental to
the present stage of civilization which still preserve to these
superstitious men a certain share of their former power.   But
there can, I think, be no reasonable doubt that the days of that
power are numbered.   And, when their reign is brought to a final
close, there will then for the first time be allowed to proceed
without interruption the successive epochs of that moral and intellectual development which we have every right to suppose will
at length conduct the human race to a state of happiness and
virtue, which a fond imagination loves to ascribe to that primitive
condition of man, of the innocence and simplicity of which we,
however, have no better evidence than what is to be found in the
traditions of the theologian and in the dreams of the poet.

### ERRORS OF VOLTAIRE.

I. He supposes that civilization has shortened the average duration of life.[1]

II. The only instance I remember in which Voltaire looks upon history as a *development*, is at tome xvii. p. 166 of his Œuvres (Essai sur les Mœurs). Generally speaking, he is too fond of assigning great events to little causes. See, for instance, xvii. 205, 246 ; xviii. 145. He evidently had no notion of it as a science. See his remarks on "the utility of history," in Fragments sur l'Histoire, article viii. Œuvres, xxvii. 216–218.

III. Voltaire may be justly charged with an unphilosophical contempt for the middle ages, and with a still more unphilosophical contempt for antiquity.

IV. If I may venture to point out what I conceive to be the errors of this great man, I should class them under three heads : an undue contempt for antiquity ; a disposition to assign great events to little causes ; and an ignorance of economical science, which he might have learnt from Hume, though Quesnai could teach him little, and Turgot had not yet written. Even in 1768 he speaks contemptuously of the middle ages.[2]

V. It appears from passages in Luther's Correspondence that, "long before the dispute with Tetzel," he was dissatisfied "with the prevailing system of theology, and the actual condition of the church." See an interesting essay on Luther in Rogers's Essays, vol. i. p. 151.

---

### ROUSSEAU AND MATERIALISM.

While the French were thus outstripping the rest of Europe in the general comprehensiveness of their views, there was unfortunately forming a school of literature which was destined to retard their progress. Indeed, it could hardly have been expected that so rapid a movement as that which followed the death of Louis XIV. could have taken place without causing serious excesses. The literary men of France, possessed of an influence of which there had then been no example, were intoxicated by

---

[1] Essai sur les Mœurs, in Œuvres, tome xv. pp. 10, 11.
[2] Pyrrhonisme de l'Histoire, in Œuvres, tome xxvi. p. 188.

their own success. At the same time, the government, which
was constantly becoming more contemptible, did everything in
its power to irritate those great writers to whom France looked
up with such respect. This tended still further to embitter their
feelings; and by the middle of the eighteenth century it was
evident that a deadly struggle was about to begin between the
literature of France and the government of France. Those who
are acquainted with the works of that age will find ample proofs
of this, which may be illustrated by a comparison of the different
writings of Voltaire. This great and good man had always shown
a disposition to keep on terms with the government, and whatever may be the prejudices of those who only know his works by
their reputation, it is certain that he was as much a lover of order
as a lover of liberty. But although he had now fallen into that
period of life of which an excess of caution is the usual characteristic, it is remarkable that the further he advanced in years
the more pungent were his sarcasms against ministers, the more
violent were his invectives against despotism. In his Life of
Charles XII., which was his first historical work, he speaks ser-
vilely of kings. In a man like Voltaire, whose sagacity has
seldom been equalled, and whose honesty of intention is indisputable, this change is well worthy of attention, and can, I think,
only be ascribed to his deep conviction that the government of
France was so hopelessly corrupt as to render its reformation
impossible. The schism between literature and the government
was aided by another schism between literature and religion.
The first notice I have met with of Rousseau having a party is in
1770.[1]

   .    .    .    .    .    .

It may however have been doubted if much could have been
effected by such men as these, whose powers were by no means
extraordinary. But there was one of a very different stamp, who
was now about to make his appearance. It was reserved for
Geneva to produce a writer who of all those in the eighteenth
century was the most eloquent, the most passionate, and the most
influential. In the same city where the great Protestant
Reformer had propagated his narrow and gloomy opinions, there
arose two centuries after his death a great social reformer, who
openly avowed doctrines from which the murderer of Servetus
would have shrunk with horror. The tenets of Rousseau were
indeed not only repugnant to all true philosophy, but were subversive of the lowest forms of civilization. In a series of works
which, for beauty of language, and for wild fervid eloquence,

[1] See Œuvres de Voltaire, tome lv. p. 177.

have never been equalled, did this great but misguided man lay down the most monstrous and revolting paradoxes.

. . . . . . .

Voltaire (lxiii. 75) justly blames Rousseau for wishing to exclude history from education. About 1773, Rigoley published an essay to show that since the time of Homer letters and morals had constantly deteriorated. This essay he prefixed to his edition of La Bibliothèque Française of La Croix du Maine et du Verdier.[1] Raynal, in his History of the Indies, extolled the innocence of primitive man.[2]

It is a striking evidence, not only of the great power of this writer, but also of the feverish condition of the national intellect, that such opinions as these were hailed with the wildest enthusiasm. Indeed, they made a progress of which few people are aware. Not only the lighter departments of literature, but even the graver branches of knowledge were tainted by them. It was even said that the celebrated Paoli wrote to Rousseau, asking him to draw up laws for Corsica. In 1776, Rétif de la Bretonne published a romance called " L'École des Pères," in which he imitates Rousseau. Le Blanc advocated his principles on the stage. Linguet supported his principles. It is said in the Penny Cyclopædia that Pestalozzi was influenced by his educational works. And in the opinion of a man eminently capable of judging, there would have been without Rousseau no revolution.

The influence of these opinions upon history may be easily conceived. If the progress of civilization is the progress of decay ; if the decline of morals is the necessary consequence of the increase of wealth ; if all government is but an impudent pretension of the few to control the acts of the many ; if these things are true, then indeed it boots little to record the general advance of that inevitable corruption which is so rapidly stealing upon us. It is not therefore surprising that the innumerable disciples of Rousseau not only abstained from writing history, but did not care to conceal their contempt for those who occupied themselves with so trivial a pursuit. As their influence was immense, and after the death of Voltaire was supreme, it necessarily followed that history would be greatly neglected. This, which was the natural consequence of the dominion of such a school, was accelerated by the approach of that great revolution which was now so close at hand. The increasing embarrassment of the French Sovereign at length compelled him to have recourse to what was

[1] Grimm's Correspondance littéraire, tomo xv. pp. 339, 340.
[2] See Alison's Hist. of Europe, vol. i. p. 174.

considered the desperate expedient of assembling the Estates of the realm. The literary men of France availed themselves of this to descend into the political arena from which they had hitherto been for the most part excluded. Within a year from the memorable day of their entrance, they were enabled to take an ample revenge for those studied insults which a foolish government had heaped upon them. But without tracing their conduct, I need only point out what is sufficiently evident, that the absorbing nature of their new pursuits was very unfavourable to those speculative and scientific habits which are essential to the historian. I will merely mention two instances in which this is particularly apparent. The younger Mirabeau was in many respects the most extraordinary Frenchman during the latter part of the eighteenth century. His wonderful speeches, which produced such an effect upon those who heard them, have perhaps obscured his reputation, for the vulgar are always unwilling to believe that a great orator can be a profound thinker. But the truth is that, in spite of the scandalous profligacy of his private life, he was not only the first of modern rhetoricians, but he had also a singular aptitude for those comprehensive investigations without which history is one of the most puerile of studies. Only a few months before the Estates were convened, he published his great work on the Prussian monarchy. This, though inaccurate in many of its details, shows that he had an idea of history far superior to that possessed by his contemporaries, and it affords, so far as my reading extends, the first attempt to illustrate the annals of a people by applying to them the science of Political Economy. This alone would form an epoch in historical literature, and there can be no doubt that in a more peaceful age Mirabeau would still further have extended its boundaries. Indeed, such was the interest he took in these subjects, that he intended to translate into French Sir John Sinclair's History of the Public Revenues of the British Empire—a work which, notwithstanding its imperfections, still remains the best we have on that important subject. But when the Estates were assembled, Mirabeau, like so many other eminent men, appeared as one of the representatives of the people. It was on his motion that the Assembly first set at defiance the royal authority, and he was soon afterwards elected president of that great body whose passions he could sway at will. Amid such excitement as this, the pursuits of philosophy were soon forgotten, and Mirabeau entirely neglected a study for which he was so admirably qualified. The other instance to which I refer is that of the Abbé Sièyes, a man of a singularly acute and penetrating intellect. This able thinker had attempted to study the laws which regulate the progress of society, the discovery of which, I need hardly say, is the end and object of all history. Indeed, his mind was so essentially speculative that there are probably many Englishmen who only know him by the undeserved ridicule with which he has been covered by Burke. But, notwithstanding this he, like Mirabeau, was seduced by the facilities afforded by the French Revolution. He entered the Assembly, where his vast powers made him supreme in the committee, as Mirabeau was at the tribune. Thus absorbed into that great vortex, he soon degenerated into a mere practical politician, and another great mind was for ever lost to the literature of France.[1]

We have thus seen that owing at first to the influence of Rousseau, and afterwards to the still greater influence of the French Revolution, a sudden check was given to the progress of history. Indeed for [many] years after the death of Voltaire there was not produced in France a single work in which an attempt was made to predict the future by studying the past.[2] This state of things was afterwards remedied, partly by the reaction against the tyranny of Napoleon and partly by the introduction into France of that great school of German literature to which Europe is so deeply indebted. But before entering into this matter we must first inquire into the progress of history in our own country.

---

## ROUSSEAU AND HIS SCHOOL.

THE first attack made by Rousseau on civilization was in 1750, when the Academy of Dijon gave him the prize for his Essay on the Mischief of Science.[3] Brougham adds that in 1753–4 he also wrote for the Dijon Academy an Essay on the Inequality of Human Conditions. In 1762, he published [the] Contrat Social, and a few weeks afterwards Émile. He died in 1778, only surviving Voltaire five weeks.[4] The opinion of Rousseau that we are degenerating in consequence of increased knowledge is expressed by him in a remarkable letter he wrote to Voltaire in 1755.[5] The influence of Rousseau was immense, and after the death of Voltaire was supreme. The influence of Rousseau was

---

[1] I think Volney would have been a great thinker but for the Revolution. Turgot, too, would have been a great thinker, but he was engrossed by politics. See Cousin, Histoire de la Philosophie, part ii. tome i. p. 251. But he died before the Revolution.
[2] Except Condorcet.
[3] Brougham's Men of Letters and Science, vol. i. pp. 157, 158.
[4] Pp. 123, 171, 180.
[5] See it in Pièces Justificatives in Œuvres de Voltaire, tome i. pp. 514, 518.

partly from the democratic movement: partly from the desire of
a reaction against materialism, and partly from that ignorant
love men naturally feel for antiquity—an explosion of discontent;
partly the old doctrine of the corruption of man.  Rousseau even
influenced travellers to exaggerate the virtues of barbarians;
this we see in the Travels of La Perouse, Dentrecasteaux and
Levaillant.[1]

The effect these opinions had upon Mably is well worthy of
observation.  This able man was the most influential of all the
French publicists of the eighteenth century; and his most celebrated work has recently been edited by a celebrated living
statesman.  His first treatise was called a Parallel between the
Romans and the French.  It was published in 1740, and in it he
speaks with great favour of the existing order of things.  But in
his latest works, which were written after Rousseau had established a reputation, he entirely changes his ground, and assails
everything that is modern.  This is the case in his Observations
upon the History of France, in his Entretiens de Phocion, and in
his Treatise upon Legislation, in all of which he pours forth
invective upon the degeneracy of the age, "all those follies to
which corrupted nations give the name of politeness, refinement,
and courtesy, are but the chains by which slaves are bound
and shackled," &c. &c.

Robespierre got his doctrines from Rousseau; and when a
youth he made a pilgrimage to visit him.  Rousseau's views
of education were adopted by Coyer and by Pestalozzi.  His
power extended to America.  On his influence over Jefferson
see Tucker's Life of Jefferson, i. 255.  Even Bailly, in his
History of Astronomy, talks of an ancient and civilized people
who preceded us, and to whom we owe all we know.[2]  In 1791,
Faust, in a work published at Brunswick, said that hernia and
a variety of other evils were first introduced by trowsers, and
were entirely unknown to innocent savages.  Sacombe not only
wrote a work to show the evil of delivering women by art, but
even established what he called the anti-Cæsarean school.  After
mentioning Roussel, say, see on the physiological bearings of
Rousseau's views Lawrence's Lectures on Man, pp. 85, 86.  I may
conclude my account of the influence of Rousseau by quoting, in
English, Raynal, who, though an historian, struck at the root of
all history; and then I may say that with such principles history
was an idle study.

[1] See the instances in Comte, Traité de Législation, tome ii. pp. 399, 424. and
tome iii. p. 339.
[2] Œuvres de Voltaire, tome 1er. p. 353.

Frederick, the well-known duke of Wurtemberg, wrote to Rousseau for advice respecting the education of his children. About 1764, Corsica, under Paoli, applied to Rousseau for a constitution.[1] Lacrételle (XVIII° Siècle, tome iii. p. 231) calls Bernardin de St. Pierre "élève de J.-J. Rousseau." The Poles applied to Rousseau for a plan of government. The writings of Rousseau greatly influenced Brissot.[2] In 1764 Linguet published Le Fanatisme des Philosophes, which, says the Biographie universelle (xxiv. p. 520), was "ouvrage un peu rechauffé du discours de J.-J. Rousseau sur le danger des sciences, mais assez plein de force et de chaleur pour être lu avec intérêt même après celui du célèbre génévois."

Dumont[3] says that Condorcet's wife had "une passion pour les écrits de Rousseau." Dumont says (p. 47) that Sièyes was a great admirer of Rousseau's Contrat Social.

---

## FRENCH LITERATURE AFTER 1750.

POETRY declined. The minds of men became physical, scientific, political. Eloquence increased. Compare Rousseau with Montesquieu. In the hands of Diderot the stage represented *common life* — just as the Republican Dutch painters. There was no selection. Everything was equally important. See also Dress. Beaumarchais and La Harpe. In 1767, Voltaire notices the decline of the theatre;[4] and in 1776, he expresses his horror of tragedies in prose.[5] The decline of the theatre is connected with dress becoming *natural*, and thus sacrificing the ideal to the *real*. In the same way in the theological art, controversy, or an appeal to the vulgar, was the most decisive evidence of its fall. The moment men *appeal* they *doubt*; and making their art practical they sacrifice the ideal and degrade it to the people instead of raising the people to it. In France after 1750, the drama first became popular and then declined, just as it has done with us, because the people rise above it. We have now no great actor, because we regard acting as a pleasure, not as a business. Sir W. Scott notices that formerly audiences were more enlightened; now only the lower classes frequent the theatre. Mably was to Voltaire what Rousseau was to Montes-

[1] Lerminier, Philosophie du Droit, tome ii. p. 229.
[2] Mémoires de Brissot, tome i. p. ii. 50.
[3] Souvenirs sur Mirabeau, p. 230.
[4] Œuvres, tome lxv. pp. 277, 352; tome lxvi. pp. 18, 50; tome xviii. pp. 124, 268.
[5] Ibid. lxix. pp. 228, 336.

quieu.[1] In Paul and Virginia the beauties of ignorance are
shown.[2] Thus, perhaps, Rousseau was properly *democratic*, for he
thought ignorance and vulgarity virtue.  Saint-Pierre who had
attempted to establish a republican colony at first on the shores
of the Caspian and then in Madagascar, published the most beautiful description of ignorance that has ever appeared.  Raynal,
Florian, Suard, Laclos, Sillery.  In France the theatre declined,
because men became too democratic and imitative.  See the
admirable remarks on the beau ideal of the theatre in Sir Joshua
Reynolds' Works, ii. 71, 72; and see my Æsthetics and Theatre.
*Our* most popular painters are Wilkie and Hogarth : *not* Reynolds,
who was too great a man, and too *ideal* for our democratic habits.
In France theatrical composers began to write solely for the
parterre.  At the end of vol. ii. of Reynolds' Works are chronological and alphabetical lists of the painters.  I think after 1700
there were no great artists in France.  Beaumarchais, the author
of Figaro, had been employed to aid the Americans in their
struggles with England.[3]  Marsy's abridgement of Bayle's Dictionary was the first great sceptical blow.[4]  I think Individuality
now rose in Literature.  See my National Character.  Even the
French Academy was seized by the philosophic spirit, and
ordered that the éloge of St. Louis should cease to be a sermon,
and be merely a dissertation on moral virtues.  The Marquise de
Crequy[5] complains that taste was corrupted and the French language destroyed by Grimm and Chamfort.  In 1756, the Protestant Fabre was arrested, and his sufferings were afterwards
represented in the drama of L'honnête Criminel, by Fenouillet de
Falbaire.[6]  In 1747, Gresset was said to have painted Choiseul in
his comedy [Le] Mechant.[7]  On Beaumarchais' Figaro see Continuation de Sismondi, xxx. 299, 300.  In 1784, Saint-Pierre, in
Études de la Nature, admires ancient simplicity, and hence finds
many arguments against the right of property.[8]  Le Blanc, about
1740, observes[9] that in France the ancients were entirely neglected, and Greek and Latin had given way to other subjects.  In
the preceding age both Corneille and Racine borrowed from the
ancients, and the combat of Corneille is due to Seneca, from
whom he borrowed, while the purer taste of Racine went to the
Greeks.  In 1774 there was a decline of taste in France.[10]  Rous-

[1] Barante, Tableau, pp. 117, 123.        [2] Ibid. p. 165.
[3] See Georgel, Mémoires, tome i. p. 457.    [4] Ibid. tome ii. p. 240.
[5] Souvenirs, tome iv. p. 101.
[6] Sismondi, vol. xxix. p. 52.        [7] Ibid. p. 191.
[8] See Villemain, Literature au dixhuitième Siècle, tome iii. pp. 390, 391.
[9] Lettres d'un Français, tome ii. p. 461 ; tome iii. pp. 478, 479.
[10] See Le Long, Bibliothèque historique, tome iv. p. 523.

seau's opera, Le Devin du Village, obtained great success on
account of its simple language, which took the Parisians by
surprise.[1] Raynal, Rousseau, &c., maintained the innocence of
original man; hence, of course, the injuries done to him by
clergy and governments. Alison well says,[2] that in consequence
of men denying a future state they applied their energies to
*present* gratification and sensuality; hence Crebillon, Laclos,
Louvet. Alison[3] says that Rousseau was to "social life" what
Voltaire was to religion. Lamartine[4] says of the French soldiers
in 1792, "On leur enseignait les hymnes des deux Tyrtées de la
Révolution, les poètes Lebrun et Chenier." Göthe has noticed the
importance of the change which took place among French *actors*,
from the stiff artificial manner of Le Kain to the *democratic* and
*natural* manner of Anfresne.[5] In painting David sacrificed *idea*
to anatomical exactness. In the hands of Colardeau, Delille, and
Saint-Lambert, poetry became *descriptive*.[6]

## ÆSTHETIC MOVEMENT AFTER 1750.

THE same love of the external and indifference to the ideal took
place in art. Tocqueville says,[7] Raphael cared little about mere
anatomy, but "David et ses élèves étaient au contraire aussi bons
anatomistes que bons peintres. Ils représentaient merveilleuse-
ment bien les modèles qu'ils avaient sous les yeux, mais il était rare
qu'ils imaginerènt rien au délà; ils suivaient exactement la nature,
tandis que Raphael cherchait mieux qu'elle." In the same way,
says Tocqueville,[8] men formerly wrote poems on gods and heroes,
but in the eighteenth century *descriptive poetry* first arose. On
the French stage there was no more yearning after the past; no
more instances of the stern patriotism of Les Horaces; of the
clemency of Augustus, or the crimes of Cinna. These were left
to an age which loved the past. But it was not till after 1750
that common life was represented. Tocqueville[9] well observes
that in the reign of Louis XIV. the dramatic writers paid too
much attention to those beauties which are observed in the closet,

[1] Alison's Europe, vol. i. pp. 168, 169.    [2] Ibid. p. 175.    [3] Ibid. p. 170.
[4] Histoire des Girondins, tome v. p. 140.
[5] Wahrheit und Dichtung, in Göthe's Werke, band ii. theil ii. p. 154. Bohn's
Translation, vol. i. p. 423.
[6] Lacrételle, Dixhuitième Siècle, tome iii. p. 328. Respecting Beaumarchais and
Figaro, see Lacrételle, Dixhuitième Siècle, tome iii. pp. 236, 237.
[7] Démocratie en Amérique, tome iv. pp. 82, 83.
[8] Ibid. p. 116.    [9] Ibid. pp. 130, 131.

but which escape attention on the stage. But *afterwards* the style became careless, because plays were written to be *seen* by the people and not read by scholars. Indeed, I think that it was only after 1750 that prose was first introduced on the stage. Our most popular artists are Hogarth and Wilkie, not Reynolds, who was too ideal for our democratic habits, and would have suited Italy. David sacrificed *idea* to anatomical correctness. In the hands of Colardeau and Delille and Saint-Lambert, poetry became descriptive. Observe the democratic minuteness of the Dutch painters. Of the famous statue of Voltaire erected by Pigale in 1772, Morellet says,[1] "Pigale, pour montrer son savoir en anatomie, a fait un vieillard nu et decharné, un squelette, défaut à peine racheté par la vérité et la vie que l'on admire dans la physionomie et l'attitude du vieillard."

---

## CLASSICAL SCHOOL.

VOLTAIRE knew little of Latin and scarcely anything of Greek literature, and even Barthélemy has made many mistakes. Schlegel pours out his wrath upon Voltaire for misunderstanding Aristophanes. Arnold[2] well observes how natural it is to ignorant and vain men to undervalue the age in which they live; "our personal superiority seems much more advanced by decrying our contemporaries than by decrying our fathers. The dead are not our real rivals, nor is pride very much gratified by asserting a superiority over those who cannot deny it. . . . . It is far more tempting to personal vanity to think ourselves the only wise amongst a generation of fools than to glory in belonging to a wise generation, where our personal wisdom, be it what it may, can not at least have the distinction of singularity."

The travels of Anacharsis perhaps formed the only exception [to the indifference in the eighteenth century in France to the classical school]; but even of these Villemain truly says,[3] "Les mœurs parisiennes, le bel esprit Francais, la société animée ingénieuse, du dixhuitième siècle, préoccupaient Barthélemy, et se reflechissaient involontairement dans ses tableaux." Even such as it was, it was too learned to be successful, and Horace Walpole says that it was little read in Paris;[4] but we learn from Grimm[5]

[1] Mémoires, tome i. p. 193.
[2] Lectures on Modern History, Lond. 1843, p. 88.
[3] Littérature au dixhuitième Siècle, tome iii. p. 286.
[4] Walpole's Letters to the Countess of Ossory, 8vo, 1848, vol. ii. p. 396.
[5] Correspondance littéraire, tome xvi. p. 135.

that great things were expected even before it was published, and that the first edition was sold in less than two months.

---

## SCEPTICISM.

BAYLE, who was born in 1647, first disturbed the theological dominion of Bossuet, and the authority of the classical literature.[1] Then came, secondly, Fontenelle, whose Histoire des Oracles and Les Mondes made him " le précurseur de Voltaire."[2]

Bayle, whose mere learning has perhaps been overrated, was a man whose singular subtlety of mind was admirably calculated to make him the founder of that sceptical school which began the great work of philosophic criticism. Most competent people will, I suppose, agree with Gibbon that Le Clerc was more learned than Bayle.[3]

In England scepticism made no head. Such men as Toland and Tindal, Collins, Shaftesbury, Woolaston, were no match for Clarke, Warburton, and Lardner. They could make no head until the time of Middleton. The works of Hume, though written in a style which has never been surpassed, could hardly find a dozen readers. The immortal work of Gibbon, of which the sagacity is, if possible, equal to the learning, did find readers, but the illustrious author was so cruelly [reviled] by men who called themselves Christians, that it seemed doubtful if, after such an example, subsequent writers would hazard their comfort and happiness by attempting to write philosophic history. . . .

Mead, I think, wrote on demons. . . .

In 1736 the celebrated Dr. Stukely published the first part of his Paleographica Sacra, in which he undertakes to show that all heathen mythology is derived from the Bible.

After Bacon, the sceptical Lord Herbert of Cherbury was our best historian.

Read Hardouin.

Middleton wrote in 1750 to Lord Radnor respecting his work on miracles, to the effect that if he had received some good appointment in the Church, he would never have given the clergy any trouble.[4] As long as the theological spirit was alive nothing

---

[1] See Villemain, Littérature au dixhuitième Siècle, tome i. p. 2; tome ii. p. 31.

[2] Ibid. p. 5.

[3] Gibbon's Miscellaneous Works, p. 437.

[4] Whiston's MS., quoted in Nichols's Literary Anecdotes of Eighteenth Century, vol. v. p. 700.

could be effected. Thus, for instance, Campanella quotes the Fathers against Aristotle, and he indignantly applies to the commentators of that great man the words—" Habent Aristotelem pro Christo, Averroëm pro Petro, Alexandrum pro Paulo."[1] In that exceedingly silly periodical, the Quarterly Review, there was published a few years ago an angry attack upon Robertson, Blair, and other eminent Scotchmen of the eighteenth century, for their liberality, in which the Christian critic calls them " betrayers of their Lord." Lord Brougham has taken the unnecessary pains of answering this foolish critic.[2] It is said in the Penny Cyclopædia (article Astrology) that in consequence of a prediction by Stœffler, that in 1524 there would be a universal deluge, all Europe was in an agony of fear, and " Voltaire mentions a doctor of Toulouse who made an ark for himself and his friends."

At the birth of Louis XIV., his mother had in her room the astrologer Morin to take his horoscope.[3]

## POLITICAL ECONOMY IN FRANCE IN THE EIGHTEENTH CENTURY.

BEFORE giving an account of political economy, relate the democratic tendencies, then say that these tendencies were furthered by political economy, which proved that a man is the best judge of his own interest.

Segur[4] says that before this [the publication of Necker's Compte Rendu] the nation had never paid any attention to the expenses of government. Segur[5] says that in 1781 the court " défendait aux journaux de prononcer le nom de M. Necker." Segur[6] mentions the great success of Necker's Administration des Finances. M'Culloch[7] says (I *think*) that Quesnai was the first who attempted to make political economy a science. Voltaire never dared to meddle with politics, and had no notion of political economy. In Essai sur les Mœurs, xvii. p. 298, he charges nunneries with what in truth is one of their great recommendations, viz., that they keep down population. Colbert forbad the exportation of corn : a prohibition which Voltaire defends.[8] He praises Louis XIV.

[1] Rénouvier, Philosophie moderne, 1843, p. 27.
[2] Brougham's Men of Letters and Science, vol. i. pp. 254, 255.
[3] See Siècle de Louis XIV. in Œuvres de Voltaire, tome xx. p. 174.
[4] Mémoires, tome i. p. 220.       [5] Ibid. p. 252.       [6] Ibid. tome ii. pp. 56, 57.
[7] Political Economy, 8vo, 1843, p. 44.
[8] Fragments sur l'Histoire, article xix. Œuvres, tome xxvii. p. 273.

for his endeavours to increase population by encouraging marriage;[1] and[2] he says that the profusion of Louis XIV., by encouraging trade, increased the wealth of France. See also p. 239, where he expresses his admiration of Colbert. Necker was called to power in 1776. His plan of finance was not so much to tax as to *borrow*: and this, says Mignet,[3] entailed the necessity of publishing accounts of finances, because where there is a mystery there can be no credit.

In 1781 Necker was dismissed, because he published a Compte Rendu, that is, informed the people of what was done with their own money.[4] In 1770, Galiani's Dialogues sur le Commerce des Blés caused great excitement in Paris.[5] Even Lavoisier studied political economy. In 1771, Voltaire writes,[6] " Le ministère est trop occupé des parlements pour songer a persécuter les dissidents de France." D'Argenson, in 1755, in a paper read before the Academy, observes that none of the modern writers had ventured to interfere with political questions, which he recommended that they should do.[7] In 1773, Voltaire[8] was angry with the economists for attacking " le grand Colbert."

In March 1789, Jefferson writes from Paris that *within two years* the French had changed their character, and become *grave* and *political.*[9] The well-known Duke de Richelieu boasted that he had always prevented the " économistes " and " philosophes " from entering the French Academy,[10] but this was soon changed.[11]

Georgel, a bitter enemy of Necker, confesses that, during his first ministry he was the idol of the people. Dupont and Roubaud were economists.[12] The Prince de Montbarey[13] mentions the popularity of Necker's Mémoire sur le Commerce des Blés. Lavallée[14] says that Necker published the Compte Rendu because he found that publicity was the great cause of English credit. Lavallée adds that this was the first instance (1781) of the public knowing anything about receipts. In 1764, Terray allowed the exportation of grain, " arrêt motivé sur les doctrines des économistes."[15] 80,000 copies of Necker's Administration des Finances were sold.[16]

[1] Fragments sur l'Histoire, article xix. Œuvres, tome xx. p. 241.   [2] Ibid. p. 278.
[3] Révolution, tome i. p. 20.
[4] Lavallée, Hist. de France, tome iii. p. 510. Beccaria, Genovesi, Filangieri, Galiani.
[5] Œuvres de Voltaire, tome lv. p. 138.        [6] Ibid. tome lxvii. p. 445.
[7] Mémoires de l'Académie, tome xxviii. pp. 640, 641, 643.
[8] Œuvres, tome lxviii. p. 293.
[9] Tucker's Life of Jefferson, vol. i. pp. 302, 303.
[10] Souvenirs de Crequy, tome iii. p. 297.        [11] Ibid. tome iv. p. 249.
[12] Georgel, Mémoires, tome i. pp. 489, 490, 505, tome ii. p. 264.
[13] Mémoires, tome ii. p. 242; see also tome iii. p. 122.        [14] Tome iii. p. 510.
[15] Sismondi, tome xxix. p. 405.        [16] Ibid. tome xxx. p. 341.

## RELIGIOUS PERSECUTION UNDER LOUIS XV.

. . . At the same time, the French government, which about
the middle of the eighteenth century seems to have reached the
maturity of its wickedness, allowed, if indeed it did not instigate,
religious persecutions of so infamous a nature that they would not
be believed if they were not attested by the documents of the
courts in which the sentences were passed. Some of these deserve
to be related as characteristic of a state of society which the
French Revolution for ever destroyed.

In 1761, a young man, named Calas, was found strangled in
his father's house at Toulouse. He had for some time been a
prey to melancholy, and there was little doubt that in a moment
of despair he had laid violent hands upon himself. But as he was
a Protestant, the French authorities affected to believe that he
had been murdered by his own father, in order to prevent his
conversion to the Catholic faith. The elder Calas was therefore
summoned before the court on this monstrous charge—a charge
not only unsupported by evidence, but full of the grossest impro-
babilities. The unhappy father brought forward ample proof of
his well-known affection for the son he was accused of having
murdered. It was shown that the deceased was in a state of
mind likely to end in suicide; that the crime, if it had been
committed, must have been known to a Catholic servant, by
whom he was constantly accompanied; and that, independently of
these considerations, it was impossible for an infirm old man to
strangle one who was young and active, and to do this without
any disturbance being heard in the house. But all was in vain.
The probability that a heretic would commit any crime was considered to outweigh every argument. The property of the family
was confiscated; the younger son of Calas was banished; and
Calas himself, in conformity with a public judicial sentence, was
broken on the wheel, protesting his innocence amid the tortures
in which he died.

In 1765, a wooden crucifix on the bridge of Abbeville was
found to have been injured apparently by blows from a sword.
The bishop of Amiens, as soon as he heard of this, formed with
his clergy a solemn procession to the scene of the outrage; and
every exertion was made to discover its authors. At length two
youths, named Barré and D'Étallonde, were arrested. It was,
however, found impossible to prove that they had injured the
crucifix, but there were witnesses ready to charge them with
other offences. It was said that they had sung irreligious songs,

that they had spoken unfavourably of the Eucharist, and that they had even passed before a procession of the clergy without taking off their hats. That which followed is a memorable lesson for those who wish to see the church reinstated in her old authority. Barré, who was a boy of eighteen, D'Étallonde, who was scarcely sixteen, were sentenced to have their tongues torn out, to have their right hands cut off, and then to be burnt alive in a slow fire. Fortunately, D'Étallonde had in the meantime effected his escape into the Prussian territories, where he received the protection of Frederick the Great. Immense exertions were made to procure the pardon of Barré, but the king would not overlook an offence against the clergy, and the unfortunate boy was publicly burnt, the only mitigation of the sentence being that he should be executed before the body was committed to the flames.

## LOUIS XV.

His harem cost more than 100,000,000 francs, and was composed of little girls.[1] He was constantly drunk.[2] "His vacillations"—from 1756 to 1763 he had no less than twenty-five ministers of state.[3] He was miserably superstitious. "Il avait laissé l'ordre des Jésuites contre ses propres affections."[4]

He hated men of letters.

In 1766, he publicly stated arbitrary principles.[5]

The king was obliged to swear to "exterminate heretics."[6]

In sixteen months Madame du Barry received money equal to more than 200,000l. Louis XV. used to turn out his own illegitimate children to prostitute themselves.[7] In 1789 the majority of the clergy declared in favour of the freedom of the press.[8]

## THE JESUITS IN FRANCE IN THE EIGHTEENTH CENTURY.

1. The destruction of the Jesuits begun by Pascal was completed by Voltaire.[9] Their abolition caused immense sensation.

2. The Jesuits were the great defenders of order and ortho-

---

[1] Sismondi, tome xxix. pp. 9, 10.
[2] Ibid. pp. 272, 341.
[3] Ibid. p. 86.
[4] Ibid. pp. 217, 272.
[5] Ibid. pp. 324, 363.
[6] Ibid. tome xxx. p. 52.
[7] Alison, Hist. of Europe, vol. i. pp. 208, 212.
[8] Continuation de Sismondi, tome xxx. pp. 451, 452.
[9] See Œuvres de Voltaire, tome lxii. p. 278.

doxy; but they had lost their abilities and now stood in the way of progress.[1]

3. In the great age of Louis XIII., the Jesuits had been attacked by Pascal and Arnauld.

4. Louis XV. loved the Jesuits;[2] and even the Pope allowed that they were suppressed contrary to his wishes.[3] The Dauphin favoured them.[4]

5. About 1761, Berryer, "Ministre de la Marine, grand ennemi des Jésuites."[5]

6. The Jesuits always aided the League against Henry IV.[6] Chatel, a Jesuit, tried to kill him;[7] and Ravaillac did kill him, as was believed, with the privity of the Jesuits.[8] Under Louis XIV. the Jesuits reigned supreme, and La Chaise and Le Tellier enjoyed the disposal of all ecclesiastical patronage. They were his confessors for forty years. La Chaise persecuted the Port Royalists, and Le Tellier destroyed them. Grégoire[9] quotes from the Lettres d'Arnaud two anecdotes characteristic of Louis XIV.'s confessors. Louis XIV. compelled members of his family to take Jesuits as confessors. Directly Louis XIV. died, Le Tellier was exiled, and when he died, the Academy, contrary to custom, did not eulogise him.[10]

---

## JANSENISM AMONG CLERGY AND EVEN STATESMEN.

1. DIRECTLY the States-General assembled in May 1789, " Le plus grand nombre des curés " voted against the upper clergy and in favour of all the orders verifying their powers in the same chamber.[11] Georgel adds,[12] " La majorité du clergé fut pour la réunion au tiers-état, et la très grand majorité du noblesse fut d'un avis contraire."

2. The Abbé Maury, the ablest among the clergy, was a bad man.[13]

3. I think the " canoniste " Héricourt opposed ecclesiastical pretensions.[14]

[1] Ranke's Päpste, vol. iii. pp. 194, 195.
[2] Flassan, Diplomatie, tome vi. p. 506.
[3] Ibid. p. 49.
[4] Ibid. pp. 316, 318.
[5] Ibid. pp. 357, 358.
[6] Georgel, tome ii. p. 326.
[7] See Lamartine, Hist. des Girondins, tome i. p. 32.
[8] See Grégoire, Histoire des Confesseurs, pp. 113, 116.
[9] Georgel, Mémoires, tome i. p. 46.
[10] Georgel, tome i. p. 61.
[11] Grégoire, Histoire des Confesseurs, p. 303.
[12] Ibid. pp. 324, 325.
[13] Ibid. p. 379.
[14] Ibid. p. 329.

4. It was on the motion of one of the clergy in 1789 that tithes were abolished.[1]  In March, 1790, it was ordered that the property of the clergy should be sold.[2]

. . . . . .

The cohesion caused by the amalgamation of ranks *settled* into clubs, by which democracy has been aided in every country.

---

## THE FRENCH GOVERNMENT ATTACKED CLERGY.

1. In 1756, the court, favouring the parliament, exiled some bishops and archbishops.[3]

2. In 1765, there appears to have been an idea of doing away with the assemblies of the clergy.[4]

3. In 1767, some edicts in favour of tradesmen attacked the church.[5]

4. Crequy[6] indignantly says that the Baron de Breteuil, in a circular letter, ordered the bishops to reside in their dioceses.

5. In 1752, the archbishop of Paris forbad dying persons to receive the sacrament unless they had a certificate of confession, signed by a Molinist priest.  Parliament replied by seizing the temporalities of the archbishop, and the king ordered him into exile.[7]

. . . . . .

9. On October 27, 1787, was issued "l'irréligieux édit" of tolerance in favour of "des non catholiques;" and this was chiefly done by the Baron de Breteuil and Cardinal de Brienne.[8]

---

## CHARACTER OF LOUIS XVI.

MARIE ANTOINETTE was an imperious and violent woman, full of personal caprices, and whose morals were doubtful; and if she were not unchaste, the report of it produced the same effect on the people as if she were.  She was very ignorant, and her beauty has been exaggerated. Lavallée[9] says that after the death of Maurepas she became the "sole councillor."

. . . . . .

[1] Georgel, Mémoires, tome ii. p. 406.　　[2] Ibid. tome iii. part ii. p. 198.
[3] Sismondi, tome xxix. pp. 39, 98.
[4] Le Long, Bibliothèque historique, tome iv. p. 298.
[5] Voltaire, Œuvres, tome lxvi. pp. 53, 54.　　[6] Souvenirs, tome v. pp. 224, 226.
[7] Lavallée, tome iii. pp. 409, 410.
[8] Georgel, Mémoires, tome ii. pp. 293, 294.　　[9] Tome iii. p. 510.

It was under these circumstances that Louis XVI. came to the throne. This feeble and amiable man had received the worst possible education, having been brought up by a courtier and a Jesuit.[1] His great amusements were carpentering and putting in lotteries.[2]

. . . . . . .

As soon as he came to the throne he refused to call to the ministry Choiseul, who had destroyed the Jesuits. He rejected Machault, and put at the head of affairs Maurepas, a feeble and frivolous man, who was supported by the Jesuits.[3] He, like Charles I., resisted the age, and like him he perished; but he was a good man, Charles a bad one : both were ruled by ambitious wives. The age was sceptical, and the prince was superstitious. He is a striking instance of the inutility and helplessness of benevolence when it is not guided by intellect. His tardy reforms showed his weakness. M. Renée[4] happily says that Louis XVI. " n'avait pas la jalousie des hommes plus grand que lui, mais en avait promptement la fatigue."

Necker and Turgot, the only two statesmen, were disgraced. Directly on the accession of Louis XVI., Maurepas, not the king, called Turgot to the finances;[5] but Renée says[6] that in 1774 the king, contrary to the wish of Maurepas, gave him the controllership. In 1774, Turgot induced Maurepas to bring into the council Malesherbes, a very liberal man. But in 1776 the king dismissed Turgot with insult.[7] A letter Turgot wrote him was returned unopened;[8] and he was succeeded as controller-general by the miserable Clugny.[9]

In 1776, Necker was made controller-general in the place of Clugny, but was, on account of being a Protestant, only called director-general. He was a great financier.[10] He, in 1781, determined not to possess responsibility without control; he demanded admission into the council, which he was told would be granted to him if he would abjure his religion. Upon [this] he indignantly sent in his resignation, to the universal regret of the country.[11] Necker was succeeded in 1781 by an ignorant man, Joly de Fleury.[12] Fleury was in 1783 succeeded by another fool,

---

[1] Continuation de Sismondi, tome xxx. pp. 13, 14.
[2] Ibid. pp. 274, 277, and see Alison's Europe, vol. i. p. 245.
[3] Sismondi, tome xxx. pp. 20, 22, 24, and Lavallée, tome iii. p. 493.
[4] Continuation de Sismondi, tome xxx. p. 232.
[5] Lavallée, tome iii. p. 493.
[6] Sismondi, tome xxx. p. 31.         [7] Ibid. pp. 56, 58, 87, 332.
[8] Georgel, Mém. tome i. p. 450.
[9] Sismondi, tome xxx. 90, 91, 236 ; Lavallée, tome iii. p. 496.
[10] Sismondi, tome xxx. pp. 98, 114, 115, 120, 412, 413.
[11] Ibid. pp. 127, 128.         [12] Ibid. pp. 235, 236, 240.

Ormesson. In 1783, the controllership was taken from Ormesson, and given to Calonne.[1] In April, 1787, Calonne was succeeded by the cardinal Lomenie de Brienne, a still weaker man.[2] The indignation against Brienne became so great that, in August, 1788, he resigned, and, by his advice, Necker was called in.[3]

. . . . . . .

Directly Louis XVI. came to the throne, Maurepas made Vergennes Minister for Foreign Affairs.[4] Vergennes was a selfish man, and procured in 1781 the dismissal of Necker.[5]

In two years, 1774 to 1776, Turgot effected the most wonderful reforms. See the list in Lavallée, iii. 494, 495. Malesherbes, minister and friend of Turgot, wished, by re-establishing the Edict of Nantes, to tolerate the Protestants, who[m] the king swore to exterminate. But he could not, and resigned before Turgot.[6] Under these circumstances the Government should, like ours, have conceded; but instead of this, Louis XV. was a selfish prodigal. Then give an account of his vices and etiquette. Then came Louis XVI., a fool. Lavallée[7] says that as men became more democratic, the pride of the court was more offensive. Absurd etiquette in 1783.[8] It was a cloud not bigger than a man's hand which swelled till it deluged the world. It was the small still voice which preceded the roar of the tempest. At a most critical moment when, in 1788, the state was nearly bankrupt, Necker made his immense private fortune responsible.[9] After the American Revolution, there took place in France a movement precisely similar to that which I have traced in the church. It was necessary that the church should fall, because men mistook the church for religion. In the same [way] it was necessary government should fall, because men mistook kings for government, and, as Lamartine says, personified in them all evils. And political knowledge had weakened the respect for royalty, just as scientific knowledge had weakened the respect for the church. We, not being prejudiced, could punish our kings without exciting our passions; but in France in the eighteenth century, the prejudices were so old that ·madness was needed to remove them. This madness was supplied by foreign powers. We have not feared to strike our kings, and we would not fear to strike them again. (Junius, at the end of his letter to the

[1] Sismondi, tome xxx. pp. 241, 287, 290 ; Lavallée, tome iii. p. 511.
[2] Lavallée, tome iii. p. 514.   [3] Ibid. p. 518.   [4] Ibid. p. 493.
[5] Renée's Sismondi, tome xxx. pp. 233, 234.
[6] Lavallée, tome iii. p. 495.   [7] Ibid. p. 512.
[8] Crequy, Souvenirs, tome iii. pp. 19, 154.
[9] Continuation de Sismondi, tome xxx. p. 429.

king expresses the general feeling, and compare Laing's Sweden,
pp. 408, 409). Louis XVI. was the first instance for centuries
in which a good man had been seen on the throne of France, and
this made violent measures necessary. When Louis refused to
sanction the decree, " sur les prêtres non assermentés," Dumouriez
in vain told him that the priests would be massacred, and that,
instead of saving religion, he would destroy it.[1] He was obstinate,
and he dismissed first Roland and then Dumouriez.[2] Lamartine[3]
observes that the first Assembly ought at once to have declared a
Republic. When, on June 20, 1792, a mob under Santerre broke
into the palace, the people still loved the king enough to be
indignant.[4] Lamartine says[5] that the Girondins, and in particular
Vergniaud, were the real authors of the death of the king. We
in England sentenced our king to die in a solemn court of high
commission, with all the forms, appliances, and paraphernalia of
justice. They in France, tempted by a brutal and besotted mob,
inflicted the last penalty on an innocent king, whose only fault
was his situation, and whose only crime was that he followed a
long line of corrupt ancestors. Spurred on by the refuse and
offal of the nation, he fell; while with us the hostility to
Charles I. came, *not* from below, but from above. Lamartine[6]
says that even at the last moment the people did not wish
Louis XVI. to be executed. The American democracy was not
bloody, for the people never loved kings, and the educated men of
the south headed the rebellion. The leaders of our revolution
met their king in the field, and, having discomfited him there,
they carried him to the block. The French had been brutalized
by slavery to an extent which those who know them at the present
day can hardly believe.[7] Even in December, 1791, Louis XVI.
was playing a double game. See his letter to the King of Prussia
in Lamartine, Hist. des Girondins, i. 228, 229.

## FRENCH REVOLUTION.

BEFORE the Revolution a long peace (?) had turned men from
war to politics. In 1789, the Abbé Maury, the ablest orator
among the clergy, was a bad man.

When the alteration of dress was introduced, the cohesion of

[1] Lamartine, tome ii. pp. 225, 228.
[2] Ibid. p. 253.
[3] Ibid. tome i. pp. 305, 323.
[4] Ibid. tome iii. pp. 2-3.
[5] Ibid. tome v. pp. 47, 48, 53.
[6] Ibid. p. 75.
[7] Ibid. tome i. p. 32.

society was increased by the amalgamation of ranks, and the cohesion *settled* into the institution of clubs.

Lamartine [1] observes that in 1791, the clergy and nobles selfishly abandoned the king, and the nobles fled.

In the hands of Diderot the stage first represented *common* life, just as the republican Dutch painters do. And *common* dress on the stage. There was no *selection*. Everything equally important. Tragedies in prose, and theatre declined. Ducis, Beaumarchais, and La Harpe.

On Louis XV.'s love of *open* vice, quote the biting remarks in Lamartine. [2]

The vices of Louis XV. were slowly producing an effect equal to that produced by the vices of our Charles II. Alison says that Maurepas, whom Louis XVI. at his accession chose for prime minister, "was overthrown by the selfish opposition of the nobles," but Mignet [3] says that Maurepas was a mere courtier. Malesherbes was called in by Maurepas, and he helped to establish liberty of commerce.

Necker, a Protestant and Calvinist, [4] was called to power in 1776. His plan of finance was not so much to *tax* as to *borrow*, and this, as Mignet says, entailed the necessity of publishing an account of the finances, because where there is mystery there can be no credit.

The clergy, who were now becoming Calvinistic, demanded the Assembly of the Third Estate ; and Necker demanded an order that when the clergy assembled the curés should be admitted, who had a majority of 208 against 48 bishops and 35 abbés or deacons. [5]

---

## NOTES FOR FRENCH REVOLUTION.

A DETAILED, but prejudiced account of Voltaire's last visit to Paris in 1778, and death, is given in Souvenirs de la Marquise de Crequy, tome v., p. 5–40. The king refused, however, to see him, and said that it was indulgence enough that he was allowed to come to Paris, p. 14.

Madame de Crequy [6] gives some interesting but too favourable details of Rousseau.

When Voltaire heard that Moncrif was made historiographe, he called him "historiogriffe." [7]

[1] Vol. i. pp. 48, 49.
[2] Vol. vii. p. 200.
[3] Mignet, vol. i. pp. 16, 17.
[4] Ibid. vol. i. pp. 18, 19.
[5] Ibid. vol. i. pp. 33, 34.
[6] Souvenirs, vol. iii. 307, 310.
[7] Souvenirs de Crequy, vol. iv. 150.

On Mémoires de Bachaumont, see Souvenirs de Crequy, tome iv. p. 157.

For a very amusing, but, I think, exaggerated account of Madame Necker, see Souvenirs de Crequy, iv. pp. 168–182.

Crequy[1] says Maurepas had little religion, though honest; but that to him and to his devotion for Necker are to be ascribed the French Revolution.

On the extent to which the revolutionary spirit under Louis XVI. seized all the departments of literature, see the very curious remarks in Souvenirs de Crequy, tome iv., chap. xi., and particularly p. 253. Madame [de] Crequy says[2] "dans la classe bourgeoise, où l'incredulité moderne et la vanité philosophique avaient fait un ravage affreux." See also Georgel, Mémoires, ii. 231, 232. Here we see the difference. In England the upper classes became sceptical; in France, never.

A whimsical description of Franklin is given by the Marquise de Crequy, who, of course was quite unable to understand his merits.[3]

For evidence of the hostility of the French clergy to the great movement even in 1782, see Crequy, Souvenirs, iv. 261–268.

Crequy says[4] that Necker published his Compte Rendu without the king's consent.

The Marquise de Crequy[5] has a very characteristic remark on Mirabeau's eloquence.

Swinburne, who was in Paris when Louis XV. died, mentions the joy of the people.[6]

On July 1, 1789, fifteen days before the dismissal of Necker, Mr. Swinburne writes from Versailles, 'Necker is very popular, and makes up to the Tiers État. Being a Calvinist, he has a horror of the French clergy, and being of low origin naturally dislikes the nobles."[7]

Swinburne, who was in Paris in 1796, mentions some striking instances of the facility with which divorces were procured,[8] and the same thing in 1793 is noticed in Burke's Works, ii. 298.

In 1796 murders were most common in Paris.[9]

On June 7, 1797, Swinburne, who was in Paris officially, writes,[10] "Everything now seems to take a turn towards tranquillity and sociableness."

At Calais, in November, 1796, "Sunday is observed here; for nobody will have anything to say to Decades;" and "a great apathy, despair, or indifference, seems to have got the better of all the French."[11]

Madame Roland—Lamartine[12] has given a strikingly beautiful account of this wonderful woman.

Coleridge[13] says the Revolution was a national act.

[1] Souvenirs, tome iv. pp. 210, 211.
[2] Ibid. tome vi. p. 29.
[3] Ibid. tome iv. pp. 258, 260.
[4] Ibid. tome v. p. 34.
[5] Ibid. tome vi. p. 77.
[6] Courts of Europe, vol. i. p. 23.
[7] Swinburne's Courts of Europe, vol. ii. p. 81.
[8] Ibid. pp. 143, 144.
[9] Ibid. pp. 150, 157.
[10] Ibid. p. 247.
[11] Ibid. pp. 116, 117.
[12] Girondins, tome ii. pp. 3, 38.
[13] The Friend, i. 246.

For a disgraceful anecdote of the French painter David on the 10th August, 1792, see Lamartine's Girondins, tome iii. p. 136.

Robespierre, the most sincere man of his time.[1]

For an account of Louvet, author of Faublas, see Lamartine, tome iv. p. 145–148.

Lamartine[2] says that Louis XV., even at his accession, could not save the throne.

Difference between seditions and revolution.[3]

Flassan says,[4] "Rien n'était moins philosophe que M. Maurépas."

Flassan quietly says[5] that Cardinal de Brienne "avait été plus heureux pour sa propre fortune que pour celle de l'état."

The declaration of Pilnitz, August 27, 1791, is in Flassan, Diplom. française, vii. 482, 483.

When Louis XV. made an infamous prostitute his public mistress, even Georgel[6] says all Paris murmured. Even Georgel says[7] that no one wept at the death of Louis XV. Even Georgel[8] allows that the "Feuillans" were a moderate party. Even Georgel, who could hardly ever see anything wrong in his own faction, gently blames the Emigrants.[9] And so does the Prince de Montbarey.[10] Georgel[11] accuses the Girondins of being privy to the massacre of September 2, 1792. The Emigrants, burning with hatred against their country, stirred up foreign princes to war. Even Georgel[12] confesses that the Revolutionists were strengthened by the Treaty of Pilnitz. Frederick William of Prussia swore at Coblentz never to lay down his arms until "l'Église de France aurait recouvré son lustre, et la monarchie française toute sa puissance et sa majesté."[13]. See at tome iii. p. 401 the impudent remarks of Georgel on the imprisonment of La Fayette. Georgel[14] says that the 10th of August and the crimes of September were caused by the presence in the French country of the Duke of Brunswick's army. See also tome v. p. 46.

Georgel[15] says that on the trial of Louis XVI. the Girondins wished to prolong the process in order to destroy both him and the Jacobins. Even in Paris the execution of Louis XVI. was unpopular.[16] Georgel[17] with unusual candour says that the attacks made on France were caused by the personal fears of kings lest they should suffer the fate of Louis XVI. I do not know the authority for the horrid list of the crimes of the Revolution in Georgel, iv. 330, 331.

Grégoire[18] says of Louis XV., "ses liasons incestueuses avec La Chateauroux et ses sœurs." Edgeworth declares that he never said "Son of St. Louis, mount to heaven." See Grégoire Hist. des Confesseurs, p. 403.

[1] Lamartine, tome iv. p. 87.  [2] Tome i. p. 25.  [3] Ibid. p. 30.
[4] Diplomatie française, tome vii. p. 115.  [5] Ibid. p. 463.
[6] Mémoires, tome i. p. 176.  [7] Ibid. p. 300.  [8] Ibid. ii. p. 496.
[9] Ibid. tome iii. pp. 286, 302.  [10] Mémoires de Montbarey, p. 229.
[11] Georgel, Mémoires, p. 339.  [12] Ibid. p. 443.  [13] Ibid. p. 445.
[14] Ibid. p. 463.  [15] Ibid. tome iv. p. 194.  [16] Ibid. p. 279.
[17] Ibid. p. 289.  [18] Histoire des Confesseurs, p. 394.

T

The Prince de Montbarey[1] says that a few years before, the suppression of the Jesuits would have been believed impossible. Montbarey[2] supposes the Cardinal de Bernis privy to the abolition of the Jesuits. The Prince de Montbarey, an eye-witness, says, that in 1756 the Marquise de Pompadour was supreme, and women of the highest rank obliged to court her.[3] The Prince de Montbarey, in two remarkable passages[4] says that by the end of the reign of Louis XV. the works of Voltaire and Rousseau were universally read. Montbarey[5] says that the Archbishop of Toulouse (Brienne?) and the Archbishop of Sens were both lovers of the "philosophical party."

Read Voltaire's Louis XV. Sismondi (xxix. 289) thinks Voltaire first introduced inoculation in France.

Georgel[6] says that Breteuil had great influence on the Queen, and prejudiced her against the Emigrants.

Even the violent Jacobins were mostly educated men. See Alison, Hist. of Europe ii. 130, 131, 218.

---

## INFLUENCE OF ENGLAND AND COALITION ON FRANCE.

EVEN Robespierre at first wished to abolish the penalty of death.[7] Directly after the unsuccessful flight of Louis XVI. in 1791, the Marquis de Bouillé writes to say, that if a hair of the head of the king was injured, there should not be left a stone in Paris. "I know the roads," said the traitor, "and I will lead the foreign armies."[8]

In 1794, the English were accused of arming an assassin against the life of Robespierre.[9] The circumstances connected with the fall of Robespierre are the worst part of Lamartine's book. He says[10] that the Reign of Terror would have ceased if Robespierre had not fallen.

---

## CONSEQUENCE OF ENGLAND INTERFERING WITH THE FRENCH REVOLUTION.

IF foreigners had not interfered, the French Revolution would have been milder, for the Girondists would not have fallen. The war declared by England injured us, but it almost ruined France.

---

[1] Mémoires, tome i. p. 212.     [2] Ibid. p. 209.     [3] Ibid. pp. 140, 142, 159.
[4] Ibid. iii. pp. 95, 108.     [5] Ibid. pp. 144, 206, 337.
[6] Georgel, Mémoires, tome iii. 106.     [7] Lamartine, Girondins, tome i. p. 52.
[8] Ibid. p. 128.     [9] Ibid. tome viii. pp. 134, 137, 207.     [10] Ibid. p. 270.

By increasing the violence of the Revolution it increased the violence of the reaction, and secured the despotism of Napoleon. The interference of England made the Revolution permanent by turning a social dispute into a national quarrel. See for evidence of the peculiar hatred against England, Alison, iii. pp. 154, 279, 432, and in particular pp. 632, 633, vi. 225, 226. Indeed, the hatred was natural when the French found they were opposed by the freest country on the earth, a country from which they had derived the inspirations of their own liberty. The result was that everything became more violent. Christianity was publicly abolished.[1] Rousseau was succeeded by Marat.[2] For the terrible crimes and loss of life during the Reign of Terror see Alison, iii. pp. 195, 209. At length the natural result followed. Anarchy was succeeded by despotism. The right of unlimited divorce was established; marriage was turned into concubinage, and France became a brothel. The genius of France now became entirely military, and this partly in hatred of England, and partly from the destruction of all other employments.[3] In 1795 fell the club of the Jacobins; and, says Alison,[4] "public opinion daily pronounced itself more strongly in favour of humane measures."

Thus the despotism of Napoleon was unnecessary, and would not have happened but for the violence with which England attempted to *force* the Bourbons on France, and the military spirit which that violence created. In 1795, the Jacobins disappeared; even dress became elegant; the laws against the Girondists and Christianity were repealed; even the faubourgs were disarmed; and "thus terminated the reign of the multitude."[5] Everything showed the returning civilization of a great people; and the Girondists swayed the Convention, which was supreme.[6] In 1792, when we first went to war, the 3 per cents were 98; but in 1797, they were 51. The funds fell; public credit was nearly destroyed; the fleet mutinied in the midst of war.[7]

In 1797, the hatred felt by the French against the English enabled the Jacobins to rally, and they re-established a military tyranny on the 18th Fructidor, which made the Directory supreme.[8] The real author of this revolution of 18th Fructidor, was Napoleon;[9] and this is "the true era of the commencement of military despotism in France." However, early in 1798, Napo-

---

[1] See the horrible details in Alison's Europe, vol. iii. pp. 178, 181.   [2] Ibid. p. 185.
[3] Ibid. pp. 404, 634; vol. iv. p. 133; vol. viii. p. 415.     [4] Ibid. pp. 585, 588.
[5] Ibid. vol. iii. pp. 589, 590, 604, 605.                     [6] Ibid. p. 627.
[7] Ibid. vol. iv. pp. 219, 233, 236.
[8] Ibid. pp. 398, 404, 405. See also Georgel, Mémoires, tome v. pp. 415, 416,
[9] Alison, vol. iv. p. 409.

leon showed great anxiety "to detach himself from the government, from his strong and growing aversion to the Jacobin party, which the revolution of the 18th Fructidor had placed at the head of the republic."[1] In 1799, the military enthusiasm was dying away, but as England continued hostile, it was absolutely necessary to revive it, and to put a great general at the head of affairs.[2] However, directly Napoleon was made First Consul he proposed peace, but England (A.D. 1799), in an insulting reply, proposed that France should restore the Bourbons.[3] The result was, as Alison confesses,[4] that in 1800, all the military enthusiasm which since 1793 had died away, was renewed. At length England had to pay the penalty of her crimes; and in 1800 the whole of Europe, which she had stirred up against France, was now by Napoleon turned against herself.[5]

About 1793, an order was issued by Robespierre forbidding quarter to be given to the English.[6] In 1803, Napoleon made a monstrous claim on us about Peltier.[7] If France had interfered with us in 1643, Charles II. would never have been restored.

In September, 1791, the king accepted the constitution, and all was cordiality between him and the Assembly;[8] but now it was, says Lamartine, that the kings and aristocracies in Europe became afraid of their own interests. Coblentz now became the centre of their counter-revolutionary conspiracy.[9] And in August the emperor and Frederick William of Prussia arrived at Pilnitz. There was then issued a proclamation, "qui fût la date d'une guerre de vingt-deux ans." This was the declaration of Pilnitz, to which all the European courts except England in some decree acceded. Louis XVI. ordered the emigrants at Coblentz to disarm, which they refused to do, and in December 1791, the emperor declared he would aid them.[10] Directly the Legislative Assembly met in 1791, there was shown a reaction in favour of Louis XVI.[11] Robespierre, who continued to increase in power, did not wish for war, and therefore he quarrelled with the Girondins; but it was in vain, for on December 21st, the Emperor Leopold, by a declaration, increased the war party in the Assembly. And on February 7, 1792, an alliance was concluded against France between Austria and Prussia, and war was ready to break

[1] Alison, vol. iv. pp. 412, 558.　　　　　　　　　[2] Ibid. vol. v. p. 165.
[3] Ibid. pp. 165, 245, 247, 248.　　[4] Ibid. p. 280.　　[5] Ibid. p. 565.
[6] Pellew's Life of Lord Sidmouth, vol. i. p. 103.
[7] See Pellew's Life of Sidmouth, vol. ii. pp. 154, 157, and see p. 177 respecting the infamous detention of the English in 1803.
[8] Lamartine, Hist. des Girondins, tome i. pp. 196-199.
[9] Ibid. pp. 205, 232.　　[10] Ibid. pp. 233-239.　　[11] Ibid. pp. 256, 259, 260.

[out], when Leopold suddenly died.  Now came military ascendency, and, says Lamartine,[1] Dumouriez was for two years supreme dictator in everything but the name.   He tried to separate Prussia from Austria, but Francis I. was eager for war, and " le prince de Kaunitz, son principal ministre, répondait aux notes de Dumouriez dans un langage qui portait de défi à l'Assemblée Nationale."   And on April 20, Louis XVI. found himself obliged to declare war against the emperor.[2]   Before the duke of Brunswick's manifesto, and *after* the declaration of war, Louis XVI. in vain requested the emigrants not to attack their own country, France.[3]   They determined to disobey him, and the duke of 'Brunswick issued that manifesto which, says Lamartine, left the French Revolution no alternative but submission or war.   The hostilities now began in Belgium " par des revers qu'on imputait aux trahisons de la cour."   The military leaders were La Fayette, who was suspected, and the duke de Lauzun (called General Biron), said to be a lover of the queen.[4]   (Early in the Revolution the nobles fled on the first alarm, and instilled their selfish fears into foreign courts. Frederick the Great and Joseph II. were recently dead).   Vergniaud, in one of his brilliant speeches in July 1792, asked how it was that at so great a crisis inexperienced men were placed at the head of French armies.[5]  This complaint was the precursor of August 10.[6]   Then came the threats from La Vendée and from Lyons, where " l'ésprit catholique et sacerdotal " was active.[7]   It was now reported that La Fayette was about to march on Paris, and that the king had fled.[8]  Then, on August 6, " la nouvelle du massacre de quatre administrateurs consterna de nouveau l'Assemblée."[9]   The power now fell into the hands of the lowest of the people ; and, on August 10, 1792, the Assembly was no longer respected.   Even then, instead of dethroning the king, they only provisionally suspended him.[10]   On August 11, the Assembly in which the Girondins were supreme, dissolved.   It was inferior to the " Assemblée Constituante," its predecessor, and to the Convention, its successor.   For, says Lamartine,[11] the first represented the *intellect* of thinking men, the last the energy of the masses, while the Legislative Assembly represented the intermediate and middle classes   And the *meaning* of the 10th of August is, that the people made a great effort to save France.[12]   At the end of August news reached Paris that La Fayette had fled ; that the

[1] Girondins, tome ii. pp. 40, 47, 50, 129, 149.           [2] Ibid. pp. 203–205.
[3] Ibid. pp. 219, 220.        [4] Ibid. pp. 239, 240.        [5] Ibid. tome iii. p. 20.
[6] Ibid. p. 33.              [7] Ibid. pp. 38, 39.           [8] Ibid. pp. 67, 71.
[9] Ibid. p. 72.             [10] Ibid. tome iii. 165, 167, 170, 171.
[11] Ibid. pp. 193, 194.       [12] Ibid. pp. 196, 221.

allied army had entered France, that Longwy was taken, that Verdun had capitulated. The result was, that from the 10th of August to the 20th of September, was nothing but the dictatorship of Danton. Still, even Danton hesitated before he would give the signal for the crimes of September.[1] After the massacres of September, the execution of the king was a very slight crime. Of these massacres a thrilling account is given by Lamartine.[2] At length the storm ceased. The assassins, drunk with blood and fatigued with crimes, reposed from their labours. But after the battle of Valmy Paris was in imminent danger. Danton still wished to save the life of the king; and the miserable prejudices of the Girondins in favour of antiquity prevented them seizing the idea of "a Christian democracy;" and they had no conception of a republic that was not modelled on that of Rome.[3]

After the bad days of September 1792, the Jacobins declined, and even Danton was tired of blood. And after the 2nd of September, Robespierre no longer appeared at the sittings of the Commune. In October the municipal elections came on, and the moderate party triumphed over the Jacobins in nearly all the sections.[4] Even in the Convention the Jacobins trembled for their favourite Robespierre. Danton desired to save the life of the king,[5] but as Fonfrede wrote,[6] it was necessary to show courage. "C'est au moment où les potentats de l'Europe se liguent contre nous que nous leur offrirons le spectacle d'un roi supplicié." (At first, I believe a republic might have been established peaceably, as in 1848.) Directly Louis XVI. was deposed, Lord Gower, the English ambassador was recalled; and the moment the news of his execution reached London M. de Chauvelin was ordered to quit England in twenty-four hours.[7] Chauvelin, returning to Paris, said that the English were preparing to rise against Pitt and George III., and *then* France declared war against England and Holland. (The rupture between England and France was the more injurious, because Dumouriez had, I think, so beaten and intimidated Prussia and Austria as to dispose them for peace.) The day after the death of Louis XVI. Catherine concluded an offensive and defensive treaty with England.[8] The execution of Louis, like that of Charles, strengthened the moderate party. See the fine remarks in Lamartine's Girondins, v. pp. 86, 87. In April, the Vendean war. In June

[1] Lamartine, Histoire des Girondins, tome iii. pp. 217, 223.
[2] Ibid. tome iii. pp. 239-275.
[3] Ibid. tome iv. pp. 32, 46, 64, 66.  [4] Ibid. pp. 84, 85, 98, 137, 138.
[5] Ibid. pp. 154, 177.  [6] Tome iv. p. 179.
[7] Lamartine, tome v. pp. 119, 120.  [8] Ibid. tome v. p. 122.

the Girondists fell, but were not executed till October. Between March and September, 1793, all Europe signed treaties against France. In August, 1793, France was in the greatest danger from the allies.[1] At the end of 1792, Dumouriez was supreme, and he wished to save the king; and Danton was weary of anarchy. After the execution of the king, famine was in the land.[2] By the issue of paper money to carry on war with England, everything was thrown into confusion.

On February 24, 1793, the people under Marat rose and plundered the rich, and a few days later came news of the movements at Lyons and La Vendee; of the defeat of Custine in Germany, of the conspiracy of Dumouriez. Commissioners were now sent to the frontiers; the theatres were shut, and the most anarchical proposals made; and a committee of insurrection organised against the Girondins;[3] and a revolutionary tribunal formed.[4] Still Danton inclined towards the Girondins, but at length turned against them; and this increased the audacity of the party of Marat.[5] The increasing success of the Vendeans and the threats of foreign generals strengthened the violent party.[6] Roland was now arrested by the Revolutionary Committee.[7] During three months after England declared war, the Girondists, last hope of their country, continued to struggle with the mob; but in 1793 "la journée du 2 Juin, qu'on appelle encore le 31 Mai, parceque la lutte dura trois jours, fût le 10 Août de la Gironde." This violent step was necessary, for, says Lamartine, if the Girondists had continued to govern, France, already half-conquered by foreigners, would have been destroyed.[8] The energy of crime was wanted to defend the nation. The Girondins, however, were received at Caen, and General Wimpfen declared that he would march against Paris,[9] and the foreign relations of France were very threatening. Danton still wished for milder measures, and was horrified at the idea of executing Marie Antoinette.[10] There was now appointed the Committee of Public Safety—the Decemvirat, which was supreme for fourteen months, and which now issued the celebrated decree raising all France against the enemy. Prices, &c. were now fixed, for, says Lamartine, "en demandant au peuple toute son energie, la Convention se crut obligée d'accepter aussi ses emportements."[11] The people cried out for pillage.[12] The revolutionary tribunals were now

[1] Alison's Abridgement, pp. 52, 54, 56.
[2] Lamartine, Girondins, vol. v. pp. 180, 183, 187, 224.    [3] Ibid. pp. 230-237.
[4] Ibid. pp. 241, 243. Vergniaud had large views of political rights, p. 247.
[5] Ibid. pp. 256-267.    [6] Ibid. tome vi. pp. 9, 10, 25, 64, 65, 70.
[7] Ibid. p. 87.    [8] Ibid. pp. 108-117.    [9] Ibid. pp. 148, 149.
[10] Ibid. pp. 202-211.    [11] Ibid. pp. 221-233.    [12] Ibid. pp. 234, 236.

reorganised, and the prisons would scarcely hold the innumerable captives.[1]  Robespierre wished to save the queen,[2] and in October, 1793, he tried to save the Girondins.[3]  Robespierre, Danton, and even Marat, were not the leaders of the Revolution: they were merely the exponents of it.  The Girondins who now fell had, says Lamartine, three great faults.  1st. That they did not dare to proclaim a revolution before August 10, the day the Legislative Assembly opened.  2nd. That they conspired against the Constitution of 1791.  3rd. " D'avoir sous la Convention voulu gouverner quand il fallut combattre."[4]  The allied sovereigns of Europe answered a manifesto by an invasion, and a theory by a fact.  How could it be expected that the old, withered, and effete aristocracies of Europe should furnish men able to struggle with a youthful republic—soldiers fighting for pay against men who struggled for liberty.  "Pourquoi," says the greatest historian of these times, " Pourquoi cette différence ? "[5]  The first great success of the French was at the battle of Wattignies.[6]  Now first appeared Napoleon, Pichegru, and Hoche.  The destruction of Lyons destroyed even in their cradle the resources of industry. After Lyons had surrendered, " Les démolitions coutaient quinze millions pour anéantir une capitale de plus de trois cent millions de valeur en édifices."[7]  The nation was drunk with crime.  At Lyons, in the midst of the massacres, jewels were worn shaped like the guillotine.[8]  In the midst of this the civil war broke out at Toulon.

At the beginning of 1794 " La guillotine semblait être la seule institution de la France."[9]  Lamartine says that the object of the new calendar was to destroy Catholicism ; for France " ne voulut pas que l'Église continua à marquer au peuple les instants de son travail ou de son répos."[10]  Immense numbers of the bishops and clergy now publicly renounced their religion, and declared that they had been carrying on a system of imposture. " Cette abdication du Catholicisme extérieur par les prêtes d'une nation entourée depuis tant de siècles de la puissance de ce culte, est une des actes les plus caractéristiques de l'esprit de la Révolution."[11]  The scenes of blood were opposed by Danton.[12]  Just before he was arrested, Robespierre was afraid to attack open crimes, but he did not hesitate to attack atheism ; and see his

---

[1] Lamartine, Girondins, tome vi. pp. 240, 246, 247.          [2] Ibid. p. 264.
[3] Ibid. tome vii. pp. 5, 6.          [4] Ibid. pp. 42, 43.          [5] Ibid. p. 61.
[6] Ibid. p. 74.          [7] Ibid. p. 136.          [8] Ibid. p. 143.
[9] Ibid. pp. 154, 206.          [10] Ibid. p. 211.          [11] Ibid. pp. 216, 219.
[12] Ibid. p. 259 ; tome viii. p. 9.

interesting speech in favour of religion.[1] Robespierre was the most cruel man, because he was the most sincere. On the 30th of March, 1794, Danton was arrested.[2] On the 29th of July, 1794, Robespierre, St.-Just, Henriot, Couthon, Coffinhal, " and all their party," were executed.[3] The men who overthrew Robespierre were little better than he, but there was now (end of July, 1794) formed a party called Thermidorians, consisting of " the moderates of all parties and the remnants of the Royalists." They began by repealing the " Law of Suspected Persons." In September they closed the Jacobin Club, and finally in April, 1795, they dispersed or imprisoned all the Jacobin leaders.[4] On June 17, 1795, says Alison,[5] "the Revolutionary Tribunal itself was quietly suppressed by a simple decree. And thus ended the reign of the multitude six years after its establishment at the storm of the Bastile. The populace, now disarmed, took no share in the further changes of government, which were brought about by the middle classes and the army." And now the government fell into its proper hands, into the hands of the middle classes, the legitimate source of power. From the States General to the Legislative Assembly, and from the Legislative Assembly to the Convention, the sources of power sunk lower and lower. Robespierre fell directly after the armies of France flourished. Lamartine[6] says that from May to July, 1794, there were most executions. Robespierre's speech in favour of religion in April, 1794, is in Lamartine's Girondins.[7]

## FRANCE IN THE NINETEENTH CENTURY.

1. THE great work of Chateaubriand was published at London in 1796, and shows, says Villemain, " combien, malgré l'originalité native de son esprit, il était alors impregné des idées et des sentiments de celui qu'il nommait le Grand Rousseau."[8]

2. Thierry and Guizot first did justice to the middle ages.

3. The religious reaction had begun before Chateaubriand. Necker published his work, De l'Importance des Opinions réligieuses, and St.-Pierre took the same side.[9] And for some of St. Pierre's opinions, which, however, were revolutionary, see pp. 389,

[1] Lamartine, Girondins, tome vii. pp. 260, 264.
[2] Alison's Abridgment, p. 71.
[4] Ibid. pp. 92, 93.
[6] Lamartine, Girondins, tome viii. p. 74.
[5] Littérature au dixhuitième Siècle, tome ii. p. 303.

[3] Ibid. p. 75.
[5] Ibid. p. 94.
[7] Ibid. pp. 123, 128, 141.
[9] Tome iii. p. 395. .

391. Alison[1] says Madame de Stael first laid down that there were only two epochs—*before* and *after* Christianity.

4. After the breaking out of the Revolution the love of antiquity began to revive. This we find in André Chenier.[2]

5. Napoleon, as Comte says, threw everything backward. Most of the literature was under his control. But there were some fiery spirits which he could not repress, and which laid the foundation of that brilliant literature which France now possesses. They were M. de Maistre and Madame de Stael. De Maistre was to theology what Napoleon was to politics. Struck with horror at the excesses of that Revolution which he had witnessed, his powerful but gloomy mind attempted to restore France to that mental slavery from which, since the death of Bossuet, she had been entirely free. It does not fall within the plan of this introduction to consider the character of his learned and eloquent works, but in another place I shall trace the influence which they have had in accelerating the progress of Puseyism. Madame de Stael in her great work on Literature asserted that in all its branches Liberty was most favourable to it. In this work she first asserted that during the middle ages man was progressive.[3] For this work Napoleon banished her forty leagues from Paris. It seemed likely that Napoleon would succeed in his infamous scheme of subjugating the intellect of Christendom. At this moment, and two centuries and a quarter after that memorable day on which Elizabeth had beaten the Armada from the shores of Britain, England again stepped forward and saved Europe from a tyranny even more dangerous than that of Philip.

Madame de Stael constantly laboured to effect an alliance between philosophy and politics. This is one of her great merits, and one of which no subsequent discoveries can possibly deprive her. But she has a merit even greater than this. She was the first writer in Europe who to a philosophic, though perhaps too scanty knowledge of history, united a knowledge of that much higher philosophy which connects liberty with religion, and literature with devotion. This, which is the brightest aspect of modern literature, owes more to Madame de Stael than to any other author with whose works I am acquainted.[4] In all her most matured writings she is never weary of insisting on the great truth that a complete, fearless, unhesitating liberty of discussion is the condition under which true religion may be most expected to flourish. The success of her works was

---

[1] Hist. of Europe, vol. ix. p. 567.
[2] See Villemain, Littérature au dixhuitième Siècle, tome iv. p. 303.
[3] Ibid. p. 355.　　　　[4] Ibid. p. 375.

scarcely inferior to their merit. She prepared France for the reception of that still higher literature which it was now to borrow from a foreign land.

6. Even M. Villemain confesses his ignorance of German.[1]

7 Ranke adopts what I may perhaps call the transcendental theory. Die Römschen Päpste, i. 35, 441. At p. 273 he seems to hold the doctrine that history is a development over which individual genius can exercise little or no control.

8. " L'école écossaise était, il y a quelques années, profondement ignorée en France. Mon illustre·prédécesseur, M. Royer-Collard, en a le premier parlé dans l'enseignement public." [2]

9. Sir J. Mackintosh [3] says, " Long after the death of Dr. Reid, his philosophy was taught at Paris by M. Royer-Collard."

Read Preface to Barante's Ducs de Bourgogne for his *artistic* mode of writing history.

10. M. Barante does not allow enough to individual genius, and he even seems to adopt the theory of cycles.[4]

11. Bonstetten was influenced by the Scotch and English school.[5]

12. Damiron [6] says that Ancillon, in his Essais Philosophiques ou Nouveaux Mélanges, has an Essay on the Philosophy of History.

13. There are three great French schools. 1st. Of *Sensation :* Cabanis, Destutt de Tracy, Garat, and Volney. 2nd. Of *Revelation :* Maistre, Bonald, and Lamennais. 3rd. *Eclecticism,* or " rational spiritualism." [7] Sensualism proceeds from sensation, Catholicism from revelation, eclecticism from consciousness.[8] The Revolution of 1789 suspended all intellectual labours until 1794-5, when the end of the Convention and the establishment of the Directory finished the movement towards *liberty* and began that towards *civilisation.*[9] The new philosophy, which was essentially that of Condillac, was taught by Garat. The Institute organised by the Directory followed the same course, and then appeared the works of Cabanis, De Tracy, De Gerando, Maine de Biran, La Romiguière, and Lancelin.[10] Everything was sensual until the first consul, hating metaphysics, banished them from the Institute. During this period, 1795 to 1803-4,

[1] Villemain, Littérature au dixhuitième Siècle, tome iii. p. 154.
[2] Cousin, Histoire de la Philosophie, part i. tome iv. p. 25.
[3] Dissertation on Ethical Philosophy, edit. Whewell, p. 318.
[4] Barante, Tableau de la Littérature, Paris, 1847, pp. 18-20.
[5] See Damiron, Histoire de la Philosophie, tome ii. p. 74.		[6] Ibid. p. 83.
[7] Ibid. tome i. p. 11.		[8] Ibid. p. 25.		[9] Ibid. p. 41.
[10] Ibid. pp. 42, 43, 44.

there was hardly any opposition to sensualism ; for Bonald, who
had not written metaphysically, had little influence.[1] Now came
the reaction.  Napoleon, who was essentially a superstitious man,
was to French philosophy what the clergy had been to the
Scotch philosophy.  Under the emperor, sensualism, hated by
Napoleon, whose mind was essentially synthetic,[2] considerably
declined.  The merit of the subsequent movement is due to
Royer-Collard, from 1811 to 1814.[3]  After the Restoration
metaphysics revived, and the theological school[4] was led by
Chateaubriand, Bonald, De Lamennais, De Maistre, Eckstein,
and Ballanche.  At the same time rational spiritualism was
advocated by Madame de Stael, who, in 1814, published her
Germany, of which she had learnt the philosophy from Benjamin
Constant, Schlegel, and Villers.  She first made Kant generally
known in France.[5]  Cousin, who at first was only a commentator
on Royer-Collard, soon added a knowledge of German to that of
Scotch metaphysics, and from the two formed eclecticism.[6]  In
1802, Cabanis published his Rapports du Physique et du Morale
de l'Homme.  His system was adopted by De Tracy, who is to
metaphysics what Cabanis is to physiology.[6]  This he did in his
Ideology,[7] and what he was to metaphysics that was Volney to
morals.  Volney in his Catechism, says that the greatest good
is health and life.[8]  The same system was adopted by Lancelin,
an able author now little known.[9]  Damiron[10] gives some account
of Broussais' system, but having no knowledge of medicine (as
he confesses at p. 165) he is very superficial.  M. Ajais is of no
particular school.[11]  Ballanche, in his Institutions Sociales, works
out the idea of the development of the human mind.  According
to him, the mind is never old, but is living and *perfectible.*
The primitive and divine tradition was first spoken, then spoken
and written, and then spoken, written, and printed.  In the same
way there was first pure poetry, which was the spontaneous
development of revealed truth, and as this only requires accent
and words, writing would be unnecessary.  But as thought
develops itself, it becomes more material, and this gives rise to
writing.  When ideas get still more abundant, writing is found
insufficient, men become impatient, and printing is invented.
Thus the three forms of tradition are oral, written, and printed.
In the first form it would have run great danger of corruption
if it were not watched over by priests and poets and the admirable

[1] Damiron, Hist. de la Philosophie, tome i p. 49.      [2] Ibid. p. 54.
[3] Ibid. pp. 55, 56, 60.        [4] Ibid. pp. 65-70.        [5] Ibid. pp. 71, 72.
[6] Ibid. p. 73.                 [7] Ibid. pp. 87, 99, 100.   [8] Ibid. pp. 117, 120.
[9] Ibid. p. 150.                [10] Ibid. pp. 162-205.      [11] Ibid. p. 218.

institution of castes. When it became written the danger was less, but still considerable, therefore, although philosophers were untitled priests and poets, remained. Since printing, the danger is no more, and therefore the authority of priests, &c., diminishes.[1] Ballanche has also put forth the first volume of a great work, La Palingénésie.[2] Among the physiologists, Virey and Bérard, by reviving the doctrine of the vital principle, began the opposition to the school of Cabanis.[3] Maine de Biran was at first a sensualist, afterwards a spiritualist. His language is obscure ; and his great merit is to have philosophized, not into the external senses— but to look upon consciousness as his science, and he considers the soul as a pure and actual force. However, his first work, his Idéologie, is only a sort of physiology. But in his article on Leibnitz he shows himself a monadist.[4] Royer-Collard began to lecture in 1811, when "rien ne semblait annoncer encore une réaction contre les doctrines de Condillac." It was he who began the great philosophic movement against Condillac. He introduced a knowledge of Reid. Besides this, he said that we have all ideas of substance and cause, and yet that ideology does not account for their existence. The real solution, he says, is this: our notions of substance, cause, time, and space all proceed from consciousness; but in different ways. 1st. As soon as the soul feels, it believes that it *is,* and that there is a connection between its *impression* and its *being.* This connection it generalises, and from this moment believes that every quality has a substance, and every substance a quality. 2nd. As the soul is active, it looks upon itself as a cause, and then generalising, believes that every effect has a cause. 3rd. As its remembers that it acted, it has the idea of its duration, which it understands by the succession of its action—hence the idea of infinite duration, time, and eternity. By an analogous method we get the idea of space, p. 147–148. Collard was as much opposed to mysticism as to sensualism.[5] Collard was succeeded as professor by Cousin, who began with the Scotch philosophy, and then studied the German. After this came his own system. He divides psychology into three points—liberty, reason, and sensibility. Liberty is the *me* in all its wholeness, and those who deny liberty deny personality (Damiron, ii. 172). In the acts of reason and of sensation there is *not* freedom, and they do not proceed from the *me,* though the *me* eventually lays hold of them. As to the reason, Cousin says that all the laws of thought may be reduced to two, causality and substance. Synthetically and in the nature

[1] Damiron, Hist. de la Philosophie, tome i. pp. 322–328.    [2] Ibid. p. 329.
[3] Ibid. tome ii. p. 23.    [4] Ibid. pp. 129–135.    [5] Ibid. pp. 141–155.

of things, the law of substance is the first; but analytically, and
in the order of the acquisition of our knowledge, the law of
causality precedes that of substance. Thus all ideas are reducible
to what *is*, and what *acts*. Indeed in reality, these two are one ;
the substance is the force which *is*, and the force is the substance
which acts. The reason is supreme when it acts *by itself ;* but
the moment the *me* intervenes—*i.e.* the moment we reflect, the
reason becomes fallible. The criterion then of truth is neither
the opinion of men nor the opinion of the individual, but it is
spontaneous perception. As to sensation, Cousin says that it is
the faculty of knowing of the exterior world whatever falls under
our senses, and he denies the existence of matter, and follows
Maine de Biran in saying that the external world only consists
of forces. Damiron thinks that Cousin is not a pantheist. According to Cousin, humanity has three epochs. 1st. When without
reflection it merely considers the *infinity* which surrounds it.
2nd. It turns its eyes on itself and considers the *finite*. 3rd.
Having still more experience, it studies the *connection* between
the infinite and the finite. Philosophy will have three corresponding epochs which are represented by the East, Greece,
and the modern era ; and in religion by pantheism, polytheism,
and theism ; in politics, monarchy, democracy, and a mixed form.[1]
Jouffroy, born in 1796, was a pupil of Cousin. He has translated
Dugald Stewart's Sketches of Moral Philosophy, in the Preface
to which he triumphantly defends the moral sciences.[2] (Constant,
the friend of Madame de Stael, introduced the German Literature
into France.) The revolutionists, after the fate of the Girondists,
anticipated the hatred of Napoleon against men who presumed to
think. In 1794 they insulted the members of the Academy,[3] and
indeed in 1793 the Academies were formally suppressed.[4] Morellet
notices[5] the dislike of Bonaparte to moral and political science.
Immediately after the final defeat of Napoleon there arose (about
1816), the great eclectic school of philosophy in France. M.
Cousin says[6] that his predecessor, Royer-Collard, first introduced
the Scotch philosophy into France.

There have been absurd exaggerations about Napoleon. In
1813, Campbell had some conversation with Herschel respecting
his interview with Napoleon. Herschel said to Campbell, "The
first consul did surprise me by his quickness and versatility on all
subjects ; but in science he seemed to know little more than any

---

[1] Damiron, Hist. de la Philosophie, tome ii. pp. 167–213.      [3] Ibid. pp. 219–223.
[2] See Mémoires de Morellet, tome ii. pp. 30, 31.
[4] Ibid. pp. 55, 58.                                      [5] Ibid. p. 217.
[6] Histoire de la Philosophie, part ii. tome i. p. 296.

well-educated gentleman; and of astronomy much less, for instance, than our own king. His general air was something like affecting to know more than he did know." [1] Lamartine is at once sentimental and picturesque. In 1802 Sir James Mackintosh, who had just returned from Paris, writes to Dugald Stewart that there was little interest felt there for metaphysics; and in 1808 Sir J. Mackintosh writes, " In the character of Corinne, Madame de Stael draws an imaginary self—what she is, what she had the power of being, and what she can easily imagine that she might have become." [2] In 1814 Sir J. Mackintosh writes from Paris, where he had seen all the most eminent persons, " Constant is the first man in talent whom I have seen here." [3] In 1802, Chateaubriand was supreme and France was evidently succumbing under a military and religious despotism. Romilly, who was in Paris in 1802, notices " in what scorn Bonaparte holds the opinions of the people." [4] In 1808 Niebuhr writes from Amsterdam, " It is now the fashion among the French themselves to decry their own literature, with the exception of the poets of the age of Louis XIV., as the production of hell." [5] Napoleon hated Madame de Stael. He forebad her to associate with Schlegel, and he (about 1811) in every way attempted to ruin the German literature. Niebuhr speaks in the highest terms of Madame de Stael's " Germany." In Morell's Philosophical Tendencies of the Age, 8vo, 1848, pp. 126, 127, there is a short account of Bonald's superstitious attempt to resolve philosophy into tradition.

*Napoleon and the injury he did.*—This great public robber levied, in 1797, £120,000,000 on Italy. [6] Besides this, notice his destruction of the Venetian Republic. [7] This forms such a catalogue of crimes as no other man has ever been able to commit. His spoliation of the Swiss Confederacy, Alison, iv. 452, 462, 562. His pillage of Rome, iv. 483. These were the things for which, when merely a military leader, he was answerable. And when he afterwards rose to supreme power, his crimes took a still wider range. Respecting the laws of conscription and their result, see Alison, iv. 544; vi. 231, 232; vii. 371; viii. 199; x. 609. The Russian campaign, xi. 199, 265, 266, 285, 287; xii. 390, 439. And yet, notwithstanding all this, such was the immense stimulus liberty had given the national intellect in

[1] Beattie's Life and Letters of Campbell, Lond. 1849, vol. ii. pp. 234, 235.
[2] Memoirs of Mackintosh, edited by his Son, Lond. 1836, vol. i. p. 406.
[3] Ibid. vol. ii. p. 296.
[4] Life of Sir Samuel Romilly, written by Himself, 1842, vol i. p. 415. See also pp. 420, 421.
[5] Life and Letters of B. G. Niebuhr, Lond. 8vo, 1852, vol. i. p. 265.
[6] Alison's Europe, vol. iv. p. 345.      [7] Ibid. p. 352.

1798, Napoleon was accompanied to Egypt by Monge, Berthollet, Fourier, Larrey, Desgenettes, Geoffroy St.-Hilaire, and Denon.[1] Napoleon's murder of the Albanians at Jaffa, iv. 624. His scandalous desertion of his own army, which he left shut up as prisoners in Egypt, iv. 650. His treachery towards Toussaint, vi. 129. His infamous arrest of the English, vi. 198, 199. His murder of the Duke d'Enghien, vi. 257, 308, 323. The murder of Palm, vii. 166. The inordinate destruction of human life, vii. 572. His seizure of the Spanish fortresses in the midst of profound peace, viii. 333 ; and subsequent occupation of the whole peninsula, viii. 388. His murder of Hofer, ix. 286. His plunder, vi. 598; xii. 187. Napoleon himself was indifferent to Christianity, but he saw that the clergy were friends of despotism.[2] In 1799, the very year he was made First Consul, he fettered the press.[3] He called the Jacobins metaphysicians, and said they ought to be thrown into the Seine.[4] In 1804 he was made Emperor; and, says Alison,[5] " In everything. but the name, the government of France was thenceforward an absolute despotism." He did not destroy the press ; he did worse ; he corrupted it.[6] Intoxicated with military glory, the French, soon after the battle of Austerlitz, presented Napoleon with the most fulsome addresses. Such was the ignorance in which France was kept by a corrupt press, that in 1814 many of the French had never heard of the battle of Trafalgar.[7] By 1807, education was entirely in the hands of the government, and of course Napoleon (like the Chinese emperors) encouraged it.[8] Napoleon, as if determined to perpetuate his infamy beyond the grave, left a legacy to the assassin who attempted to murder the Duke of Wellington.[9]

In the moment of Napoleon's fall it was soon seen what military honour was. All his marshals, the creatures whom he had raised from the dust, deserted him. After the battle of Moscow, Murat, his own brother-in-law, Berthier, his bosom friend, deserted him,[10] and so did Marmont, Ney, Augereau. Indeed Ney and Soult committed a double treachery.[11]

Napoleon hated political economists. And yet Say had just done so much.[12]

The retreat from Moscow and the battles of Vittoria and Leipsic completed that ruin of Napoleon which his own violence

[1]   Alison's Europe, vol. iv. p. 563.          [2] Ibid. p. 644.          [3] Ibid. vol. v. p. 283.
[4]   Ibid. vol. vi. pp. 8, 60 ; vol. xi. p. 262.                       [5] Ibid. vol. vi. p. 347.
[6]   Ibid. p. 365.                    [7] Ibid. vol. viii. pp. 152–159.
[8]   Ibid. pp. 203–205.              [9] Ibid. vol. ix. p. 287 ; vol. xi. p. 560.
[10]  Ibid. vol. xi. p. 424, 621 ; vol. xiii. p. 204.
[11]  Ibid. vol. xiii. pp. 191, 198, 204, 214, 625.
[12]  Ibid. vol. ix. p. 427. See also Twiss on Progress of Political Economy.

was sure to bring upon him.[1]  A century after the death of
Louis XIV., the military spirit of the French subjected them to
still greater disgrace.  The fall of Napoleon showed that the time
is long since passed, if, indeed, it ever existed, in which the
genius of a single man can permanently change the face of the
world.

Chateaubriand, directly he heard of the murder of the Duke
d'Enghien, threw up his appointment under Napoleon.[2]  In 1815,
France, besides supporting the army of occupation, had to pay
61,400,000l.[3]

Early in the nineteenth century the imagination revived, and
history, under Chateaubriand, Barante, and Thierry, become an
*art*, began to fall.  It was necessary to begin with a blunder.
Because men had loved antiquity too little, they now loved it too
much ; and in theology we have De Maistre and Lamennais.  On
the retrogressive character of Napoleon's policy, see Comte,
Philosophie Positive, v. 668, 669; vi. 386, 387.  Napoleon
favoured and rewarded Berthollet and Moreau, the great
chemists.[4]  Sismondi[5] says that Saint-Aulaire in 1817 was the first
who took a large view of the History of the Fronde.  Whewell[6]
says that Lamoriguière " was one of the first " who attacked " the
sensational philosophy" of Locke and Condillac.  Even in
Flassan's great work, Histoire de la Diplomatie française, the
authorities are rarely quoted.  Porter[7] says, on the authority of
some French merchants, that it was not till " towards the close of
the reign of Napoleon " that agriculture and industry began to
make head against the military spirit.  Georgel died in 1813,
and Napoleon's police immediately seized on his manuscript
Mémoires, which, in consequence, were not published till 1817.[8]
I suspect it is the love of the ancient writers which makes many
French historians think to imitate them by not quoting their
authorities.  The sixth and latter half of the fifth volume of Georgel's
Mémoires are important for the Life of Napoleon ; and I have
not read them.  Napoleon was very disappointed with Laplace,
whom he was so unwise as to raise to office.[9]  Monteil's Histoire
des Français des Divers États is rather curious than valuable ; the
author never generalises, and has no political economy.  However,

---

[1] Alison's Europe, vol. xii. p. 302.                [2] Ibid. vol. xiii. p. 201.
[3] Ibid. vol. xiv. pp. 99, 100.
[4] See Thomson's History of Chemistry, vol. ii. pp. 146, 150, 187, 188.
[5] Histoire des Français, tome xxiv. pp. 190, 191.
[6] History of the Inductive Sciences, vol. ii. p. 312.
[7] Progress of the Nation, vol. i. p. 288.
[8] See Georgel, Mémoires, tome i. pp. xxix, xxx.
[9] See Whewell's Bridgewater Treatise, p. 291.

he with reason complains[1] that men only write the history of kings
or of ecclesiastics.[2] Monteil tells us that this work cost him more
than twenty years' labour; and yet he fancies that modern history
begins with the fourteenth century. He says[3] that the fourteenth century was the age of feudality; the fifteenth the age of
independence; the sixteenth the age of theology; the seventeenth
of the arts; the eighteenth of reformers; but that "les siècles
antérieures ont été comme le quatorzième, des siècles féodaux;
ils ont été tous enchainés, tous stationnaires, tous les mêmes."
Monteil actually supposes[4] that the circulating specie in France
in the fourteenth century can be ascertained by the prices of
clothes, &c., and above all, by the rates of the daily wages of
labour. Sismondi[5] says he has never quoted manuscripts. He
mistakes the use of history, which he thinks a moral lesson. He
says he is Protestant, and that his history occupied him twenty-
four years.[6] Alison[7] says that, in the French Revolution, men,
being indifferent to Christianity, drew their notions of liberty
from Rome and Greece; hence, I am inclined to think, some of
the respect which the French now have for classical literature.
The French law against primogeniture is absurd. Even the
Americans do not *compel* a man to divide his property.[8] Tocqueville says[9] that an error in the French Revolution was that it not
only destroyed the power of the king, but *also* the provincial
institutions; thus falling into the error of being both *republican*
and *centralizing*. See however pp. 307–9, where Tocqueville
confesses that this centralizing spirit is not entirely the work of
the French Revolution; for that it was begun by the "légistes"
in the reign of Philip the Fair. Tocqueville, the first political
writer of the age, announces himself a Catholic.[10] Tocqueville[11]
shows himself ignorant of political economy. He says[12] that the
civil legislation of France is more democratic than that of
America, and that this was because Napoleon was willing to
satisfy the democratic passions of France in everything except his
own power; and willingly allowed such principles to govern the
arrangements of property and families, provided it was not
attempted to introduce them into the state. Thus, I think, one
great cause of the constant disorder in France is, that the demo-

---

[1] Monteil, Hist. des Français des divers États, tome i. p. 5. See also tome iv.
p. 233.
[2] Ibid. tome i. p. 6.　　[3] Ibid. p. 6.　　[4] Ibid. tome ii. p. 256, note.
[5] Hist. des Français, tome xxix. p. 511.　　[6] Ibid. pp. 513, 516.
[7] History of Europe, vol. i. p. 141.
[8] See Tocqueville, Démocratie en Amérique, tome i. p. 304.
[9] Ibid. p. 172.　　[10] Ibid. tome iii. p. 65.
[11] Ibid. tome v. pp. 43, 45. See also p. 237, note.　　[12] Ibid. p. 49.

cracy of civil life is struggling with the despotism of political
life. Tocqueville says [1] that in France, though most parties
complain of the government, they *all* call upon the government
to interfere and to do more than it is now doing. Indeed,
Tocqueville says that in *every* country centralization is increasing,
and the state gradually absorbing everything.[2] Sismondi, like
most of the French historians, knew very little of foreign literature. He hardly ever quotes our State Papers. Ranke [3] truly
says that the fullest account of the death of Henry II. is in
Forbes's State Papers, and these Sismondi, I think, never cites.
Monteil, who [was] after all merely a learned antiquary, speaks
with the greatest disrespect of Voltaire.[4] Even Capefigue takes
large views, though, like De Maistre and Lamennais, he was a
bigot. He has well seized the spirit of the sixteenth century,
and truly says that the Reformation was "action," the League
"reaction"; and the reign of Henry IV. "transaction." See his
admirable remarks in Histoire de la Réforme, tome viii. pp. 325-
363. Lamartine [5] says, "Napoléon paya, pendant quinze ans, des
écrivains et des journaux chargés de degrader, de salir, et de nier
le génie de Voltaire. Il haïssait ce nom, comme la force haït
l'intelligence." The three best historians of the French Revolution are Thiers, Lamartine, and Mignet. Of these, Thiers rarely
quotes authorities; Lamartine and Mignet never. In England,
the middle ages became popular because we disliked antiquity;
in France, from military associations; in Germany, from a love of
liberty. Capefigue [6] well says that the centralizing spirit of
France is shown by the way in which the French Academy interfered with language, attempting to destroy the provincial languages, or patois, as they are wrongly called. Napoleon revived
the mischievous example of Louis XIV. of patronising literature.
Saint-Aulaire, historian and ambassador. Lamartine, in 1848,
was placed at the head of affairs; Thiers, Cousin, Villemain.
Saint-Aulaire [7] says that offices were greatly increased under the
French kings, because it was profitable to sell them. He adds
that under Henry IV. Chancellor Paulet made them hereditary:
and in the time of Louis XIII. there were 40,000 of them.
Hallam [8] gives an instance of the ignorance of French writers

[1] Démocratie en Amérique, tome v. p. 207.
[2] Ibid. pp. 218, 225, 227, 228, 230, 241.
[3] Civil Wars in France, vol. i. p. 261.
[4] See Histoire des Français des divers États, tome viii. pp. 339-342.
[5] Histoire des Girondins, tome i. p. 181.
[6] Richelieu, Mazarin, et la Fronde, tome ii. p. 240.
[7] Histoire de la Fronde, tome i. p. 12.
[8] Constitutional Hist. of England, vol. i. p. 127.

respecting English materials for their own history. Lacretelle gives accounts of literature and philosophy and of political economy; the last very superficially. His account of art and manners is miserable.[1]

---

## GREECE.

*Foreign influence.*—THERE is no proof of " very early settlements in continental Greece from Phœnicia and Egypt."[2]

The Grecian scales for weight and money are derived from " the Chaldæan priesthood of Babylon."[3] The Greeks *certainly* derived their alphabet from the Phœnicians, and their " musical scale from the Lydians and Phrygians "; likewise their " statical system " from Assyrians.[4]

Bunsen[5] says, " Whether Plato ever was in Egypt is doubtful." In Asia, experience showed that animal food was unwholesome ; hence metempsychosis into animals. In Europe, the same doctrine, but confined to the human body. Diodorus Siculus[6] merely says the Gauls believed that " men's souls are immortal, and that there is a transmigration of them into other bodies." The Greeks arrested by that vulgar superstition which only physical knowledge can destroy. On physical geography of Greece see Journal of Geographical Society, vii. 61–74, and 81–94.

*Man.*—" The Hesiodic theogony gives no account of anything like a creation of man, nor does it seem that such an idea was much entertained in the legendary verse of Greek imagination ; which commonly carries back the present men by successive generations to some primitive ancestor, himself sprung from the soil."[7] And (at p. 598) " the intimate companionship and the occasional mistake of identity between gods and men were in full harmony with their reverential retrospect." At first the Greek artists did not presume to represent the gods as *beautiful* ; and " it was in statues of men that genuine ideas of beauty were first aimed at, and in part attained, from whence they passed afterwards to the statues of the gods." This was in B.C. 568–548.[8] The first " architectural monuments " are B.C. 600–550.[9] The

---

[1] Lacretelle, Histoire de France pendant le dixhuitième Siècle, tome ii. pp. 1, 90, 126, 286, 287, 308, 329 ; tome iii. pp. 224, 238.

[2] Grote, Hist. of Greece, vol. ii. p. 354.     [3] Ibid. vol. ii. p. 425.

[4] Ibid. vol. iii. pp. 285, 453, 454, 455 ; vol. iv. 102.

[5] Egypt, vol. i. p. 60.     [6] Book V. cap. ii. Booth, vol. i. p. 314.

[7] Grote, Hist. of Greece, vol. i. p. 88.

[8] Ibid. vol. iv. pp. 133, 134, and vol. vi. p. 29.     [9] Ibid. vol. iv. p. 134.

Argonautic expedition is a legend ; and " one of the most celebrated and widely-diffused among the ancient tales of Greece." [1]
The siege of Troy is fabulous, and there is no evidence that there
ever was a Trojan war.[2] These idle stories constituted for a time
their entire knowledge. " These myths, or current stories, the
spontaneous and earliest growth of the Greek mind, constituted
at the same time the entire intellectual stock of the age to which
they belonged." [3] The Greeks, like all barbarians, were at first
eminently and exclusively theological ; till their religion took a
*limited* form in consequence of the *curtailed* and *abridged*
physical associations. In Greece the gods were exaggerated
heroes ; in Asia, the heroes were curtailed gods. There were no
revolting miracles. Volcanoes and earthquakes rare in Greece (?).
The "return of the Herakleids" is fabulous.[4] " The great
mythical hero Theseus." [5] They placed their gods on Olympus,
the highest mountain. " In no city of historical Greece did
there prevail either human sacrifices or deliberate mutilation,
such as cutting off the nose, ears, hands, feet, &c., or castration,
or selling of children into slavery." [6] Cadmus is fabulous.[7]
" The entire nakedness of the competition at Olympia was
adopted from the Spartan practice, seemingly in 14th Olympiad." [8]
Now arose a love of discussion and oratory hitherto unknown in
the world.[9] The Fates, or Mœræ, are usually represented as
superior to the gods; and when Crœsus, king of Lydia, blamed
the Delphian god for deceiving him, "the god condescending to
justify himself by the lips of the priestess, replied, ' Not even a
god can escape his destiny.'" [10] Now were seen the first democracies of which we have any account in history ; the beginning
of that power of the people which, in spite of innumerable vicissitudes, has, on the whole, steadily increased in *Europe alone,*
and must eventually carry all before it. For the first time the
legislative and executive powers were separated, and by the
division of labour both were improved.[11] No human sacrifices.[12]
In Grecian religion none of the ferocity of Asia and America ;
but the gods are mild and even jocular. The Greek love of *man*

---

[1] Grote, Hist. of Greece, vol. i. p. 332.

[2] Ibid. vol. i. pp. 386, 435; vol. ii. p. 179.         [3] Ibid. vol. i. p. 460.

[4] Ibid. vol. ii. pp. 179, 404.         [5] Ibid. p. 29.

[6] Ibid. pp. 337, 338, and on eunuchs, see vol. i. p. 21.

[7] Ibid. vol. ii. p. 353.

[8] Ibid. pp. 338, 445; vol. ix. p. 368.         [9] Ibid. vol. xi. p. 373.

[10] Ibid. vol. iv. pp. 259, 262, 263. And so in Homer, see Mure's Greek Literature,
vol. i. p. 472.

[11] Grote, vol. iii. p. 23, and vol. v. pp. 477, 478, 497.

[12] Ibid. vol. vi. p. 218. But see Mure's Hist. of Greek Literature, vol. iii. p. 283.
and Prescott's Conquest of Mexico, vol. i. p. 66.

appears from the fact that even the best of them only studied
anatomy, physiology, and medicine; but no botany nor chemistry,
mineralogy, nor geology. In Asia, the forces of nature were too
disproportioned to the forces of man. No public oratory before
Greece. It was not till the Greek mind reacted on Asia that the
notion of divine incarnation in the form of man was able to arise,
and what shows the true origin is that Christianity, founded on
this notion, made all its great conquests in Europe, but in Asia
has always been an exotic. The Greeks had smaller temples,
partly from a contracted religion, and partly from a smaller
command of labour. Grote says,[1] "The fifth century B.C. is the
first century of democracy at Athens, in Sicily, and elsewhere."
Greece is the first country where we find historians. The
Athenians never tortured to death enemies or malefactors, but
killed the latter *painlessly* by a cup of hemlock.[2] Nor would
they mutilate the bodies of the slain in battle.[3] At Athens the
theatre held 30,000 persons, and at first everyone had to pay for
admission; but Pericles arranged that the poor should enter free.[4]
On slavery, see Grote, iv. p. 9; and vii. p. 542. Greeks "knew
no distinction of caste."[5] Homer does not mention a future state
of happiness, but only of punishment.[6] Mure[7] strangely denies
that Hesiod really believed in the existence of Pandora and Pro-
metheus. Venus fell in love with "the young Dardanian prince
Anchises,"[8] and the fruit of this intrigue was Æneas.[9]

"In so far as the face of the interior country was concerned,
it seemed as if nature had been disposed from the beginning to
keep the population of Greece socially and politically disunited"[10]
—i.e. by mountains and want of navigable rivers. Grote[11] says
that in Greece, as in Switzerland, mountain barriers made
conquest more difficult, not only from foreigners, but among
themselves; hence, "it also kept them politically disunited, and
perpetuated their separate autonomy," and "the indefinite
multiplication of self-governing towns appears more marked
among the Greeks than elsewhere; and there cannot be any
doubt that they owe it in a considerable degree to the multitude
of insulating boundaries which the configuration of their country
presented."[12] This breaking up into states is common to the
Germans, and is one of the causes of their intellectual superiority.

[1] Hist. of Greece, vol. viii. p. 462.          [2] Ibid. vol. ix. pp. 13, 14.
[3] Ibid. vol. x. p. 563.                         [4] Ibid. vol. viii. pp. 438, 439, 441.
[5] Mure, Hist. of Greek Literature, vol. i. p. 70.
[6] Ibid. vol. i. p. 496.                         [7] Ibid. vol. ii. p. 387.
[8] Ibid. p. 345.                                 [9] Ibid. vol. iv. p. 137.
[10] Grote's Hist. of Greece, vol. ii. p. 291.    [11] Ibid. pp. 298, 299.
[12] Ibid. p. 299.

"From the mountains between Achaia and Arcadia numerous streams flow into the Corinthian Gulf, but few of them are perennial, and the whole length of coast is represented as harbourless."[1] "Political disunion—sovereign authority within the city walls thus formed a settled maxim in the Greek mind. The relation between one city and another was an international relation, not a relation subsisting between members of a common political aggregate."[2] At different times, Sparta, Athens, and Thebes vainly attempted centralization. The mountains were not so large as to excite fear. They were numerous enough to diminish fear by frequency, while Asiatic civilization has always sought the table-land *skirted* by mountains. The states of Greece pressed together from *within*, and hating each other from without, were, from a sense of danger, as much as from ignorance, forced to exaggerate the importance of their own city. Hence that patriotism which, like every other virtue when predominant, is a vice; and hence the meddlesome and protective character of their government, which was most shown in Sparta, where *nature* had more isolated the people than in Athens. Neither Bœotia nor Thessaly, the two most fertile parts of Greece, could reach civilization; they were too out of the way, and Lacedæmon was too removed from other coasts, but Athens was familiarized to risk by her greater proximity to Asia Minor, and above all by the easy access of Eubœa. Grote[3] says the danger of the Persian invasion gave rise to the first *union* of Greece; but this was only a *political* union. The difficulty of communication kept the states separate, and therefore Greece independent. Custine[4] says of the Russians, "La tranquillité se maintient chez ce peuple par la lenteur et la difficulté des communications." Mure[5] says the independence of the different states "was fostered by the natural features of the country, which marked out the boundaries of the separate principalities, and interposed barriers against mutual encroachment." Hence too the Greeks, unlike every other people, not only preserved their national dialects, but so cherished them as to cultivate them for literary purposes.[6] Hence, also, until "the Alexandrian period," they had "no common national era for the computation of time."[7]

[1] Grote's Hist. of Greece, vol. ii. p. 615.
[2] Ibid. p. 340. See also vol. iv. p. 68; vol. vi. pp. 43, 312; vol. vii. p. 397; vol. ix. p. 279; vol. x. pp. 14, 71, 75; vol. xi. p. 286.
[3] Ibid. vol. iv. pp. 428, 429, and vol. v. pp. 78, 79.
[4] La Russie, vol. iv. p. 214.
[5] Hist. of Greek Literature, vol. i. p. 102.
[6] Ibid. pp. 117, 118; vol. iv. p. 113.
[7] Ibid. vol. iv. pp. 74, 75.

*Women.*—Castration and polygamy unknown.[1]  The Spartan law forbad early marriages.[2]  "Plutarch (Agis, c. 4) dwells especially upon the increasing tendency to accumulate property in the hands of the women" (of Sparta); and "Aristotle (Politik, ii. 6, 6) mentions 'a peculiar sympathy and yielding disposition towards women in the Spartan mind.'"[3]  In the mythical times of Greece women seem to have had more influence than afterwards : though even then a man bought his wife by making presents to her parents.[4]  Both then and in "historical Greece" female slaves were worse treated than male ones.[5]  However, even in the time of Homer, "Polygamy appears to be ascribed to Priam but to no one else, Iliad, xxi. 88."[6]  Aristotle says that at Spar  "it was the practice to give a large dowry when a rich man's daughter married."[7]  This assertion is contradicted by Plutarch, Ælian, and Justin : but, as Grote says,[8] Aristotle's authority is superior. In Athens, in the time of Solon, a dowry was given with wives.[9]  "Elpinike, the sister of Kimon," in the time of Pericles, "seems to have played an active part in the political intrigues of the day."[10]

Aspasia, mistress of the great Pericles, was a highly accomplished woman of the class called "Heteræ, or courtezans ;" her conversation secured her the visits of Socrates.[11]  Grote says,[12] that at Athens "the free citizen women lived in strict, and almost oriental recluseness, as well after being married as when single. Everything which concerned their lives, their happiness, or their rights, was determined or managed for them by male relatives : and they seem to have been destitute of all mental culture and accomplishments."[13]  Alcibiades received with his wife "a large dowry of ten talents."[14]  Cyrus, in the time of the "Retreat of the Ten Thousand," had with him as mistress an accomplished Phokæan lady named Milto.[15]

Xenophon[16] mentions that in the time of Agesilaus, King of Sparta, a woman of great influence lived at Anton ("a Laconian town on the frontier towards Arcadia and Triphylia"), who "spread disaffection among all the Lacedemonians who came thither, old as well as young."[17]  In Sparta women had more influence than anywhere else.[18]

[1] Grote's History of Greece, vol. ii. p. 338.          [2] Ibid. p. 510.
[3] Ibid. p. 513, also pp. 507, 508.          [4] Ibid. p. 112.
[5] Ibid. pp. 132, 133.          [6] Ibid. p. 113.
[7] Ibid. pp. 525, 540.          [8] Ibid. p. 545.
[9] Ibid. vol. iii. p. 180.          [10] Ibid. vol. v. p. 501.
[11] Ibid. vol. vi. pp. 133, 134 ; vol. viii. p. 449.          [12] Ibid. vol. vi. p. 133.
[13] See also Mure's Hist. of Greek Literature, vol. iv. p. 43, and vol. iii. p. 300.
[14] Grote, vol. vii. p. 44.          [15] Ibid. vol. ix. p. 63.
[16] Xenophon, Hellen. iii. 3, 8.          [17] Grote's Hist. of Greece, vol. ix. p. 349.
[18] Mure's Hist. of Greek Literature, vol. iii. p. 76.

Sappho flourished B.C. 600, and a little later; and "so highly did Plato value her intellectual, as well as her imaginative endowments, that he assigned her the honours of sage as well as poet; and familiarly entitled her the tenth muse."[1] "There can be no better evidence of her surpassing fame and popularity than the fact of her having figured as a favourite heroine of the comic drama of Athens, to a greater extent, it would appear, than any other histor al personage upon record. Mention occurs of not less than six comedies under the name of Sappho; and her history, rea' or imaginary, furnished materials to nearly as many. more."[2] ( 'e was a native of Lesbos, a large island in the Ægean, south of roas and west of Pergamos). Cleobulus flourished B.C. 586, a id his daughter Eumetes, surnamed Cleobuline, was celebrated 'for poetical talent, especially in the composition of metrical enigmas. The composition of such epigrammatic riddles appears to have been from an early period a favourite occupation of the Greek literary ladies," and this practice is ridiculed by several "Attic dramatists."[3]

For the first (?) time women play a great part in religion. Diana for chastity, Minerva for accomplishments. Sir W. Jones in his Commentary on Isæus, says, that among the Athenians about the time of the Peloponnesian war, dowries were so general that "a suspicion of illegitimacy was cast upon girls who were married with a small fortune in proportion to the estate of their fathers."[4] Diodorus Siculus[5] notices how the Pythian oracle was always delivered by women. In Smith's Dictionary of Mythology[6] it is said of Plato's lectures at Athens, "Even women are said to have attached themselves to him as his disciples."[7] When Greek women married, their fathers gave presents *with* them.[8] Plato in his Republic,[9] lays it down that women are to be well educated and take a share in the functions of the state; and this he repeats in Timæus,[10] and also in the Laws.[11] In the Laws[12] a man is ordered to bequeath some of his property to his daughters. At book xi. chap. xiv. p. 496, "Let a free woman be allowed to bear witness, and appear as counsel if she is more than forty years of age, and obtain by lot a trial, if she is unmarried; but, if her husband is living, let her be allowed to be a witness only." In book ix.

[1] Mure's Hist. of Greek Literature, vol. iii. p. 273.
[2] Ibid. p. 275.    [3] Ibid. 391.    [4] Jones's Works, vol. iv. pp. 204, 205
[5] Book XVI. chap. vi. vol. ii. p. 101. By Booth.    [6] Vol. iii. p. 394.
[7] Diog. Laert. lib. c. Comp. Olympiod.
[8] Herodotus, Book VI. chap. cxxii. p. 399.
[9] Book V. chap. v, vi. Works, vol. ii. pp. 139, 140.    [10] Chap. ii. vol. p. 320.
[11] Book VII. chap. xi. vol. v. pp. 277, 249.
[12] Book XI. chap. vii. vol. v. p. 474.

chap. ix. p. 379, the same penalty is inflicted if a wife kills her
husband or if the husband kills his wife ; and, in reference to slaves
it is said,[1] the laws are to be the same for men as for women.   In
the Republic [2] women are to marry at twenty, men at thirty; but
in the Laws [3] "the marriageable age of a female" is fixed at from
sixteen to twenty; and at p. 148,[4] men are to marry from thirty
to thirty-five.   See a eulogy of Aspasia in Menexemus;[5] and (at
p. 551) Burgess says in a note, "amongst the ancients not a few
women, such as Aspasia and Diotima, and others, were given to
philosophy; a list of whom has been collected by Menage, and
appended to his notes on Diogenes Laertius."

   *Progress.*—Like other barbarians, they were at first purely
theological.   "Anaxagoras and other astronomers incurred the
charge of blasphemy for dispersonifying Helios and trying to
assign invariable laws to the solar phenomena. . . . Physical
astronomy was both new and accounted impious in the time of
the Peloponnesian war."[6]  See also p. 498, where Grote quotes
Xenophon to the effect that in the opinion of Socrates, "Physics
and astronomy belonged to the divine class of phenomena in which
human research was insane, fruitless, and impious."  "Men whose
minds were full of the heroes of Homer called Hesiod, in
contempt, the poet of the Helots.   The contrast between the two
is certainly a remarkable proof of the tendency of Greek poetry
towards the present and the positive."[7]  Xenophanes, Thales, and
Pythagoras, were the three "who in the sixth century before the
Christian æra, first opened up those veins of speculative philosophy which occupied afterwards so large a portion of Greek
intellectual energy."[8]   They first threw off the theological supremacy.[9]  This went on until Socrates, "who laid open all ethical
and social doctrines to the scrutiny of reason.[10]  "The Milesian
Thales," B.C. 640, 550, was "the first man to depart both in letter
and spirit from the Hesiodic Theogony;" and he founded the
"Ionic philosophy, which is considered as lasting from his time
down to that of Socrates."[11]   He introduced the "scientific study
of nature."[12]

   Hippo came next.[13]   Contemporary with Thales Anaximander

---

[1] Book IX. chap. xvii. p. 403.
[2] Book V. chap. ix.   Plato's Works, vol. ii. p. 145.
[3] Book VI. chap. xxiii. vol. v. pp. 248, 249.
[4] Plato's Works, vol. v. p. 148, and see p. 126.          [5] Ibid. vol. iv. p. 186.
[6] Grote's Hist. of Greece, vol. i. pp. 466, 467.
[7] Ibid. vol. i. p. 487, and vol. iv. p. 101.          [8] Ibid. vol. i. p. 493.
[9] Ibid. vol. ii. p. 155; vol. iv. pp. 129, 521, 525; vol. viii. p. 468.
[10] Ibid. vol. iv. p. 129; vol. viii. pp. 466, 467, 573, 577.
[11] Ibid. vol. iv. p. 511.          [12] Ibid. p. 516.          [13] Ibid. p. 517.

tended to same direction.[1] In the eighth and seventh centuries, B.C., music and poetry conjoined were the only intellectual manifestation known among the Greeks.[2] "The interval between 776–560, is a remarkable expansion of Grecian genius in the creation of their elegiac, iambic, lyric, choric, and gnomic poetry."[3] "The poetry of Alkæus is the more worthy of note as it is the earliest instance of the employment of the muse in actual political warfare, and shows the increased hold which that motive was acquiring on the Grecian mind."[4] Grote says,[5] "Æschylus and Sophocles exhibit the same spontaneous and un-inquiring faith as Pindar in the legendary antiquities of Greece taken as a whole; but they allow themselves greater license as to the details." Æschylus takes the old mythical views of which Euripides was accused of vulgarising, and *between* the two is Sophocles, in whom "we find indications that a more predomi-nant sense of artistic perfection is allowed to modify the harsher religious agencies of the old epic." This is well noted in Schle-gel's Dramatic Literature.[6] The great dramatic development took place just after the expulsion of Xeres. Sophocles and Euripides were the followers of Æschylus, who himself was "the creator of the tragic drama, or at least the first who rendered it illustrious. . . . Sophocles gained his first victory over Æschylus in 468, B.C.: the first exhibition of Euripides was in 455, B.C."[7] Grote[8] says Æschylus is *altogether* ideal. "In Sophocles there is a closer approach to reality and common life, . . . but when we advance to Euripides the ultra-natural sublimity of the legendary characters disappears; love and compassion are invoked to a degree which Æschylus would have deemed inconsistent with the dignity of the heroic person." Aristophanes (whose "earliest comedy" was exhibited B.C. 427)[9] was a still greater lover of *common*, and even vulgar life. Even Socrates took superstitious views, and opposed physical study as impious.[10] Solon, who flourished B.C. 594, put forward his views in "easy metre," for "there was at that time no Greek prose writing."[11] Herodotus, though "a thoroughly pious man," takes a more profane view than Homer, Hesiod, or even Solon."[12] In Thucydides we see views even more *mundane* than in Herodotus, for he treats the mythical heroes as mere men, whose acts he freely criticises by a human

---

[1] Grote's Hist. of Greece, vol. iv. p. 520.
[2] Ibid. vol. iv. p. 99.
[3] Ibid. pp. 518, 519.
[4] Ibid. p. 442.
[10] Ibid. pp. 577, 578, 673.
[12] Ibid. vol. i. pp. 535, 539.

[3] Ibid. vol. iii. p. 285.
[4] Ibid. p. 122.
[5] Ibid. vol. i. p. 510.
[7] Ibid. vol. viii. pp. 434, 437.
[9] Ibid. p. 451.
[11] Ibid. vol. iii. p. 119.

standard.[1]  Grote[2] compares with Herodotus "the more positive
and practical genius of Thucydides." Before Herodotus men
were too absorbed in the wonderful and religious to think it
worth their while to record the history of human actions. Greece
was the first country that ever produced historians; and this was
an immense step, though their merit has been overrated and their
credulity was childish. Mure[3] says that before B.C. 560, "poetry
continued to be the only cultivated branch of composition."
Mure[4] well says that lyric poetry is more "subjective" or "practical" than epic. No epic poet selects his subject from present
events, but always refers to the mysterious past. On the other
hand lyric poets take *common* subjects, and always allude to
themselves. In Hesiod as compared to Homer, we first find a
lyric tendency.[5] Lyric poetry was chiefly encouraged by Sparta,
the only state whose armies were "always regulated by musical
performances," but the Spartans were not *themselves* "distinguished either as poets or musicians."[6] The first lyric poets are
Callinus of Ephesus, and Archilochus.[7] "In Homer the man is
completely absorbed in the poet; in Archilochus the poet exists
but in the man."[8] Contemporary with Archilochus is Simonides
of Amorgos.[9] Alcman, "the last of the more illustrious masters
of the Spartan school of lyric poetry" flourished B.C. 670, 611.[10]
Sappho,[11] B.C. 550, 500. Solon connects "the poetical and intellectual age of Greece," and is "the first extant author of Attic
prose composition." He was a poet; but, "as a general rule the
poet is absorbed in the philosopher and statesman."[12] In B.C. 535,
i.e. twenty years after his death, "dramatic entertainments were
first introduced into Athens."[13] The Seven Sages, "all more
celebrated as philosophers or statesmen than as poets."[14] *No
people have been so little influenced by others: therefore we can
in them best learn the normal march of the mind. In Greece for
the first time we find something like history; and I will trace
the steps through which the national intellect passed before
reaching history.*

The oldest religious sanctuary was "in the north, established,
as usual, in the early ages of paganism, on the loftiest mountain
ridge of the district preferred. This sanctuary was the oracle of
the Great Dodonæan Jove in the rugged highlands of Thes-

[1] Grote's Hist. of Greece, vol. i. pp. 540, 541.          [2] Ibid. vol. vi. p. 415.
[3] Hist. of Greek Literature, vol. i. p. 6. See also p. 168.
[4] Ibid. vol. iii. pp. 3, 5.          [5] Ibid. pp. 5, 231.          [6] Ibid. pp. 46, 49.
[7] Ibid. pp. 131, 134.          [8] Ibid. p. 156.          [9] Ibid. pp. 173, 174.
[10] Ibid. p. 198.          [11] Ibid. p. 275.          [12] Ibid. pp. 344, 345, 362.
[13] Ibid. p. 359.          [14] Ibid. p. 377.

protia."¹ Doric was "the favourite language of the higher
branches of lyric composition, and of the primitive schools of
philosophy, . . . while the new Ionic and Attic were preferred in
elegy, satire, the drama, and more popular departments of prose;"
and Herodotus, though "a native of the Dorian Halicarnassus,
prefers the Ionic for the composition of his history;" because the
Attic was not yet popular; though a little later its employment
by Thucydides gained for it "an almost universal preference in
every branch of prose composition."²

The Attic dialect now continued to progress, and by the encouragement of Philip of Macedon, became "the classical dialect
of the whole Hellenic world."³ "The old poetic Ionic or
Homeric" soon fell into disuse; but "the later Ionic is the
source whence the classical Attic of Thucydides and Plato derived its origin."⁴ Mure says,⁵ "With the exception of a few
obscure Italiote or Sicilian writers, who adhered to their native
Doric, the historians and philosophers of every district of Greece
seem to have written in Ionic prior to the ascendancy of the
Attic dialect in the latter part of the fifth century, B.C." The
fashion set by the Ionian Hecataeus was followed by the Æolian
Hellanicus, and the Dorian Herodotus."⁶ In the Penny Cyclopædia it is said of the Dorians, "Their first settlement was in
Phthiotis in the time of Deucalion; the next under Dorrus
in Hestiæotis, at the foot of Ossa and Olympus; the third on
Mount Pindus, after they had been expelled by the Cadmeans
from Hestiæotis . . . . the migration of the Dorians to the
Peloponnese, which is generally called the Return of the Descendants of Hercules, is expressly stated to have occurred eighty
years after the Trojan War, i.e. in 1104 B.C. (Thucyd. i. 12)."
Their religion rose in the most distant part of Greece and on the
highest mountains. Heyne says that "Homer always calls the
Muses Olympian, and that the Homeric gods are the Olympian
and no others."⁷ "A careful survey of the passages in Homer and
Hesiod, in which Olympos occurs, will lead us to believe that the
Achæans held the Thessalian Olympos, the highest mountain
with which they were acquainted, to be the abode of their gods."⁸
"The Greeks of the early ages regarded the lofty Thessalian
mountain named Olympos as the dwelling of their gods."⁹ As
civilization descended south it became still more *human*, and
reached its highest point in the *east*, where Athens was *accessible*

---

¹ Mure's Hist. of Greek Literature, vol. i. p. 38.
² Ibid. pp. 125, 126.
³ Ibid. p. 114.
⁷ Keightley, p. 17.     ⁵ Ibid. p. 38.
² Ibid. pp. 121, 122.
⁴ Ibid. vol. iv. pp. 112, 117.
⁶ Ibid. p. 523, et seq.
⁹ Ibid. p. 72.

and nature feeble. Keightley[1] says of Homer, "The practice of assigning birthplaces on earth to the gods does not seem to have prevailed in his age." "Pieria, in Macedonia, is said by Hesiod (Theog. 53) to have been the birthplace of the Muses; and everything relating to them proves the antiquity of the tradition of the worship and knowledge of these goddesses having come from the north into Hellas.[2] Almost all the mountains, grots, and springs from which they have derived their appellations, or which were sacred to them are, we may observe, in Macedonia, Thessaly, or Bœotia. Such are the mountains Pimplæ, Pindos, Parnassos, Helicon, the founts Hippocrene, Aganippe, Leibethron, Castalia, and the Corycian cave."[3]

Writing was known in Greece from the ninth or tenth century B.C., but "the first successful essay in popular prose literature cannot be traced beyond the sixth century B.C."[4] Herodotus first infused life and method into history,[5] but the "first Greek historian of real events was Charon of Lampsacus, B.C. 500–450."[6] Also Acusilaus and Pherecydes.[7] But the first *proper* historian is Scylax.[8] Hecatæus (B.C. 520, 479) is the only one Herodotus quotes;[9] of Homer and Herodotus Mure says,[10] "The one is the perfection of epic poetry, the other the perfection of epic prose." At pp. 352, 389 [vol. iv.], Mure has collected ample evidence of that miserable credulity of Herodotus which some writers affect to deny. He had in truth too much of the poet. He lived to late into the fifth—perhaps into the fourth century.[11] He was born at Halicarnassus in Caria.[12]

*Sea.*—"Of the Euxine sea no knowledge is manifested in Homer. . . . The strong sense of the danger of the sea expressed by the poet Hesiod."[13] However, says Grote (vol. ii. p. 152), "The extension of Grecian traffic and shipping is manifested by a comparison of the Homeric and Hesiodic poems: in respect to knowledge of places and countries—the latter being probably referable to dates between B.C. 740 and B.C. 640."

The Greek coast is full of indentations—a fact well pointed out by Strabo (ii. 293); and "Cicero notices emphatically both the general maritime accessibility of Grecian towns, and the effect of that circumstance on Grecian character;"[14] and other ancients

---

[1] Keightley, p. 159.

[2] Buttmann, Mytholog. vol. i. p. 293; Voss, Myth. Book IV. chap. iii.; Müller, Orchom. p. 381; Proleg. p. 219.

[3] Keightley, p. 159.      [4] Mure's Hist. of Greek Literature, vol. iv. p. 51.

[5] Ibid. p. 74.      [6] Ibid. pp. 72. 164, 168.      [7] Ibid. pp. 133, 134.

[8] Ibid. p. 139.      [9] Ibid. pp. 140, 141.      [10] Ibid. p. 242.

[11] Ibid. p. 245.      [12] Ibid. pp. 248, 249.

[13] Grote's Hist. of Greece, vol. ii. pp. 136, 137.      [14] Ibid. p. 295.

observe that maritime habits enlivened the imagination, and gave a greater tolerance of feeling towards strange customs and readiness to receive them ;[1] hence Lacedemonian stability and Athenian versatility.[2] Euboea " is separated from Boeotia at one point by a strait so narrow that the two were connected by a bridge."[3] Solon, B.C. 594, was the first great reformer ;[4] and he, in his business as a merchant, had " visited many parts of Greece and Asia."[5] " It is rare to find a genuine Greek colony established at any distance from the sea."[6] Greek ships always kept in sight of the coast.[7] Themistocles changed Athens " from a land power into a sea power."[8] Athens, the only maritime power, was the most intellectual ; and her intellectual splendour accompanied or directly succeeded her conversion into a sea power.

In the Peloponnesian War, Thucydides " reckons the sea as a portion of the Athenian territory ; and even the portion of sea near to Peloponnesus—much more that on the coast of Ionia."[9]

Aegean and Adriatic seas both *narrow*, hence encouraged men to navigate, for in those barbarous ages they dared not lose sight of the coast. And, though sailors are more superstitious than mechanics, or even than soldiers, still they are less so than shepherds : besides, new ideas were brought in, and the friction of minds. Thucydides[10] says, " The whole Laconian coast is a high projecting cliff, where it fronts the Sicilian and Cretan seas," and was so generally inaccessible that " the only portion of the coast of Laconia where a maritime invader could do much damage, was in the interior of the Laconic Gulf, near Helos, Gythium, &c., which is, in fact, the only plain portion of the coast of Laconia."[11] Grote[12] says, in the fourth century, B.C., " Sparta had no seamen except constrained Helots or paid foreigners (Xen. Hellen. vii. i. 13, 12)." Among the Egyptians " sea voyages were looked upon as sacrilegious."[13] Mure[14] says that the Athenians represented the " *intellect* of Greece, but wanted imagination " : and from Homer to B.C. 560, when we find " in every other part of Greece brilliant displays of imaginative genius, Attica cannot boast of a single genuine development of native poetical talent."[15] This was owing to " the ascendant of the intellectual over the imaginative faculties in that particular modification of the Greek mind which fell to the lot of the Athenians."[16] So that their development had to

[1] Grote's Hist. of Greece, vol. ii. pp. 296, 297.    [2] Ibid. p. 297.
[3] Ibid. vol. iii. p. 217.    [4] Ibid. p. 118.    [5] Ibid. p. 119.
[6] Ibid. p. 238.    [7] Ibid. pp. 476, 477.    [8] Ibid. vol. v. pp. 70, 372.
[9] Ibid. vol. vi. p. 329.    [10] IV. 54.
[11] Grote's Hist. of Greece, vol. vi. pp. 500, 501.    [12] Ibid. vol. x. p. 57.
[13] Mure's Hist. of Greek Literature, vol. i. p. 71.    [14] Ibid. vol. iv. p. 6.
[15] Ibid. pp. 7, 8.    [16] Ibid. p. 9.

*wait* for an age of prose.[1]  I think Asia produced no great prose
writers.  This first happened in Greece—the first country that
possessed *historians*.  The first Greek prose is on geography,[2]
and the two first writers on geography were Anaximander and
Hecatæus, both natives of Miletus, " a city distinguished for the
zeal and extent of her colonial undertakings."  Anaximander invented maps; and Hecatæus, his "younger contemporary"(B.C. 520,
479) " is distinguished both as a geographer and historian, and is
the first Greek prose author who obtained popularity or celebrity
as a national classic."[3]  Hecatæus was a great traveller;[4] and,
Mure says,[5] " The earliest Greek author of a prose work deserving
the name of historical in the better sense, is the geographer
Scylax of Caryanda, a town of the Halicarnassian territory ; who
may also rank (521, 485) as one of the most adventurous of Greek
navigators."  Mure says,[6] " The Ægean sea, narrow, studded with
islands and abounding in excellent harbours."  For summary of
the travels of Herodotus, see Mure, vol. iv. pp. 246–248.  Diodorus Siculus[7] says, " It is no wonder to see a man marry, but to
see him twice marry.  For it is safer and more advisable for a
man to expose himself twice to the dangers of the seas than to
the hazards of a second wife."  In Gorgias, chap. 51, Socrates
takes for granted that no one could go on the sea for pleasure, but
only to make money.

---

## DECLINE OF GREECE AND DIVERGENCE OF HIGHER AND LOWER INTELLECTS.

AIDED by circumstances, [as] I shall trace in another work, the
Greek thinkers soon outstripped the observers; and when the
divergence between people and philosophers had reached a certain
point, Greece fell.  The people sunk in brutal habits, tyrannical
to their slaves, hard masters and bad subjects.  Maritime nations,
by a law I shall presently indicate, are naturally superstitious.
Thucydides[9] mentions " how erroneously and carelessly the Athenian public of his day retained the history of Peisistratus, only
one century past."[10]  Observe popularity of Aristophanes and his
antagonism to Socrates.  The Greeks loved the theatre.[11]  In the

---

[1] Mure's Hist. of Greek Literature, vol. iv. p. 47.          [2] Ibid. p. 68.
[3] Ibid. p. 69.          [4] Ibid. p. 141.          [5] Ibid. p. 139.
[6] Ibid. p. 405.          [7] Book XII. chap. iii. vol. i. p. 442.  By Booth.
[8] Plato's Works, vol. i. p. 160.          [9] VI. 56.
[10] Grote's Hist. of Greece, vol. i. p. 603.          [11] Ibid. p. 604.

time of Lucian even the dancers were expected to know the ancient myths;[1] and they passed into the "ordinary songs of women."[2] See also at vol. i. of Grote, History of Greece, pp. 606, 608, some curious evidence of the extent of the popular superstitions.

Indeed, until the Persian War, the only point of union between the cities were religious festivals and games; and even B.C. 350, at the zenith of Greece, we find "a sacred war" of ten years. Grote[3] says, "We shall see these two modes of anticipating the future—one based upon the philosophical, the other upon the religious appreciation of nature — running simultaneously on throughout Grecian history, and sharing between them in unequal portions the empire of the Greek mind: the former acquiring both greater predominance and wider application among the intellectual men, and partially restricting but never abolishing the spontaneous employment of the latter among the vulgar." The difference between esoteric and exoteric, unknown in time of Homer, first arose between 620 and 500 B.C.[4]

So late as Solon, B.C. 594, there was no prose, and the verses of Solon were "delivered in easy metres far less difficult than the elaborate prose of subsequent writers, as Thucydides, Isocrates, or Demosthenes."[5] Mr. Grote[6] says, without ostracism the Athenian constitution must have perished. This only proves how bad the constitution was. Greek patriotism checked individuality: hence, when the foreign element of Macedonia corrupted the state everything fell. Even in the invasion of Xerxes Sparta showed her selfishness, and, though the heroism of Leonidas defended Thermopylæ, she fortified the isthmus of Corinth to defend Peloponnesus. When Xerxes retreated the Spartans would not defend the Athenians against Mardonius.[7] The Greeks were only bound together by religion and language. When these were gone the union was gone, and each state quickly fell before the Romans. Only one generation after the Persian invasion they broke out into the Peloponnesian war. See a very good note in Grote, vol. v. pp. 355, 356. The Greeks *universally* believed in supernatural intervention.[8]

On the general question of the decline of Greece, see the following passages, *none* of which will be required for my first volume, or indeed for my first work : Grote's History of Greece,

---

[1] Grote's Hist. of Greece, vol. i. p. 604.    [2] Ibid. p. 605.
[3] Ibid. vol. ii. p. 156.    [4] Ibid. vol. iii. p. 112.    [5] Ibid. p. 119.
[6] Ibid. vol. iv. p. 200.    [7] Ibid. vol. v. p. 209.
[8] Ibid. vol. viii. pp. 562, 563 ; vol. ix. pp. 312, 496. See also my note on Vices and Superstitions of Greeks, and Grote, vol. vi. p. 400 ; vol. vii. pp. 65, 84.

vol. ii. p. 361 ; vol. viii. pp. 394, 512, 514, 515 ; vol. ix. pp. 323–326 ; vol. x. pp. 53, 99, 127, 191, 435, 526, 527 ; vol. xi. pp. 280, 282, 389, 390, 406, 407, 411, 521, 522, 591. On inferiority of Xenophon to Thucydides, see Grote, vol. viii. p. 155, 379. No printing, therefore no reading; hence knowledge being *unrecorded*, Greece fell at once. Wachsmuth takes every opportunity of attacking Greeks, Grote, viii. p. 412. Greeks no physical knowledge, Grote, vol. ix. pp. 21, 22. On the badness of Aristophanes as a witness, Grote, vol. vi. pp. 661, 662, and vol. viii. pp. 454, 457. Even Mure (Greek Literature, vol. iv. p. 395) admits that the best Greek historians only related *external* events, and cared nothing for the most important part of history, as, internal polity, laws, civil institutions, &c. The Greeks eventually paid too much attention to man and neglected the operations of nature.

*Food and Diffusion of Wealth.*—Even the Helots of Laconia were sometimes wealthy.[1] Grote[2] says of Greece generally, "though the aggregate population never seems to have increased very fast." A man unable to pay his debts became the slave of the creditor : a law which filled Greece with misery until Solon abrogated it.[3] Grote says,[4] "Greece produced wheat, barley, flax, wine, and oil in the earliest times of which we have any knowledge : in the age of Pausanias, and perhaps earlier, cotton also was grown in the territory of Elis ; but the currants, Indian corn, silk, and tobacco, are an addition of more recent times." In the time of Thucydides the Lacedemonian soldiers seem to have had a good allowance of barley, meat, and wine.[5] Athens, in her great distress, B.C. 413, " with the view of increasing her revenue, altered the principle on which her subject allies had hitherto been assessed. Instead of a fixed sum of annual tribute she now required from them payment of a duty of five per cent. on all imports and exports by sea.[6] In B.C. 407, Lysander, the Lacedemonian admiral, visited Cyrus at Sardis, and requested him " to restore the rate of pay to one full Attic drachma per head for the seamen ; which had been the rate promised by Tissaphernes through his envoys at Sparta, when he first invited the Lacedemonians across the Ægean ;" but this Cyrus deemed too exorbitant, and refused.[7] He, however, consented to raise their pay

[1] Grote's Hist. of Greece, vol. ii. p. 496.   [2] Ibid. vol. iv. p. 227.
[3] Ibid. vol. iii. pp. 126, 129, 132.   [4] Ibid. vol. ii. pp. 302, 303.
[5] Ibid. vol. vi. p. 445.
[6] Thucydid. vii. 28. Grote, vol. vii. p. 489, but at vol. viii. p. 180, Grote doubts if this was really carried into effect.
[7] Grote, vol. viii. pp. 191, 192.

from three to four oboli daily.[1] In a drachma there were three oboli.[2] Bœckh[3] says that in the time of Agesilaus, king of Sparta, an Athenian, named Euripides, proposed to raise five hundred talents by an assessed property tax on the Athenians of two and a half per cent. ; but this Grote entirely doubts.[4] About B.C. 379 the Lacedemonians made war on Olynthus, and made upon their own allies an assessment by which instead of one hoplite each city might furnish "three Æginean oboli, half an Æginean drachma. . . . A cavalry soldier being equivalent to four hoplites, and one hoplite to two peltasts."[5] In B.C. 352, 351, Demosthenes estimates the price of *maintenance* independent of pay to be for "each seaman and each foot soldier ten drachmæ per month, or two oboli per day; each horseman thirty drachmæ per month, or one drachma per day. No difference is made between the Athenian citizen and the foreigner."[6] In B.C. 378, 377, a great change was introduced in the mode of taxing Athens. According to the division made by Solon, there were four classes, of which the poorest paid no "direct taxes," while the three others paid a "graduated or progressive tax" on property. This, with some modification, continued till B.C. 378, when several alterations were made, but the same principle continued of taxing the wealthier classes relatively more than the poorer, i.e. making them pay a higher per centage.[7] Homer, with only two exceptions, confines the "animal diet of the Greeks to the flesh of domestic quadrupeds, oxen, sheep, goats, hogs," and never alludes to their eating game, poultry, or fish.[8] Sir W. Jones[9] says that about the time of the Peloponnesian War "the disadvantages and odium which attended an excess of riches were considerably greater at Athens than the benefits or pleasures arising from affluence." Jones's *comprehensive* knowledge made him a good judge of the evidence supplied by laws. The Greeks were acquainted with butter, but never ate it; nor does Aristotle even allude to it, though they *did* eat cheese.[10] In the Republic,[11] "Even from Homer one may learn such things as these; for you know that in their military expeditions, at their heroes' banquets, he never feasts them with fish, not even while they were by the

---

[1] Grote's Hist. of Greece, vol. viii. p. 193.  [2] Ibid. p. 192.
[3] Bœckh, Public Economy of Athens, vol. iv. p. 493.
[4] Grote's Hist. of Greece, vol. ix. pp. 528, 530, note.
[5] Ibid. vol. x. p. 77.  [6] Ibid. vol. ix. p. 436.
[7] Ibid. vol. x. pp. 153, 154, 155, 156, 161.
[8] Mure's Hist. of Greek Literature, vol. iii. p. 486.
[9] Jones's Works, vol. iv. p. 234.
[10] Thomson's Animal Chemistry, p. 425.
[11] Republic, Book III. chap. xiii.  Plato's Works, vol. ii. p. 86.

sea at the Hellespont, nor yet with boiled flesh, but only with roast meat, or what soldiers can most easily procure." In the Laws, an interest is mentioned of sixteen and a half per cent. monthly, but this seems intended as a punishment.[1]

*Method.*—The physical conformation of Greece secured the independence of different states; but the *feebleness* of nature likewise secured for the first time a filling consciousness of human power *individually.* Food and climate *tended* to humanise the Greek religion by enabling the people for the first time in the history of the world to be *civilized* without being subjected by their rulers (for before this time only hunters and pastoral tribes had been free). Egypt pent between the impassable deserts of Africa and Arabia.

*Human.*—The religion of Greece, as it is recorded by their oldest theologians, Homer and Hesiod, stands in the strongest contrast with that of India. They do not *begin* with gods. According to Hesiod, first comes Chaos or Space, who produces Night; and this last Day. The Earth produces Heaven.[2] The celestial phenomena themselves, as thunder and lightning, are only the children of Heaven and and Earth.[3] Kronos is the offspring of the Earth and Heaven, or Uranos.[4] The offspring of Kronos is Zeus or Jupiter;[5] and now begin the Olympian gods.[6] In Homer Juno or Hera is wife or sister of Jupiter.[7] Vulcan or Hephæstos " is in Homer the son of Zeus and Hera.[8] Apollo is the son of Zeus and Leto.[9] Diana or Artemis "the daughter of Zeus and Leto."[10] Venus or Aphrodite "the daughter of Zeus and Dione."[11] Hermes or Mercury "is in one place of the Iliad called the son of Zeus."[12] There were few gloomy and impassable forests to terrify the mind into superstition ; nor earthquakes which, when they did happen, were regarded by the Greeks as omens.

Gods were exaggerated heroes, and their heroes were exaggerated men. Hercules, Theseus, Jason, Minos, Ulysses, Agamemnon, Perseus, Cecrops. Medea, even in her incantations, used human means, the fatal kettle and the poisoned robe ; the cup of Circe ; the thread and scissors of the Fates. The siege of Troy (we might as well believe Jack the Giant-killer); the labours of Hercules ; the Argonautic expedition ; Jason's search for the fleece ; the wanderings of Ulysses ; the travels of Æneas ; the

[1] Laws, Book XI. chap. v. Plato's Works, vol. v. p. 470.
[2] Keightley's Mythology of Greece and Italy, 1838, 8vo, pp. 43, 45.
[3] Ibid. pp. 45, 78. [4] Ibid. p. 43. [5] Ibid. p. 44. [6] Ibid. p. 68.
[7] Ibid. p. 96. [8] Ibid. p. 107. [9] Ibid. p. 113. [10] Ibid. p. 128.
[11] Ibid. p. 139. [12] Ibid. p. 159.

feats of Agamemnon. Gods and goddesses in love with mortals;
the loves of Venus and Anchises,[1] Cupid and Psyche,[2] intrigue
of Mercury with the daughter of Cecrops.[3] Apollo was a keeper
of oxen.[4] The box of Pandora (commonly called a box, though
more properly a jar).[5] Keightley says,[6] the gods "are susceptible of injury by mortal weapons; the arrows of Hercules
violate the divine bodies of Hera and Hades.[7] Diomedes wounds
both Aphrodite and Ares.[8] They require nourishment as men
do; their food is called Ambrosia, their drink Nectar. It is not
blood, but a blood-like fluid named *ichor*, which flows in their
veins."[9] "They mourned for the death of Adonis; and, on this
account Lobeck[10] inquires whether the ancient nations, who esteemed their gods to be so little superior to men, may not have
believed them to have been really, and not metaphorically put to
death; and, in truth, it is not easy to give a satisfactory answer
to these questions."[11]

The Greeks worshipped Fortune.[12] Hippocrates was the first
who separated medicine from those vague speculations called philosophy. Comparative anatomy now first studied. Broussais[13]
says of Aristotle, "Il est aussi le fondateur de l'anatomie comparée." Such is *now* the sense of the importance of *man*. For
an account of what Aristotle did for medicine see Rénouard,
Histoire de la Medicine, i. pp. 239-258. Rénouard[14] says, "Il
crée l'anatomie et la physiologie comparée." Rénouard says[15]
that Hippocrates was born about B.C. 460. Even Diodorus Siculus, the most credulous and unphilosophical of all the Greek historians, says, when speaking of premature births, "But such births
are not used to live, either because it is not the pleasure of the
gods it should be so, or that the law of nature will not admit it."[16]
At p. 50, book i. cap. 4, he contemptuously says of Egypt, "The
inhabitants of this country little value the short time of this
present life." At book i. chap. 6, vol. i. p. 83, "The adoration
and worshipping of beasts among the Egyptians seems justly to
many a most strange and unaccountable thing." In a speech in
Diodorus Siculus[17] — "for which of the Grecians ever put to
death those that submitted and delivered up themselves upon
hopes and belief of mercy from the conquerors?" See also in

[1] Keightley, p. 140.    [2] Ibid. p. 148.    [3] Ibid. p. 164.
[4] Ibid. p. 161.    [5] Ibid. p. 296.    [6] Ibid. p. 73.
[7] Iliad, v. 392, 395.    [8] Keightley, p. 335, 855.    [9] Ibid. 340, 416.
[10] Aglaophamus, p. 691.    [11] Keightley, p. 144.    [12] Ibid. p. 262.
[13] Broussais, Examen des Doctrines Médicales, tome i. pp. 11, 12, 63.
[14] Rénouard, Histoire de la Médicine, tome i. p. 256.    [15] Ibid. p. 133.
[16] Diod. Sic. Book I. chap. ii. vol. i. p. 29. Booth. Compare vol. ii. p. 37.
[17] Ibid. Book XIII. chap. ii. vol. i. p. 507.

book xvii. cap. 7, vol. ii. p. 214, what he says about the Persians mutilating their captives. In the learned life of Plato in Smith's Dictionary, it is said, vol. iii. pp. 402, 403, that in Plato's Timaeus important physiological and therapeutical truths are to be found; and reference is made to J. H. Martin, Etudes sur le Timée de Platon, Paris, 1841. Herodotus[1] contemptuously says, "Among the Lydians, and almost all the barbarians, it is deemed a great disgrace even for a man to be seen naked." Even Herodotus, one of the most religious of men, traces the human origin of his religion. He says,[2] "I am of opinion that Hesiod and Homer lived four hundred years before my time, and not more; and these were they who framed a theogony for the Greeks, and gave names to the gods, and assigned to them honours and acts, and declared their several forms." He says[3] that in the expedition of Xerxes against Greece, "the officers of the company from behind having scourges, flogged every man, constantly urging them forward." At viii. 105, p. 527, Herodotus says, "With the barbarians, eunuchs are more valued than others on account of their perfect fidelity." The Greeks thought it disgraceful to insult dead bodies.[4]

Plato[5] distinguishes between the legislative and judicial functions; comparing the former to gymnastics and the latter to medicine.[6] In the Republic,[7] "Not long since the sight of naked men appeared base and disgusting to the Greeks, just as now, indeed, it does to most of the barbarians." It was shameful to strip and plunder a dead enemy.[8] "At Athens there was a body of medical men paid by the state, as well as those in private."[9] The Thracians reproached the Greek physicians that they attempted to cure the body without paying attention to the soul.[10] Plato[11] attacks the notion of hereditary and aristocratic honour; and in the Laws[12] he contrasts the Greek democracy as one extreme, with the Persian monarchy as the other. At pp. 109, 138, he says men must not have office and honour because they are rich. In a passage apparently corrupt[13] he says that mankind probably always existed. Plato says,[14] "Not even a god can use force against necessity."

[1] Herodotus, Book I. chap. x. p. 5.           [2] Ibid. Book II. chap. liii. p. 116.
[3] Book VII. chap. ccxxiii. p. 487.           [4] Ibid. Book IX. chap. lxxix. p. 576.
[5] Works, vol. i. p. 130.
[6] Gorgias, chap. xliv. xlvi. clix. in Plato's Works, vol. i. pp. 156, 157, 224.
[7] Book V. chap. iii.   Plato's Works, vol. ii. p. 136.
[8] Ibid. Book V. chap. xv.   Plato's Works, vol. ii. p. 155.
[9] Note in Plato's Works, vol. iii. p. 192.
[10] Charmides, chap. ix.   Plato's Works, vol. iv. p. 118.
[11] Menexenus, chap. xix.   Plato's Works, vol. iv. p. 204.
[12] Laws, Book III. chap. xii.   Plato's Works, vol. v. p. 105.
[13] Laws, Book VI. chap. xxii.   Plato's Works, vol. v. p. 242.
[14] Plato's Works, vol. v. pp. 177, 301.

# AFRICA.

*Method.*—*Diodorus Siculus, Plutarch.* At the end of vol. i. of Bunsen's Egypt, p. 601, *et seq.*, are collected all the passages in ancient writers respecting Egypt. See p. xxxviii. Bunsen[1] speaks in highest terms of Plutarch's Isis and Osiris; which he says is based on Manetho. Diodorus Siculus is the latest of the ancients who studied Egyptian history.[2] *Diodorus Siculus* is said[3] to have "travelled over a great part of Europe and Asia," and "Scaliger has made it highly probable that he wrote the work after B.C. 8." Diodorus "did nothing but collect," and "the absence of criticism is manifest throughout the work."[4] *Herodotus* is known to have been born B.C. 484.[5] "There is no reason for supposing that he made himself acquainted with Egyptian language."[6] "He travelled to the south of Egypt as far as Elephantine." "His visit to Egypt may be ascribed to about B.C. 450."[7] *Plutarch,* "a youth or young man in A.D. 66."[8] Diodorus Siculus[9] speaks with great contempt of Herodotus's account of Egypt.

*Geography.*—In Africa, owing to bad soil, climate, &c., there was neither accumulation nor diffusion of wealth, except in Egypt, which, with part of Arabia, forms a sandy plain irrigated by the Nile and Red Sea. Southern Africa is "destitute of great rivers." Somerville's Physical Geography, vol. i. p. 141. Africa has the *smallest* "coast line" in proportion to its surface of any of the four quarters of the world—Europe has the *most.* Somerville, Physical Geog. i. p. 53. At p. 52 she says, "All the shores of Europe are deeply indented and penetrated by the Atlantic ocean, which has formed a number of inland seas of great magnitude, so that it has a greater line of maritime coast, compared with its size, than any other quarter of the world." The greater part of Africa is a barren waste;[10] and the civilization of Carthage was borrowed, planted *not* indigenous. Rain *does* fall in Upper Egypt about five or six times in the year: in Lower Egypt more frequently."[11] Hamilton[12] says that from the descriptions of

[1] Egypt, vol. i. p. 63.
[3] Smith's Biog. Dict. vol. i. p. 1016.
[5] Smith, vol. ii. p. 431.
[4] Smith, vol. iii. p. 429.
[2] Ibid. pp. 136, 152.
[6] Ibid. p. 1016.
[8] Ibid. p. 433.
[7] Ibid. p. 433.
[9] Booth's Trans. vol. i. p. 72.
[10] Somerville's Physical Geography, vol. i. pp. 148, 149.
[11] Wilkinson's Ancient Egyptians, vol. iv. p. 10.
[12] Hamilton's Ægyptiaca, p. 59.

Strabo "it is evident he never was within any of their sacred buildings." See p. 113 on the errors of Diodorus Siculus.

*Human.*—The Egyptians knew nothing of anatomy.[1] Mill[2] quotes Wilford, in Asiatic Researches, iii. 296, who says, "Nor had the Egyptians any work purely historical." Their utter ignorance of drawing man is shown by the hideous figures in Sir G. Wilkinson's valuable work, in which see the remarks at vol. iii. pp. 264, 265. Wilkinson[3] says, "Many histories of Egypt were written at different periods by native as well as foreign authors, which have unfortunately been lost." Indeed, he allows[4] that "history seems so entirely excluded from their mythological system, and so completely a thing apart from it, that we may doubt if it was admitted into it, even at the earliest periods," and this, as he well says, was the subordination of physical and historical to the *metaphysical.* Wilkinson[5] says, "Though the Egyptians were fond of buffoonery and gesticulation, they do not seem to have had any public show which can be said to resemble a theatre: nor were their pantomimic exhibitions, which consisted chiefly in dancing and gesture, accompanied with any scenic representation." It is remarkable[6] that Egyptian artists were more skilful in representing animals than in the human figure. They knew nothing of medicine.[7] Nor is Wilkinson[8] more successful in his attempt to ascribe to them a knowledge of chemistry. In war, the hands of the slain were cut off, and sometimes their tongues.[9] With the exception of the Alexandrian school, a late and foreign offshoot, they had nothing approaching to historians. Of Horapollo nothing is known. Bunsen[10] says, "Manetho, the most distinguished historian, sage, and scholar of Egypt." But he lived under Ptolemy I., and wrote in Greek.[11] Then we have Ptolemy and Apion, both Alexandrians.[12] Chæremon, also an Alexandrian, and the preceptor of Nero, also wrote a history of Egypt.[13] Bunsen[14] doubts whether he was "an Egyptian educated at Alexandria, or an Alexandrian of Greek origin" Bunsen[15] says, "The fourth Egyptian is Heraikos, a mystical saint of Alexandria, apparently about the commencement of the Neo-Platonic school in the third century. . . . This is all we hear of Manetho's Egyptian

---

[1] Rénouard, Histoire de la Médicine, tome i. p. 36.
[2] Mill's Hist. Brit. India, vol. ii. pp. 67, 68.
[3] Wilkinson's Ancient Egyptians, vol. i. p. 20.          [4] Ibid. vol. iv. p. 206.
[5] Ibid. vol. ii. p. 259.                                 [6] Ibid. vol. iii. p. 269.
[7] Ibid. pp. 389, 393, 396; vol. v. p. 460.               [8] Ibid. vol. iii. pp. 132, 133.
[9] Ibid. vol. i. p. 393; vol. iii. p. 293.   For cruel punishments, see vol. ii. p. 46.
[10] Bunsen's Egypt, vol. i. p. 66.                        [11] See *Manetho*, in Smith's Biography.
[12] Bunsen's Egypt, vol. i. p. 90.
[13] Smith's Biog. Dict. vol. i. p. 678.
[14] Bunsen's Egypt, vol. i. pp. 92, 94.          [15] Ibid. p. 95.

successors within the province of history." Herodotus[1] says that in Egypt "each physician applies himself to one disease only, and not more." The Egyptian monuments prove the barbarous treatment of prisoners of war.[2] Hoskins[3] says the Egyptians drew the human form so badly because they superstitiously copied the older figures of their deities depicted on their temples. It was not till the Egyptians were fertilised by Greek mind that they produced their only historian, Manetho.

*Immense.*—Mill[4] says, " A single king of Egypt was believed to have reigned three myriads of years. Eusebii Chronicon, p. 5, Syncelli Chron. p. 28. Bryant's Ancient Mythology, iv. 127, 8vo." Wilkinson[5] says, " The oldest monuments of Egypt, and probably of the world, are the pyramids to the north of Memphis." On their dimensions see iv. p. 26. Pliny's remark on the Pyramids seems to me very just, though it has called forth the indignation of the enthusiastic Bunsen.[6] The Pyramids, the Labyrinth, and the Lake of Mœris [see] Egypt, in Edinburgh Cabinet Library, p. 132. After these, Dendera, pp. 188, 201. At p. 237, " In no part of Egypt are more colossal sculptures seen on the walls of a public building than on the larger temple at Edfou." At p. 244, " The temples of Karnac and Luxor, the tomb of Gornoo, and the Grottos of Eleithias." *Thebes.*—On the colossal statues of Memnon see pp. 214, 217. At p. 74, it is said that Plutarch mentions that Stesicrates proposed to Alexander the Great to turn Mount Athos into a statue of him. Hamilton[7] says, " The Egyptian sculptor seems to have excelled in the gigantic style: in them the outline is bolder and more true than in the smaller compositions." He says[8] that the great temple at Thebes is even bigger than Diodorus Siculus describes it. There is a notion in Egypt that the Pyramids were built as a protection against any future deluge.[9] The finest buildings are at Philæ, 24° N. lat., where it was believed Osiris was buried.[10] He thinks[11] that the monuments are from " the granite quarries of Syene ;" but he says,[12] that in Upper Egypt they are chiefly of sandstone. The Pyramids of Merœ were *not* built for astronomical purposes, and they are even said to contain no chambers.[13] Abd Allah says of one of the

---

[1] Herodotus, Book II. chap. lxxxiv. p. 125.
[2] See Hamilton's Egyptiaca, pp. 118, 145, 146, 156, 157.
[3] Hoskins' Travels in Ethiopia, pp. 354, 355.
[4] Hist. British India, vol. i. p. 155.
[5] Wilkinson's Ancient Egyptians, vol. i. p. 19.
[6] Bunsen's Egypt, vol. i. p. 155.
[7] Hamilton's Egyptiaca, p. 89.
[8] Ibid. p. 124.
[9] Ibid. p. 29.
[10] Ibid. pp. 43-49.
[11] Ibid. p. 68.
[12] Ibid. p. 112.
[13] Hoskins's Travels in Ethiopia, pp. 70, 153.

Pyramids, " Lorsqu'on l'aborde de près et que les yeux ne voient plus que d'elle, elle inspire une sorte de saississement, et l'on ne peut la considérer sans que la vue se fatigue."—Relation de l'Egypte, p. 173.

*Stationary.* — The Egyptians hated strangers.[1] Hamilton[2] says : " The monuments of antiquity in Upper Egypt present a very uniform appearance ; aud his first impressions incline the traveller to attribute them to the same or nearly the same epoch."

*Distribution of Wealth.*—Mill[3] quoting Herodotus,[4] Strabo,[5] Diodorus Siculus[6] says : " In Egypt the king was the sole proprietor of the land ; and one-fourth of the produce appears to have been yielded to him as revenue or rent." The population at its zenith was 7,500,000 (see Wilkinson, i. pp. 216, 217, where there is a very vague statement as to the *area* ; and see vol. i. p. 180). The wealth and luxury of the higher classes was extraordinary : and " the very great distinction between them and the lower classes is remarkable as well in the submissive obeisance to their superiors as in their general appearance, their dress, and the style of their houses."[7] " Nor was any one permitted to meddle with political affairs, or to hold any civil office in the state. . . . If any artizau meddled with political affairs, or engaged in any other employment than the one to which he had been brought up, a severe punishment was instantly inflicted upon him."[8] " The fourth caste was composed of pastors, poulterers, fowlers, fishcrmen, labourers, servants, and common people."[9] They hated shepherds, and would not allow a swineherd even to enter their temples.[10] Wilkinson[11] says of the land that " a fifth part (I suppose of the *produce*) was annually paid to the government by the Egyptian peasant." At p. 263 he adopts the assertion of Diodorus, that the only landed proprietors were the king, the priests, and the military order ; the land being equally divided iuto three parts.[12]

*Religion.*—Wilkinson says :[13] " The idea of death among the ancients was less revolting than among Europeans and others at the present day, and so little did the Egyptians object to have it brought before them, that they even introduced the mummy of a deceased relative at their parties, and placed it at table as

[1] Laws, Book XII. chap. vi. in Plato's Works, vol. v. p. 519.
[2] Hamilton's Egyptiaca, p. 18.
[3] Mill's Hist. of British India, vol. i. p. 303.    [4] Herodotus, Book II. chap. xix.
[5] Strabo, lib. xvii. p. 1135.    [6] Diod. Sic. lib. ii. sec. 2, chap. xxiv.
[7] Wilkinson's Egypt, vol. i. pp. 232, 235.    [8] Ibid. vol. ii. pp. 8, 9.
[9] Ibid. p. 15.    [10] Ibid. pp. 16, 17.
[11] Ibid. vol. i. p. 74.    [12] Ibid. vol. ii. p. 2.    [13] Ibid. p. 414.

one of the guests." At p. 204, vol. iv., the Egyptians "were unquestionably the most pious of all the heathen nations of antiquity." Wilkinson says,[1] "Next to the king, the priests held the first rank, and from them were chosen his confidential and responsible advisers, the judges, and all the principal officers of state." At p. 282: "Besides their religious duties, the priests fulfilled the important offices of judges and legislators, as well as counsellors of the monarch."[2] At p. 271, vol. v.: "Even military regulations were subject to the influence of the sacerdotal caste." At vol. i. p. 262, Wilkinson says, "The priests were not obliged to make the same sacrifice of their landed property, nor was the tax of the fifth part of the produce entailed upon it as on that of the other people (Gen. xlvii. 26)." Wilkinson[3] says, "Justly did the priests deride the ridiculous vanity and ignorance of the Greeks in deriving their origin from the gods." Wilkinson[4] says, that if the Egyptians ever *did* offer human sacrifices, it must have been at a period *anterior* to all their monuments.[5] But since Plutarch quotes as his authority Manetho,[6] I do not agree with Wilkinson that "it is scarcely necessary to attempt a refutation of so improbable a tale." The Egyptians had esoteric and exoteric religion.[7] The Greeks laughed at the Egyptians for worshipping animals.[8] Indeed, they even adored "fabulous insects and fabulous quadrupeds."[9] The sense of the dignity of man prevented the Greeks from believing that *our* souls went into animals. There is plenty of evidence of their [the Egyptians] worship of animals in Wilkinson, who however sometimes attempts to invalidate testimony by the negative argument of the non-existence of evidence on the monuments. On transmigration of the soul, see Wilkinson, vol. v. p. 440–446. At p. 446 he quotes Cæsar, that "the Druids believed in the migration of the soul though they confined it to *human* bodies." *A curious proof of the European human element.* Human sacrifices are not mentioned on the [Egyptian] monuments; but there is no doubt that they *were* practised in Egypt; though they are said to have been abolished under the old empire.[10] Diodorus Siculus[11] says that the Egyptian priests "are free from all public taxes and impositions, and are in the second place to the king in honour and

[1] Wilkinson's Ancient Egyptians, vol. i. p. 257.    [3] Ibid. vol. ii. p. 23.
[2] Ibid. vol. iv. p. 169.    [4] Ibid. p. 269.
[5] Ibid. vol. v. pp. 43, 341, 344.    [6] Ibid. p. 341.
[7] Ibid. vol. iv. p. 275.    [8] Ibid. pp. 161, 162; vol. v. p. 96.
[9] Ibid. vol. v. p. 128.
[10] Bunsen's Egypt, vol. i. pp. 17, 18, 65, 441.
[11] Lib. I. cap. vi. vol. i. p. 76. By Booth.

authority." Herodotus says[1] "They are of all men the most
excessively attentive to the worship of the gods." At ii. 64,
p. 119, "The Egyptians, then, are beyond measure scrupulous in
all things concerning religion." At book ii. chap. lxvi. he says,
p. 21, of the Egyptians, "In whatever house a cat dies of a
natural death, all the family shave their eyebrows only; but if a
dog die they shave the whole body and the head." Richardson[2]
found at Ghadames, in 30° N. lat., that "the notion of the transmigration of souls lingers in these parts, but is a doctrine not
generally received." Plato[3] believed that the human soul trans-
migrated even into beasts (see the Statesman, chap. xxx.). "In
Egypt it is not permitted for a king to govern without the
sacerdotal science, and should any one, previously of another
caste of men, become by violence the king, he is afterwards
compelled to be initiated into the mysteries of this caste."[4]
Their religion is like that of India—but from similarity of
causes not from contact. "The excavated temple of Guefeh
Hassan, for instance, reminds every traveller of the cave of
Elephanta."[5] Russell[6] says that above Cairo rain, thunder, and
lightning are hardly known. The combined effect of slavery
(caused by mal-distribution of wealth) and superstition caused
by power of nature. Russell[7] remarks that the Egyptian clergy
persisted in using "imitative and symbolic hieroglyphics" long
after they became acquainted with alphabetic and phonetic
writing. The Mahometans in Kordofan "firmly believe in metempsychosis."[8] Heeren[9] says that in Upper Egypt the temples
are all built of sandstone which is found in Middle Egypt; but
that the great monuments of one piece were composed of the
"Syenite or oriental granite," found near Philæ. In India
granites are found very like those of Syene.[10]

Women.—Wilkinson says among no ancient people had women
such influence and liberty.[11] Herodotus is wrong in saying
women were never priestesses.[12] Polygamy was legal; but not
usual.[13] "A woman who had committed adultery was sentenced
to lose her nose;" the man "to receive a bastinado of a thousand

[1] Herodotus, Book II. chap. xxxvii. pp. 108, 109.
[2] Richardson's Travels in the Sahara, vol. i. p. 206.
[3] Timæus, chap. xvii. Plato's Works, vol. ii. pp. 317, 347.
[4] Plato's Works, vol. iii. p. 244.
[5] Russell's Egypt, in Edinburgh Cabinet Library, p. 21.
[6] Ibid. p. 44.                                [7] Ibid. p. 147.
[8] Pallme's Travels in Kordofan, p. 188.
[9] Heeren, African Nations, vol. ii. pp. 66, 67.
[10] Journal of Asiatic Society, vol. vii. pp. 122, 124.
[11] Wilkinson's Ancient Egyptians, vol. ii. pp. 58, 59, 61, 166, 389.
[12] Ibid. vol. i. pp. 261, 262.                [13] Ibid. vol. ii. p. 62.

blows." ¹ According to Herodotus, "If a son was unwilling to
maintain his parents he was at liberty to refuse; but a daughter
was compelled to aid them, and on refusing was amenable to
law." This, Wilkinson,² without evidence, thinks proper to
deny. Very young wives, treated as children, remain so by mere
habit. Diodorus Siculus³ says of Egyptians, "In their contracts
of marriage, authority is given to the wife over her husband, at
which time the husbands promise to be obedient to their wives
in all things." In lib. i. cap. vi.⁴: "In case of adultery the man
was to have a thousand lashes with rods, and the woman her nose
cut off." At p. 82, "The priests only marry one wife, but all
others may have as many wives as they please." Herodotus⁵
says, "No woman can serve the office for any god or goddess;
but men are employed for both offices. Sons are not compelled to
support their parents unless they choose, but daughters are compelled to do so whether they choose or not." Richardson⁶ says,
"There are several women now living more than eighty. How
long these poor creatures survive their feminine charms! A woman
in the desert gets old after thirty." Müller⁷ says that in Africa
females attain puberty in their eighth year, in Persia in their
ninth. The Arabs and Berbers of North Africa still buy their
wives.⁸ Richardson⁹ says all the Africans like not women but very
young girls. He says¹⁰ that near Lake Tchad men always buy their
wives. Mayo¹¹ says, "In the hottest regions of Asia, Africa, and
America, girls arrive at puberty at ten, even at nine years of
age; in France not till thirteen, fourteen, or fifteen; whilst in
Sweden, Russia, and Denmark this period is not attained till
from two to three years later. Habits of activity and bodily
exertion retard the arrival of puberty." At Konka on Lake
Tchad, and in the Mardara country about 10° N. lat., women are
guarded by eunuchs.¹² In Central Africa the heat is immense.¹³
At Katunga, in 9° N. lat., women are bought as wives,¹⁴ and also
north of Katunga. Russell says,¹⁵ "For various reasons, especially
the want of trees and the low elevation of the whole plain from

¹ Wilkinson's Ancient Egyptians, vol. ii. p. 39.   ² Ibid. p. 65.
³ Diodorus Siculus, Book I. chap. ii. vol. i. p. 33. Booth.   ⁴ Ibid. p. 81.
⁵ Herodotus, Book II. chap. xxxv. p. 108.
⁶ Richardson's Travels in the Desert of Sahara, vol. i. p. 362.
⁷ Müller's Physiology, vol. ii. p. 1480.
⁸ See Kennedy's Algeria and Tunis, vol. i. pp. 138, 280.
⁹ Richardson's Central Africa, vol. i. pp. 218, 219.   ¹⁰ Ibid. vol. ii. p. 103.
¹¹ Mayo's Human Physiology, 391.
¹² Denham's Central Africa, pp. 97, 130, 134, 215.
¹³ Ibid. pp. 92, 96, 107, 109.
¹⁴ Clapperton's Second Expedition, pp. 49, 92.
¹⁵ Russell's Egypt, in Edinburgh Cabinet Library, p. 43.

Rosetta to Assouan, the average degree of heat in Egypt is considerably greater than in many other countries situated in the same latitude." In Kordafan, the south-west province of Egypt, " they grow old very rapidly, and a woman in her twenty-fourth year is considered *passée*." [1] Wives bought in hot countries. In the north of Nubia, near the first cataract, girls often marry before twelve.[2] On the great heat near Shendi about 16° 30′ N. lat., see Hoskins, pp. 97, 126. " The Mohammedan law prescribes that the unmarried woman shall perform the pilgrimage " to Mecca.[3] And " in general women are seldom seen in the mosques in the east." [4]

*Sea.*—Wilkinson [5] says, " Those who traded with them were confined to the town of Naucrates." But at vol. iii. p. 191. Wilkinson *supposes* " the early existence of an Egyptian fleet." Diodorus Siculus [6] says, " It is a piece of religion, and practised among the Egyptians at this day, that these that travel abroad suffer their hair to grow until they return home." This is illustrated by Herodotus,[7] who says that this was the mark of mourning ; "The Egyptians on occasions of death let the hair grow both on the head and face." Hamilton [8] says "It was another principle with the Egyptian government to discourage foreign navigation ; and as a step to this it was necessary to check every mechanical and nautical improvement at home."

*Food.*—Dates in extreme south of Egypt.[9] At Makkarif (18° N. lat.), close to the fifth cataract, and at Dousolah, nearly in the same latitude, both in Nubia, dourah is abundant.[10] Dates the favourite and general food of Arabia.

In western part of Africa the ordinary food is Shea butter, on which see COMMON PLACE BOOK, art. 1709.

Russell [11] says, " The Phœnix dactylifera, or date tree, is of great value to the inhabitants of Egypt, many families, particularly in the upper provinces, having hardly any other food a great part of the year ; while the stones or kernels are ground for the use of the camels."

Bunsen [12] says, in Egypt "the quality of the atmosphere is particularly favourable to the generation of organic life." Loudon [13]

[1] Pallme's Travels in Kordofan, p. 63.    [2] Hoskins's Travels in Ethiopia. p. 11.
[3] Burckhardt's Arabia, vol. i. p. 359.    [4] Ibid. vol. ii. p. 196.
[5] Wilkinson's Ancient Egyptians, vol. ii. p. 76.
[6] Diodorus Siculus. Book 1. chap. ii. vol. i. p. 25.   Booth.
[7] Herodotus, Book II. chap. xxxvi. p. 108.
[8] Hamilton's Egyptinca, p. 61.    [9] Ibid, pp. 64, 71.
[10] Hoskins's Travels in Ethiopia, pp. 53, 179.
[11] Russell's Egypt, in Edinburgh Cabinet Library, p. 450.
[12] Bunsen's Egypt, vol. i. p. 104.
[13] Loudon, Encyclopædia of Agriculture, p. 173.

says, " In a good season—that is, when the rise of the Nile occasions a great expansion of its waters—the profit of the pro- prietors of rice-fields is estimated at fifty per cent. clear of all expenses." Diodorus Siculus [1] says, " In Egypt, if any tradesman meddle in civil affairs, or exercise more than one trade at once, he is grievously punished." At lib. i. cap. vi. p. 81, " For those that lent money by contract in writing it was not lawful to take usury above what would double the stock." Diodorus Siculus [2] says the greatest of the three pyramids occupied in making 360,000 men nearly twenty years. Herodotus [3] says, " Swine- herds, although native Egyptians, are the only men who are not allowed to enter any of their temples." He says [4] that in the reign of Cheops, the king " made all the Egyptians work for himself," drawing stones from quarries, &c.; and that he kept 100,000 working at the same time. In ancient Egypt men were " harnessed to the plough." [5] Although the few Greek historians who wrote on Egypt do with characteristic ignorance tell us nothing worth knowing,[6] still we have evidence of the monu- ments for the degradation of the people. When Hamilton was in Egypt, the peasants borrowed money at 25 or 30 per cent.[7] On the present horrible state of the Egyptian peasants in " the most productive country on the face of the earth," quote Hoskins's Travels in Ethiopia, p. 231 ; and as to their abandoned vices, quote Burckhardt's Arabia, vol. ii. p. 248. At Cairo, the interest of money is 30 to 40 per cent.[8]

## ASIA.

*Method.* — In Arabia and Egypt the same food—dates ; but in Arabia little accumulation of wealth ; and in pastoral and nomadic countries, where there is no accumulation, there is *always* liberty.[9] The three parts of the world where nature is most potent, are Asia, Africa, and America, and in none of them could man work out civilization. The pressure was too great,

---

[1] Diodorus Siculus, Book I. cap. vi. vol. i. p. 77.
[2] Ibid. lib. i. cap. v. vol. i. p. 60.
[3] Herodotus, Book II. chap. xlvii. p. 114.   [4] Ibid. chap. cxxiv. pp. 144, 145.
[5] Hamilton's Egyptiaca, p. 94.   [6] Ibid. p. 226.
[7] Ibid. p. 253.   [8] Burckhardt's Arabia, vol. ii. p. 246.
[9] [See] vols. vii. and viii. of Sir W. Jones. [They] are I think in Asiatic Re-searches. Colebroke's Digest of Hindoo Law. On Halhed's Code, see Wilson's note in Mill's Hist. of Brit. India, vol. i. p. 283.

and he could only do it in Europe; and first in *feeble Greece*.
Wilson [1] seems to adopt Colebrooke's estimate that the Vedas are
" about fourteen centuries prior to the Christian era." Wilson [2]
praises " the valuable works of Colonel Vans Kennedy on the
affinity between ancient and Hindoo mythology." General
Briggs [3] places the Vedas at B.C. 14.

*Diffusion of Wealth.*—Incredible numbers followed Xerxes into
Greece.[4] The gigantic works of Babylon and Nineveh were produced by slaves, squandering labour instead of economizing it
by machinery. They are proofs, not of civilization, but of
barbarism. Grote [5] says that such great works proved " a concentrated population under one government, and above all an
implicit submission to the regal and priestly sway, contrasting
forcibly with the small autonomous communities of Greece and
Western Europe, wherein the will of the individual citizen was so
much more energetic and uncontrolled." The Persian soldiers
were driven into battle by whips.[6] Xenophon describes the
luxuriant food the Greeks saw in Retreat of Ten Thousand.[7]
Enormous wealth of a Phrygian in time of Xerxes.[8] In India,
different governments succeed each other, but there was no revolution *out* of the government: the people never rose. The
Edinburgh Cabinet Library [9] says of the *present* Hindoos, " As
the rent in India usually exceeds a third of the gross produce, a
farm can yield only a very small income, which, however, enables
the tenants to keep over their heads a house that can be built in
three days of mud, straw, and leaves, to eat daily a few handfuls
of rice, and to wrap themselves in a coarse cotton robe. Their
situation may be considered as ranking below that of the Irish
peasants. The ordinary pay of a rural labourer is only from 50*s*.
to 70*s*. a year, which, indeed, compared with the price of necessaries, may be worth from 4*l*. 10*s*. to 6*l*. in Britain; but with this
small sum he must provide his whole food, clothing, and habita-
tion." In Menu,[10] " A king, even though a child, must not be
treated lightly, from an idea that he is a mere mortal; no, he is
a powerful divinity, who appears in a human shape."

[1] Note in Vishnu Purana, p. 225. And his Introduction to Rig Veda Sanhita,
p. xlviii.
[2] Vishnu Purana, p. xv.
[3] Report of British Association, for 1850, p. 169.
[4] Mure's Hist. of Greek Literature, vol. iv. pp. 399-401. Also Grote's Hist. of
Greece, vol. v. pp. 43, 48, 52.
[5] Grote's Hist. of Greece, vol. iii. p. 402.    [6] Ibid. vol. vi. p. 613.
[7] Ibid. vol. ix. p. 79.                          [8] Ibid. vol. v. pp. 38, 39.
[9] Edinburgh Cabinet Library, vol. ii. pp. 426, 427.
[10] Menu, vii. 8. Jones's Works, vol. iii. p. 242.

" That fool, who having eaten of the *fraddha* gives the residue
of it to a man of the servile class, falls headlong down to the
hell, named Calasutia." [1] The lower the class, the more the
interest they must pay. [2] One result was that justice became
*venal*; and the rich man visits the judge and bribes him. [3]
Debtors were compelled to pay by being *beaten* by their
creditors; nor was there any idea of " the equitable arrangement
of an equal dividend." [4] Wilson [5] thinks India formerly more
populous than now. Mill [6] quotes Orme that " In Indostan the
common people of all sorts are a diminutive race in comparison
with those of higher castes and better fortunes." Mill adds,
" There cannot be a more convincing proof that a state of
extreme oppression, even of *stunted* subsistence, has at all times
been the wretched lot of the labouring classes in Hindustan."
Both Medes and Persians were divided into castes. [7] At present,
says Elphinstone, [8] " bankers and merchants lend money on an
immense premium, and with very high compound interest." For
the immense wealth of a Hindoo family in 1824 see Elphinstone,
p. 188; and for the almost incredible splendour of Akber,
pp. 481, 482; and for that of Jehan, pp. 530, 531.

Plato [9] notices the love of wealth among the Phœnicians and
Egyptians. Wilson says, [10] " a creditor is authorised by the old
Hindoo law to enforce payment of an acknowledged debt by
blows, the detention of the debtor's person, and compelling him
to work in his service." On the inexhaustible fertility of the
black soil of Southern India, see Journal of Asiatic Society,
vol. viii. p. 254.

*Sea.* " Neither Egyptians, Assyrians, Persians, or Indians,
addressed themselves to a seafaring life." [11] The Institutes of
Menu [12] classes " a navigator of the ocean " among other criminals
" who are to be avoided with great care." " Nearchus, who
commanded Alexander's fleet B.C. 326, did not meet a single
ship in coasting from the Indus to the Euphrates," and we find
from Arrian that, as far as his knowledge went, there were no
Indians employed in this sea"; while from Agatharcides, who

[1] Menu, chap. iii. 249. Jones's Works, vol. iii. p. 153.
[2] Halhed's Gentoo Law, p. 2.
[3] See extract from Orme, in Mill's India, vol. i. p. 216.
[4] Mill's India, vol. i. p. 240.     [5] Note on Mill's India, vol. i. p. 320.
[6] Mill's India, vol. i. p. 477.
[7] Ibid. pp. 183, 202.     [8] Elphinstone's Hist. of India, p. 174.
[9] Plato's Works, vol. ii. p. 120.
[10] Wilson's Theatre of the Hindus, vol. i. part ii. p. 51.
[11] Grote's Hist. of Greece, vol. iii. p. 360.
[12] Chap. iii. 158, 106. Jones's Works, vol. iii. pp. 141, 142.

wrote " in the second century before Christ," it appears that the trade between India and Yemen in Arabia " was entirely in the hands of the Arabs."[1] Herodotus[2] tells a curious story illustrating the horror the Asiatic natives felt for the sea. Even the Siamese, who have so long a line of coast, are bad and timid navigators.[3] Wilson[4] has idly attempted to prove that the early Hindoos were bold navigators.

*Human.*—Rénouard[5] says of the Hindoos, " Leurs connaissances medicales se trouvent rassemblées dans un livre qu'ils nomment Vagadasasti ; " and of this he gives a short notice,[6] and says they had " des idées si ridicules sur le génération et le diagnostic des maladies."[7] The Edinburgh Cabinet Library[8] says, "The Hindoo drama was a branch of literature very imperfectly known till the important specimens and analysis furnished by Professor Wilson showed it to be one of great importance. Its productions, indeed, are very limited as to number when compared to those of European composers; and it seems doubtful if all the plays extant, even including those mentioned in literary history, much exceed sixty."[9] Sir W. Jones[10] says, " As to mere human works on history and geography, though they are said to be extant in Cashmere, it has not yet been in my power to procure them."[11] The Institutes of Menu[12] speak with the greatest dislike and contempt of "physicians."[13] Sir W. Jones[14] places the oldest Veda at B.C. 1580, and the Institutes of Menu B.C. 1280; while Elphinstone[15] assigns the Vedas to the fourteenth century B.C., and Menu about B.C. 900 ; but this, he allows, is calculated " very loosely."

Mill[16] says, " Hardly any nation is more distinguished for sanguinary laws ;" and he gives a striking list of their horrible punishments. The Hindoos preached penances compared to which the mortification of the most rigid monks were refined

---

[1] Elphinstone's Hist. of India, pp. 166, 167, who quotes Vincont's Commerce and Navigation of the Ancients.

[2] Herodotus, Book IV. cap. xliii. p. 251.

[3] Journal of Royal Asiatic Society, vol. iv. pp. 105, 106.

[4] Ibid. vol. v. pp. 137, 139.

[5] Rénouard, Histoire de la Médecine, tome i. p. 44.      [6] Ibid. pp. 44–46.

[7] See also Sir W. Jones's Works, vol. i. p. 161.

[8] Edinburgh Cabinet Library, vol. ii. p. 308.

[9] See the strange assertion of Sir W. Jones, Works, vol. vi. p. 206.

[10] Sir W. Jones's Third Discourse on the Hindoos, vol. i. p. 33.      [11] Ibid. p 147.

[12] Institutes of Menu, chap. iii. 152, 180 ; chap. iv. 212. Sir W. Jones's Works. vol. iii. pp. 140, 144, 190.

[13] See also Elphinstone's Hist. of India, pp. 42, 144, 145, and Preface to Wilson's Vishnu Purana, p. xxxviii.

[14] Sir W. Jones's Works, vol. iii. p. 56: vol. i. p. 348.

[15] Elphinstone's Hist. of India, pp. 225, 228.

[16] Mill's Hist. of Brit. India, vol. i. pp. 254, 255.

luxuries.[1] Mill[2] finely says, "The Hindoo lawgivers, who commonly mistake minuteness for precision." Wilson, though he says there *are* Hindoo histories,[3] confesses they are few and poor; for "The bias of the Hindoo mind was from the first directed to matters of speculation; and it has never attached such value or interest to the concerns of ephemeral mortality as to deem them worthy of record." Elphinstone[4] says, "The Hindus attained a high pitch of civilization without any work that at all approaches the character of a history." At p. 93, "The great Hindu heroic poem, the Maha Bharat of which Crishna is in fact the hero. . . . Crishna is the greatest favourite with the Hindus of all their divinities." Elphinstone[5] says that both in painting and sculpture "there is a total ignorance of anatomy." On the Ramayana and Maha Bharat, see pp. 206, 207, where Elphinstone says that the first poem, "when stripped of its fabulous and romantic decorations, merely relates that Rama possessed a powerful kingdom in Hindostan; and that he invaded the Deckan, and penetrated to the island of Ceylon, which he conquered." Elphinstone makes no doubt of the real existence of Rama, and of this expedition; nor of the historical value of Maha Bharat. Wilson[6] says, "The safest sources for the ancient legends of the Hindus, after the Vedas, are no doubt the two great poems, the Ramayana and Mahabharata. The first offers only a few, but they are of a primitive character. The Mahabharata is more fertile in fictions, but it is more miscellaneous, and much that it contains is of equivocal authenticity and uncertain date. Still it affords many materials that are genuine, and it is evidently the great fountain from which most, if not all the Puranas have drawn." The Mahabharata is mentioned in Vishnu Purana,[7] and therefore, of course, was written before it. Wilson[8] thinks "the war of the Mahabharata happened about fourteen centuries B.C." And at p. 385, Wilson says the Ramayana, or "heroic poem of Valmiki, seems to be founded in historical fact; and the traditions of the south of India uniformly ascribe its civilization, the subjection or dispersion of its forest tribes of barbarians, and the settlement of civilized Hindoos to the conquest of Lanka y Rama." Wilson[9] says of the Vishnu Purana, "The fourth book contains all that the Hindoos have of their ancient history." This fourth book I must read again. It

[1] See striking evidence in Mill's India, vol. i. pp. 410-412.
[2] Mill's India, vol. i. p. 444.
[3] Wilson, note in Mill's India, vol. ii. p. 67.
[4] Elphinstone's Hist. of India, pp. 10, 381.   [5] Ibid. p. 158.
[6] Wilson, Vishnu Purana, p. lviii.   [7] Ibid. pp. 275, 614, 485.
[8] Ibid. p. lxv.
[9] Preface to Vishnu Purana, p. lxiv.

is at p. 347 *et seq.* Wilson [1] thinks the date of this Purana's composition to be A.D. 1045. The most important part of the Bhagavata is the tenth book " appropriated entirely to the history of Krishna," and translated in Maurier's Ancient History of Hindustan.[2] Colebrooke thinks it is only six hundred years old:[3] and with this Wilson agrees, and says,[4] " The twelfth century is probably the date of the Bhagavata Purana ;" and this he repeats at p. 481.

According to the Hindoo medical writers there are " three humours, namely, wind, bile, and phlegm."[5] Herodotus [6] says of the Babylonians, whose civilization some people vaunt, " They bring out their sick to the market-place, for they have no physicians : then those who pass by the sick person confer with him about the disease, to discover whether they have themselves been affected with the same disease as the sick person," &c., and if so, advise him as to the treatment. Wilson [7] says the Mahometans never had any dramatic literature. Of the Hindoo plays he says,[8] " The greater part of every play is written in Sanscrit. . . . They must, therefore, have been unintelligible to a considerable portion of their audiences, and never could have been so directly addressed to the bulk of the population as to have exercised much influence upon their passions or their tastes." He says,[9] " The dramatic mythology contains curious evidence of the passion of rude people for large buildings." It is said [10] that " The first mention of the caves of Ellora is in the fourteenth century." In Indra's heaven there are thirty-five million nymphs.[11] Wilson says[12] that in the west of India the history of Rama is still " represented in the dramatic form." Ravana, who made war on Rama, had ten heads ;[13] and a king is mentioned with 60,000 sons.[14] Wilson [15] gives an analysis of " the Veni Sambara, a drama founded on the Mahabharat."[16] On the rock-cut temples of India see an elaborate essay in Journal of Asiatic Society, vol. viii. pp. 33, 34, 44, 51.

*Women.*—The jealousy felt respecting women is one of the causes of the backward state of medical knowledge.[17] Besides

[1] Preface to Vishnu Purana, pp. lxxi, lxxii.     [2] Ibid. p. xxvii.
[3] Ibid. p. xxviii.     [4] Ibid. p. xxxi.
[5] Rig Veda Sanhita, p. 95.     [6] Herodotus, Book I. cap. cxcvii. p. 86.
[7] Wilson's Theatre of the Hindus, vol. i. p. iv.
[8] Ibid. pp. v, vi.     [9] Ibid. pp. vi, vii.
[10] Elphinstone, History of India, p. 343.
[11] Wilson's Theatre of the Hindus, vol. ii. part i. p. 12.
[12] Ibid. vol. i. part i. p. 16.     [13] Ibid. vol. ii. part iii. p. 4.
[14] Ibid. vol. ii. part iii. p. 10.     [15] Ibid. vol. iii. part iii. p. 17.
[16] Journal of Asiatic Society, vol. v. p. 291.
[17] Rénouard, Hist. de la Médicine, tome i. p. 428.

this, there could be no great social and historical generalisations
when society was thus *maimed* and *imperfect*: hence *ferocity*, &c.
Another fact is, that there could be no good education; most able
men have had able mothers. The history of the influence of
women I shall hereafter trace. The Edinburgh Cabinet Library
(vol. ii. p. 343) says of the *present* Hindoo women, " Every avenue
by which an idea could possibly enter their minds is diligently
closed. It is unlawful for them to open a book: they must not
join in the public service of the temples; and any man, even
their husbands, would consider himself disgraced by entering into
conversation with them." Women even of the highest orders
have no concern with the Vedas.[1] In the advice respecting marriage,[2] sensual beauties are dwelt on, but there is no idea of *companion* or *society*.[3] Brahmins are forbidden to eat with their
wives, or even to *see* them eat.[4] Women are classed with " talking
birds."[5] Eunuchs are mentioned several times in Menu, though
possibly this meant impotent men.[6] Very jealous. " Let not a
man, therefore, sit in a sequestered place with his nearest female
relations. The assemblage of corporeal organs is powerful enough
to snatch wisdom from the wise."[7] To *talk* with the wife of a man,
or to send her flowers, or jest with her is adultery.[8] And if adultery
actually occurs, the woman is to be devoured by dogs, the adulterer
burnt alive.[9] Under *some* circumstances men buy their wives, i.e.
pay a dowry to the father of the woman. But on this point there is
some confusion, though the custom was evidently not unfrequent.
Compare Menu (in Sir W. Jones's Works, vol. iii. pp. 123, 126,
304, 347) with the note in Elphinstone's History of India, p. 33,
and Mill's History of India, vol. i. pp. 447, 456, 457. Women in
law suits " may be witnesses for women;" but the evidence of
one man " will have more weight than many women, because
female understandings are apt to waver."[10] A woman may marry,
" even though she have not attained the age of eight years;"[11] and
" a man aged thirty may marry a girl of twelve; or a man of

[1] Menu, chap. ii. 66. Jones's Works, vol. iii. p. 92, and chap. ix. 18, p. 337.
[2] Menu, chap. iii. sec. 10. Jones, vol. iii. p. 120.
[3] Mill's Hist. of Brit. India, vol. i. p. 517.
[4] Menu, iv. 43. Jones, vol. iii. p. 167.
[5] Menu, vii. 150. Jones, vol. iii. p. 261.
[6] Jones's Works, vol. iii. pp. 189, 190, 363, 364, 422.
[7] Menu, ii. 215. Jones's Works, vol. iii. p. 113.
[8] Menu, viii. 356, 357. Jones, vol. iii. p. 325.
[9] Menu, viii. 371, 372. Jones, vol. iii. p. 327.
[10] Menu, chap. viii. 68, 70, 77. Jones, vol. iii. pp. 284, 285, 286. See also Mill's Hist. of India, vol. i. p. 273.
[11] Menu, ix. 88, see also 94. Sir W. Jones, vol. iii. pp. 347, 348.

twenty-four a damsel of eight." Polygamy is distinctly allowed.[1]
" By a girl, or by a young woman, or by a woman advanced in
years, nothing must be done, even in her own dwelling-place, according to her mere pleasure."[2]　" A woman must never seek
independence ;[3] and " a woman is never fit for independence."[4]
Of *present* women Elphinstone says,[5] " Women are everywhere
almost entirely uneducated." Perhaps from physical laws genius
is hereditary on the female side. At all events I shall hereafter,
from a vast collection of evidence, prove that the popular opinion
is correct, that able men have able mothers. Women ought to
educate their children, and, in fact, nearly always do so after a
fashion ; for education is not books. The decline of public schools
and of *early* education by men I shall prove to be one cause of
our diminished ferocity of manners. Mill says, " Of all crimes,
indeed, adultery appears in the eyes of Hindoo lawgivers to be
the greatest." Among barbarians a woman labours hard ; hence
she is valuable property, and her father will not let her marry
unless *bribed* to do so. But in India women were also looked on
as *toys*. Mill[6] quotes Menu[7] that " neither by sale nor donation
can a wife be released from her husband." " This," says Mill, " is
a remarkable law ; for it indicates the power of the husband to
sell his wife as a slave ; and by consequence proves that her condition while in his house was not regarded as very different from
slavery." Mill[8] says of the Greeks, " In the time of Homer,
though the wife was actually purchased from the father, still her
father gave with her a dower."[9] Mill[10] refutes the notion that
the Hindoos borrowed their seclusion of women from the Mahommedans. Even by the Mahommedan law, " In all criminal cases
the testimony of the woman is excluded ; and in questions of
property the testimony of two women is held only equal to that
of one man."[11]

*Sattis*, or burning women for their husbands, is not in Menu,
but is said by Diodorus Siculus[12] to be as old as B.C. 300 ; and he
ascribes it " to the degraded condition to which a woman who

---

[1] Menu, viii. 28, 204 ; ix. 77, 81. Jones, vol. iii. pp. 279, 304, 345, 346. Also
Wilson's note in Mill's India, vol. i. p. 455.
[2] Menu, v. 147. Vol. iii. p. 219.
[3] Menu, v. 147. Vol. iii. p. 219, and sec. 148, p. 120.
[4] Ibid, chap. ix. sec. 111, p. 335.　　[5] Elphinstone's Hist. of India, p. 187.
[6] Mill's Hist. of Brit. India, vol. i. p. 448.
[7] Menu, ix. 46. Works of Sir W. Jones, vol. iii. p. 341.
[8] Mill's Hist. of Brit. India, vol. i. p. 451.　　[9] Hind, Lib. IX. verses 147, 148.
[10] Mill's British India, vol. i. pp. 458, 459.　　[11] Ibid. vol. ii. p. 513.
[12] Diodorus Siculus, Lib. XIX. cap. xi.

outlives her husband is condemned." [1] Elphinstone [2] says, "Murders are oftener from jealousy, or some such motive, than for gain." Elphinstone [3] says that Megasthenes [4] affirms that the Indians "bought their wives for a yoke of oxen." Polygamy was common. [5] Women who "voluntarily burned themselves with their husbands" have a very high place in heaven. [6] Women must not borrow money. [7] Nor may she be a witness, except for another woman. [8] A man may whip his wife. [9] "A man both day and night must keep his wife so much in subjection that she by no means be master of her own actions : if the wife have her own free will, notwithstanding she be sprung from a superior caste, she will yet behave amiss." [10] "The creator formed woman for the purpose that man might copulate with her, and that children might be born from them." [11] In Halhed's Gentoo Laws, [12] to talk to a woman, or send her presents, is punished as adultery. "If a woman goes of her own accord to a man, and inveigles him to have criminal commerce with her, the magistrate shall cut off that woman's ears, lips, and nose, mount her upon an ass, and drown her, or cause her to be eaten by dogs." [13] "A woman shall never go out of the house without the consent of her husband, . . . a woman also shall never go to a stranger's house, and shall not stand at the door, and must never look out of a window." [14] Polygamy common. [15] Polygamy arose because beauty soon decayed. Diodorus Siculus [16] mentions the prevalence of polygamy in India, and also wives burning themselves when their husbands died. In the oldest of the Hindoo books, the Rig Veda Sanhita (p. 281) it is distinctly said that men are to *buy* their wives. Herodotus [17] says that among the Persians "a son is not admitted to the presence of his father, but lives entirely with the women." Climate does *not* affect the proportion of sexes. Polygamy caused by hot climate. Early marriage. Comte [18] says that among the Mongolians, girls are marriageable between nine and twelve. I think polygamy is only firmly established when heat increases desire and wealth is unequally distributed. Plato [19] contrasts the

[1] Elphinstone, Hist. of India, p. 189, and see, at p. 243, the reference to Strabo.
[2] Ibid. p. 200.     [3] Ibid. p. 243.     [4] Strabo, cap. xv. p. 488, edit. 1587.
[5] See Halhed's Code of Gentoo Laws, pp. 37, 98, 178.
[6] Ibid. p. xlv. and p. 253.     [7] Ibid. p. 1.
[8] Ibid. p. 110.     [9] Ibid. p. 208.     [10] Ibid. 249.
[11] Ibid. p. 250.     [12] Ibid. pp. 237, 238.
[13] Ibid. pp. 243, 244.     [14] Ibid. p. 252.
[15] Wilson's Vishnu Purana, pp. 150, 613.
[16] Diodorus Siculus, Book XIX. cap. ii., translated by Booth, vol. ii. p. 346.
[17] Herodotus, Book I. cap. xxxvi., in Bohn's Classical Library, p. 62.
[18] Comte, Traité de la Législation, tome ii. p. 93.
[19] Plato, Works, vol. iv. p. 343.

education of the Greeks brought up by nurses with that of the Persians brought up by cunuchs. Wilson [1] says, " It seems probable that the princes of India learnt the practice of the rigid exclusion of women in their harems from the Mahommedans." For instances of polygamy see vol. iii. part i. p. 22; part iii. pp. 44, 46. Women burned on death of their husbands in B.C. 200.[2] Wilson [3] says, " To have touched the wife of another with the hem of the garment was a violation of her person." Compare the present law of Nepal; Journal of Asiatic Society, vol. i. p. 50. According to Mahommedan priests, the puberty of a girl is at nine years. See Van Kennedy's Abstract of Mahommedan Law in Journal of Asiatic Society, vol. ii. p. 101. The same high authority says (p. 98), " Amongst the Mahommedans the liberty of dissolving marriages by divorce is left entirely to the inclination or caprice of the husband." On their unwillingness to receive the evidence of women see p. 118. On state of women see Niebuhr, Description de l'Arabie, pp. 44, 63, 65, 67. In the fourteenth century Ibn Batuta (Travels, p. 108) in India, " saw those women who burn themselves when their husbands die." Herder [4] mentions that in hot countries early marriages cause wives to be treated as children. He says [5] that burning women in India was caused by the husband's being afraid that his wife, lusting after another man, would put him to death. In *all* barbarous countries, hot or cold, men despise women because they are *weak*, and, having neither knowledge nor love of society, their only standard of merit is strength, and physical, *not* moral, courage. Polygamy among the Arabs of Madagascar, see Journal of Geographical Society, vol. v. p. 241.

*Food.*—Elphinstone [6] says, " The nature of the soil and climate make agriculture a simple art. A light plough which he daily carries on his shoulder to the field, is sufficient with the help of two small oxen, to enable the husbandman to make a shallow furrow in the surface in which to deposit the grain," and " the Hindoos understand rotation of crops, though their almost inexhaustible soil renders it often unnecessary." [7] Rice not *now* general.[8] Mrs. Somerville [9] says of the Himalaya, " It is also a peculiarity in these mountains that the higher the range, the higher likewise is the limit of snow and vegetation. On the

---

[1] Wilson's Theatre of Hindus, vol. i. part i. p. 36.
[2] Ibid. part ii. p. 199.      [3] Ibid. p. 39.
[4] Herder, Geschichte der Menschheit, Band ii. Seite 148.      [5] Ibid. Seiten 151, 152.
[6] Elphinstone's Hist. of India, p. 164.      [7] Ibid. p. 165.
[8] See Wilson's note in Mill's Hist. of India, vol. i. p. 478.
[9] Mrs. Somerville's Physical Geography, vol. i. p. 97.

southern slope of the first range Mr. Gerard found cultivation 10,000 feet above the sea, though it was often necessary to reap the corn still green and unripe ; while in Chinese Tartary good crops are raised 15,000 feet above the sea. Captain Gerard saw pasture and low bushes up to 17,009 feet ; and corn as high as even 18,544 feet." But of Siberia she says,[1] " North of the sixty-second parallel of latitude corn does not ripen, on account of the biting blasts from the Icy Ocean." " China is the most productive country on the face of the earth ; an alluvial plain of 21,000 square miles formed by one of the most extensive river systems in the whole world, occupies its eastern part."[2] " The valley of the Ganges is one of the richest on the globe, and contains a greater extent of vegetable mould, and of land under cultivation, than any other country on the continent, except perhaps the Chinese empire."[3] She says[4] " Rice contains a greater proportion of nutritive matter than any of the cerealia, but since it requires excessive moisture, and a temperature of 73° at least, its cultivation is limited to countries between the equator and 45th parallel." In Ireland rice preceded potatoes.

*Religion.*—Elphinstone[5] says: "There is indeed no country where religion is so constantly brought before the eye as in India. Every town has temples of all descriptions," &c. The Edinburgh Cabinet Library (vol. ii. p. 239) says, " Doorga is the chief among the female deities, and indeed the most potent and warlike member of the Hindoo pantheon." She, at the head of 9,000,000 warriors, defeated a giant called Doorga, and took his name, her own being originally Parvati. Another great goddess is Kalee. " She is black, with four arms, wearing two dead bodies as ear-rings, a necklace of skulls, and the hands of several slaughtered giants round her waist as a girdle " (vol. ii. p. 240). " The Swerga, or superior mansion, commonly translated heaven " (p. 240). The temple of Elephanta is the " wonder of Asia " (p. 246). At the " wondrous structures of Ellora, a lofty hill is completely cut out into a range of temples. . . . We may likewise notice Mahabalipoor, known also by the name of the Seven Pagodas, situated about thirty-five miles south of Madras."[6] " Human sacrifices were anciently offered as the Vedas enjoined, but in the present age they are absolutely prohibited."[7] Grandeur of nature imposed fear. Metempsychosis is mentioned in In-

[1] Mrs. Somerville's Physical Geography, vol. i. p. 121.
[2] Ibid. p. 126.  [3] Ibid. p. 127.  [4] Ibid. vol. ii. p. 220.
[5] Elphinstone's Hist. of India, p. 86.
[6] Edinburgh Cabinet Library, vol. ii. p. 249.
[7] Sir W. Jones's Works, vol. i. p. 271. Mill's Hist. of India, vol. i. pp. 414, 415.

stitutes of Menu.[1]  Sir W. Jones[2] says of the Chinese, "Of painting, sculpture, or architecture, as arts of imagination, they seem" [like other Asiatics] "to have no idea." Mill[3] says the more ignorant a country is, the greater the power of clergy, and he adds, "The Brahmans among the Hindoos have acquired and maintained an authority more exalted, more commanding and extensive than the priests have been able to engross among any other portion of mankind." "Nowhere among mankind have the laws and ordinances been more exclusively referred to the divinity than by those who instituted the theocracy of Hindoostan."[4] "Of the host of Hindoo divinities, Brahma, Vishnu, and Siva are the most exalted."[5] Elphinstone[6] says, "The Greek gods were formed like men with greatly increased powers and faculties, and acted as men would do if so circumstanced; but with a dignity and energy suited to their nearer approach to perfection. The Hindu gods, on the other hand, though endowed with human passions, have always something monstrous in their appearance, and wild and capricious in their conduct. They are of various colours, red, yellow, and blue; some have twelve heads, and most have four hands. They are often enraged without a cause, and reconciled without a motive." At p. 38 he quotes Colebrooke[7] to the effect that in the Vedas "the worship of deified heroes is no part of the system." A sort of Pantheism in Vishnu Purana (by Wilson) pp. 6, 255, 256. See in Vishnu Purana, p. 527, a "legend having reference to the caves or cavern temples in various parts of India." Diodorus Siculus[8] says of one of the mountains near the Hellespont, "In the middle is a cave, as if it were made on purpose to entertain the gods." The Hindoos practised human sacrifices.[9] In the oldest Hindoo book[10] we find the metempsychosis into animals. At pp. 83, 111, 112, gifts to the priests are ordered. Asiatics will not change religion. Only a few years since the Hindoos believed that Vishnu had again become incarnate "in the person of a boy."[11] Human sacrifices which indicated a contempt of man are noticed by Colebrooke, Digest of Hindoo Law, vol. iii. p. 288. At vol. vi. p. 256 of Journal of Geographical Society, it is said in Guyana of a "singular rock, that the Indians, as is

[1] Jones's Works, vol. iii. pp. 81, 111, 133, 140, 146, 184, 339, 381, 443, 462.
[2] Ibid. vol. i. p. 102.          [3] Mill's Hist. of India, vol. i. p. 184.
[4] Ibid. pp. 179, 329.           [5] Ibid. p. 347.
[6] Elphinstone's Hist. of India, pp. 96, 97.
[7] In Asiatic Researches, vol. viii. p. 494.
[8] Diodorus Siculus, Book XVII. cap. i.   Vol. ii. p. 164.   By Booth.
[9] See Rig Veda Sanhita, pp. xxiv, 59.          [10] Ibid. p. 8.
[11] Journal of Asiatic Society, vol. vii. p. 109.

generally the case with phenomena of nature, make it the seat
of a demon, and pass it under fear and trembling." See also
vol. x. p. 21, for *accidents* causing superstition. Coleman [1] says,
"The Hindoos subject themselves to more devotional austerities,
penances, and mortifications, some of which are of temporary and
some of a permanent character, than perhaps any people in the
world." [2] Coleman [3] mentions "the extensive cavern temples of
Ellora, Karli, Elephanta," &c. On human sacrifices see Ward's
View of the Hindoos, vol. ii. p. 47. On metempsychosis even
into stones see Ward's View of the Hindoos, vol. ii. p. 160;
vol. iii. p. 67. For some enormous inventions in chronology, &c.,
see Ward's View of the Hindoos, vol. i. pp. xcviii. 211, 265, 266;
vol. ii. p. 179; vol. iii. pp. 3, 23; vol. iv. p. 106.

*Immense.*—The remains at Elephanta and Salsette are enormous: "The pagodas of Ellora, about eighteen miles from Arun-
gabad, are not of the size of those of Elephanta and Salsette,
but they surprise by their number and by the idea of the labour
which they cost. The Seven Pagodas, as they are called, at
Mavalipuam near Sadras, on the Coromandel coast, is another work
of the same description." [4] Mill [5] says that Bryant's Ancient
Mythology contains curious evidence of the fondness of rude
people for large buildings. It is said [6] that "the first mention
of the caves of Ellora is in the fourteenth century." In Indra's
Heaven there are thirty-five million nymphs. [7] Wilson [8] says that
in the west of India the history of Rama is still "represented in
the dramatic form." Ravana who made war on Rama had ten
heads, [9] and a king is mentioned with 60,000 sons. Wilson [10]
gives an analysis of "the Veni Samhara, a drama founded on
the Mahabharat." [11] On the rock temples of India, see an elaborate essay in Journal of the Asiatic Society, vol. viii. pp. 33, 34,
44, 51.

*Stationary.*—In Halhed's Gentoo Laws (p. 190) it is said,
"If a man of inferior cast, proudly affecting an equality with
a person of superior cast, should speak at the same time with
him, the magistrate in that case shall fine him to the extent of

[1] Coleman's Mythology, p. 165.
[2] Ibid. pp. 51, 68, 70. Also Ward's Hindoos, vol. i. pp. 21, 22, 24, 25; vol. ii.
pp. 50, 127, 128; vol. iii. p. xli.
[3] Coleman's Mythology, p. 155.
[4] Mill's Hist. of India, vol. ii. pp. 4, 5.   [5] Ibid. p. 13.
[6] Elphinstone's Hist. of India, p. 343.
[7] Wilson's Theatre of the Hindus, vol. ii. part i. p. 12.
[8] Ibid. vol. i. part i. p. 16.   [9] Ibid. vol. ii. part iii. p. 4.
[10] Ibid. vol. ii. part i. p. 20.
[11] Ibid. vol. iii. part iii. p. 17, et seq. And see Journal of Asiatic Society, vol. v.
p. 291.

his abilities." Asiatics are notoriously averse to change. And
this is shown by their retention of their old religion. It is said
that the Indian vessels which sail from the Gulf of Cutch are
now made in the same way as in the time of Alexander the
Great.[1]

*Astronomy and metaphysics.*—Before the European stage
there was no scientific knowledge except that of astronomy—the
heavens. The Hindoos have an astronomical writer, B.C. 548.[2]
Wilson[3] says, " An astronomical fact known to the author of the
Vedas, that the moon shone only through reflecting the light of
the sun." In Mirchchakati, the acquirements of an accomplished
Hindoo are thus summed up: " He was well versed in the Rig
and Sama Vedas, in mathemical sciences, in the elegant arts, and
the management of elephants."[4] In Wilson (Theatre of the
Hindus, vol. i. part ii. p. 73), the Maya or philosophy of illusion
is noticed. On the astronomical knowledge of the Hindoos, see
Journal of Asiatic Society, vol. v. p. 6.

## AMERICA—EXCLUSIVE OF UNITED STATES.

In Central America the volcanoes are frightful, and one of
them is said to have been heard " eight hundred miles distant."[5]
Stephens[6] mentions the extraordinary number of volcanoes on the
Pacific along the southern coast of Guatemala and Nicaragua.

At Palenque " the design and anatomical proportions of the
figures are faulty ; but there is a force of expression about them
which shows the skill and conceptive power of the artist."[7] See
also the hideous colossal figures in plate at p. 315 of Stephens's
Central America, vol. ii., and gigantic statue, p. 349. Stephens[8]
says, " The inference is, that the Aztecs, or Mexicans, at the time
of the conquest, had the same written language with the people
of Copan and Palenque." For an account of Mayapan ruins,
about twenty miles south of Menda in Yucatan, see Stephens's
Central America, vol. iii. pp. 131–138. For an account of Ticul,
close to Uxmal, see vol. iii. pp. 273, 277. Account of Nophat,

[1] Journal of Asiatic Society, vol. i p. 12. And compare Journal of Geographical
Society, vol. v. p. 273.
[2] Vishnu Purana, p. 206.
[3] Wilson, note to Rig Veda Sanhita, p. 217.
[4] Wilson, Theatre of the Hindus, vol. i. part. ii. p. 12.
[5] See Stephens's Central America, vol. ii. p. 37.
[6] Ibid. vol. i. p. 339.
[7] Ibid. vol. ii. p. 314.
[8] Ibid. p. 455.

see vol. iii. pp. 362, 368. And the ugly figure at p. 364. Account of Kabah, vol. iii. pp. 384, 413. At Kabah, two figures; "both have unnatural and grotesque faces." Vol. iii. p. 412. For account of Labphak, see vol. iv. pp. 159, 165. And of Chichen, vol. iv. pp. 284, 318.

For comparison of Greek and Hindoo religion Prescott[1] praises Mountstuart Elphinstone's "truly philosophic" History of India. M'Culloch's Researches concerning the Aboriginal History of America, Baltimore, 1829, "*very learned.*"[2]  Bradford's American Antiquities, "valuable."[3]  Ixtilochitl, Histoire des Chechemègues in French, by Ternaux.[4]  Squier[5] says that the aboriginal Nicaraguans were of the same stock as Mexicans, but this must be conjecture.

*Geography.*—"All along the Atlantic the country is bordered by a broad tract called the *Terra Caliente*, or hot region, which has the usual high temperature of equinoctial lands."[6]  Peru is intersected by a gigantic range of mountains. Prescott[7] says, "The empire of Peru, at the period of the Spanish invasion, stretched along the Pacific from about the second degree north to 37° S. lat.; a line, also, which describes the western boundaries of the modern republics of Ecuador, Peru, Bolivia, and Chili. . . . A slip of land rarely exceeding twenty leagues in width, runs along the whole coast, and is hemmed in through its whole extent by a colossal range of mountains which, advancing from the Straits of Magellan, reaches its highest elevation (25,250 feet), indeed, the highest on the American continent about 17° south; and, after crossing the line, gradually subsides into hills of inconsiderable magnitude as it enters the Isthmus of Panama. This is the famous Cordillera of the Andes." Prescott[8] says, "The Cordillera of the Andes, the colossal range that, after traversing South America and the Isthmus of Darien, spreads out as it enters Mexico, into that vast sheet of table-land which maintains an elevation of more than six thousand feet for the distance of nearly two hundred leagues, until its gradual decline in the higher latitudes of the north. . . . Across this mountain rampart a chain of volcanic hills stretches in a westerly direction of still more stupendous dimensions, forming, indeed, some of the highest land in the globe." Such is the scale upon which Nature does her work. In Journal of Asiatic Society (vol. ii. p. 29), it is said, I think inaccurately, that the highest peak of Himalaya is "nearly

[1] Prescott's Mexico, vol. i. p. 47.
[2] Ibid. vol. iii. p. 302.
[3] Central America, vol. i. p. 294.
[4] Prescott's Peru, vol. i. pp. 4, 5.
[5] Ibid. vol. i. p. 50; vol. iii. p. 320.
[6] Ibid. vol. i. pp. 175, 176.
[7] Prescott's Mexico, vol. i. pp. 2, 3.
[8] Prescott's Mexico, vol. i. pp. 5, 6.

five thousand feet higher than Chimborazo." Meyen[1] saw from personal observation, that Peru is very "dry, and extremely sterile;" but he was only from 16° to 19° south. On the earthquakes of Peru see Lyell's Principles of Geology, pp. 347, 453, 458, 501, 502. On the volcanoes of Central America see Squier's Central America, vol. ii. p. 101, *et seq.* On Geographical boundaries of Mexico proper, compare with Prescott, Humboldt, Nouvelle Espagne, vol. i. pp. 6, 7, 11. Human sacrifices of Peruvians, see Robertson's Works, p. 923. Walsh[2] says, " Mandioca meal is the great farinaceous food used in all parts of Brazil." The mandioc is grown in Paraguay.[3] Maize is common in South Brazil, Uruguay, La Plata, and Paraguay.[4] On the different foods grown in Brazil, see Henderson's History of Brazil, pp. 71, 100, 222, 235, 246, 265, 284, 293, 301, 314, 319, 325, 378, 405, 422, 440, 446, 489, 522. On food in western part of South America see Ulloa's South America, vol. i. pp. 36, 69; vol. ii. p. 324. Great population of Peru, see Prescott's Peru, vol. ii. p. 101, and Bullock's Mexico, p. 420. Ixtilochitl, Histoire des Chechemègues, vol. i. pp. 289, 290.

*Immense.*—Prescott[5] says that " the Peruvians, though lining a long extent of sea coast, had no foreign commerce." The Mexican temples " were solid masses of earth, cased with brick or stone, and in their form somewhat resembled the pyramidal structures of ancient Egypt. The bases of many of them were more than a hundred feet square, and they towered to a still greater height."[6] The most celebrated was " the temple of Cholula, a pyramidal mound built, or rather cased, with unburnt brick, rising to the height of nearly one hundred and eighty feet."[7]

In the Vatican are Mexican paintings " the cycles of which take up nearly 18,000 years."[8] " In casting the eye over a Mexican manuscript or map, as it is called, one is struck with the grotesque caricatures it exhibits of the human figure."[9] Torquemada says, " It was not till after they had been converted to Christianity that they could model the true figure of a man."[10] Human sacrifices formed part of the religion of Peru and Mexico.[11] The priests were very numerous and had great influence.[12] They

---

[1] See also a good description in M'Culloch's Geographical Dictionary, vol. ii. p. 313, and Ward's Mexico, vol. i. pp. 7, 8.

[2] Walsh's Notices of Brazil, vol. ii. p. 13. See also vol. i. p. 512.

[3] Azara, Amérique méridionale, tome i. p. 145.      [4] Ibid. p. 146.

[5] Prescott's Peru, vol. i. pp. 136, 137.

[6] Ibid. vol. i. p. 60, and vol. iii. p. 331.      [7] Ibid. vol. iii. p. 311.

[8] Prescott's Mexico, vol. i. p. 61.    [9] Ibid. p. 78.    [10] Ibid. p. 119.

[11] See Prescott's Peru, vol. i. pp. 31, 86, 100, 101; and Prescott's Mexico, vol. i. pp. 20, 30, 48, 53, 62, 68, 100, 163; vol. ii. pp. 8, 128; vol. iii. pp. 126, 177.

[12] Prescott's Mexico, vol. i. pp. 55, 102. Peru, vol. i. p. 96.

were cannibals[1] but *not* in Peru.[2]  In both countries the laws were extremely severe, slight offences being capital.[3]  M'Culloch[4] says of Mexico, "The base of the pyramid of Cholula is a square of 1,423 feet on each side, and its height is estimated at 177 feet;" the same size is stated in Ward's Mexico (vol. ii. p. 75).

Human sacrifices.[5]  On the remarkable fertility of the soil at and near Quito, see Ulloa's Voyage to South America, vol. i. p. 282. And on fertility of Truxillo, see vol. ii. p. 20 ; of Lima p. 26 ; of Chili, pp. 241, 242, 270.  On the dreadful earthquakes, see Ulloa, vol. i. pp. 279, 312, 319, 341 ; vol. ii. pp. 79, 138, 235.  These human sacrifices are constantly mentioned by the native historian, Ixtilochitl, Histoire des Chechemègues, vol. i. pp. 192, 214, 291, 295, 354 ; vol. ii. pp. 32, 45, 48, 120, 129.

*History.*—The Toltecs civilized Mexico,[6] but after four centuries "left the country as silently and mysteriously as they had entered it, and spread over the region of Central America and the neighbouring isles ; and the traveller now speculates on the majestic ruins of Mitla and Palenque as possibly the work of this extraordinary people."[7]  The Mexicans came from the north, " and arrived on the borders of the valley of Mexico, or states of Anahuac, towards the beginning of the thirteenth century."[8]  Early in the sixteenth century the "Aztec dominion reached across the continent from the Atlantic to the Pacific ; and under the bold and bloody Ahuitzotl, its arms had been carried from over the limits already noticed as defining its permanent territory into the furthest corners of Guatemala and Nicaragua."[9]  Prescott[10] says that " the Acothuans or Tezcucans, as they are usually called " were more civilized than the Aztecs.  The Mexicans and the Peruvians had no knowledge of each other's existence.[11]  On the inexhaustible fertility of Mexico about 20° N. lat., see the statistical evidence in Humboldt's Nouvelle Espagne, vol. ii. pp. 384, 385.  Humboldt[12] says the Toltecs introduced maize into Mexico.

*Diffusion of Wealth and Food.* — There were *two* cheap foods in Peru, and only *one* in Mexico,[13] hence Peruvians more

[1] Prescott's Mexico, vol. i. pp. 63, 131, 232 ; vol. iii. pp. 109, 126.
[2] Prescott's Peru, vol. i. p. 100.
[3] Prescott's Mexico, vol. i. pp. 29, 145.  Peru, vol. i. pp. 26, 42.
[4] M'Culloch's Geographical Dictionary, vol. ii. p. 319.
[5] Ward's Mexico, vol. ii. p. 48.
[6] Prescott's Mexico, vol. i. p. 9.                    [7] Ibid. p. 10.
[8] Ibid. pp. 11, 12.          [9] Ibid. p. 16.          [10] Ibid. pp. 137, 173.
[11] See Prescott's Mexico, vol. i. p. 104.  Prescott's Peru, vol. i. pp. 10, 116, 134. Humboldt's Nouvelle Espagne, vol. ii. p. 402.
[12] Humboldt's Nouvelle Espagne, vol. i. p. 78.
[13] [Potatos and banana in Peru ; banana only in Mexico.—ED. Note.]

populous and less free than Mexicans. Milk was used by *no* native Americans.[1] In Mexico the severity of taxation made men disaffected, and aided the Spanish conquest, and taxes were so cruelly levied that "by a stern law every defaulter was liable to be taken and sold a slave."[2] M'Culloch[3] says of Mexico, "The soil is also in most parts extraordinarily fertile: and wherever water can be procured for irrigation, the most abundant crops can be raised with very little labour." Wheat, barley, &c., succeed badly in Mexico, and indeed will not grow there "under the level of 2,500 feet above the sea."[4] M'Culloch[5] says of Mexico the capital, "There is, or at all events there used to be, an extreme disparity of wealth in this city. Many of the nobles and successful speculators in mines were excessively rich, but the bulk of the population were at once indolent and indigent." Ward[6] mentions "the lowness of wages in Mexico." He says[7] that in some states "the daily wages of the labourer do not exceed two reals, and a cottage can be built for four dollars." Ward[8] says that Humboldt is not far wrong in making the Mexican population double itself every nineteen years.

---

## OBSERVATIONS ON THE SPIRIT AND TENDENCY OF COMMERCE AND MERCHANTS.

I believe that Adam Smith, and, so far as I know, all political economists, have overlooked one cause of the decrease of mercantile profits in England since the sixteenth century—and that is, the increasing estimation in which merchants are held.

The Venetian ambassador in the reign of Mary I. reports that "there were many merchants in London with 50,000*l.* or 60,000*l.* each, that the inhabitants amounted to 180,000, and that it was not surpassed in wealth by any city in Europe."[9]

One of the most infallible marks of an improving country is a rise in wages and a fall in profits; and yet this very fall in profits, which is an evidence of national prosperity, is protested against by merchants as an evidence of national ruin.[10] This shows that merchants are bad judges of national prosperity.

---

[1] Prescott's Peru, vol. i. p. 138.       [2] Prescott's Mexico, vol. i. p. 34.
[3] M'Culloch's Geographical Dictionary, vol. ii. p. 314. Ward's Mexico, vol. i. pp. 12, 16, 36, 37 ; vol. ii. p. 228.
[4] M'Culloch's Geogr. Dict. vol. ii. p. 315.       [5] Ibid. p. 322.
[6] Ward's Mexico, vol. i. p. 14.       [7] Ibid p. 249.       [8] Ibid. pp. 20, 21.
[9] Lingard, vol. iv. p. 387, Paris 1840. He cites MSS. Barber 1208, p. 137.
[10] See Smith's Wealth of Nations, p. 38.

On their natural want of ability for government, see Smith's Wealth of Nations.[1] In April, 1554, Mary had " deulx marchands de cette ville " (i.e. of London) nailed by their ears to the pillory for some expressions they had used against her.[2] In 1563 our chief exports were cloth, wool, lead, and tin ;[3] and in 1557, wool, cloth, tin, lead, copper, coals.[4]

In estimating the importance of commerce, Smith has well observed[5] that the merchant puts less productive labour into motion than either the manufacturer or the farmer, supposing of course that all these employ an equal capital.

On the necessity of knowledge among merchants, see M'Culloch's Political Economy.[6] In 1576 Elizabeth granted to the merchant adventurers two of her great ships for an escort to Hamburg. Did she pay their expenses ? See an obscure sentence in Murdin's State Papers, p. 300. In 1576 the queen " adventured " 500l. in Martin Frobisher's attempt to discover " the North West Indies."[7] The civilizing effects of commerce are admitted by Alison.[8] For the etymology of diaper, respecting which it is said Anderson has made a mistake, see Warton's History of English Poetry, 8vo, 1840, p. 177 note.

Some of the vulgar opinions respecting wealth being among merchants the predominating object of pursuit are well refuted by Miss Martineau.[9]

Merchants have been much and justly ridiculed for holding the childish doctrine that the wealth of a nation can be measured by what is called " the balance of trade." But this, as M'Culloch truly says,[10] was a great improvement on the preceding notion that gold and silver should not be exported.[11] At p. 32 M'Culloch has a remark on the mercantile system equally witty and true. However, it was a great step in the right direction, and was due to the East India Company.[12] The mercantile system seems to have been first vigorously attacked in 1691 by Sir Dudley North,[13] and early in the eighteenth century several works appeared

[1] P. 234; see also pp. 263–266, 316, 344.
[2] Ambassades de Noailles, Leyde, 1762, tomo iii. p. 174.
[3] Haynes's State Papers, p. 409.
[4] See Report of Michele, the Venetian Ambassador, in Ellis's Original Letters, 2nd series, vol. ii. p. 219.
[5] Wealth of Nations, pp. 148, 149.
[6] Edinburgh, 1843, 8vo, pp. 331, 333, 334.
[7] Murdin's State Papers, pp. 303, 304.
[8] See his Principles of Population, 8vo, 1840, vol. i. pp. 28, 29.
[9] Society in America, Paris, 8vo, 1842, vol. ii. pp. 98–100, part ii. chap. v. sect. 3.
[10] Political Economy, Edinburgh, 1843, 8vo, pp. 29, 30.
[11] M'Culloch, p. 29.     [12] P. 38.     [13] P. 40.

z

against it.[1] However, Locke knew that labour is the constituent principle of value.[2]

In 1820 the principal London merchants presented to the House of Commons a petition in favour of free trade. It is a short and able document, and may be seen in M'Culloch's Dictionary of Commerce.[3] M. Storch says,[4] " Ce n'est point une exagération de dire qu'il y a peu d'erreurs politiques qui aient enfanté plus de maux que le système mercantile." But this is expressed much too strongly. The mercantile system, absurd as it was, was yet a great improvement on the system which it superseded. The eminent merchant Gresham, though employed by Edward and Mary in some very delicate negotiations, had not received from them even such trifling honours as princes can bestow. But one of the first acts of Elizabeth was to confer on him what was then considered the honour of knighthood, and send him to Brussels as her representative at the court of the Duchess of Parma.[5]

Morellet has published a list of fifty-five joint-stock companies established with exclusive privileges between 1600 and 1769, and it is an instructive fact that every one of these companies failed.[6] Mr. M'Culloch truly adds, " Most of those since established have had a similar fate." [7] As to the confusion in the customs' laws, see the striking picture drawn by M'Culloch, Dictionary of Commerce, p. 846. In 1531 the Exchange of Antwerp was built, and "Die Stadt zahlte jetzt einmal hundertausend Bewohner." [8] In the Egerton Papers[9] there is printed Francis Cherry's Narrative of his Voyage to Russia in 1598. In 1681, 20,000 ships were employed in commerce, of which 15,000 to 16,000 were Dutch, and 500 to 600 French.[10]

Mr. Mill has well stated the moral and economical advantages of commerce.[11] He truly says,[12] " The only direct advantage of foreign commerce consists in the imports." He finely says,[13] that commerce has succeeded war as a means of contact between nations.

The first commercial dictionary ever published in England

[1] M'Culloch, p. 43.    [2] P. 67.    [3] 8vo, 1849, pp. 384, 385.
[4] Économie politique, St. Petersbourg, 8vo, 1815, tome i. p. 122.
[5] Burgoin's Life of Gresham, vol. i. p. 279.
[6] M'Culloch's Dictionary of Commerce, 8vo, 1849, p. 386.
[7] See, however, my note in Smith's Wealth of Nations, on Joint Stock Companies.
[8] Schiller's Werke, Band viii. p. 44, Stuttgard, 1838.
[9] Camden Society, pp. 292-301.
[10] Twiss, Progress of Political Economy, 8vo, 1847, p. 74.
[11] Principles of Political Economy, 2nd edit. 1849, vol. ii. pp. 112-122.
[12] Ibid. p. 118.    [13] Ibid. pp. 121, 122.

did not appear till 1751.[1]  Even Montesquieu who has been justly accused of undervaluing commerce, confesses that it has softened the ferocity of manners.[2]  On the influence of commerce in stimulating the inventive faculties, see some very good remarks in Rae's New Principles of Political Economy.[3]  In 1599 banking in London was not a separate business, but most of the gold-smiths were bankers.[4]

Chevenix has some good remarks on the moral benefits of commerce.  He well notices " the immense addition which universal probity, the basis of commercial confidence, must make to national morality."[5]  According to the recognized principles of law at the accession of Elizabeth, it was almost impossible to recover a debt from an unprincipled debtor; for the man owing the money could defeat an action to recover the amount by waging his law—that is, by swearing that he did not owe it.  In order to put an end to this monstrous absurdity, a practice had been for some time growing up for the creditor to bring an action, not of debt, but of *assumpsit*, by which the wager of law was avoided, and the question decided on its own merits.  But this mode of proceeding, which was founded on a legal fiction, had never been recognised by the courts,[6] and there were, consequently, considerable doubts as to the validity of such an action.  These doubts, by increasing the hazard of trading transactions, tended not a little to check the growing spirit of commercial adventure.  The judges of England, who to their immortal credit, have always aided and not unfrequently anticipated the wisest efforts of the legislature, were on this occasion not wanting to their duty; and two years before the death of Elizabeth, they solemnly determined not only, that in the case of debts of simple contract, an action of assumpsit should lie, but that the party bringing the action should recover damages for the whole debt, as well as for the special loss.[7]  This important decision, which was one of the last acts in the glorious reign of Elizabeth, at once gave to a great body of commercial transactions a security not inferior to that enjoyed by the possessors of real property.[8]  A writer of very considerable learning in English law has noticed this in reference to his own immediate studies.  He says, " The

---

[1] See M'Culloch's Commercial Dictionary, 8vo, 1840, p. xxii.
[2] Esprit des Lois, livre xxi. chap. i. p. 349.        [3] Boston, 1834, pp. 237, 238.
[4] Ben Jonson's Works, 8vo, 1816, vol. ii. pp. 73, 74.
[5] Essay on National Character, 1832, vol. i. p. 153.
[6] Reeves's History of English Law, vol. v. p. 178.
[7] 4 Rep. 93, quoted by Reeves, Eng. Law, vol. v. p. 179.
[8] But it seems that independently of assumpsits an *action on the case* might be brought; see Reeves, Hist. of English Law, vol. v. p. 185.

reports of the reign contain more questions upon personal rights and contracts in one shape or other than perhaps those of all the preceding reigns put together."[1] The old common law was very severe towards insolvent debtors (?), and this was a great discouragement to persons who otherwise might have engaged in commercial pursuits. At length the 13 Eliz. cap. 7, first distinguished between bankrupts and insolvents, and gave protection to the former.[2] The same statute gave the Commissioners of Bankruptcy power to dispose of a bankrupt's lands and tenements.[3]

In 1575, Fénelon writes to the king respecting the English: " Leur principal revenu et celluy de l'Estat et de la noblesse est fondé ou bien depend du commerce."[4] Indeed, in 1568, the French and English [Qy. Spanish?] ambassadors residing at the court of London, had a long conversation on the possibility of compelling Elizabeth to become a Catholic by establishing a continental blockade against the English commerce.[5] In 1568, Fénelon writes[6] that the chief commerce of England is with Flanders and Spain. In 1569, he writes that commerce " est lo seul soubstien du pays."[7] There was a sort of stock-jobbing in London in 1569 : at least they made *bets* on the " bource," respecting political events. See Fénelon, tome ii. p. 281. In 1569, in spite of the opposition of many of her advisers, Elizabeth expressed a desire that the commerce with France should be perfectly free.[8] In November 1570, Fénelon writes[9] that the Muscovite ambassador, having left London in disgust, had caused all the English in Muscovy to be imprisoned, and that this put an end to the idea of establishing a commerce with Russia. The French ambassador was present at the opening of the Exchange in January 1571, and has given an account of it.[10] In 1571, Elizabeth asked the advice of the chief merchants of London, (iv. 204). In November 1571, the London merchants, in consequence of the heavy duties levied at Rouen, became disgusted with their commerce with France, and turned their eyes more towards that of Antwerp.[11] And in December, Fénelon writes[12] that Elizabeth was negotiating with Spain for reopening the trade with Antwerp : and he suggests to the king

[1] Reeves, Hist. of English Law, vol. v. p. 188.
[2] Blackstone's Commentaries, vol. ii. pp. 473-475, and my notes on Blackstone, p. 130.
[3] Blackstone, vol. ii. pp. 285, 286.
[4] Correspondance diplomatique, Paris, 8vo, 1840, tome i. p. xxxi. See also p. 70.
[5] See the Secret Dispatch, in Fénelon, tome i. pp. 66-73.
[6] Ibid. tome i. p. 72.                      [7] Ibid. p. 166.
[8] Fénelon, tome ii. p. 330.                  [9] Tome iii. p. 375.
[10] Correspondance de Fénelon, tome iii. pp. 450, 451.
[11] Ibid. tome iv. pp. 290, 291.               [12] Ibid. p. 313.

image
not
available

avoid thinking when he is off the field. Laing[1] observes that we respect military men less than formerly, because we find a great general may be a very weak man.

Smith says[2] that in modern Europe not more than one hundredth of the inhabitants can be employed as soldiers without ruin to the country. Hence we see the importance of his remark[3] that *gunpowder*, by rendering the habits of subordination and obedience more necessary in a soldier than individual strength, must have tended to do away with the militia, and to substitute standing armies. This, of course, would aid civilization by reducing the number of soldiers.

I suppose that no one will doubt the nautical knowledge of Sir John Ross; still less will any one accuse him of desiring to depreciate his own profession. He is, therefore, a witness worth hearing, and I shall give his own words. He is speaking of sailors. " 'The men,' as they are called, are not much given to thinking, it is certain ; though seamen of the present day (*and I am sorry to say it*) think much more than they did in the days of my junior service, and most assuredly and certainly are all the worse for it."[4] See also a similarly conceived passage in Preface, p. x. Tocqueville well says[5] that the tendency of war is to increase the power of rulers. The causes of the natural thoughtlessness of military men have been well stated by Adam Smith.[6]

I suppose Captain Marryat knows his own profession. He says,[7] " There is no character so devoid of principles as the British soldier and sailor. In Dibdin's songs we certainly have another version, ' True to his country and king,' &c. ; but I am afraid they do not deserve it : soldiers and sailors are mercenaries : they risk their lives for money, it is their trade to do so, and if they can get higher wages, they never consider the justice of the cause, or whom they fight for."

Military men commit suicide oftener than other classes, and much oftener than sailors, who are more cheerful. See my notes on Suicide.

Sailors are more liable to disease than soldiers, but they do not so often sink under it. Journal of Statistical Society, vol. iv.

[1] Tour in Sweden, pp. 401, 405.
[2] Wealth of Nations, p. 291.　　　　　　　　　　[3] Ibid. pp. 296, 297.
[4] Narrative of a Second Voyage in Search of a North-West Passage, by Sir John Ross, Paris, 8vo, 1835, p. 458.
[5] Démocratie en Amérique, tome ii. p. 26.
[6] See his Theory of Moral Sentiments, part v. chap. ii. vol. ii. pp. 37, 38, Lond. 1822, 12mo.
[7] A Diary in America, Lond. 8vo, 1839, vol. iii. p. 31.

p. 2, 3, and vol. viii. p. 78. And at vol. ix. 350, it is shown that sailors live longer than soldiers.

Mr. Rae truly says that war has been a great means of advancing mankind by disseminating arts and industry.[1] Of course the remark only holds of a barbarous state of society. Lord Brougham says,[2] "Perhaps the greatest captains have always been among the greatest statesmen in every age and in all countries." The imprudence in monarchies of giving great civil employments to military men is forcibly stated in Esprit des Lois.[3] On the tendency of civilization to diminish war, see Quételet, Sur l'Homme.[4] It is said to be a well-ascertained fact that, during the reign of Napoleon, the continued wars diminished the average height of men in France.[5] William Schlegel says: "War is much more an epic than a dramatic object."[6] See also pp. 243, 244, where he is doubtful as to the propriety of representing battles on the stage, but seems to think that it *may* be done.

The rudeness of the military character is admirably hit off in the character of Ironside in The Magnetick Lady.[7]

See Hallam's Europe during the Middle Ages.[8] During the twelfth and thirteenth centuries the Italian armies were composed of the whole population.[9] Early in the fourteenth century the proportion of cavalry was increased.[10] In 1339, Azzo Visconti dispensed with the personal service of his subjects, which in 1351 was changed into a money payment.[11] Sir John Hawkwood in the reign of Edward III. was "the first distinguished commander who had appeared in Europe since the destruction of the Roman Empire."[12] And in the fourteenth century "historians for the first time discover that success does not entirely depend upon intrepidity and physical prowess."[13] Even in the fifteenth century in Italy, battles were very bloodless.[14] The bow, indeed, *was* used before the Crusades, but armour was almost impenetrable.[15] The cross bow is *said* to have been used in the battle of Hastings,[16] but, even under Philip Augustus, was scarcely known in France.[17] Early in the fourteenth century, cannons were invented, or rather mortars, and the application of gunpowder to war was understood.[18] The French made the greatest improve-

[1] New Principles of Political Economy, Boston, 8vo, 1834, pp. 48–50, 255, 256.
[2] Political Philosophy, 2nd edit. 8vo, 1849, vol. i. p. 33.
[3] Livre v. chap. xix. Œuvres de Montesquieu, Paris, 1835, p. 225.
[4] Paris, 8vo, 1835, tome ii. pp. 291–293.    [5] Quételet, Sur l'Homme, tome ii. p. 16.
[6] Lectures on Dramatic Art and Literature, 1840, vol. ii. p. 239.
[7] Jonson's Works, vol. vi. See in particular, p. 56.
[8] Hallam's Europe, 9th edit. 8vo, 1846, vol. i. pp. 328–313.    [9] Ibid. p. 328.
[10] P. 320.    [11] P. 331.    [12] P. 334.    [13] P. 335.    [14] P. 337.
[15] P. 338.    [16] P. 339.    [17] P. 339.    [18] P. 341.

ments. (It seems that the two most important phenomena are the invention of gunpowder and the disuse of heavy armour.)

Farquhar and Steele went into the army from choice. The degree to which subordinate European soldiers reason, and the military evils which their reasoning causes, are very fairly stated by Chevenix.[1] He supposes,[2] and I think with reason, that under the same circumstances proud nations are likely to be most powerful at sea, vain nations at land. On the tendency of the mind in our present early stage of civilization to prefer military achievements to scientific discoveries, see some good remarks by Dr. Paris.[3] Jackson states with regret the decline of military enthusiasm in England.[4] He says dancing is a cause of the success of the French in war.[5] In 1589, Forman writes, " This yere, I was preste a souldiar to serve in the Portingalle voyage, whereupon I was constrained to forsake my country and dwelling and all my frindes."[6] Lord Brougham thinks that the foolish notion which still exists, that war is a very honourable occupation, is the result of feudalism. See his ingenious remarks in his Political Philosophy;[7] but I am rather inclined to assign it not to any special cause, but merely to the general ignorance of men which makes them unable to appreciate the highest order of excellence. Happily, in our times, this respect for military heroes is fast waning.

Dr. Fergusson [8] says that English soldiers, " however hideously mangled, are generally uncomplaining:" and he adds, " According to my observations, the most querulous under wounds and sickness have been the Scotch Highlanders. The Irish may be more noisy, but then it is with less plaint."

The great causes of war are : 1st. The respect paid to warriors in an age when courage is considered the first virtue. 2nd. A belief that, like the ordeal, war was a judgment of God. 3rd. In more modern times, a jealousy of each other's wealth. 4th. Religious hatred. 5th. An ignorant contempt of each other's strength. But now power is passing into the hands of the industrious classes who are pacific.

---

[1] Essay on National Character, 8vo, 1832, vol. ii. pp. 206, 207.    [2] Ibid. p. 219.

[3] Life of Sir Humphry Davy, 8vo, 1831, vol. ii. pp. 152, 154.

[4] Formation and Discipline of Armies, pp. 189-192.

[5] See COMMON PLACK BOOK, art. 619. See respecting the bayonet, COMMON PLACE BOOK, art. 2320.

[6] Autobiography of Dr. Simon Forman, from 1552 to 1602, edited by Mr. Halliwell, 4to, 1849, p. 19.

[7] 8vo, 1849, vol. i. pp. 324, 325.

[8] Notes and Recollections of a Professional Life, 1846, 8vo, p. 8.

## HISTORY OF MILITARY INSTITUTIONS AND THE ARMY.

" . . . . . their plumes of feathers and rich acoutrements, a vanity which few nations imitate the English soldiers in." (Camden's Elizabeth in Kennett, ii. 597). In 1601, Camden mentions "swords, bayonets, and pistols." (Kennett, ii. 635).

On the 1st of August, 1559, Sir Nicolas Throckmorton writes to Elizabeth from Paris that the French " suspect much the preparation and readiness of your Majesty's ships to the sea, and also the musters of men through your Majesty's realm." [1] In May 1560, Mr. Peyto writes to Throckmorton, the ambassador at Paris, that " the Quene mustereth all the realme throughout from seventeen to threescore years old," &c.; " every shire hath his muster master apart." [2]

When was *corporal punishment*, in the sense of flogging, first inflicted in the army? In Forbes [3] is a list of " orders to be observed by the English soldiers in Newhaven," to which are affixed a variety of penalties; but nothing is said of the ignominious punishment of flogging, nor is it mentioned in the list of punishments at pp. 181–183, nor in the Duke of Medina's orders to the Spanish fleet in 1588. [4] It would seem from a letter of Elizabeth in 1562, that the coats of the soldiers cost 4s. [5] In the Rebellion of 1569, the Earls of Westmoreland and Northumberland offered 16d. a day to whoever would join their standard. [6] This, no doubt, was above the average pay. The queen's levies at Barnard Castle received, common soldiers, 8d.; light horsemen and archers, 16d. a day. [7] It is said in Laing's Sweden [8] that Gustavus Adolphus invented the bayonet.

In 1563 the Lords of the Council write to the Earl of Warwick that " the choyse men " among the infantry, " being above the degree of common soldiers, may have 12d. a day, and the rest as others have." [9] However, out of their pay they had, at least when in garrison, " to make some small allowance out of the monthly wages of the soldiers towards the maintenance of surgeons, as in other garrisons hath been always used." [10]

*Arms.*—In 1563 the Earl of Warwick writes to the Council from New Haven for " 200 pickaxes, helved, and 1000 black

[1] Forbes' State Papers, vol. i. p. 184.      [2] Ibid. p. 443.      [3] Vol. ii. pp. 87, 88.
[4] See Harleian Miscellany, edit. Park, vol. i. p. 116.
[5] See Forbes, vol. ii. p. 92.
[6] Sharp's Memorials of 1569, pp. 69, 83.      [7] See the list in Sharp. pp. 216-218.
[8] P. 57.      [9] Forbes, vol. ii. pp. 446, 447.      [10] Ibid. p. 418.

bills."[1] In 1569 we find the Earl of Northumberland "armed in a previe cote under a Spanishe jerkyn, being open so that the cote might be seen, and a steele cappe covered with green velvet."[2] It appears[3] that for light horsemen, the arms were: "playte coyte, jack, bowes and arrows, and bylles" and [4] "horsemen armed in corsletts and coyts of playt."[5] At p. 80 "certain ordenance, which is a fawcon and two slyngs," and see p. 90 "a falcon of cast yron." In 1685–6, all "fire arms" could be made at Dublin cheaper than in England; and pikes could be made "and furnished into the stores for 3s. 10d. each."[6]

I have met with several things which make me believe that in the sixteenth century the *Italians* were considered the greatest masters in the scientific part of war. In July 1563, Elizabeth writes to the Earl of Warwick, that she approved of the "inventions" of "Signor Melionni" for the defence of a town, and had rewarded his ingenuity;[7] and in 1560 "an Italian is the fortifier at Dunbar."[8]

In July 1563, Lord Montague complained that so many men had been taken from Sussex as soldiers, that if more "shall be taken, the harvest of the cuntree must end itself."[9]

Chevenix says,[10] "It is not a little remarkable that in the only two battles since the days of Joan d'Arc down to 1745 in which the French obtained an advantage over the English, they were commanded, at Almanza, by the Duke of Berwick, an Englishman, and at Fontenoy, by a Saxon." In an able tract by Anthony Marten, printed in 1588, the object of which was to stir up the English against Spain, it is said : "We must consider with ourselves that the bands and cornets of horsemen, and especially of lances, have ever been, and yet are, the most necessary and puissant strength in wars, both to defend ourselves and offend our enemies."[11] Mr. Hallam says [12] that, under Henry VIII., "except the yeomen of the guard, fifty in number, and the common servants of the king's household, there was not in time of peace an armed man receiving pay throughout England. Henry VII. first established a band of fifty archers to wait on him. Henry VII. had fifty horse-guards, each with an archer, demilance, and couteillier." . . . . but on account of expense

[1] Forbes, vol. ii. p. 451.                    [2] Sharp's Rebellion of 1569, p. 15.
[3] Pp. 29. 30.            [4] P. 37.            [5] See also p. 94.
[6] Clarendon Correspondence, edit. Singer, 1828, vol. i. pp. 241, 242.
[7] Forbes, vol. ii. p. 464.                    [8] Sharp's Rebellion of 1569, p. 79.
[9] Forbes, State Papers, vol. ii. p. 464.
[10] Essay on National Character, 8vo, 1832, vol. ii. p. 229.
[11] Harleian Miscellany, edit. Park, vol. i. p. 168.
[12] Constitutional History, 8vo, 1842, vol. i. p. 46.

"this soon was given up." In 1559 it was usual in England to draw a cannon with thirty horses ; and the Council complained of the Duke of Norfolk because he used sixty.[1] In 1560 an Italian was employed as "fortifier" at Dunbar.[2] In January 1569, the French ambassador at London writes that Rochester "est le principal arsenal de ce royaulme."[3] As to the value of armour at the beginning of the fifteenth century, see a curious document printed from the Leber MSS., by Mr. Williams.[4] In 1581 Churchyard boasts that he is "one that hath used both pen and sword." See his Letter to Hatton in Wright's Elizabeth.[5] For a list of the Ordinance and Stores in the Tower in 1578, see The Egerton Papers.[6] In 1585 there were such abuses at the Ordinance Office as to excite the Queen's anger against Sir William Pelham.[7] In 1586 Walsingham proposed a method of training, by which "two pounds of powder will serve one man for four days' exercise of training."[8] In the Loseley Manuscripts[9] are preserved the first printed Regulations for the English army. Their date is 1513, and they were unknown to Grose. Henry VIII. introduced into England from Germany "the art of making body armour and offensive weapons:" and in the reign of Elizabeth, there were in London thirty-five of these armour-makers : but in the reign of James I., there were only five.[10] In 1554 the naval uniform of England for officers and marines was white and green.[11] It is said by De La Clos that Vauban's "système bastionné" was known at the end of the fifteenth century, and regularly executed in 1567 at Antwerp.[12] Respecting the employment in England in 1548 of mercenary troops, and the terms on which they served, see Tytler's Edward VI. and Mary.[13] In 1679 Locke gives an account of the uniform of the French troops.[14] In 1687 bombs and the bombarding of towns were new, being a French invention.[15] The moderns have made more rapid military marches than the ancients.[16] It is curious that even in some nautical

---

[1] Haynes's State Papers, p. 249.    [2] Ibid. p. 314.
[3] Correspondance de Fénelon, Paris, 1840, tome i. p. 158.
[4] Note in Chronicque de la Traïson de Richart Deux d'Engleterre, Londres, 8vo, 1846, p. 151.
[5] Vol. ii. p. 143.    [6] Pp. 68–74, Camden Soc.
[7] See Leycester Correspondence, p. 37, Camden Soc.
[8] Lodge's Illustrations of British History, 1838, vol. ii. p. 285.
[9] By Kempe, pp. 107–117.    [10] Loseley Manuscripts, pp. 136, 137.
[11] Machyn's Diary, Camden Soc. vol. xlii. pp. 59, 398.
[12] Grimm, Correspondance littéraire, tome xiv. p. 502.
[13] 8vo, 1839, vol. i. p. 161.
[14] King's Life of Locke, 8vo, 1830, vol. i. p. 152.
[15] See Evelyn's Diary, vol. iii. pp. 226, 341.
[16] Alison's History of Europe, vol. viii. p. 604.

matters, soldiers have been found quicker than sailors.[1]  Alison[2] agrees with Napoleon that cavalry can break an equal number of infantry.  In the middle of the reign of Elizabeth "the fighting men" in England were about 1,172,000.[3]

## HISTORY OF THE ENGLISH ARMY.

In Haynes's State Papers[4] there is a memorandum by Cecil of the arrangements made for placing the troops on the 26th of November, 1562, in eleven different counties, and in London.  The total force is 1312 horse, and 10,000 foot, of which 110 horsemen and 2,500 footmen were for London.  None of the more northern counties are mentioned.  The footmen are divided into corslets, archers, bilmen, and harquebuzers.

Hume quotes[5] Lives of the Admirals, vol. i. p. 432, to the effect that "in the year 1575 all the militia in the kingdom were computed at 182,929.  A distribution was made in 1595 of 140,000 men, besides those which Wales could supply."[6]  It appears indeed from Murdin,[7] that in 1588 the able-bodied men were only 111,513, of whom 80,875 were armed, and 44,727 were trained.  But Hume thinks that "these able-bodied men consisted of such only as were registered, otherwise the small number is not to be accounted for."  However he quotes Journals of the House of Commons, 25th of April, 1621, to the effect that Coke said, that about the same time, he and Popham, the chief justice, found on a survey that there were not more than 900,000 people in England, which would give about 200,000 to bear arms.  And yet, adds Hume, we are told by Harrison, "that, in the musters taken in 1574 and 1575, the men fit for service amounted to 1,172,674, yet was it believed that a full third was omitted."  The paper mentioned by Hume is in Murdin,[8] but it is singular that he should not have noticed that the list,[9] which he refers to as giving for all England only 111,513 able-bodied men, in reality gives that number for twenty-eight counties.  For the *expense* of the army in 1587 and 1588, see Murdin's State Papers.[10]  On the 1st of May, 1572, there was a great festival at Greenwich, on which occasion, the queen reviewed 3000 troops."[11]

[1] Alison, vol. xiii. p. 42.                    [2] Ibid. p. 139.
[3] Journal of Statistical Society, vol. iv. p. 202.      [4] Pp. 562, 563.
[5] In Appendix to Elizabeth, No. III.
[6] Strype, vol. iv. p. 221.          [7] P. 608.          [8] Pp. 594, 611.
[9] P. 608.                        [10] P. 620, et seq.
[11] Correspondance de Fénelon, tome iv. p. 415.

See my notes at the beginning of Jackson's Formation and Discipline of Armies.

The great success of the English in war had, during the four-teenth and fifteenth centuries, chiefly depended on the skill of their archers. But the invention of gunpowder and its general use, had given rise to a new feature in war, and caused the disuse of archery. One of the latest attempts made to revive archery was in a warrant issued by Elizabeth in 1596, which directed the en-forcement of an Act of Parliament, which had been passed in 1542, for the maintenance of archery in 33rd Henry VIII.[1] For evidence of the decline of archery in the reign of Mary, see Lodge's Illustrations of British History.[2] In the last year of the reign of Mary, the justices of peace for the county of Derby stated, "that in this shire, cannot be made, levied and furnished, able men above the number of 100 men, besides those who are of the inheritance or within the offices and rules of our very good Lord, the Earl of Shrewsbury."[3] Sir John Smith in his Military Discourses, which were written in 1589, seems to wish to revive archery.[4] Smith says[5] that the muskets then used were first employed in Italy about sixty years before, that is about 1529. In the south west of England, bows and arrows did not finally disappear from the muster rolls until 1599. In the meantime the musket gained ground.[6]

---

# THE RISE OF AGRICULTURE AND ITS INFLUENCE ON CIVILIZATION.

THE great importance of agriculture in increasing the material wealth of a country consists in the simple fact, that a capital em-ployed in tilling the ground puts in motion a greater quantity of productive labour than it could do if employed in any other branch of industry.[7]

As civilization advances, the progress of manufactures greatly outstrips the progress of agriculture ; because agriculture has less capacity for the division of labour than manufactures. See Smith's Wealth of Nations, p. 3. See also p. 106, where he

---

[1] See the Warrant, and Mr. Collier's note, in Egerton Papers, pp. 217–220. Cam-den Society.

[2] 1838, vol. i. p. 287.　　　　[3] Lodge's Illustrations, vol. i. p. 364.

[4] See Ellis, Original Letters of Literary Men, pp. 54–56, Camden Soc., vol. xxiii.

[5] P. 53.　　　　[6] Yonge's Diary, Camden Soc., 1848, p. xvii.

[7] Smith's Wealth of Nations, Book II. chap. v. p. 150, Edinb. 1850, 8vo.

notices the bad effects of this on the intellect and knowledge of
landed proprietors.  In America, where the inhabitants are
equally remarkable for the greatness of their wealth and the
coarseness of their manners, agricultural prejudices are very
strong.  Miss Martineau says,[1]  " It is not five years since the
President's message declared that ' the wealth and strength of a
country are its population ; and the best part of that population
are the cultivators of the soil.' "

Observe that sailors are more superstitious than soldiers, because
more dependent on nature.

The prejudices of great landlords against travelling in the reign
of Charles II. are well expressed by the rich and ignorant Sir
William Belfond.[2]

M'Culloch [3] says that, even economically speaking, agriculture
is not more important than manufactures or commerce.[4]  He
notices the inferiority of the intellect of those who cultivate the
soil.  " The spinners, weavers, and other mechanics of Glasgow,
Manchester, and Birmingham, possess far more information than
the agricultural labourers of any part of the empire ; "[5] and [6] he
mentions the dislike of agriculturists to improvements.  This
seems a sort of brute instinct, for there is no doubt that the immediate tendency of agricultural improvements is to lower rent.
M'Culloch, indeed, says [7] " There is no such opposition between his
interests and those of the rest of the community."  But this is put
much too strongly, for it is certain that the *immediate* tendency
of agricultural improvements is to diminish rent ; and it is impossible for rent to reach its former height until an increase of
population compels the cultivation of inferior soils.  Indeed
M'Culloch says as much.[8]  Landlords are perhaps the only great
body of men whose interest is diametrically opposed to the interest
of the nation.  Every agricultural improvement tends to diminish
their rents.  This was first laid down by Ricardo, and is admirably
worked out by Mr. Mill.[9]  This requires to be clearly stated.
Mill says [10] " If the assertion were that a landlord is injured by
the improvement of his estate, it would certainly be indefensible ;
but, what is asserted is, that he is injured by the improvement of
the estates of other people, although his own is included."  If,

---

[1] Society in America, Paris, 8vo, 1842, vol. ii. p. 26 ; part ii. chap. ii. sect. 1.
[2] See Shadwell's Squire of Alsatia ; Works, vol. iv. pp. 44, 45, Lond. 1720, 12mo.
[3] Principles of Political Economy, Edinb. 1843, 8vo, pp. 165–171.
[4] See also p. 173.                    [5] P. 180.                    [6] P. 463.
[7] P. 459.                             [8] P. 462.
[9] Principles of Political Economy, 2nd edition, 8vo, 1849, vol. ii. pp. 270-275.
[10] P. 275.

indeed, agricultural improvement, capital and population, advance in an equal ratio, then the landlord will be benefitted by the improvement, but in that case, he alone will gain.[1]  Thus too, emigration, which is so advantageous to a densely peopled country, entails a positive loss on the landlords.[2]  From 1688 to the Reform Bill, the landowners have been supreme in the English legislature, but have never brought forward a single measure to lessen the pressure of those burdens which weigh so heavily on their country. Mr. Mill[3] mildly calls this an "irrational hostility to improvement;" but it is rather the systematic bigotry of a body of men who are unhappily as formidable for their power as they are contemptible for their ignorance.

On the importance of towns even to agriculturists, see Mill's Political Economy.[4]

Mill says,[5] "In France, it is computed that two-thirds of the whole population are agricultural; in England at most one-third."

Towns are the great centres of knowledge; the ignorant flock to the country.  There is on the whole no fairer criterion of civilization than the proportion between the rural and civic population, and between those engaged in agriculture and those engaged in other occupations.  (Of course this would not apply to countries whose soil is ill adapted to agriculture). In Ireland the rural inhabitants are nearly seven-eighths; in England less than half of the population; and while the families chiefly employed in agriculture are in Ireland five-eighths, they are in England only one quarter.[6]  The second Pitt found it convenient to flatter the country gentlemen, but he had a real, and sometimes an undisguised, contempt for them. This is illustrated by an amusing and original anecdote related by Captain Jesse.[7]

Agriculture has made scarcely any progress.  How can agriculturists increase in civilization since they do not increase in knowledge?  Storch observes that in an advanced state of society, agricultural labour is less productive than other labour.[8]  He well says,[9] "Dans la production agricole, c'est la terre qui fait la plus grande partie de la besogne; dans les manufactures et le commerce, c'est l'homme." And again,[10] "L'industrie agricole admet le moins de division dans les travaux." He adds[11] that,

[1] Mill, p. 281.    [2] Ibid. vol. ii. pp. 303, 304.    [3] Ibid. p. 448.
[4] Vol. i. pp. 147, 148.    [5] Political Economy, 8vo, 1849, vol. i. p. 185.
[6] See Thornton on Over Population, 8vo, 1846, p. 82.
[7] Life of Beau Brummell, 8vo, 1844, vol. i. pp. 72, 73.
[8] Économie politique, St. Petersbourg, 8vo, 1815, tome iv. pp. 171-174.
[9] Ibid. p. 172.    [10] Ibid. tome i. p. 209.
[11] Ibid. p. 211, and tome ii. p. 210.

in spite of the protection and patronage of government, agriculture is not much advanced beyond the state in which the ancients
left it.    This is partly the result of the ignorance of the country
gentlemen.[1]  Mr. Rae draws an accurate picture of the operations
of an ordinary agriculturist; all of which resolve themselves into
mere observation of the economical phenomena of nature.[2]  He
well says[3] that it is impossible *à priori* to construct or even to
improve a plough.

It is well known that the immediate tendency of agricultural
improvements is to lower rent.    This truth to an economist is
almost self-evident ; but there has been found a gentleman—
a certain Rev. Richard Jones—who has not only the unparalleled hardihood to attack this principle, but who considers a
belief in it to proceed " from imperfect observation and hasty
reasoning."    See the amusing remarks in Jones's Essay on the
Distribution of Wealth,[4] and compare his remarks[5] on Ricardo,
one of the most acute and original thinkers that this age has produced.    Oldys says that the works on Husbandry and Agriculture,
published in the reign of James I. " are so numerous that it can
scarcely be imagined by whom they were written or to whom they
were sold."[6]    Mr. Alison is, I think, mistaken in saying that
capital laid out in agriculture is more productive than when laid
out in commerce or manufacture.[7]    Even *he* observes[8] that
agriculture has made little or no progress.    In towns, women
reach puberty sooner than they do in the country ; and among the
rich sooner than among the poor.[9]  Archdeacon Hare gravely says,
" The strength of a nation, humanly speaking, consists not in its
population, or wealth, or knowledge, or in any other such heart-
less and merely scientific elements, but in the number of its proprietors."[10]    On the slavish tendencies of the agricultural mind,
and the progressive spirit of cities, see Coleridge on Church and
State.[11]    Comte[12] observes that as society advances, agriculturists
must fall in the scale.    Among the ancients agriculturists were
the most superstitious.[13]  Laing[14] says, " The great difference

[1]  Économie politique, St. Petersbourg, 8vo. 1815. tome ii. p. 213.
[2]  New Principles of Political Economy, Boston, 8vo, 1834, pp. 85, 87.
[3]  P. 87.                    [4]  8vo, 1831, pp. 303, 304.                    [5]  P. vii.
[6]  Harleian Miscellany, vol. i. p. xvii.
[7]  Principles of Population. 8vo, 1840, vol. i. pp. 148, 149.            [8]  Pp. 193, 194.
[9]  See the additions of Dr. Cerise to Roussel, Système de la Femme, Paris, 1845.
pp. 337-339.
[10]  Hare's Guesses at Truth, first series, p. iii. ; 3rd edition, 8vo, 1847.
[11]  Pp. 22-26.                    [12]  Philosophie Positive, tome vi. p. 586.
[13]  See Mackay's Progress of the Intellect, 8vo, 1850, vol. ii. p. 43.
[14]  Sweden, 8vo, 1839, p. 194.

produced by agricultural improvement seems to be in the cost of production, rather than in the quantities produced from the seed." In France, two-thirds are engaged in the direct cultivation of the soil." [1] Tocqueville says [2] that rents have indeed risen, but the agriculturists, while gaining money, have thus lost interest and political power. In the plan of a " Constitution" put forward by Robespierre in the spring of 1793, " La culture des champs était le premier des travaux. Robespierre, ainsi que tous les législateurs de l'antiquité, considerait le travail appliqué à la terre comme le plus moral et le plus social des travaux de l'homme." [3] Directly after the Restoration in 1660 there began " a new system of legislation, by the landed interest, for their own immunity." [4]

Our laws, by encouraging the agglomeration of landed property into large estates, have greatly discouraged agriculture. Besides the severity of primogeniture and entail, even subinfeudation, so general in France, was checked by Magna Charta, and forbidden in 18th Edward I. by the statute called Quia Emptores. [5] Thus, too, escheats were frequent in England, because there was no power of *willing away* land. [6] There is a masterly sketch of the economic causes and tendencies of Chinese civilization in Rae's New Principles of Political Economy. [7] In 1813 Sir Humphry Davy published his Elements of Agricultural Chemistry, which, says Dr. Paris, [8] " may be considered as the only system of philosophical agriculture ever published in this country." So slow has been the progress of agriculture, that, in 1723, Lord Molesworth, having proposed that a school for teaching husbandry should be established, could find no better text book than Tusser's work, which was published in 1577. [9] Lands were not allowed to be devised by will until the 32nd Henry VIII. cap. i., which allowed *all* soccage lands, and two-thirds of lands of military tenure to be devised. These last at the restoration were turned into soccage tenure, which made all lands devisable except some copyhold. [10] The great policy of breaking up estates now went rapidly forward. By 32 Henry VIII. joint tenants were compellable, by writ of par-

[1] Laing's Notes of a Traveller, 1st series, p. 48.
[2] Démocratie en Europe, tome v. pp. 40, 41.
[3] Lamartine, Histoire des Girondins, tome v. p. 288.
[4] Campbell's Lives of the Chancellors, vol. iii. p. 194.  See also at p. 224, the impudent complaint of the Duke of Buckingham, as to a fall in rent.
[5] See Hallam's Middle Ages, 9th edition, 8vo, 1846, vol. i. p. 124.
[6] Ibid. p. 127.                                    [7] Boston, 8vo, 1834, pp. 149–155.
[8] Life of Davy, 8vo, 1831, vol. i. p. 373.
[9] See Mavor's Preliminary Dissertation to Tusser's Five Hundred Points, 8vo, 1812, p. 25.
[10] Christian's Note on Blackstone's Comment. 8vo, 1809, vol. ii. p. 12.

tition, to divide their lands. Before this statute they had no such power.[1] It is stated by a very competent authority that, among the recruits for the army, labourers in the field display more strength, and mechanics more aptitude for learning the exercises, &c.[2] As the great landowners were soon able to enslave the rest of the proprietors, the possession of land became not merely the only mark of honour, but the only title to security.[3] Posterity will not believe the extent to which this foolish respect for land-owners has carried us. Lord Brougham says, " In a manor in Essex, at this day, the power of appointing justices, who have a criminal jurisdiction over a population of 5000 souls, belongs to whoever may purchase the property."[4]

Mr. Mill truly says that " great landlords have seldom seriously studied anything;"[5] and he notices their idleness.[6] Mr. Inglis's valuable travels in Ireland contain abundant evidence that the grasping selfishness and bigotry of the landlords is one great cause of the miseries of that ill-used and lovely country. See a remarkable instance at vol. i. p. 26, 2nd edit., 8vo, 1835; and compare Thornton on Over Population.[7] See also[8] Mr. Thornton's just remarks on the shameless rapacity of the English landlords.

The fall in the value of money injured the landowners in two different ways; for while, on the one hand, they were pre-vented by the terms of their current lease from raising their rents to the full point which would restore them to their former position, so, on the other hand, the extent to which they did raise their rents exposed them to great obloquy, and seriously affected their popularity. There are innumerable attacks on landlords for raising their rents made by popular authors in the sixteenth and seventeenth centuries.[9] In Maroccus Extaticus,[10] " the covetous landlord is the caterpiller of the commonwealth." [11] Even Bancroft, in the famous sermon he preached at St. Paul's Cross in 1588, notices the charges against the landlords.[12] The decline in the value of the precious metals fell chiefly on the

[1] Blackstone, vol. ii. pp. 185, 187, 188.
[2] Jackson's View of the Formation, Discipline, and Economy of Armies, 8vo, 1845, pp. 15, 16, 188.
[3] Brougham's Political Philosophy, 2nd edit. 8vo, 1849, vol. i. p. 308.
[4] Ibid. p. 318.        [5] Political Economy, vol. i. p. 283.        [6] P. 307.
[7] 8vo, 1846, p. 97.        [8] Pp. 292, 293.
[9] See, for instance, Dekker's Knights Conjuring, 1607, p. 72, Percy Soc. vol. v. See also p. 112 of Rowland's More Knaves Yet? published about 1610, and reprinted in Percy Soc. vol. ix.
[10] 1595, Percy Soc. vol. ix. p. 15.
[11] See also to the same effect, Rich's Honestie of this Age, 1614, pp. 62, 63, Percy Soc. vol. xi.
[12] See Collier's Ecclesiastical History, 8vo, 1840, vol. vii. p. 81.

great landlords. By the common law of England (?) a lessee's
estate less than freehold might be at any time defeated by a common recovery suffered by the tenant of the freehold. But by
21 Henry VIII., the termor (i. e. he who was entitled to the term
of years) was protected against these petition recoveries, and
the consequence was that long terms of leases became frequent.[1]

In muscular employments, such as agriculture, the excess of
male over female births is greater than it is in the more sedentary ones, as commerce and manufactures.[2] So that I suppose
the more agricultural a people the fewer its women. Alison
says[3] that, in America, "the proportion of the cultivators of the
soil to the other classes of society is about twelve to one." See
also p. 549, where he says that "in 1820, out of nearly ten
millions of inhabitants there were only four hundred and twenty
thousand employed in commerce and manufactures." In the agricultural, there is about the same criminality as in the non-agri-
cultural counties.[4]

In the discouragement given to agriculture[5] the loss to the
material wealth of the country has been amply compensated by
the gain, if I may so express myself, in moral wealth. The
intellectual inferiority of farmers to traders is too manifest to
be disputed. And we find that countries—such, for instance,
as China—which have encouraged agriculture at the expense of
trade, have gained wealth without reaching civilization.[6] The
causes of this lie in the nature of their respective pursuits. Let
any man compare a merchant with an agriculturist. The range
of a great merchant is immense. His speculations cover the
surface of the world. He has to consider the wants of a multitude of markets, the feelings and habits of a multitude of people.
The casualties of war, the risks of sea, the character of distant voyages are familiar to his mind; and, if he be a man of
only ordinary apprehension, the constant consideration of such
distant topics cannot fail to enlarge his mind. With the agriculturist the case is quite different. His views are confined to
one country, and often to one place in that country. What he
gains in intensity he loses in grasp. His interests, his views, his
very aspirations are small and cramped; and, unless he be a man
of considerable natural power, he dwindles away in point of in-

[1] See Blackstone's Commentaries, vol. ii. p. 142, and my notes on Blackstone, p. 27.
See also the enabling Statute 32 Hen. VIII., in Blackstone, vol. ii. p. 319.
[2] Quetelet, Sur l'Homme, Paris, 1835, tome i. pp. 49, 50.
[3] Principles of Population, 8vo, 1840, vol. i. p. 60.
[4] See Porter's Progress of the Nation, vol. iii. p. 197.
[5] The causes of this are admirably stated by Smith, Wealth of Nations, book iii.
[6] Ibid. pp. 282, 283.

tellect to a gaping rustic who cultivates his soil. Now look at history. In every struggle for freedom, in every struggle for onward progress, the merchants and the inhabitants of towns have thrown themselves into the breach, and often have led the forlorn hope. But the agriculturists, the inhabitants of the country, always have been and still are in the rear of their age. Their voices have always been lifted against improvement; and they have but too often succeeded in drowning by clamour what they never could hope to convince by reason. Thus, too, a nation of agriculturists is more liable to superstition than a nation of traders or manufacturers. The farmer is very dependent on nature. A single unfavourable season will baffle the most scientific calculations that he can make. Hence, we find that they resort to astrology, &c. But the manufacturer is not so much operated on by the whims of nature. Whether it is wet or dry, whether it is cold or warm, little matters to the success of his operations. He learns to rely on himself. He puts his faith in his own skill and in his own right arm; nor is he very anxious about the prognostication of the astrologer, or the prayer of the priest. Besides this, in manufactures the inventive powers are infinitely more used than in agriculture. A very obvious consideration will explain the cause of this. In agriculture the principal, I may say the sole expense, is that incurred by *producing* the raw material, the corn; but in manufacture, the price of the raw material is generally much less than the value of the labour by which that raw material is worked up. Now, it is a well-known law, that the produce of land increases in a diminishing ratio to the quantity of labour employed.[1] But, to the productiveness of manufacturing labour a precisely opposite law is applicable. The consequence is that manufactures are much more susceptible of mechanical improvement than agriculture,[2] and therefore to them mechanical improvements are oftener applied.

## HISTORY OF AGRICULTURE.

In 1585, a proclamation was put forth against those who con- " verted arable lands and the richest pasture grounds " to sowing woad for the use of dyers.[3] On the 29th of November, 1569, Sir G. Bowes writes to the earl of Sussex that the rebels mean

---

[1] Mill, Political Economy, vol. i. p. 221.      [2] Ibid. p. 224.
[3] Camden's Elizabeth in Kennett, vol. ii. p. 510.

to post themselves about Stockton, where " the best country of corn joineth to those parts of this river of Tees, of both sides."[1] At p. 138, Sir C. Sharp has printed an estimate of the land and tenements of the rebels in the County Palatine of Durham. With the exception of the earl of Westmoreland's which is 574*l.*, not one reaches 70*l.* Early in Elizabeth's reign (the exact date does not appear) Sir G. Bowes bought for 980*l.* tenements worth 34*l.* a year.[2]

" It has been supposed that, if the processes and implements of industry used in the best farmed counties were generally adopted throughout the kingdom, the annual produce of the soil would be doubled."[3]

M'Culloch says[4] that, in 1571, the principle was first introduced of putting a duty on the exportation of wheat. This, of course, depressed the agriculturists, as also did the statute of apprenticeship.[5]

In 5th Edward II., we find 10*s.* allotted to the prioress and nuns of Chester, " as a compensation for acres of land in Godesbach, which they had surrendered to the king's father."[6] This is only 2*s.* 6*d.* an acre, but it does not appear what sort of land it was. In 2nd Henry VIII., Ralph Davenport of Davenport " held the manor of Davenport from Thomas Venables of Kinderton, Esq., in soccage, by the render of 18*d.* per annum, val. xls."[7] Mr. Drake says, but without quoting any authority, that in the reign of Edward VI. land " let at about a shilling an acre."[8]

In 1628, in farmers' houses the maids were employed in breaking hemp.[9] Alison says,[10] " If the annual consumption of grain by the present inhabitants of Great Britain is thirty millions of quarters, which is probably not far from the mark," &c.

It has been supposed that buck wheat—*sarrazin*—was introduced into France by the Moors, but this is denied by Dawson Turner.[11]

## HISTORY OF THE PRICES OF CORN.

In 1595, Elizabeth allowed corn to be imported from the free Hanse Towns, and thus greatly lowered its price, which had risen so

[1] Sharp's Memorial of Rebellion of 1569, 8vo, 1840, p. 80.   [2] Ibid. p. 287.
[3] Thornton on Over Population, 8vo, 1846, p. 292.
[4] Dictionary of Commerce, 8vo, 1849, p. 412.   [5] See art. APPRENTICESHIP.
[6] Ormerod's History of Cheshire, 1819, vol. ii. p. 81.   [7] Ibid. vol. iii. p. 38.
[8] Shakespeare and his Times, 1817, 4to, vol. i. p. 101.
[9] See the Mad Pranks of Robin Goodfellow, p. 19, Percy Society, vol. ii.
[10] Principles of Population, 8vo, 1840, ii. 456.
[11] Turner's Normandy, 8vo, 1820, vol. ii. p. 158.

high, that " some of the poorer sort in London began to mutiny on that account."[1]  However, in 1600, complaints were again made of the scarcity of corn.[2]

In July 1563, Lord Montagu stated, that if more men were taken from Sussex as soldiers, " the harvest of the country must end itself."[3]

On the 18th of July, 1563, Sir Francis Knollys writes to the earl of Warwick, who was then at Newhaven, " Forasmuch as I understand you have great store of wheat in the town, and no grinding for the same, I thought it good to inform your lordship that some are of opinion that the same wheat being sodden will make good victual ; and was the chiefest succour of the French soldiers in Leith."[4]

In 1645, Sir William Brereton having for some time besieged Chester, reduced it to such straits that the people began to murmur.  To satisfy them, Lord Byron asked the chiefs of the discontented to dinner, " and entertained them with boiled wheat, and gave them spring-water to wash it down, solemnly assuring them that this and such like had been their only fare for some time past."[5]

In the fourteenth century, in England, wheat was by no means so little used by the lower orders as is generally supposed.[6]  *After* the accession of Henry VII. " it ceased to form part of the food of the peasantry, and had been superseded by rye and barley, except in the northern counties, where oats, either alone or mixed with peas, had always been the usual bread corn."  But towards the end of the seventeenth century it became again general.[7]

Mr. Jacob[8] has brought forward some reasons for looking on corn as a very bad criterion of value ; but this ingenious writer, like nearly every author I have seen, underrates the consumption of wheat in England during the middle ages.

Mr. Lloyd has published the Oxford prices of corn, which, however, " present a blank from 1328 to the year 1583."[9]

In 1439, the mayor of London " sent into Prussia, causing corn to be brought from thence ; whereby he brought down the price of wheat from 3s. the bushel to less than half that money."[10]

What bread did horses eat?  We hear of " horsebread " in Maroccus Extaticus, 1595.[11]

[1] Camden's Elizabeth, in Kennett, vol. ii. p. 587.          [2] Ibid. p. 626.
[3] Forbes' Elizabeth, vol. ii. p. 464.                        [4] Ibid. pp. 467, 478.
[5] Ormerod's History of Cheshire, vol. i. p. 207.
[6] See the evidence in Thornton on Over Population, 8vo, 1846, p. 176.
[7] Ibid. pp. 202, 203.
[8] Historical Inquiry into the Precious Metals, 8vo, 1831, vol. i. pp. 339–343.
[9] Jacob on the Precious Metals, p. 76.
[10] Stow's London, edit. Thoms, 8vo, 1842, p. 42.          [11] Percy Soc. vol. ix. p. 7.

# INFLUENCE OF THE CLERGY UPON CIVILIZATION.

WHEN the clergy of any country are richly endowed, two serious evils arise : 1st. The revenue given to the clergy is taken away from the capital of the country, and thus prevented from putting into motion a great amount of productive industry. 2nd. By holding out rich prizes in the church, men are withdrawn from the universities to the church, and Smith observes [1] that in all countries where church benefices are rich and numerous, few men of great attainment remain long professors at the universities ; but that when the church benefices are poor and few, the universities are amply supplied with eminent men. Of course both clergy and professors crowd to whichever pays them best. The civilians favoured the church in reference to the oath *ex officio*, which was borrowed from their own jurisprudence, and which compelled the taker to answer all questions put to him. The common lawyers of course took the other side ; and Archbishop Whitgift could not conceal his hatred and contempt of such opposition.[2] Cranmer recanted seven times, but, finding the queen determined to take his life, withdrew his recantation at the stake.[3] Strype confesses that Cranmer recanted six times.[4]

*Fees.*—Not only did the clergy sink in estimation ; they also declined in wealth. " Before the Reformation the bishops could increase the allowance of the vicars out of the tithes of the benefice to what proportion they pleased." This was ordered by 15 Ric. II., cap. 6, and by 4 Hen. IV., cap. 12, and, though fallen into disuse, has never been repealed.[5] In the reign of Edward VI., the clergy of the Lower House of Convocation had not sat in Parliament since the reign of Henry VI. ;[6] but they now availed themselves of the weakness of government to demand a restitution of this obsolete privilege.[7]

Hallam gives the letter supposed to have been written by Elizabeth to Cox, bishop of Ely ;[8] but I have found no contemporary mention of it.

. . . . . . .

Todd [9] finds fault with Hallam for saying that the early

[1] Wealth of Nations, pp. 340, 341.
[2] Hallam's Constitutional History, 8vo, 1842, vol. i. pp. 207, 208.
[3] See Lingard's England, 4th edit. London, 1838, vol. vii. pp. 200   04.
[4] Ecclesiast. Memorials, vol. iii. pt. i. p. 395.
[5] Collier's Ecclesiastical History, 8vo, 1840, vol. v. pp. 195, 196
[6] Ibid. p. 223.          [7] Ibid. pp. 220, 221.
[8] Constitutional History, vol. i. p. 219.          [9] Life of Cranmer, vol. i. pp. 309, 310.

Anglican church held bishops and priests to be of the same order.

The fees of the clergy greatly declined. Formerly they were considerable. On the death of Jane Seymour, Sir Richard Gresham writes that "by the commandment of the Duke of Norfolk I have caused 1,200 masses to be said within the City of London for the soul of our most gracious queen."[1] In a curious work, written in 1548 by Crowsley, a complaint is made of the great fees received by the clergy.[2] It has also been published by Mr. Haslewood, who seems not to have been aware that Strype had printed it. He refers it to 1547.[3]

The Shakers and the Rappites are two flourishing sects in America, "both holding all their property in common and enforcing celibacy."[4]

A writer, whose knowledge on such subjects few will be rash enough to dispute, says that even in the middle of Elizabeth's reign "the majority of the clergy were nearly illiterate, and many of them addicted to drunkenness and low vices."[5]

An accidental circumstance greatly lessened their numbers. Almost immediately after the accession of Elizabeth there broke out one of those frightful epidemics, then so common, which carried off immense numbers.[6]

Soames[7] quotes Neal to the effect that in 1576 Elizabeth said there were too many preachers, and that three or four in each county were enough.

The Bishop of St. Asaph says that Henry VIII. transferred church property to the amount of 150,000l. yearly.[8]

The clergy have ruined Italy. In the Roman States, where the population is only 2,700,000, there are 35,000 secular clergy, more than 10,000 monks, and more than 8,000 nuns, while in England there are less than 20,000 clergy of the Established Church, and about the same number of sectarian teachers.[9] Lord Brougham says, without any authority, that Elizabeth "in 1586 made the clergy pay an assessment not voted by Convocation."[10]

---

[1] Burgon's Life of Gresham. 8vo, 1839, vol. i. p. 24.

[2] See the extract in Strype's Ecclesiastical Memorials, vol. ii. part i. p. 223.

[3] Brydge's British Bibliographer, vol. ii. pp. 291-293.

[4] See an account of them in Miss Martineau's Society in America, Paris, 8vo, 1842, vol. i. pp. 215-220, part ii. ch. i. See C.P.B. 2199.

[5] Hallam's Constitutional History of England, 8vo, 1842, vol. i. p. 195.

[6] Heylin's Hist. of Presbyterians, quoted in Soames's Elizabethan Religious History, 1839, p. 33.          [7] Ibid. p. 225.

[8] Short's History of the Church of England, pp. 146, 147, 8vo, 1847.

[9] Brougham's Political Philosophy, vol. i. p. 569, 8vo, 1849.

[10] Ibid. vol. iii. p. 259.

The queen was at one moment resolved to issue a commission to inquire into the misdemeanours of the clergy (this was in 1567), but its object would have been to inquire into the waste they had committed;[1] but more pressing matters diverted her attention. Strype, who always favours the clergy, says that in 1571 "scarce half of them understood Latin."[2]

Strype mentions the dislike of the court to the bishops.[3]  The tale about the Bishop of Ely seems to have some foundation.[4]

We learn from an official report made in 1561 to the archbishop of Canterbury, that in the archdeaconry of London only one-third of the clergy were preachers.[5]  Strype confesses that, in 1583, most of the clergy could not preach at all; "their skill extending no further than to the reading of the Common Prayer and Homilies."[6]

For proof of the poverty, ignorance, and unpopularity of the clergy in the reign of Henry VIII. and Edward VI., see Strype's Ecclesiastical Memorials, vol. i. part i. pp. 291–304; vol. ii. part i. pp. 74, 223, 590 ; part ii. pp. 27, 143.

In 1550, Lever complains that parishes are left without clergymen ;[7] and in 1552 the same thing is said in a sermon preached by the famous Bernard Gilpin.[8]

Dr. Turner, who wrote in the reign of Mary, has left us some curious evidence of the poverty of the clergy.[9]  The entire fortune of Parker, when he was chosen archbishop of Canterbury, was only 30l. ;[10] and yet such was his pomp that in a list of his yearly expenses, in 1573, his servants' wages are put down at 250l., and their liveries at 100l. ;[11] but, before he died, his servants' wages (exclusive of board wages) were 448l. a year.[12]  The archbishop of Canterbury, in 1599, estimates the value of the archbishopric at 3,000l. a year, out of which "there goeth in annuities, pensions, subsidies, and other duties to her majesty, 800l. at the least."[13] But in the very same year the steward of the archbishop stated in the House of Commons that "the revenue was but 2,200l., whereof were paid for annual subsidies 500l.[14] Aylmer, bishop of London, "kept a good house, having eighty servants with him in his family;" and "he laid out 16,000l. in purchase of lands not long before his death."[15]  In 1568, the bishop of Chester wrote to

[1] Strype's Parker, vol. i. p. 513.    [2] Ibid. vol. ii. p. 81.    [3] Ibid. p. 322.
[4] Ibid. p. 385, and Strype's Annals, vol. ii. part i. pp. 501, 502, 533, 534.
[5] Strype's Parker, vol. i. p. 189.    [6] Strype's Whitgift, vol. i. p. 240.
[7] Strype's Ecclesiastical Memorials, vol. ii. part i. p. 411.
[8] Ibid. part ii. p. 29; see also vol. iii. part i. p. 487.    [9] Ibid. pp. 420, 422.
[10] Strype's Parker, vol. i. p. 75.    [11] Ibid. vol. ii. p. 264 ; see also p. 443.
[12] Ibid. vol. iii. p. 344.    [13] Strype's Whitgift, vol. ii. p. 422.
[14] Ibid. p. 423.    [15] Strype's Aylmer, p. 127.

Elizabeth that he had "not much more than 500 marks for him to maintain himself and his poor family."[1]   Parkhurst, bishop of Norwich, died in 1574.  " He kept twenty-six men servants in his house, and also six maid-servants."[2]   In 1582, a report was made to government respecting the bishopric of St. David's, by which we learn that its net value was less than 253*l.*; but in 27 Hen. VIII. it had been 457*l.*[3]  In 1587, the Bishop of Winchester had less than 400*l.* a year *clear*, if I rightly understand the schedule in Strype's Annals.[4]   In 1595, the Bishop of Rochester, in a letter to the lord treasurer, stated that the total yearly revenue of his bishopric was 340*l.*, out of which he says nearly three-fourths—that is 250*l.* a year—was expended in hospitality, or, as he calls it, " meat and drink."[5]   The archbishop, at all events, used to be preceded by a bare-headed usher.[6]   In 1578, the Bishop of Carlisle writes to the earl of Shrewsbury, " I protest unto your honour, before the living God, that, when my year's account was made at Michaelmas last, my expenses did surmount the year's revenues of my bishoprick, 600*l.*"[7]

Voltaire [8] says that Henry I. of England " pour mettre le clergé dans ses intérêts, il renonça au droit de régale qui lui donnait l'usufruit des bénéfices vacants : droit que les rois de France ont conservé."  The celebrated letter said to have been written by Elizabeth to the Bishop of Ely is given by Voltaire.[9]

See the complaints made in Ecclesiastical Polity, in Hooker's Works.[10]

Even Archdeacon Hare allows that the clergy are more subject to pride than other men.[11]

In the Polynesian Islands generally "the office of the priesthood was hereditary in all its departments."[12]   Medicine was formerly studied by the clergy.[13]   At the end of the seventeenth century it was usual to pay the clergymen who preached the funeral sermon a guinea.[14]   In 1689, Evelyn [15] says that many

[1] Strype's Annals, vol. i. part ii. p. 266.        [2] Ibid. vol. ii. part i. pp. 508, 509.
[3] See the Report in Strype's Annals, vol. iii. part ii. pp. 226–228.
[4] Vol. iii. part ii. p. 263.
[5] See his Letter in Strype's Annals, vol. iv. pp. 316, 317.
[6] See An Epitome of Dr. Bridge's Defence, 1588, p. 53, 8vo, 1843.
[7] Lodge's Illustrations of British History, 1838, vol. ii. p. 137.
[8] Essai sur les Mœurs, chap. 50, Œuvres, tome xvi. p. 83.
[9] Ibid. chap. 168, Œuvres, tome xvii. p. 524.
[10] Vol. ii. pp. 371, 425, 431 ; vol. iii. pp. 236, 248, 249.
[11] The Mission of the Comforter, 8vo, 1850, p. 458.
[12] Ellis, Polynesian Researches, 8vo, 1831, vol. i. p. 342.
[13] See Southey's Life of Wesley, 8vo, 1846, vol. i. pp. 4, 439, 442.  On the ignorance of the clergy in the reign of Elizabeth, see ibid. pp. 271, 272, 493, 494, 496.
[14] See Calamy's Life of Himself, vol. i. p. 354, 8vo, 1829.  See also at vol. ii. pp. 217, 218, evidences of the fallen state of the clergy.        [15] Diary, vol. iii. p. 278.

clergy " in some opulent parishes made almost as much of permission to bury in the chancel and the church as of their livings, and were paid with considerable advantage and gifts for baptising in chambers." The clergy from an early period were, " generally speaking, kept better within bounds in England than in other contemporaneous states." [1]  Kemble [2] says that in the tenth century there were *absolutely* more churches in England than there are at present; and on the power of the clergy, see vol. i. pp. 145, 146. The vices of Rome, I think, gave rise to the asceticism and stoicism of Christians. Tocqueville [3] says that monasticism was the result of epicurism. Capefigue [4] says that in the fifteenth century the church possessed more than a third of the property of Europe. Hallam [5] says Elizabeth " had no regard for her bishops."

In 1574, the celebrated Sampson taunted the Archbishop of York with being called *lord*. Grindal replied " that however the title of *lord* was ascribed to him, and the rest of the bishops, yet that he was not *lordly*." [6]  In 1579, one of the Puritans taunted the Bishop of London that " he must be *lorded*, ' an it please your lordship' at every word." [7]  Flassan [8] says that Charlemagne favoured the clergy from policy, *not* from superstition. Sorbière, who was in England very soon after the Restoration, says that " the inferior clergy are mean enough, and cannot without great difficulty preach." [9]  Bishop Sprat [10] has an amusing remark on the decline of episcopacy. Until the fourteenth century, ecclesiastics were forbidden to eat at the table of princes. [11] Grégoire says [12] Charlemagne was never legally canonised. The clergy, with a few honourable exceptions, have in all modern countries been the avowed enemies of the diffusion of knowledge, the danger of which to their own profession they, by a certain instinct, seem always to have perceived.

Strype notices the impoverishment of the clergy by the cessation of pilgrimages; but he makes no attempt to estimate its extent. [13]

[1] Kemble's Saxons in England, vol. ii. p. 373.                     [2] Ibid. p. 611.
[3] Démocratie en Amérique, iv. 210, 211.
[4] Histoire de la Réforme, tome i. p. 47.                     [5] Const. Hist. vol. i. p. 206.
[6] Strype's Parker, vol. ii. p. 376, and compare Sampson's reply in vol. iii. pp. 319–323.
[7] Strype's Aylmer, p. 89. See also Strype's Annals, vol. ii. part. i. pp. 407, 410 ; vol. ii. part ii. p. 217. See also An Epistle to the Terrible Priests, 1588, pp. 68, 69, 8vo, 1843. An Epitome of Dr. Bridge's Defence, 1588, p. 59, 8vo, 1843.
[8] Diplomatic Française, tome i. p. 88.
[9] Sorbière's Voyage to England, pp. 18, 19.
[10] Observations on Sorbière's Voyage.
[11] Grégoire, Histoire des Confesseurs, p. 106.               [12] Ibid. p. 159.
[13] Strype's Whitgift, vol. i. p. 544.

In the sixteenth century the clergy married servants.[1] In the middle of the eighteenth century it was usual for livings to be conferred upon condition that the clergyman should marry the cast-off mistress of the patron.[2]

The Rev. Mr. White, who has been a clergyman in the two great Christian sects, Catholicism and Protestantism, and has, perhaps, seen more of their secret workings than any man of his day, notices "the poisonous nature of that orthodoxy, which is supported by church establishments. Doctrines being made the bond of union of a powerful body of men, whose only legal title to the enjoyment of wealth, honour, and influence is adherence to those doctrines, there must of necessity exist a bitter jealousy against every man who shakes the blind confidence of the multitude in the supposed sacredness of those doctrines."[3] On the drunken habits, &c. of the clergy, see Baxter's Life of Himself, London, folio, 1696, part i. p. 2 ; and part iii. p. 46. When in 1681, Stephen College was murdered at Oxford, some of the clergy brutally said they were pleased to have " one college more in their university."[4] In the fourteenth century, before sermon began, books were exposed and read at the doors of the churches.[5] Monteil adds[6] that in the fourteenth century the clergy were more loved in Paris than in Languedoc. For the fees received by the clergy see Monteil, ii. 300, 307 ; iv. 130. In the fifteenth century in France, even the porter of the chapter of a cathedral or abbey must be a priest.[7] In courts of law, in the fifteenth century, advocates quoted sermons.[8] In 1789, Earl Stanhope gave some curious instances of the persecuting laws of the English church.[9] And [10] he says he had " undergone the drudgery of going through the whole statute book, and found that there were no less than three hundred acts in it upon religion." Very religious men are always called atheists. In 1626, Sir B. Rudyard said " he knew two ministers in Lancashire who were found to be unlicensed ale-house keepers."[11]

---

[1] See Loseley Manuscripts by Kempe, p. 254.
[2] Menzel's German Literature, vol. i. p. 163.
[3] Letter dated Liverpool 1835, in the Life of the Rev. Blanco White, written by himself, London, 8vo, 1845, vol. ii. p. 114.
[4] Wilson's Life of De Foe, vol. i. p. 83.
[5] See Monteil, Hist. des Français des divers États, tome i. p. 32.     [6] Ibid. p. 36.
[7] Ibid. tome iii. p. 103.          [8] Ibid. tome iv. p. 92.
[9] Parl. History, vol. xxviii. p. 102 et seq.      [10] At vol. xxvii. p. 1280.
[11] Ibid. vol. ii. p. 45.

## TENDENCY OF THE LAWS RESPECTING APPRENTICES.

SEE Smith's Wealth of Nations, pp. 50–53. Apprenticeships were entirely unknown to the ancients.[1] He says[2] that the effect of the laws respecting them were to increase the wealth of towns at the expense of the wealth of the country, which they did by raising the price of manufactures. Of course, by increasing the profits of manufactures, they diverted a good deal of capital from agriculture to manufactures. Smith has given[3] a slight history of the laws respecting apprentices. Seven years was originally the term of its duration in Europe for incorporated trades, all of which incorporations were called universities. By the 5th of Elizabeth, called the Statute of Apprenticeship, it was enacted that no person should exercise any trade unless he had served to it an apprenticeship of seven years, and thus what had been only the by-law of particular corporations, became statute and general law. The words of the statute plainly mean the whole kingdom, but have been interpreted to mean only market towns, and only those trades which were established in England before 5th Elizabeth. In Paris five years is a very common term of apprenticeship; in Scotland (where corporation laws are less oppressive than in any other European country) only three years.

It is worthy of remark that this absurd statute of apprenticeship (5 Eliz.) was not repealed till 1814, and even then a reservation was made of "the existing rights, privileges, or by-laws of the different corporations."[4] How long will this contemptible spirit of corporation and of caste be allowed to predominate in our national councils? "Rights and privileges!" As if any body of men ought to have rights and privileges which are injurious to the country at large.[5]

Jacob observes that the effect of these laws was to prevent the increasing manufactures from absorbing the surplus agricultural population.[6] In that remarkable work, the Brief Conceipt of English Policy, published in 1581, the author, who was at least half a century before his age, protests with unusual freedom against the statute of apprenticeship.[7] See in the Journal of the Statistical Society,[8] evidence of "the extent to

[1] P. 51.  [2] Pp. 52, 53.  [3] Pp. 50, 51.
[4] M'Culloch's Principles of Political Economy, Edinburgh, 8vo, 1843, p. 372.
[5] See also M'Culloch's Commercial Dictionary, 8vo, 1849, p. 45.
[6] Inquiry into the Precious Metals, vol. ii. p. 111.
[7] See the passage in Harleian Miscellany, vol. ix. pp. 187, 188.  [8] Vol. i, p. 19.

which the mischievous system of compulsory apprenticeship had
been adopted in the incorporations of the counties of Norfolk
and Suffolk " from 1820 to 1835.

Early in the seventeenth century, if not before, receiving apprentices was an ordinary source of profit to great actors. The
services of such apprentices were regularly bought and sold. This
appears from Henslowe's Diary.[1]

The effects of gilds and corporations is to check population.[2]
Storch looks on the custom of apprenticeship as an unmitigated
evil; but he has fallen into the error of supposing that its effect
is to raise wages, and therefore raise price.[3] In 1643, the apprentices assisted in fortifying London against the king, and were so
important a body that Charles attempted to gain them over ; and
at Oxford, which. has always been a steady friend to despotism,
there was published an " Exhortation," the object of which was to
aid the royal efforts. It has been printed by Mr. Mackay.[4] The
old holidays being laid aside as superstitious, the apprentices in
1647 had a grand meeting in Covent Garden to oblige their
masters to grant some other times of recreation. It is hardly
necessary to say that they succeeded in their object. Mr. Wright
has printed one of the notices of meeting which the apprentices
affixed to the walls of London.[5] In 1659, they are accused of
having frequently run away with their masters' daughters.[6] On
Sundays, they were expected to accompany their masters to church;
but they not unfrequently left them at the church doors and went
to the tavern.[7] An intelligent observer, who was in England in
the year 1500, says that it was usual in London for widows to
marry the apprentices of their late husbands.[8]

---

## OBSERVATIONS UPON FREEMASONRY.

ABOUT 1820 (?) " one Morgan, a freemason, living in the western
part of the State of New York, wrote a book in exposure of
masonry, its facts and tendencies." The consequence was that

---

[1] See Collier's History of Dramatic Poetry, vol. iii. pp. 433, 444.
[2] See Mill's Political Economy, 8vo, 1849, vol. i. pp. 431, 433.
[3] Économie Politique, St. Petersbourg, 8vo, 1815, tome i. pp. 360–362 ; tomo ii.
p. 183.
[4] Songs of the London Prentices, pp. 67–69, edit. Percy Society, 8vo, 1841.
[5] Political Ballads, pp. 18, 19, Percy Society, vol. iii.
[6] Wright's Political Ballads, p. 172.
[7] See The Pleasant Conceits of Old Hobson, 1607, p. 9, Percy Society, vol. ix.
[8] Italian Relation of England, Camden Society, vol. xxxvii. p. 26.

he was arrested and carried over into Canada; "shut up in the fort at Niagara village, where the Niagara river flows into Lake Ontario . . . put into a boat, carried out into the middle of the river, and thrown in with a stone tied to his neck. For four years there were attempts to bring the conspirators to justice; but little was done. The lodges subscribed funds to carry the actual murderers out of the country. Sheriffs, jurymen, constables, all omitted their duty with regard to the rest." The upshot was, that the spirit of the Americans was roused. Anti-masonic societies were formed; in some States the law prevents the lodges taking in new members, and masonry is almost overthrown.[1]

---

## THE CONDITION AND INFLUENCE OF WOMEN.

MISS MARTINEAU[2] says, "Forty years ago the women of New Jersey went to the polls and voted at State elections. The general terms 'inhabitants' stood unqualified; as it will again when the true democratic principle comes to be fully understood. A motion was made to correct the inadvertence, and it was done as a matter of course without any appeal, as far as I could learn, from the persons about to be injured. Such acquiescence proves nothing but the degradation of the injured party." As to the present state of women in the United States, see "Miss Martineau's Society in America," vol. ii. pp. 156–178, part iii. chap. ii. Even this partial writer says,[3] "The Americans have in the treatment of women fallen below, not only their own democratic principles, but the practice of some parts of the Old World."

She says,[4] "Divorce is more easily obtained in the United States than in England." This delights her, and she adds,[5] "In Massachusetts divorces are obtainable with peculiar ease. The natural consequence follows; such a thing is never heard of. A long-established and very eminent lawyer of Boston told me that he had known of only one in all his experience." . . . At Zurich "the parties are married by a form, and have liberty to divorce themselves, without any appeal to law, on showing that they have legally provided for the children of the marriage. . . . There was some levity at first, chiefly on the part of those who were

---

[1] Miss Martineau's Society in America, Paris, 8vo, 1842, vol. i. pp. 19, 20, part chap. i.
[2] Society in America, Paris, 8vo, 1842, vol. i. pp. 104, 105, part i. ch. iii. section vii.
[3] P. 156.          [4] P. 165.          [5] P. 166.

suffering under the old system, but the morals of the society soon became, and have since remained, peculiarly pure."

Miss Martineau tells us,[1] " It is no secret on the spot that the habit of intemperance is not unfrequent among women of station and education in the most enlightened parts of the country."

Adam Smith says,[2] " The fair sex, who have commonly much more tenderness than ours, have seldom so much generosity. That women rarely make considerable donations is an observation of the civil law. *Raro mulieres donare solent.*"

The reason that the wages of women are generally lower than those of men is, that, owing to custom opening so few employments, their field of employment is overcrowded.[3] Hence, I suppose, the more agricultural a nation is, the higher will be the wages of women as compared to those of men. This is the case in France. Perhaps we may in this way discover one cause of the declining influence of women. They are less *valuable* than formerly. The advance of civilisation diminishes the proportion of those who are employed on the soil, and thus lowers their wages.

In London we have cases of women working at shirt-making, and similar occupations, eighteen hours a-day, and earning four shillings a-week.[4]

For another reason why the influence of women has declined, see art. PURITANS.

Camden says of Lady Burleigh, the daughter of Sir Anthony Cook, " She was a woman very well versed in the Latin and Greek tongues."[5] His mentioning it shows that such learning was not common.

Dr. Combe thinks that any eccentricity on the mother's side is more likely to be prevalent among the children than if it had been on the father's side.[6]

Gifford has noticed how little attention is paid by Ben Jonson to drawing female characters. This, I should suppose, was because the parts of women were played by boys.[7] But the character of the Lady Would-Be, in the Fox, shows the growing influence of the female mind. Women must have been gaining ground when it was worth Jonson's while to ridicule them by so comprehensive a satire. See also his attack on the Lady Collegiates in the

[1] Society in America, vol. ii. p. 184.
[2] Theory of Moral Sentiments, part iv. chap. ii. vol. ii. p. 19, London, 1822, 12mo.
[3] Mill's Political Economy, 8vo, 1849, vol. i. pp. 487, 488.
[4] See Thornton on Over Population, 8vo, 1846, p. 60.
[5] Annals of Elizabeth, in Kennett, vol. ii. p. 609.
[6] Principles of Physiology applied to Health, 2nd edit. Edinburgh, 8vo, 1835, p. 273.
[7] Jonson's Works, vol. i. p. 161, and iv. p. 460, but see vi. 409, and vii. 151.

Silent Woman;[1] and he allowed women of reputation to attend the meetings of his club,—I suppose at the Mermaid.[2]

Early in the seventeenth century Gifford says: "Daggers, or as they were more commonly called, knives, were worn at all times by every woman in England."[3]

At the very beginning of the seventeenth century, a lady says it is unnatural to see "books in women's hands."[4]

Chevenix[5] takes for granted the mental inferiority of women. Vico[6] observes that the wife bringing a dowry is evidence of her freedom.

Chevenix,[7] who has attempted to trace the history of women, particularly notices the effect of arts and manufactures in increasing their power.

I doubt if the attention paid to women is of northern origin. The ancient Finns treated them very badly.[8]

A writer of great observation says: "There is perhaps no instance of a man of distinguished vigour and activity of mind whose mother did not display a considerable amount of the same qualities."[9]

Lawrence well says,[10] "A nervous and hysterical fine lady and her lap dog are the extreme points of degeneracy and imbecility of which each race is susceptible."

The first work on the education of women was Fénelon's "Education des Filles," in 1688; but "he discourages too much the acquisition of knowledge by women."[11]  Sir John Reresby, who was in Germany in 1656, gives a curious account of the depressed state of the women.[12]  Charles XII. of Sweden did not care for women.[13]

Montaigne is unfavourable to their education, and says they are incapable of friendship.[14]  He adds[15] that he had known women swallow sand and ashes in order to get pale complexions. He

[1] Jonson's Works, vol. iii. pp. 346, 347.                    [2] Ibid. vol. v. p. 254.
[3] Note in Ben Jonson, vol. v. pp. 220, 221.
[4] See Middleton's Works, 8vo, 1840, vol. i. p. 163.
[5] Essay on National Character, 8vo, 1832, vol. ii. p. 316.
[6] Philosophie de l'Histoire, p. 218.
[7] Essay on National Character, vol. ii. p. 333.
[8] See Prichard's Physical History of Mankind, vol. iii. pp. 287, 288.
[9] Combe, The Constitution of Man in Relation to External Objects, Edinb. 1847, 8vo, p. 192, and see Combe's Moral Philosophy, p. 121, 8vo, 1840.
[10] Lectures on Man, 8vo, 1844, p. 163.
[11] See Hallam's Literature of Europe, vol. iii. pp. 417, 418.
[12] Reresby's Travels and Memoirs, 8vo, 1831, pp. 139, 140.
[13] Œuvres de Voltaire, tome xxii. p. 54.
[14] Essais de Montaigne, Paris, 8vo, 1843, Livre I., chap. xxiv., xxvii., pp. 73, 102, 469, 520, 521.
[15] Ibid. Livre I., chap. xl. p. 156.

says[1] that a fashion had recently grown up among women, of pulling hair out of their foreheads. In the Indian Archipelago women are better treated than generally in the East.[2] Coleridge says,[3] "The Greeks, except perhaps in Homer, seem to have had no way of making their women interesting but by unsexing them, as in the instances of the tragic Medea, Electra, &c." At vol. i. pp. 199, 200, Coleridge says : " Women are good novelists, but indifferent poets ; and this because they rarely or never thoroughly distinguish between fact and fiction." Perhaps polygamy is the first stage in the improvement of women. In Borneo women are well-treated, because polygamy makes them *dear*.[4] In England at the end of the seventeenth century women still learned Latin and Greek.[5] Mr. Marshall[6] thinks the sexual passions stronger among Europeans than among Asiatics. Catlin, who speaks so highly of the North American Indians, allows that the women are the "slaves of their husbands."[7] They neither worship nor eat with the men.[8] They marry from eleven to fifteen, and some have even had children at twelve.[9] It is " very rare " for a woman to have more than four or five children.[10] Parturition is very easy;[11] polygamy universal.[12] Schlegel[13] mentions "that high reverence for females which is everywhere inculcated in the laws and exemplified in the poems of the Hindoos." Herbert Mayo[14] says, " Girls as children are healthier than boys," because they are *nearer* to women than boys are to men, i.e. the voice and skin have less to alter. But, says Mayo,[15] their one disease is education, which is so absurd that they nearly all have diseased spines.[16] At Embomma, on the Congo, " the men will not eat the flesh of a fowl, until the woman has tasted of it, to take off the fetish as they express it ; "[17] but at the same place "the cultivation of the ground is entirely the business of slaves and women."[18]

Napoleon said everything depends on the mother,[19] and yet he

---

[1] Essais de Montaigne, Paris, 8vo, 1843, Livre I., chap. xlix. p. 186.
[2] See Crawford's History of the Indian Archipelago, Edinb. 8vo, 1820, vol. i. pp. 73, 75, 78.
[3] Literary Remains, vol. i. p. 95.　　[4] See Low's Sarawak, 8vo, 1848, p. 148.
[5] See Southey's Life of Wesley, 8vo, 1840, vol. i. p. 30.
[6] Transactions of Literary Society of Bombay, vol. iii. p. 351.
[7] Catlin's North American Indians, 8vo, vol. i. p. 51.
[8] Ibid. vol. ii. pp. 232, 233.　　　　[9] Ibid. vol. i. pp. 121, 214, 215.
[10] Ibid. vol. ii. p. 228.　　[11] Ibid. p. 229.　　[12] Ibid. vol. i. p. 118.
[13] Lectures on Literature, Edinb. 8vo, 1818, vol. i. p. 210.
[14] Philosophy of Living, 8vo, 1838, pp. 114, 115.
[15] Ibid. p. 115.　　　　　　　　　[16] Ibid. pp. 118, 123.
[17] Tuckey's Expedition to the Zaire, 1818, 4to, p. 124.　　　[18] Ibid. p. 120.
[19] Alison's Hist. of Europe, vol. iv. p. 2. See also vol. viii. p. 1, and vol. xiii. p. 200.

cared so little about women *socially* that he was in favour of the Eastern way of shutting them up,[1] but *physically*, he was very fond of women.[2] Mr. F. Newman[3] denies that Christianity has improved the position of women; and he observes[4] that "with Paul the *sole* reason for marriage is, that a man may, without sin, vent his sensual desires. He teaches that, *but* for this object, it would be better not to marry;" and he takes no notice of the *social* pleasures of marriage. Newman says:[5] "In short, only in countries where Germanic sentiment has taken root, do we see marks of any elevation of the female sex superior to that of Pagan antiquity;" and[6] "the real elevators of the female sex are the poets of German culture, who have vindicated the spirituality of love, and its attraction to character." In 1717, Lady Montagu[7] says: some of "our ladies who set up for such extraordinary geniuses upon the credit of some superficial knowledge of French and Italian." In 1572, Lady Montagu writes,[8] "To say truth, there is no part of the world where our sex is treated with so much contempt as in England." Mackay[9] says: "The ancients laid it down as incontrovertible that women are the source of all evil; an unmitigated hindrance to mankind inflicted on them by the wrath of the gods." Kemble[10] ascribes to the German element the modern respect for women. In Great Britain and Ireland there are more females than males; and in France the excess of women is still greater; but in Spain, nearly equal, and in the United States an excess of males.[11] There are rather more male than female servants.[12] Of the depositors in the Savings Banks, nearly seven in eight are women.[13] The proportionate number of female compared with male criminals is diminishing,[14] but in Scotland, the female criminals are more numerous.[15] Tocqueville[16] says, that in Protestant countries young girls always have more liberty than in Catholic ones; and that, when this is combined with a democratic state of society, the liberty becomes very great, as is the case in America. The American girls are chaste in manners rather than in mind,[17] and though, when unmarried, they have great liberty, as soon as they are

[1] Alison, vol. vi. p. 91.                [2] See vol. xi. pp. 587, 606; vol. xiii. p. 209.
[3] Phases of Faith, 8vo, 1850, pp. 162–169.
[4] Ibid. p. 163.      [5] Ibid. p. 163.      [6] Ibid. p. 165.
[7] Works, 8vo, 1803, vol. ii. p. 243.              [8] Ibid. vol. iv. p. 149.
[9] Progress of the Intellect, 8vo, 1850, vol. i. p. 419.
[10] Saxons in England, vol. i. pp. 232, 233.
[11] Porter's Progress of the Nation, vol. i. pp. 15, 16.
[12] Ibid. pp. 67, 68; vol. iii. p. 16.              [13] Ibid. vol. iii. p. 147.
[14] Ibid. p. 179.                          [15] Ibid. p. 215.
[16] Démocratie en Amérique, tome v. p. 57.       [17] Ibid. p. 58.

married they have scarcely any.[1]  For industrious and religious
nations naturally consider marriage a very grave affair.[2]  On this
account, early marriages are very rare in America; and the
American women do not marry till their reason is ripened.[3]  Göthe
says of Germany about 1772, that the influence of Richardson's
novels and Lessing's Sara Sampson had raised the standard of
female morals.[4]  Feudality treated women badly; chivalry well.[5]
English women remained Catholics longer than men did.[6]  In
1839, it is said that the effects of Sunday were principally shown
on women; there being twice as many female as male scholars.[7]
In spite of the decrease of crime, the number of female offenders
is on the increase.[8]  It has been attempted to be shown[9] that
the number of illegitimate children is in the measure of morals.
Barry, who had the best means of knowing, says of the women in
the Orkney Islands: " Though their education, as in other
places, is inferior to that of the men, their understandings are in
general superior.[10]  Until Peter I., the Russian women were kept
as secluded as those of Asia.[11]  The Indians everywhere treat their
women with contempt,[12] and so do the Burmese.[13]  Kohl says: [14]
" Female voices are never heard in the Russian Churches; their
place is supplied by boys; women do not yet stand high enough
in the estimation of the churches or of the people to be permitted
to sing the praises of God in the presence of men."  Christianity
diminished the influence of women.[15]  In 1645, women used to
preach in London.[16]  There is said to be a good article on the
state of women in Greece in No. 43 of the Quarterly Review.
According to Thirlwall,[17] " The freedom of women was not peculiar
to Sparta.  It prevailed in all Dorian states, though not perhaps
equally, and is thought to have been once universal in Greece.
It is observed, that in Homer, there is no trace of the seclusion
of women after marriage; nor do they appear to have been
insignificant or much depressed."  Mrs. Napier[18] refers to Middle-

[1] Démocratie en Amérique, tome v. p. 61.
[2] Ibid. pp. 61, 62.                                    [3] Ibid. p. 63.
[4] Wahrheit und Dichtung, in Werke, Band ii. Theil ii. p. 179.
[5] See Mill's History of Chivalry, vol. i. pp. 235, 256.
[6] Hallam, Constitutional History of England, vol. i. p. 399.
[7] Journal of Statistical Society, vol. ii. p. 67.
[8] Ibid. vol. ix. p. 182.                                [9] Ibid. vol. xiv. p. 8.
[10] Barry's History of the Orkney Islands, p. 333.
[11] See Comte, Traité de Législation, vol. iii. p. 172.
[12] See Heber's Journey through India, vol. ii. p. 71.
[13] See Symes's Embassy to Ava, vol. ii. pp. 219, 385.      [14] Russia, 8vo, 1844, p. 255.
[15] See Neander's History of the Church, vol. i. p. 252.
[16] Parliamentary History, vol. iii. p. 422.              [17] History of Greece.
[18] Rights and Duties of Women, vol. i. p. 99.

ton's Cicero, for the fact that the Romans paid great attention to having nurses who spoke pure Latin, so as not to corrupt the language of their children. At p. 163, Mrs. Napier says : " In France, where from the time of Catherine de Medicis the corruption of morals had been proverbial, it is well known that women reigned in every transaction of the empire," but I may say the French never cared for domestic life—too vain. Mrs. Napier [1] well says : " It is only in arduous pursuits the superiority of men invariably appears. In low stages of civilization it occasionally happens that the advantage is observed to be on the side of women ; for any circumstance in their habits that imposes on them the necessity of greater exercise of observation and judgment turns the balance in their favour. But in the complicated and laborious offices of civilised societies, no education would give general superiority or even equality to the female sex ; the demand for laborious investigations, and the highest power of combination and invention is too constant, both in professions and sciences." Among barbarians, *all* have the same sort of education. Intellect is more valued than ever, and knowledge more available, and yet women worse educated than ever. See Carie's Comparative Anatomy, vol. i. pp. 274, 290, 357 ; vol. ii. p. 133. Society becomes more complex, and men less impulsive ; hence *natural* divergencies increase, and *hence* increased difference between men and women, and loss of female influence. Combe [2] says : " In all countries which I have visited, I have remarked that the female head, though less in size, is more fully developed in the region of the moral sentiments in proportion to the other regions, than that of the male." Hallam [3] denies that respect for women is due to Christianity, and says that it first arose in the south of France about the end of the tenth century. He observes of Beaumont and Fletcher,[4] " The best of Fletcher's characters are female ; he wanted that large sweep of reflection and experience which is required for the greater diversity of the other sex." He says [5] of Massinger, " He has more variety in his women than in the other sex, and they are less mannered than the heroines of Fletcher." Bourgoing [6] says that Pæderasty " est absolument inconnu en Espagne." Townsend [7] says in regard to Spanish women having lovers or *cortejos*, that it was owing " to the introduction of Italian manners, on the arrival of Charles III.

---

[1] Rights and Duties of Women, vol. i. p. 282.
[2] North America, Edinb. 1841, vol. i. p. 130.     [3] Literature, vol. i. pp. 126, 127.
[4] Ibid. vol. iii. p. 113.     [5] Ibid. p. 115.
[6] Tableau de l'Espagne, Paris, 1808, tome ii. p. 345.
[7] Journey through Spain, vol. iii. p. 145.

from Naples, with the previous want of reasonable freedom in the commerce of the sexes." Mary Carpenter says:[1] "All persons who have come much into actual intercourse with boys and girls of 'the perishing and dangerous classes,' have fully agreed with my own experience, that the girls are far the most hardened and difficult to manage. A strong concurrent testimony of this was presented to me yesterday by one of the commissioners of lunacy, who had been himself for a long course of years the manager of a large institution. The females he found infinitely more outrageous than the males; and, when excited, they used language indicating a depth and intensity of wickedness which he would not have thought the heart of a man, still less, as he said, that of a woman, could have conceived." Baretti, who was in Spain in 1760, says with surprise, that Spaniards are *not* jealous.[2] See also on the cortejos, who are said to be quite innocent, vol. iii. pp. 102-111. Baretti says:[3] "In Calderon's days, it was not permitted to men to act upon the stage; so that men's characters were then acted by women; and it is but of late years that the Spaniards have obtained this permission, I cannot tell whether by the government or the Inquisition. See the whims of nations! In England, about a century ago, no women were allowed to act; and this has been during many years past, and is still the practice in the pope's capital and in Portugal." In 1806, Blanco White writes:[4] "The ancient Spanish jealousy is still observable among the lower classes; and while not a sword is drawn in Spain upon a love quarrel, the knife often decides the claim of more humble lovers." In 1776, in Valencia, the farmers would not let their wives sit with them at table.[5] In Spain, husbands are never jealous, but their wives are notoriously profligate.[6] In 1766, "In no part of the world are women more caressed and attended to than in Spain;" but very unchaste, owing partly to the Fandango dance.[7]

Knox and Buchanan were great enemies of women; and in 1567, the Scotch parliament declared that no woman should hold any authority.[8] Even Aylmer, in "The Harborow," though *defending* women against Knox, holds the coarsest language about them.[9]

[1] Transactions of Association for Social Science, 1858, p. 239.
[2] Journey through Portugal and Spain, Lond. 1790, vol. ii. p. 292.
[3] Ibid. vol. iii. p. 23.          [4] Doblado's Letters, p. 268.
[5] Swinburne's Spain, vol. i. p. 149.
[6] Townsend's Spain, vol. ii. pp. 142, 144, 147, 149-151.
[7] Thicknesse's Journey through France and Spain, Lond. 1777, vol. i. p. 236.
[8] Irving's Life of Buchanan, p. 295, Edinb. 1817.
[9] M'Crie's Life of Knox, p. 131.

Hume [1] says, coiners "are more mildly dealt with if they are males, being drawn to the gallows and hanged till they be dead. But, by a strange distinction, a woman coiner has judgment to be burned alive." In 1685, "the first trace in Scotland of systematic education of young ladies in elegant accomplishments," i.e. in boarding schools.[2] Clarendon [3] contemptuously says that many lawyers practice "the *womanish* art of inveighing against persons." Mill [4] well says that even the physical and mental inferiority of women may be partly owing to *hereditary* effect of the evil position and subordination in which they have been held. John Lysenes, " a Lutheran divine of the seventeenth century," wrote in favour of polygamy.[5] In 1641, the learned Anna Maria Schuman published a Latin dissertation, "Whether the study of literature is suitable to a Christian woman."[6] Cardan was born in 1501, and in his advice to his son he says, "A woman is a foolish animal, and, therefore, full of fraud; if you bestow over-much endearment on her you cannot be happy; she will drag you into mischief." [7] Lord John Russell [8] says, "Every one must have observed the new influence which is not being asserted or sought, but is falling to the lot of women in swaying the destinies of the world." Of *male* criminals three-fifths are under thirty years of age; but in *female* crime, age produces less effect; "the criminal tendency seems to be distributed more equally over the earlier period of active life; and when we look to the recommittals, we are tempted to infer that the comparatively small number of instances in which criminals appear as female offenders, is largely balanced by the inveteracy of the criminal tendency in that sex when once developed." [9] At p. 557, "The number of males who emigrate is, in consequence of the demand for their labour in all new colonies, much greater than females." After the middle of the seventeenth century, the Quakers set up " women's meetings," to the disgust of many, and in the teeth of St. Paul's opinion.[10] In 1616, the General Assembly at Aberdeen complained that "women take upon them to teach schools." [11] Sir David Lyndsay " everywhere speaks with a sort of Turkish contempt of women." [12]

[1] Commentaries on the Law of Scotland, Edinb. 1797, vol. ii. p. 470.
[2] Chambers's Domestic Annals of Scotland, vol. ii. p. 482.
[3] Hist. of the Rebellion, p. 123.     [4] Logic, 1846, vol. ii, pp. 444, 445.
[5] Rosa, Biog. Dict. vol. ix. p. 369.     [6] Ibid. vol. xi. p. 492.
[7] Jerome's Life of Cardan, 1854, vol. ii. p. 197.
[8] Association for Social Science, 1859, p. 17.
[9] Transactions of Social Science, 1859, p. 365.
[10] Fox's Journal, Reprint, Lond. 1827, vol. ii. pp. 212, 213, 318.
[11] Calderwood's History of the Kirk, vol. vii. p. 225.
[12] Lyndsay's Works, by Chalmers, Lond. 1806, vol. i. p. 16.

Lyndsay was born about 1490.[1] In 1655, "a reference from the
Session of Falkland to the Presbytery (of Cupar) was presented,
craving their advice: 'What should be done with a man that
strikes his wife and will not forbear it?'" They referred it to other
presbyteries; but I do not find that anything came of it, though
sessions and presbyteries were ready enough to punish.[2] An
appellation "as from a superior to an inferior, or as from an
husband to a wife."[3] "Do not likewise the Papists and Lutherans
err, who maintain that it is lawful for laics or women to administer the sacrament of baptism in case of necessity? Yes."[4]
"No vow can take away that obligation which is upon wives to
obey their husbands."[5] Hunter[6] takes for granted that "women
and children" cannot bear pain so well as men. "The blood
of males is richer in nutritive parts by nearly one and a half
per cent. than that of females."[7] Hunter says[8] that men and
women recover equally well from "local disease." He says,[9]
"Men will bear bleeding better than women." The editor of
Hunter's Works[10] says, "Probably Haller's estimate of the actual
quantity of blood in the body approaches as nearly to the truth
as any; viz. one-fifth of its weight, of which three-fourths or
more were supposed to be in the veins, and one-fourth or less in
the arteries.—El. Phys. v. i. 3." Hunter says:[11] "Too little action
arises from a disposition to act within the necessary bounds of
health, which produces real weakness and a bad state of health
with debility, without any visible state of disease, as we often see
in fine ladies. . . . . Even the habit of indolence in the mind,
joined with inactivity of the voluntary actions (which is generally
produced from an indolent state of the mind) produces the same
effects, especially as we see in women." Compare 360 on connection between this and the superstition of women. Thomson[12]
says, "The quantity of blood in a moderate-sized man is about
twenty-six pounds avoirdupois." Lithgow, about 1620, contemptuously says, "Crocodilean sex" of the tears of women.[13] Sir
Richard Fanshaw, English ambassador at Madrid, writes to
Secretary Bennet in 1663-4, from Cadiz, that the governor of

[1] Lyndsay's Works, by Chalmers, Lond. 1806, vol. i. p. 8.
[2] Selections from Presbyteries of St. Andrew's and Cupar, Edinb. 1837, 4to, p. 171.
[3] Durham on Solomon, p. 108.      [4] Dickson's Truth's Victory over Error, p. 246.
[5] Cockburn's Jacob's Vow, Edinb. 1696, p. 19.
[6] Works, by Palmer, vol. i. p. 606.
[7] Note in John Hunter's Works, vol. iii. p. 44, edit. Palmer, 1837.
[8] Ibid. p. 274.           [9] Ibid. p. 381.           [10] Ibid. p. 98.
[11] Works, vol. i. p. 312.
[12] Animal Chemistry, Edinb. 1843, p. 349.
[13] Nineteen Years' Travel, p. 451, 11th edition, Edinb. 1770.

Cadiz was very civil; and "at supper, he and his lady would bear me and my wife company, which I, accepting as a great favour, told him my wife should eat with her ladyship, retired from the men after the Spanish fashion, it being more than sufficient they would not think strange we used the innocent freedom of our own when we were among ourselves. But by no means, that he would not suffer; and, to keep us the more in countenance, alledged this manner of eating to be now the custom of many of the greatest families of Spain; and had been from all antiquity to this day, of the majestical house of Alva, the generosity whereof, particularly in the person of the present duke, he took this occasion to celebrate very highly. So, in fine, he had his will of me in this particular."[1]  "Polygamy was permitted among the Mexicans, though chiefly confined, probably, to the wealthy classes."[2]  In Peru, it was practised by the king and "great nobles."[3]  In Peru, no male could marry under twenty-four; and no female under eighteen or twenty.[4]  Mr. Ward, who was well acquainted with the Mexican Indians, says: "I do not know anything in nature more hideous than an old Indian woman."[5] M'Culloch[6] says polygamy *was* allowed to *all* Peruvians. The Mexican girls married at twelve.[7] At Leghorn, about 1660, Italian husbands were very jealous, and would scarcely let their wives go out.[8] Until the middle of the seventeenth century, it was the universal custom in Spain for women (even ladies) to take their meals separate from their husbands, or to sit on the floor.[9]

In the sixteenth century, ladies of the highest rank, incited by the example of Elizabeth, used to kill game with the crossbow.[10] Christian[11] says: "Ann, Countess of Pembroke, had the office of hereditary sheriff of Westmoreland, and exercised it in person. At the assizes of Appleby, she sat with the judges on the Bench. —Harg. Co. Litt. 326." The rise of modern literature diverted the attention of studious women from the classical authors. This, by drawing a distinction between the two sexes, made women more feminine, and enabled them to refine the coarser instincts of man. The civil law allowed husbands to beat their wives;

[1] Fanshaw's Original Letters, Lond. 1702, 8vo, p. 33.
[2] Prescott, vol. i. p. 128.
[3] Prescott's Conquest of Peru, vol. i. pp. 304, 107.          [4] Ibid. p. 107.
[5] Ward's Mexico, vol. ii. p. 74.          [6] Researches concerning America, p. 364.
[7] Ixtlilxochitl, Histoire des Chichimegues, tome i. p. 342.
[8] Lives of the Norths, vol. ii. pp. 328, 329.
[9] See Dunlop's Memoirs of Spain, Edinb. 1834, vol. ii. p. 396.
[10] See Drake's Shakespeare and his Times, 1817, 4to, vol. ii. p. 182.
[11] Note in Blackstone's Commentaries, 8vo, 1809, vol. i. p. 339.

and so did the common law, until " in the politer reign of Charles II. this power of correction began to be doubted."[1] Christian has a long and pathetic note in Blackstone, iii. 143, on the little protection which our law has given to a woman against the arts of a seducer. But I doubt if there should be any such protection at all, except in the case of a promise of marriage. The truth is, that the seduction is often on the other side; and men are as much exposed to the arts of women as women to those of men. On this, as on many other subjects, sentiment has been allowed to usurp the place of reason in our jurisprudence. M. Cousin expresses very strong opinions against female authors.[2] Muller denies that there is any evidence of gallantry towards women in the Northern Sagas;[3] but it appears[4] that this respect was paid to women by the Goths before they were acquainted with Christianity. See also some very ingenious remarks in Mallet's Northern Antiquities.[5] He says that the ancient northern nations greatly respected women; and that this was, because they valued highly every appearance of *nature*; and because women are more *natural*, more spontaneous than men. Besides this, piracy being common, women were in want of defenders and deliverers. There were even female poetesses.[6] Some of the Anglo-Saxon ladies were learned.[7] On the extent to which the increased influence of women has softened our manners, it is to be observed that the increase of towns increases the proportion of female births. On the natural mildness of women, see Roussel, Système de la Femme, p. 45, though I cannot agree with this able writer that this mildness is entirely due to her organisation.

Roussel well says that the Greeks, Jews, and Germans did not cause oracles to be pronounced by women because they respected the female sex, but because their ignorance induced them to consider as sacred those convulsive diseases to which women are peculiarly subject.[8] To this I may add, that women are more subject to insanity than men, and that many barbarous nations respect the insane. The pedantic notion that women should be scientific, or even learned, is refuted with ability and eloquence in Roussel, Système de la Femme, Paris, 1845, pp. 94–100.

In Madagascar, women pay homage to their husbands by

---

[1] Blackstone's Comment. vol. i. p. 445, who cites i. Lid. 113, iii. Keb. 433.
[2] See Cousin's Littérature, Paris, 1849, tome ii. pp. 3–7.
[3] Price's Preface to Weston's History of English Poetry, vol. i. pp. 94, 95.
[4] Ibid. pp. lii, liii.    [5] Lond. 1847, pp. 199–201.
[6] See Wheaton's History of the Northmen, 1831, p. 52. He quotes Münter, Kirchengeschichte, Band i. Seite 197.
[7] See Wright's Biographia Britannica Literaria, 8vo, 1842, vol. i. pp. 32, 33,
[8] Roussel, Système de la Femme, Paris, 1845, pp. 53, 54.

licking their feet.[1]  However, Ellis says [2] that women have more liberty than in most eastern countries, and that young people see each other before marriage.   He adds [3] that no woman ventures to marry within twelve months of her husband's death ; and a husband, on divorcing his wife, may prevent her from remarrying.

In 1812, Niebuhr, who had been reading Klopstock's Correspondence, writes respecting it : " The character of the women too is a remarkable feature of the times of Klopstock's youth.   The cultivation of the mind was carried incomparably further with them than with nearly all the young women of our days; and this we should scarcely have expected to find in the contemporaries of our grandmothers.   It was not, therefore, the work of our native literature ; for that first rose into being along with and under the influence of the love inspired by these charming maidens.   For some time after the Thirty Years' War, the ladies of Germany, particularly those of the middle classes, were excessively coarse and uneducated, as is proved beyond a doubt by a curious Book of Manners which I have bought this winter.   This wonderful alteration must have taken place, therefore, during the eighty years from 1660 to 1740, though we are quite ignorant how and when it began." [4]

Comte makes no doubt of the necessary inferiority of women,[5] but he says [6] that though inferior to men in reason and intelligence, they are superior in sympathy and sociability.   See also tome v. pp. 221–223, where he remarks that under polytheism they are first allowed to enter the priesthood, a right which monotheism abrogates.   See also pp. 440–444, where he says that Catholicism has done women great service by diminishing their political and priestly powers, and concentrating them on domestic life.   He remarks [7] that the essential differences between men and women are, like all other differences, increased by civilization.

In 1797 the celebrated Dr. Currie writes : " Women speak more distinctly than men at the same period of life. . . . . When a labouring man and his wife come to consult me, the female is always the orator." [8]

[1] See Drury's Madagascar, 8vo, 1743, pp. 64–95, and p. 222.
[2] History of Madagascar, 1838, vol. i. p. 163.          [3] Ibid. p. 174.
[4] The Life and Letters of B. G. Niebuhr, Lond. 8vo, 1852, vol. i. p. 337.
[5] Philosophie Positive, tome iv. pp. 569–574.          [6] Ibid. p. 573.
[7] Ibid. pp. 443, 444.
[8] Life and Correspondence of Dr. Currie. By W. W. Currie, 8vo, 1831, vol. ii. p. 216.

Lord Campbell[1] says of Bacon, "Like several extraordinary men, he is supposed to have inherited his genius from his mother." So did Wilberforce.[2]

In the middle of the seventeenth century, the ladies of the ancient house of Savelli, at Rome, still retained their old custom of never leaving their palace, or if they did so, only appearing in closely shut up carriages.[3]

The Mongols and Tartars "marry very young:" and as they openly buy their wives, the women of course have no portion or dowry. Polygamy is allowed, but "the women lead an independent life enough."[4]

In Siberia many of the shamans, or priests, are women.[5]

There is more water in the blood of females than in that of males.[6]

The fluid which lubricates the brain and spinal marrow is more abundant in women than in men, and in old men it is twice as plentiful as in adults, and it is very abundant in idiots.[7] In women blood contains more water than in men : and in lymphatic temperaments, there is more water than in the blood of sanguineous ones.[8] The reviving reputation of the humourist pathology gives increased importance to these facts.

The increased courtesy is shown even in the way of declaring war, in which countries now never abuse each other, but display " la plus noble décence." [9]

In the manufacturing towns males marry early, therefore they are near the same age as their wives; hence the proportion of females born is increased.[10]

It is not considered so respectable for a woman to keep a school as for a man; hence education is worse, and particularly in France and Germany, where the state interferes.

From 1836 to 1846 "the yearly average number of persons who were charged with offences in England and Wales was 25,812, viz., 20,969 males, 4,843 females, but comparatively *no* educated woman commits a crime.[11]

On the age at which in different climates menstruation occurs

[1] Lives of the Chancellors, vol. ii. p. 285.
[2] See Life of Wilberforce, 8vo, 1838, vol. i. p. 5.
[3] Ranke, Die Römischen Päpste, Band iii. pp. 60, 61.
[4] Huc's Travels in Tartary and Thibet, vol. i. pp. 184–187.
[5] Bell's Travels through Asia, Edinb. 1788, 8vo, vol. i. p. 248.
[6] See Fourth Report of British Association, p. 126.
[7] Cuvier, Progrès des Sciences Naturelles, tome ii. p. 397.
[8] Clark's Report on Animal Physiology, in Fourth Report of British Association, p. 126.
[9] Vattel, Le Droit des Gens, tome ii. p. 170.
[10] Saddler's Law of Population, vol. ii. p. 336.
[11] See Reports of British Association for 1847 ; Transactions of Sections, p. 109.

see Rep. of British Association for 1850 ; Transac. of Sections, p. 135.

We take shame to ourselves for not having sooner noticed this very interesting, and in some respects very important work ; the author unknown ; and yet the book gone through two editions, though written on a subject ignorantly supposed to be going on well. That women can be satisfied with their state shows their deterioration. That they can be satisfied with knowing nothing, &c.

The mother of Cuvier was a very able woman.[1]

Flourens[2] says that the increased desire of observing gave rise everywhere in the seventeenth century to academies of science where such facts could be registered.

In the progress of society since the sixteenth century, women have not kept their ground. Civilization increases divergence ; hence, if allowed to run its course, women must naturally decline in power. Sydney Smith, the first writer on women, erroneously says there is no original difference. In agricultural countries, as in France, women are better treated and have more wages. Compare Sparta with Athens. Women being more deductive have more sympathy with art than with science ; hence their influence in the sixteenth century, the great age of art. There is now a higher intellectual standard and a diminished regard for *manners*, once the source of women's power as giving scope to *tact*. Their excellence consists in *moral* superiority ; but morals have *not* progressed ; intellect *has*. The age of imagination has passed, and that of intellect has come. Girls are more precocious than boys ; hence coming in contact with nature, when *unripe*, they are rather imaginative than critical. Philippa, wife of Edward II., Jeanne de Montfort, Countess of Bretagne. Under Charles II., as physical science rose, the influence of women decreased. The progress of knowledge, by developing differences, has increased divergences. They have learnt to despise the arts of compounding a pleasant pudding or combining a tasty pie. They no longer wear their keys at their girdles ; nor do they carry receipts in their pockets. They have ceased to be useful, and they have not learnt to be agreeable. It is in consequence of these things that we hail with great pleasure the appearance of the present work, which is not a manifesto of rights, but a guide and a clue. Writers like Miss Martineau and Mary Wolstoncraft have done much harm. There are no such things as natural rights, and if women are ignorant and

[1] See Flourens, Histoire des Travaux de Cuvier, Paris, 1845, p. 65.
[2] Ibid. pp. 146, 147.

superstitious, the less influence they have the better. Is a woman
to have influence because she lisps broken Italian at the piano ?
Late in the eighteenth century, there rose clubs which followed
up the blow of scientific societies, and still further increased the divergence of the sexes. The great increase of nervous diseases caused
by increasing excitement makes men more irritable ; hence the
weaker goes to the wall ; and this we see among the lower orders,
where *manners* having progressed little, women are worse treated
than ever. Hence, among the higher classes, the increasing
influence of women is only *apparent*; they are no longer beaten
or kicked because kicking is not polite. Looking at the increase
of courtesy and general kindness, the respect paid to women has
not increased so fast as it ought to have done. We are more
courteous to everything. We no longer horsewhip our servants,
nor flog our children into fits. Hospitals and charities have no
other idea beyond that of protecting the weak. The encouragement given to intellect by government is happily passing away,
and women ought to confer on intellect social fame, and by this
alliance they would recover their old power. The increasing loss
of wealth, which is partly cause and partly effect of diminished
aristocracy, lessens the sympathy between the sexes and gives a
new standard of merit, and this took place in the seventeenth
century, when nobles began to marry city heiresses. The laws,
too, respecting women, have improved ; but not so fast as they
have improved on other matters. The nearest approach to
perfect equality is among savages who are *all* stupid and ignorant.
The truth seems to be that while civil and political equality are
increasing, moral and intellectual equalities are diminishing.
Men are *thinkers*, women *observers* ; but formerly there was no
thinking, and observation of trifles carried the day. In Mrs. Grey's
works are no crude notions about women having a right to vote
or sit in parliament. In the sixteenth century began the great
movement when, says Shakespeare, the heel of the courtier, &c.
That the democratic, sceptical, and inductive movement works
even now more good than harm, and eventually will work unmitigated good, is certain, but in the meantime it causes individual pain, and of this women are the natural correctives ;
hence it were to be wished their influence should increase and
women could correct the too rapid democracy and scepticism.
Classical literature is no longer studied by both sexes. Women
are physically too excitable, too prone to come into contact with
external nature, and this evil nurses painting and music and
Italian—the most enervating of all literatures, the only great
thinkers being Macchiavelli, Beccaria, and Vico. If these re-

marks are well founded, we should expect to find an increased divergence between the sexes in the seventeenth and eighteenth centuries. And such we find to be actually the case in learned societies and clubs; and in the seventeenth century, the beginning of this was coffee houses. Among the lower orders, the diminution of agriculture caused by chemical manures and increased skill in ploughing, &c., has increased the manufacturing population, and therefore has increased the number of pursuits in which women are unable to participate. Comparing barbarism with imperfect civilization, the influence of women increases; hence the hasty inference that it goes on increasing, an inference fortified by the fact that women receive an increased *external* respect. In France, twice as many agriculturists as in England; hence, women have more influence and their wages are higher. While the pursuits of men have become more great, the pursuits of women have become more little.

" Both in England and France the proportion of male to female criminals is about four to one, and that result varies but slightly during several years."[1]

Turgot[2] erroneously says, " L'asservissement des femmes aux hommes est fondé par toute la terre sur l'inégalité des forces corporelles." But women have *two* sorts of inferiority: *physical* and *mental*.

In Ireland, the number of females that cannot write is slightly greater than the number of males.[3]

Napoleon said: " My opinion is, that the future good or bad conduct of a child entirely depends upon the mother."[4] Moore[5] says that women endure pain better than men, because they have " less physical sensibility. This theory I offered to put to the test by bringing in a hot tea pot, which I would answer for the ladies of the party being able to hold for a much longer time than the men."

In 1593, in Italy, " only men and the masters of the family go into the market and buy victuals; for servants are never sent for that purpose, much less women, which if they be chaste, rather are locked up at home, as it were in prison."[6] But, says Moryson,[7] in Bergamo " The very women give and receive salutations and converse with the French liberty, without any offence to their husbands, which other Italians would never endure." In

---

[1] Report of British Association for 1839; Transactions of Sections, p. 117.
[2] Œuvres, tome ii. p. 247, Disc. sur l'Histoire.
[3] See Report of British Association for 1843; Transactions of Sections, p. 91.
[4] O'Meara's Napoleon in Exile, vol. ii. p. 100, 3rd edition, Lond. 1822.
[5] Memoirs, by Lord J. Russell, vol. vii pp. 53, 54, 1st edit.
[6] Fynes Moryson's Itinerary, part i. p. 70, Lond. 1617, folio.        [7] Ibid. p. 177.

Holland women had most freedom; they managed the shops and
looked after the accounts, while the men were idle.[1] See also
p. 288, where Moryson says that Dutch married women not only
had the right of bequest, but possessed in their lifetime the
control of their husband's common every day actions. On the
other hand, the Germans treated their wives very ill, and would
not let them eat at the same table.[2] On the influence of woman,
see J. S. Mill's Essays, vol. ii. p. 165, and p. 449 of Mrs. Mill's
Essay in the same work; also pp. 425, 435, 262. Saint-Simon,
who was in Spain in 1721 and 1722, observes[3] that greater favour
was shown to bastards in Spain than in any other Christian
country. This he ascribes to the influence of the Mahommedans.
"The natural sterility of Spanish women, who, though they may
have children by good luck, leave off child-bearing much sooner
than the women of other nations."[4] "The great and main duty
which a wife, as a wife, ought to learn, and so learn as to
practise it, is to be subject to her own husband. . . . There
is not any husband to whom this honour of submission is not due;
no personal infirmity, frowardness of nature, no, not even on
the point of religion, doth deprive him of it."[5] "The sum of a
wife's duty unto her husband is subjection." Abernethy[6] is opposed to beauty in women; for he says, "Seldom is it found that
beauty and shamefastness do agree." At p. 445, this wise man
praises persons who castrate themselves. "Humanity is the virtue
of a woman; generosity of a man. The fair sex, who have
commonly much more tenderness than ours, have seldom so much
generosity."[7] Hutchison[8] says that for husbands to inflict on
their wives "any corporal punishment, must be tyrannical and
unmanly." "Dr. Marshall Hall found that, from patients with
congestive apoplexy from forty to fifty ounces of blood might be
drawn without producing syncope; whilst in acute inflammations
the *tolerance* is usually less by about ten ounces."[9] Williams
says,[10] "Nervous diseases are most common and obstinate in the
female sex; but they are more serious in the male sex." About
nine times as many men have aneurisms as women.[11] Males are
more subject to pericarditis;[12] to pneumonia "in the proportion of

[1] Fynes Moryson's Itinerary, part iii. p. 97.                    [2] Ibid. p. 220.
[3] Mémoires, Paris, 1840-1842, tomo xxxv. pp. 240-246.
[4] History of Cardinal Alberoni, Lond. 1719, p. 250.
[5] Fergusson on the Epistles, 1656, p. 242. See also p. 356.
[6] Physick for the Soul, p. 437.
[7] Smith's Theory of Moral Sentiments, vol. ii. p. 19.
[8] System of Moral Philosophy, vol. ii. p. 165.
[9] Williams's Principles of Medicine, 1848, pp. 177, 233.    [10] Ibid. p. 449.
[11] Hasse's Patholog. Anatomy, by Sydenham Society, pp. 94, 142.    [12] Ibid. p. 110.

ten to one." [1]   Females "appear to be more prone" to "tuberculosis of the lung." [2]  But "cancer of the lung is incomparably more frequent in males than in females." [3]  On diseases of women compared with men, see Rokitansky's Pathological Anatomy, vol. iii. p. 177, vol. iv. pp. 271, 303.

<hr />

## THE CAUSES AND EFFECTS OF DUELLING.

Of all the vices natural to a modern Republic, duelling is the most brutal and the most constant.  It is the last resource of a baffled coward.  It was entirely unknown to the generous spirit of antiquity, but is most frequent in the United States of America, that wretched burlesque of an ancient Republic which possesses the forms of democracy without the spirit of liberty.  Miss Martineau [4] says : "I was amazed to hear a gentleman of New England declare, while complaining of the insolence of the Southern Members of Congress to the Northern under shelter of the Northern men not being duellists, that, if he went to Congress, he would give out that he would fight."  In the single city of New Orleans, "there were fought, in 1834, more duels than there are days in the year ; fifteen on one Sunday morning.  In 1835, there were 102 duels fought in that city between the 1st of January and the end of April ; and no notice is taken of shooting in a quarrel." [5]

It seems probable that the tendency of civilization is to increase timidity.  If this be the case, duelling may be defended on the ground taken up by Adam Smith, that it renders the restraint of anger by fear still more contemptible than it otherwise would be. [6]

In 1589, " Sir William Drury was killed in a duel by Sir John Boroughs." [7]

By the end of the sixteenth century duelling had become a regular system, and books were written in England to teach a gentleman how to give the lie in a satisfactory manner. [8]  The

[1] Hasse's Patholog. Anatomy, by Sydenham Society. p. 215.
[2] Ibid. p. 316.          [3] Ibid. p. 370.
[4] Society in America, Paris, 8vo, 1842, vol. ii. p. 108, part iii. chap. i.
[5] Ibid. vol. ii. pp. 130, 131.
[6] Theory of Moral Sentiments, part. vi. section 3, vol. ii. p. 94.
[7] Camden's Elizabeth, in Kennet, vol. ii. p. 557.
[8] See Drake's Shakespeare and his Times, 1817, 4to, vol. ii. pp. 158, 159, and Ben Jonson, 1816, vol. iv. p. 107.

famous Dr. A. Clarke thought that, in many cases, duelling is more criminal than suicide.[1]

The object of duelling was to punish injuries which the law left unpunished. This could only be done by putting the weak and unskilful on a level with the strong and skilful; thus the introduction of pistols instead of swords was a great improvement, and, I doubt not, has led the way to that better state of things when the combined authority of laws and manners will be sufficient to repress such offences.

Henry IV. of France issued edicts against duels.[2] Towards the end of the sixteenth century Ben Jonson killed a man in a duel.[3] In 1629 he attacks duelling in The New Inn; but the satire, though very moral, is also very tedious.[4]

Chevenix has well said that duelling " is more prevalent in vain than in proud nations."[5] This remark may be applied to individuals, and I believe that nothing but an ungovernable burst of passion would induce a really proud man either to send or accept a challenge.

In 1592 gentlemen seem not to have worn their rapiers, but to have made their servants carry them.[6]

In Porter's Two Angrie Women of Abington,[7] Coomes complains that the " poking fight of rapier and dagger " was becoming common, and the sword and buckler falling into disuse. Mr. Rimbault[8] says that rapiers " were introduced in England during Elizabeth's reign by a desperado named Rowland Yorke; and their lightness and convenience soon gave them a permanent footing in place of the heavy swords previously worn."

I suspect that as the trial by battle became disused, the people, clinging to their old customs, became more addicted to duelling. Blackstone says[9] that the last trial by battle waged in the Common Pleas was in 1571. I must therefore consider duelling as the *result of the decline of chivalry.* While the trial by battle was allowed, it was natural to punish those who went about armed. Thus the 2 Edward III. forbids any one to carry dangerous arms.—Blackstone iv. 149. Christian says,[10] " the last time

[1] See his Letter, dated 1732, in Mrs. Thomson's Memoirs of Viscountess Sundon, 2nd edition, 8vo, 1848, vol. ii. p. 120.
[2] See Capefigue, Histoire de la Réforme, tome viii. p. 98.
[3] See his Life, by Gifford, p. xix. in vol. i. of Jonson's Works.
[4] Ben Jonson's Works, vol. v. pp. 416–418.
[5] Essay on National Character, 8vo, 1832, vol. i. p. 159.
[6] See Park's edition of Harleian Miscellany, vol. v. p. 420.
[7] 1599; Percy Soc. vol. v. p. 61.
[8] Note to Rowland's Four Knaves, Percy Society, vol. ix. p. 132.
[9] Commentaries, vol. iii. p. 338.
[10] Note in Blackstone, vol. iv. p. 348.

that the trial by battle was awarded in this country was in the case of Lord Rae and Mr. Ramsay in 7th Car. I." But it was ordered as late as 1819, for I have read an account of the trial in Rush's Residence at the Court of London. It was afterwards got rid of by some flaw in that occasion and at once put an end to by Act of Parliament. In 1560 Cecil was so displeased with some remarks thrown out by the Bishop of Ross, in a diplomatic nego- tiation, that he challenged him to fight. "I offered in that quarrel to spend my blood upon any of them that would deny it."[1] Margaret of Austria, aunt to Charles V., mentions in 1529 the duel which was to have been fought between the emperor and Francis I.[2] Lord Brougham can only find a parallel for our wager of battle in the barbarism of a Persian law.[3] Allen says : " Private war has disappeared, and the only vestige of it that remains is the practice of duelling."[4] He adds [5] that Britton did not mention private war: "the practice was going into disuse ; and in less than half a century it was adjudged to be illegal." This, as he says, was partly owing to "the regular distribution of justice in the courts of eyre and assize." Montesquieu observes that the licence given to single combat was a consequence and a remedy of the laws which permit negative proofs. If the defen- dant could swear himself innocent, it seemed natural that the plaintiff should have some subsequent appeal.[6] If this is well founded, duelling may be connected with the use of Courts of *Conscience*, such as Chancery, or even the Court of Requests. See also respecting the trial by combat p. 448, and read the whole of livre xxviii. In 1565, Count Egmont was reproached by Philip II. for being in a company where some foolish joke was passed against Granvella. Egmont replied that no disrespect was intended to the king, and that, if he had thought any of the jokers had such intention, he would have instantly challenged him : "so würde er selbst ihn vor seinen Degen fordern."[7] In 1576 foreigners in London wore rapiers,[8] and Fleetwood says : [9] " His garments were a cloke and a rapier after the Italian fashion." " Bludgeons and bucklers " were in 1586 the ordinary weapons.[10]

---

[1] Haynes's State Papers, p. 337.
[2] See Correspondence of Charles V., edited by Mr. Bradford, Lond. 8vo, 1850, p. 224.
[3] Brougham's Political Philosophy, 2nd edit. 8vo, 1849, vol. i. p. 123.
[4] Allen on the Prerogative, 8vo, 1849, p. 118.      [5] Ibid. p. 121.
[6] Esprit des Lois, livre xxviii. chap. xiv. and xviii. Œuvres, Paris, 1835, pp. 446, 449.
[7] Abfall der Niederlande, in Schiller's Werke, Band viii. Seite 179, Stuttgart, 1838.
[8] See Fleetwood's Letter in Wright's Elizabeth, vol. ii. p. 38.
[9] Ibid. p. 40.
[10] See Leycester Correspondence, Camden Society, p. 228.

In 1580 the French Ambassador, while passing the bars at Smith-field, was stopped because his rapier was longer than the statute allowed,[1] by which we learn that there were officers sitting at Smithfield Bars whose business it was to *cut* swords that were too lengthy. In 1562 a proclamation forbad any one to carry a sword having a blade more than a yard and a quarter long.[2] Cranmer, when archbishop, challenged the Duke of Northumber-land.[3] Madame de Crequy says that the firmness of Louis XIV. had, during the last seventeen years of his reign, put an end to duels. "On n'avait pas ouï parler d'un seul duel depuis dixsept ans."[4] But she adds[5] that after his death they became frequent on account of the weakness of the regent; "La fureur des duels était si fort encouragée par la faiblesse et l'incurie du duc d'Or-léans, qu'on n'entendait parler que de jeunes gens tués et blessés." Duels were practised by the ancient Persians.[6] In 1600, the first instance in Scotland of a duellist "suffering death when nothing unfair was proved."[7] Lithgow, who was in Spain in 1620, says the Spaniards never fight duels.[8] Respecting duels fought by women, see COMMON PLACE BOOK, art. 1093.

---

## NOTES ON THE TENDENCY OF EDUCATION.

MISS MARTINEAU[9] says: "The provision of schools is so adequate [in the United States] that any citizen, who sees a child at play during school hours, may ask: 'Why are you not at school?' and, unless good reason be given, may take him to the school-house of the district." Mr. Mills says: "It is an allowable exercise of the powers of government to impose on parents the legal obliga-tion of giving elementary instruction to children."[10]

Adam Smith[11] says, probably with truth, that education at boarding-schools and colleges has seriously injured the morals of

---

[1] See Lord Talbot's Letter in Lodge's Illustrations of British History, vol. ii. p. 168.

[2] Machyn's Diary, p. 281, Camden Soc. vol. xlii.

[3] Todd's Life of Cranmer, vol. ii. p. 353.

[4] Souvenirs de la Marquise de Crequy, Paris, 8vo, 1834, tome i. p. 255.

[5] Ibid. p. 348.

[6] See Malcolm's History of Persia, 8vo, 1829, vol. i. pp. 26, 38, 39, 41.

[7] Pitcairn's Criminal Trials, vol. ii. p. 112. See for this, vol. iii. p. 502.

[8] Lithgow's Nineteen Years' Travels, 11th edit. Edinb. 1770, p. 423.

[9] Society in America, Paris, 8vo, 1842, vol. ii. p. 185, part iii. chap. iii.

[10] Principles of Political Economy, vol. ii. p. 524. See also Mill's Essays, vol. i. p. 89.

[11] Theory of Moral Sentiments, part vi. sect. 2, chap. i. vol. ii. pp. 65, 66, Lond. 1822, 12mo.

NOTES ON THE TENDENCY OF EDUCATION.　889

France and England. Southey, in a letter written in 1823, has some good remarks on the comparative advantages of public and private education. He expresses the strongest horror of boarding-schools, and greatly prefers, I think with reason, day schools.[1]

By educating a nation you increase its wealth in two different ways; for you increase the desire of accumulation, and at the same time, by making the labourer more intelligent, you make his labour more productive.[2] It also prevents over increase of population.[3]

The advantages of education to the lower orders merely in an economical point of view are well stated by Mr. Thornton, who, I think, prefers oral instruction to any other.[4]

Of the real benefits of education, Hannah More, though she did so much to impart them, had no competent idea. In 1801 she wrote a long and formal defence of her conduct to the Bishop of Bath and Wells. She says: "To teach the poor to read without providing them with *safe* books, has always appeared to me an improper measure; and this consideration induced me to enter upon the laborious undertaking of the Cheap Repository Tracts."[5] Those who have read Hannah More's works will easily understand this sentence. By *safe* books, she meant books which, under pretence of imparting spiritual knowledge, neglected intellectual knowledge and made men pious and useless. Roberts says that Hannah More, "adverting to the multitude of improving and entertaining books which were daily issuing from the press for the use of children and young persons, she added, 'In my early youth there was scarcely anything between Cinderella and the Spectator.'"[6] This was said about 1820. Hannah More in her Strictures on Female Education (the Preface to which is dated 1799) repeats her mischievous opinion that it is of no use to educate the poor, unless we tell them what to read, and "furnish them with such books as shall strengthen and confirm their principles."[7]

There is yet another point of view in which education of the poor becomes so important. It is well known to physiologists that a deficiency of nutriment affects the brain.[8] It, therefore,

---

[1] The Life and Correspondence of R. Southey, edited by the Rev. C. C. Southey, 8vo, 1849, 1850, vol. i. pp. 79, 80. See also vol. v. p. 218.

[2] Mill's Principles of Political Economy, Lond. 1849, 8vo, 2nd edit. vol. i. pp. 131–136, 202, 203, 227.

[3] Ibid. pp. 464, 465.

[4] See Thornton on Over Population, 8vo, 1846, pp. 327–377.

[5] Roberts's Memoirs of Mrs. Hannah More, 2nd edit. 8vo, 1834, vol. iii. p. 135.

[6] Ibid. vol. iv. p. 132.

[7] Works, 8vo, 1830, vol. v. p. 140.

[8] Combe's Physiology of Digestion, 2nd edit. Edinb. 8vo, 1836, pp. 247–250.

follows that the lower the real reward of the labourer, the greater
is the necessity of education, in order in some degree to obviate
the evils arising from the deficiency of his food.[1]

In and after 1557 the Quakers set up private schools both for
boys and girls.[2]

The mischievous effects on the health of young girls caused by
the absurd regulations of modern boarding-schools are scarcely to
be believed ; but they are well attested.[3]  Boys have suffered
less.[4]  I suppose then that the average life of men has increased
more than that of women.

The school books commonly used in England in the middle of
the sixteenth century are enumerated by Mr. Drake.[5]

The way, in which an increased spirit of providence among the
lower orders increases the wealth of the country to which they belong, is very clearly explained by Mr. Rae,[6] who indeed has discussed all the causes of accumulation with remarkable ability.

In that very remarkable work, The Brief Conceipt of English
Policy, published in 1581, the Doctor notices and reprobates the
increasing disregard shown to the universities.  He observes that
it had become customary to remove young men from them at an
earlier age than formerly, " whereby the universities be in manner
emptied." [7]  In 1559, Elizabeth ordered that " the parson or curate
of the parish shall instruct the children of his parish for half an
hour before evening prayer on every holyday and second Sunday
in the year in the catechism, and shall teach them the Lord's
Prayer, Creed, and Ten Commandments." [8]  In 1562 the Speaker
of the House of Commons stated, in his place in Parliament, that
" the schools in England are fewer than formerly by a hundred." [9]

The North American Indians never punish their children.[10]

The stimulus which Protestantism has given to great schools is
ably, but perhaps a little too strongly, put by M. Villers.[11]

Blackstone was in favour of compulsory education, but this, I

[1] See also Combe's Physiology applied to Health, 3rd edit. Edinb. 8vo, 1835, p. 276.
[2] See Fox's Journal, reprint, 1817, vol. ii. pp. 84, 278, 279, 357.
[3] See some evidence in Combe's Principles of Physiology applied to the Preservation of Health, Edinb. 1835, 8vo, 3rd edit. pp. 130-133.
[4] Ibid. pp. 135, 157.
[5] Shakespeare and his Times, 1817, 4to, vol. i. pp. 25-27, 57.
[6] New Principles of Political Economy, Boston, 8vo, 1834, pp. 200-204.
[7] Harleian Miscellany, edit. Park, vol. ix. p. 150.
[8] Neal's History of the Puritans, edit. Toulmin, 8vo, 1822, vol. i. p. 129.
[9] Collier's Ecclesiastical History, 8vo, 1840, vol. vi. p. 356.  See also D'Ewes
Journals of Parliament, 1682, p. 65.
[10] See Buchanan's Sketches of the North American Indians, 8vo, 1824, p. 70.
[11] Essai sur la Réformation, Paris, 1820, pp. 280-286.

fear, not from any enlightened reason; but from an over love of government interference.[1]

In 1551, Dr. Wotton promised the "searchor" at Dover (I suppose of the Custom House) that he would appoint his son to "a Roome yn our Gramer school," and expresses a wish that he should be first examined by the schoolmasters.[2]

Kant proposed that in education *no* opinions should be concealed from the student. In this noble liberality he was not only in advance of his own, but of the present age. Even M. Cousin says: " Ce serait beaucoup hasarder."[3]

Cousin speaks strongly in favour of *public* education, which he prefers to *private*; because, by placing every one under the same rule, it gives them the idea of *duty*.[4] Cousin seems to think[5] that the state is bound to *enforce* education.[6]

The tendency of Calvinism is to extend education.[7]

*Mere* education, popularly so called, that is, reading and writing, does a nation little good. The Chinese are a remarkable instance; for of this sort of education they have more than any people in the world, but yet are unable to emerge from their present ignorance. See some good remarks in Brougham's Political Philosophy.[8] This he ascribes to the " manifest intention which the sovereigns have always had to limit the literary acquisitions of their subjects,"[9] and to the efforts of the rulers to make education a political engine.[10] The influence of education in checking population is noticed by M. Quetelet;[11] but he adds[12] that merely teaching to read and write does not lessen crime so much as is supposed. Mr. Alison notices the tendency of education to " restrain the operation of the principle of increase."[13] He adds[14] that, in Ireland, " the proportion attending the primary schools is greater than in Scotland." See[15] his ill-written and ill-argued attack upon the secular education of the lower orders.[16] Reed, in a spirit far beyond his age, says: " Notwithstanding the innumerable errors committed in human education, there is hardly

[1] Commentaries, edit. Christian, 8vo, 1809, vol. i. p. 451.
[2] Haynes's State Papers, p. 113.
[3] Histoire de la Philosophie, Paris, 1846, part i. tome v. pp. 245, 255.
[4] Ibid. part i. tome i. pp. 350, 351.     [5] Ibid. part i. tome iii. p. 215.
[6] See also tome iv. pp. 300, 301.        [7] See my notes on Calvinism.
[8] 2nd edit. 8vo, 1849, vol. i. pp. 162, 167, 184.
[9] Ibid. p. 171.                          [10] Ibid. p. 185.
[11] Sur l'Homme, Paris, 8vo, 1835, tome i. pp. 108-110.
[12] Ibid. tome ii. p. 245.
[13] Alison's Principles of Population, 8vo, 1840, vol. i. p. 93.
[14] Ibid. p. 511.                         [15] Vol. ii. pp. 292-346.
[16] See also my remarks on Crime.

any education so bad as to be worse than none."[1]   Ranke observes
that it was a peculiarity of the early German literature that its
best works were written for the purposes of education.[2]   The
struggles between Protestants and Catholics must have favoured
education.   Each party wished to strengthen itself in every way,
and there was none so effective as education.

Glanvill says:[3]  "Thus, a French top, the common recreation of
schoolboys, thrown from a cord which was wound about it, will
stand, as it were, fixed on the floor it lighted."   And in Plus Ultra,
1668, p. 117, he says: "Everyone that hath outgrown his cherry-
stones and rattles."[4]   Until early in the seventeenth century, or
even later, children wore "long coats" at seven years of age.[5]
Evelyn's son went to Oxford, in 1666, aged thirteen, and "was
newly out of long coates."[6]   In 1682, Evelyn[7] mentions the vast
expence "the nation is at yearly by sending children into France
to be taught military exercises."   It used to be common for parents
to punish their children so severely as to lame them.[8]   Montaigne
had the most liberal ideas about education.[9]   Charron[10] has some
sensible remarks on education, which he seems to have taken from
Montaigne.   In the Polynesian Islands, the children used "to
resist all parental restraint."[11]   An Indian expressed his surprise
that the white people were so cruel as to whip their children.[12]
Grammar schools resulted from the dissolution of monasteries.[13]
"Like one of our schoolboys' satchels, made of wrought stuff, and
lined with leather."[14]   Locke, who was himself at Oxford, used to
express his contempt for the system of education pursued there.[15]
As to the proportion of persons educated in different countries,
see Alison, History of Europe, vol. ix. p. 221.   At the Madras
School, late in the eighteenth century, one of the masters was
dismissed because he punished children by biting their fingers.[16]
In Tartary, the discipline of the boys brought up by the priests is

[1]  Reed's Inquiry into the Human Mind, Edinb. 8vo, 1814, p. 441.
[2]  Die Römischen Päpste, Berlin, 1838, Band i. Seiten 76, 77.
[3]  Vanity of Dogmatizing, 1661, p. 80.
[4]  See also his Vanity of Dogmatizing, p. 243.
[5]  See Wordsworth's Ecclesiastical Biography, 3rd edit. 8vo, 1839, vol. iv. p. 317.
[6]  Evelyn's Diary, 8vo, 1827, vol. ii. p. 281, and see p. 282.
[7]  Ibid. vol. iii. p. 70.
[8]  Essais de Montaigne, livre ii. chap. xxxi. Paris, 8vo, 1843, pp. 448, 449.
[9]  See Montaigne's Works, edit. Hazlitt, pp. 54-76, 63, 69, 177.
[10]  De la Sagesse, Amsterdam, 1783, 8vo, tome ii. p. 177.
[11]  Ellis, Polynesian Researches, 8vo, 1831, vol. iii. p. 205.
[12]  See Catlin's North American Indians, 8vo, 1841, vol. ii. p. 241.
[13]  Nichols, Literary Illustrations of the Eighteenth Century, vol. v. p. 99.
[14]  Calamy's Own Life, 8vo, 1829, vol. i. p. 190.
[15]  King's Life of Locke, 8vo, 1830, vol. i. p. 5.
[16]  Southey's Life of Dr. Bell, vol. i. pp. 184, 186.

very severe.[1] Porter[2] says: "In the whole of England and Wales, among 367,894 couples married during three years (1839, 1840, 1841), it appeared that there were 122,458 men and 181,378 women who either could not write at all, or who had attained so little proficiency in penmanship that they were averse to the exposure of their deficiency." Colleges, properly so called, were not established in France till the end of the fifteenth century.[3] Monteil says[4] that in 1380 there were at Paris only forty schoolmasters and twenty schoolmistresses. Laing says that state interference in education has done much harm abroad.[5] In Prussia, education is compulsory to a cruel extent,[6] and the Prussians are lower in morals than any other nation.[7] In Journal of Statistical Society for 1838, vol. i. p. 47, it is said: "The endowments for purposes of education in this country possess an immense annual income, amounting, it is probable, to not less than 1,500,000. On the origin of day schools, &c., see p. 459. Fletcher says[8] of "the labouring classes" that "the day-schooling of the same classes is of yet more recent origin; for it cannot be dated earlier than 1798, when Dr. Bell published his Experiments on Education made at the male asylum at Madras, and Joseph Lancaster began practically to develope the same principles in the schools now designated British Schools. Nor was it until 1808 that the British School Society was founded on its present basis, nor until 1811 that the National Society was established. The next great step was the establishment of the first infant school in England in 1818." In England and Wales, where there are most domestic servants, there is most education. This shows the utility of luxury by increasing contact.[9] Education increases with property.[10] On the opinion of Guerry see vol. xii. 219. Giving the children at national schools a costume has done great harm by irritating the pride of the parents.[11] Vast numbers of the poor who attend schools afterward forget even how to read.[12] For a comparative list of the proportion which, in the different countries of Europe, the educated bear to the uneducated, see Journal of Statistical Soc., vol. ii. p. 386; and at p. 396 it is observed that education has diminished in Holland since the Dutch in 1830 ceased to make it compulsory.[13]

[1] See Huc's Travels in Tartary and Thibet, vol. i. pp. 58, 59, 177, 178.
[2] Progress of the Nation, vol. iii. p. 278.
[3] See Monteil, Histoire des Divers États, tome i. p. 162.
[4] Ibid. tome ii. p. 8.   [5] Observations on Denmark, p. 31.
[6] Laing, Notes of a Traveller, 1st series, p. 165.   [7] Ibid. pp. 167, 168.
[8] Journal of Statistical Society, vol. x. p. 196.   [9] Ibid. p. 207.
[10] Ibid. vol. xii. p. 235.   [11] Ibid. vol. i. p. 455. See also vol. vi. p. 213.
[12] Ibid. vol. ii. pp. 68, 73.   [13] See also vol. iii. pp. 341, 342.

After all, I think, the simplest argument against Government interfering in education is that, hitherto, whatever they have touched they have injured. They have increased crime, usury, irreligion, smuggling.

The inferior schools in Birmingham teach nothing worth learning.[1] Parents prefer sending their boys even to schools kept by women; and such schools are infinitely more numerous than those kept by men.[2] By the Visigothic Code, " If a master shall chastise his pupil so that death ensue, if he can prove that the chastisement was more severe than he intended, he shall not be punished or defamed."[3] Hallam[4] says that Hughes' Life of Barrow "contains a sketch of studies pursued in the University of Cambridge from the twelfth to the seventeenth century." He adds[5] that even Milton, notwithstanding his expression, "complete and generous education," had narrow views, and confines his course of education to "ancient writers." Locke is too rigid, and recommends that "children should be taught to expect nothing because it will give them pleasure."[6] However, he rather prefers private to public education.[7] Hallam says:[8] " No one had condescended to spare any thoughts for female education till Fénelon in 1688 published his earliest work, Sur l'Éducation des Filles. . . . His theory is uniformly indulgent; his method of education is a labour of love."[9] The foundation and free grammar schools are nearly all founded by clergymen of the Church of England, and taught by them, and for the most part arose in consequence of the monasteries being broken up. Out of 436 foundation schools, 115 date from the reign of Elizabeth; but, after this, the rate of increase gradually lessens, and, "in the long reign of George III., only twelve were founded," owing to " the religious indifference of the eighteenth century."[10] At p. 226 it is said that the first " ragged schools " in London were in 1844 ; but that " an isolated effort had been made in the country some thirty years before." On the history &c. of public schools, see M'Culloch's British Empire, 1847, vol. ii. p. 318, et seq. On legalised cruelty in education, see Hume's Commentaries on the Laws of Scotland, i. pp. 13, 45, 358, 389 ; vol. ii. p. 40. " Uneducated persons are utterly unable to separate any two ideas which have once become firmly associated in their minds ; but the cultivated being more accustomed to exercise their imagination, have experienced sensations and

---

[1] Journal of Statistical Society, vol. iii. p. 35.  [2] Ibid. vol. vi. p. 214.
[3] Dunham's Hist. of Spain, in Lardner's Cyclop. vol. iv. p. 86, Lond. 1832.
[4] Literature, vol. iii. p. 249.  [5] Ibid. p. 410.
[6] Ibid. p. 413.  [7] Ibid. p. 414.  [8] Ibid. p. 417.  [9] Ibid. p. 417.
[10] Transactions of Association for Promotion of Social Science, 1858, pp. 124-127.

thoughts in more varied combinations, and not formed inseparable combinations."[1]  "The children of the labouring classes see very little of school after the age of ten.  Their habits are so migratory that only thirty-four per cent. are found in the same school more than two years ; and of 2,262,000 children between the ages of three and fifteen who are not at school, 1,500,000 are absent without any necessity or justification.  Some learn nothing ; and more forget entirely what they have learned."[2]  At p. 63, "Among the causes to which the absence of 1,800,000 children from school are attributable, that to which the greatest prominence is given, is the indifference of parents, arising not so much from a disre ard of the welfare of their children as from a doubt whether school teaching will be of use in the daily struggles of life."  At p. 212, " During the last twenty or thirty years " great improvement has been effected in the education of the lower classes, and perhaps in that of the higher; but not in that of the middle classes.  It was to remedy this last deficiency that in 1857 or 1858 " the Statute of Examination was passed by the University of Oxford."[3]  The amiable Hutcheson[4] allows the infliction on children of " moderate chastisements, such as are not dangerous to life."  Pain sours the temper.  It has been lessened in surgery from ether and chloroform ; also from improvement in operations, and from medicine *encroaching* on surgery by curing diseases without the knife.  Sprengel[5] says that in operations for the stone, " la plupart des auteurs qui ont écrit sur la chirurgie au seizième siècle, se plurent à compliquer le grand appareil."  The famous Baulot at Paris, at the end of the seventeenth century, operated for the stone on forty-two persons, of whom twenty-five died.[6]  See also[7] the complicated way mentioned by Celsus of so simple an operation as the extraction of a tooth.  Even Avicenna would not take out a tooth that was solid in the jaw ;[8] and " till Arculanus, no one thought of stopping teeth with gold."[9]  Until the sixteenth century, castration was a common remedy for hernia,[10] and even later it was believed to be the only remedy for sarcoceles.[11]  As civilization advances, violent accidents are less common, and tetanus diminishes.  Less superstition diminishes nervous diseases.  The horrible and useless operation of ampu-

[1] Mill's Logic, 1856, vol. i. p. 268.
[2] Transactions of Association for Social Science, 1859, p. 59.
[3] Ibid. pp. 211–213.                          [4] Moral Philosophy, vol. ii. p. 101.
[5] Hist. de la Médecine, tome vii. p. 221.      [6] Sprengel, tome vii. p. 226.
[7] Ibid. tome viii. p. 235.                     [8] Ibid. p. 244.
[9] Ibid. p. 251.                                [10] Ibid. p. 229.
[11] Ibid. p. 232.

tating the bosom in cancer, Sprengel, viii. 413. Children used
to be flogged after being taken to executions.[1]  On diminution of
pain in surgical operations, see Kemble's Saxons in England,
vol. ii. p. 433.

---

## DEMOCRACY.

HUME has observed that republics are more favourable to science,
monarchies to art.  The United States seem unkind to the latter.
Miss Martineau says,[2] " I did not meet with a good artist among
all the ladies in the States.  I never had the pleasure of seeing a
good drawing, except in one instance ; or except in two, of hearing
good music."  She says:[3] " If the American nation be judged by
its literature, it may be pronounced to have no mind at all."  At
p. 212, " The periodical literature of the United States is of a
very low order.  I know of no review, where anything like enlightened impartial criticism is to be found."  As a specimen of
their taste, Miss Martineau tells us:[4] " I heard no name so often
as Mrs. Hannah More's.  She is much better known in the country
than Shakspeare. . . . Byron is scarcely heard of."  Roberts says[5]
of " Cœlebs," " Thirty editions of 1,000 copies each were printed
in that country during the lifetime of Mrs. Hannah More."  In
a letter written in 1820, Hannah More communicates to Sir W.
Pepys the great success of her works in America.  This seems to
have opened her eyes to Transatlantic virtues, for she adds : " I
am glad to have my prejudices against that vast republic softened.
They are imitating all our religious and charitable institutions.
They are fast acquiring *taste*, which, I think, is the last quality
that republicans do acquire.[6] . . . They seem to be improving in
religion, morals, and literature. . . . They treat me better than
I deserve.  They have sent me an edition of my own works
elegantly bound."[7]  Finally,[8] " The Americans have little dramatic
taste."

Adam Smith[9] has a very acute remark on the importance of
the distinction of ranks.

Mr. Mill finely says that it is more important in a democracy
than in any other form of government to restrain the power of

---

[1] Grosley's Tour to London, vol. i. p. 173.
[2] Society in America, Paris, 8vo, 1842, vol. ii. p. 177.
[3] Ibid. p. 207.                    [4] Ibid. p. 214.
[5] Memoirs of Mrs. Hannah More, 2nd edit. 8vo, 1834, vol. iii. p. 273.
[6] Ibid. vol. iv. p. 159.  See in the same strain, vol. iv. p. 217.
[7] Ibid. vol. iv. p. 278.
[8] Society in America, Paris, 8vo, 1842, vol. ii. p. 237.
[9] Theory of Moral Sentiments, part vi. section 2, chap. i. vol. ii. p. 72.

public opinion, because its tendency is to destroy originality and independence of thought.[1]   The comparative advantages of democracy and monarchy are stated by Blackstone with more fairness than one could have expected.[2]   Lord Brougham seems to deny the common idea that republics are warlike.[3]   Alison finds fault with the Americans that they have " no sort of attachment, either to the land which they have cultivated, or which they have inherited from their fathers."[4]   In the fourteenth century in France, the butchers were the recognised leaders of the mob.[5]

---

## MEDICINE.

THE rapidly increasing knowledge of medicine in England in the seventeenth century must have produced remarkable effects. The diminution of pain is, looking at things in a large point of view, the least of the benefits derived from the soothing hand of the accomplished physician.  His influence on the progress of civilization consists in being enabled to lengthen life.  During fifty years in England the expectation of life was doubled.  By this means men were enabled to perfect their discoveries with only one half the risk, before incurred, of being interrupted by death. It may be safely laid down that, supposing all other things equal, the greatest discoveries will be made by the most long-lived people.  In pure science, the results which a mighty genius has achieved, may indeed be embodied by him in a material form and handed down to posterity as a foundation on which future philosophers may build.   But the experience, the fine and subtle sagacity, the delicate perception of analogies and differences, these are the work of time as well as of genius, and these are the qualities which cannot be embodied, which cannot be bequeathed. It is in this point of view that medicine, by lengthening the average duration of life, increases the general fund of national wisdom.

Dr. Combe notices that the principle of division of labour has operated injuriously upon medicine;[6] and see to the same effect the sensible evidence of Dr. Farre, given before a Committee of

[1] Principles of Political Economy, 2nd edit. 8vo, 1849, vol. ii. pp. 511, 512.
[2] Commentaries, edit. Christian, 8vo, 1809, vol. i. pp. 49, 50.
[3] Political Philosophy, 2nd edit. 8vo, 1849, vol. i. pp. 358, 359.
[4] Principles of Population, 1840, vol. i. p. 551, and see pp. 552, 553.
[5] See Monteil, Hist. des Français des Divers États, tome ii. p. 154.
[6] Principles of Physiology applied to the Preservation of Health, 3rd edit. Edinb. 1835, 8vo, pp. 34, 35.

the House of Commons.[1] The College of Physicians, it was stated by one of the Committee (No. 3446), are so absurd as to " endeavour to discourage the union of medicine with surgery." Mr. Lawrence also gave his opinion that in the same course of lectures anatomy, pathology, and physiognomy should be combined.[2]

In 1563, the government pay to surgeons was 1s. 6d. a day, exactly three times the amount received by common soldiers. See Haynes's State Papers, p. 398. In 1588, it was also 1s. 6d.[3] The ague was very common formerly.[4] In 1568, there was no physician at Berwick, or even in the neighbouring country.[5] The increasing cultivation of medicine encouraged the rising school of metaphysics. Mr. Morell[6] well says of physicians that, " from the habit of outward observation, the general tone of their philosophy flows most readily in the sensational channel "—i.e., adapts itself to the philosophy of Locke, who had studied medicine. It is curious to observe that Reed, and, I think, most of the Scotch idealists, were *clergymen*. Wolsey's physician was a Venetian.[7] See the admirable remarks in Quetelet, Sur l'Homme.[8] He notices that the great use of medicine is to increase the average duration of life. The celebrated Gilbert, who, in some things, was in advance of Bacon, was physician to Queen Elizabeth and to James I.[9] His great point was insisting upon experiment. Whewell mentions him in the highest terms.[10] Alison says : " Perhaps the best test of public happiness is to be found in the average duration of human life." [11] If I rightly understand Mr. Green, he says that Sydenham was the first in England who united science and experience in medicine.[12] He adds [13] that Hunter's Fundamental Principles of Inflammation is " one of the most masterly performances of inductive investigation, and unprecedented in the science to which it is a contribution." Among the arts, medicine, on account of its eminent utility, must always hold the highest place. In England, an immense impulse was

[1] Report from the Select Committee on Medical Education, 1834, folio, part i. p. 223, Nos. 3443-3445.
[2] Report on Medical Education, part ii. p. 160.
[3] See Murdin's State Papers, p. 614.
[4] Haynes's State Papers, pp. 509, 527, 602. Murdin's State Papers, p. 158.
[5] See Lord Hunsdon's Letter to Cecil, in Haynes's State Papers, p. 509.
[6] View of the Speculative Philosophy of Europe, 8vo, 1846, vol. i. pp. 409, 410.
[7] See Correspondence of Charles V., edited by Mr. Bradford, Lond. 8vo, 1850, pp. 306, 307.
[8] Paris, 8vo, 1835, tome i. pp. 325, 326.
[9] Whewell's Philosophy of the Inductive Sciences, 8vo, 1847, vol. ii. p. 213.
[10] Ibid. pp. 212, 213.
[11] Principles of Population, 8vo, 1840, vol. i. p. 221.
[12] Green's Vital Dynamics, 8vo, 1840, pp. 79, 80.     [13] Ibid. p. 87.

now given to its study, which, occupied as it is with the observation of phenomena, produced most important effects on the age. Cousin says [1] that Hartley's Observations on Man is " la première tentative pour rattacher l'étude de l'homme intellectuel à celle de l'homme physique." Until the beginning of the eighteenth century there were no means in Scotland of studying medicine.[2]

In 1811, Sir James Mackintosh, who had received a medical education, writes, "Those who frequently contemplate the entire subjection of every part of the animal frame to the laws of chemistry, and the numerous processes through which all the organs of the human body must pass after death, acquire habits of imagination unfavourable to a hope of an independent existence of the thinking principle, or of a renewed existence of the whole man. These facts have a more certain influence than any reasonings on the habitual convictions of men. Hence arises in part the prevalent incredulity of physicians. The doctrine of the resurrection could scarcely have arisen among a people who burned their dead."[3] In 1784, Gibbon writes that Tissot assured him that, for gouty persons, the moisture of England and Holland is most pernicious; the dry pure air of Switzerland most favourable to a gouty constitution; that experience justifies the theory, and that "there are fewer martyrs of that disorder in this than any other country in Europe."[4] Coleridge [5] throws out a sweeping and arrogant reproach upon " the humoural pathologists in general." Not one of the so-called specifics has been discovered deductively or even been justified à priori. Medicine is still theological. A modern writer, who is in possession of some of Locke's MSS. says, "For medicine, his original profession, he had very little respect."[6] " Hierophile fut le premier qui soupçonna l'existence du système lymphatique."[7] The invention of microscopes in 1620 facilitated induction in medicine,[8] and by increasing materials, checked deductive flights. Fludd anticipated Toricelli in the barometer.[9] In 1626, Sanctorius first used the thermometer in medical observations.[10]

It is said [11] that, in 1635, Fournier discovered the lacteals. An eminent surgeon has shown statistically, that the danger of

[1] Hist. de la Philosophie, 2nde série, tome iii. p. 25.
[2] See Bower's History of the University of Edinburgh, vol. ii. pp. 128, 161.
[3] Memoirs of the Life of Sir James Mackintosh, edited by his Son, 8vo, 1835, vol. ii. p. 118.
[4] Gibbon's Miscellaneous Works, 8vo, 1837, p. 353.
[5] Biographia Literaria, 8vo, 1847, vol. i. p. 102.
[6] Foster's Original Letters of Locke, Sidney, &c., 8vo, 1830, p. cxiii.
[7] Sprengel, Histoire de la Médecine, tome iv. p. 41.    Ibid. pp. 337, 339.
[8] Ibid. tome v. p. 9.    [10] Ibid. p. 390.    [11] Ibid. tome iv. p. 205.

surgical operations is much greater than is commonly supposed.[1] After operations, there are fewer deaths in England than in any other country, and *most* in the United States of America. Persons who return from India alive are generally very healthy.[2] In West Indies, venereal disease very rare.[3] Among adults, there are more cases of diseased heart than of phthisis and the prevalence of consumption in England has been enormously exaggerated.[4] On consumption in India, see Journal of Statistical Society, vol. iii. p. 133. It is *not* true that phthisis *pulmonalis* is more fatal or more frequent in cold countries than in hot ones.[5] " Typhus fevers cannot be caused by animal or vegetable decomposition."[6] The great measure of the spread of disease is not any particular condition of the air, but the dew point.[7] Influence of age on disease, vi. 162. On the influence of employments on health, see an interesting essay in Journal of Statistical Society, vol. vi. pp. 283–304 ; " the tendency to consumption varies inversely as the amount of exertion."[8] There is no connection between sickness and mortality. Bakers are less subject to sickness than butchers, but seem not to live longer. See Statist. Soc., viii. 329, where it is also said that, in Scotland, the mortality is greater than in England, the illness less. As men get older, they are more liable to illness, but can *bear* it better.[9] All diseases, even lockjaw, which is apparently the capricious result of accident, are guided by law.[10] So far is scrofula from being a particularly English disease, that no country is so free from it, and scrofula is generally " much less prevalent than it was in the seventeenth and eighteenth centuries."[11] Blindness has greatly diminished since the decrease of small-pox ; but even now half the cases of blindness are caused by it.[12] Owing to the police, hydrophobia is becoming extinct in London.[13] Bishop Heber[14] says that in Ceylon, " Most of the workmen employed by government here are Caffres. The first generation appears to stand the climate well, but their children are very liable to pulmonary affections." Turner says that in Tibet, dropsy is the most obstinate and fatal disease to be met

[1] See Essay, by B. Philips, in Journal of Statistical Society, vol. i. pp. 104, 105.
[2] Journal of Statistical Society, vol. i. p. 282.          [3] Ibid. p. 142
[4] See Dr. Clendinning's Paper, in Journal of Statistical Society, vol. i. pp. 143, 145, 146, 147.
[5] Journal of Statistical Society, vol. ii. p. 37.          [6] Ibid. vol. iii. p. 234.
[7] Ibid. vol. vi. pp. 135, 138.          [8] Ibid. vol. vii. p. 239, see also p. 239.
[9] Ibid. vol. viii. p. 341.
[10] See Philips on Scrofula, in Statistical Society, vol. ix. p. 154.
[11] Journal of Statist. Soc. vol. ix. pp. 153, 155, 157, Essay by Benjamin Philips.
[12] Statistical Soc. vol. xiv. p. 64.          [13] Ibid. vol. xv. p. 90.
[14] Journey through India, vol. iii. p. 182.

with in the country.[1] At p. 415, he says, " Gravelish complaints and the stone in the bladder are, I believe, diseases unknown here." In the state of Salvador in Central America, goitre is very common.[2] On disease caused by wind, see Journal of Geographical Society, vol. xi. p. 63 ; and on relation between disease and state of atmosphere, see 3rd Report of British Association, Transactions of Sections, p. 461. Contagion never spreads more than a few feet.[3]

---

## CONNECTION BETWEEN MEDICINE AND HISTORY.

ABOUT one-fifth of the deaths result from specific causes—i.e. from morbid poisons, such as small-pox, typhus fever, &c.[4] Note this when I say all great plagues from the East. See No. xviii.

Chorea or St. Vitus's Dance was not known till about the fourteenth century. It is more common in girls than in boys ; and " is rarely seen after twenty."[5]

Pyrosis, or water-brash, is common in Scotland, Ireland, and Sweden, and " seldom occurs except in those who live on a low and insufficient diet."[6] But see Cullen's Works, 8vo, 1827, vol. ii. p. 412.

" The largest class of ascites arises from diseases in the kidney."[7]

Dr. Williams[8] says that insanity " has though perhaps erroneously, been supposed to be extended in proportion to the degree of civilization." In 1839, the deaths from it in England and Wales were 424—i.e. 226 males and 198 females. According to Esquirol, insanity attacks males and females in the same proportion. In about ten per cent. of the insane " there is not a trace of disease, either of the brain or its membranes," so that " insanity is merely a functional disease of the brain."[9] Above the age of fifty, it is rarely cured.[10] It used to be often treated by bleeding ; but this is now allowed to be bad, because it rather excites than calms.[11] Music produces an injurious effect.[12]

[1] Turner's Embassy to Tibet, 4to, 1830, p. 412.
[2] Stephens's Central America, vol. ii. p. 58.
[3] See Fourth Report of Brit. Association, pp. 76, 99.
[4] Williams's Elementary Principles of Medicine in Encyclop. of the Medical Sciences, p. 527.
[5] Ibid. p. 543.
[6] Ibid. pp. 552, 553.    But see Cullen's Works, 8vo, 1827, vol. ii. p. 412.
[7] Williams's Elementary Principles of Medicine in Encyclop. of the Medical Sciences, p. 608.
[8] Ibid. p. 530.            [9] Ibid. p. 531.            [10] Ibid. p. 535.
[11] Ibid. p. 535.           [12] Ibid. p. 536.

D D

The sedentary habits of civilization must diminish tetanus, which is common in armies on active service, being often the result of wounds. In civil life, it is chiefly caused by straining or contusions. It is most common in adults, and among men to women as about five to one. Larrey says that " this disease, if left to nature, is quickly fatal." [1]

Pyrosis is caused by insufficient diet ; and therefore has, I suppose, diminished. It is still common in Scotland, in Ireland, and according to Linnæus, in Sweden.[2]

Scurvy, which in the middle ages was a fatal epidemic, has now given way in consequence of the advance of agriculture enabling the farmers to kill the best meat in winter ; and, in consequence, also of a more general use of vegetables.[3]

A form of worm, called *Tricocephalus dispar*, is " common in Germany, much less so in France, and still more rarely in this country." See Williams's Elementary Principles of Medicine.[4] He adds [5] that worms are caused by an excess of vegetable food, " that diet favouring the secretion of mucus which is the nidus of these animals." The Hindoos live on rice, and nine out of ten of them suffer from worms. At p. 560, Dr. Williams says, " Three fourths of the inhabitants of Cairo are said to be infected with tænia."

I suppose diseases of the liver have increased. Dr. Williams says [6] the liver " receives nerves from the eighth pair, thus putting it under the influence of the passions. . . . Jaundice is most common in the heyday of the passions, or between twenty and forty. Women are supposed to be more liable to this affection than men."

Dr. Williams says [7]: " The kidneys are the organs by which ten-elevenths of all the azote introduced into the system as aliment is discharged." He adds,[8] " The ultimate issue of every case of diabetes is probably fatal." He says [9] that the more animals are fed with animal diet, the more loaded their urine is with lithic acid. A lady cured herself of gravel by eating more than a pound of sugar every day for six weeks. Therefore French wines and port are injurious.

Excitability by causing amenorrhœa produces insanity.[10]

Apoplexy, I suppose, has increased, being chiefly caused by excessive use of fermented liquors. In England and Wales in

---

[1] Williams's Elementary Principles of Medicine in Encyclop. of the Medical Sciences, pp. 544, 545.

| [2] Ibid. pp. 552, 553. | [3] Ibid. p. 560. | [4] Ibid. p. 558. |
|---|---|---|
| [5] Ibid. p. 559. | [6] Ibid. p. 566. | [7] Ibid. p. 576. |
| [8] Ibid. p. 580. | [9] Ibid. p. 583. | [10] Ibid. p. 587. |

1839 the deaths from apoplexy were one in thirty-three.[1] It is also the result of moral causes, as is known from the increase in France.  It is likewise caused by sudden changes in the weather, which exhaust the nervous power.  This is probably "the cause of apoplexy prevailing to such an extent at Edinburgh and Rome as to be almost endemic."[2]

Splenitis or "inflammation of the substance of the spleen" is "extremely rare" in England, and is only found for the most part in "paludal counties," as Cambridge or Essex.  Common in the East Indies, and particularly in Bengal.[3]

Inflammation of the lungs is caused by many morbid poisons. It is probably owing to the paludal poison "that although, as a general principle, diseases of the chest diminish in frequency as we approach the equator, yet that in the West Indies the inflammatory pulmonary affections greatly exceed those of this country."[4]

An animal, when domesticated, becomes more liable to tubercular disease than he was when wild.  Hence, we find that the inhabitants of towns, though they have more of the comforts of life than agriculturists, are much more subject to phthisis.[5] "The returns of the army have shown to the astonishment of everybody that phthisis is more frequent in the West Indies than even in this country."  Dr. Williams adds :[6] "Race has an influence in the production of phthisis.  In this country, the tendency of the creole and negro to phthisis is notorious."  Religious melancholy, as seen in nunneries, will cause first suppression of menses and then phthisis.[7]

Typhus fever is limited to the space between 60° and 40° N. latitude.  There is no evidence that it is caused by the putrefaction of dead animal matter, though such putrefaction by *depressing* will predispose to the disease.[8]  It prevails equally in all seasons ; but, being unknown in the tropics, it seems that the poison must be volatilised or *destroyed* at a high temperature ;[9] but [10] Dr. Williams says it is more frequent in summer and autumn than in winter and spring.  "In a large ventilated ward, a space of three feet around the patient's person so dilutes the poison that the disease rarely spreads."[11]  "The most remarkable symptom of the typhoid poison is the extreme degree of prostration, both of the physical and intellectual powers of life which it produces."[12]  In

[1] Williams's Elementary Principles of Medicine in Encyclop. of the Medical Sciences, p. 589.

[2] Ibid. p. 590.    [3] Ibid. p. 650.    [4] Ibid. p. 663.
[5] Ibid. p. 689.    [6] Ibid. p. 691.    [7] See a curious case at p. 691.
[8] Ibid. p. 721.    [9] Ibid. p. 722.    [10] Ibid. p. 723.
[11] Ibid. p. 723.    [12] Ibid. p. 725.

France, the deaths are to the attacks from 1 in 3 to 1 in 4½. "Women are supposed to have more chance of recovery than males."[1] Bleeding is most pernicious; for, when an animal is poisoned, the result is more rapid and fatal in proportion as the animal has been bled.[2]

The scarlet fever, measles, and small-pox are "supposed to have first originated in Arabia, about the middle of the sixth century.[3]

Scarlet fever is most fatal among the poor, and is "twice as fatal in towns as in the country." "Both sexes are attacked in nearly equal proportions." The infecting distance is "much greater than in typhus."[4] It is contagious, and communicated by fomites; and the susceptibility to the disease is nearly always exhausted by a first attack.[5] Formerly bleeding was always used; but it is very injurious.[6] In measles "the influence of season is exceedingly trifling."[7] Measles, as well as scarlet fever and typhus, are propagated by fomites,[8] more fatal in towns than in the country.[9] The smallpox is infectious for many yards round the person; and, as we know from inoculation, it is contagious by fomites.[10] The most amazing law relating to it is that the introduction of the variolous poison by the cutaneous tissue should produce an infinitely milder disease than when the same poison is absorbed by a mucous tissue. Perhaps one person in a hundred is attacked a second time with the smallpox.[11]

Dr. Williams says:[12] "If, however, the doctrine of a spontaneous generation of a poison by the human body be tenable, it is more probably true of erysipelas than of any other disease;" for it is often produced by the bite of a leech, or even the slightest puncture. It is infectious, contagious, and spreads by fomites.[13]

Hooping-cough is not traced earlier than A.D. 1510; now it has spread all over the world. It is very rare for a person to have it a second time. It is certainly infectious, and communicated by fomites; and probably it is contagious.[14] Out of ten fatal cases, nine belong to the poorer classes.[15]

Syphilis is entirely propagated by human contagion, and is peculiar to man; "for, in no instance, has matter taken from the primary sore produced any similar affection in animals."[16] It is milder in tropical than in northern climates; its matter will not produce gonorrhœa; nor will the matter of gonorrhœa produce

---

[1] Williams's Elementary Principles of Medicine in Encyclop. of the Medical Sciences, p. 726.

| | | |
|---|---|---|
| [2] Ibid. p. 727. | [3] Ibid. p. 728. | [4] Ibid. p. 728. |
| [5] Ibid. p. 728. | [6] Ibid. p. 732. | [7] Ibid. p. 733. |
| [8] Ibid. p. 734. | [9] Ibid. p. 736. | [10] Ibid. p. 738. |
| [11] Ibid. p. 738. | [12] Ibid. p. 475. | [13] Ibid. p. 746. |
| [14] Ibid. p. 749. | [15] Ibid. p. 751. | [16] Ibid. p. 755. |

syphilis.[1] No prior attack, however severe, will exempt the constitution from a second.[2] There was, for a long time, no satisfactory treatment for syphilitic affections of the bones and the periosteum; but the iodide of potassium is a specific remedy.[3] Gonorrhœa, like syphilis, seems to be peculiar to man. It is uncommon in hot countries; but this is probably the result of cleanliness. It is of course contagious, and we know *can* be transmitted by fomites. Susceptibility to its poison is probably never exhausted; but each succeeding attack is less violent, " till, in some cases, the danger of infection almost vanishes." [4] " The matter of gleet is supposed to be non-contagious; but this doctrine is dangerous, and is probably the cause of frequent infections immediately after marriage." [5] Copaiba was first used in 1702; latterly cubebs has been employed, but with still inferior success;[6] and in women is "entirely inert," unless the urethra is affected.[7]

A disease, I suppose, peculiar to civilization, is cellulitis venenata, which " occasionally affects the anatomist from punctures received in dissection," and also butchers, farriers, and cooks, when the animals are in a morbid state.[8]

The paludal poison, which is very destructive, must have diminished.[9] Dr. Williams adds,[10] " It appears that *race* greatly affects the liability to this class of disease;" and, while in the West Indies the white troops lose 4½ in 1,000, the black troops lose 37.

Dr. Clarke observes that negroes and Malays are more subject than other classes to tubercular phthisis; but this, says Prichard, does not show an essential difference of race, but merely arises from that change in the organic structure caused by successive generations living in a warm climate.[11]

In the Indian Archipelago the inhabitants are little liable to inflammable disease. Gout and scrofula are unknown; stone and dropsy rare; but in Java there is "a disease analogous to the venereal," and the same as the yaws.[12]

In the South Sea Islands, the small-pox, measles, hooping-cough, &c., are " unknown;" but " inflammatory tumours are prevalent," and a peculiar disease of the spine is common.[13]

[1] Williams's Elementary Principles of Medicine in Encyclop. of the Medical Sciences, p. 756.

| | | |
|---|---|---|
| [2] Ibid. p. 756. | [3] Ibid. p. 767. | [4] Ibid. p. 770. |
| Ibid. p. 772. | [5] Ibid. p. 773. | [7] Ibid. p. 775. |
| [6] Ibid. p. 788. | [9] Ibid. p. 793. | [10] Ibid. p. 798. |

[11] Prichard's Physical History of Mankind, vol. i. p. 158.
[12] Crawford's History of the Indian Archipelago, Edinb. 8vo. 1820, vol. i. pp. 33, 34.
[13] Ellis, Polynesian Researches, 1831, iii. 38, 39.

In Borneo, ague, diarrhœa, ophthalmia, and skin diseases are
common ; and " madness is said to be not uncommon " among the
Dyaks.[1]  Low[2] says of the Dyaks: " European medicines have
great effect upon their constitutions ; so that in all cases smaller
doses than usual must be prescribed for them."

Tetanus is very common in the Friendly Islands.[3]  The inhabitants of the Friendly Islands " are very subject to induration
of the liver and certain forms of scrofula." [4]

In 1700, Locke, who had studied medicine, writes : " A diabetes
is a disease so little frequent that you will not think it strange if
I should ask whether you in your great practice ever met with it." [5]

Apoplexy is caused by failure in the cerebral powers.[6]

On temperament, read the Introduction to Herbert Mayo's
Philosophy of Living.

" Although here, as well as abroad, they keep to the system of
leaving the public in the dark respecting the pestilence, things
come to light from time to time, from which the danger seems to
grow more and more decided.  The plague does not simply slay
its victims and depopulate countries; it eats away the moral
energies as well, and often quite destroys them ; thus, as I have
shown in my last public lecture before the Academy, the sudden
and complete degeneracy of the Roman world, from the time of
Marcus Antoninus onward, may be referred to the oriental plague
which then entered Europe for the first time ; just as six hundred
years earlier the plague, which was, strictly speaking, a yellow
fever, coincides too exactly with the termination of the ideal
period of antiquity not to be regarded as a cause of it.  In such
epidemics the best individuals always die, and the rest degenerate
morally.  Times of pestilence are always those in which the animal
and the devilish in human nature assume prominence.  Neither
need we be superstitious, or even pious, to regard great pestilences as something more than a conflict of the physical with the
human history of the earth.  I fear my conviction that it indicates the victory of the negative and destructive of the two contending principles, would be thought terribly Manichæan and
impious." [7]

Leigh Hunt, who was a good deal in Italy, says:[8] " The con-

[1] See Low's Sarawak, 8vo, 1848, pp. 304, 305.          [2] Ibid. p. 309.
[3] See Mariner's Tonga Islands, 2nd edit. 8vo, 1818, i. 189; ii. 242, 243.
[4] Ibid. vol. i. p. 434.   Also, to diseased testicles, &c. ; see vol. ii. pp. 246-260.
[5] Foster's Letters of Locke, Sidney, &c., 8vo, 1830, p. 71.
[6] See Mayo's Philosophy of Living, 1838, pp. 147-151.
[7] Letter from Niebuhr, dated Berlin, 1816, in the Life and Letters of Niebuhr,
London, 8vo, 1852, vol. ii. p. 27.
[8] Autobiography, 8vo, 1850, vol. iii. p. 145.

sumption, by the way, of olive oil is immense. It is probably no mean exasperator of Italian bile. The author of an Italian Art of Health approves a moderate use of it both in diet and medicine, but says that, as soon as it is cooked, fried, or otherwise abused, it inflames the blood, disturbs the humours, irritates the fibres, and produces other effects very superfluous in a stimulating climate."

In 1796, Professor Cleghorn writes from Cairo that the English consul at Alexandria has advised him, as a protection against plague, " to anoint my body with oil as a certain antidote," &c.[1]

Cullen [2] says: " A permanent grief and anxiety also, which so often excites hypochondriac disorders, will frequently cure hysterics. Thus, in the year 1745, whilst the people laboured under constant anxiety about the rebellion, nervous patients were observed in Scotland to remain remarkably free from their usual complaints."

Between 1670 and 1673, Sir W. Temple [3] says of Holland: " The diseases of the climate seem to be chiefly the gout and the scurvy."

Sir W. Temple [4] notices the great increase of gout in England within twenty years, which he ascribes to the larger consumption of wine.

Sir W. Temple [5] says : " The stone is said to have first come among us after hops were introduced here."

Sir T. Browne [6] says of rickets: " The disease is scarce so old as to afford good observation."

For some absurd notions respecting medicine in the middle ages, see Sprengel, Histoire de la Médecine, tome ii. p. 401.

No specific has been deductively proved. Indeed mercury was first employed in syphilis on account of its supposed similarity to leprosy, and its use was long confined to charlatans.[7]

Sprengel [8] says that rickets are first mentioned not by Glisson, but by Reusner, in 1582.

Huc [9] says : " The Chinese report marvels of the jin-seng, and, no doubt, it is for Chinese organisation a tonic of very great effect for old and weak persons ; but its nature is too heating, the Chinese physicians admit, for the European temperament, already in their opinion too hot." [10]

[1] Southey's Life of Dr. Bell, 8vo, 1844, vol. i. p 520.
[2] Works, Edinb. 8vo. 1827, vol. ii. p. 505.
[3] Works, 8vo, 1814, vol. i. p. 149.      [4] Ibid. vol. iii. p. 248, 272.
[5] Ibid. vol. iii. p. 303.                      [6] Works by Wilkin, vol. iv. p. 44.
[7] See Sprengel, Histoire de la Médecine, tome iii. p. 72.
[8] Ibid. tome v. pp. 598, 599.              [9] Travels in Tartary, vol. i. p. 106.
[10] See also Bell's Travels in Asia, Edinb. 8vo, 1788, vol. ii. pp. 142, 143.

In the fourteenth and fifteenth centuries, in France, bleeding was universal.[1]

The body of Charles IX. of France was opened.[2]

---

## TENDENCY, ETC., OF THE PURITANS.

THE bigotry of Puritanism has left a living sting which still corrodes the very heart of the nation. See some good remarks on the intolerant spirit of the English character in Mill's Principles of Political Economy, 8vo, 1849, vol. ii. p. 506.

Perhaps it is to the spirit of Puritanism that we owe the little influence of women and the consequent inferiority of their education. Mr. Mill truly says[3] that, in the fifteenth and sixteenth centuries women were relatively more intellectual than they are at present. This is the more to be regretted, for the civilizing effect of women is, perhaps, more felt when the division of labour is fully established. Women reap the benefit of that division without incurring its disadvantages.[4] Just before the accession of Elizabeth, Knox and his friend Goodman wrote against women.[5] This perhaps rose from the accident of the throne being occupied by Mary.

The Puritans held pleasure to be sinful; and this belief remained long after their political overthrow. At the Restoration the aristocracy were once more predominant, and their tastes mingled with the old taste of the Puritans. The result is still seen in our national character, which presents a combination of love of expense and indifference to pleasure. There, perhaps, never was a country in which was to be found so much splendour and so little gaiety as in England. This, which makes us so unamiable as a people, tends in a most extraordinary degree to increase our wealth. The indifference to pleasure makes accumulation more easy, while the love of display renders it more necessary. This has been admirably touched on by Mr. Mill,[6] who, however, seems to consider our love of display unfavourable to the increase of wealth. But this I greatly doubt. There can be no question that the unproductive expenditure of the upper classes is unfavourable to accumulation; but when united as in England with an indifference to pleasure, it gives an object and a stimulus

---

[1] See Monteil, Histoire des Français des Divers États, tome ii. pp. 78, 223 ; tome iv. p. 123.

[2] See Capefigue Histoire de la Réforme et la Ligue, tome iii. p. 340.

[3] Political Economy, 1849, vol. ii. p. 532.          [4] Ibid. vol. i. p. 157.

[5] Lingard, vol. v. p. 356.                    [6] Political Economy, 1849, vol. i. p. 213.

to labour, which, I believe, no other combination could possibly supply. The remarks which Dr. Shebbeare made a century ago are perfectly applicable at the present day. "You see more people on the roads of England than in all Europe, and more uneasy countenances than are to be found in the world besides." [1] And [2] "money is all that is zealously pursued in this nation." Again, [3] "The idea of luxury in England is ill understood; it does not deserve that name; it is profusion only, another species of self."

About and after 1570, the Catholics pretended to be Puritans, in order to weaken the church by encouraging disputes. [4] Mr. Hallam [5] says: "The first instance of actual punishment inflicted on Protestant dissenters was in June 1567." For this he quotes Strype's Parker, 242; Grindall, 114. Mr. Hallam says: [6] "It was a kind of maxim among the Puritans that Scripture was so much the exclusive rule of human action, that, whatever in matters, at least concerning religion, could not be found to have its authority, was unlawful." The monition doctrine, adds Hallam, is refuted in "the whole second book" of Hooker. In a long list of official "instructions," very early in the reign of Mary, the commissioners are charged by the queen to punish all persons who live in adultery. [7] In 1561, Knox complains, in a letter to Cecil, that "whoremongers" and "adulterers" are not punished. [8]

Leigh Hunt says: [9] "When I came to England, after a residence of four years abroad, I was grieved at the succession of fair sulky faces which I met in the streets of London. They all appeared to come out of unhappy homes. In truth, our virtues or our climate, or whatever it is, sit so uneasily upon us, that it is surely worth while for our philosophy to inquire whether, in some points of moral or political economy, we are not a little mistaken. Gypsies will hardly allow us to lay it to the climate."

Mr. Morell [10] has very well stated the "fundamental distinction between the principles of legislation and those of private morality." The Puritans, even in the reign of Elizabeth, were considered by the Catholics as the most zealous among their English persecutors. [11]

[1] Angeloni's Letters on the English Nation, 8vo, 1755, vol. i. pp. 37, 38.
[2] Ibid. p. 45.  [3] Ibid. p. 90.
[4] See the note in Hallam's Constitutional History, 8vo, 1842, vol. i. p. 119.
[5] Ibid. p. 178.  [6] Ibid. p. 212.
[7] Haynes's State Papers, p. 198.  [8] Ibid. p. 372. See art. Jansenism.
[9] Autobiography, 8vo, 1850, vol. iii. p. 179.
[10] View of the Speculative Philosophy of Europe, 8vo, 1846, vol. i. pp. 360, 361.
[11] See an extract from Gerard's MS. in Mr. Tierney's note to Dodd's Church History, vol. iii. p. 86.

Soames says that they did not bear the name of Puritan until
1564.[1]   Soames[2] mentions two instances of Catholics pretending
to be Puritans, viz., Heath, brother of the ex-archbishop of York,
and a Dominican called Faithful Cummin.   The Bishop of Asaph
says: "The declaration of open war between the high and low
church parties may be considered to have taken place in 1566,
when the proclamation of the queen gave, as it were, the sanction
of law to the advertisements, which the bishops had previously
put forth."[3]   The good effects caused by increasing luxury are
well stated in Esprit des Lois, livre vii. chap. 4, Œuvres de Montesquieu, Paris, 1835, p. 239.   He supposes that proud nations
are always idle: "La paresse est l'effet de l'orgueil; le travail est
une suite de la vanité."[4]

In 1628, it was proposed by Bayer and Schiller to establish a
new astronomical nomenclature.   The planets were to be called
Adam, Moses, and the patriarchs.   The twelve signs were to be
the twelve apostles; the constellations were to be called after
places mentioned in the Bible.[5]

The Puritans of the sixteenth century encouraged horse-
racing, "as a substitute for cards and dice."[6]   Perhaps we owe to
this some of our fine breeds of horses.

Perhaps the greatest and most beneficial work of Puritanism
was the destruction of the remains of chivalry.   The fire of the
ancient chivalry had indeed begun to dim since the end of the
thirteenth century, but its forms still lingered on, and were ready,
should circumstances allow, to be imbued with their early energy.
These forms, with the exception of the law of primogeniture,
which, to the disgrace of an enlightened age, still defaces the
statute-book, all perished in that great storm which overwhelmed
the crown, the law, and the altar.   When Charles II. returned
from exile, he could not restore feudality.

Did not blue coats for servants go out of use?   COMMON PLACE
BOOK, art. 917.   This was the last remains of the dress of
retainers.

It was usual to wear linen shirts with ornaments finely worked
by the needle.   In place of these ornaments, the Puritans used to
embroider the shirt with texts from the Bible.[7]

[1] Elizabethan Religious History, p. 52.           [2] Ibid. pp. 78, 79.
[3] Short's History of the Church of England, 8vo, 1847, p. 267.
[4] Esprit des Lois, xix. chap. ix. p. 339; and see livre xiv. chap. ix. p. 303.
[5] Whewell's Philosophy of the Inductive Sciences, 8vo, 1847, vol. ii. p. 515.
[6] Drake's Shakespeare and his Times, 1817, 4to, vol. i. p. 297; and COMMON PLACE
BOOK, art. 423.
[7] See Gifford's note in Ben Jonson's Works, vol. ii. p. 165; and see COMMON PLACE
BOOK, art. 1078.

Ben Jonson's Dedication to Sejanus, which is dated 1607, shows the bitterness of feeling between the Puritans and the stage.[1] It appears they particularly objected to starch in their linen.[2] In 1610, the Puritans lived in great numbers at Blackfriars, where they were the chief dealers in feathers, &c.[3] Banbury was particularly famous for them; and in Bartholomew Fair, acted in 1614, a Puritan is called "a Banbury-man."[4] The Puritans would not say *mass* even when the profane word was mitigated by being compounded. Thus, they called Christmas *Christtide*.[5] Ben Jonson was never weary of attacking the Puritans.[6] In Bartholomew Fair, acted in 1614, Jonson ridicules the long graces with which the Puritans used to preface their meals.[7] It would seem that they were very fond of pork.[8] In the Magnetick Lady, acted in 1632, Jonson ridicules the divisions into *doctrine* and *use* which the Puritans used to make in their sermons.[9] In the same play he has a most ungenerous allusion to the punishment inflicted on Prynne.[10] They would not say *godfathers* or *godmothers*, but witnesses.[11]

At the very beginning of the seventeenth century their hostility to the theatre is mentioned.[12]

Tocqueville[13] says, "Angleterre, le pays de l'Europe où l'on a vu pendant un siècle la liberté la plus grande de penser, et les préjugés les plus invincibles."

Early in the seventeenth century numbers of the Puritans fled to Amsterdam. This is alluded to in Middleton's Works, i. 205; iii. 255; iv. 45, 437.

The Puritans hated organs.[14] They encouraged witchcraft, I think.

"There were only three Protestant preachers in the University of Oxford in the year 1563, and they were all Puritans."[15] In Cambridge they were as strong, if not stronger. The University had a right to license twelve ministers every year to preach

[1] Jonson's Works, 8vo, 1816, vol. iii. pp. 161-165; and for other indications of the quarrel, see vol. iv. pp. 81, 191, and the amusing but bitter attack in The Alchemist, vol. iv. pp. 91-100.
[2] Ibid. vol. iv. p. 96.          [3] Ibid. vol. iv. p. 20; and vol. ii. p. 466.
[4] Ibid. vol. iv. p. 360.          [5] Ibid. vol. iii. p. 178; and vol. iv. p. 95.
[6] Ibid. vol. iii. pp. 367, 369; vol. iv. pp. 383-385, 399, 436-438; and indeed the whole of Bartholomew Fair. See also vol. vi. pp. 259-262, 342; vol. vii. p. 410; viii. pp. 163, 192; and vol. ix. p. 153.
[7] Ibid. vol. iv. pp. 383, 384.          [8] Ibid. vol. iv. pp. 400, 438, 462.
[9] Ibid. vol. vi. p. 55.          [10] Ibid. vol. vi. p. 73.
[11] Ibid. vol. vi. p. 93; and vol. viii. p. 180.
[12] See Middleton's Works, 8vo, 1840, vol. i. p. 206.
[13] Démocratie en Amérique, vol. ii. p. 111.          [14] COMMON PLACE BOOK, art. 2213.
[15] Neal's History of the Puritans. edit. Toulmin, 1822, vol. i. p. 145.

anywhere in England without episcopal license. This privilege was exercised in favour of the Puritans, and Parker in vain attempted to have it rescinded.[1] Neal says[2] that, in 1566, "in Trinity College all except three declared against the surplice, and many in other colleges were ready to follow their example." He adds[3] that, in 1571, "the University of Cambridge was a nest of Puritans."

But the Puritans at once began to advocate principles which struck at the very root of all legislative authority. Their own historian tells us that, even in 1559, they "insisted that those things which Christ had left indifferent ought not to be made necessary by any human laws."[4] They forgot that, when a government pays a sect, it has a right to stipulate in return what that sect shall do. Elizabeth bore herself high. The very year after her accession, Sandys, bishop of Worcester, complained that she had a crucifix in her chapel. To this complaint the queen replied by a threat of deprivation.[5]

In 1560, the Puritans published at Geneva a translation of the Bible with marginal notes. One of these notes laid down that disobedience to kings was allowable, and another note on 2 Chron. xv. 16, censured Asa for not having executed his mother as well as deposed her.[6] In 1562, the Puritans were so strong in convocation that their proposals to simplify the Church of England were only rejected by a majority of one.[7] This decision Neal calls "very unkind," but, if the queen had been forced to change her policy, the Catholics, then very powerful, would certainly have flown to arms, and a civil and religious war would have ensued.

It is remarkable that the chief leaders of the great separation of 1566 were "all beneficed within the diocese of London."[8]

In 1556, they "excepted to the use of godfathers and god-mothers to the exclusion of parents from being sureties for the education of their own children."[9] And in 1585 they petitioned Whitgift that "in baptism the godfathers may answer in their own names and not in the child's."[10]

In 1571, the Puritans seem to have made their first great effort in Parliament.[11]

At the beginning of Elizabeth's reign, if not before her accession, Goodman, an English Puritan, wrote a work against the government of women; and it was with great difficulty that, in

[1] Neal's History of the Puritans, edit. Toulmin, 1822, vol. i. pp. 178, 179.
[2] Ibid. vol. i. p. 180.      [3] Ibid. vol. i. p. 320.      [4] Ibid. vol. i. p. 126
[5] Ibid. vol. i. p. 132.      [6] Ibid. vol. i. p. 136.      [7] Ibid. vol. i. p. 151
[8] Ibid. vol. i. p. 197.      [9] Ibid. vol. i. p. 194.      [10] Ibid. vol. i. p. 368.
[11] Ibid. vol. i. p. 215.

1571, he was induced to recant his sentiments.[1]   The rise of the
Brownists was an important epoch.  I think the Mar-Prelate Controversy did not begin till *after* 1588.  It was apparently in 1591
that Parliament passed their most cruel act against the Puritans.[2]
In 1592 appeared Hooker's work.  His principle, that all who
are born within the confines of an established church and baptized into it are bound to submit to its laws, is, as Neal says,[3]
inconsistent with the principles of the Reformation.  This was a
slavish dogma, and it seems to me that Hooker was to the church
what Hobbes was to the state.

Fenner, a contemporary, says that, in 1586, a third of the
clergy were suspended.[4]   Neal says[5] that, in 1602, "the noncon-
forming clergy were about fifteen hundred."  Hitherto the dispute
had been merely about ceremonies and discipline; but, in 1595
and 1596, the spread of Arminianism in the church gave rise to
a controversy about doctrine, for the Puritans had always remained Calvinists.[6]   At length, the violence of the Puritans
fairly roused the civil power.  Towards the end of the sixteenth century they were prosecuted, not in the spiritual but
in the temporal courts, and Anderson, one of the judges, declared
in his charge that he would hunt all the Puritans out of his
circuit.[7]

The very tradespeople had Bibles lying on their shopboards,
which, if we may believe contemporary evidence, did not prevent
them from cheating their customers.[8]   The lowest and most infamous of mankind did not escape the moral epidemic.

In the city the clergy were nearly all Puritans; and, in 1566,
Archbishop Parker summoned before him "all the London curates
and rectors."[9]   Collier has given some extracts from the attacks
made by John Knox on female sovereigns.[10]

The Puritans now began rapidly to organise themselves.  In
1583 the Brownists first arose.[11]  Such was the horror the Puritans
had of oaths that they thought swearing as bad as, if not worse
than, murder.[12]   In 1570, Grindal, archbishop of York, wrote to
Cecil that, at Cambridge, Cartwright, who was by far the most
able opponent of the bishop, was so popular that "the youth of

---

[1] Neal's History of the Puritans, edit. Toulmin, 1822, vol. i. p. 227.
[2] Ibid. vol. i. p. 426.                    [3] Ibid. vol. i. p. 449.
[4] Ibid. vol. i. p. 382.                    [5] Ibid. vol. i. p. 463.
[6] Ibid. vol. i. pp. 451, 453.              [7] Ibid. vol. i. pp. 460, 461.
[8] See Maroccus Extaticus, 1595, p. 11, Percy Soc. vol. ix.
[9] Collier's Eccles. Hist. vol. vi. p. 429.
[10] Ibid. pp. 274–276; and see at p. 278 his insulting letter to Elizabeth.
[11] Ibid. vol. vii. p. 3.
[12] See a curious passage in Rich's Honestie of this Age, 1614, p. 56; Percy Soc. vol. xi

the university, which is at this time very toward in learning, doth frequent his lectures in great numbers."[1] In 1572, the first Presbyterian church in England arose at Wandsworth.[2] In 1583, in six counties alone, there were suspended no less than 233 clergymen.[3] In 1578 or 1579 appeared Stubbs' Gaping Gulph, an insulting puritanical work.[4] Collier[5] says : "It is somewhat remarkable that the Puritans were most active in setting up their discipline and scattering their scandalous pamphlets, when the Spanish Armada was sweeping the seas, and menacing the kingdom with a conquest." For this he cites Bancroft's Dangerous Positions. In 1592, a most illiberal act was passed, forcing, under severe penalties, everyone under sixteen to go to church. See the account given by Collier,[6] who allows that the act was directed against the Puritans. Deering, a celebrated Puritanical clergyman, in a sermon before the queen, flatly told her that her motto might be, " As an untamed heifer."[7]

The characteristic of Puritanical legislation was, I think, the confusion of public morals with private morals.[8]

Scarcely had the fears caused by the massacre of Bartholomew passed away, when the Puritans began to assume the aspect of an organised party. The French ambassador, whose voluminous despatches record every great movement in England, mentions them for the first time in October, 1573, when he writes to his court that for several days the council had been considering their demands for toleration.[9] A month later, he says that the Puritans were becoming as troublesome in England as the Huguenots in France, or the Gueux in Flanders.[10] In December, 1573, he writes that " plus de mille cinq centz personnes de qualité sont de ceste secte."[11] He again mentions them at tome vi. p. 279. It is a very curious fact that " Gorbudoc," the first tragedy in the English language, was partly written by Thomas Norton, a Puritan.[12] In 1565, Harding, a Catholic, taunts bishop Jewel : " May we not yet remember the times when, at first beginning of your sects, you rejected all doctors' authorities as writings of men, and admitted only your lyvely Word of the Lord."[13].

[1] Collier's Ecclesiast. Hist. vol. vi. 483.
[2] Neal's Puritans, vol. i. pp. 243, 244.　　　　[3] Ibid. vol. i. p. 323.
[4] Collier, vol. vi. pp. 607, 608.　　　　[5] Ibid. vol. vii. p. 74.
[6] Ibid. vol. vii. pp. 163-165.　　　　[7] Neal, vol. i. p. 283, but he gives no date.
[8] See art. Metaphysics.
[9] Correspondance de Fénelon, Paris, 1840, tome v. p. 435.
[10] Ibid. p. 456; see also p. 462.　　　　[11] Ibid. p. 470.
[12] See Collier's History of Dramatic Poetry, vol. ii. pp. 481, 482; and Warton's Hist. of English Poetry, 8vo, 1840, iii. 289.
[13] Strype's Annals, vol. i. part ii. p. 524.

Early in the reign of Elizabeth the clergy were so diminished that the bishops did not dare to enforce the law for fear of denuding the church. Sandys, afterwards archbishop of York, objected to the episcopal garments;[1] and so did Pilkington, bishop of Durham.[2] In 1588 or 1589, the Puritans began to express a confident opinion that they could overthrow the episcopacy.[3] Maskell says,[4] " The University of Oxford, during the first twenty or thirty years of the reign of Queen Elizabeth, had been remarkable for the strong leaning which it displayed towards the Puritan view of the religious questions of the day." The Puritan onslaught began directly after the Armada.[5] The Puritans appear to have had a great contempt for the civil law.[6] The bishop of Winchester declared that " men might find fault, if they were disposed to quarrel, as well with the Scripture as with the Book of Common Prayer."[7] In the same work, p. 69, the bishops are blamed for favouring the " Papists." This shows the intolerance of the Puritans. In 1586, Leicester seems to deny that he was a Puritan.[8] In 1590, the queen wrote a remarkable letter to James, warning him of the rising spirit of Puritanism.[9] As early as 1550, the Puritans began to sneer at the " Christians of the Court." See a very curious letter from Turner to Cecil, in Tytler's Edward VI. and Mary I. 333–337. Lord Fountainhall died in 1722 ; and his sitting-room in his house at Edinburgh contained a cabinet "ornamented with a death's head at the top."[10] Hallam[11] says, the Puritans under Elizabeth formed a majority of the Protestants.

John Halle, an English surgeon, in the middle of the sixteenth century, has published a prayer which surgeons should use before undertaking a difficult operation.[12]

Mr. Lewis acutely says : " It may generally be observed that the tendency of the Roman Catholics is to slide into superstition, that of the Protestants into fanaticism."[13]

It was with difficulty that Elizabeth could hold in the bishops.

[1] Sandys' Sermons, edit. Parker Society, p. xvii.
[2] See Collier's Ecclesiastical History, 8vo, 1840, vol. vi. p. 396.
[3] See the evidence for this in Maskell's History of the Martin Mar-Prelate Controversy, 1849, pp. 51–54.　　　　[4] Ibid. p. 120.
[5] See Bishop Cooper's Admonition. 1589, p. 25, 8vo, 1847.
[6] See Hay any Work for Cooper, 1589, pp. 45, 46, 8vo, 1845.
[7] See An Epistle to the Terrible Priests, 1589, p. 42, 8vo, 1843.
[8] Leycester Correspondence, edit. Camden Soc. p. 311.
[9] See it in Letters of Elizabeth and James VI. Camden Soc., 1849, p. 63.
[10] Chambers's Traditions of Edinburgh, 8vo, 1847, p. 62.
[11] Constitutional History, vol. i. p. 186, note.
[12] Historiall Expostulation, 1565, p. 49, and see p. 47 Percy Soc. vol. xi.
[13] Lewis on Irish Disturbances, 8vo, 1836, p. 401.

They did everything to insult and irritate the Puritans. All this was a serious error.

It has been often said, that by persecuting a sect you increase its power and its numbers; and the history of Christianity in the first three centuries is triumphantly appealed to as an instance. But nothing can be more shallow than such an allegation. If we did not know the clumsy eagerness with which nearly all ecclesiastical writers seize every circumstance that can be supposed to exalt the merit of their own church and blacken the reputation of their adversaries, we should be at a loss to understand how it is that the researches of Pearson, Dodwell, and Lardner have not more generally diffused a knowledge of the fact that the persecutions of the early church were slight and insignificant. The truth is, if they had been so severe as some would have us believe, it would have been hardly possible for Christianity to have survived the shock. There can be no doubt that a resolute and powerful government, by a course of consistent unflinching severity, can utterly destroy any sect which forms only a small part of its subjects; and if Augustus had possessed the spirit of Galenus(?) and Maximian(?), Christianity would in all probability be but a relic of history. London might now be studded with the gilded minarets of mosques, from which the faithful would be summoned to their daily prayers; and British subjects might be at this moment bowing the knee before the shrines of a Pagan temple. But, happily for Christianity and happily for the best interests of man, the spirit of persecution is rarely aroused until the sufferers are too numerous to be entirely destroyed. The conduct of the Pagan emperors in the third century was an exact counterpart of the conduct of the Christian bishops in the sixteenth century. The bishops neglected the Puritans until the Puritans grew so strong that they did not dare to drive them to desperation. They would not pass by their conduct with impunity; they dared not punish it capitally. They, therefore, pursued a middle course, which has always irresistible charms for weak-minded men. They irritated, but, with few exceptions, they did not strike. The treatment to which the Puritans were subject was oftener insulting than injurious. In 1573, one of them was brought before the commission. His name was White. The opportunity of a brutal joke was too tempting to be lost. The chief justice asked, " Who is this? " " White, an't please your honour," answered the prisoner. " White as black as the devil," was the reply.[1] In 1584, another unfortunate Puritan was

---

[1] Neal's Hist. of the Puritans, i. 250.

brought up before Aylmer, bishop of London, who said to him: "Thou art a very ass; thou art mad. Thou courageous! Nay, thou art impudent. By my troth, I think he is mad; he careth for nobody." "Though I fear not you, I fear the Lord," was the sturdy reply. "He hath an arrogant spirit; he can scarce construe Cato, I think," rejoined the amiable successor of the apostles.[1]

The truth is the bishops acted rather from irritability at the opposition than from conscientious motives. In their hearts they cared little about those points for which they professed such reverence. Even Sandys, archbishop of Canterbury, who was an active persecutor of the Puritans, and did not die till 1588, says that many of the rites and ceremonies of the Church of England should be reformed; and, even of those which he approves, he does not dare to say that they are necessary.[2]

The bishops drove the Puritans from the church, but they left them in the country. They sent them forth beggars, but still they left them at liberty. The consequences might have been easily foreseen. The discarded clergy were received into the houses of their lay patrons, who employed them as chaplains to their households and tutors to their children.[3] With minds burning with hatred against episcopacy, and not particularly in love with a government which protected it, they availed themselves of their position to instil into their pupils their own sentiments.

We cannot wonder that in this they succeeded. The natural docility of children renders them, for the most part, ready to believe all that they are told; and to youth, just bursting into manhood and ignorant of the wiles of the world, there is something singularly captivating in the idea that they are espousing the weaker side. The result was that, by the end of the sixteenth century, there arose a new generation, who, because they hated bishops, easily learnt to hate kings who protected bishops. The almost omniscient sagacity of Elizabeth enabled her to discern the signs of the coming storm, and to prepare against it.

But the moment James mounted on the throne all was changed.

The early Puritans were men of the most contracted and ascetic ideas. The reasons that induced them to separate from the church were of the most frivolous nature; and it was not until their union with the patriots towards the end of the sixteenth century had lent importance to their objects, that they acquired either

---

[1] Neal's Hist. of the Puritans, vol. i. p. 352.      [2] Ibid. p. 400.
[3] Ibid. p. 306.

dignity or interest. The first overt act by which the Puritans abandoned the church was in 1566 ;[1] and their own historian tells us that after this, and until Cartwright began to preach, the dispute "had hitherto been chiefly confined to the habits, to the cross in baptism, and kneeling at the Lord's Supper."[2] Nothing but a knowledge of the pettiness of theological disputes could allow us to believe that such a schism could have arisen about such insignificant trifles. Elizabeth has been often censured for not yielding on such unimportant points to the conscientious scruples of honest men. But it is singular that those who advance the argument do not see that it cuts both ways. It is true that, the more trivial the points at issue, the more absurd it was in the queen to retain them; but also the more absurd it was in the Puritans to insist on their being given up. Since then one party must yield, surely it was most proper that that deference should be paid to the majority and to the executive government.

*After* the Armada, the Brownists rapidly increased. The danger, as it diminished from without, increased from within. In 1593 Penry drew up a most offensive address to Elizabeth.[3] This, I think, is the first instance in which the Puritans insulted the queen. Another of them, Barrowe, told Whitgift to his face that he was "a monster, a persecutor, a compound of he knew not what, neither ecclesiastical nor civil, like the second beast spoken of in the Revelations."[4]

It was not till 1595 that the dispute between the Puritans and the church launched into doctrines.[5] This was the result of the spread of Arminianism in the Church of England.[6] Collier says[7] that it was not till 1570 that the Puritans "attacked the government of the church;" before that time "the habit of the clergy and the sign of the cross were formerly the only things they stuck at."

---

## HISTORY OF WITCHCRAFT, ETC.

CAMDEN, speaking of Elizabeth's affection for Dudley, suggests that it may have been caused by "something in his birth, or planets that ruled it."[8]

[1] Neal's Hist. of the Puritans, vol. i. pp. 187, 191.
[2] Ibid. pp. 210, 211.    [3] Ibid. pp. 438, 439.
[4] Ibid. p. 435.    [5] Ibid. p. 451.
[6] Ibid. p. 453.    [7] Ecclesiast. Hist. vol. vi. p. 481.
[8] Annals of Elizabeth, in Kennett, vol. ii. p. 383.  See also p. 549.

For Elizabeth's own superstitions, see MSS. Elizabeth, No. 9.

Camden [1] gravely relates that Beza, in consequence of the appearance of an extraordinary star, foretold the death of Charles IX.

Southey, who was perhaps better acquainted with what may be called occult literature than any writer of his time, says: "The books of palmistry have been so worn by perusal that one in decent preservation is now among the rarities of literature." [2]

Drake says [3] that James's Demonology "rendered a profession in the belief of sorcery and witchcraft a matter of fashion, and even of interest." Perhaps from this time the court was more superstitious than the people.

There were days on which it was lucky, and others on which it was unlucky, to buy or sell. These days were carefully noted in the almanacs, and distinguished by characteristic marks.[4] The price of these almanacs was 1d. a piece.[5]

Directly after the Restoration the Royal Society was established; in 1666, the French Academy; and in 1667 and 1675, the Observatories of Paris and Greenwich.[6]

The admirable play of The Devil is an Ass was brought on the stage in 1616. One of its main objects is to ridicule witchfinders;[7] and in Volpone, which was acted in 1605, he ridicules witchcraft.[8] In the notes to the Masque of Queens in 1609, Ben Jonson shows great reading among books on witchcraft,[9] though, as Gifford observes,[10] this no more shows that he believed in witchcraft than that he believed in the Pagan deities.

The custom of consulting conjurors is ridiculed in an amusing scene in The Family of Love, which was acted in 1607.[11]

"The disposition of ascribing all our knowledge to experience appears in Newton and the Newtonians by other indications," &c., &c.[12]

It is idle to attribute the destruction of superstition to the Reformation. Protestants were as superstitious as Catholics.

. . . . . . . .

But Protestantism is more favourable to civilization than Ca-

---

[1] Kennett, vol. ii. p. 446.   [2] The Doctor, edit. Warter, 8vo, 1848, p. 528.

[3] Shakespeare and his Times, 1817, 4to, vol. i, p. 314.

[4] See Ben Jonson's Works, 8vo, 1816, vol. iv. p. 43; and Sordido at vol. ii. p. 7.

[5] See Gifford's note in Ben Jonson, vol. ii. p. 42.

[6] Whewell's Philosophy of the Inductive Sciences, 8vo, 1847, vol. ii. p. 270.

[7] See Ben Jonson's Works, 8vo, 1816, vol. v. pp. 8, 157; and in particular the clever scene at pp. 148-154.

[8] Ibid. vol. iii. p. 321; and for other instances in which he laughs at witchcraft, see vol. iv. p. 502.

[9] Ibid. vol. vii.    [10] P. 141.

[11] Middleton's Works, 8vo, 1840, vol. ii. pp. 137-142.

[12] Whewell's Philosophy of the Inductive Sciences, 8vo, 1847, vol. ii. p. 292.

tholicism ; the Protestant believes less than the Catholic ; he has
fewer saints, fewer martyrs, fewer miracles,—in other words, fewer
ultimate facts.

On the want of harmony existing at present between science
and theology, see some good remarks in Combe's Constitution of
Man, pp. 13-16.    It will hardly be believed that, when sul-
phuric acid was first used to lessen the pains of childbirth, it
was objected to as "a profane attempt to abrogate the primeval
curse pronounced upon woman." [1]   Scepticism is shown by works
on natural theology, which attempted to *prove* what men formerly
fancied they *instinctively* believed.   The injury which the theological principle has done to the world is immense.   It has
prevented them from studying the laws of nature.

The superstitions respecting good and bad days were by no
means confined to the lower classes.   See some clever ridicule in
1619 in Middleton's Works. [2]    In 1652, there was actually published a popular ballad to ridicule the "belief in prophecies and
prognostications."   It may be found in Mr. Wright's Political
Ballads. [3]   Whenever anything was lost, the sufferer had recourse
to one of the wise men who were to be found in every town and
nearly in every village.   But their power was fast waning.   An
amusing description of one of their tricks is given in Chettle's
Kind Hart's Dream. [4]   The almanacs sold at 1*d.* each were a great
source of popular knowledge.   If there was a storm, everyone
looked to see if the almanac had predicted it. [5]    In 1603, a
"Minister of God's Word," called George Giffard, published a
very remarkable work called A Dialogue concerning Witches and
Witchcraft. [6]   The author takes an important step in advance,
for he denies the power of witches, though, by a strange confusion
of language, he recognises their existence.   Thus, to give a single
instance, he denies [7] that witches can raise a storm ; but says that
the devil, being aware that a storm is approaching, incites them
to predict it.   Here we see the first dawn of that enlightened
scepticism which eventually put an end to the belief in witchcraft.
Giffard strongly censures juries for condemning persons because
witnesses were found who declared them to be witches, and, in a
spirit before his age, asks : [8]  "If others take their oath that in
their conscience they think so [i.e. think them to be witches], is
that sufficient to warrant me upon mine oath to say it is so ? " [9]

[1] Combe. p. 138.                                    [2] 8vo, 1840, vol. v. pp. 149, 150.
[3] Pp. 123-126, Percy Society, vol. iii.        [4] 1592, pp. 52-53, Percy Society, vol. v.
[5] See Dekker's Knights Conjuring, 1607, p. 9, Percy Soc. vol. v.
[6] It has been reprinted by the Percy Society, vol. viii.
[7] Ibid. p. 91.                                           [8] Ibid. p. 106.
[9] At all events the *existence* of witches seems not to be denied, see pp. 13, 18, 30, 71.

In 1582, the whole country was convulsed with fear. Richard Harvey, brother to the great Cambridge astrologer, discovered that in the very next year there would be a conjunction of Jupiter and Saturn. What was to be done? How was the impending calamity to be averted? People were wild with horror. But Nash, in his Pierce Pennilesse, and even Elderton the balladmaker, and Tarleton the buffoon, ridiculed the popular apprehensions.[1] Neal[2] denies that the Puritan clergy claimed a power of exorcising the devil. If they believed in witchcraft, we can understand why Charles II. laughed at it.

Fortune-tellers are ridiculed in the Pleasante Conceites of Old Hobson, 1607, p. 11, Percy Soc. vol. ix.

Astronomy meant what we now call astrology. Thus, in Halle's Historiall Expostulation[3] we have: "I knowe, quoth he, by astronomy the influence of the stars, and thereby perceive when and how long any place shall be unto me fortunate."

In a draught of Discipline, bearing the name of the bishop of Exeter, and presented to Convocation in 1563, it is proposed "that witchcraft may be capitally punished,"[4] parliament having, in 1562, made it capital to use witchcraft, "whereby anybody happens to be killed or destroyed."[5]

Glanville on Witchcraft was a favourite book with Mrs. Lewis, the fashionable and lovely mother of the author of The Monk.[6] Southey allowed the advantages of knowing mineralogy and botany, but only because they "add to our outdoor enjoyments, and have no injurious effects. Chemical and physical studies seem, on the contrary, to draw on very prejudicial consequences. Their utility is not to be doubted; but it appears as if man could not devote himself to these pursuits without blunting his finer faculties." This was written in 1816.[7] Those who *observe* more than they *reflect* become superstitious. They *see* phenomena which they cannot *explain*. Even Blackstone, who in several things was before his age, is evidently half inclined to believe in witchcraft. See his amusingly cautious and, as it were, reverential remarks towards this wretched superstition in his Commentaries.[8] He says[9] that it was not till 9 Geo. II. c. 5, that it was forbidden to prosecute anyone for witchcraft; and that, though, according

[1] See Mr. Rimbault's Notes to Rowland's Four Knaves, Percy Soc. ix. 134.
[2] Hist. of the Puritans, vol. i. p. 458.        [3] 1565, Percy Soc. vol. xi. p. 9.
[4] Collier's Ecclesiastical History, 8vo, 1840, vol. i. pp. 386, 387.
[5] Ibid. vol. vi. p. 366.
[6] See the Life and Correspondence of M. G. Lewis, 8vo, 1839, vol. i. p. 28.
[7] Life and Correspondence of Robert Southey, 8vo, 1849, 1850, vol. iv. p. 191.
[8] Edit. Christian, 8vo, 1809, vol. iv. p. 60, 61.        [9] Ibid. p. 62.

to Voltaire, Louis XIV. issued an edict forbidding the tribunals
to receive informations of witchcraft, "yet Voughlans[1] still
reckons up sorcery and witchcraft among the crimes punishable
in France." After the captivity of Mary of Scotland, the jealousy
of government was excited by the astronomical and magical researches which were instituted in order to determine her fate.
See the questions put in 1571 to Robert Higforth in Murdin's
State Papers.[2] Mr. Morell[3] well says that sensualism, or, as he
calls it, sensationalism, is the natural result of a too exclusive
study of physical science. Hence, I may connect the decline
of superstition and rise of Locke. Indeed, I may trace this
back to Bacon, who analyzed *nature*, while Descartes analyzed
*thought*.

Lady Southwell, one of the maids of honour to Elizabeth,
mentions that at her death there was "discovered in the bottom
of her chair the queen of hearts, with a nail of iron knocked
through the forehead of it."[4] In the system of ecclesiastical law
which Cranmer drew up in 1552, one of the articles "imposes
punishment at the ordinary's discretion upon persons admitting
the practice of idolatry, witchcraft, and the like."[5]

The tendency of increasing civilization to lessen the habit of
accounting for phenomena on supernatural grounds is slightly
but firmly touched by M. Quetelet, who notices the analogy it
bears to the progress of an individual from infancy to manhood.[6]

Whewell says of the schoolmen,[9] "though, like the Greeks,
they thus talked of experiment, like the Greeks, they showed
little disposition to discover the laws of nature by observation of
facts."[7] It has been well observed that such words as ill-starred,
disastrous, exorbitant, a *sphere* of action, &c., show how much
our language has been affected by astrological opinions.[8] As one
religion is succeeded by another, the ritual of the old religion
supplies the form in which the witch mumbles her spells, and the
magician invokes his spirits. See this remarked by a very learned
writer, Mr. Price, in his Preface to Warton's History of English
Poetry.[9] In 1562, the Bishop of Exeter presented a paper to the
ecclesiastical synod, in which he desired "that there be some
sharp, penal, yea, capital pains for witches, charmers, sorcerers,

[1] Du Droit Criminel, pp. 353, 459.                     [2] Pp. 70, 71, 97, 98.
[3] View of the Speculative Philosophy of Europe, 8vo, 1846, vol. i. pp. 64, 65.
[4] See her relation in Dodd's Church History, edit. Tierney, vol. iii. p. 72.
[5] Soames's History of the Reformation of the Church of England, vol. iii. p. 711.
[6] Quetelet, Sur l'Homme, Paris, 1835, tome ii. pp. 273, 274.
[7] Philosophy of the Inductive Sciences, 8vo, 1847, vol. ii. p. 145.
[8] Ibid. vol. ii. pp. 490, 491.                          [9] Vol. i. pp. 44, 45.

enchanters, and such like." [1]    As early as 1574, the Puritans used to pretend to cast out evil spirits. [2]

When it was proposed to connect two rivers in Portugal by means of a canal, the Inquisition refused to allow it, on the ground that, if God had wished them to be united, he would have united them himself. [3]

For a good history of laws, &c., respecting witchcraft, see p. i.–xx. of Mr. Wright's Introduction to the Proceedings against Alice Kyteler, Camden Soc., vol. xxiv.

The Scotch and idealistic philosophy must have been favourable to the superstitions of Puseyism. M. Cousin well says that Christianity particularly relies upon à priori argument. [4]   Cousin says that all the Scotch school, from Hutcheson downwards, denied the à priori proof in favour of a God. [5]   Bower says that Robert Monson, who was born at Aberdeen in 1620, was " the first person who ever made the attempt to reduce botany to a science." [6]   At the end of the seventeenth century, Thomasius first ventured to attack the prosecutions for witchcraft, and to oppose himself to the use of torture, though in spite of this there are instances of such prosecutions as late as the end of the eighteenth century. [7]

Drury, in a religious dispute with the natives of Madagascar, gravely insisted that "a man had one rib less on one side than the other." [8]

Selden upset the theological notion of tithes, which even Hooker advocated.

Rabelais [9] ridicules judicial astrology. Since the Mahommedan dominion, the fear of witchcraft has ceased in the Indian archipelago. [10]   Coleridge [11] says: " Fanaticism, the universal origin of which is in the contemplation of phenomena without investigation into their causes." Coleridge [12] makes it an argument in favour of the inspiration of the Bible, that there is nothing in it in favour of witchcraft. The Methodists, I suspect, by encouraging the notion of witchcraft, prevented it from dying out so soon as it would otherwise have done. [13]   Indeed, in his Journal, [14] Wesley says

[1] Strype's Annals of the Reformation, vol. i. part i. p. 521 : Oxford, 8vo, 1824.

[2] Ibid. vol. ii. part i. pp. 483, 484.

[3] Storch, Économie Politique, St. Petersbourg, 1815, tome v. p. 361.

[4] Cousin, Histoire de la Philosophie, 2nde série, tome iii. pp. 372, 373.

[5] Ibid. première série, tome iv. p. 33.

[6] History of the University of Edinburgh, vol. ii. p. 326.

[7] Schlosser's History of the Eighteenth Century, vol. i. pp. 191, 192.

[8] Drury's Madagascar, 8vo, 1743, p. 181.

[9] Œuvres : Amsterdam, 8vo, 1725, tome ii. p. 93, livre ii. chap. viii.

[10] See Crawford's History of the Indian Archipelago, 8vo, 1820, vol. iii. p. 137.

[11] Literary Remains, vol. i. p. 241.        [12] Ibid. vol. iv. pp. 54, 55.

[13] See Southey's Life of Wesley, 8vo, 1846, vol. ii. pp. 89, 277–279.

[14] 8vo, 1851, pp. 602, 713.

that men who disbelieve witchcraft are deists.   Besides this, his
journals are full of monstrous stories.

The first-known instance of witches burnt in England is in the
reign of Henry II.[1]  Wright says[2] that among us, during the fourteenth and fifteenth centuries, sorcery was used *politically*; after
which began "what may be termed *par excellence* the age of
witches."  Our darkest witch-period was under James I.[3]  He
says[4] that credulity about witches "seems to have risen to its
greatest height at the time of the Reformation."  During the
fifteenth and sixteenth centuries, it was less in England than in
any country,[5] and our first statute against it was in 1541.[6]
Wright says:[7] "The great witch persecution in England arose
under the commonwealth."  He says:[8] "In general, the countries
of Northern Europe appear to have been less subject to these
extensive witch prosecutions than the South; although there, the
ancient popular superstitions reigned in great force."  Wright
says[9] that the case of Jane Wenham (in 1712) "is the last
instance of a witch being condemned by the verdict of an English
jury;" and the context shows how many of the clergy exerted
themselves to procure her condemnation.  Locke, at Montpelier
in 1676, mentions a man who "about four years ago sacrificed a
child to the devil."[10]  Even in 1699, in London, people were
terrified by an eclipse of the sun.[11]  In Scotland, the belief in
witchcraft survived the belief in England, and to deny it was
atheism.[12]  In 1691, witchcraft was punished in France.[13]  Morley[14]
says that "Andreas Alciatus, the great jurist of his age," "born
near Como, about 1493," was an opposer of torturing witches, and
apparently disbelieved in witchcraft.  He also opposed astrology,
and wished that astrologers should be punished (p. 22).

*Witchcraft.   Charles II.*—But even in point of morals, the
Restoration was by no means an unmixed evil.  The overthrow
of Puritanism by the Independents had gone far to check the
alarming progress of superstition.  The magnanimous intellect of
Cromwell was not to be imposed on by the miserable jargon of
priests; and there is little doubt that, if his life had not been

[1] See Wright's Sorcery and Magic, 8vo, 1851, vol. i. p. 15.
[2] Ibid. p. 24.        [3] Ibid. p. 179.        [4] Ibid.  p. 226.
[5] Ibid. p. 227.        [6] Ibid. p. 279.        [7] Ibid. vol. ii. p. 145.
[8] Ibid. p. 244.        [9] Ibid. p. 326.
[10] King's Life of Locke, 8vo, 1830, vol. i. p. 119.
[11] See Evelyn's Diary, vol. iii. p. 372.
[12] See Burt's Letters from the North of Scotland, 8vo, 1815, vol. i. pp. 220, 221,
268, 269.
[13] See Monteil, Hist. des Français des Divers États, vol. viii. p. 41.
[14] Life of Cardan, 1854, vol. ii. p. 21.

prematurely shortened, superstition would have been checked. But this result was hastened by the Restoration. It will be convenient to consider these results under the two heads of decline of particular superstitions and the general decline of priestly influence.

There are few superstitions which have been so universal as a belief in witchcraft. The serene theology of Paganism despised the wretched superstition, which has been greedily believed by millions of Christians. Even the early Church, encumbered with the most uncouth superstition, did not hold it so long as the Roman influence predominated in her councils. But when the Western Empire obtained her independence in the fifth century, we find the first faint indication. In our own country, it was eagerly adopted. It was reserved for the reign of Elizabeth to enter the first protest. In 1594 (?) Reginald Scott (?) boldly attacked the prevalent belief. But he made few converts.

Under the Puritans, the eagerness against witches became an awful mania. During the years of their rule, more persons were burnt as witches than in the preceding years.

But when Cromwell had gained the ascendancy all this was changed. The Puritans were religious bigots. The Independents were political bigots. So long as they retained the name of a republic, so long as they preserved the democratic element, they cared little about anything else. The course which Cromwell had pursued from knowledge, Charles II. pursued from laziness. Charles II. was thoroughly an idle man. This indifference spread rapidly from the throne to the court, and slowly from the court to the people. At length Shadwell, one of the most wretched scribblers even of that age, but a man of considerable literary influence, boldly undertook to ridicule witchcraft on the public stage. But the caution with which he found it necessary to proceed is instructive. Supported by the court, he says in his preface: "For my part, I am, as it is said of Surly in the Alchymist, somewhat costive of belief." [1] But he adds that he felt himself bound to represent actual witches; otherwise "it would have been called atheistical by a prevailing party, who take it ill that the power of the devil should be lessened." The whole of the play is on the same strain. The meanest and most foolish characters are represented as believers in witchcraft, the more enlightened ones as ridiculing it. Sir Edward Hartford treat[?] the prevailing opinion with supreme contempt.[2]

Boyle wrote The Sceptical Chemist and the Sceptical Naturalist.

[1] Shadwell's Works, vol. iii. p. 218.      [2] Ibid. p. 233.

The establishment of the Royal Society lessened superstition. It called the attention of men from theology, just as politics had done before the Restoration. The *power* of men was increased, and they despised theology. Besides this, *new* topics were introduced. The Ne Plus Ultra contains an able defence of the Royal Society, and supplies evidence of the hatred felt of it by some of the clergy.

Rogers[1] says that Bishop Parker and his patron, Archbishop Sheldon, though like the Puseyites, dogmatic as to rites, were really very sceptical. Rogers quotes Burnet for this, and as to Parker's love of Rome, he refers to the testimony of Father Petre in Dove's Life of Marvell.

## HISTORY OF THE ENGLISH NAVY.

On the 28th of April, 1560, Sir Nicolas Throckmorton writes to Cecil, "Bend your force, credit and device to maintain and increase your navy by all the means you can possible; for in this time, considering all circumstances, it is the flower of England's garland."[2] In November 1562, the Duke of Norfolk, the Earl of Pembroke, and the admiral order "that 1,000 of masters and maryners be prest upon the coast of England next to Newhaven, to be transported thither for the setting away of the principal ships first that are at this present there."[3] In April 1563, the Earl of Warwick writes from Newhaven to the Council respecting a "galley" which it is "necessary" to have, and which "will occupy nine score and twelve rowars (having forty-eight oars and four men to every owar), and thirty mariners," &c.[4] On the 10th of May, 1563, Elizabeth orders the lord admiral "to cause 300 mariners to be prested and taken up on the sea-coast next towards Newhaven, and sent thither with all spede possible."[5]

Jacob[6] says that the 14 Henry VII. cap. 10 "gave encouragement to the construction of ships, and caused the education of a considerable number of seamen."

In 1761 "copper plates were first used as sheathing on the 'Alarm' frigate," and, by the year 1780, "the whole British navy was coppered—an event which may be considered as forming an important era in the naval annals of the country."[7] It was reserved for Davy to discover the mode of arresting the corrosion of

[1] Essays, 8vo, 1850, vol. i. pp. 69, 70.
[2] Forbes's Elizabeth, vol. i. p. 416.
[3] Ibid. vol. ii. p. 172.
[4] Ibid. 382.
[5] Ibid. p. 415.
[6] History of the Precious Metals, 8vo, 1831, vol. ii. p. 17.
[7] Paris, Life of Sir Humphry Davy, 8vo, 1831, vol. ii. pp. 224, 225.

the copper by voltaic action [1]—a discovery which, as connected with others, was of the greatest importance, but which, owing to some disturbing causes, was eventually relinquished as impracticable.[2] Among the many fabulous advantages which M. Villers ascribes to the Reformation, one is that it gave rise to the English navy.[3]

The French ambassador at London, in a despatch to his own government in August, 1570, gives an account of the rapidity with which Elizabeth had made her navy ready for sea. She fitted out " vingt-neuf de ses grands navires bien artillez, et bien garnys de toutes munitions de guerre," having 5,500 men on board.[4] A month later, he mentions ten of her ships with 3,500 men on board, " dont les huict centz sont harquebouziers."[5] As to the determination of Elizabeth to have a navy, Soames[6] cites Bishop Carleton's Thankful Remembrance of God's Mercy, London, 1625, p. 4.

The extension of popular liberty gave rise to a national navy. The people soon perceived that their prince could only oppress them by calling in the aid of the military power. Of this power they therefore became jealous, and resisted all the attempts of the sovereign to increase it. But of the naval power they could have no such apprehensions; and the energies natural to a free people were dedicated to increasing that power which alone they could increase without danger to themselves. The English were the first who built frigates.[7]

On the 10th of January, 1559, the Duke of Norfolk, in a letter to Cecil, mentions " Her Majestie's navie ";[8] and on the 8th of February, 1559, the Duke of Norfolk writes that there were in the Frith (of Forth, I suppose), " her Majestie's seed navie to the number of thirteen men-of-war."[9] However, on the 11th of February, 1559, Lord Montagu and Sir Thomas Chamberlain write to the Council that even at Plymouth there was " no shipp above sixty tonnes, and these neyther furnished with ordinance, victuall, nor other munition, as is requisitt for this voyage."[10] In July, 1560, Portsmouth was the great place of assemblage for " the Queene's Majestie's ships."[11]

Hume quotes " Monson, p. 196," to the effect that Elizabeth's navy at her death consisted of 42 vessels, but that " none of these

[1] Paris, Life of Sir Humphry Davy, 8vo, 1831, vol. ii. pp. 255-256.
[2] Ibid. vol. ii. p. 270.
[3] See Villers, Sur la Réformation: Paris, 1820, p. 170.   On Impressment, see COMMON PLACE BOOK, art. 2226.
[4] Correspondance de Fénelon : Paris, 1840, tome iii. p. 260.       [5] Ibid. p. 306.
[6] Elizabethan Religious History, p. 91.       [7] See Evelyn's Diary, vol. iii. p. 290.
[8] Haynes's State Papers, pp. 221, 224.       [9] Ibid. p. 237.
[10] Ibid. p. 239.       [11] Ibid. p. 357, 358.

ships carried above 40 guns; that 4 only came up to that number; that there were but 2 ships of 1,000 tons, and 23 below 500, some of 50, and some even of 20 tons; and that the whole number of guns belonging to the fleet was 774." See in Murdin's State Papers [1] a list of the queen's navy in 1588, where it is said [2] that she had 34 ships, bearing 6,225 men, and of 12,190 tons. This was exclusive of vessels with Sir F. Drake, and also of those sent by the city of London; but the entire total of the naval force opposed by England to the Spaniards was ships 191, tonnage 31,985, men 15,272. In 1592, Elizabeth had 38 vessels, the amount of their tonnage is not added up. [3] In 1572, even the French ambassador confessed that she had "le plus beau et magnifique équippage de navyres que prince ni princesse de l'Europe." [4] In January, 1573, the French ambassador writes to his own court that Elizabeth "a faict presant d'un navyre de 600 tonneaulx, et de deux aultres de 150 tonneaulx, chacun à son admiral," and that the admiral had given the large one to his son and the other two to his relations. [5] In 1543, the bishop of Winchester and the Lord St. John write to the earl of Hertford that, although they cannot give "the peculiar declaration of the furniture of every ship in every port," yet they are "assured that there be departed from hence and ready to depart from other ports the number of 160 sail of ships." [6]

In 1544, the earl of Hertford writes to the Lords of the Council that there was not enough money in hand to pay "the month's wages now expired of the captains, soldiers, and mariners of the fleet, being about 5,000 in number." He says that 30,000l. was put aside for that purpose. [7]

It seems that in 1573 it was usual for ships, before engaging, to hoist a red cross. See Correspondance de Fénelon, tome v. p. 317; but compare p. 319, where it is said that this was done by merchant vessels in suspicious times.

Had Elizabeth in 1573 a sort of body guard of "neuf cent harquebousiers?" [8]

In 1574, the French ambassador writes to his court that Elizabeth had ordered all her great ships, except four, to put to sea; and that 3,000 mariners were already prepared to go on board; but that to pay them, she had only appropriated 35,000 "éscus," although 80,000 would be required, besides the expenses of the

[1] Pp. 615-618.                                    [2] P. 618.
[3] See Murdin, p. 619.  For the expense of the navy, see p. 620, &c.
[4] Correspondance de Fénelon, tome v. p. 146.              [5] Ibid. p. 243.
[6] Haynes's State Papers, p. 20.                          [7] Ibid. p. 30.
[8] See Correspondance de Fénelon, tome v. p. 329.

gunpowder.[1] Sixteen days later he writes[2] that, in four days, six vessels with 2,500 men would sail. Two months afterwards he again writes[3] that Elizabeth was about "mettre ses grands navyres dehors, en nombre de vingt-cinq, aultant bien équippés qu'il y en ait en ceste mer, avec les barques et aultres vnyssaulx qui suivront, oultre les particuliers qui seront bien aultant." In August, 1574, Elizabeth's "grands navires" were at Rochester.[4]

In June, 1552, the French ambassador writes that the English were fitting out "ung grand équipage de mer, lequel je pense n'estre moindre de vingt bons navires."[5] In March, 1554, he writes that all the queen's navy except five vessels were ordered to join the emperor's forces.[6] In March, 1554, Mary had in all thirty ships of war.[7] In May, 1554, the queen's ships, which were sent to Spain, put into Plymouth to be victualled.[8] In May, 1554, she had so neglected her ships that many of them were not even seaworthy.[9] In August, 1554, she completely stripped and unvictualled many of her ships, in order to supply those of Spain.[10] Indeed Nouilles was informed that she sent several of her sailors and captains to enter into the imperial service.[11]

---

## ADMINISTRATION OF JUSTICE AND INFLUENCE OF LAWYERS.

A REMARKABLE evidence of the absence of justice is supplied by a letter in Forbes's State Papers,[12] dated London, May, 1560, in which Mr. Peyto, writing to Sir Nicolas Throckmorton, the English ambassador in France, gives an account of a scuffle between Sir Thomas Sheldon and another. He says: "The matter is here afore the counsell, neither of them wantyng friendes, but *whose friendes most hable to stonde in stede, th' ende of the judgment will declare*." On January 17, 1569, the earl of Sussex writes to Cecil respecting a gentleman concerned in the rebellion. He says: "He is my wife's cousin, and therefore, if any seek to *beg*

---

[1] Correspondance de Fénelon, tome vii. p. 96.
[2] Ibid. p. 111.
[3] Ibid. p. 179.
[4] Ibid. tome vi. p. 489.
[5] Ambassades de Nouilles, Leyde, 1762, tome ii. p. 42; and see p. 48.
[6] Ibid. tome iii. p. 140.
[7] Ibid. p. 144.
[8] Ibid. p. 204.
[9] Ibid. p. 220; and see tome iv. pp. 219, 220.
[10] Ibid. tome iii. pp. 295, 296.
[11] Ibid. tome iv. pp. 80, 81.
[12] Vol. i. pp. 443, 444.

him, I beseech you to procure his stay in the queen's majesty's
hands." [1]

In Ormerod's History of Cheshire [2] there is a curious letter from
Sir Ralph Egerton, sheriff of Cheshire, to John Talbot, in which
he promises to summon a jury of his own appointment, provided
Talbot does not name any of his relations on it, as in that case
they might be challenged. The jury had to try a lawsuit respecting property, to which Talbot was one of the chief parties.
The letter is dated 3rd March, 1579. There were men who made
a trade of serving on juries and selling their verdicts. These, in
the sixteenth century, were so well known a body as to have a
distinct name, and were called "Ringleaders of Inquests." [3]

In 1601, Ben Jonson attacked the lawyers in The Poetaster. [4]
Livery of seisin was rarely effected except by open force; and
each party used to have their friends well armed. This is alluded
to in 1609 in Ben Jonson's Works. [5] In The Magnetick Lady,
written in 1632, Ben Jonson attacks the partiality of a "London
jury." [6] Indeed, false swearing was so common that a particular
word was invented for those wretches who systematically perjured
themselves for money. Such hirelings were called Knights of the
Post. [7]

In 1627, we find a complaint "that if one have ten shillings
owing him, nay, five or less, he cannot have it but by suit in law
in some petty court, where it will cost thirty or forty shillings
charge of suit." [8] Even the satiric Nash pays a high compliment
to the legal eloquence of his time. [9] Rich,[10] after speaking favour-
ably of the law, adds: "Our Inns of Court now, for the greater
part, are stuffed with the offspring of farmers, and with all other
sorts of tradesmen; and these, when they have gotten some few
scrapings of the law, they do sow the seeds of suits."

It is supposed that Calixtus, in 1630, was the first who raised
religious ethics to a science; but M. Villers says,[11] "qu'en 1577
avait déjà paru à Genève celui de Lambert Daneau ou Danæus
intitulé Ethices Christianæ libri tres, et où la morale religieuse
est traitée méthodiquement."

On horrible judicial cruelties, see Spottiswoode's History of the

[1] Sharpe's Memorials of 1569, 8vo, 1840, pp. 157, 158. In a note is another
curious begging letter.
[2] 1819, vol. ii. pp. 241, 242.
[3] See Stow's London, edit. Thoms, 8vo, 1842, p. 72.
[4] See Ben Jonson's Works, 8vo, 1816, vol. ii. p. 404.        [5] Ibid. vol. iii. p. 451.
[6] Ibid. vol. vi. pp. 60, 61.                [7] Middleton's Works, vol. v. p. 512.
[8] Harleian Miscellany, edit. Park, vol. iii. p. 211.        [9] Ibid. vol. vi. p. 176.
[10] Honestie of this Age, 1614, Percy Soc. vol. xi.
[11] Essai sur la Réformation, Paris, 1820, p. 265.

Church of Scotland, i. p. 217 ; Chambers's Domestic Annals of Scotland, vol. i. p. 471 ; vol. ii. p. 383. Buchanan's History of Scotland, vol. i. p. 911.

Mr. Trollope says that formerly in France women were always put to death by drowning ; and that " the first time a woman was hung in France was in the reign of Charles VII." [1]

The corruption of jurymen was so notorious that it enriched our language with a new word ; and to attempt to influence a jury by gifts or by promises was known as the crime of Embracery.[2]

Blackstone says, " frequenting houses of ill fame is an indictable offence." [3] For this he cites " Poph. 208." The forcible entries, so common in the reign of Elizabeth, were illegal; for, by the 5 Ric. II. Stat. I. c. 8, it was ordered that the remedy by entry should be peaceable and easy ; [4] and the 20 Hen. III. c. 2, ordered that, if in case of illegal disseisin, on which the party disseised recovered legal seisin, the disseisor shall proceed to a redisseisin, he shall be imprisoned, and by a later statute, 52 Hen. III. c. 8, shall be fined. To which penalties the 13 Edw. I. c. 26 added double damages to the party injured.[5] In 1548, the most eminent lawyers used to leave London between the terms.[6] In October, 1553, Mary caused 110*l.* " to be distributed among the judges and learned counsell that took pains in the indictment of the late duke of Northumberland." [7] " Embraceries " are mentioned in 1553.[8] Cecil, in a paper drawn up in 1579, recommends " that penal laws be not dispensed withall for private men's profits." [9] A very sagacious writer says, " Little reliance is in general to be placed on the dying declarations of criminals, although they are sought after with great eagerness." [10]

M. Cousin says of Domat: " Il est incomparablement le plus grand jurisconsulte du dix-septième siècle ; il a inspiré et presque formé D'Aguesseau ; il a quelquefois prevenu Montesquieu, et frayé la route à cette réforme générale des lois entreprise par la révolution et réalisée par l'empire." [11] We owe to him also the Calvinistic spirit of Jansenism. Frederick Schlegel regrets that, in consequence of the influence of classical association, the laws of the German nations should have been so much modified by the civil law, which, he says, were too *severely just* and did not make

[1] Trollope's Brittany, 8vo, London, 1840, vol. i. p. 172.
[2] Blackstone, vol. iv. p. 140.    [3] Comment. vol. iv. p. 64.
[4] Blackstone, 8vo, 1809, vol. iii. p. 179.    [5] Ibid. vol. iii. p. 188.
[6] See Haynes's State Papers, p. 73.    [7] Ibid. p. 189.
[8] Ibid. p. 195.    [9] Murdin's State Papers, p. 325.
[10] Lewis on Disturbances in Ireland, 8vo, 1836, p. 123.
[11] Cousin's Littérature, Paris, 1840, tome iii. p. 161.

allowances enough.[1] In the same part[2] he well points out the
real difference which is and *ought to be* between law and justice.
St. Basil orders for murder a penance of twenty years; for apo-
stasy a penance of "a whole life." This is quoted by Collier, who
considers it a model of wisdom.[3]

Bucer wished to have "those crimes capitally punished in all
commonwealths which were death by the law of Moses;" and he
particularly mentions among such crimes those who recommended
a false religion, or who broke the Sabbath.[4] As to the oath *ex
officio*, see the contemporary authorities in Soames's Elizabethan
Religious History, pp. 403–405. At the end of Elizabeth's reign
grew up the custom of stopping the ecclesiastical courts by *pro-
hibitions* from Westminster Hall.[5]

The bishop of Asaph has collected some instances of the *venality*
of justice in the reign of Elizabeth.[6] On the absurd theory of an
original compact, see Lord Brougham's Political Philosophy.[7] He
says,[8] Hobbes "was the first writer who put forth a philosophical
statement of the doctrine of the original or social compact." He
observes,[9] that even in 1314 we find the doctrine of Resistance
supposed to be originated in A.D. 1688.

Lord Brougham looks on expediency as the basis of all law and
government. Political Philosophy, 2nd edit. 8vo, 1849, vol. i.
pp. 46, 50, 494. See p. 69, where he seems to consider the judicial forces more important than the legislative power. Lord
Brougham has observed that the introduction of so beautiful and
scientific a system as the civil law tended in Europe to raise the
reputation of the men who studied it, and thus increase the dignity
of lawyers.[10] Lord Brougham asserts most positively that members
of Parliament should *not* be paid; and he notices that in other
professions men do not mind confessing that all their property is
derived from it, while no man would make such a confession as
regards politics.[11] It seems likely that the notion of an original
compact had its rise in the Saxon engagements between a man
and his hlaford.[12] When the judges were made for life, I suppose
their power lessened. Montesquieu well says: "Dans toute ma-
gistrature, il faut compenser la grandeur de la puissance par la

[1] Philosophy of History. 8vo, 1846, pp. 265, 266.   [2] Ibid. p. 265. 266.
[3] Ecclesiastical History, vol. v. p. 260, 8vo, 1840.   [4] Ibid. p. 417.
[5] Soames's Eliz. Relig. History, p. 516.
[6] History of the Church of England, 8vo, 1847, p. 283, and as to the oath *ex officio*,
see p. 301.
[7] 2nd edit. 8vo, 1849, vol. i. pp. 34–38.   [8] Ibid. p. 39.
[9] Ibid. pp. 59, 60.   [10] Political Philosophy, vol. i. p. 342.
[11] Ibid. vol. ii. pp. 30, 32.
[12] See Allen on the Royal Prerogative, 8vo, 1849, pp. 66–68.

brieveté de sa durée."[1]  With the increase of liberty penal laws
always become less severe.[2]  Montesquieu adds:[3] "C'est donc de
la bonté des lois criminelles que dépend principalement la liberté
du citoyen," and,[4] "C'est le triomphe de la liberté lorsque les lois
criminelles tirent chaque peine de la nature particulière du crime."
*Written* libels will be tolerated in monarchies; punished in aristocracies.[5]  He seems to think attainders not indefensible.[6]  As
to taxes, he anticipates Bentham.  He says:[7] "Dans l'impôt de
la personne, la proportion injuste serait celle qui suivrait exactement la proportion des biens;" and he adds that every one has a
certain sum *necessary* to him, and that this should not be taxed.
The freer the government, the more complicated the laws.[8]
Montesquieu thinks *one* witness too little, but *two* sufficient to
take away a man's life.[9]  He well says that laws have nothing to
do with repentance.[10]  I quite agree with Alison[11] that Malthus has
underrated the influence of laws.  Mr. Alison, who has had considerable experience in such matters, denies the common assertion
that transportation is not feared by criminals.[12]  Mr. Alison
gravely adds:[13] "Nothing can be more obvious than the fundamental principles of criminal jurisprudence;" but I cannot say
he has thrown much light on them.  He opposes an unpaid ma-
gistracy.[14]  He dislikes imprisonment, and recommends that "for
the second offence transportation should be invariably inflicted."[15]
Adam Smith complains of the neglect of "natural jurisprudence,
of all sciences by far the most important, but hitherto perhaps the
least cultivated."[16]

In 1585, Fleetwood, recorder of London, writes to Burghley:
"It is growen for a trade now in the courte to make meanes for
reprieves; twenty pounds for a reprieve is nothing, although it
be but for bare ten daies."[17]  In 1586, we find a letter from Walsingham, from which it would appear that the custom of sending
felons to the galleys was then very recent.  See Egerton Papers,
p. 116, Camden Sóc.  For proof of the arbitrary interference with
the course of law at the end of the sixteenth century, see Lodge's
Illustrations of British History, 1838, vol. ii. p. 386.  Read

[1] Esprit des Lois, livre ii, chap. iii. Œuvres, p. 196, Paris, 1835.
[2] Ibid. livre vi. chap. ix. p. 231.    [3] Ibid. livre xii. chap. ii. p. 280.
[4] Ibid. chap. iii. p. 281.    [5] Ibid. chap. xiii. p. 286.
[6] Ibid. chap. xix. p. 289.    [7] Ibid. livre xiii. chap. vii. p. 294.
[8] Montesquieu, pp. 226-228.    [9] Ibid. p. 281.
[10] Esprit des Lois, livre xxvi. chap. xii. pp. 426, 427.
[11] Principles of Population, 8vo, 1840, vol. i. p. 229.
[12] Ibid. vol. ii. pp. 137, 138.    [13] Ibid. p. 139.
[14] Ibid. p. 139.    [15] Ibid. pp. 140, 143.
[16] Theory of Moral Sentiments, 1822, vol. ii. p. 60.
[17] Wright's Elizabeth, 8vo, 1838, vol. ii. p. 247.

Twysden on the Government of England, Camden Society, vol. xlv.

It was usual in the sixteenth century to hang pirates at the lower water-mark at Wapping.[1] In 1562, the lord keeper advises Parliament " to make your laws as few and as plain as may be." [2] In 1584, the archbishop of York seems to taunt the House of Commons with having many young members.[3] Cousin says that the object of penal laws should be to punish crime in proportion to its viciousness, not in proportion to its effects on society.[4] Before 1710 neither the Roman law nor the municipal law of Scotland were taught in any of the Scotch universities.[5]

By the system of ecclesiastical laws drawn up by Cranmer, adultery, either in man or woman, was punished by " banishment or perpetual imprisonment." [6]

According to the Malagasy laws, a man who breaks maliciously one of his neighbour's limbs is " fined fifteen heads of cattle, which is delivered to the party injured " ; and whoever robs his neighbour of an ox or cow " is obliged to restore it tenfold." [7] Hooker [8] anticipates the argument of Coleridge against universal suffrage. In the thirteenth century we find something like the social compact laid down by a Persian moralist.[9] In 1678, Locke seems to hold it.[10] Schlegel [11] says that, during the 180 years between the consulate of Cicero and the death of Trajan, was developed the science of jurisprudence, "the only original intellectual possession of great value to which the Romans can lay undisputed claim." Alison [12] ascribes to Mackintosh the great principle that punishment should be *certain*, ignorant that Beccaria first laid it down. Lord Campbell says,[13] " in the reign of Henry VIII. there were 72,000 executions."

On the opening of the Legislative Assembly, in October 1791, " l'extreme jeunesse s'y faisait remarquer en foule." [14] Charles

---

[1] See p. 351 of Mr. Nichol's Notes to Machyn's Diary, London, 1848, p. 351.
[2] D'Ewes' Journal of Parliament, 1682, p. 66.
[3] D'Ewes' Journal of Elizabeth, p. 360.
[4] Histoire de la Philosophie, 2nde série, tome iii. pp. 189, 190.
[5] Tytler's Life of Kames, Edinburgh, 1814, vol. i. p. 15.
[6] Todd's Life of Cranmer, vol. ii. p. 29.
[7] Drury's Madagascar, 8vo, 1742, p. 240.
[8] Ecclesiastical Polity, Book I., sect. 7, Works, vol. i. p. 90.
[9] See Transactions of the Literary Society of Bombay, vol. i. pp. 29, 30.
[10] See King's Life of Locke, 8vo, 1830, vol. i. p. 217.
[11] Lectures on the History of Literature, i. 169.
[12] Hist. of Europe, vol. ix. p. 621.
[13] Lives of the Chancellors, vol. ii. p. 231.
[14] Lamartine, Histoire des Girondins, Bruxelles, 8vo, 1847, tome i. p. 252.

Butler [1] says that " the Jus Ecclesiasticum of Van Erpen, the only work perhaps which the continent has produced that can be compared with Mr. Justice Blackstone's Commentaries."

In Holstein or Schleswick "the succession by gavelkind prevails,—the youngest son, and not the eldest, succeeds to the father's land." [2] Laing says that this has been ascribed to the feudal *jus primæ noctis*, but the real fact is that holding the land was formerly a sort of bondage, and the elder son preferred being a man-at-arms in the baron's castle. Alison [3] says positively that the "Mercheta mulierum" existed in France.

On the absurdity of making laws *logically* complete, quote Tocqueville, Démocratie en Amérique, i. 209, 210. Tocqueville says: [4] "L'Angleterre n'ayant point de constitution écrite, qui peut dire qu'on change sa constitution?" The absurdity of introducing free institutions among a people not ripe for them appears from what has taken place in Mexico. [5] Tocqueville [6] is in favour of universal suffrage, in which the people elect electors as in the American Senate. He says [7] that despotism is more injurious in *preventing* production than in taking away its fruits. He well says [8] that a trial by jury is not useful, because it secures justice, but because it accustoms men themselves to be *responsible*, and to show " the sovereignty of the people." Ranke says, [9] " Louis XI. was the first monarch who decidedly recognised the fundamental doctrine that the officers of justice were not removable at pleasure." Bracton, in the middle of the thirteenth century, uses the civil law " by way of illustration, not as authority," though Lord Campbell [10] regrets that " the prejudices of English lawyers" have always prevented them making more use of the civil law. Sir William de Thorpe, in the middle of the fourteenth century, was chief justice. He, says Lord Campbell, [11] " from an obscure origin rose to power and wealth, without being a churchman—a very unusual occurrence in those days; but the law was becoming what it has since continued, one of the ties by which the middling and lower ranks in England are bound up with the aristocracy, preventing the separation of the community into the two castes of noble and roturier, which has been so injurious in the continental states." From the fifteenth century until the reign of Charles II., judges of the highest rank used to settle

[1] Reminiscences, vol. i. p. 116.
[2] Laing's Denmark, pp. 139, 140.
[3] History of Europe, vol. i. p. 199.
[4] Démocratie en Amérique, vol. i. p. 311.
[5] Ibid. vol. ii. p. 20.
[6] Ibid. p. 138.
[7] Ibid. p. 152.
[8] Ibid. vol. iii. p. 23.
[9] Civil Wars in France, 8vo, 1852, vol. i. p. 101.
[10] Lives of the Chief Justices, vol. i. p. 63.
[11] Ibid. vol. i. p. 69.

"differences privately by arbitration, on the voluntary submission of the parties."[1]  Lord Campbell says:[2] "Till Lord Coke arose in the next generation, England can scarcely be said to have seen a magistrate of constancy, who was willing to surrender his place rather than his integrity." And on the merit of Coke, see p. 239. Since 1628, "torture has never been inflicted in England."[3]  For lawyers, "the full bottom wig, and the three-cornered cocked hat were introduced from France after the Restoration.[4]  Hale was a great student of Roman law.[5]  The coif, "to conceal the want of clerical tonsure."[6]  Commercial law began under Chief Justice Holt.[7]  Holt put an end to receiving evidence respecting the *antecedents* of a prisoner.  He also procured an act to allow witnesses for the prisoner to be examined on oath ;[8] but he always employed "the French system" of interrogating the prisoner.[9] Lord Mansfield was appointed chief justice in 1756.  "His first bold step was to rescue the bar from the monopoly of the leaders."[10] "He formed," says Campbell,[11] "a very low, and, I am afraid, a very just estimate of the common law of England which he was to administer."  He almost created the law of insurance.[12]  "He likewise did much for the improvement of commercial law in this country by rearing a body of special jurymen at Guildhall, who were generally returned on all commercial causes to be tried there."[13]  Lord Campbell says:[14] "After Bacon, Mr. Justice Blackstone was the first practising lawyer at the English bar who, in writing, paid the slightest attention to the selection or collocation of words."  Descartes[15] says laws should be few, but *well kept.* Liebig[16] well says: "In times in which the means of detecting poisons with the greatest certainty were not yet known, the rack was used to make the discovery."  Tocqueville[17] well says that the institution of trial by jury is more beneficial *politically* than *judicially*: it makes men feel responsible, and gives them a sense of power.  "Je ne sais si le jury est utile à ceux qui ont des procès : mais je suis sur qu'il est très utile à ceux qui les jugent." Comte[18] opposes the abolition of punishment of death.  Mr. Mill

[1] Campbell's Chief Justices, vol. i. p. 135,
[2] Ibid. p. 392.
[3] Ibid. p. 518.
[7] Ibid. vol. ii. p. 137.
[8] Ibid. p. 174.
[11] Ibid. p. 402.
[12] Ibid. p. 407.
[13] De la Méthode, in Œuvres, vol. i. p. 141.
[14] Letters on Chemistry, 8vo, 1851, p. 293.
[18] Démocratie en Amérique, tome iii. pp. 23-26, 28, 29.
[18] Philosophie Positive, vol. iv. p. 123.

[3] Ibid. p. 207.
[4] Ibid. p. 482.
[4] Ibid. p. 72.
[8] Ibid. pp. 140, 141.
[10] Ibid. p. 398.
[11] Ibid. p. 405.
[14] Ibid. p. 566,

observes that, according to the laws of association, ideas sprung up synchronically or successively according as the sensations have been synchronous or successive; and he adds: "Of witnesses in courts of justice, it has been remarked that eye-witnesses and ear-witnesses always tell their story in the chronological order; in other words, the ideas occur to them in the order in which the sensations occurred; on the other hand, that witnesses who are inventing rarely adhere to the chronological order."[1]

Miss Wood has printed a letter from Lady Blount to Cromwell, written in 1535, which, as she says, "affords a curious specimen of an early electioneering squabble."[2] At vol. iii. p. 315 there is an order issued by Mary, in 1557, to the sheriffs, ordering them to take care that there were returned to Parliament "men given to good order, Catholic and discreet."

In 1614, it was usual to fine drunkards five shillings.[3] Early in the seventeenth century it was a standing joke to call a jury "godfathers-in-law."[4]

Before the reign of Charles II., our dramatists constantly allude to the shameless practice of selling the guardianship of wards.

In 1608 we find "I had rather give you a counsellor's double fee to hold your peace." Middleton's Works, 8vo, 1840, ii. 364; iv. 459.

"Begging for a fool" occurs in Middleton's Works, 8vo, 1840, vol. iii. p. 16, vol. iv. p. 134.

The severity of the law against sheep-stealing is indignantly noticed in Middleton's Works, iv. 460. Before the doors of the sheriffs were large posts, on which proclamations were put.[5]

Blackstone says:[6] "Experience will abundantly show that above a hundred of our lawsuits arise from disputed facts, for one where the law is doubted of." At the accession of Mary I. it was necessary again to accredit the French ambassador at her court.[7]

---

[1] Mill's Analysis of the Phenomena of the Mind, 8vo, 1829, vol. i. p. 58.
[2] Letters of Royal and Illustrious Ladies, 8vo, 1846, vol. ii. p. 167, 168.
[3] Ben Jonson's Works, vol. v. p. 130.    [4] Ibid. vol. iv. p. 489.
[5] Middleton, iii. 58.
[6] Commentaries, edit. Christian, 1809, vol. iii. p. 330.
[7] Ambassades de Nouilles, Leyde, 1763, tome ii. p. 96.

## NOTES FOR HISTORY OF MONEY AND PRECIOUS METALS.

In France, in 1563, a crown was worth 6s. 8d. English money.[1] Ormerod says:[2] "According to Stow[3] and a MS. chronicler,[4] Richard the Second selected Beeston for the custody of his treasure and jewels, to the immense amount of 200,000 marks."

Storch says[5] that in the time of Charlemagne the purchasing power of silver was four times as great as in the beginning of the nineteenth century. He adds:[6] "La découverte des mines d'Amérique a répandu dans le monde environ dix fois plus d'argent qu'il n'y en avait auparavant; cependant il n'a fait baisser sa valeur en Europe que dans les proportions de quatre à un." Jacob, who was not acquainted with the researches of Storch, says that during the sixteenth century the effect on price was as three to one.[7] Storch supposes[8] that the depreciation of the value of the precious metals reached its lowest point between 1650 and 1700. See also[9] Storch's estimate of the production and consumption of the precious metals since the discovery of America, where he seems chiefly to have followed Humboldt. See also[10] an estimate of the circulating capital of Europe. In valuing Roman money, Storch follows Garnier,[11] and he evidently thinks the price of corn is a decisive evidence of the value of money, a mistake into which he fell in common with all the earlier political economists.[12] He says[13] that just before the discovery of America, the proportionate value of gold to silver was as one to ten, or one to twelve. And he adds[14] that until 1545 Europe received more gold than silver. He says[15] that Denmark and France are the only two countries which do not add some seignorage, besides reimbursing themselves for the cost of coining. In September 1553, " 7,000 livres sterlings" were " 21,000 or 22,000 escuz sol;"[16] and a few months later, Noailles writes from London, " 20,000 livres de

[1] Forbes's Elizabeth, vol. ii. p. 470.
[2] History of Cheshire, 1819, vol. ii. p. 147.　　　[3] Annals, p. 321.
[4] Harl. MSS. 2111, 98.
[5] Économie Politique, St. Petersbourg, 8vo, 1815, tome ii. pp. 199, 200.
[6] Ibid. tome iii. p. 60.　　　　　　　[7] History of the Precious Metals.
[8] Économie Politique, St. Petersbourg, 8vo, 1815, tome iii. p. 64.
[9] Ibid. tome vi. pp. 57-70, note x.　　　[10] Ibid. pp. 76-83, note xii.
[11] Ibid. tome ii. p. 288.　　　　　[12] Ibid. tome iii. pp. 60, 64.
[13] Ibid. p. 66.　　　　　　　　[14] Ibid. p. 67.
[15] Ibid. p. 93.
[16] Ambassades de Noailles, Leyde, 1762, tome ii. p. 137.

ceste monnoye est de la notre environ 65,000 escus sol;"[1] and again,[2] "12,000 livres esterlins sont environ 40,000 escus sol." The Venetian ambassador in 1557 says that there were "many of the staplers—those to whom the exportation of wool is committed —possessed of from 50,000 to 60,000 sterling; all or the greater part is ready."[3]  In 1585, Sir Francis Drake *had* brought into the Tower 23,411 lbs. in weight of silver, and 101 lbs. of gold.[4] In 1571, 7,000 crowns Flemish were equal to 2,000*l.* sterling.[5] In 1572, "ryalls" were worth 6*d.* each.[6]  In 1572, florins were worth three shillings and fourpence.[7]  In 1573, the price of silver in England was 4*l.* 0*s.* 10½*d.* an ounce.[8]  In 1583, seven French "souse" were two groats English.[9]  In 1569, 60,000*l.* sterling were 200,000 "escuz."[10]  It is evident that one "livre" sterling was equal to 3⅓ crowns.[11]

In 1571, 2,000 marks were equal to 4,000 crowns.[12]  In 1575, 10*l.* sterling were "cent. livres tournoys."[13]  In September 1574, Fénelon writes that some Germans, Dutch, and French in England had forged 1,000,000 crowns of the coin of France, Spain, and Flanders, and that they had done this with the secret permission of some of Elizabeth's Council.[14]  These forgeries were so admirably executed that they could not be distinguished from the originals,[15] and when some of the coiners were arrested, Elizabeth's Council had them discharged.[16]  In the Egerton Papers,[17] there is an account of the money coined between 1586 and 1590.  See [18] Collier's assertion that, in 1602, "money was of about five times the value it bears at present."  Monteil, on no good authority, says [19] that the specie in France in the fourteenth century was ten millions, at six livres the silver mark.  And he adds [20] that at the end of the seventeenth century it was 500,000,000.  On the amount of gold and silver Europe has received from America, see an essay by Danson in Journal of Statistical Society, vol. xiv. pp. 11–44.  On the value of silver since 1350, see Smith's Wealth of Nations, pp. 75–88.

[1] Ambassades de Noailles, Leyde, 1762, tome iii. p. 120.

[2] Ibid. p. 205.

[3] Michele's Report in Ellis's Original Letters, 2nd series, vol. ii. p. 220.

[4] See Murdin's State Papers, pp. 539, 540.    [5] Ibid. p. 189.

[6] Ibid. p. 217.    [7] Ibid. p. 241.

[8] Ibid. p. 244.    [9] Ibid. p. 388.

[10] Correspondance Diplomatique de Fénelon, Paris, 1840, tome ii. p. 141.

[11] Fénelon, tome ii. pp. 361, 371; tome iii. pp. 112, 271; tome v. p. 313; tome vi. pp. 449, 456, 497.    [12] Ibid. tome iv. p. 215.

[13] Ibid. tome vi. p. 490, and see p. 540.    [14] Ibid. pp. 241, 242.

[15] Ibid. p. 260.    [16] Ibid. pp. 245, 246.

[17] Pp. 182-185, Camden Society.    [18] Ibid. p. 347.

[19] Histoire des Français des Divers États, tome ii. p. 256.

[20] Ibid. tome vii. p. 163.

## HISTORY AND INFLUENCE OF THE ARISTOCRACY.

ELIZABETH, at her accession, finding all the old nobility Catholics, was obliged to seek her ministers among men of a lower rank. This paved the way for the decline of the aristocracy, and the wretched insurrection of 1569 naturally induced the queen to throw all her weight into the scale opposed to those haughty nobles who had dared to dictate to her. The duke of Norfolk was a Protestant. Elizabeth put Essex to death. Leicester sprung from the very dregs of the people. His grandfather was Dudley, the wretched and base-born confidant of Henry VII. (?)

. . . . . . .

There was yet another circumstance which knit together the English aristocracy, and gave them the character of a caste. I allude to the universal custom of younger brothers of rank going to serve as pages in families of the nobility. This multiplied their points of contact, and made them more personally acquainted with each other than they otherwise would have been. See a remarkable conversation in The New Inn, acted in 1629.[1]

Dr. Paris, whose prejudices, if he has any, are certainly not democratic, says : " In England, we may in vain search amongst the aristocracy for one who feels a dignified respect for the sciences." [2] And a century has just elapsed since Dr. Shebbeare wrote : " No man of letters is acceptable to the great ; they look on him as a kind of satire on their actions, and feeling within their own vacuity, are by no means pleased with beholding in another what they want themselves." [3]

Dekker [4] says : " You mistake if you imagine that Pluto's porter is like one of those big fellows that stand like giants at lords' gates, having bellies bumbailed with ale, in lamb's wool, and with sacks, and cheeks strutting out like two footballs, being blown up with powder beef and brewis."

As the monarchical power declined, the aristocratic power rose, and the Church was not strong enough to keep it down. It remained for Elizabeth to destroy their *moral* power. Though other great sovereigns had diminished their wealth and abridged their privileges, Elizabeth was the first who systematically excluded them from her counsels. Mr. Hallam [5] says that the

---

[1] Ben Jonson's Works, 8vo, 1816, vol. v. pp. 332, 333.
[2] Life of Sir Humphry Davy, 8vo, 1831, vol. ii. p. 181.
[3] Angeloni's Letters on the English Nation, 8vo, 1755, vol. ii. p. 14.
[4] Knights Conjuring, 1607, p. 45, Percy Soc., vol. v.
[5] Constitutional History, vol. i. p. 181.

Haynes' and Murdin's State Papers show that in 1569 the duke of Norfolk actually invited Alva to invade England, and that it is probable from p. 10 of Murdin that Norfolk, on this occasion, pretended to be a Catholic. In 1557, the Venetian ambassador says that the English nobility " all live in the country, remote from the city."[1]  He adds that all the nobility kept stores of arms for their retainers, and that some of the most powerful could bring thousands of men into the field.  Aristocracy fell with chivalry.  Frederick Schlegel says: " The heroic spirit of chivalry and the whole moral character of the middle age were long paramount in England ; and hence in the poetry of no country, if we except the Spanish, is that spirit so conspicuous."[2] Northumberland was incited to the rebellion of 1569 by the queen having granted away a copper-mine found on his estate.[3]  In 1572 the duke of Norfolk was executed, and soon afterwards his eldest son, the earl of Arundel, was arrested, and in 1595 died in confinement.  The earl of Northumberland was thrown into the Tower, and in 1585 executed.[4]  Forman speaks twice of " the Duke of Arligrove "; who was he ?[5]  Lord Brougham has pointed out how it is that as the monarchy declines, the aristocracy rises in power.[6]  Lord Brougham, after giving a striking description of the savages who devastated Europe, says,[7] " The present distribution of rank and power and influence in Europe may be mainly traced to the character and habits of those savage tribes." Brougham says,[8] " The first patent of peerage was granted in Richard the Second's reign, in the year 1387."  This was, I suppose, a blow to the aristocracy.  At vol. i. pp. 344–354, Brougham has estimated with considerable ability the tendencies of an hereditary aristocracy.  And he adds[9] that as the people rise in importance, the prince finds it necessary to court the nobility. Lord Brougham says:[10] " The period in a nation's progress at which the aristocratic power is naturally established, must always be while the body of the people are in a low state of refinement."

Henry I. " employed all the energies of the law and the services of corrupt judges to entrap and convict great landowners, whose forfeited estates on their attainder he bestowed on men of the basest and most abandoned lives."[11]  He adds:[12] " The power of

---

[1] Michele's Report in Ellis's Original Letters, 2nd series, vol. ii. pp. 220–222.
[2] Philosophy of History, Lond. 1846, p. 430.
[3] Soames's Elizabethan Religious History, p. 113.        [4] Ibid. pp. 346, 347.
[5] Autobiography of Dr. Simon Forman, from 1552 to 1602, edit. Halliwell, 1849, 4to, p. 14.        [6] Political Philosophy, 2nd edit. 8vo, 1849, vol. i. p. 78.
[7] Ibid. p. 306.        [8] Ibid. p. 315.
[9] Ibid. p. 354.        [10] Ibid. vol. ii. p. 19.
[11] Ibid. vol. iii. p. 217.        [12] Ibid. p. 232.

the barons and of all landed proprietors was exceedingly increased
by the famous statute De Donis, which allowed them to entail
their real property, and thus to sustain the landed aristocracy."
During the Wars of the Roses, the old nobility was almost extin-
guished, and a further increase was given to the royal power by
the state of its finances. Almost all the concessions made by the
Crown had been the result of its pecuniary difficulties; but
Henry VII. was not thus embarrassed, for he was avaricious, and
"was the first king since Henry III. who ever lived within his
income."[1]

Mr. Alison seems to think it of Divine origin, for he gravely
says of the "gradation of ranks" that "it may safely be concluded that it is intended to answer some important purpose in
the economy of nature";[2] and yet this same celebrated Tory
writer confesses the low tastes of many of our aristocracy;[3] but
he takes for granted[4] that it is the "hereditary aristocracy which
forms the great political distinction between the eastern dynasties
and the European monarchies," and hence he infers[5] the necessity of primogeniture; but he opposes entails.[6]

Schiller ascribes to Charles V. the policy of impoverishing the
aristocracy of the Low Countries by sending them on expensive
embassies: "Unter dem scheinbaren Vorwande von Ehrenbezeu-
gungen."[7] In 1585, Leicester was charged with improperly assuming the title of "excellency," but to this he replied that
strangers had always so called him ever since he had been made
an earl.[8] In 1500, an intelligent observer remarked of the
English that "every one, however rich he may be, sends away his
children into the houses of others, whilst he in return receives
those of strangers into his own."[9] Ranke *seems* to say that in Italy,
in the sixteenth century, the aristocratic spirit was stronger in the
north than in the south.[10] See also[11] some interesting remarks on
the rise of the aristocratic principle in Italy early in the sixteenth
century, shown by the general introduction of titles, &c. In
1669, Pepys met "a country gentleman," who spoke "about the
decay of gentlemen's families in the country, telling us that the
old rule was, that a family might remain fifty miles from London
one hundred years, one hundred miles from London two hundred

---

[1] Brougham's Political Philosophy, vol. iii. p. 251.
[2] Principles of Population, 8vo, 1840, vol. i. p. 89.
[3] Ibid. vol. ii. p. 93.                    [4] Ibid. p. 50.
[5] Ibid. pp. 50, 51.                        [6] Ibid. pp. 57, 58.
[7] Abfall der Niederlande in Schiller's Werke, Band viii. Seite 66, Stuttgart, 1838.
[8] See Leycester Correspondence, p. 94.
[9] Italian Relation of England, Camden Soc. vol. xxvii. p. 25.
[10] Die Römischen Päpste, Berlin, 1838, Band i. Seite 394.          [11] Ibid. p. 489.

years, and so farther or nearer London more or less years.   He also told us that he hath heard his father say, that in his time it was so rare for a country gentleman to come to London, that when he did come, he used to make his will before he set out." [1] The porter's lodge was used in 1669 for whipping.[2]

Weld [3] says that two of the secretaries of state in the reign of Charles II., Sir Leoline Jenkins and Sir Joseph Williamson, "had both been tutors."

Combe [4] says that the sons of young parents are generally born with feeble brains; and the eldest son of a noble family has generally less intellect than his brothers.  This, of course, is an argument against primogeniture.  It cannot be concealed that the aristocracy, though, like every other class, improving, have not maintained their relative superiority to the great body of the people.  Adam Smith defended aristocracy on the ground that it is necessary for men to be led by *external* marks; but now the progress of education enables men to perceive *internal* merit.[5] In 1695, Evelyn [6] says: "Never were so many private bills for unsettling estates, showing the wonderful prodigality and decay of families."

Alison [7] says that a great misfortune in France was the title going to *all* the children, which prevented a *fusion* between the nobles and people.

Sir William Temple,[8] about the middle of the reign of Charles II., says, " I think I remember within less than fifty years the first noble families that married into the city for downright money."  The spirit of their miserable etiquette has reached its height in China.  Early in the seventeenth century, when the aristocratic power began to revive in Rome, the custom was introduced of a person stopping his carriage on meeting one of superior rank.[9]  In Sweden, there is a great passion for titles and personal decorations among the middle classes; and this has lowered their moral standard.[10]  Tocqueville [11] says that no nation ever *created within itself* an aristocracy; but that all aristocracies are the result of conquest.  The power of the French nobles was so great that Richelieu was accused of a "monstrous abuse of authority" in declaring war against their consent.[12]

[1] Pepys's Diary, 8vo, 1828, vol. iv. pp. 319, 320.          [2] Ibid. p. 328.
[3] History of the Royal Society, 8vo, 1848, vol. i. p. 263.
[4] Lectures on Moral Philosophy, 8vo, 1840, p. 115.          [5] Ibid. p. 379.
[6] Diary, vol. iii. p. 341.                    [7] History of Europe, vol. i. p. 100.
[8] Works, 8vo, 1814, vol. iii. p. 59.
[9] Ranke, Die Römischen Papste, Band iii. Seiten 63, 64.
[10] See Laing's Sweden, pp. 64, 65, 117-121.
[11] Démocratie en Amérique, tome iii. p. 260.
[12] St. Aulaire, Histoire de la Fronde, tome i. p. 10.

Aristocracy, I think, passes through the different stages of *strength, age, birth, wealth,* and *intellect.* Of strength, when men have no knowledge ; of age, when, there being no science, all knowledge is *empirical,* and experience everything ; of birth, when the accumulation of wealth or conquest raise a few families above the others.

There are hardly any really old aristocratic families in Europe.[1]

It has been shown from decisive evidence that the shortest-lived classes are kings, then nobles, then " gentry," then " professional persons "—particularly " clergy " ; while the longest lives of all are agriculturists.[2] The marriages of the aristocracy are very unfruitful.[3] The North American Indians have a remarkable respect for old people.[4] As the division of labour arose, there sprung up professions, and it was soon seen that *they* were not hereditary, and that men are not born great lawyers or good physicians. In Letters from the Baltic, 8vo, 1841, vol. ii. p. 134, it is said of the Estonians, that they pay attention solely to *birth,* and " that none of that undue preference is given to wealth, as in countries more advanced," ii. p. 134 ; and at p. 139 the authoress says : " In Russia, no one may advance in the military service, in Estonia, no one may purchase an estate, and in Weimar, no one may enter the theatre by a particular door, who has not a *de* prefixed to his name." Forbes says :[5] " I can with pleasure and with truth record that the generality of Indians, of whatever religious profession, whether Hindoos, Mahomedans, or Parsees, pay a great respect and deference to age ; the hoary head is by them considered a ' crown of glory.' " " Marriages under the age of twenty " have bad physical results.[6] Intermarriage between relatives causes congenital deafness.[7]

In the agreement between the Scotch and the duke of Norfolk in 1559, the duke has himself entitled " the noble and mighty *prince,* Thomas, duke of Norfolk."[8] The duke of Norfolk *before* his arrest assumed a high and almost independent [style]. See his Letters in Haynes's State Papers, pp. 299, 442. In January 1562, the queen's treatment of the earl and countess of Hertford

---

[1] Journal of the Statistical Society, vol. ii. p. 463.
[2] Ibid. vol. viii. pp. 73, 74, 76, 77, 306 ; vol. ix. pp. 41–43, 45, 47, 49 ; vol. x. p. 65 ; vol. xiii. pp. 313, 314, 315, 320 ; vol. xiv. p. 295.
[3] Ibid. vol. xiv. p. 79.
[4] See Buchanan's North American Indians, 8vo. 1824, pp. 71, 72.
[5] Oriental Memoirs, vol. i. p. 132.
[6] Transactions of Association for Social Science, 1859, pp. 506, 507.
[7] Ibid. pp. 544, 545.
[8] Haynes's State Papers, p. 253.

seems to have caused great discontent in London.[1]  In 1570, the duke of Norfolk was in debt.[2]

Elizabeth, immediately after her accession, appointed eight new councillors, of whom two only were men of rank, the Marquis of Northampton and the Earl of Bedford; the others were Sir Thomas Parry, Sir Edward Rogers, Sir Ambrose Cave, Sir Francis Knolles, Sir Nicholas Bacon, and Sir W. Cecil.  In 1561, she threw the earl of Hertford into the Tower because he married without her consent.  Another means by which the queen weakened the aristocracy was by her expensive visits.  Hume[3] quotes Life of Burghley, published by Collins, p. 40, to the effect that each visit she made to Burghley "cost him two or three thousand pounds."

Mary's desire to gratify the nobility was so great that it even conquered her superstition, and induced her to consent that they should not be disturbed in their possession of the church property they had acquired during the reign of Henry VIII.  That this was her reason we know from Ambassades de Noailles, iv. 36.

In September, 1571, the duke of Norfolk was thrown into the Tower "without any trouble save a number of idle rascal people, women, men, boys, and girls, running about him, as the manner is, gazing at him";[4] but what I suppose was his first arrest in 1569 very much displeased the Londoners;[5] and in 1571, he writes[6] that even the Londoners, *though they disliked him*, ran from all parts to salute him as he was going to the Tower, and censured government for arresting him.  The consequence was that the greatest precautions were used in the capital by reinforcing the watch, &c.[7]  In January, 1572, the French ambassador writes from London to his court that when the duke of Norfolk was tried, the guards were doubled at the palace, the streets lined with troops, and the prisoner himself taken to Westminster by water on account of "grande crainte de sédition par la ville."[8]

The queen several times countermanded the execution of the duke of Norfolk.[9]  This was perhaps from a fear of a rising among his dependents.

In 1585, Morgan writes to Mary of Scotland to the effect that the great families in the north of England had received "a great check" by the appointment of Sir A. Paulet as her keeper.[10]

The aristocracy, by the coolness of Elizabeth, were driven back

[1] Haynes's State Papers, p. 396.
[2] Appendix to Elizabeth, No. III.
[3] Correspondance de Fénelon, tome ii. p. 278.
[4] Ibid. p. 262.
[5] See Murdin's State Papers, p. 177.
[6] Ibid. p. 597.
[7] Murdin, p. 149.
[8] Ibid. tome iv. p. 235.
[9] Ibid. p. 346.
[10] Ibid. p. 445.

to the bosom of the church, which, in the hope of securing her favour, some of them had quitted. In March, 1586, Morgan writes to Mary of Scotland: " The earl of Arundel is now a sound Catholic, and his affliction which followed in short time after his reconciliation to the Catholic church had without doubt done him infinite good."[1]

In 1588, a colonel in the army, if " a nobleman," received 20s. a day; if he were only " a knight, or nobleman's son," he received 13s. 4d.[2]

In 1548, Sharington said that the admiral (brother to the Protector) had stated that " he could make or bring of those which be within his rules, and of his own tenants and servants, if he should be commanded to serve, ten thousand men."[3] This must be an exaggeration. In a list of instructions drawn up just after the accession of Mary, we find: " To remember the lords at London, to send away the greater part of their train."[4]

In January, 1575, the French ambassador writes to his court that the earl of Oxford was very much suspected by Elizabeth.[5]

Mary, unlike Elizabeth, discouraged the aristocracy from coming to London. This part of her policy is noticed by the French ambassador.[6] She even, on the apprehension of an insurrection ordered them to assemble their retainers in the country.[7]

Mary courted the aristocracy in order to induce them to consent to her marriage with Philip. This is noticed as her object in Ambassades de Noailles, Leyde, 1762, tome ii. p. 272. See also p. 287, and tome iii. p. 147.

Even before the rebellion of 1659 broke out, the Catholic nobility assured the French ambassador of their favourable inclination towards France.[8] This is the more observable, because at this juncture the French cabinet assumed a very hostile attitude, and made Elizabeth apprehensive of a combination of France and Spain against her.[9] The French government had just gained a victory over the Huguenots. This encouraged the English Catholics to persevere. A month before the northern rebellion broke out, the French ambassador at London writes to his court: " Les protestans de ce royaulme ont faict tenir quelques jours la nouvelle de vostre victoire si secrecte, ou bien l'ont faicte aller si deguysée, que n'en poulvant les Catholiques avoir quasi

[1] Murdin's State Papers, p. 489.
[2] Ibid. p. 615.
[3] Haynes's State Papers, p. 106.
[4] Ibid. p. 192.
[5] See Correspondance Diplomatique de Fénelon, tome vi. p. 361.
[6] See Ambassades de Noailles, Leyde, 1763, tome ii. p. 110; tome iii. p. 30.
[7] Ibid. tome v. p. 321.
[8] Correspondance Diplomatique de Fénelon, Paris, 1840, tome i. pp. 231, 333.
[9] Ibid. pp. 117, 118, 209, 217.

aulcune notice, ilz ont envoyé devers moi bien fort secrectement, mais non sans ardeur et affection, pour sçavoir ce qui en estoit." [1] The whole of Fénelon's sixty-eighth dispatch affords too many proofs of the unpatriotic feelings of the English Catholics.[2] But the reader must not fall into the vulgar error of ascribing this to their religion. If the Catholics had been in possession of the government, the Protestants would have acted the same disgraceful part.

In 1536, when Henry VIII. was at the very height of his power, the duke of Norfolk wrote to him that it was necessary that the northern borders of England should be governed by " some man of great nobility"; and his council not only confirmed this, but added that " his majesty could not be served upon his marches but by noblemen."[3]

While matters were thus tending to the consolidation of a system (Primogeniture) which, if it had been fully established, would have thrown all power into the hands of a few families, and converted England into an oligarchy, there was fortunately an influence at work which saved the nation. This was the clerical power. It is obvious that such a system was entirely opposed to its genius. The Catholics, with a wisdom which we cannot sufficiently admire, had at an early period established the celibacy of the clergy. This, indeed, was consistent with the whole course of their policy. The church, being essentially a moral power, could only hope to maintain itself by precluding the possibility of its functions becoming hereditary, which, by making their exercise the result of the accident of birth, would have degraded the hierarchy to the level of that stupid aristocracy by which it was surrounded. It was therefore with great alarm that the ecclesiastical power now saw the rise of a principle so antagonistic to their own policy.

The earl of Arundel had been one of the negotiators of the peace of Château Cambresis ; but he, in 1564, was confined to his own house.[4]  In 1569, there was a quarrel between Cecil and the duke of Norfolk.[5]

The aristocracy, repressed by Henry VII. and Henry VIII., rose in arms against Edward VI. and his uncle. In October, 1549, Lord Russell and Sir William Herbert write to the Protector

[1] Correspondance Diplomatique de Fénelon, tome ii. p. 296.
[2] See also for further evidence ibid. tome iii. pp. 18, 76.
[3] See the two very curious letters in the Hardwicke State Papers, vol. i. pp. 39–43.
[4] See Wright's Elizabeth, vol. i. p. 180.
[5] See Lodge's Illustrations of British History, 1838, vol. i. pp. 475–477.

Somerset respecting " the civil dissension which has happened between your grace and the nobility." [1]

In 1553–54, Renard, in a letter to Charles V., speaking of the English. mentions " the intestine hatred between the nobility and the people." [2]

## LAWS OF PRIMOGENITURE.

AMONG the various circumstances by which the great landed proprietors had endeavoured to secure their power, and perpetuate it in their own families, the laws of primogeniture and entail occupy a conspicuous place. The economical evil of these laws will be hereafter considered; at present, I shall merely give a view of their history, and particularly of the attempts which have been made to evade their operation.

When the whole fabric of European society was broken up by the dissolution of the Western Empire, there was introduced into Europe a system which was regardless, and indeed ignorant, of the refined wisdom of the civil code, and was only adapted to the barbarians who enacted it. In such a state of society as then existed, money being almost unknown, and trade, manufactures, and commerce being entirely unknown, land was not merely the sole wealth, but it was the sole source of power, and even of security. Those who found themselves possessed of it immediately (?) endeavoured to strike out some mode by which at their death the whole of it should be retained intact. Hence the law of primogeniture. And as it was found advisable to check the extravagance of the heir, a contrivance was hit upon to prevent him from alienating the estate which had descended to him. This contrivance was the law of entail. How much of these laws was known to our Saxon ancestors it is difficult from the fewness of existing documents satisfactorily to determine; but it is certain that the statute known as *De Donis* was the first formal recognition of them in England.

See Blackstone, 8vo, 1809, ii. 116–119. He says that the statute De Donis, though an admitted nuisance, was allowed to be unchecked nearly 200 years till 12 Edw. IV., when it was first determined by the court in Taltarune's case " that a common recovery suffered by tenant in tail should be an effectual destruction thereof. Year Book, 12 Edw. IV. 14, 19." The next step was the 32 Henry VIII. c. 36, " which declares a fine duly levied

[1] Tytler's Edward VI. and Mary, vol. i. p. 217.        [2] Ibid. 1839, vol. ii. p. 136.

by tenant in tail to be a complete bar to him and his heirs, and all other persons claiming under such entail."

In England, the declining power of the sovereign enabled the aristocracy to introduce primogeniture. By the laws of Henry I. the eldest son had only the best of his father's feuds ;[1] and even in the reign of Henry II. Glanville says that "soccage estates frequently descended to all the sons equally ; " but, under Henry III., "we find by Bracton that soccage land, in imitation of land in chivalry, had almost entirely fallen into the right of succession by primogeniture."[2] But see vol. ii. pp. 287–290, where it is said that before a law of Henry I., no man could sell lands he had himself purchased ; and even by that law he could not alienate those that had descended to him. But by *Quia Emptores*, 18 Edw. I., "all persons, except the king's tenant in capite, were allowed to alienate *all* or any part of their lands; and by 1 Edw. III. even these tenants could aliene by paying a fine to the king."

As to the *Statute of Fines*—4 Hen. VII.—about which so much has been said, it is merely a copy from a statute of Richard III. So much for the policy of Henry VII.! See Hallam's Const. History, 1842, i. 11. Mr. Hallam adds, pp. 12, 13 (on the authority of Reeves' English Law, iv. 133), that the object of this statute was not to give tenant-in-tail a greater power over his estate, but rather to check suits for the recovery of lands by establishing a short term of prescription. Indeed, "in 2 Henry VII. the judges held that the donors of an estate tail might restrain the tenant from suffering a recovery."

The mischiefs of such a law were not likely to be generally perceived ; but, when men began to inquire as well as to observe, means were adopted to evade it. These means were taken from the civil law. Fines and recoveries. The operation of fines had gradually become very cumbersome and expensive. The proclamations upon them are so numerous that no less than sixteen days in every term were occupied in making them ;[3] but the 31 Eliz. c. 2 ordered that the fines should only be proclaimed four times.[4] In the system of ecclesiastical laws which Cranmer drew up in 1552, a father is not allowed to disinherit his son unless he has received some serious injury from him.[5]

"Before the Conquest, lands in England passed by will, that having been the custom of the Anglo-Saxons and Danes, as of the

[1] Blackstone, vol. ii. p. 214.　　　　　[2] Ibid. pp. 215, 216.
[3] This is stated in 31 Eliz. c. 2, in Reeves' English Law, vol. v. p. 94.　　　[4] Ibid.
[5] Soames' History of the Reformation of the Church of England, vol. iii. pp. 718, 719.

Romans, though not of the Germans." [1]  He adds,[2] "the custom
of gavelkind existed in Ireland till it was put down by a decision
of the judges, 3 Jac. I.; and in North Wales till the Stat. 34
Hen. VIII." On the mischievous effect of primogeniture, see
vol. i. p. 320. At vol. i. p. 360, Brougham ascribes its origin to
"the influence of the monarchical principle, especially when combined with aristocracy." He adds[3] that entails were introduced
under the empire, but "Justinian confined them early in the
sixth century to four descents." In England "the law of entail
dates from 1285;" and the introduction of entails seems to have
followed the establishment of the power of alienation.

Examine the History of Borough English. Montesquieu says [4]
that in Tartary, in Brittany, and the Duchy of Rohan, the
youngest son inherited; and that this is a law incidental to the
pastoral state; for the elders had already left their father and
taken cattle with them, the youngest son only remaining at home.
In 1721, Montesquieu enters his protest against "l'injuste droit
d'aînesse."[5] In France the division of lands, so far from increasing, has actually diminished relatively to the population.[6]

It was to improve the security of these important portions of
the law that Elizabeth now directed her attention. In the twenty-
third year of her reign a law was passed ordering that no recovery
nor fine should be reversed on account of any rasure, or incon-
gruous Latin, or indeed for any want of form or words. It was
also ordered that every writ upon which common recoveries should
be suffered might at the desire of any person be enrolled in
Parliament, and kept in an office called the Office of Inrolment.[7]

The judges, mostly consisting of men who had an interest in
depressing the aristocracy (?), vigorously seconded the policy of
Elizabeth, and baffled all the attempts made by the great landed
proprietors to break down the principles which had been established.

In the same way when attempts were made to limit estates by
a proviso in a deed, the courts again interposed, and refused to
allow the limitation. In 42 Elizabeth it was decided in Corbet's
case that "a proviso to cease an estate tail, as if the tenant-in-
tail were dead, was repugnant, impossible, and against law; for
the death of tenant-in-tail was no cesser, but only his death with-

[1] Brougham's Political Philosophy, 2nd edit. 8vo. 1849, vol. i. p. 285.
[2] Ibid. p. 286.                            [3] Ibid. p. 361.
[4] Esprit des Lois, livre xviii. chap. 21, Œuvres, Paris, 1835, p. 331.
[5] Lettres Persanes, No. cxx. Œuvres de Montesquieu, p. 81.
[6] Journal of Statistical Society, vol. vi. pp. 192, 193, 196.
[7] Reeves, History of English Law, vol. v. pp. 52, 53.

out issue." [1]  Reeves says that the object of the courts was to prevent perpetuities.  This is perhaps the same case as that given by
Dyer, 351, and 1 Rep. 83,[2] where it was decided that, "To make
an estate limited to one and the heirs male of his body to cease,
as if he was naturally dead on his attempting any act by which
the limitation of the land or the estate in tail should be barred, is
not good."  It was also determined, I. Vent. 21, in Tomlin, *in
voce* Proviso (but *when?*) that in the case of a testator who devised lands to a man and the heirs male of his body, such attempt
to cease if he attempted to alien, the proviso was void.  But in
Elizabeth's reign provisos were *not* illegal in wills.[3]

The interpretation of the Statute of User was equally unfavourable to the landed proprietors.  The scholastic refinements on the
construction of that statute had been so numerous as to involve
the doctrine of uses in an almost endless labyrinth of complications.

.        .        .        .        .        .        .

The judges expressed in the strongest language their dislike to
the principle of perpetuity involved in the attempt to preserve
contingent uses.  They did not hesitate to say from their place on
the judgment bench, that, sooner than give their sanction to such
perpetuities, they would, if there had been any doubt as to the
law of this case, have grounded their decision upon the broad
ground of public expediency.[4]  Bacon put forth all his powers on
this occasion against the contingent use.[5]  This was a decision of
the greatest importance, and Reeves says: "This case became
afterwards a leading decision, not only in uses, but on all contingent limitations." [6]

In the 4 Hen. VII. it had been declared by statute that a fine
should be a bar against all claimants, unless they made claim by
way of action or lawful entry within five years ; and in the 32nd
of Henry VIII. this provision was extended so as to bar estates
tail.[7]  The great landed proprietors, unable to evade the law, endeavoured to lighten its pressure ; and laid down that if the five
years had commenced, and on the death of the ancestor the right
descended to the infant, such infant should, within five years after
he came of age, be allowed to claim the estate.[8]  Only three
years after the accession of Elizabeth this point was mooted in

---

[1] Reeves's History of English Law, vol. v. pp. 75, 77, 78.
[2] Quoted in Tomlin's Law Dict. in v. Proviso.
[3] See Reeves, English Law, vol. v. p. 78.
[4] See the remarkable passage in Reeves, vol. v. pp. 167, 168.  See also p. 194.
[5] P. 195.              [6] History of English Law, vol. v. p. 202.
[7] Tomlin's Law Dictionary, vol. i. 3 z.        [8] Reeves, English Law, vol. v. p. 53.

the great case of Stowell and Zouch, when it was decided that the infant should be barred. This case was reported by Plowden, and a very lucid abstract may be found in Reeves' English Law, v. 53–62.

The last great stronghold of the defenders of perpetuities was the provisos allowed to be inserted in "executory devises" (?). Our law had always paid a great respect to bequests; and under their shelter attempts were made to secure perpetuities. Indeed, in the 13th of Elizabeth, it was settled in the Common Pleas "that a tenant-in-tail might be restrained from alienation by the original donation." [1] But when, twenty-four years later, a similar case was brought up before the same court, a conference was held with the other judges, and it was unanimously determined that such proviso was void.[2] About the same time, the same decision was given in a similar case in the Court of Common Pleas.[3] However, in the case of Brett v. Rigden, which was a case of devise of land in 10 Eliz., it was decided that it was absolutely necessary that there should be a donec in esse capable to take the thing the moment it verted.[4]

---

## REMARKS ON THE POOR LAWS.

· · · · · · ·

MARRIAGES were made very early. In 1599, the celebrated Dr. Forman married a girl of sixteen.[5] In a lawless age, marriages are naturally early to avoid the risks of abduction. The feudal system too encouraged early marriages by making the hand of a rich ward a *property*. Even Montesquieu [6] says : " De tout ceci, il faut conclure que l'Europe est encore aujourd'hui dans le cas d'avoir besoin de lois qui favorisent la propagation de l'espèce humaine." But while population was thus outstripping capital there grew up a strange idea that a precisely opposite process was going on, and that it was necessary to encourage marriages. I believe this notion lingered till the time of Malthus. Montesquieu adopts it in his youthful work,[7] and also in his great work, the Esprit de Lois. Montesquieu notices the stimulus given to population by doing away with the celibacy of the clergy.[8]

---

[1] Reeves, vol. v. p. 168, who quotes Plowden, p. 408.
[2] Moore, p. 364, in Reeves, English Law, vol. v. p. 171.
[3] Ibid. p. 592, in Reeves, vol. v. p. 172.
[4] Plowden, p. 341, in Reeves, vol. v. pp. 73, 74.
[5] See Autobiography of Dr. Forman, edit. Halliwell, 1849, p. 30.
[6] Esprit des Lois, livre xxiii. chap. vi. Œuvres, Paris, 1835, p. 404
[7] Lettres Persanes, No. cxiii. pp. 75, 76.
[8] Ibid. No. cxviii. Œuvres, Paris, 1835, p. 80.

I have thus stated a few of the most obvious circumstances which paved the way to the depression of the people and the increase of the poor. But there is yet another cause, which, though less obvious, is more important than any I have stated, which is in full operation at the present moment, and which, as it seems likely to become more efficient, is almost the only real inconvenience which man has sustained in passing from barbarism to civilization.

The feelings and passions of the mind, which are so complicated in their first appearance, are still more complicated in their ultimate effects. Thus, the advance of general benevolence, which is perhaps one of the most unerring tests of civilization, has produced one serious mischief,—I allude to the establishment of foundling hospitals. To provide for those who are left destitute by no fault of their own, and who are utterly unable to provide for themselves, is a labour so soothing to our sympathies that it may appear a refined political paradox to point out its inconveniences. And yet those inconveniences are great and permanent. The love of a mother for her offspring is one of those feelings which not only ennoble our common nature, but which forms one of the most certain protections to the whole of an organised society. The establishment of foundling hospitals, by removing the apprehensions of a mother as to the fate of her child, is a direct incentive to bastardy and to concubinage. This is evident on a mere view of the nature of things, and is supported by the most decisive statistical evidence.

M. Quetelet suggests [1] that the religious ceremonies performed in Catholic countries at the bedside of a patient may often accelerate or even cause his death. If this is true, the mortality must be greater in Catholic than in Protestant countries.

In Alison's Principles of Population, 8vo, 1840, there are some singularly superficial remarks upon the poor laws and population. See, for instance, vol. i. p. 36, where he quite forgets the necessity of cultivating inferior soils. He says [2] with truth that artisans and men engaged in commerce must be fed by the labours of agriculturists; hence he supposes that the increase of trade and commerce in England is a proof that productiveness is gaining ground upon population; and he adds [3] that the same thing is shown by the low interest of money. He charitably says [4] that the attacks made on the poor laws proceed from the vexation of the selfish at being *obliged* to contribute towards the support of the

---

[1] Sur l'Homme, tome, i. p. 229.     [2] Principles of Population, vol. i. pp. 58, 59.
[3] P. 63.     [4] Vol. ii. p. 190.

poor. Alison, who has had good opportunities of observing, says that the poorer the labouring classes are, the greater the number of their marriages.[1]  Amid all this nonsense, Alison has *one* good remark.  He says that, while slavery existed, the land-lords were obliged to feed their slaves; but when that was done away with, it was necessary for government to feed them, *hence* poor laws; and, while in Russia, Poland, Hungary, and Moravia there are no poor laws (because the poor, being the *property* of their masters, have a claim on them), yet we find them in every civilized country, in England, Scotland, France, Flanders, Austria, Prussia, Switzerland, and Norway.[2]

## HISTORY OF PRICES.

In 1569, military horsemen paid "one penny a meale, and one penny night and day for haye."[3]  At pp. 333, 334, of Sharp's Memorials of the Rebellion, is a list of the expenses incurred in 1571 and 1572 for the earl of Northumberland.  Among them is, "for iij post-horses from Alnwick to Morpeth, 3s. 4d.," and the same from Morpeth to Newcastle, and from Newcastle to Durham. Mention is made in 1560 of "the ordynarye bordes heare at vid. the meale."[4]  This seems to have been at one of the towns of the north of England; but Sir C. Sharp does not say which.

Jacob[5] has published the contract prices at the Royal Hospital at Chelsea for 1730 to 1732, and 1791 to 1793, both inclusive, by which it appears "that, in the sixty years, the advance on bread, beef, mutton, cheese, and butter had been at the rate of 20 per cent.; that on pease and oatmeal more, and that on coals still more.[6]

In Woodchurch church, Cheshire, there is "suspended a large table, containing a list of the benefactors to the parish," in which "appears the name of James Goodier, of Barnstow, who gave 20 marks in 1525 to buy 20 yoke of bullocks for the poor of the parish, afterwards set apart for the purchase of cows, to be hired out to the poor at 2s. 8d. per annum."[7]

Early in the sixteenth century, Goodman's Fields had a farm, at which Stow, when a young man, used to buy milk, "three ale pints for a halfpenny in the summer, nor less than one ale quart

---

[1] Alison's Principles of Population, 8vo, 1840, vol. ii. pp. 206-214.
[2] Ibid. pp. 170-175.
[3] Sharp's Memorials of the Rebellion, 8vo, 1840, p. 24.            [4] Ibid. p. 378.
[5] History of the Precious Metals, vol. iii. p. 393.            [6] Jacob, vol. ii. p. 219.
[7] Ormerod's History of Cheshire, 1819, vol. ii. p. 288.

for a halfpenny in the winter." [1] In 1533, it was ordered in London that beef should be sold for a halfpenny, and mutton for a halfpenny farthing a pound, very much to the displeasure of Stow, who says that before that time the price of beef was 1*d.* for 3 lbs.; a fat ox, 26s. 8*d.*; a fat wether, 3s. 4*d.*; a fat calf, the same; and a fat lamb, 12*d.*[2] In 1547, the price of Malmsey wine was one penny halfpenny the pint.[3] At the beginning of the sixteenth century, the price of soap varied in London from $\frac{3}{4}$*d.* to 1$\frac{1}{4}$*d.* the pound.[4] In 1531, Stow gives a list of prices in London: a "great beef," 26s. 8*d.*; "carcass of an ox," 24s.; and a "fat mutton," 2s. 10*d.*; a "great veal," 4s. 8*d.*; pigeons, 10*d.* a dozen.[5] The rise of prices is noticed in a proclamation by Elizabeth in 1560;[6] but is solely ascribed to the depreciation of the currency. In Stafford's Brief Conceipt of English Policy, published in 1581, the rise of prices is frequently mentioned.[7] Of labourers, we are told : "All things are so dear that by their day wages they are not able to live";[8] and[9] "such of us as do abide in the country still cannot with 200*l.* a year keep that house that we might have done with 200 marks but sixteen years past." Again : "I have seen a cap for 13*d.* as good as I can get now for 2s. 6*d.*; of cloth, ye have heard how the price is risen. Now a pair of shoes cost 12*d.*, yet in my time I have bought a better for 6*d.* Now I can never get a horse shooed under 10*d.* or 12*d.*, where I have also seen the common price was 6*d.*"[10] He says[11] that within thirty years the price of "the best pig or goose that I could lay my hand on" had risen from 4*d.* to 12*d.*; that a good capon, which could then have been purchased for 3*d.* to 4*d.*, had doubled or trebled in price; and that the same proportional rise had taken place in hens, which had been 2*d.* each, and chickens, which had been 1*d.* each. He adds[12] that a man with 300*l.* a year could scarcely live so well as his father would have done on 200*l.* a year. Dekker notices the rise in prices, but ascribes it to the increase of population.[13] In Giffard's Dialogue concerning Witches,[14] one of the speakers says of a friend of his : "He lost six hogs, he would not have took fifteen shillings a hog for them"; and[15] we hear of a "gelding worth ten pounds." Croke, in his will, dated 1554, says: "I bequeath to every

[1] Stow's London, edit. Thoms, 8vo, 1842, p. 48.
[2] Survey of London, 8vo, 1842, p. 71.          [3] Ibid. p. 90.
[4] Ibid. p. 94.                                   [5] Ibid. p. 145.
[6] See it in Harleian Miscellany, edit. Park, vol. viii. pp. 68–71.
[7] See it in vol. ix. of Harleian Miscellany.     [8] P. 147.       [9] P. 149.
[10] P. 154.              [11] P. 156.              [12] P. 173.
[13] A Knight's Conjuring, 1607, p. 39, Percy Society, vol. v.
[14] 1603, Percy Society, vol. viii. p. 9.          [15] At p. 19.

of my servants, men and women, a black livery at 7*s*. or 8*s*. the yard, the men to have coats, the women gowns." See Documents relating to the Croke Family, p. 63 in Percy Soc., vol. xi. At p. 64, we hear of black gowns at 10*s*. the yard. In 1573, "the hire of two hacknies from Sittingbourne to Canterbury" was 4*s*.; from Rochester to Sittingbourne, the same; and, from Canterbury to Gravesend, also for two hacknies, 10*s*.[1] In 1576, the hire of a horse was from 18*d*. to 20*d*. a day;[2] but in 1582 it had advanced to 2*s*. See at p. 183, four entries for that amount. In 1573 flannel was 9*d*. a yard.[3] In 1578 "cotten candles" were 4*d*. a pound, and "cearing candle" 12*d*.;[4] and in 1580 "cotten candells" were 4*d*. a pound.[5] In 1574 coals were 8*d*. "the sack,"[6] and in 1576 they were 9*d*.,[7] and the same price in 1578.[8] In 1580 they had risen to 10$\frac{1}{2}$*d*.,[9] and in 1580 they were 1*s*.,[10] and also in 1581 they were 1*s*.[11] In 1573 they were 22*s*. a load.;[12] in 1580 they were 26*s*.;[13] but in 1581 they were only 18*s*.[14] In 1586 Charles Paget writes from Paris to Mary of Scotland that "everything is excessive dear." See Murdin's State Papers, p. 507, and again at p. 540, "all things being unreasonable dear."

The French Ambassador, in a letter to his own court written at London in May 1574, complains bitterly of the dearness of everything; and that in one year the price of all provisions had risen 50 per cent., and some 100 per cent.;[15] but the context shows that the French Ambassador was afraid that the French court would cut down his salary. Early in Elizabeth's reign the usual allowance to ambassadors for their diet was 3*l*. 6*s*. 8*d*. a day.[16] In 1586, provisions at "Margat, in Kent," were much dearer than in London.[17] In 1469 the price of the best sheep in Nottinghamshire was something above 13*d*. each.[18] In 1481, "fat oxen" cost 18*s*. each.[19] In the Rutland Papers[20] there is a curious list of articles with their prices in 1521. "Bieffes" are 40*s*., "muttons" 5*s*., "veales" 5*s*., "hogges" 8*s*. In 1516, the price of lead was from 4*l*. to 4*l*. 6*s*. a fother; the fother was 2000 pounds.[21] In

---

[1] See p. 45 of Mr. Cunningham's very valuable Extracts from the Accounts of the Revels at Court, Shakesp. Soc., 8vo, 1842.

[2] See several entries at pp. 111, 112 of Cunningham's Revels.

[3] See Cunningham's Revels, p. 54.    [4] Pp. 131, 132, 144.

[5] P. 157.    [6] P. 87.    [7] P. 119.    [8] P. 124.    [9] P. 166.

[10] P. 164.    [11] P. 174.    [12] See two entries at pp. 63, 70.

[13] Pp. 157, 158, 171.    [14] P. 180, and another entry at p. 181.

[15] Correspondance de Fénelon, Paris, 1840, tome vi. p. 119.

[16] See Wright's Elizabeth, 8vo, 1838, vol. i. p. 449.

[17] See Leycester Correspondence, Camden Society, p. 51.

[18] See Plumpton Correspondence, Camden Society, p. 21.

[19] Ibid. p. 41.    [20] Camden Society, p. 41.

[21] See Lodge's Illustrations of British History, 1838, vol. i. pp. 20, 29.

1575, at Rouen, diaper cost 8*s*. 2*d*. the ell; and "whited canvass" 3*s*. 5*d*. the ell.[1] In 1575, Ralph Barber, who seems to have been a commissioner or merchant, enters in his accounts, "Two shirts for my man at 3*s*. 4*d*. a piece."[2] In the same year, he puts down 16*d*. per week for three weeks "for my horse grass at Rye."[3] In 1548, candles cost 2*d*. a pound.[4] In 1548 (?) "muttons" cost 5*s*. a piece.[5] In 1593, the provisions necessary for the Royal Household were contracted for at fixed prices.[5] " Fat and great veals of the age of six weeks and upwards 6*s*. 8*d*. a piece; fat and good lambs 12*d*. each; capons 4*s*. a dozen; hens 2*s*. a dozen; pullets 18*d*. a dozen; geese 4*s*. a dozen; and chickens 1*s*. the dozen."[6] See also at pp. 276, 277, a letter in which Elizabeth's fishmonger proposes to Sir William More to buy some of More's carp for which he offers 12*d*. to 18*d*. each. In 1556, coals cost 16*s*. the load.[7] In 1552, a proclamation was issued commanding all butchers in London to sell " beef, mutton, and veal, the best, 1½*d*. the pound, and necks and legs at ¾*d*. the pound, and the best lamb the quarter 8*d*.[8] In 1553, three tuns of beer cost together 3*l*. 1*s*. 8*d*.; a quarter of beef, weighing 110 pounds, cost 9*s*. 2*d*.; a side of beef, weighing 145 pounds, cost 12*s*. 1*d*.; " a veal, 4*s*.; half a veal, 2*s*. 4*d*.; two muttons, 9*s*. 4*d*."[5] In 1621, the price of everything was low, except corn.[10] The rise of prices is noticed in a letter from Hooper to Cecil in 1551.[11] He says[12] that " the body of a calf is in the market, 14*s*.; the carcass of a sheep at 10*s*." See also[13] a paper on the " Causes of the Universal Dearth in England," dated 1551, in which it is said[14] " The purveyor alloweth for a lamb worth 2*s*., but 12*d*.; for a capon worth 12*d*., 6*d*.; and so after that rate." In 1775, Captain Topham writes from Edinburgh, " the necessaries of life are almost as dear as in London."[15] In 1550, Sir John Mason writes from Paris to the English Council; " It is a marvelous thing to see the dearth of this country. I assure your lordship that all kinds of victuals bear double the price of what they do in England."[16] See also[17] the complaint in 1551 of Bishop Hooper, that in consequence of enclosures, prices even of meat had greatly risen. On

[1] See Lodge's Illustrations, vol. ii. p. 69.       [2] Ibid. p. 72.       [3] P. 71.
[4] Loseley's Manuscripts, edited by Kempe, p. 81.       [5] Ibid. p. 179.
[6] Ibid. p. 273.       [7] Ibid. p. 12.
[8] Machyn's Diary, Camden Society, vol. xlii. p. 24.
[9] Chronicle of Queen Jane and Mary, Camden Society, 1850, p. 112.
[10] Yonge's Diary, Camden Society, vol. xli. p. 52.
[11] Tytler's Edward VI. and Mary, vol. i. pp. 364–367.       [12] P. 365.
[13] At pp. 367–371.       [14] P. 369.
[15] Letters from Edinburgh, 8vo, 1776, p. 111.
[16] Tytler's Edward VI. and Mary, 8vo, 1839, vol. i. p. 298.       [17] P. 365.

the rise of prices in consequence of the discovery of America, see
Blanqui, Histoire de l'Économie politique, tome i. pp. 329, 330.
For lists of prices, see Monteil, Histoire des Français des Divers
États, tome i. pp. 145, 146, 156; tome iii. p. 41 ; tome iv. p. 43 ;
tome v. p. 216 ; tome vi. p. 240 ; tome viii. pp. 100–117.    In
Journal of Statistical Society, vol. ii. pp. 214–216, there is a
curious list of prices at Penzance, in Cornwall, from 1746 to 1813.
In Journal of Statistical Society, vol. xiii. p. 213, is stated the
interesting fact that the lower classes, both in food and dress, ask
for things of a certain price, as 3*d.* of cheese, &c., so that a rise in
price affects not their *pockets*, but their *comforts*.    In 1741, the
ordinary price of cherries at Birmingham was "a halfpenny a
pound."[1]    Keith's Church and State in Scotland, vol. ii. p. 387.

.        .        .        .        .        .        .

# HISTORY AND INFLUENCE OF THE COLONIES.

IT was not till 1607 that the English first formed a permanent
colony.  This small beginning of so great an empire was at
Jamestown in Virginia.[2]    In 1611 Moll says, "Take deliberation,
sir ; never choose a wife as if you were going to Virginia."[3]    Lord
Brougham agrees with the general opinion that democracies treat
their colonies worse than monarchies treat theirs.[4]    He truly
adds[5] that the mother country should willingly give up the
colonies, and thus part with them in a kindly spirit.    Dawson
Turner says, that the sailors of Dieppe "established a colony for
the promotion of free trade in Canada, if indeed they were not the
original discoverers of that country."[6]    Twiss[7] observes that
colonies, by creating a demand for labour, stimulate population in
the mother country.

While the domestic administration of Elizabeth had secured
internal tranquillity, her foreign administration had excited public
spirit.  The nation burned with energy.  The great Queen well
knew how to employ the spirit of her people.  Spain groaned
under the devastation of the English cruisers.  In the Atlantic,
in the Baltic, in the Mediterranean, in the Pacific, foreign flags

[1] Hutton's Life of Himself, 8vo, 1816, p. 48.
[2] McCulloch's Dictionary of Commerce, 8vo, 1849, p. 335.
[3] Middleton's Works, 8vo, 1840, vol. ii. p. 472.
[4] Brougham's Political Philosophy, 8vo, 1849, vol. i. pp. 510, 511, and vol. iii.
p. 135.                         [5] Ibid. vol. ii. p. 20.
[6] Turner's Tour in Normandy, in 2 vols. Lond., 8vo, 1820, vol. i. p. 20.
[7] Progress of Political Economy, 8vo, 1847, p. 220.

lowered their pennons to the English flag (?). Drake, Gilbert, and Raleigh extended the boundaries of geographical knowledge, and the whole nation was rife with hope. But the great Queen was gathered to her fathers, and was succeeded by a whining pedant. James I. loved peace, not from policy but from fear. It was not so much that he cherished tranquillity as that he hated enterprise. The national vigour which he would not direct against the spoliators of his daughter he was equally afraid of encouraging at home. But it was too late to repress the spirit of the nation, and the reign of James I. is the epoch of colonisation. The advantages were incalculable. On the one hand wages were kept up, which an unprecedented increase of population had seriously lowered. Besides this, we owe to the colonists the first sound principles of legislation.

\* \* \* \* \* \* \*

---

## HISTORY, ETC. OF WAGES.

THE wardrobe book of Margaret of Anjou, wife to Henry VI., extends from 1452 to 1453. By it we learn that " her herbman, or gardener, received 100s. a year ; her valet of the washing house (called *scalding* house) 40s. ; her twenty-seven armour-bearers or esquires, 143l. 4s. 4d. in all; and her twenty-seven valets 93l. 15s. 6d.[1]

In 1533, the wages of English soldiers in Calais were 8d. a day,[2] or sometimes 6d.[3] In 1541 "the board wages of a woman attending upon the late Countess of Sarum within the Tower" were paid for eighty-three weeks at 18d. a week.[4] In 1537 the maids-of-honour at the court of Anne Boleign received 10l. a year, out of which they had to provide a wardrobe and keep a maid.[5]

In 1379, the wages, in London, of labourers to clear out ditches seem to have been 5d. a day. But this was, perhaps, unusually high; and in 1519 they were also only 5d., while every " vagabond " (by which, I suppose, is meant the lowest sort of casual labourers) received "one penny the day, meat and drink."[6] In 12th of Edward II. the keeper of the King's leopards in the Tower received

---

[1] Miss Wood's Letters of Royal and Illustrious Ladies, 8vo, 1846, vol. i. p. 98.
[2] Ibid. vol. ii. p. 87.    [3] Pp. 227, 228, 307.    [4] Ibid. vol. iii. p. 94.
[5] Ibid. vol. ii. p. 314.
[6] Stow's London, edit. Thoms, 8vo, 1842, p. 8.

"three half pence a day for diet."[1]   In 14th Edward II. the
allowance fixed for prisoners in the Tower was, " a knight 2*d.* a
day, an esquire 1*d.* a day, to serve for their diet."[2]   In 1532
West, bishop of Ely, had a hundred servants " continually in his
house."   Half of them received for wages 53s. 4*d.*, the other half
40s. each yearly, besides a winter and summer dress.[3]   In 38th
Henry VIII. it was arranged between the king and the city that
" the vicar of Christ's Church was to have 26*l.* 13s. 4*d.* the year ;
the vicar of Bartholomew 13*l.* 6s. 8*d.* ; the visitor of Newgate
(being a priest) 10*l.* ; and five priests who aided in administering
the sacrament, &c., each 8*l.* ; two clerks, each 6*l.* ; and a sexton,
4*l.*[4]   In The Devil is an Ass, which was acted in 1616, Pug offers
himself as a servant without wages ; an offer which Fitzdottrel,
" a squire of Norfolk," accepts, and he says he will turn away his
other man " and save four pounds a year by that."[5]   This makes
it evident that wages of servants were 4*l.* a year, and as the scene
is laid in London, this probably applies to the metropolis.

In a curious tract in 1538, directed against the monks, it is
said : " Who is she that will set her hands to work to get three
pence a day, and may have at least twenty pence a day to sleep an
hour with a friar, a monk, or a priest ?   What is he that would
labour for a groat a day, and may have at least twelve pence a
day to be a bawd to a priest, a monk, or a friar ?"[6]   In the time of
Tusser it was estimated that one-tenth of the produce of a farm
went for rent, and another tenth for wages.[7]   It is stated in a
proclamation of Elizabeth, in 1560, that just before the reformation of the coinage, wages of soldiers and serving men were from
20s. to 20 nobles " and so upward by the yere."[8]   Money wages
did not advance in the same proportion that the value of money
fell.   In 1581, Stafford writes of labourers, " all things are so
dear that by their day wages they are not able to live "[9] and we
are told [10] that the chief sufferers in the rise of prices were those
who had " their livings and stipends rated at a certainty, as common labourers at 8*d.* a day. . . . serving men to forty shillings a
year ;" and again [11] " where 40s. a year was honest wages for a
yeoman afore this time, and 20 pence a week board wages was
sufficient, now double as much will skant bear their charge."

[1] Stow's London, edited by Thoms, 8vo, 1842, p. 19.                    [2] Ibid. p. 20.
[3] Ibid. p. 34.                     [4] Ibid. p. 119.
[5] Ben Jonson's Works, 8vo, 1816, vol. v. pp. 21, 22.
[6] Harloian's Miscellany, edited by Park, vol. ii. p. 541.
[7] See Five Hundred Points of Husbandry, edited by Mavor, 1816, pp. 195, 196.
[8] Harleian Miscellany, vol. viii. p. 70.
[9] Brief Conceipt of English Policy in Harleian Miscellany, vol. ix. p. 147.
[10] Ibid. p. 154.                     [11] Ibid. p. 174.

In a song, published in 1609, we have :

> " The serving man waiteth fro' street to street,
> With blowing his nails and beateth his feete,
> And servoth for forty shillings a yeare." [1]

In 1571 the wages of porters were 12*d.* a day ; [2] and in 1580 we find an entry, [3] under the year 1580, " the porter at 12*d.* the daye, and as moche the night." In 1584, plumbers received 16*d.* a day. [4] In 1580, " wyerdrawers " from 16*d.* to 20*d.* [5] In 1573, painters had from 20*d.* to 12*d.* ; [6] and in 1574 they are all put down at 20*d.* [7] In 1572, common carpenters 12*d.* a day ; [8] in 1573, 16*d.* [9] and 14*d.* ; [10] in 1580, 16*d.* ; [11] in 1582, also 16*d.* ; [12] and the same in 1584. [13]

In 1573-74, the wages of tailors were 20*d.*, 16*d.*, and 12*d.* a day. [14] In 1576, 12*d.* and 20*d.* ; [15] in 1577 the same ; [16] and they remained the same in 1582 and 1584. [17]

In Haynes's State Papers [18] there is an account of the expense in 1563 of the East, West, and Middle Marches, by which we learn that the soldiers and the gunners received each 6*d.* a day. The wages of household servants are put down at 6*l.* 8*s.* 4*d.* a year, [19] and " one surgeon " at 1*s.* 6*d.* a day. [20] In 1588, the surgeon still had only 1*s.* 6*d.* [21] In 1588, the wages of seamen in the queen's navy was 14*s.* a month. [22] In the 20th of Richard II., the following daily wages were paid to those who had the custody of the castle and city of Porchester. The door-keeper and one lad under him 4½*d.* ; the artilleryman, 6*d.* ; the guard, 3*d.* [23] In 1580, Dr. Dee paid a female servant, Jane, 6*s.* 8*d.* a quarter, and a nurse 10*s.* a quarter ; [24] but another woman, who perhaps was a wet nurse, received 6*s.* a month. [25] However, in 1595, he engaged a " dry nurse," who is to have " 3*l.*, her yere's wagis, and a gown cloth of russet." [26] In 1592, he writes: " Richard cam to my service, 40*s.* yearly and a livery." [27] In 1602, workmen received 18*d.* a day ; labourers, 12*d.* ; and diggers of gravel, 10*d.* ; also " cutters of berche," 10*d.* Bricklayers received 18*d.* a day. [28] In 1585,

[1] Songs of the London Prentices, edited by Mr. Mackay for the Percy Society, 8vo, 1841, p. 150.

[2] See the Revels at Court, edited by Mr. Cunningham, Shakespeare Society, 8vo, 1842, p. 2.    [3] P. 156.    [4] P. 190.    [5] P. 156.

[6] P. 69.    [7] P. 81.    [8] P. 40.    [9] P. 52.

[10] P. 69.    [11] Pp. 156, 160.    [12] P. 178.    [13] P. 190.

[14] Pp. 62, 77, 81.    [15] Pp. 102, 115.    [16] Pp. 143, 151.    [17] Pp. 178, 189.

[19] Pp. 397-401.    [18] P. 400.    [20] P. 398.

[21] Murdin's State Papers, p. 614.    [22] Ibid. p. 620.

[23] Rot. Parl. 20, Richard II. p. 2 ; 1st February quoted by Mr. Williams in the note at p. 184 of his edition of Chronicque de Richart Deux d'Angleterre, Lond. 8vo, 1846.

[24] Dee's Diary, Camden Society, vol. xix. p. 8.

[25] Pp. 15, 34, 36.    [26] P. 54.    [27] P. 40.

[28] See Sle's account in the Egerton Papers, Camden Society, p. 348.

soldiers received 8*d*. a day.[1]  In 1521, the hire of labourers was 6*d*. a day.[2]  In 1557, the English soldiers received 6*d*. a day for the infantry, and 9*d*. for the cavalry; but the council in the north proposed that, on account of the "dearth of things," they should be raised, "the footmen to 8*d*. and the horsemen to 12*d*."[3]  In 1589, it was ordered that "every soldier, at all musters and trainings, shall have, over and besides 8*d*. a day for his wages, a penny a mile for the wearing and carriage of his armour and weapon, and other furniture, so that it exceed not six miles."[4]  In 1540, the wages of painters for the king's revels were "12*d*. per diem."[5]  In 1551, we find carpenters receiving 1*d*. per hour; bricklayers the same; labourers, ½*d*. an hour; plasterers, 11*d*. a day; painters, 7*s*. 6*d*. a day.[6]  In 1548(?), Sir Thomas Cawarden paid his servants 40*s*. a year.[7]  In 1621, the labour market was in England so overstocked that many persons offered "to work for meat and drink only."[8]  In 1512, Sir Edward Howard received as admiral 10*s*. a day, and the captains 18*d*.; the men 5*s*. every lunar month for wages, and another 5*s*. for victuals.[9]  In 1541, workmen at Calais received 8*d*. a day, and the commonest labourers 6*d*.[10]  In 1841, Bishop Copleston writes to Archbishop Whately that he wishes more notice to be taken "of my speculations on the origin and occasion of the first poor laws in this country. The depreciation of money, I am persuaded, was the main cause, wages not rising with the price of provisions and other necessaries."[11]  In 1686, there was such jobbing in Ireland that, though the king allowed 6*d*. a day, the soldiers had only 2*d*. to live upon.[12]  In 1705, the common wages of a labourer were 9*s*. a week; those of a tile-maker 16*s*. to 20*s*.[13]  In 1676, at Montpellier, "wages for men 12 sous, for women 5 sous at this time" (in January); "in summer, about harvest, 18 for men and 7 for women;"[14] and in the Grave country, in 1678, peasants received 7 sous a day.[15]  In 1680, the English silkweavers received

[1]  See Leycester Correspondence, Camden Society, p. 27.
[2]  Rutland Papers, edit. Camden Society, p. 42.
[3]  Lodge's Illustrations of British History, 1838, vol. i. p. 323.  See also p. 330.
[4]  Ibid. vol. ii. p. 403.        [5]  Loseley Manuscripts, by Kempe, 1835, p. 70.
[6]  Ibid. p. 96.        [7]  Ibid. p. 179.
[8]  Yonge's Diary, Camden Society, vol. xli. p. 52.
[9]  Chronicle of Calais, Camden Society, vol. xxxv. p. 67.        [10]  Ibid. pp. 198, 199.
[11]  Memoirs of Edward Copleston, Bishop of Llandaff, by W. J. Copleston, Lond. 8vo, 1851, p. 85.
[12]  See Clarendon Correspondence, 1828, 4to, vol. i. pp. 340, 341.  See also the details at pp. 379, 380.
[13]  See Wilson's Life of De Foe, vol. ii. pp. 311, 313.
[14]  King's Life of Locke, 8vo, 1830, vol. i. p. 102.
[15]  Ibid. pp. 146, 147.

1*s.* a day.[1]  Comte[2] says Hallam has shown that the real reward of labour has diminished since the fourteenth century.  For a list of wages from 1800 to 1836, see Porter's Progress of the Nation, vol. ii. pp. 251–254 ; Monteil, Histoire des Français des Divers États, tome i. pp. 117, 119, 147 ; tome v. pp. 217, 284 ; tome vi. p. 124.  In Cornwall, early in the reign of Elizabeth, the wages of the labourers in the tin mines were 4*d.* a day, out of which the labourer had to spend more than 2*d.* to find himself "meate and drinke."  In 1601, Raleigh said that, since "the granting cf my patent" in 1585, wages had risen in Cornwall from 2*s.* to 4*s.* a week.[3]  On the wages at Penzance, from 1565 to 1770, see Journal of Statistical Society, vol. ii. pp. 217, 218.  In 1787, Jefferson travelled through the south of France and north of Italy.  He says, at Beaujolois, "The wages of a labouring man here are five louis ; of a woman, one half."[4]  Near Montelimart, in Dauphiné, "Day labourers receive sixteen or eighteen sous a day, and feed themselves."[5]  At St. Remis, "a labouring man's wages here are one hundred and fifty livres ; a woman's half, and fed."[6]  At Aix, near Marseilles, "the wages of a labouring man are one hundred and fifty livres the year ; a woman, sixty to sixty-six livres, and fed."[7]  At Bordeaux "they never hire labourers by the year ; the day wages for a man are thirty sous, a woman fifteen sous, feeding themselves."[8]  On wages and prices, see Tytler's History of Scotland, Edinburgh, 1845, vol. i. p. 63 ; vol. ii. pp. 216–221.

---

## CHIVALRY.

Miss Wood has printed a letter from a Mrs. Creke to Cromwell, about 1536, which, as she says, affords "a curious illustration of the system of wardship which was prevalent even in the middle and lower classes of society."[9]

Puritanism destroyed chivalry.

Chevenix truly says that the progress of military arts alone was enough to destroy chivalry.[10]

[1] See Twiss's Progress of Political Economy, 8vo, 1847, p. 58.

[2] Philosophie Positive, tome vi. p. 336.

[3] See Journal of Statistical Society, vol. i. pp. 71, 72, and Parliamentary History, vol. i. p. 928.

[4] Correspondence of Jefferson, by Randolph, vol. ii. p. 119.      [5] Ibid. p. 122.

[6] Ibid. p. 125.      [7] Ibid. p. 127.      [8] Ibid. p. 153.

[9] Letters of Royal and Illustrious Ladies, 8vo, 1846, vol. ii. pp. 267, 268.

[10] Essay on National Character, 8vo, 1832, vol. ii. pp. 387, 388.

Among the various circumstances which resulted from the decline of chivalry, one of the most important was the rise of duelling, which, though unnecessary, and even barbarous in a refined age, has contributed not a little to refining the manners of Europeans.

At the end of the sixteenth century the minstrels declined so much in fame that, by the 39th of Elizabeth, they were classed among "rogues, vagabonds, and sturdy beggars." " This Act," says Percy, " seems to have put an end to the profession," [1] though the *name* is sometimes used.[2] Percy has published[3] a curious poem, " The Turnament of Tottenham," in which chivalry is ridiculed. He does not mention the date, but from the language I should assign it to the fourteenth century. There is another ballad, called " The Dragon of Wantley," which is a satire on works and romances of chivalry, and was written early in the seventeenth century.[4] Even in the reign of Elizabeth the minstrels were exceedingly well paid.[5]

William Schlegel says: " From a union of the rough but honest heroism of the northern conquerors and the sentiments of Christianity, chivalry had its origin, of which the object was, by holy and respected vows, to guard those who bore arms from every rude and ungenerous abuse of strength, into which it was so easy to deviate."[6] Schlegel adds:[7] " The spirit of chivalry has nowhere outlived its political existence so long as in Spain."

Warton says[8] that in 1237 we have " the most early notice of a professed book of chivalry in England." It has been supposed that Milton was a great reader of the romances of chivalry, but this is doubted by Mr. Keightley, a very competent authority.[9] Ever since the foundation of the Order of the Garter by Edward III., there had been held on St. George's Day a grand feast, which lasted for three days. But in 1567, Elizabeth, with the view apparently of doing away with the custom, ordered that for the future it should be kept wherever the sovereign might happen to be.[10] In A.D. 1600, a gentleman in Shropshire died, and his widow actually offered the Secretary of State 1,000*l*. to be permitted to

---

[1] Percy's Reliques, 8vo, 1845, pp. xxi. xxii.
[2] See p. xxxviii.
[3] Pp. 92, 95.                    [4] Pp. 268-271.                    [5] P. 132.
[6] Lectures on Dramatic Art, Lond. 1840, vol. i. p. 14.
[7] Vol. ii. p. 355.
[8] History of English Poetry, 8vo, 1840, vol. i. p. 118.
[9] See Keightley's Tales and Popular Fictions, Lond. 1834, p. 25.
[10] Lodge's Illustrations of British History, 1838, vol. i. p. 443.

have the wardship of her own son.[1] Early in the sixteenth century the Spanish aristocracy was, I suppose, the only one then existing which could have produced a Loyola.[2]

.    .    .    .    .    .    .

## TOWNS AND CITIES.

In a curious Discourse, written in 1578 by a friend of Stow's, it is said : "Navigation, I must confess, is apparently decayed in many port towns, and flourisheth only or chiefly at London";[3] and early in the seventeenth century it had become so usual to sell the paternal acres and live in London, that the practice is noticed in Every Man out of his Humour.[4] In a tract called The Present State of England, published in 1627, complaint is made of the eagerness with which people flocked to London from the country.[5] In Stafford's Brief Conceipt of English Policy, 1581, it is said that "the most part of all the towns of England, London only excepted," is "fallen to great poverty and desolation."[6] This rush to London is ascribed[7] to the great rise in prices which compelled several country proprietors to break up their establishments "and get their chambers in London or about the court, and there spend their time."[8] Early in the seventeenth century, Rich notices that those whose ancestors lived in stately palaces like princes in their country, bravely attended by a number of proper men, now come and live in the cittie."[9] Bertie, in a letter to Cecil in 1569, contrasts the opulence of husbandmen with the poverty of artificers.[10]

Mr. Alison is very severe upon cities, and says that the increase of crime in England is the result of their increasing population.[11] Animal decomposition is not dangerous, and the salubrity of the country has been overrated.[12]

[1] Sydney Letters, edit. Collins, folio, 1746. vol. ii. p. 197.

[2] See the admirable remarks in Ranke, Die Römischen Päpste, Berlin, 1838, Band i. pp. 179, 180.

[3] Stow's London, edit. Thoms, 8vo, 1842. p. 205.

[4] Ben Jonson, Works, edit. Gifford, 8vo, 1816, vol. ii. pp. 30, 31.

[5] Harleian Miscellany, edit. Park, vol. iii. p. 210.

[6] Ibid. vol. ix. p. 147.      [7] P. 173.      [8] See also pp. 179, 186.

[9] Mr. Cunningham's Introduction to Rich's Honestie of this Age, Percy Society, vol. xi. p. xviii.

[10] See Haynes's State Papers, p. 519.

[11] Alison's Principles of Population, 8vo, 1840, vol. i. pp. 4, 46, 47, 140, 141, 517, 518, 568.

[12] Mayo's Philosophy of Living, 2nd edit. 8vo, 1838, p. 214.

Comte[1] points out the beneficial effects arising from the condensation of population.[2] The Anglo-Saxons had no idea of
citizenship like that of the Athenians and Romans, but made the
possession of land and not birth the full qualification.[3] Kemble[4]
observes that situation is the most powerful element of the prosperity of cities, as we see in Munich and Madrid. He says[5] at
first those who assembled in cities were under the authority of
the castellan; and " in truth *burh* does originally denote a castle,
not a town." In France, in the fourteenth century, none but
artisans and tradesmen lived in towns; the clergy and nobles remained on their estates.[6] Monteil[7] says that about the time of
the crusades, at the very end of the eleventh century, citizens
began to free themselves. It seems to be doubtful[8] whether
Laon or Noyon is the first commune; that of Noyon dates from
the beginning of the reign of Louis le Gros. Alison[9] says with
great simplicity that cities are always democratical. Tocqueville[10]
thinks that for the future, cities will increase according to the
increase of political rights. In the battle of Crecy and Poitiers,
the French nobles were almost annihilated, and this aided the
civic communities, which were also favoured by the kings of
France.[11] Louis XI. did immense things for the towns.[12] This
shows the unimportance *nationally* of morals; for a bad prince
like Louis XI. did great good. Henry III. was the first king
who regularly lived in Paris, and under him the city wonderfully
increased.[13] In 1588, the population of Paris was half a million.[14]
In the middle of the fifteenth century the " bourgeoisie " of Paris
were becoming important enough to be courted by kings.[15] Cities
are not in themselves unhealthy; but the mortality is great
because in them many persons follow unhealthy occupations.[16] In
London, bricklayers are more subject to fever than persons who
clean the sewers and collect the night soil!!!![17]

---

[1] Philosophie Positive, vol. iv. pp. 642–644.
[2] See also tome vi. p. 96.
[3] Kemble's Saxons in England, vol. i. pp. 88, 89.          [4] Ibid. vol. ii. p. 307.
[5] P. 323.
[6] Monteil, Histoire des Français des Divers États, tome i. pp. 18, 19.
[7] Vol. iii. pp. 122, 123.                          [8] Pp. 123, 125.
[9] History of Europe, vol. i. p. 224.
[10] Démocratie en Amérique, vol. ii. p. 206.
[11] See Ranke's Civil Wars of France, 8vo, 1852, vol. i. pp. 60, 61.  See also p. 63.
[12] Ibid. vol. i. p. 101.               [13] Ibid. vol. ii. p. 108.
[14] Ibid. vol. ii. p. 191.               [15] See Monteil, Divers États, vol. iv. p. 307.
[16] Journal of the Statistical Society, vol. viii. p. 312.
[17] Ibid. vol. xi. pp. 73, 75, 76, 77, 80.

## BEGGARS IN ENGLAND.

EVEN as late as the end of the sixteenth century Gifford supposes beggars who were diseased or infected used to go about with a *clap dish*, a wooden vessel with a moveable cover by clapping which they gave notice of their state.[1] And in 1607, see Middleton's Works, 8vo, vol. ii. p. 169.

In Every Man in his Humour, acted in 1598, Brainworm, wishing not to be known, takes as the most natural disguise the character of a mendicant soldier;[2] and in Every Man out of his Humour, acted in 1599, there is a character who goes about begging, pretending to be a soldier. Indeed it was so common for soldiers to beg, that there was a particular word invented for those who solicited charity under the pretence of having been in the army. Such begging was called *skeldring*, and is repeatedly mentioned by Ben Jonson.[3] These disbanded soldiers, when pleading for charity, used to say "God pays." This seems to have become almost proverbial.[4]

In The Roaring Girl, in 1611, when Trapdoor begs, he disguises himself as a poor soldier.[5] Those who were sent to Bridewell in 1608 were obliged to "beat chalk, make linen," &c.[6] In 1669, the pillars of the Temple were "hung with poor men's petitions."[7] Were there many mendicant Irish in London? Dekker[8] has, "more bare than Irish beggars." In 1578, Googe writes: "Sir William Drury, a paragon of arms at this day, was wont, I remember, to say that the soldiers of England had always one of those three ends to look for: to be slaine, to begge, or to be hanged."[9] Rich has preserved the formula of complaint used by the London beggars early in the seventeenth century.[10] By the common law apparently (*but query*) it was felony for soldiers and sailors to wander about the realm, or for persons to pretend to be such.[11] In 1575, Sir Thomas Smith mentions, "the common rowtes nowadays of roging beggars by the highway side, naming themselves soldiers of Ireland lately discharged."[12] In 1641,

[1] Note in Ben Jonson's Works, 8vo, 1816, vol. i. p. 44.
[2] Jonson's Works, vol. i. p. 54.
[3] Ibid. 8vo, 1816, vol. ii. pp. 8, 396, 397, 401, 453, 514.
[4] See Ben Jonson's Epigram, Works, vol. viii. p. 158.
[5] Middleton's Works, 1840, vol. ii. pp. 534, 535. [6] Ibid. vol. iii. pp. 221–236.
[7] Rowley's Search for Money, Percy Society, vol. ii. pp. 27, 47.
[8] Knights Conjuring, 1607, Percy Society, vol. v. p. 40.
[9] Mr. Cunningham's Introduction to Rich's Honestie of this Age, in Percy Society, vol. xi. p. viii.
[10] The Honestie of this Age, 1614, Percy Society, vol. xi. p. 18.
[11] Blackstone's Commentaries, vol. iv. 165. He quotes 3 Inst. 85.
[12] Smith's Letters to Burghleigh in Wright's Elizabeth, vol. ii. p. 29.

Evelyn[1] was struck by the admirable arrangements made in Holland for the poor.

On the poor laws in France, see Monteil, Histoire des Français des Divers États, tome vi. pp. 88–92. A sort of one seems to have been known in A.D. 1530.[2] Foundling hospitals increase illegitimate births.[3] "The Foundling Hospital of Palermo receives all children deposited in the wheel, without inquiry, and without distinction of sex. About half of the foundlings die within the second year."[4] The poorer people are, the more they marry.[5] In Frankfort, persons are not allowed to marry unless they have a certain income; hence, says Colonel Sykes,[6] an immense increase of illegitimate children. The bad influence of foundling hospitals is noticed by Comte.[7] In 1592, the House of Lords made "a contribution for the relief of such poor soldiers as went begging about the streets of London."[8]

---

## HISTORY OF RENTS.

In a "supplication" to Henry VIII., printed in 1544, it is said that "scarce a worshipfull man's lands, which in times past was wont to feed and maintain twenty or thirty tall yeomen, a good plentiful household for the relief and comfort of many poor and needy, and the same now is not sufficient and able to maintain the heir of the same lands, his wife, her gentlewomen, a maid, two yeomen or lackeys."[9] So that the rise of rents did not meet the rise of prices.

In a very curious pamphlet, published in 1627, it is stated that within sixty years rents had quintupled.[10] The rise of rents is mentioned by Greene in 1592.[11] But there is no doubt that the rise was not equal to the rise in prices. In Stafford's Brief Conceipt of English Policy, 1581, the knight says that he is compelled to raise the rents of those lands 'which fall in, but that he has comparatively little opportunity of doing so. "I do either receive a better price than of old was used, or enhance the rent thereof, being forced thereto for the charge of my household, that it is so increased over that it was; yet in all my lifetime I

---

[1] Diary, 8vo, 1827, vol. i. pp. 28, 29.  [2] Monteil, vol. vi. p. 91.
[3] See Journal of the Statistical Society, vol. ii. p. 109.
[4] Ibid. vol. v. p. 200.  [5] Ibid. vol. vi. pp. 152, 153, and vol. i. p. 170.
[6] Ibid. vol. vii. p. 344.  [7] Traité de Législation, tome i. p. 506.
[8] Parl. History, vol. i. p. 864.
[9] Harleian Miscellany, edit. Park, vol. ix. p. 464.
[10] Ibid. vol. iii. p. 207.  [11] Ibid. vol. v. p. 400.

look not that the third part of my land shall come to my disposition, that I may enhaunce the reut of the same; but it shall be in men's holding either by lease or by copy granted before my time and still continuing, and yet like to continue in the same state for the most part during my life and percase my sonnes." [1]

Dr. Lingard strangely supposes that the rise of rents in the middle of the sixteenth century was caused by a rise in the value of produce, which in its turn was caused by a depreciation of the currency.[2] In 1746, Mr. Pilkington took " a pretty decent room at 3l. a year in Great White Lion Street, at the sign of the Dove, near the Seven Dials." [3]

---

## ROYAL REVENUE AND TAXES.

Sir Robert Naunton says that during the war with Spain and Ireland, the military expenses of Elizabeth " 300,000l. per annum, at least, which was not the moiety of her other disbursements and expenses." [4] He mentions [5] an instance of the care with which she superintended the finances of the country. In the Brief Conceipt of English Policy, 1581, Stafford says of taxes, " And yet that way of gathering treasure is not always most safe for the prince's surety; and we see many times the profits of such subsidies spent in the appeasing of the people that are moved to sedition partly by occasion of the same." [6] There is no doubt that the " loans " demanded by Elizabeth were in reality compulsory. There is proof of this in a letter written in 1597 copied from the Harleian Manuscripts by Mr. Hallam; [7] but Hallam adds [8] that the queen always faithfully repaid them, and "incurred no debt till near the conclusion of her reign." Lingard [9] says : " From the report of the Senator Barbaro in the senate of Venice (communicated by H. Howard of Corby, Esq.), it appears that the king's (i.e. Edward VI.) income greatly exceeded his ordinary expenditure in time of peace; the former being about 350,000l., and the latter about 225,000l. ;" but a year's war in Scotland, adds Lingard, " had plunged him deeply in debt," and forced him to borrow money from Antwerp at very high interest. In

---

[1] Harleian Miscell. vol. ix. pp. 148, 149. See also p. 173.
[2] History of England, Paris, 1840, vol. iv. p. 250.
[3] Richardson's Correspondence, 8vo, 1804, vol. ii. p. 147.
[4] Harleian Miscellany, edit. Park, vol. ii. p. 85.     [5] P. 86.
[6] Ibid. vol. ix. p. 155.
[7] Constitutional History, 8vo, 1842, vol. i. p. 239.     [8] P. 240.
[9] Paris, 1840, vol. iv. p. 260.

September, 1553, Mary *borrowed* of the Londoners "24,000 ou
25,000 escuz sol." [1] In the same letter Noailles says [2] that 7,000*l.*
sterling are 21,000 or 22,000 escuz sol.  But five months later,
we find her so poor that she could scarcely pay the purvevors of
her own palace ; [3] and yet in the very same month s_e lent
money to the emperor to enable him to fit out his fleet with
greater rapidity. [4]  Philip was himself surprised at her poverty, [5]
to remedy which she adopted the ruinous expedient of borrowing
money at high interest. [6]  In October, 1555, parliament granted
her 16 deniers in the pound, which Noailles estimates [7] would
amount to " environ un million d'or."  Butler [8] quotes Andrews,
History of Great Britain, vol. ii. p. 35, to the effect that Elizabeth received yearly 20,000*l.* from the rich Catholics as the price
of dispensations permitting them to abstain from church.  Montesquieu, from whom so many political writers have stolen
without acknowledgement, says: "Regle générale ; on peut
lever des tributs plus forts à proportion de la liberté des sujets." [9]
See Wright's Elizabeth, 8vo, 1838, vol. i. p. 143, and vol. ii.
p. 361.  In the Egerton Papers [10] there are printed the instructions issued in 1600 respecting the sale of crown lands.  For an
account of the revenue of Henry VII. in the year 1500, see
Italian Relation of England, Camden Soc. vol. xxxvii. p. 47 *et seq.*
Alison [11] says Cromwell raised nearly 5,000,000*l.* a year, " or
more than five times as much " as that raised by Charles I.

In Haynes's State Papers [12] there is one of the queen's privy
seals for a loan of money, dated 1569.  In it the amount is
guaranteed to be repaid within twelve months after it is received.
For the expense of the army and navy in 1587 and 1588, see
Murdin's State Papers, p. 620, &c., and p. 619, where the yearly
expense of victualling the ships and of the wages is 113,438*l.*
This, of course, is exclusive of the cost of repair and the chance
of loss.  The accounts which follow are very confused.

In 1571, the queen could not pay the loans borrowed under
the seal when they became due ; and she therefore thought it
necessary to apologise, and to request that her creditors would
" be content to forbear payment for such a time as seven months
is." [13]  In 1579 [it was] proposed that there should be regular

[1] Ambassades de Nouille, Leyde, 1763, tome ii. p. 136.          [2] P. 137.
[3] Ibid. tome iii. pp. 96, 97.          [4] Tome iii. p. 120.
[5] Tome iv. p. 80.          [6] Tome v. p. 171.          [7] Tome v. p. 187.
[8] Historical Memoirs of the Catholics, 8vo, 1822, vol. i. p. 292.
[9] Esprit des Lois, livre xiii. chap. xii. Œuvres, p. 290
[10] Camden Society, pp. 285-287.
[11] History of Europe, vol. vii. pp. 3, 4.          [12] P. 518.
[13] Murdin's State Papers, p. 181.

loans made and kept for the government in banks, whereof there should be one in each shire.[1]

In 1580 the expenses of the queen in Ireland alone were "above 10,000*l*. a month."[2] See also p. 664 where Raleigh writes to Sir Robert Cecil in 1593 : "Her majesty hath good cause to remember that a million hath been spent in Ireland not many years since."

In Haynes's State Papers[3] there is a minute made by Secretary Paget, from which it appears that in 1545 the military and naval expenses were for six months 104,000*l*. and that an intended "benevolence" was expected to produce 50,000*l*. to 60,000*l*. He suggests that "lands" should be sold for 40,000*l*. In Haynes's State Papers[4] there is presented a minute by Secretary Cecil, from which it appears that in 1552 the king owed nearly 220,000*l*. The embarrassed Secretary suggests all sorts of expedients for meeting the deficiency.

In April, 1575, Elizabeth borrowed by privy seal 60,000 "livres esterlin (qui sont 200,000 escus) ;" of this London paid half, the clergy one-sixth, and the other two-sixths, "le commun du royaulme."[5] In 1570 the queen found great difficulty in raising "l'émprunt de trois mil privés scelz qu'elle a naguières imposez," and would not use force, fearing another insurrection.[6]

---

## PROGRESS AND TENDENCY OF ENCLOSURES.

GREENE says :[7] "and first I alledge against the grasier that he forestalleth pasture and medow grounds for the feeding of his cattall, and wringeth leases of them out of poor men's hands."[8] But the fullest view I have seen of the tendency of enclosures is in Stafford's Brief Conceipt of English Policy, published in 1581, and reprinted in the Harleian Miscellany.[9] The author says: "I have known of late a dozen ploughs within less compass than six miles about me, laid down within these seven years, and where three score persons or upwards had their livings, now one man with his cattell hath all."[10] The great increase of enclosures is said to have been within thirty years, and chiefly in Essex,

---

[1] Murdin's State Papers, p. 327.   [2] Ibid. p. 346.
[3] Pp. 54-56.   [4] Pp. 126-128.
[5] Correspondance Diplomatique de Fénelon, Paris, 1840, tome vi. pp. 413, 414.
[6] Ibid. vol. iii. p. 160.   [7] Quip for an Upstart Courtier, 1592.
[8] Harleian Miscellany, edit. Park, vol. v. p. 418.
[9] Vol. ix. pp. 139-192.   [10] P. 147.

Kent, and Northamptonshire.[1]  The reason is clearly stated:[2]
" So long as they find more profit by pasture than by tillage, they
will enclose and turn arable land to pasture;" and it is proposed[3]
to reduce the profits on pasture lands by putting a duty on the
export of wool, and at the same time[4] allow the free exportation
of corn.  Mr. Lewis[5] seems to consider that the enclosures in the
sixteenth century were beneficial by destroying the cottier system,
and thus relieving the peasants from a " state of quasi-villenage."
In Tytler's Edward VI. and Mary[6] there is a letter from John
Hales, one of the commissioners appointed to investigate the
causes of the conversion of arable into pasture land.  It is dated
July, 1548, and addressed to the protector ; but contains nothing
of moment.  See also[7] a letter in 1551 from Hooper to Cecil in
which the bishop complains that the price of meat had become
immense because cattle were no longer bred, but only sheep ; and
" they be not kept to be brought to market, but to bear wool,
and profit only to their master."  In 1551 it was estimated that
there were in the realm " thirty hundred thousand sheep " of
which 1,500,000 were " kept on the commons, and rated at 1d.
the piece."[8]

---

## PROGRESS OF TOLERATION.

NEAL says:[9]  " In the first eleven years of her reign (Queen
Elizabeth) not one Roman Catholic was prosecuted capitally for
religion," and that during the next ten years there were only
twelve priests executed.  In 1591(?) a law was passed which
Neal calls the most cruel that had yet been enacted against the
Puritans.[10]  In 1584, Whitgift, archbishop of Canterbury, drew
up twenty-four articles for the use of the Court of High Commission.[11]  These articles were so violent that Burleigh wrote to him
stigmatizing them in the strongest terms.  He says:[12] " I find
them so curiously penned, so full of branches and circumstances,
that I think the Inquisition of Spain used not so many questions
to comprehend and trap their priests."  Two months later—September, 1584—the lords of the Council remonstrated with the
archbishop;[13] and a treatise to the same effect was written by

[1] Brief Conceipt of English Policy, Harl. Misc. vol. ix. p. 160.
[2] P. 161.          [3] P. 162.          [4] P. 163.
[5] Irish Disturbances, 8vo, 1836, pp. 314, 315.
[6] Tytler's Edward VI. and Mary, 8vo, 1839, vol. i. pp. 113-117.          [7] Ibid. p. 365.
[8] Ibid. p. 370.
[9] History of the Puritans, vol. i. p. 444.          [10] Ibid. vol. i. p. 426.
[11] Ibid. vol. i. p. 337.          [12] Ibid. vol. i. p. 339.          [13] P. 341.

Beale, clerk of the queen's council.[1] He would certainly not have
ventured on this course without feeling certain of Elizabeth's
approbation.  In 1584, Aylmer, bishop of London, wrote an
angry letter to the council, but the only notice they took of it
was to remonstrate with that violent prelate.[2]  Punishments
gradually became milder.  It is stated by Barrington[3] that
" exile was first introduced as a punishment by the legislature in
the 39th of Elizabeth."  Parliament has created 160 felonies![4]
An act of parliament[5] ordered poisoners to be boiled to death,
and Coke[6] mentions several persons who suffered this frightful
punishment.[7]  In the seventeenth century—but *when* (?)—a boy
eight years old was hung for setting fire to two barns.  See
Blackstone,[8] who quotes Emlyn on 1 Hal. P. C. 25.  He adds, on
the authority of Foster, 72, that " in very modern times," a boy
of ten was hung for murdering his bedfellow.  Lingard accuses
Elizabeth of introducing the Inquisition into England.[9]  It is a
remarkable proof of the effect of intolerant laws that " the ratio
of Catholics to Protestants in Ireland has, therefore, gone on
regularly increasing from the period of the Revolution." [10]  Mr.
Lewis well adds [11] that religious persecution fails because it is not
sufficiently energetic.  Lewis [12] quotes Kohlrausch, Deutsche Geschichte, p. 470, to the effect that Gustavus Adolphus treated just
in the same way both Catholics and Protestants.

In a paper addressed in 1597 by an English Catholic to Philip II.,
it is stated that there are " four hundred secular priests in the
kingdom." [13]  Hunter, a Jesuit, states that under Elizabeth there
were not more than five or six Jesuits at any one time in England.[14]
In 1550, it was Cranmer who at length succeeded in inducing
Edward to sign the warrant ordering Joan Butcher (or Joan of
Kent) to be burned for heresy in Smithfield.[15]

Even the Puritans, whom Elizabeth hated, she would not
allow Parker to persecute.[16]  In 1576, Elizabeth made Grindal
archbishop of Canterbury, which, as Soames says, was a very

[1] Neal's History of the Puritans, vol. i. p. 342.        [2] Ibid. pp. 346, 350, 351.
[3] Ancient Stat. p. 269, quoted by Christian, note to Blackstone's Commentaries,
vol. i. p. 137.                              [4] Blackstone, vol. iv. p. 18.
[5] 22 Henry VIII. c. ii.                      [6] 3 Inst. 48.
[7] Blackstone, vol. iv. p. 196.                [8] Vol. iv. p. 24.
[9] History of England, Paris, 1840, vol. iv. p. 351.
[10] Lewis on Irish Disturbances, 8vo, 1836, p. 346.
[11] Pp: 374, 375.                            [12] P. 379.
[13] Dodd's Church History, Appendix, vol. iii. p. lxviii.
[14] Ibid. edit. Tierney, vol. iii. Appendix, p. clxii.
[15] Collier's Ecclesiastical History, vol. v. p. 386.
[16] Soames's Elizabethan Religious History, 8vo, 1839, p. 42.

conciliatory measure towards the Puritans.[1] In 1579, Hammond was burned at Norwich for denying the Trinity, &c.[2] In 1581, Campion was executed—but the usual butchery was prevented by Charles Howard, the Lord Admiral, who would not allow him to be cut down till he was dead.[3] In 1588, Francis Kett, " a master of arts, and probably a clergyman," was burnt at Norwich for his opinions on Christ ; but, says Soames, " his case was the last in which Elizabeth's government answered reflections upon its catholicity by fire and faggot." [4] In the reign of Elizabeth, five persons were burned as Unitarians (two in London and three in Norwich), and five Protestants, Nonconformists, were hung.[5] Soames says,[6] that only five persons in the reign of Elizabeth were " actually condemned as religious offenders."

It was in an age of dissoluteness that toleration grew up. The dissoluteness passed away ; the toleration remains. The Regency, which, as Mr. Macaulay has observed, presents a strong analogy to the court of our Charles II., seems to have given rise in France to toleration.[7]

A strong argument against severe laws is their needless cruelty; but a still stronger one is the impossibility of administering them. M. Quetelet, who has made a curious calculation from the criminal statistics of France, shows that if an individual is accused of crime against persons, the chances are 477 to 1000 that he will be condemned ; but in an accusation for crime against *property*, the chances of condemnation rise from 655 to 1000.[8] I may add that this inequality, which can only arise from a reluctance to inflict severe penalties, is in reality more than 655 to 477, because we naturally look with more severity on murder than on robbery, so that *à priori* the chances of punishing a murderer would be greater than of punishing a robber. The influence of sympathy on the executive is shown by the fact that women have a much better chance of acquittal than men.[9]

In 1585, the archbishop of Canterbury ordered inquiries to be made if the minister " once every Sabbath day put the church-wardens in mind of their duty to note who absented themselves from divine service, and upon the goods and chattels of such to

[1] Elizabethan Religious History, p. 220.      [2] Ibid. p. 234.
[3] Bartoli, p. 214, quoted in Soames's Elizabethan Relig. Hist. p. 306.
[4] Elizabethan Religious History, p. 354.
[5] Ibid. p. 595.            [6] Ibid. p. 598.
[7] See a remarkable passage in No. lx. of Lettres Persanes, published in 1721, Œuvres de Montesquieu, Paris, 1835, p. 41.
[8] Quetelet sur l'Homme, Paris, 1835, tome ii. p. 297 *et seq.*
[9] Ibid. pp. 299, 600.

levy 12*d.* a piece."[1]  Strype says that in 1560, the queen at the prayers of the bishops first ordered images to be removed from the churches.[2]

At the merciful and politic proceedings of Elizabeth the bishops and clergy were seriously displeased. With the bigotry which, unhappily for the interests of religion, seems almost characteristic of their profession, they endeavoured to goad the queen into a general persecution of the Catholics.

In 1565, the Prince of Orange, himself a Catholic, laid down in the clearest language the principles of religious toleration. See his remarkable speech in Schiller's Abfall der Niederlande.[3] He says: [4] "Eine so lange Erfahrung sollte uns endlich uberweisen haben, das gegen Ketzerei kein Mittel weniger fruchtvoll als Scheiterhaufen und Schwert." I suspect that the *impolicy* of persecution was perceived before its wickedness. The first great consequence of the decline of priestly influence was the rise of toleration.

In 1595, Robert Southwell, a Catholic priest, was executed at London, and the hangman wished to cut the rope before he was dead, in order as usual to butcher him alive; but this the people would not allow.[5] An unfeeling expression was current : " make this letter a heretic," i.e. burn it.[6] Sir Henry Wotton, who wrote at the end of the sixteenth century, expresses himself in favour of toleration.[7]  " Le dernier auto-da-fé célébré à Madrid est de 1680; "[8] but in Portugal the last was in 1755; and that this was the last is perhaps owing to the eloquent chapter of Montesquieu.[9]  Cheke's letter to Mary in 1556, declaring his readiness to change his religion is in Ellis's Original Letters of Literary Men.[10]  M. Cousin, who on the whole takes a very unfavourable view of Locke, still admits that he has the great merit of always appealing to *reason*.[11]  See the remarkable sophistry with which Todd [12] has attempted to clear the archbishop of the stain of intolerance.

The duke of Northumberland died a Catholic in 1553, and yet little more than twelve months before his execution, he writes to

[1] Strype's Whitgift, vol. i. p. 462, vol. iii. p. 179.
[2] Annals, vol. i, part i. pp. 330-332.
[3] Werke, Band viii. pp. 217-220.                    [4] P. 218.
[5] See Challoner's Missionary Priests, Manchester, 8vo, 1803, vol. i. p. 177.
[6] See Leycester Correspondence, edit. Camden Society, p. 342.
[7] See Wotton's State of Christendom, Lond. folio, 1657, p. 129.
[8] Villemain, Littérature au xviii* Siècle, tome iii. p. 165, Paris, 1846.
[9] Ibid. p. 170.                    [10] P. 19, Camden Society, 1843.
[11] Histoire de la Philosophie, 2nde serie, tome iii. p. 67.
[12] Life of Cranmer, vol. ii. pp. 331, 332.

Cecil declaring that he had been a Protestant more than twenty years.[1] This I may add to the case of Sir John Cheke, who also became a Catholic at the accession of Mary.

Drury, who was fifteen years in Madagascar, says that religious persecution is unknown, and this he ascribes to the absence of any separate order of priesthood.[2] Ellis observes that the king of Madagascar is the high priest.[3] Mr. Newman [4] observes that, with the exception of the Persians and Jews, all the ancient nations were to a certain degree tolerant—i.e. they had none of the proselytizing spirit: but "this kind of toleration by no means gave scope for inquiry or progressive amendment. It was a toleration of public religions or sects, not of individuals";[5] and [6] he says that the toleration known to paganism was not "conducive to the advance of truth." Charron[7] opposes toleration on religious grounds. In Bohemia, in 1508, it was first publicly laid down that a Christian ought not to compel any one to embrace the true faith.[8] Even Fuller thought the magistrate ought not to punish error.[9] Coleridge truly says that Whitgift and Bancroft were more criminal than Bonner and Gardner.[10] The murder of Servetus was approved by Melanchthon and the Protestants generally.[11] Coleridge [12] makes the curious admission that "toleration then first becomes practicable when indifference has deprived it of all merit." Even Locke in his first work, written in 1660, is inclined to deny the right of complete toleration, but in 1667, he had very liberal sentiments.[13] Mr. F. Newman, who looks on toleration as the result of *intellectual progress*, says,[14] "Nevertheless, not only does the Old Testament justify bloody persecution, but the New teaches that God will visit men with fiery vengeance *for holding an erroneous creed.*" The popes were the first who attempted to secure toleration for the Jews.[15] Read Zeuss, Die Deutschen und die Nachbarstämme, Munich, 1837, praised very highly in Kemble's Saxons in

[1] Tytler's Edward VI. and Mary, vol. ii. p. 148.
[2] See Drury's Madagascar, 8vo, 1743, pp. 188, 231.
[3] History of Madagascar, 1838, vol. i. p. 359.
[4] Lectures on the Contrasts of Ancient and Modern History, 8vo, 1847, pp. 37–42.
[5] P. 39.    [6] P. 40.
[7] De la Sagesse, Amsterdam, 1782, 8vo, tome ii. p. 13.
[8] See Talvi's Languages and Literature of the Slavic Nations, New York, 1850, p. 190.
[9] See Coleridge's Literary Remains, vol. ii. p. 384.
[10] Ibid. vol. ii. pp. 388, 389.
[11] Ibid. vol. iii. p. 74, and vol. iv. p. 379.        [12] Ibid. vol. iii. p. 189.
[13] See King's Life of Locke, 8vo, 1830, vol. i. pp. 11–15, 289, 290.
[14] Phases of Faith, 8vo, 1850, p. 168.
[15] Kemble's Saxons in England, vol. ii. pp. 89, 90.

England, vol. i. p. 4. Parr, in a letter to Charles Butler[1] says: " I pay great deference to Thuanus, and I think his preface a most admirable defence of toleration." Capefigue[2] says, " La grande transaction de Passau, l'acte le plus important dans l'histoire du droit public, parceque, proclamant pour la première fois la liberté de conscience, il fit passer l'Allemagne sous l'empire d'un principe tout politique." Calvin had predetermined to put Servetus to death.[3] In 1607, it was laid down that the king, if he conquer an infidel country, " may massacre all the inhabitants."[4] Bishop Tomline[5] says, " The reigns of James II. and of George III. are the only reigns since the time of Queen Mary, in which some additional severity was not enacted against Roman Catholics." Orme[6] says that Owen, in his treatise Of Toleration, " has the honour of being the first man in England who advocated, *when his party was uppermost*, the rights of conscience, and who continued to the last to maintain and defend them."

The principle of toleration, so far as the Catholics were concerned, is clearly laid down in what appears to be a proclamation of Elizabeth in 1569;[7] but in 1571, the queen writes to the archbishop of Canterbury, declaring that she will have " a perfect reformation of all abuses attempted to deform the uniformity prescribed by our laws and injunctions, and that none should be suffered to decline either on the left or on the right hand from the direct line limited by authority of our said laws and injunctions."[8] In 1579, Lord Burghley proposes as a remedy against the "comfort of obstinate Papists," that there should be ".penalties increased upon recusants."[9] In a letter from Thomas Morgan to Curle, dated the 25th of January, 1586, that arch-conspirator says that Elizabeth " hath banished within these twelve months a hundred priests, or thereabouts, whereof some of them have lived many years close prisoners in England, and some of them be grown lame and impotent."[10]

In August, 1575, the French ambassador writes to his court, without expressing any surprise, that some Dutchmen had been burned in London for heresy.[11] After the failure of Wyatt's rebellion, the French ambassador at London writes to his court, " Il n'y a par toute la ville triomphe que de gibets et testes de

---

[1] Butler's Reminiscences, vol. ii. p. 235.
[2] Histoire de la Réforme et la Ligue, tome i. p. 348.
[3] Ibid. tome ii. p. 72.
[4] Campbell's Lives of the Chief Justices, vol. i. p. 236.
[5] Life of Pitt, vol. ii. p. 402, note.    [6] Life of Owen, pp. 102, 103.
[7] Haynes's State Papers, pp. 591, 592.    [8] Murdin's State Papers, p. 183.
[9] Ibid. p. 331.    [10] Ibid. p. 461.
[11] Correspondance de Fénelon, vol. vi. p. 490.

justiciez par-dessus les portes."[1]   In February, 1554, he writes
to his court that the burning the heretics gave great delight to
the people, and even to the very children;[2] but in May, 1556, he
says that the executions had reached such a height as to disgust
the people.[3]  In October, 1573, the French ambassador writes from
London: " Ces libelles que les angloys qui sont à Louvein en
avaient envoyé semer ung nombre, ont mis du trouble beaucoup
en ceste court."[4]

An able but eccentric writer says: " Genuine belief ended with
persecution.  As soon as it was felt that to punish a man for
maintaining an independent opinion was shocking and unjust, so
soon a doubt had entered whether the faith established was unquestionably true.  The theory of persecution is complete.  If it
be necessary for the existence of society to put a man to death
who has a monomania for murdering bodies, or to exile him for
stealing what supports them, infinitely more necessary is it to put
to death, or send into exile, or to imprison, those whom we know
to be destroying weak men's souls, or stealing from them the
dearest of all treasures.  It is because—whatever we choose to
say—it is because *we do not know, we are not sure*, they are doing
all this mischief; and we shrink from the responsibility of acting
upon a doubt."[5]

A writer greatly attached to Christianity, says: " It is a fact
not to be disputed that some of the most enlightened minds of
the day have nurtured a secret opposition to the doctrines of
Christianity, owing to the intellectual intolerance of its abettors."[6]
And [7] he adds, " We cannot conceal our fear that should the theological odium pursue the spirit of philosophy with the rancour
which has too often been experienced, the result must in time be
fatal to the best interests of morality and of religion itself."  Again,[8]
Morell says: " In England, a distrust and contempt for reason
prevails amongst religious circles to a wide extent; many Christians
think it almost a matter of duty to decry the human faculties as
poor, mean, and almost worthless: and thus seek to exalt piety at
the expense of intelligence.  Delusive hope !  Is not Christianity
itself a matter of intelligence ?  Must not its claim to authority
be weighed by the human reason ? "

Mr. Butler, who from his religious bias had a natural tendency

---

[1] Ambassades de Noailles, Leyde, 1762, tome iii. p. 83.
[2] Ibid. tome iv. p. 173.                    [3] Tome v. p. 370.
[4] Correspondance Diplomatique de Fénelon, tome v. p. 424.
[5] Froude, Nemesis of Faith, 8vo, 1849, pp. 84, 85.
[6] Morell's History of Speculative Philosophy, 8vo, 1846, vol. ii. p. 225.
[7] Ibid. p. 227.                          [8] Ibid. p. 505.

to exaggerate the persecutions of the Catholics by Elizabeth, says that the 35 Eliz. c. 2, " was the first penal statute made against popish recusants by that name, and as distinguished from other recusants."[1] He adds[2] this " closed the penal code of Elizabeth against her English Catholic subjects." In 1581 and 1582, fifteen priests were sentenced to die. Twelve of them, who refused to deny the right of the Pope to depose Elizabeth, were executed ; the remaining three, who consented explicitly to deny such right, were pardoned.[3] Butler says,[4] " Between the Armada and the death of Elizabeth, more than one hundred Catholics were hanged and embowelled, merely, we must repeat, for the exercise of their religion." Between 1558 and 1563, Butler can only find three acts against the Catholics.[5] But of these the first, which protected the queen's supremacy, only affected persons who held ecclesiastical or civil offices ; the second " affected only the Protestant clergy, and persons in general who should speak against the Common Prayer-Book." The third act was passed in the fifth of Elizabeth, and extended the penalties for not taking the oath of supremacy to all who had said or heard mass. But even this was evidently a mere vindication of the civil power against the Church, and at the same time Butler confesses[6] that " it was far from being generally carried into execution." In Dodd's Church History[7] there is an elaborate list of those Catholics who suffered capitally in the reign of Elizabeth ; but in it I do not find that any one was executed before 1573, and then only one, Thomas Woodhouse.[8] But I think there is an earlier instance.

In the system of ecclesiastical laws drawn up by Cranmer, in 1552, the punishment of death is pronounced against heretics. For this Lingard quotes the Reformatio Legum Ecclesiasticarum. This Soames cannot deny, but he asserts that by heretics were meant those who rejected Christianity.[9] Indeed, he adds,[10] that it was not intended to punish capitally opinions which in the Reformatio Legum are called heresies. It is certain[11] that those who reject " the Christian religion " are to be " put to death and forfeit all their property." Soames himself expresses on this subject[12] the most illiberal opinions.

Broughton, one of the most learned men of the age, held some opinions respecting the word *gehenna* which did not please Arch-

[1] Butler's Historical Memoirs of the Catholics, 8vo, 1822, vol. i. p. 293.
[2] Ibid. vol. ii. pp. 42-44.          [3] Ibid. vol. i. pp. 424-431.
[4] Ibid. vol. ii. p. 11.        [5] Ibid. vol. i. pp. 345-347.          [6] P. 347.
[7] Edit. Tierney, vol. iii. pp. 159-170.          [8] See p. 165.
[9] History of the Reformation of the Church of England, vol. iv. pp. 314-316, note.
[10] Ibid. p. 318.          [11] Ibid. p. 317.          [12] Ibid. vol. iii. p. 722.

bishop Whitgift, who therefore sent officers to apprehend him, to avoid whom Broughton fled the realm. Eventually the archbishop adopted that very opinion for maintaining which he had persecuted Broughton, but refused in any way to further the ecclesiastical promotion of the man he had so cruelly injured. For the particulars of this disgraceful affair see Strype's Life of Whitgift.[1] The reputation of Broughton was so great, that the Turks offered him the use of the temple of Sophia, if he would go to Constantinople and read in Hebrew or Greek.[2]

Grindal, in 1559, asked the celebrated Peter Martyr to write to Elizabeth not to continue the crucifix in her chapel. But Peter knew better; and politely refused.[3]

In consequence partly of the general increase of knowledge, and partly of the diminished influence of the clergy, there had been gradually growing up in the minds of men an indifference to mere rites and dogmas of religion. Sir John Cheke, the learned tutor of Edward VI., in order to save his life, publicly recanted his religion during the reign of Mary.[4] Men became less superstitious and more moral.

Strype, whom no one will accuse of loving the Catholics, fully exonerates Elizabeth from the charge of having an undue regard for their religion.[5] In 1558 and 1559 Elizabeth deprived in all 192 spiritual persons, of whom fourteen were bishops.[6]

Bonner, ex-bishop of London, was kept in prison for his own safety. Indeed he was so hated by the people, that when he died, it was found advisable to bury him in the middle of the night, "to prevent any disturbances that might have been made by the citizens."[7]

In 1587, some justices of the peace were Catholics.[8]

In Strype's Annals[9] there is a list copied from a book, printed at Antwerp, of the Catholics executed in London from 1570 to 1587. For evidence of the intolerant spirit of the bishops, see Strype's Parker, vol. ii. p. 120.

Alphonso de Castro, confessor to Philip II., preached in England in favour of tolerance.[10]

In order to check violent recriminations, Elizabeth, in 1558, forbad any one to preach without a licence. Lingard represents

---

[1] Vol. ii. pp. 220–222, 320, 355, 389.　　　[2] Vol. ii. p. 407.

[3] Strype's Life of Grindal, p. 48.　　　[4] Strype's Life of Cheke, pp. 111–127.

[5] Strype's Annals, vol. i. part i. p. xi.　　　[6] Ibid. p. 106.

[7] Ibid. part ii. p. 298.

[8] Ibid. vol. iii. part ii. pp. 462, 463. See also vol. iv. p. 402, and Strype's Life of Whitgift, vol. i. p. 514.

[9] Ibid. vol. iii. part ii. pp. 494, 495.

[10] See White's Evidence against Catholicism, p. 250.

this as directed against the Catholics, but he ought to have known that she punished Protestant clergy who presumed to disobey it.[1]  In 1578, the bishop of Ely said "that he much rejoiced that her majesty was somewhat severe against her enemies the papists.  Would God that all her magistrates, high and low, would follow diligently her godly view.  I trust, hereafter, her highness and her magistrates will prosecute severely the same trade."[2]  In 1580, the archbishop of York wrote to the treasurer, requesting him "to deal roundly with all the obstinate, of what calling soever, noble as well as mean."[3]

These, and similar acts, have been often assigned to a partiality which Elizabeth is supposed to have had for the Catholic worship. But after a long and careful study of her reign, I think myself authorised to say that this supposition is entirely gratuitous.  No historian has advanced any evidence to support what has now become a traditional hypothesis : and so far as my reading extends, it is not warranted by any contemporary document which has come down to us.  The truth seems to me that in religious matters she was naturally tolerant.  Her mind, bent on great objects, cared little for polemical dispute ; and it was not until a later period, when her temper was soured by opposition, that she descended to the level of such men as Bonner and Cranmer.  Protestant historians who, with two or three brilliant exceptions, have always been intolerant, choose to represent this as the popish inclination of Elizabeth.

## HISTORY, ETC. OF THE THEATRE.

THE Puritans, who had been employed twenty years in maturing their power, now first began to make head against the theatre. In 1577 appeared the first attack on the stage, Northbrooke's Treatise against Dancing, Dicing, Plays.  In 1579, Gosson's School of Abuse; in 1581 or 1582 his "Plays confuted in Five Actions ;" in 1583 Stubbe's Anatomy of Abuses; in 1587 Rankin's Mirror of Monsters; in 1599, Dr. Rainold's Overthrow of Stage Plays; in 1610 Histriomastix; in 1615 the "Refutation of the Apology for Actors."[4]  In spite of these attacks dramatic literature advanced with a rapidity of development for which it would be difficult to find any parallel.  It would seem

---

[1] Strype's Annals, vol. i. part. i. p. 63.
[2] Ibid. vol. ii. part ii. p. 196.          [3] Ibid. p. 341.
[4] See some account of these works in Preface, pp. v-x. to the Shakespeare Society's reprint of Gosson's School of Abuse.

as if even the imagination of the Puritans was captivated by that splendid array of genius which toward the end of the reign of Elizabeth adorned the theatre. At all events, it is remarkable that after the work of Rainold's in 1599 there was, with the exception of the two anonymous tracts I have just alluded to, no formal attack on the stage for thirty-four years, when Prynne's Histriomastix was published.[1] But in the meantime a still more formidable opponent appeared. It is remarkable that the Lord Mayor and Aldermen of London had from the beginning so steadily opposed the stage that neither the players nor their patrons could ever succeed in obtaining a fixed place of exhibition within the limits of the city.[2] They were therefore driven to the liberties and suburbs, from whence they not unnaturally made war upon their persecutors, and covered them with ridicule. The friends of the city magistrates were not slow to retaliate, and a bitter and long-continued enmity grew up between the two parties, and the citizens were ready to aid the Puritans in overthrowing the theatre.

Heywood observes with regret that it had become usual in plays to satirize great persons.[3]

In 1805, Southey writes : " Fifteen years ago, the more melancholy a tale was, the better it pleased me ; just as we all like tragedy better than comedy when we are young."[4]

Mr. Cunningham, whose valuable works upon our early literature are so well known, says that James I. "saw five times as many plays in a year as Queen Elizabeth was accustomed to see."[5]

In the middle of the sixteenth century, the Dutch Protestants availed themselves of the stage to ridicule their opponents.[6] Hooft at the beginning of the seventeenth century created the Dutch drama, which has, however, always been poor in comedy.[7] Like the Greek, its chorus was very important.[8] Just before the breaking out of that great Protestant rebellion which secured the independence of Holland, the Dutch ridiculed the clergy on the stage.[9]

[1] See Introduction to Shakespeare Society's Reprint of Heywood's Apology for Actors, p. i.

[2] See some evidence in Mr. Collier's Introduction to Northbrooke, pp. xi. and xii.

[3] Apology for Actors, edit. Shakesp. Soc. p. 61, and see note at p. 66.

[4] Life and Correspondence of Robert Southey, edited by the Rev. C. C. Southey, 8vo, 1849, 1850, vol. ii. p. 322.

[5] Revels at Court in the Reigns of Elizabeth and James, edit. Shakespeare Society, 8vo, 1842, p. xxxiv.

[6] See Van Kempen, Geschiedenis der Letteren in de Nederlanden, Gravenhage, 8vo, 1821, deel i. blad 70, and Schiller's Werke, Band viii. p. 54, Stuttgart, 1838.

[7] Ibid. vol. i. pp. 128, 129.          [8] Ibid. p. 131.

[9] Abfall der Niederlande in Schiller's Werke. Band viii. p. 186.

Mr. Collier thinks Northbrooke hardly a Puritan.[1] His is the first regular attack on the stage.[2] This attack on it is at pp. 84–403. Sir Walter Scott notices that the French, who are so lively, have made their stage very declamatory : " while the Spaniard, grave, solemn, and stately, was the first to introduce in the theatre all the bustle of lively and complicated intrigue ;—the flight and the escape, and the mask, and the ladder of ropes," &c.[3] Of this peculiarity in the French drama Scott attempts no explanation ; and as to the Spanish, he merely ascribes it to the unceasing wars either between the Spaniards and Moors, or between the Castilians and Arragonese.

The immediate consequence of the outburst of dramatic talent was the rise of a body of profound and original thinkers.[4] We know from the experience of history that in every country the dramatists have preceded the metaphysicians. It is thus that the taste is first cultivated, and is soon developed into original thought. M. Cousin has well observed that genius is only taste in action.[5] He finely adds :[6] " L'art est la reproduction libre de la beauté, et le pouvoir en nous capable de la reproduire s'appelle le génie." Cousin[7] refutes the common notion that the business of art is to copy nature ; and he finely says that art is superior to nature because it gives a greater development to moral beauty. " La nature peut plaire davantage, l'art touche plus, parcequ'il s'addresse plus directement à la source des émotions profondes. L'art peut être plus pathetique que la nature, c'est le signe et la mesure de la grande beauté."[8] Cousin rejects the idea that the great object of art is illusion, and that the drama, for instance, to be perfect, should make the spectator believe that it is real. In fact, as he says, its business is to raise the dignity of man by transporting him above the realities of existence.[9] The theatre refined manners. It was to the people in the sixteenth century what chivalry was to the nobles in the thirteenth century, and the pomp and *forms* of chivalry, which were in full force till Puritanism, must have favoured it. M. Quetelet[10] has made a very curious statistical comparison between the dramatists of France and England. The English authors have been rather

[1] Introduction to Shakesp. Soc. reprint, p. xvi.  [2] Ibid. p. v.
[3] Life of Le Sage, in Scott's Miscellaneous Prose Works, 8vo, Paris, 1837, vol. iii. p. 210.
[4] Note this under James I.
[5] Histoire de la Philosophie, part i. tome ii. p. 150.  [6] Ibid. p. 172.
[7] Ibid. pp. 174-179.  [8] Ibid. pp. 175, 176.
[9] Quote a fine passage, pp. 179, 180 ; see also p. 186.
[10] Sur l'Homme et le Développement de ses Facultés, Paris, 1835, tome ii. pp. 112-120.

more precocious than the French,[1] but in both countries the dramatic power has gone on increasing until the age of fifty or fifty-five, when it has diminished, both in regard to the value and the number of the works produced.[2] Quetelet makes the important remark[3] that the tragic talents (in France, at least) develop themselves more rapidly than the comic—that is to say, that the greatest French tragedies have been written by younger men than the greatest French comedies.

In 1563, the bishop of London wrote to Cecil, expressing a wish to put an end to the performances of plays in London.[4] In 1584, Fleetwood, recorder of London, was violently opposed to theatres.[5] In France, there have been more great actresses than great actors. This is ascribed to the greater sensibility of women, to their greater flexibility of voice and movement, and to their general superiority in tact and address.[6] On the slavish manner in which the dramatic writers of Italy early in the sixteenth century copied the ancients, see Ranke.[7] This, I think, only applies to Italy.[8] Menzel[9] says the Germans have never had a great theatrical literature, because they have no great metropolis.

It is said by the author of the well-known Commentary on Voltaire, that his Merope in 1743 was " la première pièce profane qui réussit sans le secours d'une passion amoureuse."[10] In 1760 appeared Voltaire's Tancred, which, says the Biographie Universelle,[11] reminds us of Zaïre ; but *after* this, his tragic genius degenerated. Voltaire says,[12] " La coûtume d'introduire de l'amour à tort et à travers dans les ouvrages dramatiques, passa de Paris à Londres vers l'an 1660 avec nos rubans et nos perruques." Coleridge says,[13] " The talent for mimicry seems strongest where the human race are most degraded." " With all theatrical representations, not only are the Persians, but the Moslems of every country, perfectly unacquainted."[14] In 1576, Henry III. introduced the Italian theatre.[15] In Germany, the theatre has no influence, and the people do not care for it.[16] At

[1] Sur l'Homme et le Développement de ses Facultés, Paris, 1835, tome ii. p. 115.
[2] Ibid. p. 115.   [3] Ibid. p. 118.
[4] Wright's Elizabeth, 1838, vol. i. p. 167.   [5] Ibid. vol. ii. pp. 227, 229.
[6] Roussel's Système de la Femme, Paris, 1845, p. 39.
[7] Die Römischen Päpste, Berlin, 1838, Band i. pp. 65, 66.   [8] Ibid. p. 68.
[9] German Literature, vol. iii. p. 161.
[10] Œuvres de Voltaire, Paris, 1820, tome i. p. 399.
[11] Biographie Universelle, tome xlix. p. 486.
[12] Sur les Anglais, lettre xviii., Œuvres, tome xxvi. p. 112.
[13] Biographia Literaria, 8vo, 1847, vol. i. p. 74.
[14] Transactions of Literary Society of Bombay, vol. ii. p. 101.
[15] See Sismondi, Histoire des Français, tome xix. p. 386.
[16] Laing's Notes of a Traveller, 1st series, pp. 269-271.

Petersburg it is everything, and the authoress of Letters from the Baltic[1] says, " From the national enjoyment which Russians of all classes take in every description of scenic diversion, the theatre is particularly a popular amusement."

It has been supposed that the introduction of scenery was a *cause* of the decline of dramatic poetry ; but I rather believe it to be an *effect* ; for, when the mind was less stimulated, the eye must be more pleased.

In the next volume, in which I shall relate the decline, and, I fear, the final fall of the English drama, I shall examine the causes which regulate the fluctuations of dramatic genius ; at present, I shall give merely a hasty view of its rise and the influence which it exercised on our national civilization.

Under Charles II., all our great masters were forgotten. Shakespeare was neglected ; for how could his merits be appreciated by a corrupt and ignorant court ? Ben Jonson was neglected, for his powers chiefly consisted in depicting national manners which had already become obsolete.[2] Schlegel says[3] that the Germans have not had a theatrical literature because they are too *speculative*, and that for the drama a *practical* spirit is necessary. He adds,[4] " In Italy and Germany, where there are only capitals of separate states, but no general metropolis, great difficulties are opposed to the improvement of the theatre." He forcibly states the influence of the stage on the *mind* of a people.[5] Schlegel says that tragedy is more moral than comedy ;[6] in tragedy, the powers are more concentrated ; in comedy, more dispersed,[7] and it has a much lower ideal.[8] Tragedy delights in *unity*, comedy in exuberance.[9] See also [10] where he says that tragedy deals with *fate*, comedy with *accident*, and comedy " connects together, like tragedy, events as causes and effects ; but it connects them by the law of experience, without any reference, as in tragedy, to one idea." He says [11] that as soon as we sympathise with the characters, comedy is at an end ; for its business is not moral instruction, but to increase our experimental knowledge.[12]

The first regular tragedy is the Sophonisba of Trissino ; but the author was a " spiritless pedant," and in the middle of the sixteenth century, the pastoral drama of Tasso and Guarini forms a new epoch.[13]

[1] Letters from the Baltic, 8vo, 1841, vol. ii. pp. 249, 250.
[2] Schlegel's Dramatic Literature, 8vo, 1840, vol. ii. p. 298.　　[3] Ibid. vol. i. p. 29.
[4] Ibid. p. 324.　　[5] Ibid. pp. 34–39.　　[6] Ibid. pp. 42–45, 78.
[7] Ibid. 196, 197.　　[8] Ibid. pp. 198, 199, 204.　　[9] Ibid. p. 200.
[10] Ibid. 242, 243.　　[11] Ibid. p. 256.　　[12] Ibid. pp. 257, 258.　　[13] Ibid. p. 296.

Perhaps the patronage of James I. corrupted the taste of the drama; and I should not be surprised if this explains the retirement of Shakespeare. Schlegel well says that the taste of a court is nearly always bad.[1] The first French tragedies are those of Jodelle.[2] I have already observed that the decline of the clergy was fatal to architecture; and by an analogous process, the decline of the aristocracy was fatal to the drama. As the nobility sank and the spirit of caste fell before the levelling hand of democracy, the theatre necessarily fell. Schlegel well says of the time of Shakespeare, "the distinction of rank was yet strongly marked; and this is what is most to be wished for by the dramatic poet."[3] But our democracy was *religious* as well as *political*; this was another motive that the Puritans had in attacking the drama. There are yet other reasons. The Catholic religion favoured the drama. The stage also will naturally decline as history advances and becomes more philosophic and less picturesque; also, when a sense of the ridiculous increases, and audiences become more fastidious. Schlegel[4] notices the advantage of chronicles. And[5] Schlegel says, " If the effeminacy of the present day is to serve as a general standard of what tragical composition may exhibit to human nature, we shall be forced to set very narrow limits to art, and everything like a powerful effect must at once be renounced." Schlegel adds,[6] " It is deserving of remark that Shakespeare, amidst the rancour of religious parties, takes a delight in painting the condition of a monk, and always represents his influence as beneficial."

As to the rise of the drama, Schlegel is very superficial. Indeed, he does not examine the cause, but gets over the difficulty by *stating* it. See vol. ii. p. 273, where he says, " There are periods in the human mind," &c., but *why* are there? Schlegel says[7] that Elizabeth desired Shakespeare to represent Falstaff in love, hence the Merry Wives of Windsor; but for this I believe there is no good authority.

Schlegel says[8] that the Greeks always played with masks. Sophocles was almost the only Greek dramatist who was not an actor.[9] Schlegel accounts for the decline of dramatic art by a metaphor.[10] With Euripides, the Greek drama declined,[11] and this was because he copied human nature too exactly.[12] He ridicules women.[13] Aristophanes alone saw his real faults.[14] " The

[1] Schlegel's Dramatic Literature, vol. i. pp. 306, 307.  [2] Ibid. p. 327.
[3] Ibid. vol. ii. p. 113.  [4] Ibid. p. 121.  [5] Ibid. p. 142.
[6] Ibid. p. 174.  [7] Ibid. p. 237.  [8] Ibid. vol. i. p. 66.
[9] Ibid. p. 122.  [10] Ibid. p. 142.  [11] Ibid. pp. 144, 145.
[12] Ibid. p. 147.  [13] Ibid. p. 152.  [14] Ibid. pp. 157-222.

history of ancient tragedy ends with Euripides," [1] who became too *utilitarian*, for tragedy should not give *practical* instruction.[2] In Greece, tragedy was "exhausted"; it died a natural death; but comedy was cut short by the hand of power,[3] which silenced Aristophanes and killed Socrates.[4] The Greek women were certainly present at tragedies, but *probably* not in the old comedy.[5] The plays of Aristophanes suppose prodigious knowledge in the audience.[6] The middle comedy has no personal satire nor chorus,[7] but it is in fact only a transition to the new comedy,[8] which last is the old "tamed."[9] It imitates Euripides, but studies what is *natural*, and ridicules objects themselves.[10] The old comedy is "a pleasant dream"; the new comedy is "serious in form,"[11] and represented the manners of the day,[12] and is nearer to tragedy than the old comedy was.[13] Our clowns are like the old comedy.[14] Perhaps Ben Jonson, by representing *manners*, laid the foundation of the corruption of our stage.

Plautus and Terence are not original.[15] The Greeks respected authors: the early Romans despised them.[16] The Romans sometimes played without masks: the Greeks never.[17] In tragedy, the Romans (less mild than the Greeks) show their own contempt of pain and death.[18] The only specimens left are those of Seneca.[19] As to the unities, see vol. i. pp. 331–356. Of the unities, the only one of which Aristotle "speaks with any degree of fulness" is the unity of action: of the unity of place he says nothing,[20] and Aristotle himself knew little of the theory of the fine arts.[21] There is as much *real* unity in Shakespeare's tragedies as in Æschylus and Sophocles.[22] The French are right in prefering a comedy in verse to one in prose.[23] The English and Spanish theatres are essentially similar.[24] The romantic drama, like painting, unites what is dissimilar and mixes together seriousness and mirth.[25] Schlegel, who speaks of Seneca's tragedies with well-deserved severity, says that both Corneille and Racine have borrowed a great deal from him.[26] He says that the French have taken more from the Spaniards than from the Italians,[27] and adds [28] that of the French, "Racine is perhaps the oldest poet who seems to have

[1] Schlegel's Dramatic Literature, vol. i. p. 191.
[2] Ibid. p. 205.
[3] Ibid. p. 212.
[4] Ibid. p. 206.
[5] Ibid. pp. 237, 238.
[6] Ibid. p. 240.
[7] Ibid. p. 241.
[8] Ibid. p. 208.
[9] Ibid. p. 239.
[10] Ibid. p. 244.
[11] Ibid. p. 252.
[12] Ibid. p. 242.
[13] Ibid. p. 261.
[14] Ibid. pp. 261, 262.
[15] Ibid. pp. 253, 254.
[16] Ibid. pp. 291, 292.
[17] Ibid. p. 293.
[18] Ibid. p. 287.
[19] Ibid. pp. 331, 335.
[20] Ibid. p. 345.
[21] Ibid. p. 333.
[22] Ibid. pp. 100, 101.
[23] Ibid. pp. 102–104.
[24] Ibid. vol. ii. p. 40.
[25] Ibid. pp. 297–328.
[26] Ibid. p. 392.
[27] Ibid. vol. i. p. 296.

been altogether unacquainted with the Spaniards, or at least who was in no manner influenced by them." He says[1] that the Italians were much indebted to the Spanish theatre. It is to the influence of Seneca that we must attribute many of the most serious faults of Corneille.[2] Schlegel says[3] that comedy is "morality in action, the art of life." He says[4] that neither the Spanish nor English dramatists have borrowed from each other. "The formation of these two stages is equally independent of each other; the Spanish poets were altogether unacquainted with the English; and in the older and most important period of the English theatre, I could discover no trace of any knowledge of Spanish plays (though their novels and romances were certainly known); and it was not till the time of Charles II. that translations from Calderon made their appearance." He adds,[5] "Calderon had many predecessors; he is at once the summit and almost the conclusion of the dramatic art among the Spaniards." As masks were disused, perhaps the theatre naturally became more moral; for masks hide the blushes of women. Schlegel is very unsatisfactory as to the causes of the change which took place in our drama after the Restoration.[6] He adds, however, I think with truth,[7] "Pope, who, however, passes for a perfect judge of poetry, had not even an idea of the first elements of the dramatic art." Schlegel supposes[8] that Beaumont and Fletcher "entertained no very extravagant admiration" of Shakespeare. He speaks in the highest terms of Calderon,[9] and adds[10] that after him nothing of the least value appeared; but "I recollect having read a Spanish play, the object of which was to recommend the abolition of the torture." Lessing was the first in Germany who praised Shakespeare.[11] Perhaps the æsthetic investigations of the Germans prevent their having a great dramatic literature.[12] In the seventeenth century, Shakespeare was hardly known out of England.[13] The best comedies in England have been written by young men; but there is hardly an instance of an inexperienced writer writing a good tragedy.[14] The Count of Lauraguais, afterwards Duke de Brancas, introduced the custom of making actors dress on the stage according to their characters.[15]

Cibber states that the Maid's Tragedy of Beaumont and

---

[1] Schlegel's Dramatic Literature, vol. i. p. 316.            [3] Ibid. p. 296.
[2] Ibid. vol. ii. p. 47.            [4] Ibid. p. 95.            [5] Ibid. p. 105.
[6] Ibid. p. 272.            [7] Ibid. p. 285.            [8] Ibid. p. 303.
[9] Ibid. pp. 348, 349.            [10] Ibid. p. 363.            [11] Ibid. p. 374.
[12] Ibid. p. 400.            [13] Ibid. p. 368.
[14] See Prior's Life of Goldsmith, 8vo. 1837, vol. i. p. 24.
[15] Mémoires de Segur, tome i. pp. 134, 135.

Fletcher was forbidden to be acted in the reign of Charles II.[1] Beaumont and Fletcher seem to have enjoyed a great popularity in the beginning of the eighteenth century;[2] and respecting their reputation in the first half of the seventeenth century, see the Shakespeare Society's Papers, vol. iii. p. 94. In the same volume is an interesting article[3] headed "Salmacis and Hermaphroditus not by Francis Beaumont."

I have already noticed the rise of the English drama; I have now to consider its decline—perhaps its final fall. It will be found an universal rule that as a nation advances, its taste for theatrical amusement declines. With the progress of civilization there arise new tastes and new resources. Books are multiplied, and the diffusion of education increases the desire of reading them. The advance of liberty throws open to all the arena of speculative politics which before had been confined to a few. The facilities of travelling create an excitement before unknown, and instead of journeys being made only for business they are also made for pleasure. All these things drive from the theatre the active, the voluptuous, and the gay.

Such was the state of things at the Restoration. Under Elizabeth and James I. immense sums had been paid for entertainments. The profits of actors were enormous. Men of character paid for having their pieces acted, and Sir Walter Scott notices the character of the pieces, which can only be accounted for on the ground of a superior class of audience. Under Charles II. the dissolute and the ignorant crowded the theatres, where amid thunders of applause was performed the miserable ribaldry of Shadwell and Killigrew. As a proof that the decay of taste was only in the court and at the theatre, though Shakespeare and Ben Jonson were neglected on the stage for the wretched plays of Dryden, the Paradise Lost of Milton was received with raptures by the people.

Perhaps in our own times Hannah More did something to lower the reputation of the theatre. Her bigoted attack on the stage is reprinted by Mr. Roberts.[4] Her main argument is, that it gives too high notions of honour, false honour, as she calls it.[5] It is hardly necessary for me to say that this, which she considers a decisive objection to the theatre, is precisely the means by which it has aided in civilizing and unbrutalizing man. The drama has done in modern times what chivalry did in the

[1] See Cibber's Apology for his Life, 8vo, 1756, vol. i. p. 250.
[2] See The Postman Robbed of his Mail, Lond. 12mo, 1719, p. 149.
[3] No. xiii.
[4] Memoirs of Hannah More, 8vo, 1834, vol. iv. pp. 381-393.          [5] Ibid. p. 386.

twelfth and thirteenth centuries. Under Charles II., for the first, and, as I trust, for the last time in England, the theatre became a professed engine of vice. Contrary to the ordinary principles of mankind, the more degrading were the sentiments and the more indecent the language, the more tumultuous was the applause.

" It is unfair to take the stage as a proof, and to ask why we have not Molières and Shakespeares starting up at every period. The preceding age has gleaned all the twenty or thirty characters of strong and extravagant humour which lie upon the surface of society, not because it had greater talents for humour, but merely because it *was* the preceding age. The blustering captain, the inebriated and witty rake, the obese alderman, the squire in London, slaving poets, homicide physicians, chambermaids, valets, and duennas, are all gone; employed by dramatic writers who had the first of the market. These characters cannot be re-introduced on the stage; they are worn out there; but they exist in real life, and of course *must* exist, while men are what they have been." [1]

There were two causes of its decline: 1st, The increase of other amusements, such as travelling, &c. ; 2nd, Political excitement. An attempt was made early in the seventeenth century to introduce political characters on the stage. If the same licence had been allowed that was allowed to the early Greek dramatists, it is likely that our theatre would have continued to flourish just as Menander followed Aristophanes. But the combined authority of the court and the master of the revels was too strong. The consequence was that a large amount of ability was carried from the stage to the senate, where it soon shook the throne. The folly of James in all this is inconceivable. He should have allowed the *safety valve* of the theatre. A government is never so secure as when it allows to its opponents the liberty, and even the abuses of the press. The more people talk, the less they will do.

## BALLADS.

Mr. WRIGHT, who is a very high authority on such matters, has observed that after the Restoration, even the very ballads became more indecent.[2] Indeed, some verses are so coarse that Mr.

---

[1] Elementary Sketches of Moral Philosophy, delivered at the Royal Institution, in the years 1804, 1805, and 1806, by the late Rev. Sydney Smith, M.A. 8vo, 1850, p. 148.

[2] Political Ballads, published by the Percy Society, vol. iii. p. xiii.

Wright has felt himself obliged to omit them.[1] Mr. Chappell[2] says: "From very early times down to the end of the seventeenth century, the common people knew history chiefly from ballads. Aubrey mentions that his nurse could repeat the history of England from the Conquest down to the times of Charles I. in ballads." In the reign of Edward VI. Protestant ballads began to be written. Percy's Reliques, 8vo, 1835, p. 117. As to the *duration* of tradition, see COMMON PLACE BOOK, arts. 1191 and 1198. In our own country, I believe, none of the ballads sung by the Saxons before they were acquainted with letters are extant; but we know that, in what I have called the second stage of ballads, they became in England, as elsewhere, quite unfit for historic purposes. Thus we are told that the minstrels "made no scruples of changing the names of the personages they introduced to humour their hearers."[3] Percy, in an ingenious, but in point of learning, superficial dissertation on the Ancient Metrical Romances, says, "It was not probably till after the historian and the bard had long been disunited that the latter ventured at pure fiction."[4] The Finns were ignorant of the art of writing until they were conquered by the Swedes in the twelfth and thirteenth centuries,[5] but hardly anything was written in it before the sixteenth century.[6] The question as to whether the early Germans were acquainted with letters seems to depend on the meaning we assign to a sentence of Tacitus: "Literarum secreta viri pariter ac feminæ ignorant."[7] Blackwell[8] says that the Scandinavians were acquainted with Runic letters in or before the sixth century, but few are remaining before the eleventh century. The Anglo-Saxons, before their conversion, had a Runic alphabet which indeed they used in MSS. as late as the twelfth century, but "their form rendered them inconvenient for writing extensively."[9] Clarke says that the Latin poets drew many of their details from specimens of ancient art, as sculpture, &c.[10] Is is possible that European poetical history has been corrupted by an unfaithful sculpture and painting? Clarke says that the Laplanders "have no national poetry, not even so much as a

---

[1] Political Ballads published by the Percy Society, vol. iii. p. 250.

[2] Introduction to the Crown Garland of Golden Roses, Percy Society, vol. vi. pp. vii. viii.

[3] Percy's Reliques, p. 30.  [4] Ibid. p. 188.

[5] See Prichard's Physical History of Mankind, vol. iii. p. 284.

[6] Ibid. p. 289.

[7] Mallet's Northern Antiquities, 8vo, 1847, pp. 222, 223.

[8] Additions to Mallet, pp. 228-231.

[9] Wright's Biographia Britannica Literaria, 8vo, 1842, vol. i. p. 105.

[10] Clarke's Travels, 8vo, 1817, vol. iii. p. 101.

song;"[1] neither have they the least knowledge of music.[2] Mr.
Keightley has noticed the great deficiency of fairy tales, &c., in
Spain.[3] M. Van Kampen positively says that the Germans were
ignorant of the art of writing: " Dat de oude Deutschers in den
Heideuschentyd in de schryfkunst onbedreven waren schynt
voldongen te zijn ; slechts in het Noorden vindt men Zekere
schryfteekenen Runen genaamd."[4] The first Dutch historian
seems to have been Miles Stoke, at the very end of the thirteenth
century ;[5] but there was one who wrote in Latin (Sigebert) as
early as the twelfth century.[6] His work is "vol fabelen in de
oude tijden."[7] The widely-spread story of the Seven Sleepers is
an evidence of the want of invention.[8] Aubrey says : " My nurse
had the history from the Conquest down to Charles I. in ballad."[9]
Read Thornton Romances, Camden Society, vol. xxx. In the
middle of the eighteenth century, the police in Paris used "to
take up ballad-singers who presume to sing any songs that have
not been licensed."[10] It is curious to observe how little use our
early historians have made of the Anglo-Saxon ballads. This, I
suspect, arose from our being a conquered and despised people.
The same cause would make our forefathers cling more to their
traditions ; and I doubt if in any civilized country ballads lingered
so long among the people as in England.

The Russians have traditions similar to those of Charlemagne
and his Twelve Peers.[11] Talvi says [12] that in Teutonic ballads
there are few instances of talking animals, but that in the Slavic
songs they are very common; while in the Spanish they are
unknown. The ballads of the Servians have been only recently
printed, but are very old.[13] The present Dalecarlians are better
acquainted with the history of the appearance of Gustavus Vasa
among them than is Geyer himself.[14]

---

[1] Travels, 8vo. 1824, vol. ix. p. 386.          [2] Ibid. pp. 440. 547, 518.
[3] Keightley's Fairy Mythology, Lond. 1850, p. 456.
[4] Van Kempen, Geschiedenis der Letteren in de Niederlando, Gravenhage, 1821, 8vo,
deel i. blad 2.          [5] Ibid. p. 14.          [6] Ibid. blad 28.          [7] Ibid. blad 29.
[8] See Gibbon's Decline and Fall, pp. 552, 553, end of chap. xxxiii.
[9] Thoms's Anecdotes and Traditions, p. 102, Camden Society, 1839, vol. v. p. 102.
[10] The Police of France, London, 4to, 1763. p. 51.
[11] See Talvi's Slavic Nations, New York, 8vo, 1850, p. 64.
[12] Ibid. p. 327.          [13] Ibid. p. 379.
[14] Laing's Sweden, p. 215.

## HISTORY OF THE PRESS, ETC.

In 1585, Whitgift obtained an order from the queen that there should be no printing press except in London and in the two universities; and that even there no book should be printed that had not been read by the archbishop or bishop of London, or by their chaplain.[1] And in 1586, he allowed Ascanio, an Italian merchant, to import certain Roman Catholic books.[2]

In 1534, the 25th Henry VIII. c. 15, says that there are Englishmen who can print as well as any foreigners, and, on this account, "forbids the sale of bound, books imported from the continent."[3] Even M. Cousin is in favour of limitations on the freedom of the press.[4] The influence of a free press has been estimated by one of the most original inquirers of our time.[5] M. Quetelet observes that its tendency is to deprive revolutions of their violence by hastening the period of reaction. I do not know if every reader will immediately understand this; but it is impossible to give an abridgment of his weighty but very compressed remarks.

In 1572, Day, the printer, wished to set up a shop against the walls of St. Paul's; but the mayor and aldermen would not allow him to have it in the churchyard.[6] On the power of the press, see some original remarks in Tocqueville, Démocratie en Amérique.[7] In 1563 there was in France a rigid censorship of the press.[8]

Essai historique sur la Liberté d'Écrire chez les Anciens et du Moyen-Âge; sur la Liberté de la Presse depuis le quinzième Siècle, par Gabriel Peignot, Paris, 1832, 8vo. In this work, consisting of 218 pages, Peignot has given scarcely anything beyond bibliographical anecdotes. The following facts I note as being exceptions.

By a statute in 1323, confirmed in 1342 and in 1405, it was ordered "que les *escrivains* des livres n'en pouvaient communiquer aucun soit par vente, soit par louage, qu'il n'ait été préalablement examiné, corrigé et approuvé par l'une des facultés de l'Université."[9] Peignot says of printing:[10] "Ce bel art dont le berceau est definitivement fixé à Mayence malgré les préten-

---

[1] Neal's History of the Puritans, 8vo, 1822, vol. i. 369, 370.      [2] Ibid. p. 285.
[3] Hallam's Constitutional History of England, vol. i. p. 81.
[4] Histoire de la Philosophie, Paris, 1846, part i. tome iii. pp. 340, 341.
[5] Quetelet, Sur l'Homme, Paris, 1835, tome ii. pp. 289, 290.
[6] See Wright's Elizabeth, 1838, vol. i. p. 447.
[7] Tome ii. pp. 98-110, and tome iv. pp. 177-182.
[8] See Journal of Statistical Society, vol. iii. p. 376.
[9] Peignot, p. 20, and Dubreuil, Antiquités de Paris, p. 118.      [10] Ibid. p. 31.

sious de Haarlem et de Strasbourg."!!! He does not offer the slightest argument to support his positive assertion respecting a subject which has been, and still is, warmly disputed. Peignot states : [1] "En 1543 on publia à Venise le premier *Index* des livres défendus, qui soit connu : il a pour titre : Index generalis Scriptorum interdictorum, Venetiis, 1543." He says that the first index was published in Spain in 1559.[2]

In p. 58, Peignot says, "Voici l'un des premiers actes de l'autorité qui exige une sorte de garantie relativement à la publication des ouvrages. C'est une déclaration de Henri II, du 11 Décembre 1547, 'qui ordonne que le nom et surnom de celui qui a fait un livre soit exprimé et exposé au commencement du livre, et aussi celui de l'imprimeur avec l'enseigne de son domicile.'"

In p. 76, Peignot says : "Il nous semble que c'est de l'ordonnance de 1629 qu'on peut dater la véritable origine des censeurs nommé par le chancelier, et pris parmi les hommes des lettres et les savants." This order is given in pp. 74, 75, in which, after expressing the great inconvenience arising from the extreme liberty of the press, it proceeds to forbid any book being printed before it has been seen in manuscript and approved by such persons as the chancellor or guard of the seals may appoint for that purpose. Respecting this order Peignot however remarks,[3] " Ce n'est pas que la censure proprement dite ait commencé à l'ordonnance de 1629 dont nous parlons ; elle était exercée, comme nous l'avons vu, par l'université, dès le treizième siècle ; et pendant très-longtemps ce corps, qui s'était rendu si formidable, a fait valoir ses droits exclusifs à la censure universelle, comme les tenant du pape. Mais depuis Charles IX et les troubles qui ont signalé le règne de Henri III, and surtout la Ligue, l'université ayant un peu perdu de son crédit et de sa puissance fut insensiblement réduite à la censure des écrits sur la religion."

Peignot says [4] that the first statute respecting the liberty of writing is in A.D. 1275. In pp. 104, 105, Peignot says that it is a very difficult, *not to say impossible* thing to remedy the licentious evils of the press without trespassing on the rights " d'une sage liberté." Monsieur Peignot then proceeds to observe that "this difficulty has been perfectly felt and very well expressed by a celebrated Englishman, Samuel Johnson, in his reflections upon the Areopagiticus of Milton ;" a work, adds Peignot, "où ce *fougueux républicain*, cité déjà dans la note précédente, soutien la liberté indéfinie de la presse." Thus he

[1] Peignot, p. 55.    [2] Ibid. 61.    [3] Ibid. p. 77.    [4] Ibid. 14.

speaks of Milton !!! in p. 107. After quoting Johnson's remarks, he observes : [1] " Ces réflexions sont fort judicieuses. Elles doivent d'autant plus nous frapper, qu'elles partent d'un écrivain, très-attaché a tous les genres de liberté dont son pays est si renommé pour offrir le modèle." Milton then is nothing but a " fiery republican "; and Johnson, the Tory bigot, is a man " attached to every sort of liberty for which his country is celebrated "!!!

Peignot [2] says that in 1547, a proclamation issued by Henry II. was one of the first acts of authority directed against the liberty of the press. However Leber, in pp. 8, 9 of his De l'État Réel de la Presse et des Pamphlets, 8vo, 1834, Paris, has given some earlier instances.

In Le Clerc, Bibl. Choisie, xxvi. 246, et seq., are some interesting remarks on the laws of the ancient Romans respecting usury.

Leber, De l'État de la Presse. Great restrictions on the liberty of the press in the sixteenth century.[3]

It was the Reformation which induced Francis I. to destroy the liberty of the press.[4] The preachers in the sixteenth century were directed as to the manner in which they should handle the topics of the day.[5]

## ORIGIN OF THE MIDDLE AND MONEYED CLASSES.

Rich [6] says: " In former ages, he that was rich in knowledge was called a wise man ; but now, there is no man wise but he that hath wit to gather wealth." In the preceding chapter, I have traced the history of the decline of aristocratic power : and in the ordinary course of events, the decline would have been accompanied by a corresponding increase in the authority of the Crown. But, happily, there arose in England during the sixteenth century another body which was more than able to balance the power of the prince, and which twice during the seventeenth century saved England from a despotic sovereign, and once saved it from the still gloomier horrors of a military tyranny. All this was effected by the middle class; a class of which the slightest vestige is not to be found in the records of antiquity, nor indeed has ever been known to exist except in a few of the most favoured countries of Europe, and in that mighty republic of America. Elizabeth

[1] Peignot, p. 108.　　[2] Ibid. p. 68.　　[3] Leber, p. 4.
[4] P. 7.　　[5] P. 12.
[6] The Honestie of this Age, 1614, p. 14, Percy Society, vol. xi.

destroyed villenage ; at all events, at the accession of James I.,
there was hardly a trace of it.[1]

Montesquieu finely says: " Règle générale: dans une nation
qui est dans la servitude, on travaille plus à conserver qu'à acquérir ; dans une nation libre on travaille plus à acquérir qu'à
conserver."[2] Mr. Alison has well observed that it is the middle
classes which prevent the increase of wealth being fatal to a
country.[3]

---

## ARMINIANISM.

THE first four books of Hooker's Ecclesiastical Polity appeared in
1594, and in 1597 the fifth.[4] In 1595, the disputes between the
Puritans and the Church *first* became doctrinal—the former
maintaining the divine origin of the Sabbath and predestination.[5]
In 1595, to appease this, the Lambeth Articles were drawn up
and consented to by Whitgift, by the archbishop of York, and by
Fletcher, bishop of London, &c.[6] In them, it was laid down that
the number of the predestined was *fixed*. Neal says[7] that, before
this dispute, " the articles of the Church of England were thought
by all men hitherto to favour the explication of Calvin." Even
Collier confesses that when in 1594 Arminianism arose, " the
Puritans held the Calvinistic side, and here it must be confessed
they were abetted by no small number of the conforming clergy."[8]
He makes no doubt[9] that Whitgift believed the Lambeth
Articles, but he undertakes to show[10] " that these Lambeth
Articles were not the general doctrine of the English Reformation." But Collier promises more than he performs. His first
quotation is from Jewel's Apology, and is not decisive. Dr. Baroe,
indeed, professor in Cambridge in 1574, attacks the Calvinian
doctrine of predestination ; and Harsnet, in a sermon at Paul's
Cross in 1584, " takes occasion to break out with some warmth
against the Calvinian doctrine of reprobation." Collier observes[11]
that in 1595 the University of Cambridge " began to make a
stand upon the predestinarian novelties, to throw off the impositions of Calvinism, and recover the old doctrine of the Re-

[1] Brougham's Political Philosophy, 8vo, 1849, vol. i. p. 292.
[2] Esprit des Lois, xx. chap. iv. Œuvres, Paris, 1835, p. 351.
[3] Principles of Population, 8vo, 1840, vol. i. pp. 118, 119.
[4] Neal's History of the Puritans, 8vo, 1822, vol. i. p. 446.
[5] Ibid. pp. 451-453.    [6] Ibid. pp. 454, 455.              [7] Ibid. p. 453.
[8] Ecclesiastical History, 1840, vol. vii. p. 184.            [9] Ibid. p. 186.
[10] Ibid. pp. 188-191.              [11] Ibid. p. 195.

formation." See also the account of this quarrel in Soames's Elizabethan Religious History, p. 463–478, and Short's History of the Church of England, 8vo, 1847, p. 308.

Cheney, bishop of Gloucester, died in 1578. He was "a Lutheran and a free-willer."[1] The ignorance of the clergy caused many, such as Campion, to join the Church of Rome ; and by the end of the sixteenth century the Church of England was in imminent danger of dissolution. At this moment, the rising fame of Arminius suggested the formation of a party which might stand midway between Calvinism and Popery. To this party James I. inclined, for he was disgusted with the Scotch Calvinists, and the bishops found many things in the writings of Arminius favourable to their order. The presence of many Dutch in London also favoured this. I suspect that much of the Arminianism was brought from Scotland. At the end of the sixteenth century, there was constant communication between Holland and Scotland and the Scotch were often educated in Holland.[2]

---

OBSERVATIONS UPON SUICIDE.

De la Manie du Suicide et de l'Esprit de Révolte. Par J. Tissot, Professeur de Philosophie à la Faculté des Lettres de Dijon. Paris, 8vo, 1840.

M. Tissot thinks that suicide is scarcely known to barbarous nations, and that the more a people reflect, the more likely they are to commit it.[3] He well explains[4] why suicides are uncommon among barbarians: "C'est tout simplement parceque leurs passions féroces se portent au dehors, qu'ils réflechissent peu sur eux-mêmes," &c. He supposes[5] that if there were more convents suicides would be less frequent; and he remarks[6] "que le suicide est dû plus souvent à des causes morales qu'à des causes physiques." At all events, there seems no doubt from the statistical evidence brought forward by M. Tissot that in the present century the number of suicides has greatly increased.[7] Indeed, he says:[8] "S'il faut en croire M. Schoen,[9] on a fait en France et en Prusse à l'époque des guerres de la république et du consulat l'horrible découverte des sociétés de suicides dont les statuts

---

[1] Strype's Annals, vol. ii. part ii. p. 52.
[2] See Bower's History of the University of Edinburgh, vol. i. pp. 259, 260.
[3] Tissot, pp. 2, 34, 151.    [4] Ibid. p. 47.    [5] Ibid. p. 132.
[6] Ibid. p. 77.    [7] Ibid. pp. 31, 43, 150.    [8] Ibid. p. 32.
[9] Statistique générale et raisonnée de la Civilisation Européenne, p. 151.

obligeaient les membres à se donner la mort. En Prusse, le dernier membre de cette affreuse tontine a, dit-on, terminé ses jours en 1819." It is probable, but not certain, that as civilization advances, suicides increase.[1]

Tissot says[2] that animals never intentionally kill themselves. Comte says that suicide *is* known to animals; but this is denied by Lewis.[3]

At p. 15, M. Tissot quotes Schoen, Statistique de la Civilization, p. 156, to the effect that suicide is more common among Protestants than among those of the Greek and Romish Churches.

Tissot says[4] that suicide is much more common in towns than in the country. Indeed it is said that, when other things are equal, the proportion is 14 to 4.[5]

It has been supposed that climate has much to do with suicides, and that they are most common in cold, damp countries; but this Tissot denies,[6] because there are fewer at St. Petersburgh than at Paris, and more in summer than in winter. See also the evidence,[7] from which it is evident that they are more common in summer than in spring, and in spring than in winter. See also evidence to the same effect in Quetelet, Sur l'Homme, Paris, 1835, tome ii. pp. 152, 158.

Tissot says[8] that the greatest number of suicides are between the age of 20 and 30, and, according to Esquirol, particularly from 20 to 25.[9] Tissot[10] quotes M. Broussais to the effect that " les deux tiers de suicides sont des hommes." In Berlin, the suicides committed are in the proportion of five men to one woman; in Geneva, four to one.[11] Most of the women who commit suicide are married; most of the men are single.[12] Tissot[13] says that according to Falset, quoted by Broussais " les deux tiers des suicides sont célibataires "; but M. Prevost " n'en trouve que sept contre six."

Tissot says:[14] " Nous devons signaler ce qu'il est convenu d'appeler l'onanisme comme une des causes éloignées les moins équivoques des suicides. Les médecins sont unanimes à ce sujet."

In the above work, Tissot has attempted an exhaustive analysis of the causes of suicide. Blackstone says, " the attempting it

---

[1] Quetelet, Sur l'Homme, vol. ii. p. 151.
[2] Observation in Politics, 8vo, 1852, vol. i. p. 25.
[3] Quetelet, Sur l'Homme, tome ii. pp. 147, 152.
[4] Ibid. pp. 149, 150.
[5] Ibid. 161.
[6] Quetelet, tome ii. pp. 152, 153.
[7] Tissot, pp. 147, 148.
[8] Tissot, p. 20.
[9] Tissot, p. 21.
[10] Tissot, p. 50.
[11] Ibid. p. 60.
[12] Ibid. p. 149.
[13] Ibid. p. 151.
[14] Ibid. 142.

seems to be countenanced by the civil law," and quotes Ff 49, 16, 6.[1]  Christian adds:[2] " the instances of females attempting or committing suicide are now very numerous."

Montesquieu, who had been in England, says : " Les Anglais se tuent sans qu'on puisse imaginer aucune raison qui les y détermine ; ils se tuent dans le sein même du bonheur."[3]

In France, from 1827 to 1831 inclusive, the proportion of suicides to the entire population was 1 to 18,000.[4]  In 1835, the proportion was 1 to 20,000.[5]

Men commit most suicides between 35 and 45 ; women between 25 and 35.[6]

Napoleon, after abdicating in 1814, tried to poison himself.[7] Rousseau is suspected to have killed himself.[8]

Comte[9] says the ancients admired it ; but Catholicism has the great merit of discouraging it.

Tocqueville[10] says that in America suicide is rare ; insanity common.

Tallemant des Reaux,[11] who wrote in the middle of the seventeenth century, says the English are melancholy and very prone to it.

Lerminier[12] takes for granted that suicide is unknown to animals.

There are more suicides in summer than in winter.[13]

In 1836, the population of New York was nearly 300,000, and and the yearly suicides 42.[14]

There are more suicides among military men than among civilians.[15]  It is said that sailors, being more lively and cheerful than soldiers, are less prone to commit suicide.

In Prussia, in 1838, out of 100,000 deaths, 370 were by suicide.[16]

Among convicts of Norfolk Island suicide is very rare.[17] Buchanan, who appears to have seen a good deal of the North American Indians, says of them : " Suicide is not considered by

[1] Commentaries, edit. Christian, 1809, vol. iv. p. 189.      [2] Ibid. note, p. 190.
[3] Esprit des Lois, livre xiv. chap. xii., Œuvres de Montesquieu, Paris, 1835, p. 305.
[4] Quetelet, Sur l'Homme, tome ii. p. 148.      [5] Ibid. p. 158.
[6] Ibid. vol. ii. p. 159, but see p. 155.
[7] Alison's History of Europe, vol. xiii. pp. 207, 208.
[8] Villemain, Littérature au xviii^e Siècle, tome ii. p. 301.
[9] Philosophie Positive, tome v. p. 438.
[10] Démocratie en Amérique, Bruxelles, 1840, tome iv. p. 217.
[11] Historiettes, vol. ii. p. 122.      [12] Philosophie du Droit, tome i. p. 185.
[13] See Journal of Statistical Society, vol. i. pp. 102-108.
[14] Ibid. vol. ii. pp. 5, 25.
[15] Ibid. p. 253 ; see also vol. iv. 12, 13.
[16] Ibid. pp. 366, 367.      [17] Ibid. viii. 33.

the Indians either as an act of heroism or of cowardice ; nor is it
with them a subject of praise or blame.  They view this desperate act as the consequence of mental derangement ; and the
person who destroys himself is to them an object of pity.  Such
cases do not frequently occur." [1]  At and near Benares, suicide
(independently of the suttees) is very common.  The usual way
is by drowning, and this is done sometimes with religious views,
sometimes after a quarrel, that their blood may lie at their
enemy's door. [2]  In Kamtschatka and in the Kurile Islands,
suicide is very common, and this not on religious grounds, but
simply because " they think it more eligible to die than to lead
a life that is disagreeable to them." [3]  Kohl [4] says : " There are
fewer suicides in St. Petersburgh than in any capital in Europe.
On an average, not fifty occur in a year ; for every 10,000 inhabitants, therefore, not more than one yearly lays violent hands
upon himself."  Among the earlier monks, there were several
cases of suicide. [5]  But in the sixth century, the Church exerted
itself against suicide. [6]  Ford [7] says that in Spain " suicide is
almost unknown."  Suicide was rare among " the lively Greeks,"
but common among " the proud Romans." [8]

## IMPROVEMENT OF MORALS.

The lord had the right of *selling* his female tenant until wardship
was abolished.  It is remarkable that her lord lost the benefit if
the marriage was delayed till she was sixteen ; and that the
18 Eliz. c. 7, which makes it capital crime to abuse a consenting
child under ten " seems to leave an exception for these marriages
by declaring only the *carnal* and *unlawful* knowledge of such
woman-child to be a felony.  Hence, the abolition of the feudal
wardship and marriage at the Restoration may, perhaps, have
contributed not less to the improvement of the morals than of
the liberty of the subject." [9]  What distinguishes Ireland from
all other civilized countries is that crimes intended to produce

[1] Buchanan's North American Indians, 8vo, 1824, p. 184.
[2] Heber's Journey through India, vol. i. pp. 353, 389.
[3] Grieve's History of Kamtschatka, pp. 176, 200, 238.
[4] Russia, 8vo, 1844, p. 194.
[5] See Neander's History of the Church, vol. iii. p. 337.        [6] Ibid. vol. v. p. 141.
[7] Handbook for Spain, 1847, p. 337.
[8] Smith's Theory of Moral Sentiments, vol. ii. pp. 157, 159.
[9] Christian's note in Blackstone's Commentaries, 8vo. 1809, vol. ii. p. 131.

a *general* effect, such as threatening notices, murders to intimidate *others*, &c., are more numerous than crimes committed with a view to benefit the criminal, such as robbery, or murder as an act of *personal* revenge.[1] For horrible cruelty in punishment, see Tytler's Hist. of Scotland, Edinburgh, 1845, vol. i. pp. 201, 227, 229, 230; vol. iii. p. 150.

## HORSES.

FROM an early period great attention had been paid in England to encouraging the breed of horses. Indeed, I believe there was no personal chattel so protected.[2] In 1555, the French ambassador in London writes to the king of Navarre that he had endeavoured to procure for him " des juments blanches de ce pays pour mettre en son parc de Pau ; " but after inquiring in all the English fairs, he had not been able to meet with any ; but he was given to hope that they might be procured in the north.[3] In 1559, there were no horses " for the draught of grete ordynaunce " to be found north of Yorkshire and Nottinghamshire.[4] The Venetian ambassador, who was a very intelligent observer, writes in 1557 that England " produces a greater number of horses than any other country of Europe. But the horses being weak and of bad wind, fed merely on grass, being like other cattle and animals kept in field or pasture, which the temperature of the climate admits of, they are not capable of any great exertion, and are held in no estimation. . . . . The horses which we commonly see in the cavalry are all foreign, imported from Flanders."[5] Alison says:[6] " Each horse requires as much food as eight persons. . . . . In the expedition to Russia it is calculated that Napoleon lost 200,000 horses, and France contains 2,500,000." Egwin of Worcester, who died about 718, " before leaving Mercia ordered a smith to make for him heavy fetters of iron, closed with locks ' such as they fixed about the feet of horses.' "[7] In 1578, Gilbert Talbot writes to his father, the earl of Shrewsbury, from Charing Cross: " There are two Friesland horses, of a reasonable price for their goodness. I have promised the fellow for them 33*l.* I think them especial good

[1] See Lewis on Local Disturbances in Ireland, Lond. 8vo, 1836, pp. 94-97.
[2] See Blackstone's Commentaries, 8vo, 1809, vol. ii. p. 451.
[3] Ambassades de Noailles, Leyde, 1763, tome v. pp. 63, 64.
[4] See Hayne's State Papers, pp. 230-242.
[5] Michele's Report in Ellis's Original Letters, 2nd series, vol. ii. p. 224.
[6] Principles of Population, 8vo, 1840, vol. i. p. 198.
[7] Wright's Biographia Britannica Literaria, 8vo, 1842, vol. i. p. 224.

for my ladyship's coach."[1]   In 1687, the bishop of Chester
"bought two horses, one for eleven guineas, and the other
5*l*. 1*s*. 0*d*."[2]  In 1747, " Yorkshire is esteemed the best county in
England for horses."[3]  In Great Britain, more than 600,000
horses.[4]

## HEREDITARY AND DIVINE RIGHTS OF KINGS.

It is very curious that to assert that the king and parliament
cannot limit the crown was " a high misdemeanour, punishable
with the forfeiture of goods and chattels," during the *whole* of
the seventeenth century.  Indeed the 13 Elizabeth, c. 1, made it
high treason during the life of that queen.[5]  In 1593 was
published " A Conference about the next Succession, by R. Dole-
man."  In this work, which is attributed to the famous Parsons,
it is distinctly laid down that the right of succession to any
government does *not* depend on natural and divine laws, but
merely on human and positive laws.[6]  On the accession of
Edward VI., Cranmer, archbishop of Canterbury, in the coronation sermon, said that the king's " crown being given him by
God Almighty, could not, by a failure in the administration, be
forfeited either to church or state."[7]  In 1549, the king's council
ordered Dr. Hopkins, chaplain to Mary, to tell her that Edward
" is king by the ordinance of God."[8]  Calvin at different times
expressed different opinions respecting passive obedience.[9]  At
vol. i. pp. 99-101 of his Political Philosophy,[10] Lord Brougham
has given a good though popular account of the tendency of
civilization to convert an elective into an hereditary monarchy.
The comparative advantages of hereditary and elective monarchies
are very temperately discussed by Lord Brougham.[11]  He, like
most able political writers, prefers the hereditary form.  The
great increase of the royal authority under the Tudors is shown
by the number of parliaments they summoned as compared with
the Plantagenets.[12]  Allen says, " Under the Saxons, the crown

[1] Lodge's Illustrations of British History, 8vo, 1838, vol. ii. p. 99.
[2] Cartwright's Diary, Camden Society, 1843, p. 68.
[3] Nichols's Literary Illustrations of the eighteenth Century, vol. iii. p. 356.
[4] Alison's History of Europe, vol. x. p. 247.
[5] Blackstone's Commentaries, edit. Christian, 1809, vol. iv. p. 92.
[6] Butler's Memoirs of the Catholics, 8vo, 1822, vol. ii. p. 22.
[7] Collier's Ecclesiastical History, 8vo, 1840, vol. v. p. 181.          [8] Ibid. p. 313.
[9] See the note in Soames's Elizabethan Religious History, 8vo, 1839, p. 36.
[10] 2nd edit. 8vo, 1849.          [11] Ibid. vol. i. pp. 363, 364.
[12] See the List in Brougham's Political Philosophy, vol. iii. p. 252.

was elective."[1] He adds[2] that Richard III. "is the first king of England who can be said to have ascended the throne without the form at least of an election, and without any interval having elapsed between the death of his predecessor and his own accession. There are public acts in his name dated in the first year of his reign, before his coronation had taken place." Hemingford says that Henry III. was regularly elected, and the nine days that elapsed between his father's death and his own coronation are "considered as an interregnum during which the throne was vacant;[3] and even the accession of Edward I. was dated, not from his father's death, but from his own recognition.[4] However, "since the accession of Edward I. there has been no interregnum unless when the line of succession has been broken," and, at the accession of James I., "it was declared to be the law of England 'that there can be no interregnum within the same.'"[5] Allen says,[6] "There is no trace among the Anglo-Saxons, as among the Franks, of a general oath of fealty to the king from all his subjects," and the oath taken by an Anglo-Saxon to his hlaford "contains no reservation of fealty or obedience to the king."[7] But William I. procured a law which "obliges every freeman in his dominions to take an oath of fealty to his person without reserve or qualification."[8] Allen follows Lye in saying that the etymology of king is *not* the same as *can*, but "cyning is derived from *cyn*, which means kindred, family, tribe, nation," and in Anglo-Saxon "is manifestly a patronymic."[9] On hereditary bishops, &c., see COMMON PLACE BOOK, art. 991. Sir Henry Wotton, who wrote at the end of the sixteenth century, clearly, though cautiously, affirms the right of resisting bad princes. The resistance, he says, must be made by parliament; but, if the sovereign refuse to summon a parliament, the nation has the right of compelling him to do so.[10]

Early in the sixteenth century, a design seems to have been seriously entertained of making the papacy hereditary.[11] Voltaire[12] says the Visigothic Vamba "est le premier roi qui ait crû ajouter à ses droits en se fesant sacrer, et il fut le premier que les prêtres chassèrent du trône." Hooker's view seems to be the right one though on shallow grounds.[13] Even Chillingworth held the mon-

[1] Rise of the Royal Prerogative, 8vo, 1849, p. 44.      [2] Ibid. p. 45.
[3] Ibid. p. 46.                                          [4] Ibid. pp. 46, 47.
[5] Ibid. p. 47.      [6] Ibid. p. 64.      [7] Ibid. p. 69.      [8] Ibid. p. 70.
[9] Ibid. pp. 175, 176.
[10] Wotton's State of Christendom, Lond. folio, 1657, pp. 201-207.
[11] See Ranke, Die Römischen Päpste. Berlin, 1838, Band i. pp. 45–59.
[12] Essai sur les Mœurs, chap. xxvii. note in Œuvres de Voltaire, tome xv. p. 483,
[13] Ecclesiastical Polity, book i. sect. 10, Works, vol. i. p. 109.

strous doctrine of passive obedience.[1] Lord Dartmouth[2] says it was not heard of before James I. The language of Montaigne is most unfavourable to divine right.[3] In Java there is no hereditary nobility, and the sovereign is supreme.[4] Charron distinctly says the kingly power is limited.[5] At the end of the sixteenth century, the Jesuits denied the divine right, and said that all power proceeded from the people.[6] The protestants, on the other hand, affirmed the divine right.[7] Ranke[8] says that in the works of Holtmann, a Frenchman, in the reign of Henry III., "the idea of the sovereignty of the people makes its appearance in French literature." See also Capefigue.[9] Calvin distinctly upholds the doctrine of passive obedience:[10] and the divine right is supported by the French Protestants early in the seventeenth century.[11] Indeed Amyrant wrote a work expressly to advocate passive obedience.[12]

## OBSERVATIONS ON METAPHYSICS.

THE increase of Puritanism was increased by that school of Jansenists and Mystics which asserted that things were only just because God willed them to be just. This dangerous error in morals is well refuted by M. Cousin.[13]

Hobbes, who first ( ? ) laid down the idea of government being founded on an original compact, added that if the government broke the compact the governed were nevertheless bound by it.[14] Subsequent writers, such as Locke, recognised the original compact, but denied the right of infraction. The idea of an original compact which was the foundation of government now began to be generally advocated. This idea, though utterly false, was, like many other errors, of signal advantage.

[1] Religion of Protestants, 8vo, 1846, p. 372, and Des Maizeaux, Life of Chillingworth, 8vo, 1725, p. 298.

[2] Note in Burnet's History of His own Time, vol. iii. p. 382.

[3] See Essais de Montaigne, Paris, 8vo, 1843, livre iii. chap. vi. p. 573.

[4] Crawfurd's History of the Indian Archipelago, Edinburgh, 8vo, 1820, vol. iii. p. 16; see also Ellis's Polynesian Researches, 2nd edit. vol. iii. p. 94.

[5] De la Sagesse, Amsterdam, 8vo, 1782, tome ii. pp. 13, 38.

[6] Ranke, Päpste, vol. ii. pp. 186-190.      [7] Ibid. pp. 193, 194.

[8] Civil Wars in France, 8vo, 1852, vol. ii. p. 62.

[9] Histoire de la Réforme et la Ligue, tomo iii. p. 311.

[10] Medley's History of the Reformed Religion in France, 1832, vol. i. p. 110.

[11] See Quick's Synodicon in Gallia, Lond. folio, 1692, vol. i. p. 412, and vol. ii. p. 387.

[12] Biographie Universelle, tome ii. p. 81.

[13] Histoire de la Philosophie, Paris, 1846, part i. tome ii. p. 278, &c.

[14] See Cousin's Histoire de la Philosophie, Paris, 1846, part i. tome iii. p. 282.

The less beautiful the climate, the more likely are thinkers to arise.  See COMMON PLACE BOOK, art. 1854.

See in Cousin's Histoire de la Philosophie,[1] a magnificent and, as I think, decisive vindication against Kant of the capacity of metaphysics for affording proofs as certain as those of mathematics.

Perhaps Hutcheson was the first who clearly saw that government was *not* founded on a contract.[2]

Morell, an enthusiastic student of German philosophy,[3] says, "The great peculiarity which distinguishes the modern philosophy of Germany from that of every other country is the use of the ontological instead of the psychological method."  Contrary, he says, to Bacon, Descartes, and Locke, they "begin by laying down the most primitive and abstract *notion* we have of existence, as though it were a reality, and proceed onward until step by step they have constructed the whole universe.  Morell says of the Germans, "They have not been willing to tolerate anything whatever that is merely experimental, or even that includes an inductive process."[4]  See also vol. ii. p. 378, where Morell says that the Germans always prefer the ancient deductive synthetical method to the Baconian inductive, analytical method.

Frederick Schlegel says, "The second corruption of Christianity was from Arianism, which corresponds to what in modern times is called rationalism," &c.[5]

Morell says, "By the tendencies of a metaphysical system we mean the whole mass of ultimate consequences which can be fairly and logically drawn from its acknowledged principles."[6]  This shows his ignorance of the application of metaphysics to history.  The real tendency of a system is not what *can* be *logically* inferred from it, but what is likely to be inferred.

Whewell well refutes the popular notion that discoveries are accidental.[7]

Lord Brougham says that in metaphysics "we must be content with evidence of an inferior kind to that which the mathematical sciences employ."[8]

Whewell[9] says, "In the inductive sciences a definition does

[1] Paris, 1846, part i. tome v. pp. 240-244.
[2] See Cousin's Histoire de la Philosophie, 1846, part i. tome iv. pp. 186, 187.
[3] History of Speculative Philosophy, 8vo, 1846, vol. ii. p. 180.      [4] Ibid. p. 494.
[5] Philosophy of History, Lond. 8vo, 1846, p. 313.
[6] History of Speculative Philosophy, 8vo, 1846, vol. ii. p. 442.
[7] Philosophy of the Inductive Sciences, 8vo, 1847, vol. ii. pp. 23-26.
[8] Political Philosophy, 2nd edit. 1849, vol. i. p. 2.
[9] Philosophy of the Inductive Sciences, vol. i. p. 575.

not form the basis of reasoning, but points out the course of investigation." There appears to be no doubt that Schelling *à priori* anticipated the discovery that electricity was producible from common magnetism.[1] It has been observed, and I think with great truth, that there are more false facts than false theories in the world.[2] A very competent authority, Mr. Green, says that Schelling's speculations " cannot but be admitted to have had an invigorating influence on the progress of natural science." [3] Even in physical science it is allowable as it were to *feel one's way*, and to draw inferences from analogies.[4] Metaphysics, as it must be the end of all knowledge, so it was the beginning of all knowledge. Coleridge well says, " Thus in the thirteenth century the first science which roused the intellects of men from the torpor of barbarism was, as in all countries ever has been and ever must be the case, the science of metaphysic and ontology." [5] Lord Brougham is certainly mistaken in supposing that Hume was the first who asserted " that we only know the connection between events by their succession one to another in point of time ; and that what we term causation, the relation of cause and effect, is really only the constant precedence of one event, act, or thing to another." [6] Brougham talks [7] of "the necessarily imperfect nature of inductive evidence." On the nature of axioms and on logic, read Cousin, Histoire de la Philosophie, 2nd series, tome iii. pp. 272–340. Cousin says that Locke's system leads to scepticism and materialism.[8] Baxter, who lived in Scotland, appears to have directed Lord Kames's attention to metaphysics.[9] In 1751, Kames published Essays to show that the laws of morality are certain and unchangeable.[10] Bower says,[11] " The University of Edinburgh possesses the high honour of having been the first public seminary in Europe in which the Newtonian philosophy was publicly taught." This was by David Gregory, about 1690.[12] Hooker [13] anticipates Locke in denying the existence of innate ideas. Glanville very clearly saw that the senses do *not* deceive

[1] Whewell, vol. i. pp. 371, 372.    [2] Mayo's Outlines of Medical Proof, 1850, p. 13.
[3] Green's Vital Dynamics, 8vo, 1840, p. 38.
[4] See the rules for ascertaining causes laid down in Herschel's Discourse on Natural Philosophy, 8vo, 1830, pp. 152, 164, 165.
[5] Hints towards the Formation of a more comprehensive Theory of Life, by S. T. Coleridge, edited by Dr. Watson, Lond. 8vo, 1848, p. 28.
[6] Brougham's Lives of Men of Letters and Sciences, 8vo, 1845, vol. i. p. 200.
[7] Ibid. p. 391.
[8] Histoire de la Philosophie, 2 de série, tome iii. pp. 243-253.
[9] See Tytler's Memoirs of Kames, Edinburgh, 1814, vol. i. pp. 31–37.
[10] Ibid. p. 183.
[11] History of the University of Edinburgh, vol. ii. p. 81.    [12] Ibid. p. 82.
[13] Ecclesiastical Polity, book i. sect. 6, in Works, vol. i. pp. 85, 86.

us.[1] Mr. Lawrence speaks in the highest terms of the applicability of Brown's "Cause and Effect" to the physical sciences.[2]
For some curious cases of "double consciousness," see Mayo on
the Truth in Popular Superstitions.[3] Coleridge [4] erroneously
supposes that the senses sometimes deceive us. He thinks, but
doubtfully, that Jeremy Taylor is the first good English writer
before 1688 who uses the word *idea* as a mental image.[5] Coleridge says [6] that what is *objectively* a law is *subjectively* an idea.
He insists on the great importance of distinguishing between the
reason and the understanding, and between ideas and conceptions.[7]
De Foe has some acute remarks on "never inquiring after God
in those works of nature, which, depending upon the course of
things, are plain and demonstrative." [8] In 1679, Locke mentions
contemptuously "an Hobbist." [9] In a letter written in 1734, Voltaire [10] clearly states the absurdity of thinking that a materialist
must be an atheist. Dr. Whewell has attempted, I think unsuc-
cessfully, but certainly with great ability, to confirm the truth of
the idea of substance by the history of physical knowledge.[11] The
Romans as thinkers were infinitely inferior to the Greeks.[12] Tocqueville says,[13] " Une idée fausse mais claire et précise aura
toujours plus de puissance dans le monde qu'une vraie idée mais
complexe." Herbert Mayo well says that a great truth always
goes through three stages. Napoleon says, " A man, before
doing anything of consequence, ought to digest his dinner and
sleep a night upon it; and then, if he is of the same opinion the
following day, it is the real determination of his mind; if not, it
is only a caprice or whim." [14]

## SUBSTANCE.

JAMES MILL says, " But what is the rose, besides the colour, the
form, and so on ? Not knowing what it is, but supposing it to be
something, we invent a name to stand for it. We call it a *sub-*

[1] The Vanity of Dogmatizing, 8vo, 1661, pp. 91–94.
[2] Lawrence's Lectures on Man, 8vo, 1844, p. 56.
[3] Combe's Elements of Phrenology, Edinburgh, 6th edit. 1845, p. 149.
[4] Literary Remains, vol. iii. p. 350.          [5] Ibid. p. 380.
[6] Church and State, 2nd edit. 1830, p. 7.     [7] Ibid. p. 71.
[8] Wilson's Life of De Foe, vol. ii. p. 269.
[9] See King's Life of Locke, 8vo, 1830, vol. i. p. 191.
[10] Œuvres, tome lvi. p. 392.
[11] Philosophy of the Inductive Sciences, vol. i. p. 401–419, and 407, 408.
[12] See Whewell's Philosophy of the Inductive Sciences, vol. ii. p. 137.
[13] Démocratie en Amérique, vol. ii. p. 18.
[14] Forsyth's Captivity of Napoleon, Lond. 1853, vol. ii. p. 277.

*stratum.* This substratum, when closely examined, is not distinguishable from cause. It is the cause of the qualities; that is, the cause of the causes of our sensations. The association then is this. To each of the sensations we have from a particular object we annex in our imagination a cause; and to these several causes we annex a cause common to all, and mark it with the name substratum." [1] Again, [2] he says: " The term 'quality,' or ' qualities of an object,' seem to imply that the qualities are one thing, the object another. And this in some indistinct way is no doubt the opinion of the great majority of mankind. Yet the absurdity of it strikes the understanding the moment it is mentioned. The qualities of an object are the whole of the object. What is there beside the qualities? In fact, they are convertible terms : the qualities are the object, and the object is the qualities." Reid's mode of proving a substance is whimsical enough. He says that because we *call* a phenomenon a quality, and because qualities must have a subject, *therefore* substance exists. [3] Locke, in his Essay, seemed to doubt the existence of *substance* ; " but in his first letter to the bishop of Worcester he removes this doubt, and quotes many passages of his Essay to show that he neither denied nor doubted of the existence of substances both thinking and material." [4] Reid, with singular presumption, says that a man who denies the existence of substance " is not fit to be reasoned with." [5] Mr. Newman[6] truly says that " we should not attain greater accuracy by expunging the two words " (substance and matter) " from our vocabulary." But I do not know of any metaphysician who has proposed to expunge them. The real question, I apprehend, is not whether *substance* is a useless word : but whether it is expressive of that which has an objective existence, or whether it is a mere verbal generalization.

---

## LEASES.

THE Statute of User, 27 Hen. VIII. c. 10, turned user into possession by making cestui qui use terre tenant. The courts in interpreting this laid down that as the statute only spoke of those who were *seised* to use, it did not extend to term of year or any other chattel interest of which the termor cannot be *seised*, but only *possessed*; " and therefore if a term of 1,000 years be

[1] Analysis of the Mind, vol. i. p. 263.   [2] Ibid. vol. ii. p. 53.
[3] Essays on the Powers of the Mind, Edinburgh, 1808, vol. i. p. 276.
[4] Reid's Essays, Edinburgh, 1808, vol. ii. p. 278.   [5] Ibid. vol. i. p. 38.
[6] Natural History of the Soul, 8vo, 1849, p. 92.

limited to A, to the use of or in trust for B, the statute does not execute this use, but leases it at common law."[1] This, I suppose, would encourage long leases.

---

## CHANCERY AND ITS EQUITABLE JURISDICTION.

FOR this, I suppose, the way was paved by the Courts of Requests. They were established by an act of the Common Council in the reign of Henry VIII., but were not legal till 3 Jac. I.[2] The bishop of St. Asaph says that Sir T. More is the first instance of a layman being made Lord Chancellor.[3]

---

## ÆSTHETICS AND HISTORY OF THE ARTS.

MARY employed a painter named Nicolas, who, though born in France, had been thirty-two years in England, and was patronised by Henry VIII. and Edward VI.;[4] but his business seems merely to have been to paint the standards, &c., of the army.[5] In 1568, in a conversation between Mr. White and Mary of Scotland, a question was raised as to whether carving, painting, or "working with the needle" was "the most commendable quality." Mary inclined towards painting, but Mr. White seemed to lean the other way.[6] On the difference between the *real* and the *true*, see Cousin, Histoire de la Philosophie, Paris, 1846, part i. pp. 385, 386. Cousin says that Hutcheson was the first who revived the Platonic theory that all beauty was referrible to moral beauty.[7] He adds[8] that Hutcheson first placed sentiment above sensation; and Reed first placed reason above sentiment. He says:[9] "Fille de la scholastique, la philosophie moderne est demeurée long-temps étrangère aux graces, et les Recherches d'Hutcheson pré-sentent, je crois, le premier traité spécial sur le beau, écrit par un moderne. Elles ont paru en 1725 (je ne vois avant la Re-cherche que l'ouvrage fort ennuyeux de Crouzas, 'Traité du

---

[1] Blackstone, vol. ii. p. 336, who quotes Bacon, Law of Uses, p. 335, Jenk. p. 244, Poph. 76, Dyer, 369.
[2] Ibid. 8vo, 1809, vol. iii. p. 82.
[3] Short's History of the Church of England, 8vo, 1847, p. 95.
[4] Ambassades de Noailles, Leyde, 1762, tome ii. p. 255; see also tome iv. p. 61.
[5] Ibid. tome iv. pp. 155, 156.
[6] See White's Letter to Cecil in Haynes's State Papers, pp. 509-511.
[7] Histoire de la Philosophie, Paris, 1846, part i. tome iv. p. 527.
[8] Ibid. p. 540.        [9] Ibid. tome iv. p. 84.

Beau,' Amsterdam, 1712). Cette date est presque celle de
l'avènement de l'esthétique dans la philosophie européenne.
L'ouvrage du père André en France est de 1741, celui de Baumgarten en Allemagne est de 1750." He adds [1] that in æsthetics
Hutcheson's great merit is having distinguished the faculty
which perceives pure beauty from the two which were generally
supposed to comprise the entire soul, viz., understanding and
physical sensibility. He says [2] that the theory that beauty is the
agreement of beauty and variety was borrowed by Hutcheson
from Plotinus. Cousin [3] says, " Le dix-huitième siècle d'un bout
de l'Europe à l'autre n'a pas produit un artiste de génie, et il a
manqué la grande poesie parcequ'il a ignoré la vraie morale et
la grande metaphysique." But I believe that when metaphysics
began art would decline, because men became hypercritical. The
influence of chivalry upon the arts is noticed in Schlegel's Philosophy of History. [4] Lord Brougham says of despotism, " The
arts of poetry, painting, and sculpture may well flourish under its
influence." [5] He adds that it is not tyranny, but want of cultivation, which has prevented them flourishing in the east; [6] but
surely many parts of Asia were more cultivated than England at
the time of Chaucer. I rather ascribe it to a want of imagination
in the Asiatic mind. Brougham says [7] that under *free* governments the fine arts " have at all times flourished the most steadily
and abundantly." M. Quetelet thinks that among the moderns
art has suffered from a too servile imitation of the ancients. [8]
Dr. Whewell has an ingenious idea that the middle ages owed
their feebleness in science to the indistinctness of their ideas;
and that it was the arts, peculiarly the fine arts, which first remedied this evil. On their indistinctness of ideas, see his History
of the Inductive Sciences. [9] He well says [10] that one of the proofs
of this is " the fact that mere collections of the opinions of physical philosophers came to hold a prominent place in literature." [11]
He then observes [12] that " in all cases the arts are prior to the related sciences;" and [13] he gives a view of the architecture of the
middle ages; and says [14] that the "indistinctness of ideas
which attended the decline of the Roman empire, appears in the
forms of their architecture;" but by the twelfth century "every-

[1] Histoire de la Philosophie, Paris, 1846, part i. tomo iv. p. 99.
[2] Ibid. p. 98.          [3] Ibid. p. 101.
[4] Lond. 8vo, 1846, pp. 371–374.
[5] Political Philosophy, 8vo, 1849, vol. i. p. 155.
[6] Ibid. p. 155.          [7] Ibid. p. 156.
[8] Quetelet sur l'Homme, Paris, 1835, tome ii. pp. 256, 257.
[9] 8vo, 1847, vol. i. pp. 253-279.    [10] Ibid. p. 255.    [11] Ibid. p. 280.
[12] Ibid. p. 351.      [13] Ibid. tome i. 360-369.      [14] Ibid. p. 361.

thing showed that, practically at least, men possessed and applied with steadiness and pleasure the idea of mechanical pressure and support." [1]  He denies [2] the Arabic origin of Gothic architecture. Whewell says: [3] " And thus the natural process of vision is the habit of seeing that which cannot be seen; and the difficulty of the art of drawing consists in learning not to see more than is visible.  But again, even in the simplest drawing, we exhibit something which we do not see.  However slight is our representation of objects, it contains something which we create for ourselves.  For we draw an *outline*.  Now an outline has no existence in nature."  He says: [4] " It appears probable that neither poetry nor painting, nor the other arts which require for their perfection a lofty and spiritualised imagination, would have appeared in the noble and beautiful forms which they assumed in the fourteenth and fifteenth centuries, if men of genius had at the beginning of that period made it their main business to discover the laws of nature, and to reduce them to a rigorous scientific form."  He adds [5] that some of the earliest attempts to found in the sixteenth century a rational philosophy were made not by men of science but by men of art, such as Leonardo da Vinci.  I suspect civilization is generally unfavourable to the fine arts. Reed says : " They are nothing else but the language of nature, which we brought into the world with us, and have unlearned by disuse, and so find the greatest difficulty in recovering it.  Abolish the use of articulate sounds and writing among mankind for a century, and every man would be a painter, an actor, and an orator." [6]  He adds [7] that the fine arts are all founded upon the connection between signs and the things signified by them. [8]  At p. 165 he remarks that painting is the only profession in which it is necessary to distinguish " the appearance of objects to the eye from the judgment we form by sight of their colour, distance, magnitude, and figure."  William Schlegel says of Winkelmann, " No man has so deeply penetrated into the innermost spirit of Grecian art." [9]  Mr. Green observes that the motions of our different parts "all tend to the circular and curvilineal in their movements, a circumstance which mainly tends to confer on human motion the character of beauty." [10]  But may not the fact

[1] History of the Inductive Sciences, 8vo, 1847, vol. i. p. 263.      [2] Ibid. p. 364.

[3] Philosophy of the Inductive Sciences, 8vo, 1847, vol. i. pp. 114, 115.

[4] Ibid. vol. ii. p. 176.      [5] Ibid. pp. 205, 206.

[6] Reed's Inquiry into the Human Mind, Edinburgh, 8vo, 1814, pp. 97, 98.

[7] Ibid. p. 111.      [8] Ibid. see also p. 210.

[9] Lectures on the Dramatic Art, Lond. 1840, vol. i. p. 47.

[10] Green's Vital Dynamics, 8vo, 1840, p. 77.

that they *do* tend to the circular have given rise to the notion that the circular has the character of beauty? In his Mental Dynamics [1] he says that, although the ancients invested the *Finite* with beauty, yet we have the merit in the fine arts, poetry, and the drama of the expression of the Infinite. Schiller says, I think truly, "Mit kürzen Worten; die Katholische religion wird in Ganzen mehr für ein Künstlervolk, die protestantische mehr für ein Kaufmannvolk taugen." [2] Ranke ascribes the decline of art in Italy, in the latter half of the sixteenth century, to the decline of religious enthusiasm.[3] He adds [4] that when, at the end of the sixteenth century, the church of Rome recovered its power, the fine arts began to revive, and there arose in poetry Tasso, in painting Caracci. Adam Smith [5] observes that in painting we may, but in sculpture we may not, imitate mean and disagreeable objects. Sir J. Reynolds (Works, vol. ii. p. 24), could not understand the reason. The reason is [6] that in statuary there is not a sufficient disparity between the imitated and the imitating object; for, he observes,[7] the exact resemblance of two objects of art always lessens the merit of both. Thus, colouring is unpleasant in sculpture, because it still further lessens the disparity.[8] Hence we often grow tired of looking at the most beautiful artificial flowers, but never of looking at a beautiful painting of flowers. This is because the first are too like.[9] Thus, the pleasure we receive from painting and sculpture, so far from being connected with deception, is incompatible with it, and is altogether founded upon wonder at seeing how well art has surmounted the disparity nature has put between the two things.[10] In painting the disparity is greater than in sculpture; hence we are pleased at many subjects when represented in a painting which would afford no pleasure in sculpture.[11] Schlosser says that Baumgarten "is the well known inventor of a new philosophical science, æsthetics, which was afterwards transplanted to Berlin by his disciple Schulze." [12] Grimm observes that the more is *written* on the fine arts the less they flourish.[13] Morellet supposes that the more men *reason* the less they are alive to mere artistic beauty;

[1] 8vo, 1847, pp. 24, 25.
[2] Abfall der Niederlande in Schiller's Werke, Stuttgart, 1838, Band viii. p. 53.
[3] Die Römischen Päpste, Berlin, 1838, Band i. pp. 491, 492.
[4] Ibid. pp. 496-498.
[5] Essays on Philosophical Subjects, Lond. 4to, p. 138.
[6] Ibid. p. 140.
[7] Ibid. p. 136.
[8] Ibid. p. 140.
[9] Ibid. p. 141.
[10] Ibid. pp. 145, 146.
[11] Ibid. p. 147.
[12] History of the eighteenth Century, vol. ii. p. 173.
[13] Correspondance Littéraire, tome iii. pp. 98, 99.

and he gives himself as an instance.[1] Cousin thinks that modern sculpture is impossible.[2] Gibbon says:[3] "All superfluous ornament is rejected by the cold frugality of the Protestants; but the Catholic superstition, which is always the enemy of reason, is often the parent of the arts." Archdeacon Hare says:[4] "In Coleridge's Remains[5] this fondness for fantastic and verbal analogies, which was so prevalent in a large portion of our Jacobite and Caroline divines is ascribed to their study of the fathers. There may be some truth in this remark; at least, a large part of the fathers are tainted with the same fault; but it is much the same thing as we find in so many poets of Charles the First's time, who in like manner substitute fanciful images and fantastical combinations for imaginative impersonation and harmonies. Nor is this practice confined to the poets. Indeed, this is an ordinary characteristic of the state of transition between an imaginative or spiritual age, and one under the predominance of the reflective critical understanding." The Aztecs have so odd a notion of beauty that they flatten the heads of their children at birth.[6] Lieber, whose admiration for Niebuhr was unbounded, says of him: "Though he loved the fine arts and was delighted by masterworks, still I believe he had no acute eye for them."[7] See some ingenious remarks in Hare's Guesses at Truth, first series, pp. 48–70, 3rd edit. Lond. 8vo, 1847. Archdeacon Hare says[8] that "a taste for the picturesque" must always arise late in a country, because it is the result of "looking at pictures." On the fine arts, and on wit, humour, &c., see Coleridge's Literary Remains, vol. i. pp. 100, 131–138, 155, 174, 216–230, 266–273, vol. ii. pp. 7–83. Townley, who by his collections, &c., did so much for the arts, was a Catholic;[9] and so, I suppose, was Lord Arundel, his ancestor.[10] It is remarkable that Swiss scenery has never been represented by any great poet or painter.[11] Laing[12] says: "All Swedes are performers on some musical instrument,

---

[1] Mémoires de Morellet, Paris, 8vo, 1821, tome i. pp. 56, 57.
[2] Histoire de la Philosophie, part ii. tome ii. pp. 13, 14.
[3] Life of Himself in Miscellaneous Works, 8vo, 1837, p. 72.
[4] The Mission of the Comforter, 8vo, 1850, p. 221.
[5] Vol. iii. pp. 104, 117, 175.
[6] See Lawrence's Lectures on Man, 8vo, 1844, p. 251.
[7] Reminiscences of B. G. Niebuhr, Lond. 8vo, 1835, p. 60.
[8] Hare's Guesses at Truth, p. 48.
[9] See Nichols's Literary Illustrations of the eighteenth Century, vol. iii. p. 721 et seq.
[10] Ibid. p. 735.
[11] See Alison's History of Europe, vol. iv. pp. 432–433.
[12] Tour in Sweden, 1839, p. 68.

and understand music ;" and he adds [1] "that the taste of the
Swedish people for the beauty of form in the fine arts is far more
advanced and developed than ours." Protestantism unfavourable
to the arts.[2] Sir J. Reynolds, "at a very early period of his life,"
showed taste for the arts ;[3] but to the end of his life never knew
anatomy.[4] Reynolds says [5] that taste is acquired, and some good
judges do not at first admire Raphael. Reynolds first came into
note in 1752, when he was twenty-nine.[6] From Henry VIII. to
George I. all the painters in England were foreigners ; and even
under George I. and George II. there were, with the exception of
Hogarth, no better ones than Richardson, Thornhill, and Hud-
son.[7] But in 1760 the first public exhibition was opened,[8] though
in 1711 an attempt had been made to establish an academy.[9] It
was in consequence of the exertions of Boydell that we first exported instead of importing engravings.[10] Sir J. Reynolds always
says "artists must *not* imitate nature ;"[11] for he says : [12] "The end
of art" is not to imitate nature, but "to produce a pleasing effect
upon the mind ;" and "the great end of art is to strike the imagination."[13] A painter "must compensate the natural deficiencies
of his art ;" and as "he cannot make his hero talk like a great
man, he must make him look like one."[14] And I may say that in
the drama where they *do* talk, we are hurried for *time*. In
painting we have *time* but no *voice*. Reynolds observes that *all*
accessories should be sacrificed ; but that *we* do not esteem art
sufficiently to make "the sacrifice the ancients made, especially
the Grecians, who suffered themselves to be represented naked,
whether they were generals, lawyers, or kings."[15] Sculpture
having only "one style," can only correspond to "one style" in
painting ; and the sole object of sculpture is *beauty*.[16] Reynolds's
remarks [17] on architecture are unsatisfactory. From Angelo to
Maratti the Italian painters constantly declined.[18] The Dutch
painters only address the eye ; [19] and for a list of the great Dutch
painters, see p. 206, and see vol. i. p. 358, 359 ; vol. ii. p. 128.
See also at the end of Reynolds's works [20] a chronological and alphabetical list of painters. Neither Scotland nor modern Germany
have produced great painters. Why ? Metastasio said that the

[1] Tour in Sweden, 1839, p. 73.
[2] See the remarks of Beechey in Sir J. Reynolds's Works, vol, i. pp. 7–12 ; see also
Reynolds's own Observations, vol. ii. 189, 190.          [3] Ibid. vol. i. p. 37.
[4] Ibid. pp. 6, 48.          [5] Ibid. pp. 62, 63, 67.          [6] Ibid. pp. 115, 118.
[7] Ibid. pp. 25, 26.     [8] Ibid. p. 143.     [9] Ibid. p. 147.          [10] Ibid. pp. 183, 184.
[11] Works, vol. i. pp. 329, 336, 394 ; vol. ii. pp. 68, 127.          [12] Ibid. vol. ii. p. 74.
[13] Ibid. vol. i. p. 347.     [14] Ibid. pp. 348, 349, 439.          [15] Ibid. p. 420.
[16] Reynolds's Works, vol. ii. pp. 6, 7, 12.          [17] Ibid. p. 75.
[18] Ibid. p. 129.          [19] Ibid. 205.          [20] Ibid. p. 428 *et seq.*

Improvisatori had done much harm to poetry.[1] In 1793, the French, merely from hostility to Christianity, waged war against the fine arts.[2] Vico [3] says that in an early state of civilization poetry is sublime, because reason is weak.[4] Vico says [5] that the art of engraving metals must precede the art of painting, because the latter is most abstract. In the fourteenth century the ode was still hardly known in France.[6] In the fourteenth century it was laid down [7] that in sculpture all personages must be clothed *except angels*, who were allowed to be naked. In the fourteenth century great opposition was made in France to the "new taste" for painting.[8] Monteil thinks[9] that oil-painting did not become general till the beginning of the fifteenth century. Lamartine [10] says: "La musique, le moins intellectuel et le plus sensuel de tous les arts." See some ingenious remarks in Comte, Traité de Législation, tome ii. pp. 34, 38. He says that every race thinks perfect beauty consists in an *exaggeration* of its own peculiarities. "Mr. Hamilton used to observe that Burke knew every subject of human knowledge except two, gaming and music."[11] Between the city of Guatemala and the Pacific there are some beautiful waterfalls, very accessible, but "nobody ever visits them."[12] He adds [13] that near Leon, in Nicaragua, is a fine volcano which nobody ever goes to see. The Biographie Universelle [14] says that Beaumarchais' Eugenie has "une espèce d'interêt dont Diderot avait donné l'exemple dans son Père de Famille." See a most striking article on music in Fraser's Magazine, October, 1857 (containing review of my book). The writer observes that music, among other things, increases sympathy and diminishes cruelty. The Spaniards have no landscape painters, and none of their writers on America describe scenery.[15] Inglis [16] says "the state of modern sculpture in Spain is more promising than that of painting." Ford [17] says: "In Spain, as among the classical ancients, *landskip* was only an accessory or conventional, and seldom treated

[1] Works of Sir J. Reynolds, vol. ii. p. 46.
[2] See Georgel, Mémoires, vol. iv. p. 387.
[3] Philosophie de l'Histoire, p. 117.        [4] Ibid. p. 268.        [5] Ibid. p. 260.
[6] See Monteil, Histoire des Divers États, vol. i. p. 223.
[7] Monteil, Histoire des Français, tome i. p. 240.
[8] Ibid. tome ii. pp. 311, 315.        [9] Ibid. vol. iv. p. 161.
[10] Histoire des Girondins, vol. vii. p. 81.
[11] Bisset's Life of Burke, 2nd edit. 1800, vol. i. p. 108.
[12] Stephen's Central America, vol. i. p. 292,
[13] Ibid. vol. ii. p. 14.        [14] Tome iii. p 636.
[15] Ticknor's History of Spanish Literature, vol. ii. p. 436; vol. iii. p. 22; and Hoskin's Spain, 1851. vol. ii. pp. 174-176.        [16] Spain, vol. i. p. 249.
[17] Handbook for Spain, 1847, p. 341.

as a principal, either in art or literature." At p. 432 " the pen
and pencil were sculpturesque rather than picturesque." Tom
Moore was born and died a Catholic; and his mother, who had
great influence over him, was "a sincere and warm Catholic." [1]
Sir Walter Scott " confessed that he hardly knew high from low
in music," and " Lord Byron knew nothing of music." [2]

The essential difference between ancient and modern art is that
the first is *plastic*, the other *picturesque*, and as Hemsterhuys
says, the "ancient painters were probably too much sculptors." [3]
Schlegel applies the remark to poetry. Greek art is the perfection of beauty, but too sensual,[4] and "among the Greeks human
nature was in itself all sufficient." [5] The poetry of the ancients was
the poetry of enjoyment, ours is that of desire." [6] "The moderns
have never had a sculpture of their own." [7] This, as Schlegel
well says,[8] accounts for the ancients having so great a love for
the "unities." Sculpture fixes our attention on a group regardless of external accompaniments, whereas painting delights in
secondary objects. Thus the *plastic* spirit of antiquity is different from the *picturesque* spirit of romantic poetry. Schlegel
well says [9] that "genius is the almost unconscious choice of the
highest degree of excellence, and consequently it is taste in its
greatest perfection."

In 1814 Campbell writes from Paris: " Any little *taste* in
painting I know full well I have not got; but the pleasure of the
paintings grows upon me; though still far, far, inferior to that
of the *statues*." [10] Dr. Beattie, the intimate friend of Campbell,
says of him, " He was always fond of music: particularly those
airs with which he had been familar in early life." [11] In 1838,
Campbell writes that Burney has not done justice to the early
English musicians: " Handel studied Purcell and looked up to
him as a master. . . . The fact is that England, until fifty years
ago, was fertile in great musical poets. Witness her Purcell, her
Bull, her Locke, her Lawes, and Arne." [12]

Crawford [13] says that the Javanese, " in common with all semi-
barbarians, are good imitators; but in this respect they fall short

[1] Moore's Memoirs by Lord J. Russell, vol. i. pp. xxii. 29; vol. iv. p. 305; vol. vii.
p. 61.
[2] Ibid. vol. iv. p. 342, Lond. 1853.
[3] Lectures on Dramatic Art and Literature, by A. W. Schlegel, Lond. 1840, vol. i.
pp. 9-70.
[4] Ibid. p. 12.          [5] Ibid. p. 15.          [6] Ibid. p. 16.
[7] Ibid. p. 18.          [8] Ibid. p. 357.         [9] Ibid. pp. 7, 8.
[10] Beattie's Life and Letters of Campbell, 8vo, 1849, vol. ii. p. 268.
[11] Ibid. vol. iii. p. 362.          [12] Ibid. p. 265.
[13] History of the Indian Archipelago, Edinburgh, 8vo, 1820, vol. i. pp. 47, 203.

of the Hindus." See also respecting the Javanese theatre, vol. i. pp. 127–132.

In 1811, Sir James Mackintosh writes : " It is, you know, a favourite notion of mine, that the sensibility to the beauties of natural scenery is a late acquirement of civilized taste. Mr. Twining, in his translation of Aristotle's Poetics, observes that there is no single term, either in Greek or Latin, for 'prospect.'"[1]

Leigh Hunt[2] observes that poetry flourishes best in an inclement climate ; painting in a beautiful one. Hence, while we have such fine poets, our painters are indifferent. I may shortly express Hunt's idea by saying that poetry derives its materials from *within* ; painting from without. He says : " It is observable that the greatest poets of Italy came from Tuscany, where there is a great deal of inclemency in the seasons. The painters were from Venice, Rome, and other quarters ; some of which, though more northern, are more genially situated. The hills about Florence made Petrarch and Dante well acquainted with winter ; and they were also travellers and unfortunate." ·

Alison, in his " Beauty," follows the sensual school of æsthetics, and resolves beauty into association. His views, and many of his illustrations, are adopted by Mr. James Mill, who, however, points out an error of his in relation to form.[3] Wilkie " has been heard when his fame was high to declare that he could draw before he could read, and paint before he could spell."[4] Wilkie as a child disliked arithmetic,[5] but was very mechanical, and loved to construct mills, carriages, &c., and even the arts of shoe-making and weaving.[6] Wilkie was born in Fifeshire in 1785 ; therefore, he was only twenty-one when, in 1806, the appearance of the Village Politicians raised him to the height of fame.[7] We find Wilkie constantly insisting upon the superiority of painting from nature to imagination.[8] In 1805, when nineteen, he writes, " I am convinced now that no picture can possess real merit unless it is a just representation of nature."[9] And for similar expressions, see p. 158 ; but in 1836, when he was fifty-one, he writes : " If art were but an exact representation of nature, it could be practised with absolute certainty and assurance of success ; but the duty of art is of a higher kind. . . . Art is

[1] Memoirs of Sir J. Mackintosh, vol. ii. p. 125.
[2] Autobiography, 8vo, 1850, vol. ii. p. 297.
[3] Analysis of the Phenomena of the Mind, 8vo, 1829, vol. ii. pp. 203, 204.
[4] The Life of Sir David Wilkie, by Allan Cunningham, 8vo, 1843, vol. i. p. 11.
[5] Ibid. p. 13.                    [6] Ibid. p. 15.
[7] Cunningham's Life of Wilkie, vol. i. p. 115.
[8] Ibid. p. 58.                    [9] Ibid. p. 76.

only art when it adds mind to form."[1]  In 1825, at the age of
forty, he complains that after Michael Angelo paintings seem to
have been made "more for the artists and connoisseur than for
the untutored apprehension of ordinary men."[2]  In 1827 and
1828, when he was in Spain, he notices the striking similarity
between Velasquez and the best English paintings.[3]  But, he
observes,[4] that among all classes in Spain, Murillo was the
favourite.  Wilkie was never fond of painting portraits.[5]  Allan
Cunningham says[6] that Wilkie did not care for the "picturesque"
in scenery, but preferred men.  Wilkie is said *once* to have been
in love; but that is doubtful.[7]  Early in 1825, Wilkie, then
aged forty, was seized with a "nervous debility" which prevented
him from painting, or, indeed, attending to anything more than
five minutes at a time, and yet otherwise he remained in perfect
health.[8]  At length, in April 1827, he writes, "I have again
begun to paint."[9]  He afterwards recovered, but died apparently
rather suddenly in 1841, aged fifty-six.[10]  Allan Cunningham
says[11] that Wilkie's first style was copying nature; the second
style, which he did not live to work, was grander and more
historic.  Wilkie thought colour one of the very first things.[12]
Wilkie says that the Catholic religion is more favourable to art
than the Protestant.[13]  He thinks[14] that the Greek sculptors
began by learning painting.  In 1840 he writes from Constantinople that the Turkish religion was so unfavourable to art
that he found no one there who took any interest in it.[15]  Wilkie
observes that none of the great Christian painters had taken the
trouble to go to the Holy Land.[16]  Dr. Burney, who was a friend
of Herschel, mentions that that great astronomer told him in 1797,
"that he had almost always had an aversion to poetry," unless
"truth and science were united to fine words."[17]  Dr. Burney,
who knew Pitt, writes in 1799 that he was indifferent to music.
"Mr. Pitt neither knows nor cares one farthing for flutes and
fiddles."[18]

M. Comte[19] has admirably shown that the love of imaginative
expression is the result of personification, characteristic of the
early forms of superstition.  On the rise of the æsthetic principle,

---

[1] Cunningham's Life of Wilkie, vol. iii. p. 131.
[2] Ibid. vol. ii. 197.    [3] Ibid. pp. 486, 519.    [4] Ibid. p. 516.
[5] Ibid. vol. iii. p. 62.    [6] Ibid. pp. 477, 478.    [7] Ibid. vol. ii. pp. 54, 55.
[8] See the interesting details in vol. ii. pp. 219, 251, 252, 286, 287, 303. 323. 343,
345, 349.        [9] Ibid. p. 414.            [10] Ibid. vol. iii. pp. 472, 473.
[11] Ibid. pp. 494, 495.    [12] Ibid. vol. ii. p. 443.    [13] Ibid. pp. 223, 437.
[14] Ibid. p. 269.        [15] Ibid. vol. iii. p. 354.    [16] Ibid. pp. 415, 438.
[17] Madame D'Arblay's Memoirs of Dr. Burney, 8vo, 1832, vol. iii. pp. 253, 254.
[18] Ibid. pp. 274, 275.    [19] Philosophie Positive, vol. v. pp. 47-49.

see also tome v. pp. 104–161, where are some ingenious remarks
on the influence of religion on the fine arts. At tome vi. p. 158,
he says that the abstract character of monotheism is unfavourable
to the fine arts.[1]

Mozart was born in January, 1756. "At four years of age,
or earlier, he composed little pieces which his father wrote down
for him."[2] At the age of six " Mozart knew the effect of sounds as
represented by notes, and had overcome the difficulty of composing
unaided by an instrument."[3] In April, 1764, when Mozart was eight
years old, there used to be placed before him difficult pieces by
Bach, Handel, Paradies, &c., "which he played off not only at
sight and with perfect neatness, but in their exact time and
style."[4] His organisation was so delicate that in 1763 not only
the sound of a trumpet, but even the sight of one, caused him
great alarm.[5] Holmes says[6] of Mozart that, "when travelling
with his wife through a beautiful country, he would at first gaze
attentively and in silence on the view before him; by degrees,
as the ordinary serious and even melancholy expression of his
countenance became enlivened and cheerful, he would begin to
sing, or rather to hum, and at last exclaim, 'Oh! if I had but
the thema on paper.' . . . Mozart always composed in the
open air when he could." Mozart, though often exhilarated by
wine, is said by his sister-in-law never to have been drunk.[7] A
short time before Mozart died, he had an idea amounting to
monomania, that he had been poisoned.[8] He died in 1791, "at
the age of thirty-five years and ten months."[9] Holmes adds: [10]
" Mozart's notion that he had been poisoned was always treated
by those about him as a fantastic idea; and in fact the post-mortem
examination discovered nothing extraordinary beyond inflammation of the brain." From the account given by Holmes, Mozart,
so far from having the irritability generally ascribed to artists, was
a man of the most remarkable mildness, and of a very forgiving
temper. His generosity was almost criminal profusion.

Keats greatly preferred *association* to *scenery*. He says:
"Scenery is fine, but human nature is finer."[11] Wordsworth says:
"Poetic excitement, when accompanied by protracted labour in
composition has throughout my life brought on more or less

---

[1] Philosophie Positive, vol. vi. pp. 170, 171, 196–208, 231, 232, 251–259.
[2] The Life of Mozart, by Edward Holmes, Lond. 8vo, 1845, p. 9.
[3] Ibid. p. 18.          [4] Ibid. p. 32.          [5] Ibid. p. 20.
[6] Ibid. p. 231.          [7] Ibid. p. 300.
[8] Ibid. 8vo, 1845, pp. 344, 345.    [9] Ibid. p. 349.      [10] Ibid. p. 349.
[11] See his letter from Teignmouth in 1818, in Life, Letters, and Literary Remains of
John Keats, by R. M. Milnes, 8vo, 1848, vol. i. p. 218.

bodily derangement ;" and he mentions that when he wounded
his foot, a cure could not be effected until he left off composing.[1]
He adds :[2] " Nevertheless, I am at the close of my seventy-third
year, in what may be called excellent health ; so that intellectual
labour is not necessarily unfavourable to longevity. But, perhaps,
I ought here to add that mine has been generally carried on out
of doors." In 1822, Wordsworth had an accident, from the effects
of which he rapidly recovered, which, says his nephew, Dr.
Wordsworth, " was owing, humanly speaking, to his very temperate habits. To the same cause it may be ascribed, that
during his long life, he was scarcely ever confined to the house
by so much as a day's illness."[3]

" Sculpture had always languished in England, even while painting had flourished under Vandyke and his successors."[4] In 1773, Dr.
Brown published his Dissertation on Poetry and Music, " to show
that music, dance, and poetry, were united in the savage state of
man, have been separated by civilization, and ought to be reunited."[5]

Comte says[6] that the real cause of the decline of the æsthetic
principle is that owing to a diminution in the theological spirit
we cease to sympathise with its *objects*.

Lord Campbell[7] says, " Few poets deal in finer imagery than
is to be found in the writings of Bacon ; but if his prose is sometimes poetical, his poetry is always prosaic."

Huc[8] says of the Tartars, west of China, " The Lamas are
far better sculptors than painters." In 1780 an intelligent
German says of the Bohemians, " Their fondness for music is
astonishing."[9] Laing[10] well says that we overrate the fine arts
because we associate them with great persons, i.e. we see them
favoured by kings, nobles, &c. Laing says,[11] " The Swiss appear
to be a people very destitute of imagination and its influences ;
remarkably blind to the glorious scenery in which they live.
Rousseau, the only imaginative writer Switzerland has ever produced, observes ' that the people and their country do not seem
made for each other.'" This, Laing ascribes[12] to the fact that
they have always been hirelings, as warriors, or as domestic
servants. Laing[13] is very severe on music as a civilizing medium.

[1] Memoirs of William Wordsworth, by Christopher Wordsworth, 8vo, 1851, vol. ii.
p. 55.                    [2] Ibid. pp. 55, 56.                    [3] Ibid. p. 211.
[4] Pictorial History of England, vol. iv. p. 757.                    [5] Ibid. vol. v. p. 637.
[6] Philosophie Positive, vol. vi. p. 184.
[7] Lives of the Chancellors, vol. ii. p. 430.
[8] Travels in Tartary, Thibet, and China, vol. i. p. 90.
[9] Riesbeck's Travels through Germany, vol. ii. p. 140.
[10] Notes of a Traveller, 1st series, 8vo, 1842, p. 13.          [11] Ibid. p. 320.
[12] Ibid. pp. 320, 321.                    [13] Ibid. 2nd series, pp. 348–358.

Mr. Martineau finely says that ideas of pleasure or of pain being more strongly associated than other ideas, and all associations being either synchronous or successive, and pain and pleasure being more strongly felt in the synchronous than in the successive, it follows that "in minds of strong organic sensibility, synchronous impressions will predominate, producing a tendency to conceive things in pictures:" hence *artists*; "while persons of more moderate susceptibility to pleasure and pain will have a tendency to associate facts chiefly in order of their succession," and become men of science.—Mill's Logic, 1856, vol. i. pp. 525, 526. See also vol. ii. p. 433, where it is observed that this is the difference between observing *objects* and events. On æsthetics see J. S. Mill's Essays [Dissertations], vol. i. pp. 63 to 94.

## HISTORY, ETC., OF LITERATURE.

In 1553, the French ambassador, writing from London, mentions " ung libraire François qui se tient içy de longtemps." [1] In 1571, London booksellers sold so few books that they were obliged to lend their services in writing letters for other people. This was the case with Henry Cockayne, a bookseller in Fleet Street. [2] Dr. Whewell says that when Bacon wrote "scarce any branch of physics existed as a science except astronomy." [3] Schlegel observes that in France, the sense of the ridiculous which is the result of high social cultivation, has been fatal to poetry. [4] He adds [5] that in the northern literature, there is little intrigue ; for that life is there founded on mutual confidence ; while the southerns, though they have stronger passions, also possess greater powers of dissimulation. Schlegel adds : [6] "The Spanish poets were not, as was usual in other European countries, courtiers, scholars, or engaged in some civil employment ; of noble birth for the most part, they led a warlike life." On the influence of literature on the progressiveness of man, see some able remarks in Greene's Mental Dynamics. [7] The celebrated Clarke observed that the north of Europe has produced great naturalists and chemists, " because natural history is almost the only study to which the visible objects of such a region can be referred ; and

[1] Ambassades de Noailles, Leyde, 1763, tome ii. p. 274, and see p. 292.
[2] Murdin's State Papers, pp. 121, 122.
[3] Whewell's Philosophy of the Inductive Sciences, 8vo, 1847, vol. i. p. 11.
[4] Lectures on Dramatic Art, 8vo, 1840, vol. i. pp. 381, 382.
[5] Ibid. vol. ii. p. 325.     [6] Ibid. p. 356.
[7] 8vo, 1847, pp. 22, 23.

almost all its men of letters are still natural historians or chemists."[1] And[3] "since the days of Aristotle and of Theophrastus, the light of natural history had become dim until it beamed like a star from the north." At p. 462 he says of a Swedish clergyman, "Like almost all the literary men of Sweden, he had attended more to natural history than to anything else." At vol. x. p. 32, he says of the natural history of Sweden, "This branch of science is more particularly studied than any other. There is hardly an apothecary or a physician who has not either a collection of stuffed birds, or of insects," &c. A writer, very learned in European mythology, says, respecting the different tales of dwarfs, "Like the face of nature, these personifications of natural powers seem to become more gentle and mild as they approach the sun and the south."[3] Of the Celtic race he says,[4] "Its character seems to have been massive, simple, and sublime, and less given to personification than those of the more eastern nations. The wild and the plastic powers of nature never seem in it to have assumed the semblance of huge giants and ingenious dwarfs." Lord Burghley never patronised literature; and in a letter written in 1575 to the earl of Shrewsbury, sneers at "human learning."[5] Paper and printing were so dear in London that, in 1538, Coverdale and Grafton went to Paris to print their Bible there. See the account from manuscripts in the Chapter House at Westminster in Todd's Life of Cranmer, vol. i. pp. 228–234. In 1675, Evelyn[6] says of Sir W. Petty's Map of Ireland, "I am told it has cost him near 1,000l. to have it engraved at Amsterdam." In 1686, Evelyn mentions[7] "that Milton wrote for the regicides"!!! Kemble[8] says: "The genius of the Anglo-Saxons does not indeed seem to have led them to the adoption of those energetic and truly imaginative forms of thought which the Scandinavians probably derived from the sterner natural features that surrounded them." On the state of public libraries in 1848, and the ratio which, in the different countries of Europe, the number of volumes bears to the number of inhabitants, see Journal of Statistical Society, vol. xi. pp. 251, 252.

[1] Clarke's Travels, vol. ix. pp. 108, 109.    [3] Ibid. p. 212.
[3] Keightley's Fairy Mythology, Lond. 1850, p. 264.    [4] Ibid. p. 361.
[5] Lodge's Illustration of British History, 1838, vol. ii. p. 56.
[6] Diary, 8vo, 1827, vol. ii. p. 403.    [7] Ibid. vol. iii. p. 210.
[8] Saxons in England, vol. i. p. 405.

## TRAVELLING.

IN 1593, the Lords of the Council wrote to the Lord-Lieutenants of Sussex, directing them to make inquiry as to what persons had gone abroad. Those who were Protestants were not to be molested, but the friends of those who were Catholics were to be called on to give security for their appearance on a certain day.[1] This letter seems to have been a circular; for a copy of it addressed to Burghley is in Murdin's State Papers, pp. 667, 668.

A very able statistical inquirer says of Europe, " On pourrait dire qu'on trouve le plus de lumières là où il existe le plus de communications, et où coulent de grands fleuves comme le Rhin, le Seine, la Meuse, &c."[2] As travelling increased, political economy arose.

Perhaps the immediate effect of the acts passed by Mary were bad. A very intelligent traveller who was struck with the excellent state of the roads in Sweden and Denmark, ascribes it " to the emulation and rivalship excited among the inhabitants to excel each other in their respective shares of the work." There, as formerly in England, each peasant has to repair some particular part of the road, a plan, Clarke thinks, which " might be imitated advantageously in Great Britain."[3] In 1557, all the waggons between York and Newcastle and all the sacks within twenty miles of Newcastle, were insufficient to convey about five hundred quarters of wheat from Newcastle to Berwick.[4] The Swedes mend their own roads; but the moral inconveniences of this are considerable.[5] For some very curious information respecting the wretched travelling, 150 years ago, see Clarendon Correspondence, edited by Singer, 4to, 1828, vol. i. pp. 193, 198, 202, 203. See also p. 269, where we find that in 1686 there was no packet-boat between Scotland and Ireland, but correspondence had to go through London. At vol. i. p. 197, the earl of Clarendon writes in 1685 from St. Asaph, " There is in the city, as it is called, two very pretty inns who have room for fifty horses." In Italy, in 1655, it was " extraordinary to get clean sheets."[6] For the mode of travelling in France, and expenses in 1677, 1678, see King's Life of Locke, i. 149. For the cost of travelling in France in the

[1] Ellis's Original Letters, 2nd series, vol. iii. pp. 171–174.
[2] Quetelet, Sur l'Homme, Paris, 1835, tome ii. p. 185.
[3] Clarke's Travels, vol. ix. p. 268 ; vol. x. pp. 134, 478, 479, 8vo, 1824.
[4] Lodge's Illustrations of British History, 1838, vol. i. pp. 346, 347.
[5] See Dillon's Winter in Lapland and Iceland, 8vo, 1840, vol. ii. pp. 13–15.
[6] Reresby's Travels, 8vo, 1831, p. 103.

sixteenth century, see Monteil, Histoire des Divers États, tome v.
pp. 30-33.  In 1625, parliament requested, and the king promised, that no one should be allowed to have their children
educated abroad.[1]  The formation of roads in the Highlands has
lessened crime.[2]

Even in our own times, the importance of travelling is obvious,
and we rarely find an untravelled man who is not full of prejudice and bigotry.  But in the sixteenth century its importance
was much greater ; for, as there were no authentic accounts of
foreign countries, it was impossible to know them except by
*seeing* them.

A writer early in this century, quoted by Mr. Lewis,[3] says that
in Ireland " to horsewhip or beat a servant or labourer is a frequent mode of correction.  But the evil is not so great among the
gentlemen of large property, whose manners have generally been
softened by education, *travelling*," &c.

---

## FRENCH IN ENGLAND IN THE SIXTEENTH CENTURY.

Such great numbers of French Protestants fled to England that
in 1568 Cecil was obliged to apologise to the French ambassador
for allowing them to settle in London ;[4] and immediately after
the massacre of St. Bartholomew, a great number of French came
to London.[5]  This caused continued remonstrances from the
French cabinet ; but Elizabeth positively refused to send them
from England.[6]  However, they soon began to return to France.
In October, 1573, more than five hundred of them left London for
that purpose,[7] and in November, 1574, they were followed by " la
pluspart de toutz ces françoys qui restoient icy."[8]  And yet in 1575
they were so numerous that the French ambassador complained
of the rejoicing they publicly made in London for a defeat sustained by the French king.[9]  Indeed, there were four ministers
settled in London as " conseil d'estat de ceulx de la nouvelle
religion de France et de Flandres."[10]  In 1563, a sermon was

---

[1] Parliamentary History, vol. ii. p. 23.
[2] See Porter's Progress of the Nation, vol. ii. p. 10.
[3] Local Disturbances in Ireland, 8vo, 1836, p. 53.
[4] Correspondance diplomatique de La Mothe Fénelon, Paris, 1840, tome i p. 74 ;
see also tome iii. p. 311.
[5] Ibid., tome v. pp. 136, 162, 177, 202, 362, 410; tome vi. pp. 0, 59.
[6] Ibid. p. 231.          [7] Ibid. p. 426.          [8] Ibid. tome vi. p. 230.
[9] Ibid. p. 394.          [10] Ibid. p. 380.

preached by the bishop of Winchester, at which 45*l.* was collected for the French refugees in England.[1]  Prescott[2] says: "On the 12th of March, 1558, the diet having accepted the renunciation of Charles, finally elected Ferdinand as his successor.  It is another proof of the tardy pace at which news travelled at that day, that the tidings of an event of so much interest did not reach Yuste till the 29th of April.  One might have thought that this intelligence would have passed from mouth to mouth in less than half the time that it is stated to have taken to send it by courier.  That this was not so can only be explained by the low state of commercial intercourse in that day, and by the ignorance of the great mass of the people, which prevented them from taking interest in public affairs."

---

## PUBLIC AND INTERNATIONAL LAW.

On the death of Charles IX., Elizabeth told the French ambassador that his powers had expired, and that he must have fresh ones from the new king;[3] and in spite of his protestations, she persevered in this view.[4]  Lord Brougham says that the law of nations arose out of the federal union of Germany.[5]

---

## THE SPIRIT, ETC., OF JANSENISM.

Cousin observes[6] that Hutcheson's Manual of Logic was only an abridgment of the Port Royal Logic; and he says[7] that Hutcheson, like Fénelon, made *love* the basis of all religion; and[8] that his theory inclined to mysticism.  Indeed, Cousin says[9] that Hutcheson borrowed from the Logic of the Port Royal his celebrated division of the faculties of the understanding.  Mr. Morell strangely says, "Pascal's scepticism is all aimed against the *abuses* of philosophy."[10]

Cousin well says that mysticism is "le coup de désespoir de la raison humaine, qui après avoir cru naturellement à elle-même,

[1] See Machyn's Diary, Camden Society, vol. xlii. p. 305.
[2] Additions to Robertson's Charles V. p. 568.
[3] Correspondance diplomatique de Fénelon, tome iv. p. 153.
[4] Ibid. pp. 166, 170, 186.
[5] Political Philosophy, 2nd edit. 8vo, 1849, vol. i. pp. 490–492.
[6] Histoire de la Philosophie, Paris, 1846, tome iv. p. 45.
[7] Ibid. p. 156.        [8] Ibid. p. 153.        [9] Ibid. p. 414.
[10] Morell's View of Speculative Philosophy, 8vo, 1846, vol. i. p. 252.

et débutée par le dogmatisme, effrayée et découragée par le scepticisme, se réfugie dans le sentiment, dans la pure contemplation et l'intuition immédiate." [1] It is therefore, as Cousin well says,[2] that mysticism naturally came *after* sensualism, idealism and scepticism.

## STATISTICS.

COUSIN has a foolish note on statistics, in which he depreciates what he does not understand.[3] The metaphysician despises the statistician, the statistician laughs at the metaphysician ; and to these petty quarrels are sacrificed the interests of knowledge. In France, 100 marriages produce 408 births.[4] Quetelet[5] agrees with Malthus that if there were no checks, population would increase geometrically. In 1835, the homicides in France were estimated to be annually to the whole population as 1 to 48,000.[6] In consequence of the general advance of civilization during the seventeenth century, there sprang up those habits of prudence which so eminently distinguish civilized men from savages. This gave rise to the desire to equal the vicissitudes of life, and hence the origin of insurances, which can only exist in a people far advanced in the scale of society. Young rams perhaps have most female offspring. See some experiments recorded in Combe's Constitution of Man in relation to External Objects, Edinburgh, 1847, pp. 483, 484. When old men marry young women, the offspring are generally daughters, hence the reason why in the east, where polygamy is practised, more females are born than males.[7] In 1757, Voltaire[8] writes : " C'est à Breslau, à Londres, et à Dordrecht, qu'on commença il y a environ trente ans à supputer le nombre des habitants par celui des baptêmes. On multiplie dans Londres le nombre des baptêmes par 35, à Breslau par 33." In 1686, there were great disputes about the population of London and Paris.[9] Comte[10] peremptorily rejects the application to sociology of the doctrine of chances. Porter says[11] that the diminution of births and marriages is *not* owing to increased prudence, but to " the increased duration of life," which increases

[1] Cousin, Histoire de la Philosophie, 2nde série, tome iii. p. 13.   [2] Ibid. p. 17.
[3] Histoire de la Philosophie, Paris, 1846, part i. tome iv. p. 173.
[4] Quetelet Sur l'Homme, tome i. p. 80.   [5] Ibid. p. 273.   [6] Ibid. tome ii. p. 158.
[7] See Combe's Lectures on Moral Philosophy, 8vo, 1840, pp. 134, 135.
[8] Œuvres, tome. lx. p. 326.
[9] See Ray's Correspondence, edited by Dr. Lankester, 8vo, 1841, p. 189.
[10] Philosophie Positive, vol. iv. pp. 512-516.
[11] Progress of the Nation, vol. i. p. 33.

the number of those who *cannot* become parents. The average inhabitants to a house in England are 5·6. In Middlesex, 7·4.[1]

Alison[2] says that in Paris the illegitimate births are to the legitimate as 10 to 19, but there is nothing more absurd than to make this a test of morals, for prostitutes and men given to venery have few children.

Capefigue[3] gives an account of the very important statistical labours undertaken by Louis XIV. from 1695 to 1700, which he says[4] remain in manuscript, and have never been consulted. The statisticians think that political economy is inductive, and is based on figures.[5]

"The greatest numbers of births are found in the first months of the year."[6] Among the poor who nurse their own children there is generally an interval of two years before the birth of the next child.[7]

In 1783, the native king of Burmah "took a census of the population of the Burmese empire."[8]

The French suppose that in illegitimate births, the proportion of females is greater than in legitimate ones ; but according to the Report of the Registrar-General for 1843, the reverse of this is the case in England : "the legitimate boys being as 105·4 to 100 girls, while the illegitimate are 108 to 100."[9] But Colonel Sykes adds :[10] ". The Frankfort returns support the French view, and so do the Prussian."[11] It is *possible* that the climate of India influences the proportion of sexes born.[12] Read Works of Casper and Villermé, and Quetelet, Statistique Morale, 1846, in tome xxi. of Mémoires de l'Academie Royale de la Belgique, Statist. Soc. xii. 231. Bishop Heber[13] says : "The population of Lucknow is guessed at 300,000. But Mussulmans consider every attempt to number the people as a mark of great impiety, and a sure presage of famine or pestilence ; so that nothing can be known with accuracy." Comte[14] says : "Dans les pays orientaux on ne tient aucun régistre des décès ni des naissances." For a curious instance even of the present imperfect state of statistics see Talvi's Slavic Nations, New York, 8vo, 1850, p. 226.

[1] Porter, vol. iii. p. 8.   [2] History of Europe, vol. i. p. 215.
[3] Louis XIV. tome ii. pp. 85–88.   [4] Ibid. p. 86.
[5] See Journal of Statistical Society, vol. i. p. 317; vol. ii. 104; vol. vi. 322.
[6] Ibid. vol. ii. p. 110.   [7] Ibid. vol. iii. p. 320.   [8] Ibid. vol. iv. p. 325.
[9] Sykes, On Statistics of Frankfort, in Statistical Society, vol. vii. p. 345.
[10] Ibid. p. 345.   [11] Ibid. see vol. ix. p. 81, and vol. x. p. 161.
[12] Ibid. vol. viii. pp. 50, 51.   On the proportion of illegitimate births in different countries see vol. x. p. 162.
[13] Journey through India, vol. ii. p. 90.
[14] Traité de Législation, vol. iii. p. 105.

## POLITICAL ECONOMY.

THE foundation of this great science, without which it could not
for a moment exist, is the supposition that men are the best
judges of their own material interests.    Mr. Morell strangely
says, " The axiom, that men follow their interest whenever they
know it, cannot, we contend, be sustained with any approach to
plausibility ; " and this he makes out by adding that many men
have desires contrary to their own interests.[1]    But whoever said
that *all* men follow their own interest?    It is a *general*, not an
universal rule, and no mixed sciences have universal rules for
their base.

In 1721, Montesquieu distinctly says that an increase of money
would not be an increase of wealth.[2]  Alison actually supposes " that
prices  inevitably rise in the old and wealthy community from the
great quantity of the precious metals in the existing currency which
their opulence enables them, and their numerous mercantile transactions compel them, to keep in circulation ; and consequently,"
&c. &c. ! ! ![3]    In 1829, Southey writes to Dr. Gooch :  " As for the
political economists, no words can express the thorough contempt
which I feel for them.    They discard all moral consideration from
their philosophy, and in their practice they have no compassion
for flesh and blood."[4]    As to Southey's knowledge of political
economy, see[5] his remarks on Malthus.    A living philosopher,
whose extraordinary abilities have even ennobled the name of
Herschel, speaks in a very different way of political economy.[6]

Foreign travels, by showing a greater number of political
phenomena, made men *think*, and gave rise to political economy.
It is thus, for instance, at a later period, that Malthus collected
the materials for his great work on population when travelling in
the north of Europe with the celebrated Clarke.[7]

Mr. Keightley has an ill-suppressed sneer at political economy.[8]
Ferguson gravely says, " To increase the number of mankind may
be admitted as a great and important object."[9]

[1] History of Speculative Philosophy, 8vo, 1846, vol. ii. pp. 464, 465.
[2] Lettres Persanes, no. cvi. Paris, 8vo, 1835, p. 71.
[3] Alison's Principles of Population, 8vo, 1840, vol. ii. p. 409.
[4] Life and Correspondence of R. Southey, 8vo, 1850, vol. vi. p. 58.
[5] Ibid. p. 100.
[6] See Herschel's Discourse on Natural Philosophy, 8vo, 1831, p. 73.
[7] See Clarke's Travels, 8vo, 1824, vol. ix. p. 43, and compare on Malthus, Otter's
Life of Clarke, vol. i. pp. 442, 476.
[8] See Keightley's Tales and Fictions, Lond. 1834, p. 8.
[9] Ferguson on the History of Civil Society, Lond. 8vo, 1786, p. 96.

The *first* great work on commercial legislation is the Discorso Economico of Antonio Bandini, addressed in 1737 to the Grand Duke of Tuscany, but not published till 1775.[1] In 1769, "Pillo Verri, a Milanese, in his work 'Sulle Leggi Vincolanti,' maintained the doctrine of absolute and universal freedom of commerce."[2] Brougham[3] refers to the learned article on political economy in Penny Cyclopædia, vol. xviii. p. 339. In 1758 appeared the Tableau Économique de Quesnay; and in 1768, his Physiocratie.[4] At p. 138, Lord Brougham has some very superficial remarks on wages. Lord Brougham seems not to be aware that Anderson was the first who put forward the doctrine of rent.[5] I suspect Adam Smith was well acquainted with the Italian economists. At all events, in 1755 he was very familiar with foreign literature.[6] The study of political economy in France must greatly have favoured free discussion. Madame du Hausset, who was a friend of Quesnai, says, "Il recevait chez lui des personnes de tous les partis, mais en petit nombre, et qui toutes avaient une grande confiance en lui. On y parlait très hardiment de tout."[7] She adds[8] that Quesnai considered De La Rivière to be the only man fit to conduct the French finances. Schlosser well says that the real authors of the destruction of the provincial divisions of France were the economists.[9]

In 1757, Grimm[10] writes from Paris that the Ami des Hommes by Mirabeau, which had just appeared, had made a great sensation. In 1759, Grimm writes from Paris:[11] "Autrefois nos mauvais auteurs faisaient des romans et des vers détestables; aujourd'hui tout le monde veut écrire sur l'agriculture, sur le commerce, sur la population." In 1763 he writes, "On a vu ériger par tout le royaume des sociétés d'agriculture."[12] In 1550, Sir John Masone, in a letter to Cecil, strongly states the impossibility of fixing prices by laws.[13] Coleridge was so ignorant of political economy as to suppose that if tithes were done away with rents would rise.[14] He evidently despised it,[15] and Southey

[1] Brougham's Men of Letters, vol. ii. p. 91.　　[2] Ibid. p. 91.
[3] Ibid. p. 92.　　[4] Ibid. p. 95.
[5] Brougham's Historical Sketches of Statesmen, 16mo, 1846, vol. iv. p. 21.
[6] See Stewart's Life of Adam Smith, p. xx. prefixed to Smith's Philosophical Essays, 4to, 1795.
[7] Mémoires de Madame du Hausset, Paris. 8vo, 1824, pp. 57, 58.　　[8] Ibid. p. 123.
[9] History of the eighteenth Century, vol. ii. p. 159.
[10] Correspondance Littéraire, tome ii. p. 213.　　[11] Ibid. pp. 404, 405.
[12] Ibid. tome iii. p. 385 : see also p. 534.
[13] See his letters in Tytler's Edward VI. and Mary, vol. i. p. 311.
[14] Biographia Literaria, 8vo, 1817, vol. i. p. 235; and Church and State, p. 91.
[15] Literary Remains, vol. i. pp. 348, 349.

makes the same error.[1]  De Foe's economy is sometimes sound
and sometimes the contrary.[2]  Combe[3] ignorantly supposes that
when profits fall, wages will fall.  He adds[4] that "the leading aim
of the economists has been to demonstrate the most effectual
means of increasing wealth."  Alison[5] says of Paul of Russia,
"his prodigalities-even contributed to the circulation of wealth."
Fox "had never read the Wealth of Nations."[6]  Comte speaks of
political economy with the greatest contempt.[7]  Sir W. Temple[8]
shows a complete ignorance of political economy.  Manufactures,
&c., carried on by the Danish government, were a pure loss, but
falling into private hands they became profitable.[9]  Whewell[10]
calls political economy an *inductive* science.  Ricardo objects
that a legacy duty is bad, because it falls on the capital; but to
this Porter replies that *because* it falls on the capital it is not
felt, and is therefore so far good because it does not engender
irritation.[11]  Laing[12] shows a complete misapprehension of one important point in political economy.[13]  Our political economists,
by showing that each man was the best judge of his own affairs,
thus extended the suffrage.  Tocqueville thinks[14] that the
Americans construct instruments, such for instance as ships, very
slightly, because they are constantly expecting new improvements.  But I believe the real cause is a high rate of profits.
In the middle of the seventeenth century, Tonti, an Italian, proposed what are now called tontines.[15]  For a curious instance of
the way in which great crimes were caused by an economical
blunder of the Sicilian Government, see Journal of the Statistical
Society, vol. ii. p. 454.  The first chair of political economy in
Europe was founded at Naples, and occupied by Genovese.[16]  On
the influence of the price of food on revolutions, see a remarkable
essay in Journal of Statistical Society, xiii. 152–167, and quote

[1] Life of Wesley, 8vo, 1816, vol. i. p. 264.
[2] Wilson's Life of De Foe, vol. ii. pp 309, 310.
[3] Lectures on Moral Philosophy, 8vo, 1840, p. 225.          [4] Ibid. p. 254.
[5] History of Europe, vol. v. p. 547.
[6] See Alison's History of Europe, vol. vii. p. 172, and for another piece of ignorance see vol. xiii. p. 294.
[7] Philosophie Positive, tome iv. pp. 264–280, 645; tome v. p. 447, 756; tome vi.
332, 334, 440.
[8] Works, vol. i. p. 176; vol. ii. pp. 117, 118; vol. iii. p. 2–58.
[9] Laing's Sweden, pp. 15, 16.
[10] Philosophy of the Inductive Sciences, vol. i. p. vii.
[11] Porter's Progress of the Nation, vol. ii. pp. 312, 313.
[12] Denmark, 8vo, 1852, p. 189.              [13] Ibid. p. 307.
[14] Démocratie en Amérique, vol. iv. pp. 53, 54.
[15] Monteil, Histoire des Français des divers États, tome vii. p. 103.
[16] See Mr. Goodwin's valuable papers on the Two Sicilies, in Journal of Statistical
Society, vol. v. p. 57.

Porter, xiii. 216, who says that when all the earnings of the labourer are employed in procuring food, there can be no society or moral progress. In 1799, Malthus travelled with Clarke to gather materials for his work on Population, of which however, says Otter, he had already published a first edition.[1]

At the end of the sixteenth century, Sully restored the French finances.[2] He was a great friend to agriculture,[3] and repealed those taxes which pressed on the cultivation of the soil, but he forbad the exportation of specie and coin,[4] and violently opposed manufactures and commerce.[5] England set the example of allowing the exportation of the precious metals.[6] This was chiefly effected by Thomas Mun and Sir Dudly Diggs.[7] This gave rise to the commercial system;[8] but it was not till 1663, that full permission was given by Parliament to export the precious metals.[9] Twiss thinks that the mercantile system introduced a spirit of commercial jealousy, and a disposition to interference on the part of the statesmen.[10]

After the death of Henry IV., France was in confusion till 1661, when Mazarin died, having recommended to Louis XIV. Colbert, who was entirely opposed to the economical views of Sully, and who looked upon agriculture as subordinate to manufactures and commerce.[11] He forbad the exportation of coin,[12] and the result was that its price fell one-half, and half the land was put out of cultivation.[13] In his tariff of 1664, he encouraged the exportation of French raw materials, and discouraged the importation of foreign manufactured goods.[14] In 1667, he raised the import duties still higher, but lowered them by the peace of Nimeguen in 1678.[15] He encouraged commerce, and allowed the exportation of the precious metals.[16]

In 1667, Sir William Petty laid down that labour was the foundation of value;[17] and in 1697, Sir Dudley North "made an able statement of the true principles of commerce."[18] Locke distinguishes between *natural* value or utility, and *actual* value, and ascribed the difference to the amount of labour required to produce them. But by the *value*, he meant "the capacity of satisfying the wants of men," and "greater value with him was identical with greater usefulness."[19] He *seems* to have known

[1] Otter's Life of Clarke, vol. i. pp. 412 and 476.
[2] Twiss, Progress of Political Economy, 8vo, 1847, p. 38.      [3] Ibid. p. 39.
[4] Ibid. p. 40.          [5] Ibid. pp. 42, 44.          [6] Ibid. p. 46.
[7] Ibid. pp. 47, 48.          [8] Ibid. p. 48, 53.          [9] Ibid. p. 49.
[10] Ibid. p. 56.          [11] Ibid. pp. 67, 68.          [12] Ibid. p. 68.
[13] Ibid. p. 70.          [14] Ibid. p. 71.          [15] Ibid. p. 71.
[16] Ibid. p. 74.          [17] Ibid. p. 81, 82.          [18] Ibid. p. 83.          [19] Ibid. pp. 86, 87.

the difference between value in use and value in exchange ; but he wanted the clearness of Petty ;[1] and Law, in 1705, was the first who broadly laid down the difference between value and utility.[2] His fundamental error was confounding money with capital.[3] On account of the fluctuations in the precious metals, he proposed to substitute land, and at the same time save expense by making paper supply the place of coin.[4] Owing to the different methods of taxation, the economists of England paid more attention to the production, those of France to the distribution, of wealth.[5]

The failure of Law weakened Colbertism, and paved the way for Quesnai's system.[6] Quesnai proposed only one tax, levied at once on the real produces of the land.[7] De Gournay, too, aided Quesnai in attacking the mercantile system.[8] Turgot was the greatest of the economists or physiocrats ; their great opponent was Necker.[9] In 1768, Beccaria, and, in 1771, Vein also opposed them ; but did not fall into the errors of the mercantile system.[10] The establishment of the mercantile system was an event of the greatest importance. According to its expounders, labour employed in manufacture was more productive than labour employed in agriculture.[11] This was an error, but an error productive of the best effects ; for, by weakening the influence of agriculturists, it accelerated the march of civilization. I have no doubt that the influence of Quesnai's school has retarded the progress of general knowledge in France as compared with England ; for though the French want some natural advantages we possess, the deficiency is not enough to account for the prodigious excess of their agricultural population. The first stimulus was given by Sully, who laboured to destroy the French manufactures. Respecting Malthus, see Twiss, Progress of Political Economy, pp. 203–225, and 213, 222. On the economical policy of Sully, see Blanqui, Histoire de l'Économie Politique, tome i. pp. 347–361. He despised manufactures,[12] but freed France from debt.[13] On the system of Colbert, see Blanqui, tome i. pp. 362–378, and, in particular, pp. 363, 366, 368, 372. He exempted from all taxes a father of ten children.[14] M. Blanqui[15] is not afraid to say that without smuggling commerce would have been destroyed. ' C'est à la contrabande que le commerce doit de n'avoir pas péri sous l'influence du régime prohibitif." M.

---

[1] Twiss, Progress of Political Economy, pp. 88, 89.    [2] Ibid. p. 93.
[3] Ibid. p. 98.            [4] Ibid. pp. 96, 99–101.        [5] Ibid. p. 130.
[6] Ibid. p. 141.          [7] Ibid. p. 148.                 [8] Ibid. p. 152.
[9] Ibid. p. 153.          [10] Ibid. p. 153, 155.          [11] Ibid. p. 182.
[12] Blanqui. op. cit. tome i. p. 349.       [13] Ibid. p. 361.       [14] Ibid. p. 374.
[15] Ibid. tome ii. p. 25.

Blanqui [1] says that our navigation laws have not been beneficial, even in a political point of view; and of course economically there is no doubt as to their evil results. On origin of banks, see Blanqui, tome ii. pp. 38–41. Blanqui [2] observes that Quesnai was a natural reaction after the failure of Law; and for a view of his school, see pp. 75-95. I think I may say Law was for the state; Quesnai, for the people. Law for *accumulation*; Quesnai for *distribution*. Blanqui [3] has some good remarks on the importance of *distribution*. For account of Malthus, see Blanqui, tome ii. pp. 131-142. Lord Brougham, at the beginning of his Life of Adam Smith, gives a pretty good account of the history of political economy, and observes that in the eighteenth century the French began to study it, *not knowing* that the Italians were working at it at the same time. This shows how its study depended on general causes.

---

# ETHICS.

Morell [4] says that the best ethical inquiries in modern times are those of Jouffroy in his Mélanges Philosophiques.

The sensual school of metaphysics fail in æsthetics: but, I think, they fail still more in ethics. James Mill, for instance, resolves friendship and kindness into association; and says: "We never feel any pains and pleasures but our own." [5] His analysis of the origin of parental affections, though inducted in the same manner, is perhaps more satisfactory, [6] but still I strongly suspect that something has been overlooked. [7] At pp. 244, 245, Mill observes that we know that our own virtue is the reason why men are virtuous to us; and, therefore, with the idea of our own acts of virtue are associated the ideas of the great advantage we derive from the virtuous acts of our fellow creatures. "When this association is formed in due strength, which it is the main business of a good education to effect, the motive of virtue becomes paramount in the human breast." In the same way he accounts for the desire of posthumous fame, [8] and see in particular [9] his ingenious attempts to explain why we often prefer praiseworthiness to praise.

[1] Blanqui, Histoire de l'Économie Politique, tome ii. pp. 33-35.
[2] Ibid. p. 75, 76.   [3] Ibid. p. 127.
[4] History of Speculative Philosophy, 8vo, 1846, vol. ii. p. 414.
[5] Analysis of the Mind, 8vo, 1829, vol. ii. pp. 174, 175.
[6] Ibid. pp. 177, 183.   [7] See what he says at p. 212.
[8] Ibid. pp. 246, 247.   [9] Ibid. p. 249.

Jeremy Taylor took great pains with the Ductor Dubitantium, which he looked on as his capital work, and which he published in 1660.[1] At p. cclxxii. Heber ignorantly says of Taylor's Ductor Dubitantium, " he has preceded in the same track the labours of Tucker and of Paley."[2]  " Sous le règne même de Louis XIV, tromper au jeu n'était pas une action déshonorante dans la bonne société."[3] Neander[4] says Ambrose of Milan was the first who applied ancient ethics to Christian morals.  " Fortune favours fools," is a proverb " in all the languages of Europe."[5]  Melmoth published notes on Cicero's De Amicitiâ in which " he refuted Lord Shaftesbury, who had imputed it as a defect to Christianity that it gave no precepts in favour of friendship, and Soame Jenyns, who had represented that very omission as a proof of its divine origin."[6] The New Testament overlooks the importance of *pride* and *individuality*, and takes a gross view of women.

## CHURCHES.

In 1594, London churches were used as prisons.[7]  We know from a sermon preached in 1561 by the bishop of Durham, that it was common in St. Paul's church for persons to be " talking, buying, and selling, fighting and brawling."[8]  In 1561, the queen was obliged to issue a proclamation forbidding persons to " shoot any handgun or dag within the cathedral church of St. Paul."[9]  In 1571, the archbishop of York was obliged to order throughout his diocese that no minstrels or morrice dancers should be allowed to perform in the churches during " the time of divine service or of any sermon."[10]  In 1562 the bishop of Exeter presented a paper to the ecclesiastical synod in which he requested " that there be some order taken for the punishment of them that do walk and talk in the church at time of common prayer and preaching, to the disturbance of the ministers, and offence to the congregation."[11]

[1] See Heber's Life of Taylor, in vol. i. of Taylor's Works, 8vo, 1828, pp. lxxvi. and xcvi.
[2] See King's Life of Locke, 8vo, 1830, vol. ii. pp. 122, 123.
[3] Comte, Traité de Législation, vol. i. p. 64.
[4] History of the Church, vol. iv. p. 365.         [5] Mill's Logic, 1856, vol. ii. p. 335.
[6] Rose's Biog. Dict. London, 1848, vol. x. p. 85.
[7] Stonyhurst MS. in Mr. Tierney's edit. of Dodd's Church History, vol. iii. p. 115.
[8] Pilkington's Sermon in Strype's Parker, Oxford, 1824, vol. i. p. 187, and Strype's Grindal, p. 81.          [9] Strype's Grindal, p. 84.          [10] Ibid. p. 250.
[11] Strype's Annals, vol. i. part i. p. 522.

## CALVINISM.

It is often said that speculative principles do not influence the conduct; and this is undoubtedly true of many subjects, particularly of morals. However, we know that a belief in predestination does influence the conduct of the Turks.[1] Those infamous assassins the Thugs are fatalists. "Fatalism is a prominent dogma of the creed of the Thugs."[2] On the democratic tendency of Calvinism, see Esprit des Lois, livre xxiv. chap. v., Œuvres de Montesquieu, Paris, 1835, p. 408.

The doctrine of justification by grace, and a contempt of good works made immense progress in the sixteenth century, even among those who had no regard for Luther and who venerated the pope.[3]

The Calvinists reciprocated the hatred of the Catholics.

At the end of the sixteenth century, Rollock was very active in spreading Calvinism in Edinburgh.[4]

Todd boldly says that the tenets of the Church of England, as settled by Cranmer, have been but little altered and are essentially anti-Calvinistic (Life of Cranmer, vol. ii. p. 268). See also pp. 301–318, where, on the authority of Waterland, he denies the Calvinism of the Seventeenth Article,[5] and he quotes[6] Archdeacon Tottie, who says that the Liturgy is the best comment upon the Articles! In 1543 Cranmer says, "Men are to themselves the authors of sin and damnation;"[7] and it is supposed[8] that Cranmer required the pre-existence of good works as necessary to salvation.

In 1636, Knott, an English Catholic, says that Calvinism "once a darling in England, is at last accounted heresy; yea, and little less than treason."[9]

Coleridge says,[10] "And this, I fancy, is the true distinction between Arminianism and Calvinism in their moral effects. Arminianism is cruel to individuals, for fear of damaging the race by false hopes and improper confidences; while Calvinism is horrible for the race, but full of consolation to the suffering individual." Southey[11] has a most violent remark on Calvinism.

---

[1] Brougham's Political Philosophy, 2nd edit. 8vo, 1849, vol. i. p. 404.
[2] Illustrations of the History and Practices of the Thugs, 8vo, 1851, p. 113.
[3] See Ranke, Die Römischen Päpste, Berlin, 1839, Band i. pp. 138–146.
[4] See Bower's History of the University of Edinburgh, vol. i. p. 104.
[5] Life of Cranmer, p. 303.          [6] Ibid. p. 308.
[7] Ibid. p. 309.          [8] Ibid. p. 310.
[9] Des Maizeaux, Life of Chillingworth, 8vo, 1725, p. 112.
[10] Literary Remains, vol. iii. p. 303.          [11] Life of Wesley, 8vo, 1846, vol. i. p. 321.

The Church of England till 1620 was Calvinistic.[1]
On the bad effects of the doctrine of election, see King's Life
of Locke, 8vo, 1830, vol. ii. pp. 98, 99. In the sixteenth century
the Protestants became more Calvinistic; the Catholics more
Arminian.[2] Arminianism was chiefly held by the Jesuits, who
by their support of free will injured their influence in Spain
when they were attacked by the Inquisition and Dominicans.[3]
The Dominican doctrine was favoured by Clement VIII.,[4] who,
however, did not venture to give any decision.[5] It was also
favoured by Paul V.[6]

On Calvin's miserable bigotry see Ranke, Civil Wars of France,
8vo, 1852, vol. i. pp. 216, 218. Orme says:[7] "Previous to the
Synod of Dort, though individuals might have believed and
taught differently, Calvinism was the prevailing theological system of this country. The complexion of the Thirty-nine Articles
is evidently Calvinistic."

Mr. Morell[8] says that "Hartley and Priestley drew the doctrine
of philosophical necessity from their peculiar psychological principles." This was followed up by Goodwin, Belsham, and Bray.[9]
According to Morell, this school holds that man is born without
moral principles, and that what produces pleasure is good, what
produces pain is evil,[10] that pleasure in contemplation is *desire* or
*will*, which is therefore never free.[11] Morell adds[12] that the
Calvinistic metaphysician would consider crime almost entirely
as the result of bad government. From this, I suppose, would
follow sympathy with the criminal, and perhaps mildness in laws
which punished *civil* offences; *severity* in those which punished
*state* offences. Hence the Calvinistic school would value highly
education as well as laws; for they are the most effective modifications of the *will*. Indeed Morell[13] says that Socialism "is the
fullest development of philosophical necessity which the present
age has known;" and adds[14] that the great error of Socialism is
to deny the freedom of the will, and exaggerate the advantages of
education. Mr. Morell, I regret to say, has made very improper
remarks on Mr. Owen.

Dr. Jackson, who had seen and thought a great deal of the
military profession, accounts for the courage of the Scotch by

---

[1] See Nichols, Literary Illustrations of the eighteenth Century, vol. iv. p. 326.
[2] Ranke, Päpste, vol. ii. pp. 296, 297.                    [3] Ibid. p. 301.
[4] Ibid. p. 306.          [5] Ibid. p. 307          [6] Ibid. p. 355.
[7] Life of Owen, p. 32.
[8] View of the Speculative Philosophy of Europe, 8vo, 1846, vol. i. p. 367.
[9] Ibid. pp. 367, 368.          [10] Ibid. p. 369.          [11] Ibid. p. 370.
[12] Ibid. p. 383.          [13] Ibid. p. 386.          [14] Ibid. pp. 386, 396.

their religion : " The Scotch are Calvinists in religious belief ; and Calvinists believe that everything which happens in life is pre-ordained by Providence to happen ; consequently that individual life is as secure in the rage of battle as in the shades of peace. Such opinion influenced the conduct of the Lowland Scot, fortified his mind in the dangers of war," &c.[1]

" Jansenism is a sort of Catholic Calvinism. It affords a new instance of the more pure and severe moralists naturally adopting a doctrine of self-debasement, and in Pascal's language, of self-hatred, and of their referring every action, enjoyment, and hope, exclusively to the all-perfect Being. The Calvinistic people of Scotland, of Switzerland, of Holland, and of New England, have been more moral than the same classes among other nations. Those who preached faith, or in other words a pure mind, have always produced more popular virtue than those who preached good works, or the mere regulation of outward acts. The latter mode of considering Ethics naturally gives rise to casuistry, especially when auricular confession makes it necessary for every confessor to have a system, according to which he can give opinion and advice to his penitent. The tendency of casuistry is to discover ingenious pretexts for eluding that rigorous morality and burdensome superstition which, in the first ardour of religion, are apt to be established, and to discover rules of conduct more practicable by ordinary men in the common state of the world." These admirable remarks were made by Sir J. Mackintosh in 1808, and are in Memoirs of Mackintosh, edited by his Son, 8vo, 1835, vol. i. p. 411.

In Scotland, the Episcopalians liked ornaments in their churches ; the Presbyterians hated them.[2]

---

## MANUFACTURES.

THE influence of the Civil Law, I suppose, increased the disrespect with which an ignorant age naturally treated manufactures. I have already pointed out how the effect of the feudal system was to create a powerful nobility; and it is evident that the same cause must have given a factious dignity to agriculturists. Because property in land was the original source of nobility, men, by the influence of association, continued to respect the possession

---

[1] Jackson's View of the Formation, Discipline, and Economy of Armies, 8vo, 1845, p. 109.

[2] Burton's History of Scotland, 1853, vol. ii. p. 547.

of it, even when its possession ceased to confer rank.[1]  At the
same time the dread of novelty made men look with contempt on
the innovations of manufactures and commerce.  The influence of
feudal association in making men respect landowners still exists
among the unreflecting part of modern politicians.  It is seen in
the language that is held by some men respecting the supposed
importance of the agricultural interest ; and it is seen in the
insane laws of primogeniture and entails which are still permitted
to deform our statute book.

In 1568, Sir Francis Knollys writes to Cecil: "I am glad of
your bettered news of the matters of Count Lodowyke.  I must
needs commend the artificial usage of your copper mines."[2]  In
1549, it was proposed that a law should be passed compelling
every possessor of a certain number of acres of ground to sow
some of them with flax and hemp.  It was also proposed that the
families of all farmers should not be allowed to wear any shirts
except those spun within their own houses, or at least in the
country.[3]  In the same paper[4] it is proposed that whoever fells
a tree shall be obliged to sow and maintain another for it.  At
p. 284 there is a letter dated 1598 from Sir John Popham to the
queen respecting tin, in which he says that for five years together
"there was yearly brought to the coinage xii$^e$ thousand pounds weight
of tin," of which about a fourth was spent in England ; and about
"ix$^e$ thousand pounds" exported.  The usual price was 48s. the
hundred.  On the extraordinary adaptability of iron to the wants
of man, see a good passage in Prout's Bridgewater Treatise, 8vo,
1845, p. 127.  In 1562, a petition from Kingston upon Thames
complains that an iron mill in the neighbourhood has consumed
so much wood that the price of it has been raised from 3s. to 4s.
a load ; and that of charcoal from 10s. to 20s.  The petitioners
request that the mill may be put down by act of parliament.[5]
In 1575 the council orders that no more iron ordnance shall be
made in Surrey, because it had been exported to foreigners, and
because iron mills and forges had "greatly consumed the woods."[6]
In 1586 the inhabitants of the neighbourhood of Guilford complained " of an Italian having erected a glass-house in those parts,
whereby the woods are likely to be consumed to the prejudice of
the whole country."  In consequence of this petition the council
ordered that the Italian should appear before them, and that in

---

[1] Brougham's Political Philosophy, vol. i. p. 319.
[2] Wright's Elizabeth, 8vo, 1838, vol. i. pp. 293, 294.
[3] Egerton Papers, Camden Society, 1840, p. 12.          [4] Ibid. p. 13.
[5] Losely Manuscripts, by Kempe, p. 488.                  [6] Ibid. p. 490.

the meantime the working of the glass-house should be stayed.[1] Several bills were passed against iron mills, because it was feared that the working of them would destroy our woods.[2] The general use of coal by doing away with this fear must have given a great stimulus to our iron manufactures. In 1686, a manufacture of velvet was set up in Ireland.[3] In 1675, Locke saw at Pont St. Esprit in France, "the way of winding silk by an engine that turns at once 134 bobbins."[4] Copper was not found in Great Britain to any extent till about 1700.[5] It is doubtful if manufactures are prejudicial to health, and it is certain that those who work at them are *not* particularly liable to consumption.[6] Bishop Heber[7] gives a very clear account of the way they make attar of roses near Benares.

## THE REFORMATION AND PROTESTANTISM.

IT has been calculated that in France the loss in the productiveness of industry caused by the celebration of Catholic holidays amounted in the last century every year to nearly 2,500,000l. sterling.[8] The Reformation gave an air of ferocity even to literature. This is confessed by a great Protestant (?) writer.[9] "La Suisse fut le premier pays hors de l'Allemagne où s'étendit la nouvelle secte qu'on appelait la *primitive église*."[10] This, Voltaire says, was the work of Zwinglius. On the vulgar idea that the Reformation secured the liberty of conscience, see some good remarks by Lord King.[11] The Reformation lowered wages by doing away with holidays, and this gave rise to the poor laws.[12] Comte[13] says that Luther did nothing; but that everything was already prepared; and respecting the injury done to morals by the Reformation allowing divorce, see pp. 686, 688. Even Ranke does not venture to explain the success of the Reformation

[1] Loseley Manuscripts, p. 493.
[2] See D'Ewe's Journals of Parliament, folio, 1682, pp. 30, 31, 55, 289, 305.
[3] See Clarendon Correspondence, edit. Singer. 1828, 4to, vol. i. p. 321.
[4] King's Life of Locke, 8vo, 1830, vol. i. p. 96.
[5] See Journal of Statistical Society, vol. i. p. 65.
[6] Ibid. vol. v. pp. 277, 278, 279, 280 ; see also vol. vi. p. 200.
[7] Journey through India, vol. i. p. 250.
[8] Dupin's Note in Œuvres de Montesquieu, Paris, 1835, pp. 413, 414.
[9] Abfall der Niederlande in Schiller's Werke, Stuttgart, 1838, Band viii. p. 194.
[10] Essai sur les Mœurs, chap. cxxix. Œuvres de Voltaire, xvii. p. 217.
[11] Life of Locke, 8vo, 1830, vol. ii. pp. 68, 69.
[12] See on this Blanqui, Histoire de l'Économie Politique, Paris, 1845, tome i. p. 288 et seq.
[13] Philosophie Positive, tome v. pp. 643, 644.

in some countries, and its failure in others. He merely says [1] " es verdiente wohl," &c. Ranke [2] seems to ascribe the failure of the Reformation in France to the alliance between the crown and the church. The emperor Maximilian acknowledged that he had no power over his own subjects.[3] Connect this into the success of the Reformation in Germany. Ranke [4] candidly confesses that : " Many had adopted the reformed system in the expectation that it would allow them greater freedom in their personal habits." [5] He says, " The rise of German protestantism was possible only because a number of the princes and cities had been permitted by resolutions of the Imperial diet to refuse the aid of the secular arm to ecclesiastical laws." This remark had already been made by Capefigue.[6] Ranke [7] thinks that the traditions of the Waldenses *did* favour the Reformation in Southern France ; but, he adds, this is a point not yet proved. In the sixteenth century the great vassals used to sign their letters in France with all the pomp of the king.[8] Capefigue truly says that the Reformation, under the pretence of freedom, compelled men to adopt its opinions.[9] Reformation connected with the Albigenses.[10] On the coarseness of Luther, see Capefigue, i. 337, 338 ; and on his enormous influence in Germany, p. 340. Capefigue [11] says that the Interim of Charles V. having a *political* view, was attacked by both parties. He says[12] that the Act of Passaw is the first proclamation of liberty of conscience. On the encouragement to political inquiry, see iv. p. 160. Capefigue [13] says that probably Lutheranism, so far from emancipating the multitudes, merely took property from the clerks to give it to the barons, and thus *reconstructed* feudality. Capefigue [14] says that in 1615 the Diet of Ratisbon cared nothing for *material* interests, but only for religion. " At the beginning of the sixteenth century, the principal booksellers came from Basle in Switzerland." [15] The objection of English Roman Catholics to marry during Lent is gradually diminishing.[16]

[1] Päpste, vol. ii. p. 23.
[2] Civil Wars of France, 8vo, 1852, vol. i. p. 188.
[3] Ibid. p. 150.    [4] Ibid. vol. i. p. 214.    [5] Ibid. p. 228.
[6] Histoire de la Réforme, tome i. p. 62.    [7] Civil Wars of France, vol. i. p. 234.
[8] Monteil, Histoire des Divers États, tome v. p. 162.
[9] Histoire de la Réforme, tome i. p. 164 ; tome viii. p. 336.
[10] Ibid. tome i. pp. 192, 193.
[11] Ibid. pp. 345, 347.    [12] Ibid. p. 348.
[13] Ibid. tome viii. p. 330.
[14] Richelieu, Mazarin, et La Fronde, tome i. pp. 142, 143.
[15] Journal of Statistical Society, vol. iii. p. 165.
[16] Ibid. vol. iv. p. 41.

# CIVILIZATION COMPARED WITH BARBARISM.

" On a remarqué cependant que l'homme civilisé est généralement
plus fort que l'homme pris dans l'état sauvage." [1]  And the same
thing is said still more positively by Archbishop Whately. [2]  Even
Reid, who was far too acute a thinker to fall into the paradox of
Rousseau, supposes that barbarians are stronger than civilized
men. [3]  The error of supposing that old times are better than the
present ones is amongst uninformed men almost universal.  Mr.
Price, who has ably examined its causes, observes that it is precisely in the same way that a belief has arisen that men were
formerly giants and long lived. [4]  Ranke allows that there is an
essential difference between ancient and modern civilization. [5]  He
says [6] that the ancient civilization is in a great measure owing to
a union of Church and State.  Lawrence [7] observes that civilized
men are more powerful than savages.  Ritter has noted the connection between the extent of sea-coast and civilization. [8]  Archdeacon Hare oracularly tells us, without a word of explanation,
that "The ultimate tendency of civilization is towards barbarism." [9]  Ellis [10] observed that English sailors were stronger
than South Sea Islanders.  We need not be afraid of retrograding.
There are many things which distinguish us from the ancient form
of civilization.  We have public opinion, and printing to dissemi-
nate it.  Political economy first taught us that nations gain by
each others gain. [11]  While Europe is secure against internal decay,
the chances of an inroad of barbarians is still less.  The invention
of gunpowder and the successive improvements in the manufacture
of weapons, and chemical art being concentrated on gunpowder,
makes war, barbarous as it is, depend upon acts too delicate in their
origin and scientific in their application for barbarous nations.  In
every instance where Europeans have come into contact with barbarians they have fled before us, and great empires have been
founded by a handful of men.  Besides, the barbarians are de-

[1] Quetelet, Sur l'Homme, Paris, 1835, tome ii. p. 272, and see p. 67.
[2] Lectures on Political Economy, Lond. 8vo, 1831, p. 59.
[3] See Reid's Inquiry into the Human Mind, Edinburgh, 1814, pp. 439, 440.
[4] Price's Preface to Warton's History of English Poetry, 8vo, 1840, vol. i. pp. 23, 24.
[5] Die Römischen Päpste, Berlin, 1838, Band i. p. 34.        [6] Band i. pp. 3, 4.
[7] Lectures on Man, 8vo, 1844, pp. 274–276.
[8] Prichard's Physical History of Mankind, Lond. 8vo, 1837, vol. ii. pp. 354, 355.
[9] Guesses at Truth, second series, 2nd edit. 8vo, 1848, p. 234.
[10] Polynesian Researches, 8vo, 1831, vol. i. p. 98.
[11] See Johnson's absurd remark.

creasing. Finally, our experience is greater, and we have no slavery.

Democracy is no longer dangerous. The influence of mind increases in three distinct ways: 1st. Those classes who oppose it are losing their power. 2nd. Civilization, as Comte says, increases the difference of men. 3rd. Education increases the ease into which that difference is perceived. Even Alison [1] confesses that after Napoleon's expedition of Egypt, our decisive superiority over barbarians is no longer a disputable point. Alison [2] thinks nations *must* decay. Porter says,[3] "Of 5,812,276 males twenty years of age and upwards, living at the time of the census of 1831, there were said to be engaged in some calling or profession 5,466,182," &c. Laing [4] thinks Europe is tending towards federalism. Tocqueville[5] denies the existence of a stationary state. The *regular* labour of a policeman is immense, certainly greater than any exercise savages can go through.[6] The only peculiarity I have found common to *all* barbarous nations is improvidence—indifference to the future. The assertion of Whately, &c, that civilized men are stronger than barbarians must not be put too generally.[7]

Polygamy has been succeeded by adultery.[8] Insanity is, like crime, more often cured than formerly, because treated more mildly. The *wants* of men have increased faster than their *resources*, so that countries have not *spare strength* enough to go to war.[9] Lord Mahon [10] says, "Drunkenness, a vice which seems to strike deeper roots than any other in uneducated minds." One of the most intelligent of modern missionaries very frankly says, that the introduction by the Christians of vaccination into Thibet would probably overthrow Lamanism.[11]

---

## CRIMES, THEIR STATISTICS, ETC.

IN France, for every 4,463 inhabitants, one is yearly accused of crime,[12] and out of 100 accused 61 are condemned.[13] In the Low Countries, the proportionate number accused is nearly the same,[14]

[1] History of Europe. vol. iv. pp. 652, 653.   [2] Ibid. vol. vi. p. 120.
[3] Progress of the Nation, vol. iii. p. 2.
[4] Notes of a Traveller, first series, pp. 26–28.
[5] Démocratie en Amérique, tome ii. pp. 87, 88.
[6] See Journal of Statistical Society, vol. ii. p. 104.
[7] See Comte, Traité de Législation, tome iii. p. 327 *et seq.*   [8] Ibid. p. 432.
[9] See Laing's Sweden, p. 417.   [10] History of England, vol. ii. p. 187.
[11] Huc's Travels in Tartary and Thibet, vol. ii. p. 199.
[12] Quetelet, Sur l'Homme, Paris, 1835, tome ii. p. 165.   [13] Ibid. pp. 165, 166.
[14] Ibid. p. 171.

but there are fewer crimes against persons.[1] In France, during 1828 and 1829, the more intellectual the classes, the greater was the proportion which crimes against persons bore to crimes against property;[2] but from this no general conclusion can be drawn against education.[3] In winter we have the *minimum* of crimes against persons, and the *maximum* of crimes against property: in summer, precisely the reverse.[4] For every 100 men accused in France, there are 23 women accused;[5] but for crimes against property the proportion is 26 to 100, for those against persons only 16 to 100.[6] This perhaps is the result of *weakness*, for in cases of poisoning the numbers are equal for the two sexes,[7] so that the difference in morality is not so great as is generally supposed.[8] In men at the age of twenty-five, in women at thirty, the tendency to crime is at its height,[9] but the tendency to theft *always* remains.[10] Of all the circumstances which control the tendencies to crime, age is the most active.[11] Alison speaks of "the prodigious increase of crimes in England."[12] He adds[13] that in Lanarkshire "crime is increasing six times as fast as the number of people"; and he quotes Moreau to the effect that "the number of individuals charged with serious offences is in England five times greater than it was thirty years ago; in Ireland, six times; but in Scotland, twenty-nine times."[14] He adds[15] that "since 1820, commitments for felonies and other serious crimes have increased about 185 per cent. in England"; in Ireland, 200; in Scotland, 250 per cent.; and as population has not advanced more than 50 per cent., "over the whole empire serious crime is augmenting four times, in Scotland five times, as fast as the number of the people." See the table at p. 326, where I find that the commitments are nearly *equal* in England and Ireland; in 1820 they were in each country every year from 12,000 to 13,000; in 1838, 23,000 to 25,000. In Sweden and Norway, the crime is even greater.[16]

Alison notices[17] that in America education does *not* prevent crime; in France, it increases it. In Iceland, suicide is scarcely known;[18] indeed, almost the only crimes known are offences against property, "and even these are both rare and trivial."[19] In

---

[1] Quetelet, Sur l'Homme, Paris, 1835, tome ii. p. 172.
[2] Ibid. pp. 176, 177.   [3] Ibid. pp. 176–179.   [4] Ibid. p. 211.
[5] Ibid. p. 213.   [6] Ibid. p. 214.   [7] Ibid. p. 217.
[8] Ibid. p. 219.   [9] Ibid. pp. 230, 231.   [10] Ibid. p. 235.   [11] Ibid. p. 242.
[12] Principles of Population, 8vo, 1840, vol. i. p. 156.
[13] Ibid. vol. ii. pp. 97, 98.   [14] Ibid. p. 317.   [15] Ibid. pp. 325, 326.
[16] Ibid. p. 327.   [17] Ibid. p. 320.
[18] Dillon's Winter in Lapland and Iceland, 8vo, 1840, vol i. p. 142.
[19] Ibid. p. 139, and see p. 296.

Sweden, highway robberies are hardly known.[1]  In 1553, Renard
seems to say that the English committed more violent crimes in
summer than in winter.[2]  Combe says:[3]  "Thus a public execution, from the violent stimulus which it communicates to the
lower faculties of the spectators, may within twenty-four hours of
its exhibition be the direct cause of a new crop of victims for the
gallows."  At pp. 372–374, he has some clever remarks on the
bad working of the jury system.  Mr. Wright[4] says positively
that crime diminished from the Reformation to the end of Elizabeth, increased under James I. and Charles I, and since then has
been constantly diminishing.  Combe[5] thinks punishment should
be *entirely* addressed to reforming the criminals, and not as an
example.  Plint[6] says:  "The absolute ratio of crime for all
England in 1801 is shown in the table to have been 54 in 100,000,
and in 1845, 156 in 100,000—nearly threefold."  He says[7] that
many people, owing to ignorance of the method of calculation,
believe that the increase has been greater.  When food is dear,
crime is increased and marriages diminished.[8]  However,[9] Plint
quotes, and apparently believes, some evidence to show that crime
is now decreasing.[10]  Increased longevity must, I suppose, lessen
crime; for, says Plint,[11]  "Mr. Neison has shown in an elaborate
paper in the Statistical Magazine for October, 1846, that about
64 per cent. of all criminal offences in England and Wales is
committed by persons from fifteen to thirty years of age."  Alison[12]
actually supposes that the increasing crimes in England are the
result of diminished punishment.  Laing[13] says that Sweden is
" in a more demoralized state than any nation in Europe."  But
Laing's coarse and slovenly estimate[14] of " persons convicted of
some criminal offence " is worth nothing until we know what the
laws punish as criminal.  The only precise statements of Laing
are that in 1836 the rural population of Sweden was 2,735,487,
which supplied " 28 cases of murder, 10 of child murder, and 4 of
poisoning ; 13 of bestiality, 9 of robbery with violence."[15]  From
1 in 140 to 1 in 134 are yearly convicted of " criminal offence,"[16]
while in England and Wales, in 1831, 1 in 707 were accused, and
1 in 1005 convicted.[17]  In 1836, the rural population of Sweden,

[1] Dillon's Winter in Lapland and Iceland, 8vo, 1840, vol. i. pp. 154, 155.
[2] Tytler's Edward VI. and Mary, 8vo, 1839, vol. ii. p. 334.
[3] Constitution of Man, 8vo, 1847, p. 353.
[4] St. Patrick's Purgatory, 8vo, 1844, p. vi.     [5] Moral Philosophy, 8vo, 1840. p. 301.
[6] Crime in England, 8vo, 1851, p. 11.           [7] Ibid. p. 12.            [8] Ibid. p. 46.
[9] Ibid. p. 27.                                  [10] Ibid. p. 138.          [11] Ibid. p. 86.
[12] History of Europe, vol. ix. pp. 623, 624.
[13] Tour in Sweden, 8vo, 1839, pp. 108, 109.                                [14] Ibid. p. 109.
[16] Ibid. p. 110.               [15] Ibid. pp. 109, 110.                     [17] Ibid. p. 111.

2,735,000 ; committed 3,328 crimes, of which 1,176 were thefts, 2,080 assaults, and 7 perjury.[1] This only makes 1 in 822, and yet [2] Laing says that, "in 1837, of the country population of 2,735,487, 1 in 460 has been punished for criminal offence." This shows the absurdity of the expression "criminal offence." Female criminals "are in the proportion of about 1 in 3."[3]

In the province of Gifle, 120 miles from Stockholm, the country population is 95,822, of whom "1 in 595 has been condemned in 1837 for moral offences, not including as such the police transgressions or offences against conventional laws ; " and of these five were murders.[4] The illegitimate births in Stockholm are 1 to $2\frac{1}{10}$,[5] while in Paris they are 1 in 5, and in the other towns of France 1 in $7\frac{1}{2}$ ; in London and Middlesex 1 in 38 ! ! ! No women who can afford it ever nurse their children.[6] And yet, with the exception of Denmark, no country is so educated as Sweden.[7] Laing[8] ascribes this to "their low civil condition, their state of restriction and pupillage in all that relates to the free use and enjoyment of their industry and property, which works out a low moral condition which even religious knowledge and education cannot elevate ; " and masters may beat their servants.[9]

But the influence of the clergy is immense. We find[10] "one in every 126 of the whole population living by the teaching the Swedish people their religious and moral duties." In Gothland there is "one minister of religion to every 435 individuals ; "[11] and crime there is immense.[12] And the Swedish clergy are powerful as well as numerous. Laing[13] mentions a case of one of them flogging a woman for having an illegitimate child. "In no country in Europe is the church establishment so powerful and perfect."[14]

Porter[15] has vainly attempted to make out that education lessens crime. He says[16] that Guerry[17] has shown that "in the departments where the greatest amount of instruction had been imparted, there the greatest amount of crime was found to exist ; " but Porter pertinently observes that the crimes were *committed* by the uninstructed ; and this was natural, because, where many persons were instructed, they would monopolise em-

---

[1] Tour in Sweden, 8vo, 1839, p. 126.          [2] Ibid. pp. 134, 135.
[3] Ibid. p. 140.          [4] Ibid. p. 213 ; and as to Gothland, see pp. 322, 323.
[5] Ibid. p. 113.          [6] Ibid. p. 116.          [7] Ibid. pp. 186, 242, 243 275, 425.
[8] Ibid. p. 276.          [9] Ibid. p. 276, and see p. 430.          [10] Ibid. p. 245.
[11] Ibid. p. 321.          [12] Ibid. pp. 322, 323.
[13] Ibid. p. 278.          [14] Ibid. pp. 425, 426 ; see also for its intolerance p. 324.
[15] Progress of the Nation, vol. iii. pp. 200–221.          [16] Ibid. . 211 212.
[17] Statistique Morale de la France.

ployment, and poverty would drive the ignorant to crime; besides, in an *instructed* community offences would not be so readily overlooked as in an ignorant one. But [1] Porter seems to say that education will *not* diminish crime. "The great end of all punishment, the deterring of offenders." [2] *More* than ⅓ of persons in gaol have previously been in prison. [3] During 1834 nearly 100,000 persons were in prison in England and Wales. This includes *all* the most trivial offences. [4] Porter says: [5] "In England and Wales the number of persons now committed for trial is five times as great as it was in the beginning of the century." "The number of convictions in proportion to committals is now much greater than formerly." [6]

In the fifteenth century, in France, all criminal prisoners were kept on bread and water alone, unless the judge made an order to the contrary. [7] In 1785, the solicitor-general, in bringing forward a new police bill, said "it was a certain truth that of the whole number hanged in the metropolis, 18 out of every 20 were under the age of 21." [8] In 1785, Alderman Townshend, [9] insisting on the necessity of certainty in punishment, said, "So it was with thieves; their calculation was that, for every offender convicted, one out of thirty-three only was executed." Comte [10] positively says crime is constantly decreasing. Comte [11] observes that drunkenness is promoted by an ignorance of the results; but Liebig [12] says that it is the *effect* of poverty, deficient nutriment requiring the *compensation* of alcohol. Laing [13] says that no men are so moral as Londoners; for none have to struggle so much with temptation; and what is virtue but temptation conquered? Should we praise a savage for not committing burglary where there are no houses, or not picking a pocket where there are no clothes? Crime is increased: 1st. By increased ability in the thief; 2nd. By greater number of things to steal; 3rd. By more artificial wants. "It is ascertained that three-fourths of the criminals under seventeen years of age are the children of bad parents." [14] At p. 86 it is said that crime is caused by drunkenness, and that "by foul air and the depressing influence of bad localities, bringing with it a fierce desire for stimulants; and by bad and deficient water." [15] "Bad water and bad air" the two causes of crime. [16]

[1] Progress of the Nation, vol. i. pp. 220, 221.　　[2] Ibid. p. 133.　　[3] Ibid. p. 140.
[4] Ibid. pp. 140, 141.　　　　[5] Ibid. vol. iii. p. 172.　　　　[6] Ibid. p. 179.
[7] Monteil, Histoire des Français des Divers États, tome iv. p. 58.
[8] Parliamentary History, vol. xxv. p. 889.　　　　　　[9] Ibid. p. 907.
[10] Traité de Législation, tome i. pp. 53, 54.　　　　[11] Ibid. pp. 58, 59.
[12] Letters on Chemistry, p. 255.
[13] Notes of a Traveller, first series, pp. 281, 282.
[14] Transactions of Association for promoting Social Science, Lond. 1859, p. 15.
[15] Ibid. pp. 88, 89.　　　　　　　　　　　　[16] Ibid. p. 91.

At Liverpool, the recorder " disallows the expenses of prose-
cutors who have been robbed through their own carelessness in
exposing goods at the doors of their shops; but the only effect is to
render the shopkeepers indifferent about prosecutions in any subsequent loss." [1] In England and Wales one fourth of the criminals
are between 20 and 25 years old, and " nearly three-fifths between
15 and 30." [2] At p. 389, " Upwards of 30 per cent. of our criminal
population range between the ages of 16 and 45." At p. 396,
" With regard to the causes of crime in Baden and Bavaria, each of
the governors *assured* me that it was *wine* in one country and
*beer* in the other which filled the gaols." A reformatory where
" music and singing are cultivated as much as possible, and have
much tended to eradicate the low and vulgar propensities of the
lads." [3] At p. 643, " Very rarely do you find a man who is fond
of flowers taken up for misdemeanour of any kind."

---

## PHILOLOGY.

" LANGUAGE is often called an instrument of thought, but it is also
the nutriment of thought; or rather it is the atmosphere in which
thought lives," &c., &c. [4] Reinier Prodinius, who died in 1559, was
a celebrated Dutch philologist. " Hy war ein von de voornaarmte
beoefeuaars der spraak afterding (*etymologie*) der Latiynsche tale
op uiens grouden Vossius naderhaud bouwde." [5] Contrary to the
general opinion, Cousin says disputes are generally *not* about
words, but about things. [6] Lord Brougham supposes that Tooke's
Diversions of Purley contains original discoveries. [7] Coleridge [8]
has some admirable remarks on the tendency of words to *desyno-
nymize.* To *resent*, which now only means to *take ill*, formerly
also meant to *take well.* See an instance in Pepys's Diary, 8vo,
1828, vol. iv. p. 247. Prichard [9] says of Mount Altai: " The
Turkish name of *Alta-in-oole* means the Golden Mountains." In
the Australian and Polynesian languages there is a singular, dual,

---

[1] Transactions of Association for Social Science, 1859, p. 355.
[2] Ibid. p. 365.    [3] Ibid. p. 408.
[4] Whewell's Philosophy of the Inductive Sciences, 8vo, 1847, vol. i. pp. 270, 271.
[5] Van Kampen, Geschiedenis der Letteren in de Niederlanden, Gravenhage, 8vo,
1821, deel i. blad 75.
[6] Histoire de la Philosophie, 2nde série, tome iii. p. 218.
[7] Brougham's Historical Sketches of Statesmen, Lond., 1845, vol. iii. p. 142 *et seq.*
[8] Biographia Literaria, 8vo, 1847, vol. i. p. 80.
[9] Physical History of Mankind, vol. iv. p. 281.

and plural.[1]  Prichard says:[2] "In a barbarous state of society, and principally in one of early and imperfect, but growing refinement of mind, the imagination has more influence in the formation of language than in a more advanced stage." Lemontey, in his "Louis XIV.," says that first in this reign *honnête* changed its meaning, and "that till the latter half of the reign of Louis an 'honnête homme' was the name for an upright, not for an inoffensive man."[3]  Father Nobili, early in the seventeenth century, was the first European who well understood Sanscrit.[4] Burton[5] says that the inhabitants of Scinde "have no proper name for the Indus in general and vulgar use: the Mitho Daryan or 'Sweet Water Sea' is the vague expression commonly employed." It used to be thought that lunacy was caused by the moon; hence the word; and now the word is used to justify the opinion.[6]  Georgel[7] says that in 1790 the crime "lèse nation" was a "mot nouveau."  See some very ingenious remarks on the Latin language in Vico, Philosophie de l'Histoire, pp. 125–131, and 140–143, and 222-226. He says (p. 244) that as the Romans did not know what luxury was until they saw a native of Tarentum, they called a perfumed man "un Tarentin," &c.  Compare this with Adam Smith.  At the end of the fourteenth century in France, "le nom de serf commence à devenir une insulte."[8] Monteil says:[9] "Le mot de financier, qui vient de *finer*, payer, est d'origine moderne.  Je doute qu'il ait été en usage avant le treizième ou douzième siècle : mais il l'était au quatorzième, ainsi qu'on le voit dans les ordonnances de ce temps." Kiel, the Tekelia of Ptolemy, is said to be still called by the Platt Deutsch peasantry Tokiel or Tomkiel.[10]  Laing says:[11] "Mediatise is a word which came into use at the Congress of Vienna of 1814–15." Tocqueville[12] says: "Le seul Milton a introduit dans la langue anglaise plus de six cent mots, presque tous tirés du latin, du grec, et de l'hebreu." He says[13] that as nations become democratic, their love of generalisation is shown even in their language.  Thus the Americans carry the abstraction so far as to

---

[1] See Prichard's Physical History of Mankind, vol. v. p. 276.    [2] Ibid. p. 319.

[3] Stephen's Lectures on the History of France, 8vo, 1851, vol. ii. p. 442; and see note in Des Réaux, Historiettes, vol. v. p. 213.

[4] Ranke, Die Päpste, Band ii. p. 494, note.

[5] Sindh and the Races in Indus, 8vo, 1851, p. 380.

[6] See Georgel, De la Folie, p. 440.

[7] Mémoires, tome iii. p. 94.

[8] Monteil, Hist. des Français des Divers États, tome ii. p. 178.    [9] Ibid. p. 180.

[10] Laing's Denmark, 8vo, 1852, p. 22.

[11] Notes of a Traveller, first series, p. 122.

[12] Démocratie en Amérique, tome iv. p. 103.    [13] Ibid. pp. 109-110.

talk of " the capacities " for capable men, or of " eventualities " for
everything that can happen.   For two curious instances in which
the Greeks were led into error by foreign language, see History
of Maritime and Inland Discovery (by Cooley), 8vo, 1830, vol. i.
p. 67.   In 1797 "circulating medium" was a new expression.[1]
" Cowper Law " is said to be derived from " Cupar, a town where
little mercy was shown to the Highland rovers."[2]   Lord Mahon[3]
wishes " Fatherland," a " Teutonic " word, to be used in English.
The word *riotte* is lost in French, but from it we have *riot*.[4]   In
1798 " uncandid " is spoken of as a new word, or at all events " a
word in fashion."[5]   In 1689 it is said[6] that " by the employment "
of a man, was not good English ; but that it should be " by the
*employ*."   In 1738 " *socking*, which is a cant term for pilfering
and stealing tobacco from ships in the river."[7]   The Danish language is still understood in part of Westmoreland.[8]   Comte[9] well
says that one reason why conquerors adopt the manner and language of the conquered is that they marry their women, and that
the next generation prefers the language, &c., of their mothers
(with whom they are constantly) to that of their fathers.   In
1764, Dr. Grieve, in translating the valuable Russian account of
Kamtschatka, says at chapter xx. : " This chapter in the original
contains an account of three different dialects of the Kamtscha-
dales, which, as they are very unintelligible to an English reader,
we think proper to omit."[10]   This is the whole of the chapter ! ! !
Lake Peten is in Yucatan.   " In this lake are numerous islands,
one of which is called Peten Grande, Peten itself being a Maya
word, signifying an island."[11]   For a blunder caused by language,
see Journal of Geographical Society, vol. xii. p. 32.

[1] See Parliamentary History, vol. xxxiii. pp. 340, 343, 548.
[2] Mahon's Hist. of England, 1853, vol. i. p. 198, and vol. ii. p. 44.
[3] Ibid. p. 213.
[4] Notes in Lettres de Madame de Sévigné, 1843, tome i. p. 120.
[5] Parliamentary History, vol. xxxiv. p. 48.
[6] Ibid. vol. v. p. 463.       [7] Ibid. vol. viii. p. 1274.
[8] Journal of Statistical Society, vol. ii. p. 334.
[9] Traité de Législation, tome iii. pp. 62, 63.
[10] Grieve's History of Kamtschatka, p. 222.
[11] Stephens's Central America, vol. iv. p. 192.

## MANNERS (*for Preface*).

WILLIAM SCHLEGEL goes so far as to consider taste in dress "a criterion of social cultivation or deformity."[1]  Dawson Turner says that in the country about Caen the dress of the women is like that worn in England in the fifteenth and sixteenth centuries; and "as to the cap which the Cauchoise wears, when she appears *en grand costume*, its very prototype is to be found in Strutt's Ancient Dresses."  See Turner's Tour in Normandy, London, 8vo, 1820, voL i. p. 8, where he also gives a representation of this high cap.

## POPULATION.

—"Scantly you have two miles without a town or a village inhabited."[2]  In 1563, when the plague was in London, Cecil writes to Sir Thomas Smith: "They dye in London above one thousand in a weke."[3]

## PHYSIOLOGY, ETC. (*for facts.*)

THE Icelanders are tall, fair, but "white hair, instead of being universal, is by no means as common as in Scotland and Denmark."[4]

In 1774, Captain Topham says that in Scotland he "never saw either an exceedingly deformed person or an aged, toothless, paralytic highlander."[5]  Ellis[6] says that in the South Sea Islands the chiefs are superior to the common people in height and in physical strength.  But this is explained by Williams[7] as the result of superior diet.  Catlin[8] observes the peculiarity of their heads, which, he adds,[9] "is produced by artificial means in infancy."[10]  For their stature, &c., see pp. 225, 226.  High training, &c., does *not* wear out the frame; but, on the whole, "looking to the human race, it is certain that the average exer-

[1] Lectures on Dramatic Art, Lond. 1840, vol. ii. pp. 327, 328.
[2] Cooper's Admonition, 1589, p. 92, 8vo, 1847.
[3] Wright's Elizabeth, 8vo, 1838, vol. i. p. 138.
[4] Dillon's Winter in Lapland and Iceland, 8vo, 1840, vol. i. p. 133.
[5] Letters from Edinburgh, 8vo, 1776, p. 79.
[6] Polynesian Researches, 8vo, 1831, vol. i. p. 82.
[7] Missionary Enterprise in the South Sea Islands, 8vo, 1837, pp. 512, 513.
[8] North American Indians, 8vo, 1841, vol. i. p. 193.
[9] Ibid. vol. ii. p. 41.          [10] Ibid. pp. 110–112.

cise used is excessive, and more harmful than beneficial."[1] Alison talks very confidently about the difference of race, but contradicts himself.[2] In the retreat from Moscow the French bore the cold better than the Russians, and the survivors "almost all were Italians or Frenchmen from the provinces to the *south* of the Loire."[3] In 1675 it was considered remarkable that the blood of a negro should be red instead of black.[4] On *race*, see Comte, Philosophie Positive, tome iii. p. 355. Dr. Prichard[5] says: "According to Burton, the offspring of parents advanced in years are more subject than others to melancholy madness." Laing[6] takes it for granted that "the Gothic" care more than "the Celtic race" for the "enjoyments and luxuries of civilized life." In Leeds the lowest classes have most children ; then the outdoor "handcraftsmen ;" then the indoor; then tradesmen ; and "independent and professional people" the fewest of all.[7] Hutchinson, in his Paper on Vital Statistics, says :[8] "The pugilists, without exception, are the finest class of men I have examined." The Indians are less subject to cholera than the Europeans ; but this is said to arise from their greater temperance.[9] "A sufficient proof that the Malay race is never likely to become assimilated to the climate of Ceylon."[10] In India all the lower classes of native women are short, but the better sort are the average European height. This was told Heber by Dr. Smith.[11] Heber[12] observes that the Brahmins are superior in intellect, and have *fairer complexions* than the other castes.

Murray[13] says of Bruce, the traveller's, father : "It may be remarked as an instance of the transmission of bodily as well as mental qualities, through a long line of descendants, that the features and character of Robert Bruce, the firm and haughty leader of the Scottish church in the reign of James VI., were retained by his representatives at the distance of two centuries." Kohl[14] says of St. Petersburgh : "In no other towns are there so few cripples and deformed people ; and this is not merely owing to

[1] Mayo's Philosophy of Living, 2nd edit. 8vo, 1838, pp. 125, 126, 131.
[2] See Alison's History of Europe, vol. ii. pp. 336, 338 ; see also vol. vi. p. 136; vol. viii. pp. 525, 526.        [3] Ibid. vol. xi. p. 183.
[4] Ray's Correspondence, by Dr. Lankester, 8vo, 1848, p. 120.
[5] Treatise on Insanity, 8vo, 1835, p. 159.
[6] Observations on Denmark, p. 154.
[7] Journal of Statistical Society, vol. ii. pp. 423, 424 ; see also note at vol. iii. pp. 252, 253.
[8] Ibid. vol. vii. p. 203.    [9] Ibid. vol. x. pp. 121, 122, 123.    [10] Ibid. p. 258.
[11] See Heber's Journey through India, vol. ii. pp. 509, 510.
[12] Ibid. vol. i. p. 120.
[13] Life of Bruce, p. 24.
[14] Russia, 8vo, 1844, p. 30.

their being less tolerated here than elsewhere, but also, it is said, to the fact that the Slavonian race is less apt than any other to produce deformed children." Kohl, near Odessa, "found the wife of the Bulgarian, who, as it usually happens with women, had preserved the national features more unaltered than her husband." [1] On the absurdity of *vis vitæ*, see Liebig's Letters on Chemistry, 8vo, 1851, p. 13. The ancient Celts in England had very small hands.[2] In 1846, Sir Benjamin Brodie told Moore "that among the many dying patients he had attended he had but rarely met with one that was afraid to die." [3] " The negro race is remarkably exempt " from calculus ; but so are *all* the inhabitants of " tropical countries." [4] Chossat "found that defective nourishment notably reduced the weight of all the structures of the body except only those of the nervous system, which were wonderfully little diminished by it." [5] The pale globules of the blood were known to Hewson.[6]

---

## TENDENCY OF CLASSICAL LITERATURE.

COMBE[7] suggests that great injury has resulted from teaching children to admire the literature and history of Greece and Rome. Even Lawrence [8] says : " Let us never forget that the principal and richest portion of our intellectual treasure consists of the literature and history of two nations of antiquity, whose astonishing superiority seems to have arisen principally from their having enjoyed freedom." Even Milton recommends hardly anything but the ancient writers.[9] Sancroft, in 1663, notices the decline of " Hebrew and Greek learning." [10] On the absurdity of studying so much classics, and on the low civilization of the Greeks and Romans, see Combe's Lectures on Moral Philosophy, 8vo, 1840, pp. 74, 75, 108, 109. In 1693, Evelyn [11] mentions that his daughter " has read most of the Greek and Roman authors and poets." Lewis [12] has collected some evidence of the slow diffusion of *news*

[1] Kohl's Russia, p. 435.
[2] See Report of British Association for 1850. Transactions of Sections, p. 145.
[3] Moore's Memoirs, by Lord J. Russell, Lond. 1856, vol. viii. p. 22.
[4] Erichsen's Surgery, 1857, 2nd edit. p. 946.
[5] Williams's Principles of Medicine, p. 169.
[6] See Gulliver's edition of Hewson's Works, p. 282.
[7] Constitution of Man in relation to External Objects, Edinburgh, 1847, 8vo, p. 264.
[8] Lectures on Man, 8vo, 1844, pp. 332.
[9] Hallam's Literature of Europe, vol. iii. p. 410.
[10] D'Oyly's Life of Sancroft, 2nd edit. 8vo, 1840, p. 78.
[11] Diary, vol. iii. p. 324.
[12] Method of Observation in Politics, vol. i. p. 431.

among the ancients.  Even Sir W. Temple, the great admirer of the ancients, will not allow that they generally were wiser than we.[1]  Laing[2] has some very severe remarks on the boasted civilization of the Romans; and Tocqueville[3] speaks contemptuously of their great works, as aqueducts, &c.  The ablest writers now never make classical allusions or quote ancient authors ; therefore a great inducement to study the classics is taken away.  In the sixteenth century ambassadors were obliged to harangue princes in Latin.[4]  Ancients ignorant of geography.[5]  Mills[6] mentions the absurdity of ascribing the progress of Europe to the revived study of classical literature.  The Venetian family, Cornaro, derived their descent from the Roman Cornelia.[7]  For instance of the classical pedantry of Beza, see Smedley's History of the Reformed Religion in France, vol. i. p. 213.  On the vices of the ancients and absurd respect felt for them, see some striking remarks in Comte, Traité de Législation, tome i. pp. 51, 52, 402 ; tome iii. p. 470; and on their contempt for commerce, p. 501 *et seq.*, and tome iv. pp. 7, 15.  On the absurdity of admiring ancient languages for their synthetic and inflexional state, see Report of British Association for 1852, Transactions of Sections, p. 82.

----

## THEOLOGY AND RELIGIOUS SUPERSTITIONS.

ONLY women and eunuchs are allowed to see the king of Dahomey eat or drink.[8]  The Javanese robbers think that they can cause deadly sleep by throwing into a house they intend to plunder earth from a newly opened grave.[9]  Low[10] says of the Dyaks of Borneo, " death to their ignorant and unenlightened minds displays no terror."  The inhabitants of the Friendly Islands believe that men were formerly giants.[11]  On the connection between lust and religion, see Southey's Life of Wesley, 8vo, 1846, vol. i. p. 173.  Vans Kennedy thinks[12] that the "indelicacy" of a part

----

[1] Temple's Works, 8vo, 1814, vol. i. p. 14.
[2] Notes of a Traveller, first series, pp. 386, 406.
[3] Démocratie, tome iv. p. 85.
[4] Monteil, Histoire des Français, tome iv. p. 154.
[5] See History of Maritime and Inland Discovery, by Cooley, 1830, vol. i. p. 89.
[6] History of Chivalry, vol. ii. p. 170.
[7] Lettres de Patin, vol. iii. p. 697.
[8] See Forbes' Dahomey and the Dahomans, 8vo, 1851, vol. i. p. 79.
[9] Crawford's History of the Indian Archipelago. Edinb. 8vo, 1820, vol. i. p. 56.
[10] Sarawak, 8vo, 1848, p. 263.
[11] See Mariner's Tonga Islanders, 2nd edit. 8vo, 1818, vol. i. p. 313.
[12] Transactions of Literary Society of Bombay, vol. iii. p. 155.

of the Hindoo religion " has no effect on their morals." A writer
who has seen the religious customs of many different nations
observes that the most ignorant are " the most fixed and stubborn " in religion.[1]   On the origin of superstition Locke has
some ingenious but, I think, unsatisfactory remarks.[2]   For an
instance of the mischief caused by an established church, see
Combe's Lectures on Moral Philosophy, 8vo, 1840, p. 82.   Many
Protestant theologians have maintained that prayer produces no
effect on the Deity.[3]   Alison,[4] has well observed that the difficulty of Protestantism is to keep scepticism from the uneducated, the difficulty of Popery to keep it from the educated ;
because popery appeals to the senses, Protestantism to the intellect.   Comte observes that miracles are an evidence of the
decline of the theological spirit.[5]   At tome v. p. 44, he says, I
think with truth, that animal worship is not so common as is
generally supposed.   Archbishop Whately [6] thinks that what we
call the *cause* of a superstition is in reality its *effect*.   Sir W. Temple [7] thinks comets may affect mind and body.   Sir T. Browne [8]
believes that oracles were supernatural.   The diminution of
superstition will take away one cause of madness.[9]   Kemble [10]
seems to think that the process is that myths, as they become
popular, deteriorate and "assume traits of the popular humorous
spirit."   The Saxons, and even many ecclesiastics, believed that
hell was cold.[11]   Kemble says (vol. i. p. 47), " It is indeed probable
that all capital punishments among the Germans were originally
in the nature of sacrifices to the gods."   At Marseilles, in 1646,
Monconys [12] was told that seven of the 11,000 virgins were buried ;
he also heard that the Queen Blanche, by entering the chapel
and making a vow to the Virgin, recovered her sight.[13]   In 1663,
Monconys [14] was shown at Oxford a horn which the Jews said was
made like those with which the walls of Jericho were blown
down.   In 1648, it was still the common opinion that an eclipse
or comet always preceded any accidents to kings or empires.[15]
Göthe says that men soon give up a superstition when they find it

[1] Catlin's North American Indians, 8vo, 1841, vol. i. p. 183.
[2] See King's Life of Locke, 8vo, 1830, vol. ii. p. 101.
[3] Combe's Moral Philosophy, 8vo, 1840, pp. 434–438.
[4] History of Europe, vol. x. p. 240.
[5] Philosophie Positive, tome iv. pp. 673, 674, 679, 683–685.
[6] Errors of Romanism, 8vo, 1830. p. 178.
[7] Works, 8vo, 1814, vol. iii. p. 45.            [8] Works, vol. iii. p. 329.
[9] See Prichard on Insanity, 8vo, 1835, pp. 19, 20, 30, 187, 198 ; and Pinel, Traité
sur l'Alienation Mentale, pp. 41–45, 108, 119, 151, 164, 165, 431, 457, 479.
[10] Saxons in England, vol. i. p. 382.            [11] Ibid. p. 394, 395.
[12] Voyages, 1695, 12mo, tome i. p. 195.            [13] Ibid. tome iv. p. 22.
[14] Ibid. tome iii. p. 96.            [15] Ibid. tome v. pp. 103, 104.

contrary to their interest.[1] The mortality among children is. greatly increased by carrying them to church to be baptized. See Quetelet, Sur l'Homme, tome i. p. 167; and at p. 229 it is observed that religious ceremonies at the bedside of a patient cause death. Pilgrimages are eagerly followed . by the Mahometans even now. Doctrine of a God not universal. Of the Orkney Islanders, in 1805, Barry says:[2] "Thursdays and Fridays are the days in which they incline to marry; and they scrupulously and anxiously avoid it at any other time than when the moon is waxing."[3]

"Toutes les religions font des promesses ou des menaces dont il n'est pas facile de vérifier l'accomplissement."[4] The negroes believe that the devil is white.[5] Telling fortunes by palmistry is practised by the Tibetans.[6] Symes says:[7] "The Birmans have a superstitious abhorrenee of any person's passing over them when they are asleep." The Kamtschatkans "are very great observers of dreams, which they relate to one another as soon as they are awake in the morning, and judge from thence of their future good or bad fortune; and some of these dreams have their interpretation fixed and settled. Besides this conjuration they pretend to chiromancy, and to foretell a man's good or bad fortune by the lines of his. hand; but the rules which they follow are kept a great secret."[8] Blanco White says:[9] "I am inclined to believe that the illuminated grottoes of oyster-shells, for which the London children beg about the streets, are the representatives of some Catholic emblem, which had its day as a substitute for a more classical idol." Neander looks on Christianity as a development. See his History of the Church, vol. i. pp. 4, 6, 20, 38, 60, 61, 269, 379, 465; vol. ii. pp. 118, 132, 157, 164; vol. iii. p. 488; vol. vi. p. 412. At. vol. i. p. 100, and vol. iii. p. 71, Neander has some unfair and uncritical remarks. In the fifth century a number of hypocrites became Christians.[10] He says:[11] "The nomadic life, which prevailed over the largest portion of Arabia, ever presented a powerful hindrance to the spread of Christianity." In the fourth century images were first used in churches,[12] and "heathen melodies" introduced into "church psalmody."[13]

[1] Wahrheit und Dichtung, in Göthe's Werke, Band ii. Theil ii. p. 145.
[2] History of the Orkney Islands, p. 342.   [3] Ibid. p. 342.
[4] Comte, Traité de Législation, tome i. pp. 275, 276.   [5] Ibid. tome ii. p. 37.
[6] See Turner's Embassy to Thibet, p. 284.
[7] Embassy to Ava, vol. iii. p. 255.
[8] Grieve's History of Kamtschatka, Gloucester, 1764, 4to, p. 206.
[9] Doblado's Letters from Spain, p. 302.
[10] See Neander, vol. iii. pp. 139, 140.   [11] Ibid. p. 166.
[12] Ibid. p. 413.   [13] Ibid. p. 451.

Neander[1] says : " The weavers, an occupation which from its peculiar character has ever been a favourite resort of mystical
sects." Formerly in France a man who died on Good Friday was
deemed a saint.[2] White meat *mortifies the flesh* by its want of
iron.[3] Laing, who is anything but sceptical, says there is no
country in Europe where there is so much morality and little
religion as Switzerland.[4] He says[5] the Swiss are remarkable
" for a sense of property ; " and[6] that the Catholics are more religious than the Protestants. He says[7] that now Rome is busily
engaged in educating the people and propagating knowledge.

## NATIONAL CHARACTER OF THE DUTCH.

BURNET, who was in Holland in 1664, says : " There seemed to be
among them too much coldness and indifference in matters of
religion."[8] Hallam[9] calls Holland " the peculiarly learned state
of Europe during the seventeenth century." Burnet says :[10] " I
was never in any place where I thought the clergy had generally
so much credit with the people as they have there." In 1716,
the Dutch were remarkable for cleanliness.[11] Sir W. Temple's
Observations upon the United Provinces were written between
1669 and 1673. He mentions the great simplicity of living even
among the highest ranks,[12] but luxury was creeping in.[13] The
lower people fond of drink, but the highest classes more temperate ;[14] but none ate much. " Their great parsimony in diet
and eating so very little flesh, which the common people seldom
do above once a week."[15] The people are " cold and heavy ;"[16]
" so little show of parts and of wit, and so great evidence of
wisdom and prudence."[17] " I have known some among them that
personated lovers well enough, but none that I ever thought were
at heart in love."[18] He mentions[19] their remarkable cleanliness.
He says[20] of rich families, " Their youth, after the course of their
studies at home, travel for some years as the sons of our gentry

[1] History of the Church, vol. vi. p. 358.
[2] Liebig's Letters on Chemistry, 8vo, 1851, p. 433.
[4] Notes of a Traveller, first series, pp. 323, 324, 333.
[5] Ibid. p. 430.
[6] Own Time, Oxford, 1823, vol. i. p. 357.
[9] Literature of Europe, vol. iii. p. 243.
[10] Own Time, vol. iii. 293.
[11] See Lady Mary W. Montagu's Works, 8vo, 1803, vol. i. p. 201.
[12] Works, 8vo, 1814, vol. i. pp. 113, 116.
[14] Ibid. pp. 142, 143.
[15] Ibid. p. 147.
[17] Ibid. p. 115.
[18] Ibid. p. 141.
[19] Ibid. p. 132.

[3] Ibid. vol. vii. p. 457.
[6] Ibid. p. 354.
[7] Ibid. pp. 349, 440.
[13] Ibid. p. 184.
[16] Ibid. p. 114.
[20] Ibid. p. 135.

use to do; but their journeys are chiefly into England and France, not much into Italy, seldomer into Spain. . . . . The diseases of the climate seem to be chiefly the gout and the scurvy."[1] In Holland the clergy *never* had any jurisdiction,[2] and there was great toleration.[3] Temple mentions[4] their burning nutmegs to raise the price. As late as 1669 and 1670 "there was hardly any foreign trade among them." After England, there is no country so badly off for pauperism as Holland; and this is owing "to the existence of so many thousand endowed institutions for the relief of the poor."[5] Laing[6] says that the importance of the Dutch herring fisheries has been greatly exaggerated. He supposes[7] that the *sole* cause of the ruin of Holland was that she was the broker and carrier of Europe; but, as the nations advanced, they did this business themselves. After Descartes, Holland was the great refuge of scepticism.[8] Laing says:[9] "The Dutch people eminently charitable and benevolent as a public, their country full of beneficial institutions, admirably conducted and munificently supported, are, as individuals, somewhat rough, hard, and, though it be uncharitable to say so, uncharitable and unfeeling."

## NATIONAL CHARACTER OF THE FRENCH.

FROM phrenology it appears that the French are remarkable for vanity, and the English for pride.[10] All the ancient writers notice the "boldness, levity, fickleness," and unchastity of the Gauls;[11] and Prichard adds:[12] "Of all Pagan nations the Gauls and Britons appear to have had the most sanguinary rites." In 1818, Dr. Combe observed at Paris that the heads of Frenchmen "sloped backwards from the nose" more rapidly than the heads of Frenchwomen; and, says George Combe, this difference in the reflective organs not being found among the sexes in England, accounts for the greater influence women have in France.[13] In 1753, Voltaire[14] candidly allows that the French are not inven-

[1] Sir William Temple's Works, 8vo, 1814, vol. i. p. 149.          [2] Ibid. p. 157.
[3] Ibid. pp. 159–162.                                              [4] Ibid. p. 183.
[5] Porter's Progress of the Nation, vol. i. p. 113.
[6] Notes of a Traveller, first series, pp. 7, 8.          [7] Ibid. p. 9.
[8] See Lamartine, Histoire des Girondins, tome i. p. 221.
[9] Notes of a Traveller, first series, p. 14.
[10] See Combe's Elements of Phrenology, 6th edit. Edinburgh, 1845, pp. 87, 90.
[11] Prichard's Physical History of Mankind, vol. iii. p. 178.          [12] Ibid. p. 187.
[13] Combe's Life of Dr. Combe, Edinburgh, 8vo, 1850, p. 71.
[14] See Correspondance in Œuvres, vol. lix. pp. 313, 314.

tive.[1] M. de Barante[2] says the vanity of the French is chiefly the result of men of letters being indignant at the absence of political power. Richelieu, in his Mémoires[3] mentions the particular levity of the French. Sir J. Reynolds[4] observes that in art they are very quick *extempore* for invention, but not for finishing their paintings. Laing[5] says that the French are more honest than the British. He praises[6] their subdivision of property. "The French, with all their centralisation, have roads infinitely inferior to ours."[7] Laing says :[8] "In France, at the expulsion of Louis Philippe, the civil functionaries were stated to amount to 807,030 individuals." The Prince de Montbarey says :[9] 'Il faut le dire avec toute la vérité que je professe, le Français dans toutes les classes et dans toutes les circonstances, ne sait jamais garder un juste milieu." Tocqueville[10] says that the Americans, notwithstanding the wildness of their lives, value women so highly as to make rape a capital offence, while in France, such is the "mépris de la pudeur" and "mépris de la femme," that it is difficult to get a jury to convict on such a charge. In France there are 138,000 functionaries.[11] He says[12] that there is no country where the social distance between master and servant is so slight as in France ; nowhere is it so great as in England. The lower order of French are more civilized than the lower order of English, while the lower order of Germans are at the bottom of the scale. This is explained by the *language*, which in Germany is like Latin or Greek, synthetic, not calculated for the *diffusion* but for the *preservation* of knowledge. See in Journal of Statistical Society, vol. iii. pp. 376, 377, "a classification of new works" (i.e. books) "in France from 1829 to 1833." I believe one reason why the French have so many memoirs is because they are a vain people, and dare not write on political subjects. The French historians, long accustomed to memoirs, are now, like Thierry, Barante, and Capefigue, become too *personal* and *anecdotical.* Comte[13] says there is nothing remarkable in the Code Napoléon, and nothing not to be found in preceding laws. And on the retrogressive spirit of Napoleon, see Comte, Traité de Législation, iv. 269.

[1] See also tome lxi. pp. 41 ; lxvi. p. 466.
[2] Littérature Française au xviii* Siècle, p. 80.    [3] Tome ii. pp. 132, 133.
[4] Works, vol. ii. pp. 57, 58.
[5] Notes of a Traveller, first series, p. 54.    [6] Ibid. p. 53.
[7] Laing's Notes, 2nd series, pp. 118, 119.    [8] Notes, 2nd series, p. 185.
[9] Mémoires, vol. i. p. 162.
[10] Démocratie en Amérique, tome i. p. 82.    [11] Ibid. tome i. p. 220.
[12] Ibid. tome v. p. 23.    [13] Traité de Législation, tome i. pp. 356–357.

## NATIONAL CHARACTER OF THE SPANISH.

SCHLEGEL [1] says : " In general, ever since its first commencement, the poetry of Spain has always been more cultivated by nobles and knights than by mere *literati* and authors." There was no country where entails had been so general and injurious as in Spain ; [2] and ecclesiastics were very numerous and influential.[3] Charles V. arrested the development of towns.[4] Villemain [5] says that, except Herodotus, all Greek historians were public men, and so were Machiavelli, Guicciardini, Davila, Fra Paolo, and De Thou. I believe this was the point where Spain stopped. There was no division of labour.

Keightley [6] notices the great deficiency of fairy tales, &c., in Spain. Little is known about the statistics of Spain ; but there is an interesting paper on mortality, &c., of Cadiz, in Journal of Statistical Society, vol. iv. p. 131.

In Spain, to be a physician, it was necessary to be able to defend the doctrine of the Immaculate Conception.[7] See also [8] the absurd treatment of the Spanish colonies. Blanco White, in 1798, says,[9] " The influence of religion in Spain is boundless. It divides the whole population into two comprehensive classes, bigots and dissemblers." See also [10] the extraordinary loyalty of the Spaniards. And [11] their absurd love of titles and of numerous Christian names. For their absurd etiquette, see p. 51. Men of high rank are rewarded for fighting with bulls; and preachers who assail the theatres never venture to preach against bull-fights.[12] In 1801, no Spaniards travelled for amusement.[13] In Seville twelve sermons preached every day.[14] Religious melancholy disease.[15] Jealousy of women has left the upper classes, but is still an active passion among the lower.[16] Blanco White [17] speaks in the highest terms of Moratin as a dramatic genius. He adds [18] that the Spanish language is too grand and not flexible enough for poetry; that since the beginning of the sixteenth century " our best poets have been servile imitators of

---

[1] Lectures on the History of Literature, vol. ii. p. 92.
[3] Alison's History of Europe, vol. viii. p. 407.        [5] Ibid. p. 410.
[4] See Blanqui, Histoire de l'Économie Politique, Paris, 1845, tome i. p. 282.
[6] Littérature au xviiie Siècle, tome ii. pp. 391, 392.
[9] Fairy Mythology, 8vo, 1850, p. 456.
[7] Comte, Traité de Législation, tome iii. p. 497.        [9] Ibid. tome iv. p. 118.
[8] Letters from Spain, by Doblado, 1822, p. 8.        [10] Ibid. pp. 11, 12.
[11] Ibid. pp. 32, 44, 323.        [12] Ibid. pp. 142, 148.        [13] Ibid. p. 160.
[14] Ibid. p. 220.        [15] Ibid. p. 252 *et seq.*        [16] Ibid. p. 268.
[17] Ibid. p. 379.        [18] Ibid. p. 381.

Petrarch, and the writers of that school." Respecting the " suppression of the Jesuits in Spain," see Doblado, Appendix, p. 445 *et seq.* A celebrated traveller, Mr. Kohl, says : " The environs of St. Petersburgh are more sterile and unproductive than those of any capital in Europe, Madrid excepted." [1]

After the conquest, Guatemala " remained in a state of profound tranquillity as a colony of Spain," and the Indians *all* became Catholics ; but, early in the nineteenth century, " a few scattering rays of light penetrated to the heart of the American continent ; and in 1823 the kingdom of Guatemala, as it was then called, declared its independence of Spain," and formed a republic with San Salvador, Honduras, Nicaragua, and Costa Rica. But there were quickly formed two parties, " the aristocratic, central or servile," and the " federal, liberal or democratic ; " " the latter composed of men of intellect and energy, who threw off the yoke of the Romish Church." [2] The clergy excited the people to murder the liberals as " heretics ; " and the most horrible excesses were committed at the capital, Guatemala. [3] Stephens went there in 1839, and he says : [4] " From the moment of my arrival I was struck with the devout character of the city of Guatemala," i.e., churches were filled. He says : [5] " There was but one paper in Guatemala, and that a weekly, and a mere chronicler of decrees and political movements ; " " the priests always opposed to the liberal party." [6] He says the brutal and ferocious Carrera had " a strange dash of fanaticism ; " [7] and [8] " Carrera's fanaticism bound him to the church party." Stephen's [9] gives an extraordinary account of the religious mania he witnessed at Quezaltenago, in 1840. At Palenque he met a padre who had been severely punished because " his surplice had been soiled by the saliva of a dying man." [10] In 1840, Stephens, being becalmed in a Spanish vessel, the sailors ascribed it to the presence of heretics on board. [11] Stephens, who had great opportunities of observing, says : [12] " But the countries in America subject to the Spanish dominion have felt less sensibly perhaps than any other in the world the onward impulse of the last two centuries." In Yucatan, " forty or fifty years after the conquest, the Indians were abandoning their ancient usages and customs, adopting the rites and ceremonies of the Catholic church, and

[1] Kohl's Russia, p. 138.
[2] Stephens's Central America, vol. i. pp. 194, 195.
[3] Ibid. p. 196, 197.
[4] Ibid. p. 210.      [5] Ibid. p. 222.      [6] Ibid. 225.
[7] Ibid. p. 234.      [8] Ibid. p. 245.      [9] Ibid. vol. ii. pp. 214, 215.
[10] Ibid. p. 366.      [11] Ibid. pp. 464, 467.      [12] Ibid. vol. iii. p. 190.

having their children baptized with Spanish names."[1]  Stephens [2]
gives a disgusting account of a bull-fight he saw at Merida in
1841.   In Yucatan most of the " padres " have recognised mis-
tresses.[3]  On the great mineral treasures of Spain, see Liebig's
Letters on Chemistry, 8vo, 1851, p. 499.

At Salamanca, in 1806, says Bourgoing : [4]  " Quand on sait au
reste que Salamanca outre cette cathédrale a encore vingt-sept
paroisses, vingt-cinq couvents d'hommes, quatorze de filles, on
n'est plus étonné de sa pauvreté et de sa dépopulation."

Under Philip II., Spain, with about 10,500,000 inhabitants, had
58 archbishops, 684 bishops, 59,500 convents and monasteries,
" 312,000 prêtres séculiers, 200,000 ecclésiastiques de moyen ordre,
et plus de 400,000 religieux."[5]

According to the official returns of the census of 1787, the ecclesiastics of all descriptions, including 61,617 monks, 32,500
nuns, and 2,705 inquisitors, amounted to 188,625 individuals.[6]
And it appears from the official returns published in the Coreo
Literario of Madrid, in 1833, that notwithstanding the attacks
made upon the ecclesiastical state during the French war and
subsequently, it then comprised 175,574 individuals, of whom
61,727 were monks, and 24,007 nuns.  In Laborde's Spain [7] it is
said that, in 1787-88, the population was 10,143,975, of which
125,000 were " secular and regular clergymen."  This is exclusive of 22,337 " nuns or friars."[8]  Laborde says [9] that in 1788
Spain, with a population of 11,000,000, had 147,657 spiritual
persons, i.e. one sixty-ninth, while France actually had 460,078,
which, with a population of 25,000,000 makes one fifty-second of
the whole.  According to the government returns of 1787, the population was 10,268,150, of which those devoted to religion were
188,625, and of them 61,617 were monks in prime of life ; [10]  and
even in 1833 there were 61,727 monks.  Cook [11] estimates the
clergy at 130,000.   In 1830, says Inglis,[12] " 130,000 friars."
Avila, with 1,000 houses, had sixteen convents and eight parish
churches.[13]   In Segovia less than 2,000 families had 25 churches
and 21 convents.[14]

[1] Stephens's Central America, vol. iii. p. 270.
[2] Ibid. pp. 26–38                         [3] Ibid. vol. iv. pp. 114–116.
[4] De l'Espagne, tome i. p. 62.            [5] Sempéré, tome i. p. 266.
[6] Townsend, vol. ii. p. 213.              [7] Vol. iv. pp. 25, 28, 40, 41.
[8] Ibid. p. 28.                            [9] Ibid. vol. v. pp. 15, 16.
[10] M'Culloch, vol. ii. p. 711, and Townsend, vol. ii. pp. 213, 214.
[11] Spain, vol. i. p. 222.                 [12] Spain, i. 295.
[13] Townsend, vol. ii. p. 98.              [14] Ibid. pp. 117, 118.

*Income.*—M'Culloch [1] says: "According to an official statement drawn up in 1812, it appears that the clergy were in possession of about one-fourth part of the landed property of the
kingdom, exclusive of tithes and other casual sources of income,
producing in all a total gross revenue of about eleven millions
sterling a year. In 1749, in Castile, [2] "L'état séculier possédait
61,196,166 mesures de terre, dont les produits s'élevaient à
817,282,098 réaux ; l'état écclesiastique possédait 12,209,053
mesures de terre, dont les revénus étaient 161,392,700 réaux." [3]
In 1555, Alva stated, "Que dans les seuls royaumes d'Espagne,
les ecclésiastiques possèdent pour plus de deux millions de ducats
en fonds de terre." [4] Dunham [5] says that soon after the accession
of Ferdinand VI. (which was in 1746) the returns of a commission showed that, comparing "the relative possessions of the
lay and clerical orders, the whole annual income of the former
was 1,630,296,143 reals ; of the latter, 340,890,195. The absorp-
tion of one-fifth by an order which could contribute nothing to
the community, but, on the contrary, derived its support from
the other, was a lamentable state of things. In England, where
the whole ecclesiastical revenues do not yield three millions,
while the returns from land, manufacture, commerce, funded property, &c., certainly return 250 millions, we are sufficiently inclined to join in condemnation of the enormous wealth of the
church ; what shall we say to the proportion of not one eightieth,
but one fifth ?"

In 1403, the archbishop of Toledo was "le plus riche de toute
la chrétienté." [6] Wealth of the clergy. [7]

About 90 days are feast days. [8]

Cook estimates the clergy at 130,000. [9] San Felipe, population 12,000 and ten convents. Medina Rio Seco, population
8,000, and three parish churches and six convents. Lerida, population 18,000, and eleven convents. Tarragona possessed
eleven convents, though its population was under 8,000. Valla-
dolid, with 20,000 souls, boasted of forty-six convents and fifteen
parish churches; and we are assured that Segovia, in 1826, with
a population of 10,000, had twenty-one convents and twenty-six
churches. In Toledo, the population being in 1786 under
25,000, there were twenty-six parish churches and thirty-eight
convents. In Valencia there were, in 1786, 100,000 people and

[1] Geog. Dict. vol. ii. p. 711.                   [2] Ibid. p. 102.
[2] Sempéré, Monarch. Espag. vol. ii. p. 162.
[4] Ibid. vol. i. p. 247.                              [6] Vol. v. p. 282.
[5] Fleury, tome xxi. p. 16.                        [7] Prescott, vol. iii. p. 435.
[8] Laborde, vol. iv. pp. 42, 43.                 [9] Spain, vol. i. p. 222.

forty-four convents; in Granada, 80,000, and forty convents; in Malaga, 42,000, and twenty-five convents. In Xeres, in 1776, the population was 40,000, of whom 2,000 were ecclesiastics. Alicante contained 18,000 inhabitants, and eight convents; Onhuela, 21,000 and thirteen convents. In Guadix we find 6,000 souls, with four churches and seven convents; in Ecija, 28,000, with six churches, eight chapels, and twenty convents; and Seville, possessing a population of barely 100,000, was bounteously provided with 100 convents. On Madrid, Laborde, tome iii. p. 93, and Barretti, tome ii. p. 300. In Cordova, 32,000 souls and fortyfour convents; Baza, 15,000, and five convents.

These convents, churches, and chapels were for the most part richly endowed, it being considered that the clergy having rendered vast services to Spain by keeping the faith pure, they should be well paid. The court was drained and bankrupt, the people were slaves, but the church must be upheld. The archbishop of Toledo, in 1786, had more than 90,000l.; and, " besides the archbishop, there are forty canons, fifty prebendaries, and fifty chaplains. The whole body of ecclesiastics belonging to the cathedral is 600, well provided for."

As partly cause and partly consequence of this, the people retained and still retain their ignorance; for the clergy knew that on it was based their own power.

In 1690, in Cadiz, there were thirteen convents.[1] In 1679, the archbishop of Compostella, in Galicia, had "70,000 écus de rente," [2] i.e. " 60,000 ducats."[3] Southey[4] says there are fewer clergy in England than anywhere else. Alison[5] says that, in 1787, there were " 22,480 priests and 47,710 regular clergy belonging to monasteries or other public religious establishments." On Toledo, see Laborde, tome iii. p. 84. In 1786, Barcelona, with a population of 95,000, contained thirty-seven convents. " There were no fewer than 12,000 Franciscan convents before the invasion of Spain by Napoleon's troops."[6] At Alicant, in Valentia, there were, in 1694, "six convents for men and two nunneries." [7]

Prescott[8] says: " The archbishop of Toledo, by virtue of his office primate of Spain and grand chancellor of Castille, was esteemed after the pope the highest ecclesiastical dignitary in Christendom. His revenues at the close of the fifteenth century

[1] Labat, Voyages en Espagne, vol. i. p. 90.    [2] Ibid. p. 164.    [3] Ibid. p. 314.
[4] Southey, Common Place Book, vol. iii. p. 635.
[5] History of Europe, vol. viii. p. 410.
[6] Quin's Ferdinand. vol. vii. p. 157.
[7] Travels through Spain, by a Gentleman, Lond. 1702, p. 66.
[8] Ferdinand and Isabella, vol. i. p. lxix.

exceeded 80,000 ducats. He could muster a greater number of
vassals than any other subject in the kingdom, and held jurisdiction over fifteen large and populous towns, besides a great number
of inferior places."

---

## NATIONAL CHARACTER OF THE IRISH.

In Clarendon Correspondence, 4to, 1828, vol. i. p. 373, there is a
very curious account of the wretched state of the Irish in 1686,
between Dublin and Kildare. See also p. 536, where the earl of
Clarendon writes that the old English planters were in Ireland
the most important. In 1686, kitchen gardens began to be
common in Dublin.[1] The Bible was not translated into Irish
" till nearly the middle of the seventeenth century " by Bishop
Bedell.[2]
In 1760, there were German colonies near Limerick.[3] Wesley
mentions[4] the " fickleness " of the Irish. In 1771, he expresses
his surprise[5] at the improvements made in Ireland " within a few
years." In 1747, he says[6] that in Ireland there were no Protestants except those " transplanted lately from England." Heber
says[7] that, unfortunately for Ireland, " among the English clergy
who were the first heralds of Protestantism to her shores, a large
proportion were favourers of the peculiar system of Calvin, a
system of all others the least attractive to the feelings of a Roman
Catholic." In 1725, Lady Mary W. Montagu writes:[8] "Wit
has taken a very odd course, and is making the tour of Ireland."
On Ireland, read works of Sir William Temple, vol. iii. p. 1-28.
Laing[9] observes that in Ireland the *division* of land goes on
without the sense of ownership. In 1799 it was observed that
the Irish were always superior when abroad to when at home.[10]
In Limerick extremely early marriages, even at thirteen.[11] The
Irish, it is well said, are idle, because wages are too low.[12]

---

[1] Clarendon Correspondence, vol. i. p. 407.
[2] See Southey's Life of Wesley, vol. ii. p. 149.
[3] See Wesley's Journals, 1851, 8vo, p. 464.          [4] Ibid. p. 557.
[5] Ibid. p. 649.                                       [6] Ibid. p. 258.
[7] Life of Jeremy Taylor, p. cxx. in Taylor's Works, 8vo, 1828, vol. i.
[8] Works, 8vo, 1803, vol. iii. p. 146.
[9] Notes of a Traveller, 2nd series, p. 82.
[10] Parl. History, vol. xxxiv. p. 222.
[11] Journal of the Statistical Society, vol. iii. pp. 322, 323, and for their admirable
patience under the sufferings of starvation, see p. 326.
[12] Statistical Society, vol. vii. p. 24.

## ITALIANS, THEIR NATIONAL CHARACTER, ETC.

Burnet[1] mentions the indifference of the Romans to religion. In 1655, Sir John Reresby[2] says that the Italians never got drunk. In the time of Montaigne the Italians still preserved their reputation for ability.[3] In 1759, Lady M. W. Montagu writes[4] that a great change had taken place among the Italians, who were no longer jealous of their women, and that this change "begun so lately as the year 1732, when the French overran this part of Italy." She writes in 1718[5] that the fashion of Cicisbeos, which had begun at Genoa, "is now received all over Italy." In 1740, "the Abbé Conti tells me often that these last twenty years have so far changed the customs of Venice that they hardly know it for the same country."[6] And in 1752, she writes from Brescia:[7] "The character of a learned woman is far from being ridiculous in this country." In 1740, many Italians were "atheists."[8] In 1741, lotteries had become general.[9] In 1741, Italian husbands were no longer jealous.[10] In 1777, Swinburne writes:[11] "There is no place where music seems to be in less esteem than Naples, or where so little is heard." A writer well acquainted with Naples says: "The Neapolitan peasants are a rough but kind-hearted set of people, who only require to be well used and honestly treated to become good subjects and hard labourers;"[12] but even the better classes are miserably ignorant.[13] An author of the fourteenth century regrets the progress of luxury in Italy.[14]

---

## CHARACTER OF THE SCOTCH.

Mr. Chambers says:[15] "It is quite remarkable, when we consider the high character of the popular melodies, how late and how slow has been the introduction of a taste for the higher class of musical composition in Scotland. The earl of Kelly, a man of

[1] Own Time, vol. iii. p. 163.
[2] Travels. 8vo, 1831, p. 103.
[3] Essais de Montaigne, Paris, 8vo, 1843, livre iii. chap. viii. p. 586.
[4] Works, 8vo, 1803, vol. v. p. 89.   [5] Ibid. vol. iii. p. 51.
[6] Ibid. p. 199.   [7] Ibid. vol. iv. p. 148.
[8] Correspondence between Ladies Pomfret and Hartford, 2nd edit. 8vo, 1806, vol. i. p. 234.   [9] Ibid. vol. ii. p. 330.   [10] Ibid. vol. iii. p. 259.
[11] Courts of Europe, 8vo, 1841, vol. i. p. 164.
[12] Journal of the Statistical Society, vol. v. p. 177.   [13] Ibid. p. 203.
[14] See Comte, Traité de Législation, tome i. p. 462.
[15] Traditions of Edinburgh, 8vo, 1847, pp. 245, 246.

yesterday, was the first Scotsman who ever composed music for an
orchestra. This fact seems sufficient. It is to be feared that the
beauty of the melodies is itself partly to be blamed for the indifference to higher music." Wesley made little or no impression
in Scotland.[1] In 1788, Wesley[2] writes: "When I was in Scotland first, even at a nobleman's table, we had only flesh meat of one
kind, but no vegetables of any kind; but now they are as plentiful
here as in England. Near Dumfries there are five very large public
gardens, which furnish the town with greens and fruit in abundance." Dr. Cullen[3] says it has long been usual in Scotland for
people of all ranks to wash their children with cold water from the
time of their birth. As to the supposed freedom of Scotland from
crime, an eminent Scotchman suggests[4] that this arises from an
indifference about the Scotch people respecting the detection of
criminals. In Scotland there are more wills and bequests of property than in England.[5] Laing says,[6] "It is a peculiar feature
in the social condition of our lowest labouring class in Scotland,
that none perhaps in Europe of the same class have so few
physical and so many intellectual wants and gratifications." On
the management of the poor in Scotland, read Journal of the
Statistical Society, vol. iv. pp. 288-319. At p. 314, it is said of
the Scotch, "The great cause of pauperism is the custom of mar-
rying young." In 1628, Sir Benjamin Rudyard said of Scotland,
"Though that country be not so rich as ours, yet they are richer
in their affection to religion."[7] In August, 1650, all Scotchmen
were ordered to leave England.[8] Scotland has had a public
system of "religious instruction since 1696;" and "England is the
only civilized European country which in 1857 has no nationally
organized plan of education."[9] See also pp. 185, 186, 202, 203,
where it appears that this was due to Fletcher of Saltoun. At
p. 202, "In 1696 a law was passed by the Scottish Parliament,
ordaining that there should be, in all time coming, and in every
one of the thousand parishes of Scotland, an endowed school for
teaching the elementary branches of education. This enactment
has been in force ever since;" but[10] this system was the work of
the "Presbyterian clergy," and under it "there was little health-

[1] See Southey's Life of Wesley, 8vo, 1846, vol. ii. pp. 138, 145, 146.
[2] Journals, 8vo, 1851, p. 866.
[3] Works, Edinburgh, 1827, vol. ii. p. 626.
[4] Laing's Sweden, p. 128.
[5] See Porter's Progress of the Nation, vol. iii. p. 130.
[6] Notes of a Traveller, first series, p. 272.
[7] Parliamentary History, vol. ii. p. 387.     [8] Ibid. vol. iii. p. 1353.
[9] Transactions of Assoc. for Social Science, 1858, p. 181.
[10] Ibid. p. 203.

ful exercise of the intellect."[1]  Scotland is a healthy country, and the people cautious and frugal ; hence the mortality in " country districts " is remarkably low, " less than fifteen annual deaths per 1000."[2]

For the ignorance of women in Scotland, see Burton's Life and Correspondence of Hume, vol. i. pp. 196–198, and Hume's Philosophical Works, vol. ii. p. 59.  George Combe[3] says of his father : " His education extended only to reading, writing, mensuration, and book-keeping.  He never learned either grammar or the art of spelling.  In the middle of the last century even the gentry of Scotland were not in general better educated."  In 1786, Lord Buchan writes from Scotland : " The middling class of people here are either too poor or too much occupied in professional engagements to prosecute any inquiry that does not promise a pecuniary reward."[4]  There was no middle class, and many gentlemen educated at the universities used to be obliged for a living to keep public-houses.[5]  Much greater crime in Scotland than in England.[6]  The total offences seem to be less than in England, but murder and robbery with violence is much more common.[7]  The Scotch consume two times as much spirits as the English![8] and the illegitimate births are immense.[9]  On the present immigration of Scotch into England, see Statist. Soc. vol. xv. pp. 88, 89 ; Grenville Papers, vol. iv. p. 340 ; curious letters on Scotland in Forster's Life of Goldsmith, vol. i. pp. 446–448 ; Parr's Works, vol. vii. p. 558 ; Correspondence of Sir J. E. Smith, vol. i. p. 66 ; Russell's Memorials of Fox, vol. iii. pp. 344, 361 ; Bedford Correspondence, vol. iii. p. 55 ; Albemarle's Rockingham, vol. ii. p. 300.  Finish the chapter by saying that, when the cholera broke out, the Scotch irreligiously, and to the disgrace of an enlightened age, petitioned Palmerston.  Then was seen the difference between the two countries.  The English minister, a great lover of power, and though an able man by no means a remarkable one, took a large view, and England supported.  But we do not find that Scotland protested against the impiety.  Conclude by saying that, happily, the Scotch, though superstitious, are not loyal, and are therefore saved from being like Spain exposed to both evils.

On the *present* animosity of the Scotch clergy against all in-

[1] Transactions of Assoc. for Social Science, 1858, p. 203.          [2] Ibid. p. 359.
[3] Life of Dr. Andrew Combe, Edinburgh, 8vo, 1850, p. 6.
[4] Nichols's Literary Illustrations, vol. vi. p. 514.
[5] See Burt's Letters from the North of Scotland, vol. i. p. 66.
[6] Journal of Statist. Soc. vol. vi. p. 236.          [7] Ibid. vol. x. pp. 326, 329, 330.
[8] Ibid. vol. x. p. 330 ; vol. xiii. pp. 359, 360.          [9] Ibid. vol. xiv. p. 68.

nocent amusements, and on the connection between this and the drunkenness of the people (stimulus being the only amusement), see and quote a curious letter in p. 5 of the Times of Friday, September 10, 1858. In the eighteenth century the Presbyterians hated genius, and the wits and the clergy were so incessantly at war, that it became an acknowledged function of literature to attack the clergy; and, as this was unpopular, literary men became a degraded class, as in Smollett and Burns.[1] Dr. Archibald Pitcairne was at the head of these profane wits.[2] In the eighteenth century some of the best Scotchmen " connected themselves with other countries."[3] Burton[4] says: " Burns, with all his strong democratic tendencies, was a sentimental Jacobite." On the *separation* of intellectual and practical classes, see Burton, vol. ii. pp. 552–555, where it is said that in the time of Knox and in the seventeenth century " it was felt that the Scotch tongue was becoming provincial, and those who desired to speak beyond a mere home audience wrote in Latin." " Those who are acquainted with the epistolary correspondence of learned Scotchmen in the seventeenth century will observe how easily they take to Latin, and how uneasy and diffident they feel in the use of English." At the end of the seventeenth century " Scotland had not kept an independent literary language of her own, nor was she sufficiently expert in the use of that which had been created in England. Hence the literary barrenness. The men may have existed, but they had not the tools." " Not till Burns came forward did the Scottish tongue claim an independent place in modern literature." But much earlier " one distinguished man wrote in Scotch, Allan Ramsay."[5] Thomson shook it off, " and became the most characteristic painter of English rural life and scenery."[6] In 1799, Niebuhr writes from Edinburgh: " Scotland stands far and wide in high repute for piety, and has done so from the commencement of the reformation. The clergy in general are not good for much; that is allowed by every one who knows the country. The piety of the people is, for the most part, mere eyeservice; an accustomed formality without any influence on their mode of thinking and acting."[7]

In 1696, for, I think the first time, the Church *consulted* with the " State " about " appointing fasts and thanksgivings."[8] On the history of the Scotch Church in the eighteenth century, see

[1] Burton's History of Scotland, vol. ii. p. 561.　　[2] Ibid. pp. 559, 560.
[3] Ibid. p. 563.　　[4] Ibid. p. 418.
[5] Ibid. p. 554.　　[6] Ibid. p. 555.
[7] Life and Letters of Niebuhr, 8vo, 1852, vol. i. pp. 440, 441.
[8] Acts of General Assembly, from 1638, p. 253.

Spalding Miscellany, i. 197 *et seq.* and p. 227 *et seq.* At vol. iii. p. 22, Lord Grange writes in 1733 : " neither for our own sake nor for our country's ought the divines to be suffered to meddle beyond their own sphere."

McCulloch [1] says, " Scotland, from being about the middle of the last century one of the worst cultivated countries of Europe, is now one of the best. At this moment, indeed, the agriculture of the best farmed counties of Scotland is certainly equal, and is by many deemed superior, to that of Northumberland, Lincoln, and Norfolk, the best farmed counties of England. The proximate cause of this extraordinary progress must be sought for in the rapid growth of manufactures and commerce, and consequently of large towns, and the proportionally great demand for agricultural produce since the peace of Paris in 1763, and especially since the close of the American war. . . . . . Down to the close of the American war, the farm buildings in most parts of Scotland were mean and inadequate in the extreme," and filthily dirty. " The dunghill was universally opposite the door, and so near it that in wet weather it was no easy matter to get into the house with dry feet." (Hence perhaps the custom of going about without stockings.) " The change that has taken place in these respects during the last half century has been signal and complete. In none but the least accessible and least improved districts are any of the old houses now to be met with. See McCulloch's Geog. Dict. vol. ii. p. 655, and see his British Empire, vol. i. pp. 428, 488. At p. 656, " In respect of farming implements, Scotland has very much the advantage over England." At p. 657, the arable land in Scotland is inferior to that of England ; but in the former country rent is *decidedly higher*, owing to the greater skill and economy of Scotch farmers. " Rent has increased much more rapidly in Scotland than in England : so rapid an increase of rent is probably unmatched in any old settled country, and indicates an astonishing degree of improvement. . . . . . We have, indeed, no hesitation in affirming that no old settled country of which we have any authentic accounts, ever made half the progress in civilization and the accumulation of wealth that Scotland has done since 1763, and especially since 1787." [2] For these changes since 1760 McCulloch refers [3] to Robertson's Rural Recollections. McCulloch [4] says of Roxburghshire or Teviotdale, that " Dawson, the great improver of Scotch husbandry, occupied

[1] M'Culloch's Geog. Dict. vol. ii. p. 655.    [2] Ibid. p. 657.
[3] Ibid. p. 657 note.
[4] British Empire, vol. i. p. 276.

*image not available*

Europe." And yet in that very year, and indeed " *in that very month*," the Scotch persecuted witches and infidels, and put to death Thomas Aikenhead, a boy of eighteen, for blasphemy.[1] In and after 1470, we find the first " corporations of trades." [2]

(What follows was written in September, 1859.)

The land was inclosed, drained, and manured. The same spirit of industry, method, and perception of regularity and sequence which was shown in manufactures now for the first time also appeared in agriculture, though, from the greater incapacity of farmers, the improvement was slower : but its early traces are clearly discernible. Chalmers, in his learned work but detestable style, says: [3] " The star of agricultural melioration began to twinkle at the Union. In 1723, a Society of *Improvers in the Knowledge of Agriculture* was formed at Edinburgh, consisting of all who were either high, or opulent, or learned, or ingenious in Scotland." [4] At vol. ii. p. 32 Chalmers says: " In 1698 was printed at Edinburgh, Husbandry Anatomized, or several Rules for the better Improvement of the Ground. In 1706 was given to the public by Lord Belhaven, Advice to the Farmers of East Lothian how to Improve their Grounds. In 1724, the Society of Improvers at Edinburgh published A Treatise on Fallowing, Raising Grasses, &c. And other works followed in 1729, 1733, and 1743. In Roxburghshire, " before 1743, the practice of draining, inclosing, summer fallowing, sowing flax, hemp, rape, turnip and grass seeds, planting cabbages after and potatoes with the plough in fields of great extent was generally introduced." [5] At vol. ii. p. 868, Chalmers says: " The year 1723, when the Society of Improvers was established, may perhaps be deemed the true era. From this period, a sort of enterprise may be traced in every shire." Of Galloway he says: [6] " One of the first steps towards improvement, which was marked with insurrection, was inclosures in 1724." At p. 286, "the real improvement of the soil in this district began effectually in 1740, where shell marle was discovered, or at least attended to, as a useful manure." At vol. iii. p. 796, " Potatoes, almost the only green crop, and almost the only instance wherein drill husbandry is practised, were introduced to Paisley and Renfrew about the year 1750 from Kintyre, and were at that time first planted in the field."

In the county of Aberdeen, in the parish of Kennellar, says

---

[1] Macaulay's History, vol. iv. pp. 781-784.
[2] Pinkerton's History, vol. ii. pp. 410, 411.
[3] Caledonia, vol. i. p. 873.          [4] Ibid. vol. ii. pp. 311, 312, 734.
[5] Ibid. pp. 143, 869.          [6] Ibid. vol. iii. p. 285.

Sinclair, " Grass seeds had not been seen in this parish in any considerable quantity before the year 1750; till about that time they were not kept for sale by the merchants in Aberdeen, and consequently could not be much known among our farmers."[1]  " Improvements of land by inclosing, planting, and raising artificial grasses, cabbages, and turnips."[2]  At vol. iv. p. 11, "it is only about twenty years ago that the farmers began to clean their land by sowing turnips and to sow grass seeds."  " Turnip for twenty years past has been sown in the fields, and clover and rye-grass have become a constant part of the rotation."[3]  " Artificial grass, as clover and rye-grass, begins to be more cultivated with more attention."[4]  " About 1740," the proprietor of Dankeith (in the parish of Symingham, in the county of Ayr) " was among the first who introduced rye-grass into Ayrshire."[5]  At vol. vi. p. 193, " The people begin to see the advantage of sowing grass seeds, and adhering to a regular rotation of crops."  In counties of Haddington and Berwick " Improvements in husbandry have within these last thirty years made rapid progress, especially in fallowing their lands, clearing it of stones, regular rotations of crops with turnips and grass."[6]  In county of Aberdeen, " Potatoes, turnips, flax, and artificial grasses were introduced about fifty years ago (i.e. 1743) by the late Lord Strichen."[7]  At vol. vi. p. 439, "Before the introduction of the turnip husbandry and the raising of clover and rye-grass, the farmers were frequently obliged in the winter season to drive their sheep into the low country and purchase hay for them. . . . . The introduction of the use of lime as a manure has been of great benefit to the arable grounds.  Very considerable crops of oats, barley, and pease have by means thereof been raised from land which in its natural state was of little or no value.  It not only occasions a more plentiful, but also a much earlier crop."  *Finish by saying that all this let loose and made available more hands for manufactures; so that the improvements in agriculture diminish the influence of the agricultural classes.*  " Sir John Dalrymple, grandfather to the present baronet, was the first person who introduced into Scotland the sowing of turnips and the planting of cabbages in the open field."[8]  In the parish of Toryland, in the county of Kirkcudbright, it is said,[9] about 1730 John Dalywell saw "the advantage of inclosing, subdividing, and improving land.  He was the first who discovered and made use of marl.

---

[1] Sinclair's Statistical Account of Scotland, vol. iii. p. 497.

[2] Ibid. p. 553.  [3] Ibid. vol. iv. p. 395.  [4] Ibid p. 444.

[5] Ibid. vol. v. p. 396.  [6] Ibid. vol. vii. p. 403.  [7] Ibid. p. 417.

[8] Ibid. vol. ix. p. 282.  [9] Ibid. p. 314.

By this manure he raised upon the poorest land the most luxuriant crops of different kinds of grain, to the astonishment of all the country around. He meliorated the soil, and raised the finest crops of natural and artificial grasses."

In part of Ayrshire " within thirty years " (i.e. 1764) " all the arable and a great part of the pasture lands have been inclosed." [1] About 1720, the earl of Haddington " introduced the sowing of clover and other grass-seeds " into the county of Haddington in the synod of Lothian.[2] At Salton in county of Haddington, " so early as the beginning of this century, lime was adopted as a manure; but was gradually discontinued and at length totally laid aside, from an opinion that it was of no advantage in the improvement of land." [3]  " When grass was introduced as a crop, the old tenants were much offended, and said, ' It was a shame to see *beast's meat* growing where *men's meat* should grow.'" [4]  "Grass seeds, such as rye-grass and clover." [5]  " In 1740, shell marl was discovered in Galloway, and abundant crops produced by the use of this manure." [6]  In county of Haddington, " the first example of fallowing ground, in the beginning of the eighteenth century." [7] In county of Aberdeen, lime was used about 1734.[8]  In 1749 " the cultivation of potatoes " in the county of Ross. [9]  " Benefit of inclosures and green crops." [10]  " Cultivating and planting large tracts of waste moor ground, making substantial regular fences, and liming his lands." [11]  " The grasses sown are rye-grass, red, white, and yellow clover, and narrow plantane or rib grass." [12] " Little waste ground in the parish. What is wet they are draining, what is uncultivated and arable they are bringing into tillage; what is not arable they are planting." [13]  " About 1750, potatoes began to be planted " at Northmaven in the county of Orkney.[14]  In county of Fife, " in the beginning of the eighteenth century, Lord St. Clair began to plant and enclose." [15]  In county of Aberdeen in 1745 " began plantations." [16]  " Kelp was totally unknown in the Highlands until about 1735." [17]  " Waste land drained, levelled, and enclosed." [18]  In county of Forfar " some years before 1750 he first of this parish (of Monifeth) began to enclose land; and between 1750 and 1752 to use lime as a manure." [19]  " When the use of marl or lime as a manure was

[1] Sinclair's Statistical Account of Scotland, vol. x. p. 38.

| | | |
|---|---|---|
| [2] Ibid. p. 171. | [3] Ibid. p. 253. | [4] Ibid. p. 612. |
| [5] Ibid. p. 630. | [6] Ibid. vol. xi. p. 65. | [7] Ibid. p. 85. |
| [8] Ibid. p. 412. | [9] Ibid. p. 425. | [10] Ibid. p. 503. |
| [11] Ibid. p. 565. | [12] Ibid. p. 601. | [13] Ibid. vol. xii. p. 191. |
| [14] Ibid. p. 354. | [15] Ibid. p. 508. | [16] Ibid. vol. xiii. p. 181. |
| [17] Ibid. p. 305. | [18] Ibid. p. 463. | [19] Ibid. p. 491. |

unknown, and that of dung was the sole one, a certain quantity
of it arising from the confinement of the cattle during winter
could only be obtained." [1] "Tracts of common and barren land
brought into culture." [2] "Green crops—viz., potatoes, turnips, and
sown grass." [3] At vol. xiv. p. 505, "Before the Union, Scotland
had no foreign market for her sheep and black cattle; and consequently had no motive to raise more of these than her own
domestic consumption demanded, which was extremely small, as
little butcher's meat was used. But after the Union the price of
cattle rose, and landlords perceived that it would be as profitable
to cultivate land for rearing and feeding cattle as for raising
grain. They therefore enclosed their grounds and united several
of their small farms." [4] Rae [5] says that at the end of the eighteenth century "The construction of the plough in Scotland was
so improved that two horses did the work of six oxen. The
diminution of outlay thus produced, giving the farmer from a
smaller capital an equal return, encouraged him to apply himself
to materials which he would otherwise have left, as his forefathers
had done, untouched. He carried off stones from his fields, built
fences, dug ditches, formed drains, and constructed roads. Lime
was discovered to be a profitable manure. The additional returns
which the hard clay thus converted into a black loam yielded
were spent in the cultivation of land, before waste. The cultivation of turnips was introduced, and instead of useless fallows, the
farmer had a large supply of a nutritive food for his cattle.
This reacted on the inhabitants of towns, and their industry
was augmented by the increased returns yielded by the country
and by the new demands made by it. Rocks were quarried, the
metal left the mine, large manufacturing establishments arose,
wharfs, docks, canals, and bridges were built, villages were
changed into towns, and towns into cities." In the county of
Kirkcudbright "shell marl was first discovered and used" about
1732. [6] In Kincardine "in so little repute was farming before
the year 1712, that the proprietor of Brotherston found it necessary to give premiums in order to induce tenants to rent his
farms." [7] In 1722, the first kelp made in the Orkneys. [8] Lime
in Aberdeenshire about 1750. [9] "Enclosing, draining, and clearing the ground of stones." "Clear his land of weeds either by
applying proper manure, or by raising potatoes, turnips, and other

---

[1] Sinclair's Statistical Account of Scotland, vol. xiv. p. 9.
[2] Ibid. p. 104.  [3] Ibid. p. 156.  [4] Ibid. p. 505.
[5] New Principles of Political Economy, p. 261.
[6] Sinclair, vol. xv. p. 82.  [7] Ibid. p. 220.  [8] Ibid. p. 395.
[9] Ibid. vol. xvi. p. 471.

green crops, or by exerting himself in summer fallowing." [1] In Perthshire, " the first marl-pit was partially drained and opened for public sale about the year 1734." [2] In part of the county of East Lothian there was in 1700 little planting, " it being supposed no trees could grow because of the sea air and north-east winds ; " but " in 1707 the enclosing and planting of the moor were begun." [3] At Kelsyth in county of Stirling, potatoes were first cultivated in the fields in 1739. They had previously been " raised in gardens, and there was a common prejudice that they could be raised nowhere else to advantage." [4] Even natural manure was difficult to get, though always abundant in the large cities, for " it was not till after the year 1750 that carts came to be in general use, at least to the west of Edinburgh, though they had been long employed on the east side ; the conveyance of all materials having been before that period in sacks, hurdles, or creels upon the backs of horses. About 1730, the offals and manure of the streets of Edinburgh sold at 2d. per cart ; at present the cart load sells sometimes for 1s. 6d. or upwards." [5] Adam Smith [6] says : " It is not more than a century ago that in many parts of the Highlands of Scotland, butcher's meat was as cheap or cheaper than even bread made of oatmeal. The Union opened the market of England to the Highland cattle. Their ordinary price at present is about three times greater than at the beginning of the century, and the rents of many Highland estates have been tripled or quadrupled at the same time. In almost every part of Great Britain a pound of the best butcher's meat is in present times generally worth more than two pounds of the best white bread, and in plentiful years it is sometimes worth three or four pounds." [7] At p. 63 Adam Smith says : " The use of the artificial grasses, turnips, carrots, cabbages, and other expedients to make a greater quantity of land feed a great number of cattle, reduces the superiority of the price of butcher's meat compared to that of bread." See also p. 93 a and b on the low price of cattle in Scotland before the Union, owing partly to the ignorance of manure. At p. 94a Adam Smith says, " Of all the commercial advantages, however, which Scotland has derived from the union with England, the rise in the price of cattle is perhaps the greatest. It has not only raised the value of all Highland estates, but it has perhaps been the principal cause of the improvement of the low country." On application of chemistry to agriculture in 1749, see Thomson's Life of Cullen, vol. i. p. 62.

[1] Sinclair's Statistical Account of Scotland, vol. xvii. p. 229.
[2] Ibid. p. 469.     [3] Ibid. p. 576.          [4] Ibid. vol. xviii. p. 282, 283.
[5] Ibid. p. 363.     [6] Wealth of Nations, p. 626.
[7] See Cairns, On Butcher's Meat in Australia, in Fraser's Magazine, On Gold.

.        .        .        .        .        .        .

In 1710, " The greatest number of the Episcopalians continue
under the direction and influence of the exauctorate bishop of
Edinburgh, who is entirely in the interest of the Pretender, and
will allow none of his followers to pray for the queen." [1]

In 1693, by virtue of an act of parliament, no one could sit in
the Assembly unless he took an oath to William. This the
church furiously resisted as Erastianism, and William at the last
moment was forced to give way.[2] This mollified the Assembly,
and " from this time there was a full reconciliation between the
established church and King William." [3] " The seeds which in
their ripening brought on the Church of Scotland the reproach of
lukewarmness, if not of a slight degree of scepticism, were thus
sown in the reaction against stern fanaticism." [4] In 1703, Anne
being queen, alarm was excited by the inclination of government
to favour episcopacy.[5] In 1706, during negotiations for the
Union, Presbyterianism was secured by a clause " specially excluding the discipline and government of the church from the
deliberations of the commission," [6] and it was understood that
" each nation must keep its own church." [7] And by the Act of
Presbyterianism was declared " unalterable, and the only government of the church within the kingdom of Scotland." [8] This
made " the moderate Presbyterians favour the Union " ; [9] but the
zealous Covenant men and Cameronians opposed it as involving
an alliance with the idolatrous church of England.[10] In 1706–7,
" the comfortable established clergy were different men from the
theocrats of Dunbar and Bothwell Brig; and the sagacious Car-
stairs, though no longer their moderator and chairman, led them
by his counsel." [11] In 1710, government slighted the Assembly so
much as to despise the fasts it ordered.[12] In 1712, even the
" patronage act," so unfavourable to the scriptural classes, failed
to rouse the church ; [13] and " it was clear that the Assembly was
now a very different body from that which twenty years earlier
had offered dangerous defiance to King William." [14] But in 1711–
12, Mac Millan " organised the first secession from the church of
Scotland." [15] In 1714 the General Assembly deposed two clergymen for not praying for the king ; [16] but the episcopalians were
the great Jacobites ; and " it was from the rebellion of 1715 that

[1] Ellis's Original Letters, first series, vol. iii. p. 356.
[2] Burton, vol. i. pp. 231–233, 234.                     [3] Ibid. p. 236.
[4] Ibid. p. 256.          [5] Ibid. pp. 354, 355.          [6] Ibid. pp. 394, 424.
[7] Ibid. p. 401.          [8] Ibid. pp. 466, 467.          [9] Ibid. 429, 430.
[10] Ibid. pp. 431, 432 ; compare, respecting the Cameronians, pp. 32–55.
[11] Ibid. p. 445.          [12] Ibid. pp. 39, 40.          [13] Ibid. p. 55.
[14] Ibid. p. 56.          [15] Ibid. p. 69.          [16] Ibid. p. 90.

the British government was awakened to, and acted on, the fact that the Hanover settlement had a great friend in the Scottish Presbyterian Establishment, and a bitter enemy in Scottish episcopacy." [1]

In 1715–17, " the church of Scotland was becoming daily more important as an ally of the Hanover government, and a friend of the landed gentry." [2]   But the old Covenanting spirit was active, and at length caused dissent, [3] and claimed the power of working miracles. [4]   Burton [5] says priestly power decayed *because* the state protected the church.   I think the fact was that the clergy relaxed their zeal for the people, because they ceased to need the people.   The first great proof of decay of the church was the rise of a lay and sceptical philosophy.   " Much as has been said about the fervent religion of the Scotch, very little of it has ever existed among the upper classes." [6]   Burton says : [7]   " The decrease of discipline was one of the main grievances which created dissent in the eighteenth century."   Between 1720 and 1730 disputes broke out between the General Assembly and presbyteries. [8]   In 1732, everything was aggravated by disputes respecting patronage, the complaint being that " no absolute power of rejection was given to the congregation"; and now Ebenezer Erskine formed his body of seceders. [9]   In Scotland dissent assumed a very different and more *rampant* character than in England. [10]   The followers of Erskine reproached the church of Scotland with its toleration, and not rebuking " great men " as of old. [11]   The seceders, however, always refused to unite with the Cameronians, [12] and the secession was not completed till 1740. [13]   " Their church was particularly that of the humbler classes." [14]   They discouraged attacks upon government, [15] and when the Jacobites approached Edinburgh in 1745, " there was a marked zeal among the seceders to help in the defence of the city." [16]

After 1715, " the episcopalian non-jurors were not hard pressed by the government " ; [17] but " in the rebellion of 1745 the Scottish episcopal church came forth again so flagrantly in support of the Stuarts that severe restraints could no longer be avoided." [18]
Respecting " the secession which took place in 1732," see Bogue

---

[1] Burton, vol. ii. p. 220.        [2] Ibid. p. 282, and see p. 311.
[3] Ibid. pp. 290, 291.        [4] Ibid. p. 295.        [5] Ibid. p. 298.
[6] Ibid. p. 303.        [7] Ibid. p. 301.        [8] Ibid. pp. 314–316.
[9] Ibid. pp. 321, 322, 324, 325, 327.
[10] Ibid. see some good remarks in pp. 328, 329.        [11] Ibid. pp. 332, 333.
[12] Ibid. p. 336.        [13] Ibid. p. 337.        [14] Ibid. p. 341.
[15] Ibid. p. 344.        [16] Ibid. p. 452.        [17] Ibid. p. 357        [18] Ibid. p. 358.

and Bennett's Hist. of Dissenters, vol. iv. p. 57 *et seq.* Martineau's
Hist. of England, vol. ii. pp. 318, 583.

McCulloch [1] says: "At present, and since 1712, the privilege
of appointing clergymen to parishes has been vested in the crown
or in private patrons"; but this "right of patronage has long been
exceedingly unpopular, and its enforcement in spite of public
opinion occasioned the great secession from the church in 1741.
The General Assembly, by the *Veto Act* in 1834, gave the congre-
gations belonging to parishes a right to reject a presentee if he
were not acceptable to them; but it was decided by the House of
Lords in 1839 that the General Assembly had no power to pass
the Veto Act, and that all proceedings under it were null and
void." This roused the General Assembly, who met in 1843, and
*protesting* that "the courts of the church are coerced by the civil
courts," an immense number seceded and formed The Free Church
of Scotland.[2] All the seceding ministers voluntarily gave up
"their homes and incomes," but the greatest liberality was shown
in Scotland in building and endowing churches. In 1845, 570
new churches had been built, and "the total numbers within the
pale of the free church may be estimated at 600,000";[3] so that,
as McCulloch says:[4] "the established church is no longer the
church of a decided majority of the people, and religious animosities and fanaticism have been widely diffused."[5] It is said
that the Scotch clergy have become more bigoted since the
French Revolution.[6]

On persecution of Simson, see Index to Wodrow's Analecta,
vol. iii. p. 235; on Webster and Pitcairn, Analecta, vol. iii. p. 307.
In 1711, Wodrow writes,[7] "At Edinburgh I hear Dr. Pitcairn
and several others do meet very regularly every Lord's day, and
read the Scripture in order to lampoon and ridicule it."[8] Wodrow
says that this even extended among the clergy; "young
preachers" also began in the eighteenth century to insist on
*reason* and *inquiry*, and to oppose church judicatories.[9]

After 1688, the moderation of the crown attempted to dissolve
the alliance between the people and the clergy, but only checked
fanaticism *for a time*, thus showing how weak *political* causes
are in the presence of *social* ones. The two great evils of the
church complained of in and after 1712 by Wodrow were "tole-

[1] Geog. Dict. vol. ii. p. 662.
[2] See also McCulloch's British Empire, vol. ii. pp. 288-291.
[3] Geog. Dict. p. 662.      [4] Ibid. p. 663.      [5] British Empire, p. 294.
[6] Combe's North America, vol. iii. pp. 227-234, 424, 425.
[7] Analecta, vol. i. p. 323.
[8] Ibid. vol. ii. p. 256; see also on this increase of scepticism, vol. iii. pp. 129, 184;
vol. iv. p. 63.          [9] Ibid. vol. iii. 147, 155, 167, 169, 178, 239, 240, 412.

ration" and "patronages."[1] However, in 1731, the most powerful Scotch nobles were determined to retain the patronage.[2]

Pitcairn[3] says there is a curious account of the marriage of James IV. by John Young, Somerset Herald, in Leland's Collectanea, vol. iv. p. 258. Pitcairn says[4] that in Archæologia, vol. xxii. p. 7, are "Observations upon a Household Book of James V., by Henry Ellis." The clergy mourned over the declining power of the kirk after 1688.[5] On black-mail, see Mackenzie's Criminal Laws, p. 165. A servant could not be punished for committing a crime in obedience to his master's orders.[6]

Phrenology being deemed too *dangerous* in England, found its boldest advocates in Scotland—Combe and Spurzheim.[7] On Scotch bigotry *within the last year*, see Fraser's Magazine for December 1859, pp. 680–683. External gaiety being repressed, incest and other crimes more hideous still grew rife, and were safely and securely practised. Insufferable dulness and taciturnity.

. . . . In Scotland, as in France before 1789, the tyranny and impudent pretensions of the clergy made educated men Deists.[8] A clergyman says,[9] "In this part of the country it is only fashionable for the lower classes of the people to attend the church. The higher orders are above the vulgar prejudices of believing it necessary to worship the God of their fathers." [10] How could educated men listen to their stuff? In 1696, clergy losing ground over educated classes.[11] Topham[12] says that in Scotland "Deism is the ruling principle." The middle class of tradespeople were ignorant and poor.

Stephen[13] says, "The unchaste vices have been more universally practised in Scotland in all periods of her history than in any other Christian country in the world." In the middle of the eighteenth century, the Scotch clamoured for penal laws against the Catholics.[14] On hostility between theology and physical knowledge, see Wodrow's Correspondence, vol. i. pp. 95, 96; vol. ii. p. 361.

[1] Analecta, vol. ii. pp. 39, 133.        [2] Ibid. iv. 246.
[3] Criminal Trials, vol. i. p. 118.
[4] Ibid. vol. i. p. 209.        [5] Howre's Biog. Scoticana, p. 579.
[6] Mackenzie's Criminal Laws, p. 170.        [7] Elliotson's Physiology, p. 403.
[8] Life of Adam Smith, in Rose's Biog. Dict. and Chalmer's Biog. Dict.
[9] Sinclair's Statist. Account, vol. x. p. 606.        [10] To the same effect, see vol. xi.
p. 165.
[11] Cockburn's Jacobins, pp. 348, 377.
[12] Letters from Edinburgh, 1776, p. 238.
[13] History of the Church of Scotland, vol. i. p. 41.
[14] See Russell's History of the Church in Scotland, vol. i. p. 286; also Stevenson's Hist. of the Church of Scotland, p. 55; see also Burton's Hist. of Scotland, vol. i. p. 201.

In 1709, it began to be noticed that the clergy were less respected.

Sir William Hamilton says that nowhere has there been so little classical learning as in Scotland.[1]

In 1706, Blair of Dundee held some remarkably sound views on the nervous system.[2]

Pitcairn tried to apply to medicine " the rigid rules of mathematical demonstration." [3]

. . . . From a general point of view we might expect that the works of the great northern thinkers would have exercised a favourable influence over the literature of England, written as they were in our own language, and frequently published at our own capital. But unfortunately the hatred between the English and the Scotch at this period was as great as it had been before they were finally united into one empire. The old feelings of animosity, so far from being assuaged by the Act of Union, seemed to be increased by the mutual recriminations with which the passing of that act was accompanied. The English taunted the Scotch with their poverty; the Scotch reproached the English with their ignorance. In 1682, the celebrated Sir Thomas Browne writes to his son in disapproval of a charter which had just been granted to the physicians of Edinburgh. His great fear was that this concession would induce too many Scotchmen to leave their own country. For, he says, " If they sett up a colledge and breed many physitians, wee shall bee sure to have a great part of them in England." The university of Oxford was so vexed with the union with Scotland that it refused to congratulate Anne on its completion.

In London, those satires were greedily read which were directed against the inhabitants of Scotland by Johnson, Wilkes, Churchill, Junius, &c.; and during the administration of Lord Bute, and indeed long after it, every tale against him was willingly circulated because he was a native of that abhorred country. In Edinburgh the great writers who adorned that capital could not conceal the contempt with which they regarded their southern neighbours. They derided the greatest efforts of our genius. Indeed, nothing but national prejudice could make a man of such fine taste as Adam Smith depreciate the greatest poet the world has ever seen. Hume said [4] that the Epigoniad of Wilkes was equal to Paradise Lost, and that Home's play of Douglas was

---

[1] Discussions in Philosophy, pp. 329, 338, 379, and see p. 341.
[2] Wagner's Physiology, p. 528.
[3] Thomson's History of Chemistry, vol. i. p. 208.
[4] See remarks on Shakespeare in History of England.

superior to Macbeth. Lord Monboddo is perhaps the last man of any reputation who has attacked the Newtonian philosophy. His attacks, which were made in 1779, I only know from the notice in Whewell's Philosophy of the Inductive Sciences.[1] Wilkes was burnt in effigy at Edinburgh. Lord Monboddo, who as a scholar possessed considerable reputation, said that the Douglas of Home was not only superior to any of Shakspeare's plays, but was better than anything Shakspeare could have possibly written.

Hume, whose open disposition prevented him from concealing his opinions, says in one of his letters from Paris, " It is probable that this place will be long my home. I feel little inclination to the factious barbarians of London." On another occasion, he writes to Blair respecting England, " The little company there that is worth conversing with are cold and unsociable; or are warmed only by faction and cabal : so that a man who plays no part in public affairs becomes altogether insignificant, and if he is not rich, he becomes even contemptible. Hence that nation are relapsing fast into the deepest stupidity and ignorance." When Gibbon's Roman Empire was published, the astonishment of Hume was unbounded. In 1776, he writes to the great historian, " I own that if I had not previously had the happiness of your personal acquaintance, such a performance from an Englishman in our age would have given me some surprise. You may smile at this sentiment ; but as it seems to me that your countrymen for almost a whole generation have given themselves up to barbarous and absurd faction, and have totally neglected all polite letters, I no longer expected any valuable production ever to come from them." Indeed, violent as were the animosities between the French and English, it seemed to be understood that every patriotic Englishman ought to hate a Scotchman even more than he hated a Frenchman. After the quarrel between Hume and Rousseau, Adam Smith wrote to Hume to dissuade him from publishing an account of it ; for, said he, your opponent " will have a great party, the church, the Whigs, the Jacobites, the whole wise English nation, who will love to mortify a Scotchman, and applaud a man that has refused a pension from the king."

Such sentiments as these were fully reciprocated by the English. But as our countrymen had always inflicted great injuries upon Scotland, it was natural that they should hate the Scotch even more than they were hated by them. Even in the slightest things this prejudice was allowed to appear. Horace Walpole was almost the only Englishman of any reputation who ventured to utter a word in their favour. But for doing this he was severely attacked in the North Briton and in the Public Ledger, the two most influential periodicals which were then published in London.

On one occasion, Home offered for performance a tragedy which he had just written ; but it was considered so hazardous to act in London a play written by a Scotchman, that Garrick refused to accept it unless the author would conceal his name, and would allow to have it attributed to' an Englishman. To this Home agreed, and during twelve nights the tragedy was received with universal applause. But on the thirteenth night, the secret having by some means transpired, the piece was not only condemned, but Garrick was threatened with having his house burnt down for having dared to bring on the English stage the production of a Scottish author.

A few years before this occurred, Macklyn wrote a farce called Love à la Mode, the merits of which are anything but remarkable. But as it contained a character in which the Scotch were turned into ridicule, it met with immense success, and not all the influence of Lord Bute could prevent it from being constantly acted. Nor was it merely by the mob of a theatre that such feelings were displayed. Rawlinson, who early in the eighteenth century was an historian and antiquary of some repute, had bequeathed a considerable property to the Society of Antiquaries. But by a subsequent clause he revoked the whole of the gift, and one of the reasons which he assigned for doing so was that a Scotchman had been elected secretary to the society. Indeed, the national prejudices were so strong that they more than once threatened to embroil the two countries. In 1713, the disputes respecting the extension to Scotland of the malt tax caused such mutual recriminations that a motion made in the House of Lords to bring in a bill for repealing the Union was only lost by a majority of four votes. In 1736, a tumult having arisen at Edinburgh, Captain Porteous, who commanded the town guard, ordered his men to fire on the mob. For this wanton outrage, which caused the death of several persons, he was brought to trial, found guilty, and condemned to die. The English government, instead of allowing the sentence to be carried into execution, granted a reprieve ; but the Scotch, who were determined that the murderer of their countrymen should not escape, rose in arms, seized the gates of the city, burst open the prison in which Porteous was confined, dragged him to the Grassmarket where criminals usually suffered, and there hanged him deliberately, and with all the formalities of a legal execution. In our own time such an act, if it could possibly occur, would be only considered as an infraction of the law, would be punished, and would soon be forgotten. But such were the feelings that a century ago existed between England and Scotland that so slight a matter was found sufficient to threaten the most dangerous results. The Scotch took it up as a national question, and unanimously declared that they would protect the murderers of Porteous. The English were as determined to revenge his death; and the ministers of the crown openly stated that, if resistance were offered, the punishment should extend to the whole country; and the queen, who was then acting as regent, threatened so to desolate Scotland that it should be turned into a hunting-field. Parliament, which was then sitting, displayed the greatest warmth; and it was actually moved in the peers that the lord-justice of Scotland should be brought as a criminal before the bar of the house. This monstrous proposition, which, if persisted in, would probably have caused a civil war, was by the influence of more moderate men with difficulty rejected; but to the great offence of the Scotch, their judges were eventually compelled to come to London, and to appear as witnesses before what they considered a hostile and almost a foreign jurisdiction. At the head of English affairs there was at this time Sir Robert Walpole, a man of great abilities and of still greater moderation. He was one of the ministers of the crown during three successive reigns, and was its chief adviser for more than twenty years. But the Scotch looked upon him as their declared enemy, and hated him with a bitterness which still further exasperated the national animosities. He indeed was driven from office in 1742; but three years afterwards broke out that great northern rebellion which he is said to have predicted, and in which the Scotch, as is well known, penetrated to the centre of England. They were afterwards entirely defeated; but the infamous cruelties of their English conquerors left a deep impression on their minds, and the names of Cumberland and Culloden long remained the by-words of national hatred. In the Highlands these feelings have lingered even to our own time; and although in the Lowlands they gradually died away, still they left a soreness which frequently embarrassed the English government. Towards the end of the reign of George II., the lord-chancellor, in his place in Parliament, complained that the Scotch seemed absolutely determined not to pay the imperial taxes, and he submitted to the house whether some measure could not be adopted to compel them to do so. For his own part, he said that he was not acquainted with any means by which so desirable a result could be effected.

After the death of George II., the same prejudices long predominated. Sir Nathaniel Wraxall, who, although a weak man,
was an attentive observer of passing events, has made the remark
that the unpopularity of George III. during the first twenty years
of his reign was chiefly caused by the indignation which the
English felt at seeing a Scotchman placed at the head of affairs.
This, if true, is a remarkable proof how inveterate the hostility
must have been; for the king dismissed Lord Bute only three
years after his accession, and never ventured again to place a
Scotchman at the head of his government.   Even Lord Chatham
was violently attacked because he entrusted a Scotchman with
the Privy Seal of Scotland.   Indeed, so late as 1804, when Barrow
was made one of the secretaries of the admiralty, Lord Melville
expressed his delight at finding that he was an Englishman; for,
said he, "Mr. Pitt and myself have been so much taunted for
giving away all the good things to Scotchmen, that I am very
glad on the present occasion to have selected an Englishman."
And in 1805, so lenient a judge as Wilberforce, after highly
praising Dundas, mentions it as a remarkable fact that, instead of
sending to India as governor-general one of his own countrymen,
he actually "appointed the fittest person he could find, Sir John
Shore."   And into such matters did this spirit descend, that even
early in the present century, the Scotch farmers rejected "as an
old English practice" that plan of folding sheep on the land,
which they now generally adopt.[1]

The intercourse between the two nations, it may easily be supposed, was neither cordial nor frequent.   The Scotch, indeed,
flocked to London, because it was a wealthy city, and because
they hoped to participate in the riches of its inhabitants, whom
they considered to be more remarkable for their money than
for their wit.   But the Londoners themselves did not care to return the attention.   Pennant, the well known antiquary, visited
the southern part of Scotland in the middle of the eighteenth
century.   He was very proud of having accomplished what he
considered so hazardous a feat; and in his minute account of
Edinburgh, he tells us that he was the first Englishman whom
motives of curiosity had ever carried to that city.   Indeed, several
years later, when the facilities of travelling were so much greater,
there were few Englishmen who ventured to imitate so bold an
example; and Captain Topham, who, in 1774, passed some
months in Edinburgh, says that the Scotch were greatly surprised
when they learnt that this Englishman intended to spend the
winter in their capital.

[1] Laing's Denmark, p. 134.

Although the Scotch universities were in the middle of the eighteenth century infinitely superior to those of England, and were possessed of men whom European reputation placed far above the professors at Oxford and Cambridge, there was hardly to be found a single Englishman who would send his sons to be educated in so hated a country.

The existence of such feelings as these tended to prevent that fusion of the two literatures by which both countries would have been greatly benefited. But this was not all. In addition to these national prejudices, the almost exclusively inductive, and, if I may so say, mechanical, character of the English still further indisposed them to welcome the large and philosophical investigations of their northern neighbours. The consequence was that the few productions of Scotch literature which in our own country met with much attention were of a less elevated character than those which were treated with comparative contempt. The profound investigations of Adam Smith, which he published at an early period of his life, excited in England but little curiosity, although they were set off with every charm that language and fancy can afford. Even the master-piece of his intellect, the Wealth of Nations, was not only neglected, but was treated with contempt by such men as Johnson and Warburton.

In the same way the History of England, by Hume, for some time scarcely found a single purchaser; and yet the History of Scotland, by Robertson, which is infinitely its inferior, was received with transports of applause, and was considered superior not only in learning but also in style. Indeed, the long prevalence of mere practical pursuits had perverted our national taste to an almost incredible extent. One of the most popular books of the age was Smollett's History of England, a work which at the present day scarcely any one would begin to read, and which, I suppose, no one who made the attempt would ever live to finish. The discouragement thus given to the greatest efforts of Scotch genius, must in the ordinary course of affairs have produced injurious results, and have tended to degrade the national literature.

The Heritable Jurisdiction Bill, in 1747, was violently opposed by the Scotch. Three years after the battle of Culloden, the Scotch pride was still further wounded by a law forbidding the Highlanders to wear their national garb. Ridicule was thrown on the speech of George III. that he was "born a Briton." During the Wilkes' riots in 1768, the inhabitants of London were particularly indignant that a "Scotch regiment" should be called to quell the disturbances.

Wedderburn, afterwards celebrated as Lord Loughborough, was
the first educated man in Scotland who ventured to practise at
the English bar; and this was considered so hazardous an enterprise that, nearly twenty years after his first arrival in London,
we find Lord Chatham expressing a fear that his country would
prevent his promotion. And when Lord Bute first received his
appointment, the Spanish ambassador, then residing in London,
foretold the speedy demolition of his administration " on account
of the circumstance of his country."

Indeed, to say *a man acted like a Scotchman* became a proverbial expression for a base action.

.        .        .        .        .        .        .

" Learning and philosophy " made " atheists," said in her " last
words " Lady Coltness, the idol of the faithful.[1] In 1648, Baillie,
the most learned and one of the most moderate of the clergy,
wonders what any one can see in Descartes, " a very ignorant
atheist." The Rev. J. Scrimzeor " often wished that most part
of books were burned, except the Bible and some short notes
thereon." [2] Wodrow calls Locke one of the main props of the
Socinians and Deists. For men to be conscious of their own
abilities was blasphemous. An eclipse sent to prevent men
knowing too much. If a youth got on too fast in his studies the
Lord sent him a fever. Tutors at the universities should not
read classics, for the fathers were better; and " philosophy is
more prejudicial to piety than handiwork or manufacture." An
eclipse of the sun was sent sometimes to prevent men studying
astronomy. From the passing of the Perth Articles (which caused
a deluge) there were twenty years of barrenness, when the ground
refused to yield until the Covenant restored its fertility. We
laugh at this, but look at our queen and ministers offering up
prayers for cholera and for war!!! In 1621, there was an inun-
dation at Perth " on account of the five episcopalian articles
passed there by the General Assembly three years before. " There
is nothing by which a man will be more readily puffed up than
the inward gifts of the mind, if they be not sanctified, such as
wit, knowledge, eloquence, memory," &c.[3] History was only
studied with a theological view, to know all about Antichrist.
The clergy wished to stop people from reading *unknown* books.
Abernethy [4] says that for the study and solace of the heart, " In
old times philosophers did supply this place; but now amongst

[1] Select Biographies, vol. ii. p. 504.            [2] Howie's Biog. Scot. p. 131.
[3] Fergusson on the Epistles, p. 354.            [4] Physicke for the Soul, p. 16.

Christians the fittest man is a true theologue." The clergy hated
statistics; and Abernethy [1] says Satan " caused David to number
his people." The grass refused to grow not on account of soil or
chemical laws, but because incest was committed there. They
insisted on humility, for that secured their own power; but
they had none of it themselves. All geological speculations as
to the origin of the world before man existed were criminal.[2]
Nothing known in arts and trades since Jubal and Tubal Cain.[3]
Until man fell, he had great reason; but now nothing is left
save " some little spunk or sparkle." [4] " We have some remnant of
reason in us that hath some petty and poor ability for matters
of little moment, as the things of this life." " Believing
ignorance is much better than rash and presumptuous knowledge." To be even *silently* conscious of superior abilities is
" a loud blasphemy in God's ear." [5] " Whatever wanton and las-
civious reason can object against absolute reprobation." [6] On the
winnowing machine, see Burton's History, vol. ii. p. 396 ; Penny's
Traditions of Perth, p. 147. It is very foolish for men to try " to
be accounted wise and learned," " seeing that our days are so few,
and that we are of so short continuance in the world." [7] Cockburn
says [8] men are foolishly occupied " in curious inquiries about the
motions and transactions of some remote prince which little concerns them." The Scotch clergy bemoaned the " general ignorance ; " and to relieve it, they recommended the most trumpery
theological books.[9]

## CHARACTER, ETC., OF THE RUSSIANS.

AFTER forty, the lower class of the Russians look old. This is
caused by the vapour bath.[10] The Russians are the greatest dis-
simulators and negotiators in Europe.[11] The Russians show their
improvidence by the rapidity and want of durability with which
they build their palaces.[12] Kohl says [13] of St. Petersburgh : " There
is no other European capital where the inhabitants are content to

[1] Physicke for the Soul. p. 190.            [2] Binning, vol. i. p. 194.
[3] Cowper's Heaven opened, p. 301.          [4] Binning, vol. i. p. 29.
[5] Ibid. vol. i. pp. 30, 143; vol. ii. p. 427.   [6] Rutherford's Christ Dying, p. 416.
[7] Cockburn's Jacob's Vow, p. 131.          [8] Ibid. p. 305.
[9] See A Cloud of Witnesses, p. 56.
[10] See Mayo's Philosophy of Living, 2nd edit. 8vo, 1836, p. 176.
[11] Alison's History of Europe, vol. vi. p. 594 ; xi. 119 ; xiii. 220.
[12] See Kohl's Russia, 8vo, 1844, p. 9.            [13] Ibid. p. 49.

make use of goods of such inferior quality, or where, consequently,
they have such frequent occasion to buy new articles, or to have
the old ones repaired. . . . . A Russian seldom buys anything
till just he wants to use it ; and, as he cannot then wait, he must
have it ready to his hand."

The "fickleness" of the Russians in their purchases is extraordinary.[1]  Kohl says:[2] "The Russian is by nature a light-
hearted creature, and by no means given to reflection." Even
the population of St. Petersburgh is constantly changing, so fluctuating and uncertain are Russian movements.[3]  A great passion
for reading has lately sprung up among the lower orders ;[4] and
Russian authors are highly paid.[5]  Extraordinary superstition of
the Russians.[6]  But the Greek church is, however, tolerant.[7]
Kohl[8] says : "Nearly all the charitable institutions in Russia are
presided over by Russians." The merchants are German or English ; for "no Russian either in St. Petersburgh or any other part
of the empire engages in maritime trade; he has neither the
knowledge nor the connection necessary thereto, still less the true
commercial spirit of enterprise."[9]  Kohl[10] says : "The Russians
know so little of those prejudices against illegitimate births which
have descended to us from the middle ages, that there is scarcely
a word in their language to express the idea." Kohl[11] mentions
the "extraordinary uniformity of dialect through the empire."
The Russians *like* being commanded.[12]  Eccentric persons are
found most commonly in England ; hardly ever in Russia.[13]  Extraordinary loyalty.[14]  The ablest governors, merchants, &c., in
Russia are from the Baltic provinces.[15]  Walk is between Riga
and Dorpat; and "In Walk, the Lettish dialect is still spoken ;
but just beyond it begins the territory of the Esthonians. The
Lettes and Esthonians are two very different races, and they hate
one another with all the bitter animosity of contiguous nations.[16]
Kohl says :[17] "The peninsula of Courland, and the country round
the mouth of the Dwina, and that bordering on the Aa, are the
districts inhabited by the Lettes. A line drawn through Livonia
from the south point of the Peipus lake, through Verro and Walk
to the Gulf of Riga, would be about the boundary between the
two races. The Esthonians occupy the whole of Esthonia, the

[1] Kohl's Russia, 8vo, 1844, 227.                          [2] Ibid. p. 51.
[3] Ibid. pp. 51, 52.
[4] Ibid. pp. 88, 223, 393.              [5] Ibid. pp. 132, 133.
[6] Ibid. pp. 53, 56, 61, 131, 132, 136, 160, 229, 250, *et seq.* 262, 269, 354.
[7] Ibid. pp. 267, 396, 397.        [8] Ibid. p. 111.        [9] Ibid. pp. 117, 118.
[10] Ibid. p. 113.                      [11] Ibid. p. 283.        [12] Ibid. p. 279.
[13] Ibid. pp. 286, 287.               [14] Ibid. pp. 289, 290.   [15] Ibid. pp. 344, 345.
[16] Ibid. p. 342.                      [17] Ibid. p. 366.

Œsel Archipelago, and the northern parts of Livonia." And,[1]
" The country bordering on the Niemen, and on its various tribu-
tary rivers, is inhabited by Lithuanians. The country around
the mouth of the Dwina, the whole of Courland, and the southern
half of Livonia, is inhabited by Lettes." This was in 1840. At
p. 397, Kohl has a striking passage on the eminently religious
character of the Russians.

## CHARACTER, ETC., OF THE GERMANS.

In 1669 it was supposed that, on account of taking opium, " the
Germans are, of all nations, most continent and least addicted to
women."[2] In Germany, the fine arts, music, and painting, are
the only points of contact between the higher and lower intellects; hence they flourish, as they did in Greece. Kohl[3] says :
" The Germans are the most loyal people in the world. They
cling to the present ; and, whatever may be the origin or nature
of the governing authority for the time being, they always show
themselves faithful to it." Neander[4] says that, about the thirteenth century, the German bishops became *political* and too
secular. Bancroft[5] says that, in 1756, the question was whether
Prussia, "a Protestant revolutionary kingdom," should be allowed
to exist in the Europe of the middle ages ; and that it was to
settle this question that " France and Austria put aside their
ancient rivalry, and joined to defend the Europe of the middle
ages," with its traditions and ecclesiastical influence, against Frederick the Great. In 1758, Washington took great interest in
the fortunes of Frederick.[6] In 1762, the reactionary character of
our George III. showed itself in attempting to weaken Prussia.[7]
At vol. ii. p. 1, Bancroft says : " The successes of the Seven
Years' War was the triumph of Protestantism."

## AMERICA.

THE fault of the Americans is the opposite of the French. With
them liberty has outstripped scepticism. Read the long account
of America in vol. xiii. of Alison's History of Europe ; and for

[1] Kohl's Russia, p. 372.
[2] Ray's Correspondence, by Dr. Lankester, 8vo, 1848, p. 52.
[3] Russia, 8vo, 1844, pp. 395, 396.
[4] History of the Church, vol. vii. p. 296.
[5] History of American Revolution, vol. i. pp. 315-317.
[6] Bancroft, vol. i. p. 359.                    [7] Ibid. p. 495.

proof of the great influence of the clergy, see p. 317. Hence we find that their only original works have been on jurisprudence.[1] On the intellectual independence natural to the democratic mind, see Wahrheit und Dichtung in Göthe's Werke, Band ii. Theil ii. p. 192.

In 1775, Congress undertook an expedition against Canada, and Colonel Arnold summoned De la Place to surrender " in the name of the great Jehovah and the Continental Congress."[2] In 1774, General .Lee writes that, latterly, even the manners and appearance of New Englanders had been changed, their slouching appearance having become erect and firm.[3] In 1778, it was said that not one in one hundred of the American merchants knew anything of French.[4] In 1838, the Americans were greatly impressed with the importance of spreading education.[5] See[6] a classification of the works published on the United States in 1835. The Americans have more newspapers than all Europe put together, but the style is wretched.[7] The United States are unhealthy; and, little attention being paid to improving their' towns, the Americans are short-lived; hence the prevalence of *young* men with violent passions, &c.[8]

The Americans have done much for establishing public libraries.[9] On the extraordinary increase of the United States between 1840 and 1850, see Statistical Society, vol. xv. pp. 65, 66. The white population is increasing more rapidly than the black.[10] The Americans, in 1851, had 10,289 miles of railroad, while in Great Britain and Scotland there were only 7,000.[11] Comte[12] well says that the reason why slave states, as Virginia, have produced great politicians, is because ability being never turned into manufactures, trade, &c., has no vent but in politics. Segur, who was in America in 1782, speaks very highly of the elegance of American women.[13]

Bancroft[14] says that, in 1754, Washington, by " repelling France from the basin of the Ohio," began the revolution by beginning the movement which freed America from France and the

---

[1] Alison's History of Europe, vol. xiii. p. 345.
[2] Adolphus's History of George III. vol. ii. p. 233.
[3] Burke's Correspondence, vol. i. p. 518.
[4] See Parliamentary History, vol. xix. p. 940.
[5] Journal of the Statistical Society, vol. i. p. 383.     [6] Ibid. vol. iii. p. 382.
[7] Ibid. vol. iv. pp. 120, 121.     [8] Ibid. vol. vii. pp. 26, 27, but compare p. 48.
[9] Ibid. vol. xi. p. 274.
[10] Ibid. p. 67.     [11] Ibid. p. 111.
[12] Traité de Législation, vol. iv. p. 243.
[13] See Mémoires de Ségur, tome i. p. 387.
[14] History of the American Revolution, 8vo, 1852, vol. i. p. 133.

"institutions of the middle ages."[1] On the *proportions* of American population in 1754, see Bancroft, vol. i. pp. 144, 145. In 1754, the English clergy sent out to America to hold livings were "too often ill-educated and licentious men."[2] The English forbad the Americans to print a Bible; and "no trace of an American edition of the Bible, surreptitious or otherwise, previous to the Declaration of Independence, has been found."[3] In 1765, John Adams says, "A native American who cannot read and write is as rare an appearance as a comet or an earthquake."[4] Bancroft[5] says, "The exceedingly valuable history of the American Revolution, by Gordon." An able American writer, who is unfavourable to slavery, says that a belief in the inferiority of *race* is "an opinion which the most philosophical of the citizens of the South conscientiously maintain."[6] The greatest astonishment was felt at an African girl being able to read in eighteen months.[7] Lord Brougham[8] says, "The never-ceasing state of party agitation, there being no office from the highest to the lowest, from president to penny-postman, which may not be changed at each renewal of that high functionary's term." This must *educate* the people in the art of organisation, &c. Lord Shaftesbury says, "All the powers of government are consigned to the younger persons;"[9] and he mentions a letter from a friend of his, who writes, "I have travelled over a considerable part of the Union, and I do not hesitate to say that during the last two months I have not met with a single old man who was in a hale condition."[10] On the energy shown by the Americans in codifying their laws, see pp. 195–197. On persecution of Quakers in America about 1660, see Fox's Journal, vol. i. pp. 498, 499. This was *hearsay*; and Fox, who was in America in 1672, and gives an account of his visit (which ends at vol. ii. p. 167), does not mention any persecution.

---

## GENERAL REMARKS ON NATIONAL CHARACTER.

HARE[11] observes that Thirlwall and Schlegel notice the importance of the great extent of coast possessed by Greece, as compared with the entire surface of the country. Hare adds[12] that

[1] History of the American Revolution, 8vo, 1852, pp. 524, 525.
[2] Vol. i. p. 151; see also p. 156.   [3] Ibid. vol. ii. pp. 302, 303.
[4] Bancroft, vol. ii. p. 368.   [5] Ibid. vol. i. p. 430.
[6] Tucker's Life of Jefferson, vol. i. p. 122.
[7] Abdy's United States, vol. i. p. 166; and see vol. iii. p. 237.
[8] Transactions of Social Science Association, 1859, p. 41.   [9] Ibid. p. 90.
[10] Ibid. p. 90.
[11] Guesses at Truth, first series, p. 100.   [12] Ibid. p. 101.

the same advantage is possessed by Italy and England. Malcolm says of Kurdistan,[1] " I travelled through the entire country in 1810; and should judge from what I have read and seen of its inhabitants that they have remained unchanged in their appearance and character for more than twenty centuries." See some ingenious remarks in Laing's Denmark, pp. 204–207. He says the Irish, French, and Scotch have a national character very strongly marked in each individual, but have " very little individuality of character among them." The English, Americans, Danes, Norwegians, and Dutch have both national character and individuality; while the Austrians, Prussians, &c., have neither individuality nor nationality.

Laing says "nationality of character" depends on the same people being knit together by common interests, &c., while " individuality of character" proceeds " from a higher source," and depends on men being *let alone* by government. Therefore, in the French and German drama we find no individuality, but always the type of some class, and the same thing in painting.[2] And in his Second Series of Notes[3] he says that, from Tacitus to the present time the Germans have had no nationality, for " the social cement which binds populations together into one nation is their mutual material interests. . . . . What common interest, for instance, have the people of Bavaria, on the Danube, or on the shores of the Lake of Constance, with the people on the Vistula, or on the shores of the Baltic ? They have nothing to exchange with each other."[4] See also Notes of a Traveller, first series, pp. 477–481, where Laing says this is the reason the Italians have no nationality; their soil and climate are too good.

## INCREASE OF HUMANITY AND VIRTUE.

BECAUSE Sir Matthew Hale would not receive a present of game from a gentleman whose cause he had to try, his refusal " was somewhat censured as an affectation of an unreasonable strictness."[5] And Burnet[6] mentions it, as a " remarkable instance of his justness and goodness," that when he had received bad money he abstained from passing it to other people.

The real difference between this and any other age is the edu-

[1] History of Persia, 8vo, 1829, vol. i. p. 82.
[2] See also Laing's Notes of a Traveller, first series, p. 268.
[3] 8vo, 1850, pp. 518–522.    [4] Ibid. pp. 520–521.
[5] Life of Hale in Burnet's Lives, edit. Jebb, 8vo, p. 48.    [6] Ibid. p. 98.

cation of the people. This is the only guarantee against a return to barbarism. Not only is the light of civilization more brilliant than ever, but its basis is larger and more secure.

Evelyn, one of the most humane men of his time, went in 1650 to see a child cut for the stone;[1] and, a few months later, he, actuated by mere curiosity, went to see the most horrid tortures inflicted on a criminal.[2]

In 1650, the Marquis of Montrose was executed, and the Marchioness of Argyle was present with her family to see him die; but, before the last moment, "the marchioness expressed her spite at the fallen hero by spitting at him."[3] Montaigne[4] says that he never opens letters addressed to other people. De Foe says, "When you would speak well of a man, you say he is an honest, drunken fellow, as if his drunkenness was a recommendation of his honesty."[5] The Duke de la Rochefoucault, "un des plus nobles caractères d'un beau siècle," wished to assassinate Retz.[6] Charles Comte[7] observes that the progress of morals has been aided by *analytic* studies.[8] The breed of cultivated plants and of domestic animals has been improved by "constant elimination of imperfect types, and the selection of the finest individuals." This applies in some degree to man; for neither idiots, cretins, nor great criminals often marry; but the beautiful, the healthy, and the good are attractive and *do*. Hence, perhaps, the race is improving.[9] Even to the beginning of the eighteenth century, "hitherto the utility of hospitals as curative institutions had been exceedingly equivocal. We had actually diseases in hospitals which exist nowhere else, diseases named after hospitals, hospital gangrene, hospital erysipelas, hospital pyæmia, hospital fever."[10]

## DIMINISHED SUPERSTITION.

Burnet, in his Life of Hale, says, "In the year 1666, an opinion did run through the nation that the end of the world would come that year."[11] In 1652, an eclipse of the sun "so ex-

[1] Diary, 8vo, 1827, vol. ii. p. 17.    [2] Ibid. pp. 29, 30.
[3] Chambers's Traditions of Edinburgh, 8vo, 1847, p. 285.
[4] Essais, Paris, 8vo, 1843, livre ii. chap. iv. p. 224.
[5] Wilson's Life of De Foe, 8vo, 1830, vol. i. p. 37.
[6] Saint-Aulaire, Histoire de la Fronde, tome ii. p. 141.
[7] Traité de Législation. vol. i. pp. 56, 60.    [8] See also p. 114.
[9] See interesting remarks by Dr. Farr in Transac. of Association for Social Science, 1859. pp. 508, 509.    [10] Ibid. p. 536.
[11] Lives, &c. edit. Jobb, 8vo, 1833, p. 108.

ceedingly alarmed the whole nation that hardly any one would work nor stir out of their houses."[1] The Duke of Monmouth was executed in 1685. In his pockets were found charms and spells in his own handwriting.[2] In 1687, Bishop Cartwright, one of the most corrupt of men, writes,[3] "Being my birthday, I made my last will and testament."

## DECLINE OF IGNORANCE.

In the reign of James II., Lord Conway, one of the ministers, on hearing of "the circles of the empire," wondered "what circles should have to do with politics."[4]

## MAHOMETANISM.

The Mahometan missionaries are very judicious.[5] Ranke[6] thinks that but for the Carlovingian kings France would have been conquered by the Mahometans.

## INSANITY.

There are four kinds—Moral Insanity, Monomania, Mania, and Incoherence.[7]

According to Heinroth, all insanity is referrible to the feelings, the understanding, or the will.[8] Prichard says,[9] "MORAL INSANITY consists in a morbid perversion of the feelings, affections, and active powers, without any illusion or erroneous conviction impressed upon the understanding; it sometimes co-exists with an apparently unimpaired state of the intellectual faculties." Prichard says :[10] "The existence of moral insanity as a distinct form of derangement has been recognised by Pinel, Traité sur l'Alienation, p. 156," and is now generally admitted.[11] And yet

---

[1] Evelyn's Diary, 8vo, 1827, vol. ii. p. 52.
[2] Reresby's Memoirs, 8vo, 1831, 3rd edit. p. 312.
[3] Diary, Camden Society, 1843, p. 76.
[4] Mackintosh's Revolution of 1688, 4to, 1834, p. 6.
[5] See Crawford's History of the Indian Archipelago, Edinb. 8vo, 1820, vol. ii. p. 307.
[6] Civil Wars and Monarchy in France, 1852, 8vo, vol. i. p. 16.
[7] Prichard on Insanity, 8vo, 1835, p. 6.          [8] Ibid. p. 8.
[9] Ibid. p. 12.          [10] Ibid. p. 14.          [11] Ibid. see p. 21, 47, 50.

in another work Prichard [1] claims for himself the first recognition
of moral insanity, though he allows [2] that Georgel recognised its
existence. He says,[3] " The prognosis in cases of moral insanity
is often more unfavourable than in other forms of mental derangement."

MONOMANIA is often preceded by moral insanity.[4]

MANIA or RAVING MADNESS is distinguished from Monomania,
first by its violence, and secondly, by the fact that " the derangement of the intellect is not partial." [5] In this condition, the
muscular strength is great ; the memory remains unimpaired, and
the patient escapes contagious and epidemical diseases.[6]

INCOHERENCE or DEMENTIA.—The " ultimate tendency of insanity is to pass" into this state.[7] The mind is occupied by unconnected thoughts, sometimes " without any symptoms of other
insanity."[8]

" Insanity does not consist in disease of the sensitive or per-
ceptive powers," [9] but " in disturbance of the understanding " ; [10]
though, says Prichard,[11] " Perhaps we may observe in general that
the power of judging and of reasoning does not appear to be so
much impaired in madness as the disposition to exercise it on
certain subjects." There seems reason to think " that the primary
seat of mental alienation is generally in the region of the stomach
and intestines." [12] If we except congenital predisposition, the
moral causes of insanity are more frequent than the physical
ones.[13] Insanity is often connected with disorders of the heart,[14]
but not with the liver.[15] Madness is not a disease of the mind,[16]
and Prichard thinks [17] that even " moral insanity depends in some
instances at least on disease of the brain." Insanity not dangerous
to life.[18] Often hereditary,[19] and aided probably by the marriage
of persons near akin.[20] It is rare before puberty,[21] and the longer
men live the more likely they are to be subject to it.[22] In insanity the skull is generally natural, and the brain without disease.[23]
Insanity is, on the whole, more common among women,[24] but male
lunatics are most numerous in the south of France, and in Italy
(particularly in Naples) and in Great Britain ; and it is said that
the excess of male lunatics is greater in the higher than in the

[1] Insanity in relation to Jurisprudence, p. 36.
[2] Treatise on Insanity, p. 25.  [4] Prichard, p. 28.
[5] Ibid. pp. 77, 78.  [7] Ibid. p. 79.
[9] Ibid. p. 116.  [10] Ibid. p. 118.
[12] Ibid. p. 122.  [13] Ibid. pp. 173, 174, 177.
[15] Ibid. p. 232.  [16] Ibid. p. 235.
[18] Ibid. p. 146.  [19] Ibid. p. 158.
[21] Ibid. p. 165.  [23] Ibid. p. 168.
[24] Ibid. pp. 162, 163, 164.
[3] Ibid. p. 39.
[5] Ibid. pp. 71, 72.
[6] Ibid. pp. 83, 85.
[11] Ibid. p. 120.
[14] Ibid. pp. 228, 229.
[17] Ibid. p. 247.
[20] Ibid. pp. 160, 161.
[23] Ibid. pp. 210, 211, 213

lower classes,[1] while it seems to be greatest of all in the United States.[2] Winter is most fatal to the insane.[3] Sir A. Halliday, who paid the greatest attention to the subject, said that in 1826 there were more than 8,000 lunatics in England and Wales;[4] in Scotland, 3,700; in Ireland, 3,000.[5] But in 1829 Halliday says 14,000 in England, and 2,500 in Wales.[6] In France the insane are one in 1,000, " a proportion less than that believed to exist in Great Britain and some other countries."[7] Among savages mental diseases are hardly known.[8] As to recovery, the most unfavourable form of insanity is complication with general paralysis.[9] Most recoveries are in summer.[10] In *recent* cases, at least seven out of eight recover,[11] but there is a case of a lady recovering after being mad twenty-five years.[12] " Esquirol observes that the most favourable age for recovery is between the twentieth and thirtieth year, and that few are cured after the fiftieth;[13] "insanity is, generally speaking, more curable in women than in men."[14] Perhaps in *all* cases one-third recover.[15] There is a great difference of opinion respecting the propriety of bleeding in insanity,[16] but Prichard is in favour of it.[17] Purgatives are very useful,[18] and digitalis and other narcotics,[19] and rotatory motion to cause nausea and diminish the nervous power.[20] Pinel[21] has suggested that perhaps in women reason, as well as the aberration of reason, are sooner developed than among men. Georgel[22] says that at least ninety-five per cent of the insane cases result from moral causes. Georgel[23] agrees with Esquirol that the moon has no connection with it any more than that the patients are frightened by its clearness. Even Patin never mentions insanity as nervous disease.[24] We find from the Commission in Lunacy that among paupers the female insane exceed the male by one-third; but among " private patients " the number of females " falls short of that of the males by nearly a ninth."[25]

Among both paupers and private patients, more males die than females.[26] At vol. iv. p. 18 of Journal of the Statistical Society,

[1] Pritchard, Treatise on Insanity, pp. 163, 164.
[2] Ibid. p. 164.          [3] Ibid. p. 152.          [4] Ibid. p. 331.
[5] Ibid. p. 332.          [6] Ibid. p. 333.
[7] Ibid. p. 343, where however there seems to be a misprint.
[8] Ibid. pp. 174, 175, 349.    [9] Ibid. p. 127.    [10] Ibid. pp. 136, 152.
[11] Ibid. 129.          [12] Ibid. p. 134.          [13] Ibid. p. 135.
[14] Ibid. p. 135.          [15] Ibid. p. 138.          [16] Ibid. pp. 252-257.
[17] Ibid. p. 258.          [18] Ibid. p. 265.          [19] Ibid. p. 268.
[20] Ibid. pp. 273, 274.
[21] Alienation Mentale, p. 415.          [22] De la Folie, p. 160.          [23] Ibid. p. 440.
[24] See Lettres de Gui Patin, tome i. p. xvi.
[25] Journal of Statistical Society, vol. iii. p. 148.
[26] Ibid. pp. 148, 149, and vol. vii. p. 311; see also on the mortality, vol. iv. pp. 20, 24.

it is said, " At the Middlesex Asylum, no straight waistcoats, straps,
or other instruments of personal coercion have been used since September 21, 1839." It is said that out of 500 English one is insane.[1]
Insanity is more common among men than among women ; and
Esquirol and other writers who follow him in asserting insanity to
be more frequent among women, have erroneously conducted their
statistical analysis, having, in the first place, neglected to consider
that adult females are more numerous than adult males ; and, in
the second place, having estimated not the *occurring* cases, but
the *existing* cases.[2]   In Scotland, one in every 1,139 is mad ;[3] in
England and Wales one in 1,120.[4] At pp. 59-60, it is wrongly said
that women are more prone to insanity than men.   At p. 61, Dr.
Stark ascribes the frequency of insanity in Scotland to intermarriage ; hence less insanity in Catholic countries,[5] and in Ireland.[6]

Marsden[7] says of the Sumatrans, " When a man is by sickness
or otherwise deprived of his reason, or when subject to convul-
sions or fits, they imagine him possessed by an evil spirit."   In
Western India (about the Rajpoot country), Bishop Heber[8] saw
a mad woman, and " all the people called her a Moonee or inspired person, and treated her if not with respect, at least with forbearance." [9]   The phenomena of insanity were formerly surveyed
with a theological eye,[10] and fanaticism ascribed them to possession
by demons.[11]   Even within fifty years, madmen were shown as a
curiosity.[12]   Among barbarous people the insane are respected as
inspired.   Then comes the second stage, when they are believed
to be possessed by demons.   Hence formerly the keeper of the
insane became hardened into cruelty.[13]   Pinel says [14] that prejudice
and ignorance made men believe insanity incurable.[15]

## SLAVERY.

Tocqueville [16] says that even the negroes themselves often believe the inferiority of their own race.   In the Northern States,
slavery has been abolished because the masters saw it was their

---

[1] Journal of Statistical Society, vol. iv. p. 278.
[2] See the interesting essay, On the relative Liabilities of the two Sexes to Insanity,
in Journal of Statistical Society, vol. vii. pp. 310-316, and in particular, pp. 310,
311, 312, 314.
[3] Journal of Statistical Society, chap. xiv. p. 52.     [4] Ibid. p. 53.
[5] Ibid. p. 62.                               [6] Ibid. pp. 53, 54.
[7] History of Sumatra, p. 156.
    Journey through India, vol. ii. p. 471.          [8] Ibid. p. 477.
[10] Quote Georgel, De la Folie, p. 10.      [11] Ibid. p. 68.      [12] Ibid. p. 294.
[13] Pinel, Alienation Mentale, p. 360.      [14] Ibid. pp. 404, 405.
[15] See also pp. 445, 476, and pp. 263, 264, 312.
[16] Démocratie en Amérique, vol. iii. p. 110.

interest to do so; while Christianity merely attacked slavery on the ground that it was contrary to the rights of the slave.[1] I believe that slavery was necessarily abolished as soon as labour ceased to be disgraceful, for then it was found contrary to the interest of the master; and as we approach the South we find idleness held in honour.[2] Tocqueville[3] has confirmed from experience the theoretical conclusion of Adam Smith that slavery is more costly than free labour. In France, the diminution of slavery was slower in the domains of the church than anywhere.[4] On the history and different kinds of slavery, see Comte, Traité de Législation, tome iii. pp. 469–535, and the whole of tome iv. Mr. John Stanley in 1791, spoke against abolishing slavery on the ground that St. Paul and "several other saints" had not opposed it.[5] Slavery is allowed by the French Protestants in 1637.[6] In 1799 it was attempted to show that Christianity *did* forbid slavery.[7] Comte[8] says that neither Macchiavelli nor Montesquieu nor Rousseau say anything against slavery. In 1790, the celebrated Hugh Blair writes to Bruce from Restalrig, "I am in the same sentiments with you about what you call the paroxysm of modern philanthropy respecting the slave trade; but I do not see that you had much occasion to enter into that controversy."[9]

---

[1] Tocqueville, vol. iii. pp. 156, 164.    [2] Ibid. pp. 166, 173.    [3] Ibid. p. 181.
[4] See note in Monteil, Hist. des Français des Divers États, tome vi. p. 101.
[5] Parliamentary History, vol. xxix. p. 315.
[6] See Quick's Synodicon in Gallia, 1692, vol. ii. p. 348.
[7] Parliamentary History, vol. xxxiv. 1136, 1137.
[8] Traité de Législation, vol. iii. p. 515.
[9] Murray's Life of Bruce, p. 279.

# LORD MACAULAY'S WORKS.

*Kept on sale in the following Editions :—*

## HISTORY *of* ENGLAND, *from the* ACCESSION *of* JAMES *the* SECOND :—

Library Edition, 5 vols. 8vo. £4.
Cabinet Edition, 8 vols. post 8vo. 48*s.*
People's Edition, 4 vols. crown 8vo. 16*s.*
Student's Edition, 2 vols. crown 8vo. price 12*s.*

## CRITICAL *and* HISTORICAL ESSAYS :—

Student's Edition, 1 vol. crown 8vo. 6*s.*
Library Edition, 3 vols. 8vo. 36*s.*
Cabinet Edition, 4 vols. post 8vo. 24*s.*
People's Edition, 2 vols. crown 8vo. 8*s.*
Traveller's Edition, ONE VOLUME, square crown 8vo. 21*s.*

## SIXTEEN ESSAYS, *reprinted separately* :—

Addison *and* Walpole, 1*s.*
Frederick the Great, 1*s.*
Croker's Boswell's Johnson, 1*s.*
Hallam's Constitutional History, 16mo. 1*s.* fcp. 8vo. 6*d.*

Warren Hastings, 1*s.*
Pitt *and* Chatham, 1*s.*
Ranke *and* Gladstone, 1*s.*
Milton *and* Machiavelli, 6*d.*
Lord Bacon, 1*s.*   Lord Clive, 1*s.*

Lord Byron *and* the Comic Dramatists of the Restoration, 1*s.*

## *The* COMPLETE WORKS *of* LORD MACAULAY.

Edited by his Sister, Lady TREVELYAN. Library Edition, with Portrait.
8 vols. 8vo. £5. 5*s.* cloth ; or, £8. 8*s.* bound in calf.

## LAYS *of* ANCIENT ROME :—

Illustrated Edition, fcp. 4to. 21*s.*
With *Ivry* and *The Armada*, 16mo. 3*s.* 6*d.*
Miniature Illustrated Edition, imperial 16mo. 10*s.* 6*d.*

## SPEECHES, *corrected by* Himself :—

People's Edition, crown 8vo. 3*s.* 6*d.*
Speeches on Parliamentary Reform, 16mo. 1*s.*

## MISCELLANEOUS WRITINGS :—

Library Edition, 2 vols. 8vo. 21*s.*
People's Edition, ONE VOLUME, crown 8vo. 4*s.* 6*d.*

## MISCELLANEOUS WRITINGS & SPEECHES :

Student's Edition, in One Volume, crown 8vo. price 6*s.*

London : LONGMANS and CO. Paternoster Row.

www.ingramcontent.com/pod-product-compliance
Lightning Source LLC
Chambersburg PA
CBHW021929110726
47901CB00003B/774